THE RUNNER

Hyde heaved his frame against the running KGB man,
lifting him off his feet, turning him into a dark lump
facedown against the snow. Then he heard a voice, seeming
to come from the man on the ground.

"Stop him—kill him if you have to," in unaccented
English. It was no Russian voice, yet it was coming from
the pocket transceiver clipped to the lapel of the unconscious
man's coat. English, spoken by a native. *Collusion*, Hyde
had time to register. MI 5 and the KGB. *Collusion*.

His eyes cast about on the gravel, but he failed to
locate the recorder. Distant figures were running toward
him. *The recorder!*

No *time!*

He began running. Panic and survival controlled him.
He mounted the last steps onto the terrace of the Belvedere.
Two men below, another two converging.

Kill him if you have to. . . .

Hyde was stunned by the collusion. Now they wanted
him dead. He had seen and heard. He must be eliminated.
Driven by his own fear, Hyde ran toward the gates onto
the Prinz-Eugen strasse, toward Vienna.

Kill him if you have to. . . .

Lion's Run

The new bestseller by the author of
Firefox and *Firefox Down!*

CRAIG THOMAS

CRAIG THOMAS
Lion's Run

BANTAM BOOKS
TORONTO • NEW YORK • LONDON • SYDNEY • AUCKLAND

LION'S RUN

A Bantam Book

Bantam hardcover edition / December 1985
2nd printing . . . January 1986
Bantam rack-size edition / December 1986

Library of Congress Cataloging-in-Publication Data

Thomas Craig.
  Lion's run.

  I. Title.
PR6070.H56L56 1985   823'.914   85-47653
ISBN 0-553-25824-9

Bantam Books are published by Bantam Books, Inc. Its trademark, consisting of the words "Bantam Books" and the por-
trayal of a rooster, is Registered in U.S. Patent and Trademark
Office and in other countries. Marca Registrada. Bantam
Books, Inc., 666 Fifth Avenue, New York, New York 10103.

the tenth, like the first,
is for
JILL
with all my love

ACKNOWLEDGMENTS

Apart from my habitual thanks to my wife for her editing of this, my longest novel to date, I wish to especially thank Peter Matthews for his invaluable assistance with the theft of information from the KGB's central computer, which appears in Part Three of the book. Any errors, distortion, or license of method or terminology are my responsibility, not his.

Time hath, my lord, a wallet at his back,
Wherein he puts alms for oblivion,
A great-sized monster of ingratitudes:
Those scraps are good deeds past: which are devoured
As fast as they are made, forgot as soon
As done.

Shakespeare, *Troilus and Cressida*, III, 3

Preludes

I have done the state some service and they know't:
No more of that.

Shakespeare, *Othello*, V, 2

Quick.

Remember what they told you, the front cover of the file first. Camera joggle. Remember that too. You must be in a hurry, and nervous. . . . It must all be slightly out of focus, especially at the beginning.

The electronic flash flared onto the paper he could see through the lens, a small sunburst but much whiter than sunlight. *Teardrop*, the file proclaimed in the Cyrillic alphabet. The other words and reference numbers signified its importance, and the fact that it was consigned for immediate incineration, its contents having been transferred to tape and stored in Moscow Centre's principal security computer.

Teardrop. A man's history.

He turned the cover of the file, exposing the first of the pages it contained. A digest. Photograph that, they had said. No matter the urgency or the effects of your fear, you would have obtained at least that much in the way of bona fides. The earliest date was 1946, the last as recent as a month before. And the file was still not closed.

Camera joggle, he reminded himself. It had already become too mechanical, too skilled and unhurried. Pages one to five without a break, without a tremor. Perhaps practice did not make perfect. How many times had he done this . . . ?

Make certain the gray metal shelving appears in the top corner of some of the shots. Authenticity. Skip pages . . .

He flicked over the seemingly ancient sheets, the torn-out pages of notebooks, the letters, the carbons of signals received, splaying them like cards against the background of the buff folder and the dusty floor of the cold records basement.

3

No need for induced joggle, induced fear; he was shivering with cold now.

Live it—they will ask you about these moments, again and again. . . . They will ask, seeking to verify, to prove . . .

Fear—footsteps? He tried to imagine the hostile ring of bootsteps in the concrete, strip-lit corridor outside the door. Flip through the pages. Flash, flash, flash—white light glaring on the passing, momentary sheets of paper. His knee would be at the edge of one shot—he congratulated himself for that simple, authentic touch. Part of the series of interrogations from 1946. Then he flicked on quickly, the pages now becoming very distressed, spread untidily on the concrete between the racks of gray metal shelves. . . .

Then it was no longer 1946, it was the last two years. . . . Joggle the camera—but not too much. . . .

Remember what you feel at each moment; associate feelings and experiences with some of the pages. . . .

What was that? A meeting in Helsinki last year. Footsteps on the concrete outside, halting . . . ? He managed to frighten himself in the darkness, his eyes still dazzled from the last exposure.

On again, flash, flash . . .

The last page. *No, not the last one or the penultimate, not even the one before that . . .*

Then he had finished. He shivered with the cold and the returning darkness. His legs, up to the bent knees, were invested with an aching cramp. He could hear his own breathing. It might, after all, have all been real.

He sighed aloud.

"Well done," came a voice from the darkness. So he had been convincing, he told himself, his body jumping at the sudden words. "You'd like a drink now, I expect?"

The last white sheets in the *Teardrop* file had acquired a faint, snow-reflected gleam as he recovered his night vision. Yes, you are committed now, he told himself. Your fate is in these pages, with his.

Him. The subject of the *Teardrop* file.

"Yes," he replied, clearing his throat in the echoing dark. "I would like a drink."

Patrick Hyde watched Kenneth Aubrey as he and the Russian left the ferry in the wake of vacationers intent on reaching the gates of the zoo. Hyde disliked the fact that Aubrey was not wired for sound, in deference to the Russian's unaccustomed nervousness. He felt cut off from his superior, hampered in his task of protecting Aubrey.

He waited until the ferry was empty of passengers. There did not appear to be any contradiction between Deputy Chairman Kapustin's given word that he was alone and Hyde's own surveillance. If there were KGB bodyguards, they were unusually unobtrusive. Hyde strolled down the gangplank and along the quay toward the pine trees that masked Helsinki's Korkeasaari Island Zoo. Behind him, across the breeze-ruffled, gleaming water, Finland's capital was white and pink and innocent in the summer afternoon.

Hyde was still irritated by the fact that Aubrey had forbidden him to search Kapustin for a weapon or a microphone. Aubrey's face, as he unwound the lead from his waist and unclipped the microphone from his shirt, had been smug with trust. Hyde's blunter sensibilities did not enable him to trust Kapustin, even though these meetings were almost two years old.

Nothing new. A long, unfruitful courtship. Kapustin, by his words but not his actions, wished to defect to the West. A full Deputy Chairman of the KGB, Inspector-General of First Chief Directorate, Operations and Personnel. The glittering prize that dazzled Aubrey.

Ahead of him, fifty yards away against a backcloth of summer shirts and bright dresses, Aubrey and Kapustin strolled toward the turnstiles at the entrance to the zoo. A lion roared in the distance. Children gasped or squeaked with anticipation. Nothing dangerous moved beneath the heavy, aromatic pines, yet Hyde could not relax. There was no danger, nothing more than his persistent, recurring sense of wrongness. Everything was wrong about this—what, perhaps the tenth or even fifteenth meeting between Aubrey and Kapustin? Kapustin, the reluctant virgin. Kapustin vacillating, refusing to commit himself, worried about the money, the new identity, the place of residence. Leading Aubrey by the nose.

A red-and-yellow ball rolled across the path at Hyde's feet. A small boy in shorts, freckled and pale blond, chased it, then trotted away toward his parents picnicking beneath the trees on wooden benches where sunlight poured down on them. Midges hung in the air like visible motes of their laughter.

He stayed twenty yards behind Kapustin and Aubrey as they walked the narrow paths between goat pens. A llama watched Hyde with the superior stare of a civil servant, and bison grazed against a high mesh fence. Perhaps he was just disgruntled. Fed up with acting as Aubrey's bodyguard on this periodic tour of European capitals. The meetings were arranged to coincide with Kapustin's visits of inspection to the Soviet embassies of Western Europe—Berlin, Vienna, Bonn, Stockholm, Madrid, London, Helsinki. Each time Kapustin supplied high-level gossip, Politburo insights, evidence of shifts of power and opinion—and excuses for not coming over. Demanding twice the money or twice the security, perhaps even twice the flattery.

Kapustin and Aubrey had halted in front of a monkey cage. Small, furry, whiskered faces watched them, small hands clutched toward them through the bars. Aubrey appeared earnest; Kapustin, taller and heavier, seemed to lean over him, a schoolmaster over a pupil trying to rush at a solution. Aubrey's expression was a mirror of the cross, pinched face of a Capuchin monkey that watched the two men through the bars. Hyde watched the crowd around them, watched the cameras and the eyes. Nothing.

The exasperation was clear on Aubrey's face, beneath the straw trilby. Kapustin gestured broadly, a noncommittal shrug. Hyde moved closer to the barrier in front of the cage. A small, gray monkey skittered away from him along a branch that led nowhere, as if he represented a palpable threat.

"Double agent? We are not asking you to be that, Dmitri," Aubrey was saying in a quiet, urgent voice. "Why do you persist with the idea? It was your request—*you* contacted *me*, Dmitri. Directly. Personally."

"As if I were waking a sleeper?" Kapustin murmured.

"Quite." Aubrey refused to smile at the remark. "Ever since then, you have toyed with us, with me."

"I apologize." Kapustin watched Hyde for a moment as the Australian drifted closer, his eyes looking away from the monkey cage. In the distance, the lion roared again. Then Kapustin returned his attention to Aubrey. "You have been very helpful, you have done everything . . ." he murmured.

"My duty, no more than that," Aubrey observed stiffly. "What you offered could not be ignored. But why hesitate now—again and for so long?"

"I cannot decide between you and the Americans."

"Money? Is that it?"

"Would it be money with you?"

"No. The situation would not arise."

"Obviously not, now that Cunningham is to retire."

"You know, of course."

"You are expected to take his place, as the Director-General. You will, of course?"

Aubrey brushed at the air with his hand. "That's irrelevant."

"Your real work can begin then."

"Perhaps. Listen to me, Dmitri. The period of courtship is over. You must decide. You must act. . . ."

Hyde drifted away from the two men. Their voices became lost in the screeching of the monkeys and the noise of the children. The same conversation, the endless tape loop of persuasion and hesitancy. Kapustin playing with Aubrey, wasting everyone's time. Elaborate verbal games, continual amusements . . .

Hyde let the thought go in the babble of a school party of pigtailed girls and crop-headed boys, bustled past him by an efficient schoolmistress. A high of vanilla ice cream melted and

·

·

·

"This is now the actor, from yesterday?" Kapustin asked in the darkness at the back of the room. The film whirred in the projector. Cigarette smoke drifted in the beam of white light that reached toward the wall screen.

"Yes, Comrade Deputy Chairman."

"The cloud shadows don't look right to me. You have the right time of day, and the glare of the sun. But there was more of a breeze today. There aren't enough shadows."

Kapustin watched his own back moving away from the camera, accompanied by a figure apparently that of Kenneth Aubrey. The actor bore little facial resemblance to the Englishman, but from this viewpoint he was identical. The walk was good, very good, the attitude of the shoulders and the head slightly on one side, like a listening bird. The straw trilby was habitual summer wear with Aubrey, and it was fortunate he had worn it that afternoon.

"We'll make a computer comparison, Comrade Deputy Chairman," the leader of the technical team offered. "We can do something about the shadows, I'm certain—even if there

... ... the film for a moment longer, then said: "Show me the film from this afternoon."

The projector slowed into silence. A second projector alongside it threw images at the screen, then he and Aubrey were again walking away from the camera. Sunlight, yes. Clothing to be copied, naturally. Manner. The actor would have to be rehearsed. There was an irritation about Aubrey that was infrequently displayed but was here now, on this piece of film, shaping his body, moving his limbs. The Australian drifted along the path behind them, hands in his pockets, apparently bored.

"Okay, sir?" the team leader asked at his elbow. Kapustin nodded.

"Not bad."

"We can solve the problems. The film quality will look identical, once the computer's finished setting up its comparisons." The man was less ingratiating than proud—of his skills and his equipment and reputation, presumably. "We'll be able to stitch in anything you want, as long as the actor's right."

"He will be."

"Yes, sir."

on his brown corduroy trousers, took them away. The idea of ice cream appealed to him as he vented his irritation on the two old men behind him.

Teardrop. Kapustin's codename, suggested by the Russian himself at that first meeting in Paris. He looked back. The two men were surrounded by the shuffling party of schoolchildren. The strident voice of their teacher lectured them. The image of Aubrey and Kapustin was harmless, even risible. Nothing would come of *Teardrop.* Hyde did not expect the KGB Deputy Chairman to defect—not this year, not next year or the year after that. Aubrey was still not certain of the man's motives for wishing to defect. A vague disillusion seemed insufficient to explain it. *Teardrop.* It didn't mask some personal tragedy, as far as SIS could establish. It meant nothing, just a codename.

Mechanically, Hyde watched the cameras and the eyes, then the paths and the trees. Nothing. He yawned, felt bored, and wished for action.

Kapustin and Aubrey passed him then, returning to the gates, deep in urgent conversation. Unimportant. Nothing. *Teardrop* was a waste of everyone's time.

Slowly, unalert, he began to follow the two old men.

Kapustin and Aubrey were now standing in front of the monkey cage, engaged in what was evidently an urgent conversation. The distance the cameras had had to adopt because of Hyde's presence assisted the deception. No one could blow these images up enough to lip-read. They could identify Aubrey when he was full on or in profile, but they'd not be able to lip-read what he was saying. It was good. On the tapes, they could make Aubrey say anything they pleased.

"It looks good," Kapustin murmured, tapping his teeth with his thumbnail. The smoke from his cigarette caught the gleam from the projector. "Yes, good . . ." he luxuriated. He could almost hear in his mind the doctored, edited, stitched-together conversation that would accompany the film. When Aubrey had agreed, at Kapustin's pretense of nerves, not to be wired for sound, it had been difficult for the KGB Deputy Chairman not to pat his own tiny microphone in self-congratulatory pleasure at the Englishman's trusting naiveté. At the recollection of it, Kapustin chuckled quietly. "Let me have a look at the next bit of rehearsal film," he said.

The projector slowed and stopped. The other projector threw an image of Kapustin and the actor onto the screen. Yes, the film was necessary, he told himself. Of course, Aubrey was officially logged to meet Kapustin in Helsinki, and the film was not necessary as proof that they met. But—

Kapustin smiled. The actor had paused. He passed a package to Kapustin. There was guilt in the angle of the head, the set of the shoulders. Kapustin, on the screen, acted gratitude and almost immediately satisfaction, followed by assertiveness, command. The tiny scene was over in perhaps six or seven seconds. It unmistakably portrayed Aubrey as a double agent—a traitor.

Teardrop.

"Okay—satisfactory so far. Let's go to the tape, shall we?"

The lights came on. The image on the screen faded, as if seen through a curtain of light or snow, and then the projector was switched off. Kapustin studied the young, eager, competent faces that turned toward him like plants toward the sun. His own technical team. His special *Teardrop* team.

"What do you want, sir?"

"The boat, first. The ferry. What did you get there, and what have you done with it?"

"You'll like it, sir." The young man grinned. There was

suddenly complete silence in the room as he switched on the cassette players. Japanese. Expensive. Commercial tapes of rock music lay heaped beside it on the table, amid the mikes and leads and in front of the reel-to-reel recorder and tape editor. His young men had been buying in Helsinki.

"I'd better," he said good-naturedly, fatherly.

Seagulls, then voices. The team leader handed him a typed transcript. In underscored letters were the questions and observations he had previously recorded and which had been edited into his conversation with Aubrey. Kapustin listened intently.

"It is increasingly difficult for me," Aubrey insisted from the speakers. Seagulls, water, wind, the noise of the ferry's engines. He had gone on, in reality, to explain to Kapustin that his vacillations were irritating London, that Aubrey was having difficulty persuading his colleagues that Kapustin was serious about defecting. Now, with an inserted question regarding Cabinet papers and the minutes of the Foreign Affairs Committee, it appeared that Aubrey was providing his KGB control with highly secret information.

Kapustin smiled, tapped his teeth, and listened.

"I realize that," he heard himself saying. "But this information is very important." Beneath the words he could hear his own heartbeat, fainter than the pulse of the ferry's engines. "You must try . . ." he insisted.

"I am doing everything asked of me!" Aubrey replied with querulous and frightened anger. At least, it could have been fear. Where had that conversational snippet come from—Paris, Vienna, Berlin? This year, last year?

"No," he announced. "Switch off." The team leader appeared stoical, other and younger faces were crestfallen, one or two distinctly irritated in the hot, smoky room. "Sorry, lads—my heartbeat's not exact in the inserts. And there's something about the perspective of Aubrey's voice—he's got to be a little nearer."

"What about the background sound?" someone asked.

"That's okay—no difference. That's good. I'm sorry, but Finnish Intelligence is going to be given this when the time is right, and the first thing they're going to suspect is that it's a fake. They're going to try to find what's been put in and what's been taken out. I can *hear* it. It's not good enough. Okay—run on to the zoo. . . ."

The cassette tape whirred, then the Play switch clicked again. The lion roared as if on cue. The monkeys chattered at the children, the children at the monkeys. Kapustin listened.

"Your real work can begin then," he heard himself saying.

"No more than my duty," Aubrey replied stiffly. Then he continued: "I've waited patiently—for a very long time, Dmitri—now it's within our grasp. . . ."

"Again!" Kapustin snapped, clipping the excitement from his voice.

Rewind, then Play. He listened. Snippets of conversation from Berlin, from Vienna, from Rome. Background filtered out, new background supplied. The zoo. He listened. All that chatter—he had not believed they could do it. They wanted it to disguise the initial filtering out of traffic, of wind or rain. Yet he had disbelieved them. Until now. This was . . .

"Marvelous," he breathed. A collective sigh of relief seemed to fill the room. Lion, monkeys, children. A seamless, flowing background, natural, lifelike. Undoctored.

It had happened. This was the best it had ever been, on all the tapes they had doctored. The best in the last two years. The most crucial moment; the springing of the trap.

Aubrey was *Teardrop*—was, for certain, *Teardrop*. Aubrey was a traitor to his service and his country. It was there, on the tape. *Teardrop* unmasked.

"Again," he whispered, luxuriating in his sensations of complete, infallible success. "Again."

There was a video projection screen at the far end of the first floor of the shop. On it, in somewhat blurred colors, a ballet dancer impersonating Squirrel Nutkin bounced across a leaf-carpeted glade to the inappropriate accompaniment from wall speakers of a disco tune. The image caused him to smile, then he turned his back on the screen and ascended to the cassette department. He was early for his appointment, for this final contact in the HMV Shop in Oxford Street.

He had come out of the Bond Street tube station into a hot September afternoon that made the whole of crowded, sweltering Oxford Street seem to smell of frying onions from an invisible hotdog stall. Ground floor, he had been told. At four precisely. At four, you come over. A pity you couldn't have been posted to Washington or even New York—but, from Oxford Street we can get you the couple of blocks to the embassy in Grosvenor Square. The HMV Shop's always good and crowded. That'll be the pickup point. Be early, move around the shop. We'll want time to look for any tail. Be careful.

He should not have felt real tension, he knew. There should be only the feelings he had practiced and learned in readiness for this moment. *Remember, they will expect fear, tension, sweating. Just as with the file, you must be sure of your emotions. They must be correct—the feelings of a defector on the point of going over.* The smell of frying onions after the smell of hot dust in the tube station had turned his stomach. It was an image to hold, to bring out later like a pressed flower. A proof of honesty.

A hard-looking boy with pink hair, eye makeup, and an earring sat lounging behind the cash desk. Grigori Metkin moved slowly along the racks of cassettes, appearing to browse, finger running along the shelving, following the alphabet of pop singers and rock bands that were, almost without exception, unfamiliar to him. His eyes sought and found his shadow from the Soviet embassy, intently studying the bargain-priced cassettes. He carried two green Marks & Spencer bags. There was nothing Russian about him. He was dark and pot-bellied enough to be an Arab or an Iranian. Metkin glanced at his watch. Two minutes before four.

A man in a light suit brushed past him and stared knowingly into his face. There was the merest hint of an encouraging smile, then he was gone. After a moment, Metkin followed him downstairs. On the video screen, to the accompaniment of Bach supported by the alien groundswell of electric guitars from the floor below, Raquel Welch in an animal-skin bikini fled from a dinosaur. Again, Metkin smiled. Then, as he looked back from the stairs leading to the ground floor and the wailing guitars, he saw his shadow with the green bags coming unconcernedly after him. For the briefest moment, he understood intensely what he was leaving behind and the dangers of his new role; his stomach became hollow and weak.

The man in the light suit was waiting for him. There was a second man, then a third. All in well-tailored suits, perhaps intending to advertise the benefits of America to him, their newest recruit. The conflicting noises of three or four different hit records seemed to increase in volume as he hesitated on the bottom step. The sunlight glared outside the doors of the shop.

Make it good, he thought. *Make it convincing*, he remembered. Where was his instructor now, from which Oxford Street window would he be watching this? Then Metkin saw a flicker of recognition on the face of one of the Americans. His shadow had given himself away. The light suit moved toward him, and a strong brown hand grabbed his arm. The man's other hand began reaching into the breast of his jacket. A second American had moved swiftly toward the doors. Metkin could smell the frying onions again. He felt nauseous.

"Come on, come on," the American urged. Men in patterned shirts, all highly colored, moved toward himself and the CIA officer. The necessary counteractivity, the threat that the prize might yet be snatched away. The American bustled him to the doors, his right hand still inside his jacket as if seeking a missing wallet. "Come *on*—"

Sunlight, hard and dusty, collided with Metkin as he emerged. He bumped into an Arab woman and knocked over her child. He recognized that he would possess all the necessary emotions to recall under debriefing interrogation. A cry from behind them. Three suits, one next to him and two guarding the black limousine. The rear door was opened. He was bundled in like a bag of washing. The American who had pushed him, the one in the light suit, slid into the seat next to him.

Look around, look frightened, he remembered. He saw the sweating, angry faces gather on the pavement. The Arab woman picked up, dusted off her child. The patterned shirts retreated, then disappeared as the car turned out of Oxford Street. The Americans were arguing.

"Neither of you picked those guys up—neither of you!"

"Sorry—"

Thank them, he remembered, *thank them profusely.* . . .

"Thank you! Thank you!" he exclaimed breathily, feeling the sweat run freely beneath his arms, on his chest. "Oh, thank you, thank you . . ."

The American next to him smiled, then nodded. "You're safe now, pal. Safe."

And suddenly, ahead of the car, the weather-stained white concrete of the U.S. embassy, surmounted by the eagle with its spread wings. To Metkin, it possessed the appearance of a prison and the associations of a minefield. Safe? His danger was only just beginning.

Their hands moved in and out of the pool of light that fell upon the desk, attacking the heap of photographic blowups. The ceiling of the darkened room was washed with pale light, much of it filtering through the uncurtained windows from the moonlit snow lying deep on that part of the Virginia countryside. Their shadows bobbed and eddied on the ceiling.

"How much of this can you verify?" The Deputy Director of the CIA sounded skeptical.

"A lot of it."

"From Metkin, our defecting friend?"

"No. He knows nothing about this. He grabbed it as a bargaining lever. It was too secret for him to handle. But, look here—" Hands shuffled the gleaming, frequently overexposed pictures, then tapped one of them. "We know this style of classification and secrecy grading has never been used by the KGB. It belonged to the NKVD, at least thirty years ago. And this . . ." The hands shuffled once more. The Deputy Director was struck by their confident, trained movements. The hands were indeed dealing cards—a bad hand. ". . . this is his handwriting all right. It's been checked by a lot of experts. It's been scanned and examined by computer. It may be almost forty years old, but it's his handwriting."

"I see." The Deputy Director looked into the shadowy corners of his spacious office, then at the silvery snowgleam on the ceiling. His shadow and that of his companion seemed hunched and diminished and sinister, crouching over the photographs on his rosewood desk. He could smell his cigar butts still in the ashtray—no, they were on the pile carpet, upended there by someone reaching for the sheaf of blowups. "I see," he repeated.

"The history fits, too. As far as we can check, all these 1946 dates can be corroborated."

"What about the recent dates—the last two years?"

"It all checks out. At least, as far as we can go without asking London direct."

"Then all this was garbage about a KGB Deputy Chairman wanting to defect . . . ?"

"We think so."

"What else do you think?"

"Aubrey's been a sleeper for more than thirty-five years. Two years ago, when he was within an ace of the top job, they woke him up."

"You say you haven't talked to London?"

"No, sir. We need to talk to MI 5, sure—but that's the Director's decision, not ours."

"Okay." The Deputy Director's finger tapped at the blowup of the file's summary sheet, near the bottom. On the ceiling, his shoulders seemed to move spasmodically in unison, as if he were vomiting. "You believe this defector—and *this*?"

"We've tried him every way. Even under drugs and hypnosis. He comes up smelling of roses every time. Same story. As a cipher clerk, he'd heard the rumors everyone else had heard. Important files about to be incinerated—topmost secrecy. He knew it could be his ticket on the first-class gravy train, so he took his Japanese camera to work—and found *Teardrop*."

"Aubrey's an old man now. . . ."

"And he's just become Director-General of British Intelligence."

"Dammit, Bill, I know that. . . ."

"Well, sir?"

The Deputy Director's large hands rearranged the sheaf of photographs, irresolutely. "Hell, I don't know—I just don't know!"

"Sir, I'd stake my reputation on the fact that *Teardrop* is a genuine highest security file from Moscow Centre. More than that, these reference numbers on the cover show that it has been transferred to their main security computer. Also, access is limited to the Chairman and six Deputy Chairmen of the KGB. No one else, with the exception of Nikitin himself, can get to see it. These pictures come up genuine under every test we can make. The story they tell—however appalling—holds up under investigation. . . ." Once more, the pictures were dealt like cards, fanned open across the whole desk. One or two slid to the carpet, out of the pool of strong white light. "And it all means that Kenneth Aubrey is a Soviet agent. It means he's *the* Soviet agent of all time!"

"And he's just been made head of British Intelligence."

The Deputy Director sighed once, but the sound became a stifled belch. "Okay—we'll take this to the Director first thing in the morning."

"I am using President Nikitin's own words, Kapustin. Let it begin in earnest, the destruction of Kenneth Aubrey . . . and with him, the destruction of British Intelligence. Does the President exaggerate?"

"He does not, Comrade Chairman . . . thank you. Your health, Comrade Chairman—"

"I prefer to toast the success of this operation."

"Very well—to *Teardrop*, then."

"*Teardrop* . . . which will *succeed*, of course, Kapustin?"

"I give you my word on it. The timing is perfect—perfect. I assure you—"

"And you intend Aubrey to be arrested by his own people at your next, and final meeting with him . . . ?"

"Yes—Vienna."

"And you are certain that his *friends*—will arrest him? That they will swallow your fiction and arrest him, believing him guilty?"

"Absolutely, Comrade Chairman. I am convinced of it—just as you are not, I see."

"I am backing you, Kapustin. *I* placed the operation in your hands, remember? The timing, however, was your decision, not mine."

"The timing is right!"

"Aubrey has *friends* . . ."

"And enemies in his own service, in the British Cabinet, in the civil service. The British Prime Minister is said not to like him, Sir William Guest does not, nor do other powerful men. Aubrey is not of their class, Comrade Chairman, and that rankles. Also, for too many years he has been spectacularly successful—the cleverest boy in school, which has earned him enmity on a scale only the British Establishment could show toward intelligence, skill, success. . . ."

"Yes, yes—I am aware of the mores of the British upper classes—but haven't you been carried away by their significance?"

"No, Comrade Chairman. The media coverage will be overwhelming, and destructive. Apart from that, Guest and the other members of the Joint Intelligence Committee wish to reorganize the intelligence and security services under one roof. Aubrey has consistently opposed this, and made enemies there, too. Powerful men will see Aubrey's disgrace as their opportunity to put through the reforms they desire. Further, Aubrey has been promoting his own people, most of them young, thereby alienating many old hands since he became Director-General. The people he disappointed will not forgive him, and those he has helped are young enough to be more concerned with keeping what they have than risking everything to help Aubrey. . . . He will be, I assure you, without powerful allies. Without such, he must fail—*we* must succeed."

"Mm. Perhaps you are right. I have made my reservations clear to the Politburo and to the President . . . but, you still have my backing for the operation."

"I understand you clearly, Comrade Chairman."

"Then, in the spirit of your unshakable confidence, let us drink to success?"

"Certainly—a pleasure."

"Let us wish Sir Kenneth Aubrey, KCVO, a Happy New Year—eh? A *very* Happy New Year!"

One by one, the rows of windows of the Belvedere Palace in Vienna turned from bronze to orange in the setting afternoon sun, as if invisible servants were going from room to room lighting great chandeliers. Kenneth Aubrey and the Russian were almost in darkness as they patrolled the terrace of the Upper Belvedere beneath the great windows: two shadowy, unsubstantial, and isolated figures. Patrick Hyde sat perched on the stone plinth beneath the enigmatic, crouching statue of a sphinx. Its companions ranged away from him along the terrace, each of them staring out of Maria Theresa faces and from beneath eighteenth-century hair down toward the city. Hyde looked up at his sphinx as Kapustin continued his explanation to Aubrey. Yes, the smile on that face was alluring as much as mysterious—lewd, even, as it retreated into cold winter darkness. Appropriate to the conversation that he could tinnily hear through the earpiece of the portable recorder in the pocket of his dark overcoat. This time, Aubrey was wired for sound and Kapustin seemed unworried at the prospect.

In a pause in Kapustin's halting, almost embarrassed explanation, Aubrey exploded with anger. Hyde had never heard him so enraged, so undiplomatic, so unreserved before.

"You cannot tell me now that you refuse to come over?" his voice asked in mocking, venomous disbelief. "After more than two years, you simply cannot mean that!"

The silence hummed. The KGB Deputy Chairman, *Teardrop*, was backing away. Hyde had known it for more than half an hour now, ever since the first moments of the meeting. Almost from the moment Kapustin had greeted Aubrey and Hyde had drifted to a more useful surveillance distance, he had sensed a new and even more reluctant mood.

And it was a woman. An inducement to remain in the Soviet Union that Aubrey would be incapable of understanding or accepting.

"I—I do mean that, my friend," Kapustin explained. "I—am sorry, but I can say it in no other way. I—cannot come with you."

"Everything is arranged!" Aubrey stormed. "You agreed to everything at our last meeting. It was to be *next week*, dammit!"

Hyde watched the two almost undiscernible figures reach the far end of the terrace, turn and begin toward him again. The orange color of the windows was now uniform, as if the early sunset had stalked after them along the terrace. Hyde saw the pale blotch of Wilkes's trench coat drifting like a patch of fog behind the two men. He and the rest of Vienna Station were in control of security. Once more Hyde felt himself, as Aubrey's traveling companion and bodyguard, flatteringly unused. Wasted. He rubbed his ungloved hands. His breath smoked in the last of the light. To the east, the pale sky darkened toward purple. The gardens of the Belvedere glittered with yesterday's snow.

"But, this woman—" Aubrey persisted. "You say you have known her only for a matter of a few months. . . ."

"That is correct."

"Then, then—then I do not *understand*!"

"You have never been moved by such a passion, my friend?"

"Bring her with you!" Aubrey blurted out.

"I cannot. She—has a family. I do not need to tell you what former colleagues of mine would do to them were the two of us to emerge in the West. No, my friend, it cannot be. . . ."

"Dammit, you're sixty-one!"

Hyde smiled and tossed his head. Aubrey, the man devoid of sexual passion, simply could not comprehend. Deputy Chairman Kapustin would not come out to play, now or ever. To Hyde, it was a matter of indifference. The cold impinged more keenly. Only for the loss of Aubrey's coup was he regretful. And even that wasn't important—Aubrey already had it all: knighthood, Director-Generalship, honor and glory, world without end. . . .

"And should know better?" Kapustin asked mockingly.

"Evidently I do not."

"You could be blown—"

"I do not think so. And you, my friend, you would not betray me just for disappointing you. I am truly sorry. There is much in the West that I still covet, and much at home that sickens and disgusts me. But—I am in love. . . ."

Hyde heard Aubrey's snort of derision and saw Kapustin spread his arms in a gesture of pleasurable hopelessness. Aubrey's stunted figure beside him, now that they were close again, looked feeble and old and bemused.

"Then this is our last meeting. We have nothing more to say to one another." Aubrey's voice was still hurtfully contemptuous.

"It would appear so. You have been patient and you have been secure. When I came to you, I asked a high price. You have, eventually, granted it. You have satisfied me in the matter of a new identity, a new life. And now that I have everything, it means nothing to me. I can no longer go down these steps— " They were standing just above Hyde now, at the head of a flight of stone steps. Hyde's sphinx seemed to smirk with superiority in the gloom. "—with you, or get into one of your cars parked outside the palace gates. London is an impossible distance away. Washington is another planet—for me, at least."

"Very well. I shall report the matter. . . ."

"Ah, yes. You will give a most withering description of my sudden—weakness?" Kapustin laughed. To Hyde, the KGB Deputy Chairman sounded like an actor, overplaying his role.

"I—it's simply that I do not understand," Aubrey admitted.

Hyde jumped down from his stone perch. It was almost dark now, the time of maximum danger when everything was shadowy and confusing and suspicious. Sunset is a trap, someone had once told him. He picked out Wilkes in his ghostly trench coat, and two of the others. And no enemy activity. *Teardrop* could move about Western cities much as he liked. That kind of seniority was what had made him such a valuable catch, the fish of the season.

And Aubrey had failed to land him. . . .

"Good-bye, my friend."

"Good-bye."

The two men shook hands briefly and stiffly, and then Kapustin came down the steps and passed Hyde without a glance in his direction. Aubrey descended much more slowly, as if greatly tired. His face, in the frosty almost-dark, was abject.

"Sorry, sir—" Hyde began.

"God in Heaven, what's got into the man?" Aubrey exclaimed.

"Sex, that's all it is," Hyde replied with assumed disgust.

"I found the whole business—so hard to believe," Aubrey complained. "And kindly don't mock me, Patrick."

"Sorry, sir."

"But to have *lost* him!" Aubrey burst out again as Wilkes approached. The senior field officer of Vienna Station backed away at the tone of Aubrey's voice. "Two years since he first approached us—two years of meetings, negotiations, arrangements, assurances—of *courtship*, dammit!"

"And then he dumps you for another woman," Hyde could not resist observing, immediately regretting that he had done so. Aubrey turned to face him, his eyes gleaming like chips of ice in the last of the light. Then the old man shrugged.

"If he had arranged the whole charade for my personal embarrassment," Aubrey remarked, "he could not have had more success. My enemies—on both sides of the Atlantic—will say of me that I am finally too old to cope. Washington contains few people I have worked with in—sensitive matters. They will be *delighted* at Langley with our success here!" Aubrey's pale features twisted in irony. "Sir Kenneth Aubrey, KCVO, Director-General of SIS, falls flat on his face. How *pleased* so many people will be to hear of it! The Cabinet Office and MI 5 will have a field day. . . ." He sighed as he choked off the sentence, then waved his hand toward Wilkes's hovering form, dismissing him. "Back to the hotel, Patrick," he murmured tiredly.

"Okay, sir."

Their footsteps crunched on the gravel of the path as they moved down the slope toward the high hedges that bordered the more formal and enclosed part of the gardens. The huge ornamental pool in front of the Upper Belvedere was a sheet of glassy ice. A sliver of moon had appeared above the horizon, and the first stars were like gleams of frost. Hyde realized that Aubrey was still wired for sound. He could hear his breathing and his heartbeat faintly in his earpiece. He took the plug from his ear and thrust it and its cord into his pocket. Kapustin, usually so wary of recordings of his conversations with Aubrey, had seemed indifferent on this occasion. Doubtless, out of a sense of fair play, Aubrey would order him to wipe this tape. Kapustin was dead to Aubrey, the matter closed as a mortuary drawer.

They reached a shorter flight of steps, then the tall hedges and trimmed firs and statuary of the lower gardens. Hyde touched Aubrey's elbow, offering him his support on the slippery steps. Aubrey did not refuse the assistance. The weight of his arm was birdlike, fragile. Wilkes was twenty yards away, on another gravel path, and his three men were farther off, forming a screen. Aubrey's breathing was almost like a crackle of static close to him. . . .

The recorder clinked on the gravel as Hyde dropped it.

Crackle of static?

"Sorry, sir—dropped the bloody tape," Hyde said in an unnecessarily loud voice. Aubrey clicked his tongue in disapproval. Shut up, Hyde thought. Quiet . . .

Wilkes's shoes on gravel. He scrabbled one hand over the path as if searching for the recorder, which he had already retrieved from near his left knee. The gravel was sharp and cold through his corduroy trousers. His woolen scarf felt damp against his mouth as he held his breath.

"Come along, Patrick. . . ." Aubrey sighed impatiently.

Shut up—

Crackle of static, and nearer than their own men . .

Radio—two-way?

Aubrey took a step toward him—footsteps as Wilkes drew nearer. Other footsteps, a small party of men. Wilkes hurried close to Aubrey.

What?

Where the hell had Kapustin gone? Hyde hadn't even watched him leave the gardens of the Belvedere. Damn—

Hyde's hand reached into his coat.

"Sir Kenneth? It's Andrew Babbington—" one of the approaching knot of men—four, no, five of them—called out.

"Babbington?" Aubrey replied confusedly, moving toward the group. "Babbington—Andrew, what are you doing here?"

Hyde remained on one knee, his hand gripping the butt of the Heckler & Koch the embassy had issued him that afternoon. Its molded plastic was warm from his body. He could not ignore the crackle of static.

Then Aubrey said, "It is you—what is it?"

Crackle—legs, there, beneath the trees. He saw them through a diseased, thinned part of the hedge. Wilkes and the others had closed up now, forming a group of men in dark overcoats and light trench coats, surrounding Aubrey. Must be an emergency? The legs he could see through the hedge rose to a dark, bulky coat. He could not see the man's face. Aubrey had been joined by the Director-General of MI 5 and the Vienna Head of Station. It had to be an emergency. Highest priority.

The legs remained still. Did the body have a familiar shape?

Another pair of legs arrived silently. *Two* watchers. Hyde got to his feet and moved slowly and quietly off the gravel path. His hand held the recorder and its lead and the earpiece. He thrust the recorder into his pocket and the plug back into his ear.

". . . it's extremely embarrassing, Sir Kenneth," someone was murmuring deferentially. Parrish, Head of Station in Vienna.

"I simply do not understand why you are here, Andrew," Aubrey snapped as Hyde again bent low by the hedge. The two watchers had not moved. Their stance betrayed their interest in the group on the path. They were unaware of him.

"Mr. Babbington—I'm sorry, Sir Andrew has given me very precise instructions, Sir Kenneth. I'm very sorry. . . ." Why wasn't Babbington speaking for himself? Why the hell was Babbington in Vienna anyway? MI 5 was internal security, not intelligence. He was on Aubrey's patch. "I must ask you to accompany us, Sir Kenneth."

"Why, may I ask?" Aubrey asked waspishly. "And why won't you speak for yourself, Andrew? What is it? What is the matter?"

Hyde slipped along the grass verge, his back brushing the tall hedge. A statue loomed, and the hedge opened in decay behind it. He slipped through into the deeper darkness beneath the trees.

". . . this is very awkward for me, Sir Kenneth," Parrish was protesting. "Very awkward for all of us . . ."

"Where is your man Hyde?" Babbington suddenly asked. Hyde was chilled by the tone of command, the sense of urgency. It was a palpable threat. He *knew* it as such and was unnerved by disbelief. Ahead of him, he could see the two watchers beneath the trees. They were perhaps thirty yards from the group on the path. Who were they?

"I—have no idea where Hyde is," Aubrey said cunningly. "He was here a moment ago. . . . What do you want of me, Andrew?"

"You'll return to London in our company, Kenneth—and there you will remain incommunicado at your flat until such time . . ."

"*What?*"

Hyde was rigid with shock, almost unaware of the watchers even though they were now moving in his general direction.

"Kenneth—" Babbington warned.

"What is it, man? What in the devil's name are you talking about?" Aubrey stormed.

"Treason, Sir Kenneth," Babbington replied coldly. Hyde gasped with incredulity. *Aubrey?*

"What did you say?"

"Sir Kenneth, I must warn you that there are grounds for the strongest suspicion—there are matters which *must* be investigated. . . ."

Footsteps to Hyde's left, coming through the trees. Noises on gravel, farther off.

Kapustin . . . Kapustin . . .

He recognized the man. He had been the first watcher he had spotted beneath the trees. He hadn't left the gardens—he had *known* . . .

Known it would happen.

Hyde's breath escaped in a cloud. Kapustin saw him. Almost immediately, he bent his head to one side and whispered furiously into a small transceiver. Kapustin had known it would happen, that Aubrey would be . . .

Arrested.

Running footsteps, and the noises of Aubrey's group moving off, as if abandoning him.

"This is blatantly ridiculous," Aubrey was saying, his voice seeming to grow fainter. "You know why I'm here, what this is about."

Hyde was alone. Running footsteps on gravel, closing in. Kapustin watched him, expectant and confident. A body brushed through low fir branches, a slithering sound. Kapustin's transceiver suddenly crackled with voices. In his ear, Aubrey continued to protest, his voice and circumstances now irrelevant. Kapustin was about to speak. Hyde felt his legs become heavy. The adrenaline coursed in his veins, but he seemed powerless to employ it.

A body blundered against him, slipping on a patch of ice in a hollow in the leaf mold and hard earth. The collision freed him. He tugged the pistol from his overcoat and struck out, catching the man across the temple. The KGB man staggered back, clutching at the sudden rush of blood. It seeped between his fingers, ran into his eyes. Hyde heaved him out of his path and ran.

He burst from beneath the trees, skidded on the frosty, sparkling gravel, then recovered his balance and fled toward the Upper Belvedere, aware that he was moving away from Aubrey and the men who had arrested him. Then he was aware only of the sheen of snow on the gardens, the glint of the frozen pool, the sparkling steps, and his breath beginning to labor as he ran up the long slope toward the darkened, deserted palace.

The air was chilly against his cheeks, his mouth gasped at its coldness, tasting and wetting the wool of his scarf. He heard footsteps behind him. On the end of its lead, the earpiece of the recorder bounded like a fusillade of tiny pebbles against his shoulder.

He saw a form converging, racing across the moonlit white lawn, and he checked then heaved his frame against that of the running man. His breath exploded, and Hyde's shoulder lifted him off his feet, turning him into a dark lump facedown against the snow. Hyde staggered, lurched, felt the recorder drop from his pocket, and heard it land on the gravel.

Then he heard a voice, seeming to come from the man on the ground, and for a moment he was unable to move.

"Stop him—kill him if you have to," in unaccented English. It was no Russian voice, yet it was coming from the pocket transceiver clipped to the lapel of the unconscious man's coat. The words were muffled by the man's body, but they were audible on the chilly air. English, spoken by a native. *Collusion*, he had time to register. MI 5 and the KGB. Collusion.

His eyes cast about on the gravel, but he failed to locate the recorder. Distant figures were running toward him. *The recorder!*

No *time!*

His body began running again, even as he knew he ought to continue the search. Panic and survival controlled him. He mounted the last steps onto the terrace of the Belvedere. Again, the ghostly features of the sphinx grinned and smirked with superiority. His hand slapped against her stone hair as he regained his balance and looked behind him. Two men below, another two converging.

Kill him if you have to . . .

He was stunned by the collusion, but it was the threat that was now predominant. They wanted him dead. He had seen and heard. He must be eliminated. Not simply isolated, left alone, but eliminated. Driven by his own fear, he ran toward the gates onto the Prinz-Eugen strasse, toward Vienna.

Kill him if you have to . . .

His shoes pounded on the icy pavement. Lines of lights and parked cars stretched ahead of him down the hill toward the city. He ran on, the idea of collusion fading in his mind like the distanced noises and cries behind him.

PART ONE
Fall Like Lucifer's

. . . O how fall'n! how chang'd
From him, who in the happy Realms of Light
Cloth'd with transcendent brightness didst outshine
Myriads though bright.

Milton, *Paradise Lost*, Bk. 1

1
After the Fall

Paul Massinger balanced his whiskey on the small table and then eased himself, left leg extended, into the deep armchair. His face creased into lines of irritated pain for a moment until he settled his arthritic hip to greater comfort. Ridiculous. He had felt so much younger since his marriage to Margaret. He had belied his fifty-nine years; defeated them. Now his body persisted in its reminders of his physical age; it was pertinent yet false, just as the elegance of the Belgravia flat occasionally reminded him how easily he, a mere American, could be charged with having married for money. In many eyes he had at first been—still was to some people—little better than a colonial buccaneer, a gold digger. At least, that was what other gold diggers said. None of it hurt or even affected him. Margaret had entered his long widowerhood firmly and purposefully, and opened a new door.

The Standard lay still folded on the arm of the chair. He dismissed the thought that he must arrange to have an operation on his worsening hip—not yet, not yet—and pressed the button of the remote control handset. The television fluttered to life. Margaret was not yet home. A sense of absence filled him to the accompaniment of the signature tune of the early evening news. Alistair Burnet's comfortable features filled the screen. Paul heard a key in the lock, and surrendered to the small, joyous sensation at Margaret's return. He turned in his chair in order to see her the moment she stepped into the drawing room. There was an excited tightness in his chest. His hip twinged savagely, as if envious of his emotions and the object of his attention. In the same complex moment he was young and old.

The long fox fur coat and the matching fur hat; a high

color from the evening drop in temperature made her younger than her forty-three years. The confident, unselfconscious step . . . The smile faded from his lips. Alistair Burnet's voice was that of a brutal intruder upon the scene. She had halted abruptly in midstep, and the color had blanched from her cheeks. One gloved hand played about her lips. Her eyes looked hurt, bruised. Massinger turned his head toward the television set, and gasped.

A grainy monochrome picture of a man of forty or so, fair hair lifted by a breeze, half-profile, lips parted in a smile, eyes pale and intent. Handsome. Massinger did not hear what Alistair Burnet said to accompany the photograph. He did not need to hear the appalled, choked word that Margaret uttered:

"Father!"

He knew it already. Robert Castleford, almost forty years dead.

Margaret dragged the fur hat from her head, disheveling her fair hair. Her mouth was slightly open, as if there were other things she wished to say. Massinger said, stupidly:

"Margaret, what's going on . . . ?"

She moved to his chair but did not touch him, except to brush his hand as she snatched the remote control handset from the arm of the chair. Burnet's voice boomed in the drawing room.

". . . the accusations, said to have been made to the CIA by a Russian defector, now in America, involve the circumstances surrounding the death in 1946 in Berlin . . ."

"Why?" was all Massinger could think to say. He looked up at his wife, but she was staring at the screen, her body slightly hunched like that of a child expecting to be struck.

". . . the Foreign Office has declined to comment on the matter, and will neither confirm nor deny that any investigation of the head of the intelligence service is under way, as this evening's edition of *The Standard* newspaper claims. . . ."

Her hand scrabbled near his sleeve like a trapped pet. The crackling of the folded newspaper was followed by a deep gasp that threatened to become a sob. Massinger, suddenly, could not look at her.

Why hadn't the authorities issued a D-notice and clamped down on the story, his mind asked irrelevantly, and answered itself almost casually, like a voice issuing from a deep club armchair of worn leather, The British have let it come out. For some reason, they want it known. . . . Aubrey has enemies, then. . . . He loathed his own detachment and wanted to clutch her hand. Alistair Burnet passed to another news story. Bombs in Beirut.

"What—what does it say?" he asked throatily. She did not reply. Aubrey, he thought. Aubrey knew Castleford in Berlin in 1946. But Castleford disappeared in Berlin. . . . His remains were found in—in 'fifty-one, beneath the ruins of a house. He'd been murdered, but no one ever thought . . .

Aubrey?

"Darling," he said with ponderous, eager gentleness, "what does it say?"

She let the paper fall into his lap, and crossed the room to the sideboard. He heard a drink being poured, and breathing like that of someone close to death. Castleford's picture was alongside the headline WHERE IS "C"? Beneath that, a sub-heading, *Intelligence Furor—Who Killed Who?* He could feel the pain each word must have inflicted upon her, but he could not turn his attention from the article.

> *Exclusive.* Arrest of the Head of Intelli-
> gence, "C," expected at any moment
> . . . CIA sources in London . . . White-
> hall refuses to . . . Soviet embassy
> sources angered by the accusations of
> complicity in Castleford's death . . .
> Castleford's background, senior and
> distinguished civil servant, brilliant
> university scholar, veteran of the Span-
> ish Civil War, until now believed mur-
> dered for some undiscovered personal
> reason—or motivelessly done to death
> . . . information in our possession,
> fourth man, fifth man . . . Blunt and
> Long and the others all small fry . . .

Massinger checked back, tracing his finger up the column. The subject had changed. Aubrey was not merely suspected of Castleford's murder. Russian agent, Russian agent, he read . . . information in our possession, Russian defector in the U.S., CIA file delivered to MI 5, MI 5 to act . . . arrest of "C" expected at any moment, pending a full investigation of the charges. . . .

He read on until he reached the demonic folklore, and the old devils of Philby, Burgess, MacLean, and Blunt came to occupy their familiar places. Then he threw the newspaper from him and it fluttered heavily to the pale blue velvet carpet. He turned to look at his wife.

"Well?" she said in a tight, strained voice. He sensed the malevolence in her tone.

"Well?" he could only repeat hopelessly.

"It is *Aubrey* they're talking about, isn't it? Your *friend* Aubrey?" He could do no more than nod in admission. "To think that he's *been* here! *Here!* Sat here with us, with you . . . !" Evidently, she believed every word of the report.

"Darling . . ." he began, hoisting himself out of his chair with the aid of his stick. When he looked up, her face wore an appalled expression, as if his movements were some further species of betrayal. "I can't defend him," he said shakily, moving toward her. She seemed to back away slightly along the sideboard. Her large cuff slid against the crystal of a decanter, and her gold bracelets rattled against the glass. "I can't tell you anything, anything at all. . . ."

"You've known him . . . for years you've known him!"

"Not then . . ."

"He's your *friend!*"

"Yes . . ."

"He murdered my father!" Her face was young, urchinlike, abandoned.

"They say he betrayed your father to the NKVD. . . . I don't know what to say to you—it's no more than a *rumor*."

They wanted it known, he reminded himself, and the future became clear to him in a moment of insight; it loomed over him like a cloud—no, more solid than that, like a great stone that would crush him if he could not learn to carry it. "Only a rumor," he repeated huskily. They wanted it known. The Joint Intelligence Committee, the Cabinet Office, the Foreign Secretary, even the PM—they've all allowed the witch hunt. Everyone must want Aubrey's head. . . . Then, he realized the truth. . . . They believe it. They believe Aubrey's guilty . . . they even believe he's a Russian agent.

He opened his arms. She moved into them with the sullen step of reluctant surrender. Her body heaved with sobs. His neck was wet from her tears. Thirty-five years late, she was overcome by the emotions of a bereaved daughter. Her world, her certainties, had been altered irrevocably, thrown into shadow.

His eyes roamed the large room. He noticed, as if for the first time, the number of framed photographs of her father on the walls, the sideboard, the occasional tables. Almost as if the place were a roadside shrine to a little-known local saint. A portrait of the young Castleford stared down at him from one of the walls. Margaret's mother, of course, had been mostly responsible for the veneration her daughter still felt; the unalloyed, immutable admiration of a child remained with her even now. *Especially* now—

Margaret had been flung back down some time tunnel to the moment when Castleford had first disappeared, to the moment he had died.

Silently, Massinger cursed the bad fortune that had raised Castleford from the dead. Once more, he was back to distress their domestic life.

At the sight of her father's face Margaret had regressed as suddenly as if brought out of a mild trance by the click of a hypnotist's fingers. The past two years, the span of their marriage, might at that moment not have occurred. She had become as he first found her—lost, precariously unstable, survivor of a quest in which she had ceased to believe but which she could not forsake—to find a man enough like her father to make her happy, keep her safe.

Massinger had accepted that role, then changed it. He had brought her with him, or so he thought, to a new sense of herself, a new confidence and equanimity—even to a joy she had not previously experienced. Her father—whose dead hand she still clutched, forty years after his death, thirty years after her own childhood—had faded, become less important to her, little more than a memory . . . the portrait in oils, and a collection of framed photographs that littered the rooms of their apartment. But until this moment—Massinger ground his teeth—until *this* moment, he had ceased to pose any threat, any rivalry for Margaret's loyalties and affection.

"There, there . . ." he breathed, stroking her hair from crown to neck. "There, my darling, my darling . . ."

"After all this time," she murmured, sniffing. He felt her swallow hard, and then her voice was firmer. "I wasn't prepared for anything like this—his face on the screen, suddenly to know that he had been betrayed, not just murdered, but betrayed deliberately. . . ."

He continued to stroke her hair gently. "I know, I know. . . ." He glanced up, into the mirror behind them. He saw a face that had been quickly, and perhaps permanently aged. Deep lines, hunted eyes. His own features. His hip ached with the premonition of effort. He was unready; it was unfair, grossly unfair. . . .

He knew it was false. All of it. Not Aubrey. Aubrey could not be a Russian agent. Never.

But Margaret . . . ?

Massinger inwardly quailed from the path he saw before him, winding into some obscure and dangerous distance. He could not help Aubrey, much as friendship might demand it. He had no power to help him . . . but Aubrey, by telling the truth, could help the Massingers, the couple, the married couple who were themselves threatened. Massinger could see, with utter clarity and certitude, like a doctor diagnosing a patient with an incurable disease, the slow collapse of his fragile, newfound happiness and contentment, battered by the waves of the past like a rotting, hollowed cliff.

Margaret would retreat, would go back to her old devotions, and he would begin to lose her. Dear Christ in Heaven, she had been *five years old* when Castleford disappeared!

He couldn't let that happen to her, not again. He'd saved her from it once, and he couldn't lose her now. He had to see Aubrey, get at the truth about Castleford. Because if Castleford had been murdered, and by Aubrey, he had all the makings of a martyr. Sainthood would surely follow, and Margaret would become the votary at the shrine, tending Castleford's sacred flame. He couldn't let that happen, either to her or to himself. Aubrey had some questions to answer. . . .

"Come in, Andrew—come in, my dear fellow!" Even in a room as large as Sir William Guest's sitting room, his voice echoed and rumbled like a distant storm.

Sir Andrew Babbington passed Mrs. Carson, Sir William Guest's housekeeper, after handing her his hat and coat. Guest rose from his armchair, wreathed in cigar smoke. A room of dark paneling, faded curtains, a rich but worn carpet highlighted by Chinese and Afghan rugs; a room littered with antique furniture either bought or inherited, its settees and deep chairs covered with well-worn chintz. The room might have been put together by a team of female relatives, mistresses, women friends, and other men's wives over a long period of time. Which was probably what had happened, Babbington reflected.

"Sit down, sit down," Guest urged. He was wearing a thick dressing gown over his shirt and trousers. There were old, comfortable slippers on his feet. The smell of the cigar assaulted Babbington's nostrils. Guest's heavy jowls shook as he moved his head from side to side. "Bad business, bad business," he murmured. Mrs. Carson was dismissed with a wave of his hand. "Scotch, my dear fellow?" Guest offered.

"Thank you." Guest poured the single malt sparingly, miserly in his pleasures when sharing them with others. Babbington took the crystal tumbler with its small splash of pale liquid. Sipped. He had seated himself opposite Guest, who resumed his armchair, the quiet violence of his bulk causing the springs to protest. His host sipped at his own more generous measure, puffed at his cigar, watched the smoke ascend leadenly toward the ceiling and the chandelier.

"Oh, Andrew," Guest sighed, "were we not just a little precipitate in informing our friends of the press?" The sigh, Babbington decided, was pure theater, without real meaning.

"Cold feet, William?" he asked with evident irony.

"Not at all, dear boy—not at all! It just drags all of us through the mud, don't you see?"

"Ashes, rather. From which Security and Intelligence Directorate rises like a phoenix . . . mm?"

Guest laughed, his jowls shaking, his ample stomach rising and falling to a quicker rhythm than his breathing.

"Maybe. Oh, I still find it hard to believe, you know . . . not that matter of 'forty-six, but this long-term sleeper thing. Are you *certain* we're right to believe it?"

Babbington sipped at his whiskey, contemplating his answer. Eventually, he said: "It is almost too fantastic to believe, I grant you that. But when I was at Langley last week I saw *all* the tests, heard *all* the theories. Our CIA friends are convinced—*angry* and convinced, William." He paused, but Guest waved him on, his eyes narrowed in concentration. "We have to proceed. The investigation is already under way. And . . ."

"Yes, yes—the PM's peculiar nonconformist sense of morality has led to a feeling of outrage. She wants this matter pursued—*vigorously pursued*, were her words."

"She dislikes Kenneth, of course."

"He has the trick of making her feel slow of thought, without intuition—and without humor. A very telling point with her. Yes, I am certain she is prepared to believe in Aubrey's guilt. You're right, of course. We must do the same—just in case. Aubrey will be replaced anyway; *you* will replace him in due course. The reorganization is certain to come."

"I hate the manner of achieving it—"

"But you will serve, of course." Guest laughed. The noise echoed from the paneling, seemed to glance like arrows of light from the crystal.

"Yes," Babbington answered quietly. "But, William, what if it is all a ghastly setup, just to trap Aubrey, have him out of the way?"

"You believe that?"

"I'm playing devil's advocate, shall we say?"

"They get rid of Aubrey just to help us build a more efficient, unpenetrated, *clean* intelligence service—rubbish, Andrew! No, Andrew, the more one looks into this thing, the more one comes to the inevitable conclusion that Kenneth must be guilty. As to the man's motives, who can say? That's up to your people to discover. All I will say is thank *God* we found out in time! Left alone, Aubrey could have given the Russians everything concerning the new organization while it was in the planning and discussion and changeover period—everything!"

After a lengthy pause, Babbington swallowed the rest of his drink, scanned the room as it retreated into the shadows of poor lighting and thick cigar smoke, then said, "Will our masters want a trial?"

"I think so. The PM would be well disposed toward one. Symbolic cleansing of the stables, that sort of thing. A large *gesture*, a decisive *act* . . . oh, yes, if there's proof, he goes on trial."

"The Russians are denying everything, of course—"

"Hardly likely not to, are they?"

"I suppose not."

"More whiskey?" Guest asked in a reluctant voice. "A small one for the road?"

Babbington glanced down into his empty tumbler. Then he looked up.

"You know, William, I think I will—yes, please. I think I need another drink."

Guest rose ponderously from his chair, took Babbington's glass, then stood over him.

"Find out the truth, Andrew—and quickly! If Kenneth Aubrey has been a sleeper who's never yet been used by the KGB but who's been on their payroll for almost forty years, *find out*! You won't encounter any resistance or reluctance, none at all, if you do find he's guilty—I can promise you that. *Our* concern is the future."

"And a clean break with the past, via Aubrey's guilt and trial and sentence—would not be frowned upon."

"The PM is outraged, Andrew, outraged. Another intelligence scandal, after all the others—let's make this the last. And for Aubrey there will be no immunity from prosecution, I promise you. *No more Blunts*, the PM told me. No more Blunts."

"Very well, William. I assure you of my best efforts, MI 5's best efforts, in the matter. I'll see poor Kenneth tomorrow."

"Good, good. Ah, now, you wanted another drink—just a small one, was it?"

Hyde finished the last mouthful of Wiener schnitzel and washed it down with a glass of thin red Austrian wine. The café was noisier now, more crowded with regulars interested only in wine and beer and coffee. He was almost the last person to have ordered a meal. Now, his stomach was full and his mind had slowed to a half-amused, cynical walking pace. He could no longer seriously accept the idea of collusion between Kapustin and MI 5. It was patently ridiculous, even after only a small carafe of wine. Someone had wanted him dead, yes. . . .

But that had been because it was a setup. Kapustin's game plan depended upon getting rid of Hyde. Leaving Aubrey alone to face the music. It was neat, clear, hard-edged in his mind, like a piece of colored glass. No witnesses, no corroboration for Aubrey from the one man who had been at most of the meetings with *Teardrop*. Efficiency.

He dabbed at his lips with the paper napkin, studied the remaining few sautéed potatoes, and decided against them. He was replete, calm—certain. He looked at his watch. Just after ten. Almost time to call in, arrange to be picked up by the embassy.

Aubrey was accused of treachery. Kapustin was cast, no doubt, as his control. A clever KGB setup, one which Aubrey had danced along with for two years. Babbington and MI 5 had swallowed the story. Clever. Specious, but clever. Aubrey had enough enemies in MI 5 and JIC and the Cabinet Office for it to tip the scales against him; a cloud was all they needed, not a prosecution.

He must recover the recording of Aubrey's conversation with Kapustin. It would prove that it was the Russian who was refusing to come over, that Aubrey had been engaged in a proposed defection by Kapustin to the West. He must find it—Vienna Station *must* find it—

He studied the bill, counted notes onto the table, and then moved toward the back of the café and the telephones. Now, he was possessed by an urgent curiosity to discover how clever the KGB had been, to talk to Aubrey and even to Babbington. Also, part of him wanted to see Aubrey wriggle and scratch his way out of his dilemma.

He dialed the Vienna Station number, and when the switchboard answered, he supplied the current code identification. Almost immediately, he heard Wilkes's voice, breathy and urgent, at the other end of the line.

"Patrick? Where have you been, man?" Wilkes exclaimed, his urgency creating a ringing suspicion in Hyde that was immediately subdued by Wilkes's next words. "The old man's been crying out in his sleep for you! Where the hell did you get to?"

"I—a little local difficulty," Hyde replied, reading the felt pen graffiti on the mirror in the phone booth. Punk rock, the inevitable swastika, telephone numbers promising sodomites' paradise. He closed the door of the booth against a burst of laughter from the café. Outside, in hard-and-shadowed lighting, tipsy jollity suggested normality. He had been stupid. Even in danger of his life, he had been stupid.

"He's all right?" he asked.

"Furious—you know him," Wilkes replied confidentially. There was a chuckle in his voice. So *normal*—

A gale of laughter from the café was like a concussion

against the glass. A waitress passed the booth in a checked apron that matched the row of tablecloths.

"What's going on?"

"Christ—Babbington and his merry men haven't confided in me. They're in a huddle with Aubrey now. All sorts of charges are flying around."

"The KGB tried to kill me—"

"What?" Wilkes was incredulous.

"It's their setup, has to be. *Teardrop* was watching from the wings. . . ." Wilkes was silent for a moment. Hyde added: "It's all Kapustin's game—the tape will prove that."

"What tape, Patrick?" Wilkes asked eagerly.

"Aubrey was wired—"

"Yes—we saw that. Where's the tape?"

"I dropped the bloody thing in the Belvedere."

"We'll take care of it!" It sounded like relief, even to the sigh that followed the words. Hyde was puzzled. Then Wilkes removed the impression as he said with urgent concern: "Come in, Patrick. This is just what the old man needs. We'll find that tape—*you* talk to Babbington."

"Have they arrested the old man?"

"Christ knows! The mutual embarrassment's like a fog in here. But everyone looks serious—deadly serious."

"Okay."

"Where are you?"

For a moment Hyde studied the number on the dial of the telephone, and the location information. Another gust of laughter concussed the glass. He turned his head. Normal. Aubrey needed his information.

"Okay," he said. "Small café, in the Goldschmidgasse, near the cathedral. I'll be inside."

"Hang on. We'll have a car there for you in ten minutes. Anyone suspicious in the area?"

"No. I wasn't followed, once I shook them off."

"Good. Thank God you're all right. Everyone was worried. . . ."

"Okay, Wilkes. Hurry."

"Ten minutes at the outside."

Hyde put down the receiver. The scrawled-upon mirror was cloudy, and the glass of the booth had become dulled with the raised temperature. He folded back the door and stepped into the café. Strangely, the laughter had a mocking rather than comforting ring. He shivered, and returned to his table. The notes had been collected. He left the pile of change and pulled his overcoat from the back of his chair. He hesitated with one arm thrust into a sleeve, because the café was warm and because he realized that all he had to do was to wait. A matter of a few minutes. Outside there was the same sleet riding on a fresh wind as when he entered the café. Then he continued to put on the coat because he felt shaken into wakefulness by his instincts. He should check the area around the cathedral square. Someone still wanted him dead. Someone who spoke accentless English. That unwelcome realization bobbed out of the dark at the back of his mind, more real than the lights and the laughter and talk and the reassurances of Wilkes's voice.

He closed the door behind him. Sleet blew down the narrow Goldschmidgasse and through the halo of white light around a streetlamp in the Stephansplatz. The wind had strengthened, and it eased itself through his overcoat. He shivered, then turned toward the lights of the square, shoulders hunched, collar turned up, the melting sleet from his hair insinuating itself between his collar and skin. The west door of the Stephansdom was a gap of dark shadow in the sooty facade of the cathedral. Light burst from the metro entrance to his right. Hyde eased himself into the doorway of a shop and surveyed the square. Three minutes by his watch since he had put down the receiver. He had only to wait.

A group of people emerged from the mouth of the metro station, most of them young and noisy. He watched them bait each other, bait an old man, reel. One youth blundered against the shop's grilled window, pressing his nose flat as he tried to resolve the blurred souvenirs into distinct objects. Then he rolled on, bumping against Hyde before moving on. Hyde's body had flinched from the contact, and he was aware of his heightened nerves. The youth expelled beery breath and a hard laugh and almost returned to reproduce the fear he sensed, but then was towed by the laughter of his friends toward the north side of the cathedral. Couples drifted or were blown like black scraps across the square. Bodies crouched beneath umbrellas. Hyde's breathing returned to normal.

"Come on, come on," he murmured. Six minutes, and his feet were cold through the suede boots. His hands seemed numb in his pockets. "Come on . . ."

An old woman tottered down the steps into the metro

station. The light coming from it appeared now like the open mouth of a furnace as Hyde became colder. He could wait there.

He moved out of the doorway. Sleet slapped against his cheek. He hurried across the square, head bowed, into the darkness beneath the archway of the cathedral's west door. He pressed his back against the wood, then scanned the square once more.

And saw the first of them. He had been looking for surveillance, something that might prevent his reaching the car. Someone stumbling upon him by chance. He found purpose. He found informed opinion. Knowledge. The car in the Goldschmidgasse, coming from the far end of the narrow street, extinguished its lights perhaps seven seconds before it turned into a parking space. And the man he had seen on foot, moving from the Rotenturm toward the side street, had signaled to it. He shuddered, pressing his arms against his sides to still the quivering of his body. Overcoat, sports jacket, woollen shirt, skin. He was intensely aware of his vulnerability.

Second man, third man . . .

One had come out of the mouth of the metro station in a dark hat and overcoat. The other had come from the cathedral's south side, moving purposefully across the still-lit windows of a men's outfitters. Dark hat, dark overcoat. Dressed for the weather but umbrellaless in the sleet. Erect, unaware of the weather, heads turning like pieces of machinery—oiled, regular, thorough. Point of convergence, the Goldschmidgasse. The first man he had seen paused in the shop doorway where Hyde had first placed himself.

Eight minutes. These people had come for him—by arrangement.

Hyde could not bring himself to admit the idea, even though the accentless voice cried in his head, *Kill him, kill him. . . .* He was able, just, to hold the idea of *collusion* simply as an unfamiliar word in his awareness. It did not burgeon into acts, arrangements, betrayals, pain, faces. Eight minutes, thirty—

Move, he told himself. Go now. Fourth man. He scanned the Stephansplatz. A dark figure beneath a streetlamp, then another passing across the lights from a coffeehouse window. Point of convergence, the Goldschmidgasse—

Then a knot of men appeared at the corner of the narrow

street, moving urgently. The figures he had identified spread outward, like seed cast from a hand. The net spread; men began running. A second earlier, they had been evident by their immobility in the wind that hurried the innocent across the square like leaves; now, they were moving more swiftly, projectiles rather than detritus. In that moment, it was already too late. Hyde was trapped in the doorway of the cathedral, the door locked against him.

His thoughts raced but held no form. Adrenaline offered itself, but with the crudeness of a one-swallow drink. Dark overcoat moving to the cathedral's north side, dark overcoat to the south side, skirting the square. Doorways checked. Two men coming across the square toward the west door and its concealing shadow, two more descending into the light of the metro station. Other, disregarded shapes drifted or hurried across the Stephansplatz, as unimportant as the sleet blown through the light of the lamps. Two men coming toward him, north side man closer than the man on the south side. Eight men altogether; nothing being left to chance. Substitution, *collusion*—now when he didn't want them the images came to accompany the word. Wilkes's voice, the accentless English in the palace grounds, Kapustin watching, Babbington arresting Aubrey for treason—the arrangement of his own capture and murder.

Now—

South side man perhaps thirty yards from him, the two men crossing the square, one taller than the other, broader, striding more quickly—they were fifteen yards, fourteen, twelve . . .

He ran.

Hyde's boots skidded on the little accumulation of sleety snow on the bottom step, then he turned to his left, thrust away from the sooty, crumbling stonework, head down. A shout, other shouts like answering hunting horns. The south side man hurrying almost at once, without noticeable shock delay. Hyde rounded the west facade into deeper shadow, hearing the footsteps behind him over the pounding of his heart; over the drumming realization that he was running into a narrowing canyon behind the cathedral where the pedestrianized streets on the north and south sides converged. At that instant, men were running along the north side, beneath the unfinished, capped tower of the Stephansdom, to head him off. It was a race. There would be no doubling back, no luck of deception. Point of convergence—himself. He would have to outrun them.

Lights from fashionable, expensive apartments above fashionable, expensive shops. Shoes gleamed in a soft-lit window. A couple huddled in chilly passion in the shop's doorway. The shadows along the cathedral wall were deep, almost alive. Hyde skidded again, and his hand rubbed against cold stone as he righted himself. He could hear the beat of footsteps ahead and behind him.

Shop window, doorway, couple, dark side street . . .

He turned, saw the three men bearing down on him, and then fled down the narrow street, away from the cathedral. Their pursuit resounded from the blank, gray walls of the tall houses. Left into a narrow alley with light at the other end, then right and across the street, hearing a car moving away from him and the sudden, chilling screech of a cat, then another alley, then a lightless street after the loom of a church.

He paused and listened. The car's noise had faded. There was the noise of someone blundering into a trash can, music from an upstairs window, and the beat of footsteps—splitting up, the noises moving away. He crossed the street and walked swiftly, hands in his pockets. A man emerged from the alley into the dark street. He was alone, and nothing more than a shadowy lump. Then he moved off in the opposite direction.

Sausages hung in the unlit window of a delicatessen; fat, ripe, Daliesque. His dark, narrow features stared out at him in reflection. He looked abandoned, inadequate. He had no cover, no luggage, no hotel, no backup. Wilkes had set the KGB on him.

A Mercedes roared past, startling him, making his hand reach instinctively in to the breast of his overcoat toward the butt of the gun. Then he relaxed, and looked again at his slight, hunched figure and the sallow reflection of his face. He began walking slowly on, with no purpose other than to conceal himself.

"Is this to be the beginning or the end of this—*lunacy*?"

Sir Andrew Babbington, Director-General of MI 5, lowered himself with studied casualness into the armchair opposite Aubrey, and then looked up into the older man's face as if assessing the visible symptoms of a disease. Aubrey waved his glance aside with an angry gesture that underlined his enraged question.

"Kenneth—"

"Babbington, I asked you a question. Pray do me the courtesy of replying."

"This is Colonel Eldon," Babbington said, indicating his companion, "of our Counterespionage Branch." His smile indicated that he considered he had answered Aubrey's inquiry. Eldon nodded.

"Sir Kenneth," he murmured. Eldon, behind his military moustache, was sleek, handsome, clear-eyed; he was also tall. And Aubrey sensed a tough doggedness just beneath the surface of this senior interrogator. For a moment, Aubrey's heart beat with a ragged swiftness. He gripped the arms of his chair to suppress the quiver of his hands. The game had begun in earnest. There was no room for mistakes, no margin for error.

"I have been held under what I can only consider to be house arrest for two days. My telephone has been tapped, there have been guards at my door. My housekeeper has been allowed to go shopping only after a humiliating search. She is searched again when she returns. Oh, sit down, Eldon!" He waved his hand toward the unoccupied sofa. Eldon sank into its deep cushions. The interruption had defused Aubrey's angry protest.

Babbington said, "You wish the charges against you to be clarified?" There was something sharp gleaming through the man's urbanity, and it worried Aubrey.

"What charges?"

"Charges of treason," Babbington snapped.

"So you said at the Belvedere, and again at the embassy—and again on the aircraft and in the car from Heathrow. You must be more explicit," Aubrey added with a calm acidity he did not feel.

Babbington grinned. Apparently, a moment for which he had been waiting had arrived. Eldon, too, seemed pleased that a point of crisis had been reached. He was stroking his moustache in a parody of the military man he had once been. His eyes appeared blank and unfocused, and Aubrey realized that the man was dangerously intelligent, dangerously good at his job.

"Very well, Kenneth," Babbington sighed.

"You'll have to try very hard, Babbington—even were I guilty!" Aubrey snapped, surprised at his own rage.

"Oh, we realize it will be a very long job, Sir Kenneth," Eldon murmured.

"Why have I been denied all access to the Minister, to the Chairman of the JIC—whom I might expect to be here in your stead, incidentally—and even to the Cabinet Office?"

"Because for the present, and until this matter is resolved—the power of all three lies in me."

"I see," Aubrey replied. He controlled the muscles of his face, which wished to express apprehension, even shock. "Yet another rearrangement of our peculiar hierarchy, I gather," he murmured contemptuously.

Babbington merely smiled. Aubrey had been appointed as "C" after the retirement of Sir Richard Cunningham. The appointment had coincided with the changes in the Joint Intelligence Committee that the Franks Report on the Falklands campaign had urged. The Chairmanship of the JIC had been lost by the Foreign Office and MI 5, under Babbington, had seized its chance to bask in the sun. MI 5 had survived the Blunt, Hollis, Long scandals and emerged in the ascendent under a younger, more virile leadership. SIS was regarded as a country for old men, Aubrey being the oldest among them. Everyone was waiting for his retirement. Sir William Guest, as Chairman of the JIC and with the ear of the PM, had his own plans for a combined security and intelligence service. And Aubrey knew that he intended Babbington to head the new service, SAID.

Everyone—friends and enemies alike, simply *everyone*—was waiting for Aubrey's retirement. He was the single stumbling block between them and their plans and dreams, because he would not agree, even in principle, to the amalgamation of the security and intelligence services of his country. His opposition had earned him little short of the enmity of the PM, the Cabinet Secretary, the Home Secretary, Guest, and the JIC . . . almost the whole group. But he would not bow to pressure.

He dismissed the futile anger, the righteous self-justification. It was part of the past already. History. It would not serve him now, surrounded as he was by people who wished him gone, like a dinner guest outstaying his welcome. This accusation, this frame-up, had fallen into their laps. His enemies would be eager to believe it—they all wanted to be rid of him!

He could almost see the impatience in Babbington's eyes,

sense it in the room. He would be removed and the new service would be inaugurated, and Babbington would have his place in the sun.

Aubrey controlled his features once more. They had him now. Another Russian agent. Babbington was outraged, even vengeful, being an old family friend of the Castlefords.

Evidently his face had again betrayed his thoughts, because Babbington smiled and said with silky threat: "Whatever else may or may not be true, Kenneth—if you betrayed Robert Castleford to the NKVD in 1946, I will have your head. I promise you that." The anger was cold, well-savored. It was an emotion that had become a motive, a mainspring of action. Aubrey avoided glancing toward Eldon's glittering eyes.

Then Eldon said: "Sir Kenneth . . ." Aubrey looked venomously in his direction. "Perhaps you would prefer that these conversations . . ." His hands moved apart, suggesting the passage of a great deal of time; a time without specified term. ". . . take place at one of our—residences out of town?"

Aubrey shook his head. "I'm sure you realize that I would prefer to cling to the familiar?" he replied with an acid smile. "In this case, however, I would be using my surroundings as a constant reminder of what is at stake for me—what I might lose. You would prefer to remain here, too, I suspect—comfort and familiarity can be great betrayers." Eldon nodded his head in acknowledgment. "No, we'll stay here, I think. Coffee?" he added brightly.

"Please."

Aubrey lifted the small silver bell which Mrs. Grey had instructed him to buy and use as a proper means of summoning her, and it tinkled softly in the comfortable room whose window looked north over Regent's Park. The central heating clunked dully. The morning's headlines lay exposed and sharp on the table beside Aubrey's chair.

When he had ordered coffee, Aubrey said: "Why wasn't the press kept quiet, Babbington? Why the hue and cry? I can't see how that can be to your advantage. . . ."

"Not us. The Americans, we're pretty sure. They're impatient for answers, for proof."

"Ah. They'd prefer to see the ascendency of your service completed." His face folded into bitter creases, and his hand plucked for a moment at the fringing on the armchair. "As would HMG, now that there is the slightest doubt about myself. No country for old men, mm?" He looked up at Babbington, whose face was as immobile as if he had suffered a stroke. One eyelid flickered for a moment. Then Aubrey laughed, a short, derisive bark. "My God, Babbington, you really *do* have a lot to gain from my guilt!"

"And are you guilty, Sir Kenneth?" Eldon interjected.

Aubrey threw down his challenge. "I was using more sophisticated techniques of interrogation when you were still wondering about the birds and the bees, Eldon."

"I'm well aware of your reputation, Sir Kenneth."

"Ah, coffee—excellent. Thank you, Mrs. Grey."

Mrs. Grey deposited the silver tray on the sideboard, bestowed glances of proprietorial malice upon Aubrey's visitors, and then left the room. Aubrey poured the coffee, fussing over it in a caricature of aged bachelorhood. He flexed mental muscles as he did so. Then he returned to his seat.

"Well, gentlemen?" he asked brightly. "I have the last forty-five years to lose, and the emperor's new clothes. . . ." He indicated the large room and its furniture. "Perhaps you'd better begin."

Immediately, Eldon said: "Sir Kenneth, did you know that at your last Helsinki meeting your controller was wired for sound, even though you were not . . . by his request, if I remember your report correctly."

Aubrey was silent for some moments. The information had winded him. Suspicions crowded in his mind, just out of the light. "Wired for sound? *Controller!*" He squeezed contempt into his voice.

"Your KGB contact, if you prefer," Eldon corrected himself. "Yes, wired for sound. We have the tape."

"Then—"

"It seems very conclusive."

"Where is it?"

"We'll let you hear it, Kenneth," Babbington soothed, savoring Aubrey's failure of nerve.

"Conclusive, you say. Then why the need for . . . ?"

"Conclusive of treason, perhaps I should have said, Sir Kenneth."

"Then it's faked! Where did you get it?"

"The Finns. They have people in the Soviet *apparat* in Helsinki. One of them got it out, the Finns handed it straight on to us—to Sir William and the Cabinet Office. . . ."

"You bloody fools—you *dangerous* fools!" Aubrey snapped.

"We're in the process of submitting it to the most stringent technological tests, Sir Kenneth," Eldon continued, unperturbed. "I may say that, thus far, it holds up. It would appear to be genuine. The meeting took place at the zoo. Near the monkey house, from the background noises."

"Kenneth," Babbington interrupted with what might have been genuine concern, "it's not good. This tape holds up just like the file that fell into the hands of the CIA. They're convinced that file is genuine—and so are we." His voice hardened on the last few words, as if he were pressing them in a vise.

"My God . . ." Aubrey whispered. He saw the way ahead very clearly; a dark path between close, high trees in failing light. It was the only path, and his feet were already upon it.

"The file indicates quite clearly that you were the instrument of Robert Castleford's betrayal," Babbington insinuated. The use of his name brought the man himself back vividly to Aubrey; not the photograph in the newspapers or on the television, but a haggard, defeated, cunning face—the last time he had seen Castleford alive. An older, surprised, appalled, finally dangerous Castleford. Careful of your face, your eyes, Aubrey reminded himself, as if afraid that the memories would become visible.

"I'm afraid that is precisely what the *Teardrop* file indicates, Sir Kenneth," Eldon agreed.

"What did you call it?" Aubrey demanded, stunned.

"*Teardrop*." Eldon appeared to permit himself a smile, and a catlike smoothing of his moustache. His eyes glinted with concentration. "Your codename, apparently."

"*My* codename? My *God*!" Aubrey half raised himself from his chair. "You know it was *his* codename, dammit!"

"Do we? The file now in Washington has *Teardrop* upon its cover. It was opened in 1946, Sir Kenneth."

"But you've checked the records—dammit, you know that Kapustin was *Teardrop*. . . ." His jaw dropped. "The records are ambiguous," he admitted in a hoarse whisper. "I could just as easily have been meeting—my controller from Moscow. . . ."

"Precisely, Sir Kenneth."

"And you—have drawn that conclusion."

"Let's say we're proceeding on that assumption, Kenneth," Babbington supplied. "It will be up to you to disprove it, if you can."

"I might add, Sir Kenneth, that we have some film with the Helsinki tape. We're examining that, too, for signs that it might be a forgery. We don't think it is."

Aubrey shook his head weakly, and then looked at them, his eyes moving from face to face. He felt as close to pleading with them as he felt distant from their sympathy and understanding.

"Where's Hyde?" he asked unexpectedly. "Why did he flee the scene?"

Babbington appeared taken aback.

"We—we're looking for him now."

"He hasn't called in?"

"No."

"Why not? What smell's in his nose, Babbington?"

"Hyde could be on a binge for all we know, Sir Kenneth," Eldon said dismissively.

"Good God, man—you're not even interested!" His outburst was directed at Babbington. "I have been cleverly— very cleverly—framed, and you are going along with it out of personal ambition!"

Babbington stood up quickly. His eyes glared at Aubrey.

"If you want a *personal* motive, Kenneth," he said, "then I should try revenge rather than ambition. You betrayed Robert Castleford—you've betrayed everybody and everything for the last thirty-five years and more!" Babbington's mouth clamped into a thin line, then he added in a quieter voice: "We'll leave you for a few hours now, Kenneth. Shall we say two-thirty this afternoon? We'll be taping, naturally."

Babbington strode to the door. Eldon followed him with an easy, relaxed step. At the door, however, the colonel turned to Aubrey and said: "You will recall, Sir Kenneth, that the emperor had no new clothes." Then he shut the door behind him.

Aubrey heard Mrs. Grey usher the two men coldly from the apartment, and consciously suppressed his sudden desire for alcohol. A large cognac would be craven, not medicinal. The wall lights in the lounge, switched on because of the lowering gray sky outside, glinted on the crystal decanters next to the silver coffee pot.

For two days they had left him alone and unvisited. And uninformed. Alone with his growing suspicions and his imaginings. Now, a series of detonations had damaged, perhaps destroyed, his foundations. He was like an old building that tottered from the concussions. Tapes, films, files—*Teardrop*. Above all, that clever, clever, *clever* codename—*calm down*. . . .

All he had known before that morning had been gathered from the newspapers, and the television the previous evening—early news, *Nine O'Clock News*, *News at Ten*, *Newsnight*, the endless repetition of a growing nightmare.

Two species of treachery, separate yet interwoven. In December 1946, he had betrayed Robert Castleford, a distinguished civil servant working for the Allied Control Commission in postwar Berlin, and ever since then he had been a double agent, at first for the NKVD, then later the MVD, finally the KGB. For more than thirty-five years he had led a secret life. He was Philby, he was Blunt, he was Burgess—he was worse than any of them.

Mrs. Grey's head appeared at the door, and hastily withdrew as he turned a baleful glance upon her.

And he could never prove his innocence.

He could never tell the truth, not about December 1946, not about Castleford.

Impatiently, leadenly, he paced the room. *The emperor had no new clothes.* Silver, white napery, jade; velvet, wool, crystal, china, porcelain, oak, walnut. *The emperor had no new clothes.* KCVO. Sir Kenneth. Director-General. *The emperor had no new clothes.*

He could never tell the truth. There was a crime, but he could never reveal it. He would not be believed. He would never be believed innocent. He would only compound his guilt if he told the truth, because he had killed Robert Castleford.

In a gray tin box, in the safekeeping of one of the few people who had never lost his trust, his motives lay bound in leather, inside a buff envelope. He had written the account immediately in the wake of Castleford's murder. After the war, it had lain in a deposit box in his bank. His secret, his bane. His leather-bound guilt and conscience. Then, in 1949, when he had met Clara Elsenreith once again, in Vienna during his service there with the Allied Control Commission, he had surrendered the journal—confession?—into her safekeeping. She still possessed it. All the reasons were there, he had fully explained them; but now those reasons would never excuse the crime. The truth would finish him as effectively as the KGB's lies. He had killed Robert Castleford.

The emperor had no new clothes, he thought bitterly, anger vying in his chest and stomach with growing fear, so that he felt inflated. Asphyxiated. His head had suddenly begun to pound, and the chill gray light from the tall windows pained his eyes. The trap was perfect. *Teardrop*—Deputy Chairman Kapustin—had set him up to perfection, had led him by the nose for two unsuspecting years while his damnation was arranged. His heart pumped, his head beat with his impotent rage and accusations of failure and gullibility. He had been tricked—*he* had been tricked. . . .

He banged his fists against his thighs as he paced back and forth across the length of the lounge. The icing on the cake was to make him appear to have been activated as a Soviet agent; it clinched the guilt they had suggested for him in 1946. *The emperor had no new clothes*.

The KGB had him. *Teardrop* was now *his* codename, the codename of a traitor, a traitor who was Director-General of SIS. The trap had closed.

Crystal, jade, silver: presents for the nativity of his promotion. The emperor's clothes. Unreal, like the new apartment overlooking Regent's Park, like the new housekeeper, like the new office at Century House, overlooking the river; like his knighthood, which he had been so long in taking. He had been moated with fulfilled ambitions, but now they had him, inescapably, finally. For he had killed Castleford, and the Russians evidently knew that, and upon their knowledge the whole strategy turned. He had killed him and had hidden the crime for thirty-five . . . for so *many* years. . . .

His heart pumped and his head throbbed. His body felt too frail to support his emotions and their physical manifestations. The doorbell rang, startling him. He heard his old, weary breathing in the silence that followed, and surrendered to hopelessness. Mrs. Grey answered the door as he experienced dread at the possible return of Babbington and Eldon with all the virulence of an aging woman unprepared by makeup and rest for the arrival of visitors.

Into Aubrey's mind a clear, high, pure treble voice floated, an almost unearthly sound. A boy's voice. The words of the hymn or anthem, whichever it was, were indistinguishable in the echoing innocence of the voice. Perhaps *Abide with me*, perhaps the *Nunc Dimittis*. He knew only that he was singing in his vividly remembered childhood. A cathedral nave crowded in upon him. White surplices ghostly in an incensed gloom. His father, the disgruntled, vicious, bigoted cathedral verger, was there, smiling; his lips drawn back over his teeth in the demonstration of a snarl.

Aubrey was frightened of the memory; not because of its potency, but because it seemed to herald an incontinence of mind that endangered him. It was an involuntary retreat from the present when he needed all his energies, all his concentration, simply to survive.

He looked up, visibly shaken, as Paul Massinger appeared at the door, unannounced. Aubrey's eyes narrowed in calculation and surprise. He saw Massinger's handsome face register shock and he recalled Massinger's wife: Castleford's daughter. Then Aubrey pushed himself firmly to his feet.

"Paul, my dear fellow! How good of you to come. . . ."

"Kenneth—you're all right? You look—"

"Yes, yes," Aubrey replied testily. "A little tired. Sit down, sit down."

Massinger chose Eldon's place on the sofa, opposite Aubrey. Aubrey noticed the walking stick and the moment of discomfort as Massinger lowered himself into the cushions. The man's breath escaped in a sigh.

"I—" Massinger began.

"A drink?" Aubrey suggested, almost involuntarily beginning to control the situation.

"Thank you. Scotch and soda—heavy on the soda." When Aubrey had poured the drinks and returned to his seat, he sensed, what was it? A shiftiness, evasion like a mist around his friend. Why had he come? What did he want here? Sympathy—or *aid*? Aubrey caught his breath. Then felt his optimism sag and fold like a deflating balloon. Paul Massinger had no official status and little influence. He could do nothing. Yet Aubrey could not prevent himself from snatching at hope, however futile.

Into the silence between their raised glasses, Massinger blurted: "I—I came to offer my, my sympathies. . . ."

Then he had no help to offer, Aubrey reflected bitterly. Mere sympathy, which he despised, especially since the sympathy of a close friend affected him, however much he resisted it, with contempt.

"Thank you, Paul," he managed to say. There was something else; the shifty look would not leave the American's eyes. . . . He was embarrassed by his motives for being there.

Castleford's daughter . . . of *course*. Aubrey kept the bitter sneer from his features. Paul had come to find out whether he had murdered the woman's father! It was too much, really too much!

Aubrey wanted to embarrass, even wound. He said, with studied gentleness, "I'm grateful, Paul, to an old friend . . . but what is it? Something seems to be worrying you? What is it?"

Massinger's face flickered with pain at each of the soothing ironies. He looked down at his shoes, then up again into Aubrey's face, his eyes searching for something—an answer which would avoid a spoken question. Aubrey maintained a blank, gently smiling expression, eyes widely innocuous.

"It's—Margaret . . ." The words seemed excavated from some deep mine within him. "Margaret and her father!" It was a plea for assistance, as if it were Massinger who found himself trapped and alone. Afraid. Aubrey could feel only a heaviness in his chest, his thoughts filled with a wish to fling up mental arms against the anticipated blow of Massinger's honesty and doubt.

"What—about Margaret?" he asked, sighing, beginning to manipulate the situation almost by instinct rather than in expectation. Massinger could do nothing for him, after all—

"There's nothing in this nonsense, of course!" Massinger cried. His hand swept in front of him, the gesture of a blind man feeling for obstacles. The sight angered Aubrey, but his voice was level, spiced with the right amounts of sincerity, gravity, and affection as he replied.

"Paul, I give you my solemn word on it. I did not betray Robert Castleford to the NKVD. That is a complete fabrication."

He had molded his features to an expression of pained but determined honesty. His eyes expressed the intimacy of long friendship and the lack of deception between two such old friends. Massinger studied his face for a long time, then he finally nodded.

"Thank God," he whispered, "thank God."

"Why did you come, Paul?" Aubrey asked more briskly, patting Massinger's knee. "What's happened?"

Massinger's eyes were eager for understanding and even sympathy. They reflected the depths of a private world such as Aubrey had never experienced, and created envy, and irritation. No—Massinger would be of no assistance to him. . . .

At last, he sighed. "God, Kenneth, you know the old, old story!" Despite his irritation, Aubrey responded sympathetically to the painful sincerity, the anguish. Yes, he knew. By a mere coincidence, it had been he who had introduced them, Massinger, the long-time widower, and Margaret, though he had not known Margaret Castleford well. She had always had money, all the trappings appropriate to a real life, but nothing of the inner certainty, the sense of identity, to really live. Aubrey had never much liked her. Dinner parties at the Massingers' had been prickly with a possessive tension on her part, a defensiveness—as if Aubrey were a rival for her husband's affections. She clung to Paul almost as to a life raft.

Yet, the Massingers had seemed happy, at least until now. They had married and spectacularly failed to fulfill the anticipations of onlookers by being and remaining happy. Now . . . now, it seemed that Massinger feared his wife would adopt her past like old and familiar clothes. He had to be reassured—anger rose in Aubrey and he quelled it with difficulty . . . *he had to reassure Massinger of his innocence!* The lie was easy—it was the demand for it that pained him.

"I know," he soothed. "I'm just sorry this business has brought it back to her so vividly and abruptly. She—yes, she would believe me guilty, of course?"

Massinger nodded. "She's—in a state of shock, of course," he murmured, as if it excused something. "But—her father's very special, still."

"I understand. She won't stop to question whether or not she has heard the truth. I'm sorry for that."

"I—maybe if I explain to her, tell her what you've said?"

"Perhaps," Aubrey sighed, impatient with the incoming tide of this private life so deep and intense that it made him envious even as it irritated him. It was not Margaret Massinger, suddenly, who had skated across the pond surface of life for so many years . . . it was himself. He dismissed the image. In this mood, Massinger was *dangerous to him*!

Margaret Massinger would be demanding, irrational, selfish. Paul would be forbidden to help him, would abandon him as everyone else had done . . . *self-pity*, he warned, eschewing it with a violent distaste. *Not yet, things aren't that bad yet*. . . .

"Kenneth, I'm sorry," Massinger said then, surprising

Aubrey—as if he had apologized for the abandonment Aubrey had been imagining.

"Yes?"

"By rights, you should have kicked me out the moment I asked." He essayed a warm, almost boyish grin. Aubrey forgave him; began to consider his usefulness even as Massinger added: "It's not your problem. . . . I'm only sorry Margaret will blame you. . . ." He shook his head. "It's not your problem, you're innocent—" It was as if the idea had struck him forcibly, a new concept he had not previously entertained. "What do *they* believe, Kenneth?" he asked.

"They've abandoned me, Paul. The Cabinet Office, the Foreign Secretary, JIC, the PM herself—abandoned me."

"The ingratitude of princes? Surely they don't *believe* any of it?"

"Margaret does," Aubrey snapped waspishly, and Massinger colored quickly. "I'm sorry, Paul—that was unforgivable." And it was. Paul was enthusiastic in his defense, and might be used, in that mood. Don't wound the man! Perhaps he could fulfill the role of contact, messenger? "They want me out of the way, of course," he continued levelly. "They want the reins in Babbington's hands."

"But *why*?"

Aubrey did not answer immediately, but crossed to the sideboard and returned with the whiskey decanter. He began speaking as he refilled their glasses, his mind racing, calculating how he could use Paul's new sense of indebtedness. There were other, professional debts, too, which he hoped Massinger would have in mind as he listened. He talked urgently, eagerly, the story tumbling out. It took only minutes.

". . . and the original *Teardrop* was the Deputy Chairman himself. He set me up for this. For all of it." Massinger had remained silent throughout his narrative. Even as he spoke, Aubrey had watched the American's face, seeing, to his great relief, behind the quick flicker of emotions, the recurring signals in his eyes. Paul Massinger was remembering, was aware of the debt he owed Aubrey; wished to avoid repayment, wanted to leave . . . but the sense of obligation was increasing, weighing on him. Aubrey hoped it was heavy enough to prompt the American to action, even in the face of his wife's undoubted hatred of Aubrey himself. . . .

"And JIC really believes this cock-and-bull story?" Massinger finally asked.

"Down to the last fabricated detail, I'm afraid," Aubrey replied, sipping at his drink, watching Massinger's clouded face. His jaw worked slightly, as if the American were trying to masticate the information prior to swallowing it.

When he looked up, he asked: "Why should the KGB want you so thoroughly disgraced?"

Aubrey controlled his breathing. Massinger's eyes were brighter, *involved!* He was alert, almost eager, confronted with the mechanism of an intelligence operation. He had been a good CIA operative: intelligent, quick, decisive. Now, a former professional self seemed to be breaking through the layers of the academic and the married man like something through the walls of its chrysalis. *Thank God for it—*

Now, Massinger might help him. In small ways, of course—furtively and behind his wife's back—but he might assist . . . there was, too, that certain, strong loyalty to friends and a priggish sense of right and wrong. Combined, a heady brew. It might prompt Massinger now into vigorous mental life, into excitement, like strong drink. And there was the debt. Aubrey had once saved the man's career by establishing the presence of a double agent in one of Massinger's networks. The double had betrayed the network. It had not been lost, as had originally been suspected, because of Massinger's incompetence or neglect. The debt had never been repaid, except in loyal friendship. Now, however, something more concrete might be offered . . . but he would have to tread with the utmost caution. Margaret Massinger and her bright new hatred of him waited in ambush at every turn of the conversation. Aubrey was certain that, forbidden by her, Massinger would not help him.

"To sow confusion?" Aubrey replied. "For revenge or mischief or both. If, after all the witch-hunts of the past decade we have indeed cleansed the stables and our security and intelligence services conceal no traitors in high places—then it would suit Moscow Centre's book to replace substance with shadow, would it not? I really don't know, Paul, I really don't!"

Massinger was silent for a time, then he said: "If Charlie Buckholz was alive, he'd never have let JIC see that file."

Aubrey remembered, vividly, Massinger's arm supporting him as they stood together at the damp, chilly graveside. The military chaplain had hurried his words, Buckholz's coffin had been lowered, and the Deputy Director of the CIA had vanished from their lives. Their mutual friend. Aubrey could have turned to him now, could have—

Massinger's eyes were heavy with memory, the dark stains of sleeplessness beneath them appearing like the underlinings of a purpose, a decision. Good—

"If I can do anything . . ." he said.

Aubrey suppressed a small shiver of success. "Thank you, Paul."

"How are you fixed here? What access do you have?"

"None. The telephone is tapped. I am guarded night and day. Fortunately, Babbington has been kind enough to keep the press away from my door. There are no other advantages to my isolation." His tone was bitter, mocking.

"Then what can you do?" Massinger asked. Aubrey recognized his reluctance, his sense of doubt. He could be a messenger, but little more—dammit!

"If only Hyde were here!" Aubrey burst out. "If only I could make contact with him, perhaps through Shelley . . ." Aubrey laid out the route for Massinger to take.

"Who's Hyde?"

"A good field man."

"Would he help?"

"Yes—if only I could reach him!"

"Where is he?"

"He was with me in Vienna when I was arrested. He—fled."

"Why?"

"I don't know. He must have had good reason. If only he would come in . . ."

"And Shelley might be able to contact him?"

"Peter Shelley has East Europe Desk now. I promoted him. He could help."

"Won't he have been warned off?"

"Yes. Yes, I think everyone will have been warned off. The situation is extreme—I am not believed. But I think Peter will come through. He *has* to—"

"Very well, Kenneth. I'll—see him for you. He must know where Hyde is, what happened in Vienna. I can do that for you. . . ." The last remark was almost shamefaced, as if there was more that should be offered. But Massinger recognized his lack of freedom to act. This much he could do without Margaret's anger, even knowledge.

"Invite him to lunch, that's safest—today," Aubrey instructed with a dry, hungry eagerness.

"As you wish. From a phone booth, naturally," Massinger replied with a grin. In a small way, he had rediscovered his addiction to the secret life. "Who's running our show?"

"Babbington. Keep out of his way."

"Andrew?" *A friend of Margaret and her family.* The thought was as tangible as words.

"The Cabinet Office—William Guest that is—has dumped everything in his lap. Director-General of MI 5, chief investigating officer in the case of yours truly, acting DG of SIS. An unparalleled array of finery!" he concluded with surprising venom.

"Could I talk to him unofficially, as a friend of Margaret?"

"Would that do any good? He wants my head and my job. . . . Like your dear wife, Paul, Babbington is convinced I'm guilty!"

"Okay, okay. What is it you want from Shelley—precisely?"

"He must find Hyde for me—and I must have access to the files on me . . . everything they're using to convict me. Peter can get his hands on it. I need everything. And tell him he must find Hyde!"

"Can you prove your innocence, without the shadow of a doubt?"

"I must. I must break the mirror and show the reality behind it. I am not *Teardrop*. I must prove that. Otherwise—" He waved his hands to indicate the room and its possessions. Motes of dust danced uncertainly in a beam of watery sunlight. Aubrey's face was gray in its pale light. "—all is lost. *I* am lost."

"You have to prove you controlled *Teardrop*, not he you."

"Exactly."

Massinger looked at his watch, then hoisted himself stiffly out of his chair, levering his body upright with the aid of the stick. The image of infirmity alarmed Aubrey. Leaning on his stick, he looked down at the older man.

"Okay, Kenneth. I'll see Shelley for you. It's the least I can do. . . ." *It's all I can do.* Aubrey reinterpreted the sentiment. Margaret evidently nagged at his thoughts, his conscience, even before he began. "I'll be in touch."

Aubrey shook Massinger's hand. Light flashed from the face of an expensive gold watch Margaret might have supplied.

"Thank you, Paul, thank you!" Aubrey said.

The upstairs room of Antoine's in Charlotte Street was almost empty. Peter Shelley watched Massinger over the rim of his glass, and then sniffed the Armagnac. He sipped at it, savored it, and sensed his moment. He shook his head firmly. Massinger's hand, about to pick up his demitasse of black coffee, quivered. The tiny cup rattled in its saucer.

"I'm sorry, Professor Massinger—there's nothing I can do. There's a shutdown order on everything. Christ, I'd like to help the old man—but he's out of bounds. They're watching me, for God's sake!"

"Who?"

"Babbington's chums. I'm near the top of the list of potential help the old man might try to employ. I couldn't fart without them knowing about it."

Massinger stared into his coffee, then absently swilled the pale Armagnac in his glass. From the moment the lobster had been served, he had known this would be the outcome. Aubrey's fall had left Shelley still in the directorship of East Europe Desk, but his hold upon his new office was precarious. He was an Aubrey man. He might yet go. Shelley was keeping his head down until the gunfire stopped.

"Babbington intends to control both services, finally?"

Shelley nodded. "Oh, yes. He's ambitious, and he's favored. It's happened before, in the 'sixties, and since then. One man doing both jobs. Babbington's the man, apparently."

"You must owe Aubrey a great deal," Massinger suggested.

Inwardly, he winced at his own indebtedness, which he knew he was afraid to honor. He felt guilty even sitting down to lunch with Shelley. Margaret was convinced—and it was not an irrational conviction, since it was shared by Aubrey's superiors and most senior colleagues—that Aubrey was a traitor and that he had murdered her father. That conviction was unshakable, dangerous to their future if he were seen to be doing anything to aid Aubrey. He looked up at Shelley, his eyes reflecting his self-criticism, appearing aloof to Shelley. "You owe him," Massinger repeated.

"I do," Shelley replied frostily, his face twisted into an ugly grimace as he drained his glass. He evidently disliked being reminded of his debts, especially by someone outside his service, and an American, at that. Massinger controlled his anger.

"And I'm aware of it, and I'm grateful. But I can do *nothing*." He leaned confidentially toward Massinger. "To begin with, JIC has impounded all the papers, the tapes, everything. Sir William sent in some people and they took stuff away by the truckload. And I just *can't* get you a transcript of the *Teardrop* file. It's much too hot and much too jealously guarded. I haven't even *seen* a copy. Any one of the few copies in existence would be missed immediately. I can't do it. The old man's being sent to the wall, Professor. There's nothing to be done about it."

Massinger sighed impatiently, admitting inwardly that Shelley was right. He was not even craven, simply right. "What about Hyde?"

"Mm. Vienna Station says he's disappeared. They've heard nothing from him."

"You don't believe that, do you?"

"Patrick Hyde's a funny bloke—but he wouldn't leave the old man up to his eyeballs in the shit without a very good reason."

"Then what does he know or suspect? What did he see or hear that night?"

"I've no idea."

"And you're not curious?"

"I can't get hold of him without going through Vienna Station. And I can't do that with any hope of secrecy. Hyde's cut off. He might even be dead."

"Why should he be dead?"

"I don't know," Shelley whispered fiercely with growing exasperation. "But unless he calls in, no one is ever going to find out what spooked him."

He owed Aubrey. It had become a chorus in his head, a refrain he could not quiet. Shelley's reluctance threw his own lack of assistance into sharp relief. He ought to do more. . . . Aubrey had saved his career before he had taken to the academic life, moved to England. Perhaps even here Aubrey had pulled strings for him, gotten him the contacts and the interviews and the *esteem* that had led to his professorship . . . he didn't know. He had to do *more*, a *little more*, at least!

"What's Hyde's home address?" he blurted out, afraid of his own new resolve.

"I—" Shelley paused, then said: "I'll write it down for you." He scribbled on the back of an envelope. Massinger pocketed it without reading the address. "He won't be there."

"Would there be anyone else at home?"

Shelley looked thoughtful. "There's a woman upstairs—she actually owns the place. His landlady. I've no idea *what* their real relationship is. Most odd . . ." He shrugged.

"Would he trust her? In trouble, would he try to contact her?"

"I don't know. Perhaps . . ."

Massinger leaned forward. "Look," he said, "you don't believe any of this nonsense against Aubrey, do you?"

Shelley shook his head. He looked young and cunning and ambitious and embarrassed. "No, of course not—"

"Then?"

"I *can't!*" he protested. His long index finger tapped the tablecloth, then stirred the crumbs from his bread roll as he continued. "There's nothing that can be done to help him, Professor. I *know* that. I'm there every day. No one is going to help him buck JIC, the Cabinet Office, and HMG. No one wants it to happen, but they can't fight it." He looked up from the curling comet's tail of crumbs on the white cloth. He shook his head emphatically. "Nothing can be done. The old man's beyond saving."

In the foyer of the InterContinental Hotel, Hyde passed a row of long mirrors that reflected a man perhaps he might not have recognized had he not created him. The glass windows of the souvenir shop mirrored him more palely than wide-skirted dolls and curved wooden pipes. Then the window of the newspaper shop caught and held him again. The face that stared back at him from the front page of the evening newspaper suddenly exposed the inadequacy of the moustache he wore as a disguise, with the clear spectacles and the three-piece business suit. His own face—the familiar one that confronted him in his shaving mirror and the face of the man who had slept rough for two nights in Vienna, by the river and then in an alley behind a restaurant—stared at him from the rack. His disguise was at once useless and foolish. Gingerly, he took one of the newspapers, flinching as a large, middle-aged Austrian did the same before passing into the shop to pay for it. Hyde opened the paper. The small headline and the story lay below the photograph. The snapshot was official. It matched his passport photograph. It *was* his passport photograph. SIS must have supplied it.

Drugs. Wanted for suspected drug offenses.

KGB—SIS—Viennese police.

He felt the weight of the falling net upon his shoulders.

Upstairs, in the suite he had booked with the passport he had stolen on the metro, the rest of his new clothes, the too-large suitcase that was part of his cover, the new toothbrush and comb and aftershave all waited like props he could no longer use because the play had closed. He had booked into one of Vienna's most expensive hotels because it would be among the small hotels and pensions that they would look for him first.

Now, drugs. He was a police matter. He shuffled the clear-glass spectacles on the bridge of his nose, fingered the pads in his cheeks; his disguise seemed pitiful, amateurish. He thrust the newspaper back into the rack, and walked away from the shop. Arabs lingered over coffee in the foyer; a group of Americans lined up at the registration desk; there was laughter from the bar. He reached the lifts, then paused.

What? Who?

He had not dared attempt to hire a car, or try the airport or the railway stations. Now, he might have to. Now he had to get out of Vienna before his face began to stare nightmarishly at him from lamp posts and newspaper and metro station walls and trolley car windows. This was only the opening bombardment. The pressure would increase, the crimes grow in enormity, his capture become more essential.

Savagely, he stabbed his finger on the button to summon the elevator. He needed to retreat to the hideously expensive suite on the tenth floor that he could not use any of his own credit cards to pay for. The doors sighed open and he stepped in. The elevator ascended, smooth and swift, as if rushing him away from possible identification and arrest. He felt fear—pure, undiluted, and inescapable. He knew he was beaten.

Train, car, bus, boat . . .

The elevator doors sighed open. He hurried along the corridor, passing an open suite door. Two Arab women and two children sat there, a tray of fruit and biscuits outside the door. They were prisoners of the hotel, like himself. He fumbled his key into the lock, opened the door, and closed and locked it behind him.

His breathing was loud and ragged. His body was heavy, wanting only to sink into the cushions of the sofa or lie upon the bed in the next room. His hands were shaking. There was no way out, his body urged. Give it up. . . .

Train, car, bus, boat, aircraft . . .

All watched. All watched.

The telephone lay on the writing desk. He could ring, call Parrish or Wilkes at the embassy, play along, ask them what they wanted—

Or just walk in. They couldn't execute him in cold blood. Whatever they wanted or didn't want from him, he could listen to them, agree to do it, forget what had happened. . . .

That would be easy—as easy as telling them about the tape he had dropped, the tape they undoubtedly had by now. He damned his stupidity, his gullibility, once more. Easy—

For them, killing him would be just as easy.

"Christ!" he exclaimed in an explosion of breath. "*Christ!*"

Then, involuntarily, he picked up the telephone and flicked over the directory of international code numbers on the desk, running his finger down the column of figures. He began dialing, first the code for the UK, then the London number. He could see the telephone—perhaps his cat was sitting by it, or looking lazily up at its summons. It was no doubt ensconced in Ros's apartment, above his own.

"Come on, come on . . ." he breathed.

Give up, some part of him suggested seductively.

"Screw that," he muttered, then: "Come on, Ros, come on, girlie . . ."

She knew where the other passports were, the money, the credit cards in another name. Would she bring them? At least she could send them.

"Come on, darling . . ." he muttered urgently as the telephone went on ringing in his apartment in Earl's Court.

2
Meat Market

The taxi dropped Paul Massinger at the corner of Philbeach Gardens and the Warwick Road and he walked quickly, his limp easing with exercise, along the crescent of the Gardens. Through the spaces between the houses he glimpsed the Earl's Court Exhibition Building, which lay behind the crescent. St. Cuthbert's Church, though elaborately Gothic, seemed shrunken and dwarfish by comparison as he passed it.

He felt a cold tickle of danger in his stomach as the afternoon closed in. Gaps in the darkening clouds were blue-turning-black already. There was a chilly sliver of fear in the small of his back. What he had suspected in the taxi was now confirmed. He had collided with reality and the impact had snatched away his breath and his wits, but he was certain that he was under surveillance.

The blue Cortina had stopped by the church. It had pulled out behind his taxi in Charlotte Street, and from time to time, he had seen it during the journey to Earl's Court. Now, there could be no fudging, no postponement of certainty. He could not remember having seen the same car in the vicinity of Aubrey's apartment, or on the way to Antoine's. But it had been there when he and Shelley had left, and it was still with him.

God, he had done no more than call on an old friend and eaten lunch with a second man, and someone already thought him worth tailing—

Shelley? he thought, and dismissed the idea. Babbington? The KGB? Who?

He shook his head, ridding himself of the questions as a dog might have done water from its coat. He studied the house numbers in the crescent. Bare trees flanked the railings of the gardens themselves, trunks black as iron. The grass beyond them was patchily white with old snow.

He climbed three steps to a front door, and studied the discolored cards below each doorbell. *P. Hyde* claimed one of them. On the second floor, he was informed in a more flowing script, lived *R. D. Woode*. He pressed the top floor bell. There was a delay, and then a tinny voice with a distinct Australian accent issued from the grille of the speaker above the bells.

"My name is Massinger—a friend of Kenneth Aubrey," he enunciated clearly in reply to the inquiry. "Am I speaking to Patrick Hyde's landlady?"

"You are, sport. He's away on business." Even through the distortions of the speaker, the voice seemed pinched and tense with knowledge.

"I know that. You know the name Aubrey, maybe?" Shelley knew nothing of Hyde's relationship with the woman. But he had felt Hyde trusted her—she might know Hyde's work . . . ?

"I know it."

"He's in trouble. He wants to know Mr. Hyde's whereabouts, urgently." Massinger felt the cold of the late afternoon seeping into him, mingling with the chill knowledge of the watchers in the blue Cortina. He was tempted to turn around, but remained hunched near the grille of the speaker.

"I know that, too," the voice admitted. Then, rallying: "Shit, what do you want, mister?"

"I'd like to talk to you. I assure you Kenneth Aubrey, Patrick Hyde's, er, employer sent me."

There was a long silence. Massinger heard a crow coughing in one of the naked trees. Then, in a graceless, churlish tone, the woman said: "I'll meet you outside his apartment. Second floor." There was a buzz, and he pushed open the door, letting it close behind him on its security springs. The hall smelled of cooking, but was carpeted and quiet. He went up the stairs as confidently as he could, wincing at the pain each tread caused in his hip.

Hyde's door was painted a garish crimson. Standing in front of it was a woman of perhaps two hundred pounds in a kaftan that billowed around her. She appraised him with keen brown eyes. Her dark hair was pulled back from a broad forehead and held in a ponytail. She held a bunch of keys in her hand.

"Massinger?" she asked.

"Yes." He held out his hand.

"Ros Woode," she acknowledged, gripping his hand firmly and then letting it drop. He studied her face. It was impassive almost to the point of boredom, but he sensed that the expression was adopted. A mask.

"Glad to meet you."

"You'd better come in."

She unlocked and opened the door into Hyde's apartment. The doors on either side of the tiny hall were closed, but the one ahead was open. A tortoiseshell cat appeared in the open doorway, stretching first its front then its back legs. Then it ingratiatingly rubbed itself against the woman's legs as she passed into the main living room. The cat followed her, then jumped back into an impression it had made in one of the sofa's cushions. An ironing board stood in front of the empty fireplace, a shirt draped over it, the iron standing sentinel. The woman allowed him to enter the room, then turned on him.

"Right, sport, let's begin with who you are, shall we?" she snapped.

"As I explained," Massinger began, leaning on his stick, "I'm a friend of Kenneth Aubrey, Mr. Hyde's—"

"I know what Hyde does."

"He trusts you that much?"

"Apparently. Now, this is his apartment, and as you can see for yourself, he isn't here."

"You read the papers?"

The woman's mouth twisted for a moment, and there was some secret knowledge gleaming in her eyes.

"So?"

"Hyde wasn't arrested at the same time as Kenneth Aubrey—but, of course, you already know that . . . ?"

"What the bloody—?" Then her mouth clamped shut in a line that emphasized self-reproach. Then she said: "Sorry, sport, I don't know what you're talking about."

"I see." He glanced around the room. He registered the reproductions, mostly of French Impressionists, the velvet curtains, the pale carpet, the honey-painted fireplace, the green plants, the good pieces of furniture. It was an unexpected impression of Hyde.

"In case you're wondering, I chose most of the stuff. I wouldn't let Hyde buy the place, and I wouldn't let him put the junk he brought with him in one of my apartments. So, he bought new—on my instructions."

Massinger studied the woman. Like Shelley, he had no inkling as to her relationship with Hyde. He wanted not to consider her too fat, too plain to appeal sexually, but the thought continued to intrude. What did she feel for Hyde, he for her?

Carefully, he said: "Could I ask you to do something for me?"

"Depends."

"Just listen, then," he instructed. "If you should hear from Mr. Hyde—" He held up his hand to stifle her protest. "—if you should hear from him, would you please tell him of my visit, and tell him also that I have been asked by Sir Kenneth Aubrey to try to contact him. Sir Kenneth has to talk to your—tenant, it's a matter of the utmost urgency. Hyde may hold the key to Aubrey's predicament. The KGB have framed Aubrey. Tell him that, and tell him that I firmly believe it to be the case." Massinger cursed inwardly. He needed something that would convince this woman, but he had nothing to offer. . . . He did not want to help, he wanted to leave—if only he could say to himself, with some semblance of conviction, that he had done what was asked of him. Done enough. But he could not. More immediately, he needed a password, a token of good faith that would convince Hyde to contact Aubrey through himself. Yet he knew nothing about the man. What—

"Has Hyde worked for Aubrey long, do you know?"

"He has. Why?" The woman seemed subdued now. She appeared to wish to believe him. He realized she must have been in touch with Hyde and had been warned against visitors.

"I'm trying to find something that will convince him I'm a genuine friend, not a trap. But I can't. All I can tell you is that I am the husband of the daughter of the man Aubrey is supposed to have betrayed to the Russians. I am working behind my wife's back in trying to arrange this contact for Aubrey."

"Christ, mate . . ." the woman breathed.

"Which either makes me Aubrey's bitter enemy or his one real friend. Hyde must decide if I can be trusted. If he contacts you again, or if you can reach him, tell him everything

I've said . . . and that he must contact me so that I can relay what he knows to Aubrey. That's—all I can do, but it may help Aubrey. Will you do that?"

The woman hesitated for a long time, and then she finally, reluctantly, nodded.

"I'll do it—*if* I hear from him," she grudgingly agreed.

"Thank you. Now, I'll leave you. Good afternoon, Ms. Woode." He inclined his head, and turned to leave the room. The woman made no effort to recall him, and Massinger was dubious as to his success. She might just warn Hyde off.

He closed the door of the apartment behind him and went down the stairs. A young woman passed him in the hallway, then opened the door of the ground-floor apartment. The commentary of a cricket game issued into the hall, together with the smell of pipe tobacco. The radio informed him of an imminent batting collapse by the England team before the door was closed upon the commentator's voice. He had never learned the English trick of passionate interest in such a sleepwalking game, especially not in a recording of a game being played on the other side of the world.

He opened the front door.

The blue Cortina was clearly visible in the failing light, against the black railings of the gardens. Two men, driver and passenger. He noted the number, then descended the steps.

He had walked three or four yards in the opposite direction from the parked car when he heard its engine start. A noise harsher than the crow's coughing earlier. His body suffered a violent spasm of shock, as if he had been dreaming and then suddenly awoken. The car passed him. He forced himself to turn his head, and felt a chill of recognition. A type, not an individual. A professional. The driver's glance was vivid with threat.

The car turned out of Philbeach Gardens, and disappeared. Massinger walked on in the chill dusk, his heart refusing to adopt a calmer, more regular rhythm.

Margaret was perched on the edge of the armchair that faced the door of the drawing room. Her hands comforted and strengthened each other on her lap. Babbington was in half-profile to Massinger until he turned his head in greeting. Or perhaps it was no more than an acknowledgment of his presence. Massinger felt himself an intruder, the shoulders of his overcoat sparkling with melted snow that had blown along the orange-flaring darkness of the street outside. The warmth of the central heating seemed a barrier—a border he had yet to cross.

Babbington stood almost at once, and held out a hand. Massinger moved toward him, conscious of an ache in his hip. Margaret's features betrayed anxiety. Babbington seemed to weigh and discard him, and to be almost amused at his infirmity.

"My dear Paul," he murmured.

"Sir Andrew," Massinger replied stiffly. Babbington smiled sardonically and with infinite confidence.

Margaret stood up jerkily, her body that of a faint-hearted conspirator in the moment of flight. "I—I'll leave the two of you to talk," she murmured. Massinger allowed a look of pain to cross his face. It was evident Babbington and she had been talking. She knew—if not everything, then a great deal about how he had spent the day. He could not but be hurt, and guilty, in the moment before other thoughts crowded in. *Blue Cortina*. Babbington's people? Why? He felt breathless. "Don't forget to leave yourself time to change," Margaret added as she moved to the door.

Flowers—he was aware of a number of new flower arrangements that must have been delivered that afternoon. The sideboard was laden with drink and glasses.

"Why?" he asked stupidly.

"The Royal Opera House," she murmured in a tight little voice, indicating displeasure. Then she closed the double doors to the dining room behind her. Immediately, he could hear her supervising the activities of the butler and the housekeeper.

"Sit down, my dear Paul," Babbington murmured, indicating a chair. It might have been the man's own room. Massinger lowered himself into his armchair as vigorously as possible, casting the stick and his removed raincoat aside. Babbington watched him with what might have been greed rather than curiosity. "You're not well?"

"Fine, thank you, Andrew—and you?"

"Good health, thank God."

Massinger quailed inwardly. It was not knowledge of Babbington's position, authority, and reputation that made him do so. Rather, Babbington exuded those things; they were palpably present in his frame, his features, the room.

"You seem serious, Andrew," he commented as lightly as he could.

"I am, Paul—I am. This Aubrey business. This affair of your friend Aubrey. Deeply distressing." Babbington shook his head as an accompaniment to his words. The scent of winter roses from near the windows, where the central heating was opening the tight buds, was sharp and warm in Massinger's nostrils. He had not noticed the scent when he had come in from the cold, wet street. Now, he heard the sleet patter against the windows behind the heavy curtains, and through one window at the far end of the room where the curtains had not been drawn, he saw it blow in a gust through the orange light of a streetlamp. The image was almost identical to that of one of the two Turners on the wall above the sideboard.

"Yes. My friend, as you say." It sounded like a confession of weakness or guilt.

"I'm sorry for you, Paul. It must be very upsetting, caught in the middle as you are."

"Yes."

"Especially when one is impotent, useless." The words had been carefully chosen. "When one can do nothing to help, even though one wishes to—however much one wishes to." Babbington spread his hands on his thighs.

"You think nothing can be done?"

"I'm certain of it," Babbington replied sharply. His eyes held Massinger's. "I'm sure of it," he repeated softly.

"You think he's guilty?"

"It doesn't look good. In fact, it looks very bad, from whichever angle the light strikes it. Very bad."

"But you *know* he's not a traitor!"

"I know nothing of the sort, neither do you. You don't *believe* he is. Nothing more than belief."

"Nonsense."

"My God—if he is allowed to remain as DG of the intelligence service, Paul—the *havoc*, the absolute, irreparable *harm* of it!"

"I don't believe it. Any of it. You shouldn't believe it either."

"Aubrey's day is over, Paul, whatever the final outcome. I assure you his sun has set." Babbington's eyes gleamed with an undisguised ambition.

"Whatever the truth really is?"

"I'm sorry," Babbington murmured insincerely. "I realize he is a very close friend . . ."

"And if it is a KGB setup, as Aubrey believes?" Massinger asked, feeling warmth ascend to his cheeks. He felt foolish, hot and angry and not in control of his situation. And he felt insulted and unnerved by the threats that had underlain each of Babbington's remarks. "Don't you wonder why the KGB might want to help you achieve your ambitions—why *they* should want Aubrey ditched like this?"

Babbington was silent for a time, as if considering Massinger's theory. Then he studied the cornice, and the central molding above the chandelier. Plaster pastoral, shepherds and shepherdesses against pale blue, like a piece of Wedgwood. Then he returned his gaze to Massinger.

"You're not going to go on with this, of course?"

"What?"

"This misguided attempt to assist someone who cannot be helped."

"The truth doesn't matter?"

"That is the second time you have asked me that. It still sounds just as naive."

"My God—"

"Aubrey is as guilty as hell!" Babbington snapped. It was not an outburst of anger, or irritation. It expressed a genuine conviction. Aubrey had been right—they were *all* convinced, just as Margaret was. Babbington's powerful hands bunched on his knees as he leaned forward in his chair. "You'll see," he continued more softly, "when we get to the bottom of all this—to the center of the web—that I'm right. I don't take his guilt lightly. It's a heavy burden. But I've seen all the evidence. It's all but impossible to refute, quite impossible to regard it as false or faked. Aubrey's been a Soviet agent for nearly forty years. More than that, he betrayed your wife's father to the NKVD and had him disposed of by his new masters!"

"Why should he have done that?" Massinger disputed hotly, his face burning with anger and with Babbington's stinging reminder of his disloyalty to his wife.

"Proof of loyalty—or because Castleford was on to him, to save his own skin . . . take your choice."

"That's crazy—"

Babbington sat back, as if weary. His eyes, unlike his

cheeks and lips, were not angry, but studied Massinger coldly.

"As you will," he said. "But he did it. Killed a man whose bootlaces he wasn't fit to tie! My God, Paul, do you realize how much you've upset Margaret just by *seeing* Aubrey? She damn near broke down altogether when I told her—"

"Then why tell her?"

"I came to see you—to put the record straight, to explain to you that you couldn't help Aubrey. . . . Margaret got me to explain it to her. . . . I'm sorry, I didn't realize it would cause such distress—such a problem between you. But you should have been more *sensible*, Paul! Margaret wouldn't forgive your meddling any further. Of that I'm convinced, just from talking to her today." He leaned forward. "Paul, other people won't take kindly to your interference. . . . You will find offers of city directorships withdrawn, other lucrative appointments failing to materialize, that kind of thing. It's the way things happen here, you know that. Just *think* for a moment before you vault onto your white horse to ride to Aubrey's defense. . . . Don't ruin your own life, Margaret's future, I beg you as an old friend. . . ."

"Blackmail," Massinger sneered at once.

Babbington's face suffused with anger. "Pigheaded!" he barked. He stood up. "Don't bother to see me out. Say goodbye to Margaret for me. Tell her that Elizabeth will be in touch—dinner, perhaps? Good evening, Paul. Please think carefully on what I've said."

And he was gone before Massinger could clear his throat of accumulated bile and fear. He watched the door close, as if half-fearful the man would not leave. He felt his hands twitching on his thighs, but did not look at them. His body felt hot and without energy. Babbington had threatened to take his wife from him.

The doors to the dining room opened, and she posed, the light and bustle behind her like a natural setting. He was terrified, as if she had shown herself to him before being taken away to some place of confinement; or before she voluntarily departed. The butler and the housekeeper busied themselves behind her, part of the *tableau vivant*. Crystal, gleaming napery, silver. Candlesticks and candelabra. Caviar, smoked salmon, canapés, asparagus. Champagne, Burgundy, claret, hock.

She released the door handles and moved out of her setting toward him. Her face began to mirror his as he moved, and she hurried the last few steps, then knelt beside his chair, taking his proffered, quivering hand at once.

"Oh, my dear, my dear . . ." she murmured over and over, her cheek against the back of his hand. Massinger listened to the note of sympathy in her voice, clinging to it, afraid to lose it. And he heard, above the sympathy, like static spoiling broadcast music, something he could only comprehend as necessity. She knew what had been said, and she knew it had been necessary to her happiness. She had allowed Babbington to threaten and blackmail, to frighten him off. Her father existed in some sacrosanct part of her memory, deeper-rooted than himself.

Class, too, he thought miserably. Damned English class. She had taken sides, and she expected him to join her. Nothing else would make sense to her. Aubrey had been a verger's son, and a scholarship boy. A choral scholar with a brilliant first-class degree. A verger's son.

He shifted in his chair. "It's—all right, my dear," he muttered. She looked at him, the gleam of her satisfaction slowly becoming absorbed in affection.

"I know, darling. I know." She stood up. "Are you—ready to change?"

"Yes, of course," he replied with studied lightness. His hip stabbed him like a painful conscience as he moved, and his limp was more pronounced. Without looking at her, he said as he reached the door: "There'll be no trouble, my love. No trouble." He heard her sigh with satisfaction.

He crossed the hall to the dressing room, avoiding the long, gilded eighteenth-century mirror on the wall above the telephone, avoiding the cheval glass in one corner of the dressing room. The long modern mirror on the inside of the fitted wardrobe door caught him by surprise, revealing the irresolute, dispirited shame on his features. He turned away from it, slamming the wardrobe door. He took off his jacket and tie, uncrooked his arm, and dropped his overcoat to the carpet. The hard seat of the divanette looked inviting.

The telephone rang, startling him out of his recriminations. He looked at the extension on the wall, then snatched at the receiver.

"Professor Massinger?"

Peter Shelley's voice?

"Yes. Who is that?"

"Shelley, Professor."

Massinger's head turned so that he could guiltily watch the door. The shadows in the dressing room enlarged, moving across the carpet like the progress of a conspiracy. He slumped onto the divanette.

"What—what do you want?"

He listened for the second click of an eavesdropper. His hand shook.

"I—I'd like to help," Shelley blurted. "I—think I can get you the file, just for a couple of hours, you can photocopy it and I can get it back. . . ." The plan spilled out. Shelley had gone over and over it, it was obvious, overcoming his reluctance and ambition and fear. "It's a transcript, of course, not a copy of the original photographs in Washington. It's all I can do, I won't be able to do anything more."

Massinger listened. No one else seemed to be listening on another extension.

"I—"

"Professor—you said you wanted it. Do you want it?"

"I—"

Click? Telephone being picked up? *Margaret?* Massinger was enraged, and his anger spilled onto Shelley. Shelley was part of the conspiracy to separate him from Margaret—

"I don't require it now," he said as unemotionally as he could. "I'm sorry, but it's nothing to do with me. Thank you for calling."

Shelley put down his receiver at once. Massinger listened. Above the purring tone, he heard a slight click as one of the extensions in the apartment was replaced. He slapped his own receiver onto its cradle as if it burned his hand. Then he waited for Margaret to open the door, a smile of sympathy and congratulation on her lips. Misery occupied his chest and stomach like water that threatened to drown him.

Margaret glowed. There was no doubt of it. Happy, confident, secure once more. She received the sympathies of her guests concerning the news of her father's betrayal and murder almost with equanimity. Order had returned to her universe. Massinger watched her moving amid the guests at her après-opera gathering with a love that seemed renewed. Refreshed. And as a perpetual stranger to this kind of social intimacy.

Eugene Onegin, with a Russian soprano and conducted

by the soprano's more famous husband, had failed to lift him from his mood. Only Margaret's silent glances of approval and satisfaction throughout the evening in their box had stilled the nagging self-criticisms. Yet now, after whiskey and good Burgundy and very little to eat, he could begin to accept and live with the choice he had made. His priorities were reasserted. He had slightly adjusted the focusing ring of his moral and emotional lens, and Margaret's image was precise and clear in the eyepiece. He could only hope he was wrong about losing her to Castleford.

He was standing near the windows, and the scent of the roses was clearer than the cigar and cigarette smoke. Already, two or three people had spoken warmly to him of directorships; another had murmured an inquiry concerning an imminent Royal Commission and his willingness to serve; yet another had dangled the prospect of a lucrative Quango appointment. All of it had pleased Margaret immensely; all of it appealed to some hidden instinct in himself to increase his Anglicization—to become, now that he was no longer a respected university teacher and merely an emeritus professor of King's College, London, a useful, even powerful member of the closed community in which he moved. He felt a need to strengthen his roots in England, to give himself a more appropriate *weight* as Margaret's husband. Now, it was beginning to happen. Anything was possible now. Were he younger, and a British citizen, he might have sought, and found, a safe parliamentary seat. He was being courted. Everyone knew, and everyone was pleased with him. He smiled bitterly into his glass.

The scent of the roses was momentarily nauseous and the room too hot. Then Sir William Guest, senior Privy Councillor, formerly head of the Diplomatic Service and presently security and intelligence coordinator in the Cabinet Office and Chairman of the Joint Intelligence Committee, was standing beside him. Caviar speckled the corner of his mouth until the tip of a pink tongue removed it. Moselle glowed palely in his tall glass. He was beaming at Massinger with evident satisfaction. Of all people, of course, Sir William would know he had withdrawn from the contest—given Aubrey up. Sir William's eyes moved to Margaret, who waved over heads to him and Massinger. Margaret, waving to her godfather and her husband.

"You are blessed, my boy," Sir William murmured.

"I know it."

"Your continued—your *uninterrupted* happiness." Sir William raised his glass and drank off a toast. "My god-daughter's looking so well, so— *happy* these days." He sighed like a large dog before a blazing hearth.

"Yes, William."

"Lucky man—lucky to have been able to draw that much from a woman." Sir William chuckled. His jowls moved slightly out of sequence with the sound. Then he appraised Massinger. "Can't imagine how you've done it. It must be something you Americans have." He laughed. The noise seemed bellicose. "A great shame this business of her father ever reached the public domain," he continued. "Very upsetting for Margaret."

"I think she's coping," Massinger replied, studying his glass.

"Naturally, as her godfather, I worry about her. Her father was my closest friend, and he would have been a great man. A future head of the Diplomatic Service—he might even have kept me out of the job!" He laughed again, briefly. "A bloody disgrace—"

"If it's true."

"Oh, of course, if it's true." Sir William's heavy eyebrows almost touched above his nose as he frowned at Massinger. The expression was a warning. "Even so, very upsetting. As for the thought that one of our people . . . Still, this is not the occasion. Leave it to time, eh?"

"And Babbington?"

Sir William's eyebrows closed upon each other again. His eyes were hard as he shook his head slightly. "We'll leave that. It's out of our hands, mm?" He watched Massinger over his glass. A gold-rimmed Venetian glass, a little florid for his own taste. Apparently, Castleford had bought a set in Venice before the war. There were four left. Sir William might almost have chosen it deliberately to further his arguments and threats.

The piano sounded in the next room. A soprano began a Schubert song, slow and delicate and moving. "An der Mond," Goethe's song to the moon.

"We must lunch soon," Sir William announced. "My bank requires one or two new directors—fresh blood, and all that. I want men I can trust." He smiled and patted Massinger's arm. What remained of the Aloxe-Corton in Massinger's glass stirred but refused to catch the light. "An der Mond" continued. One of the Covent Garden chorus singing, perhaps? A small, sweet voice. The noise in the room slowly stilled, as if every guest had been caught in the fine mesh of the melody—or because they wished to overhear the catalogue of Sir William's bribes.

"And that Royal Commission," Sir William continued, "just the sort of thing you should be seen to be doing at the moment." He drained his glass and added: "Schubert— overrated, I'm afraid. Far too flighty for me." The bellicose laugh moved away with him, into the crowded room.

Massinger finished his wine, and listened. The room applauded as the song ended, and there were calls for others— Mozart arias that the singer would be wise not to attempt, Schubert again, Wolf, Victorian fireside ballads. Massinger propelled himself through his wife's guests in search of the Aloxe-Corton. A young man hired for the evening by Stephens, the butler, refilled his glass. He turned toward the sound of the soprano, now singing a modern pop song, "The Way We Were." She followed Streisand's floating and swooping more than adequately.

The KGB Rezident at the Soviet embassy was standing in front of him, smiling and raising a glass of cognac in salute.

"Pavel!" Massinger exclaimed in surprise, almost with pleasure. Pavel, ostensibly the Russian Cultural Attaché, was usually drunk at social gatherings, and often amusing. Massinger had found him attached, even bound, to Margaret's musical and cultural set almost from the time he had met her. Everyone seemed to know his real position. Massinger believed that Pavel used Margaret's parties not for intelligence gathering but for relaxation, under the pretense to his masters, no doubt, that important people, people with secrets and with influence, frequented Margaret's *salon*.

"Paul, my good friend!" Pavel exclaimed thickly. It was evident that he was drunk again. Yet he was neither aggressive nor morose in his cups. Only louder. The Russian beneath the Party man.

The girl in the next room caressed past and present without touching them.

"You're enjoying yourself, Pavel?" Massinger inquired archly, nodding at the brandy balloon.

"Of course, of course! Your parties are always splendid— splendid! So good for spying!" He burst into laughter again.

His English was good, cosmopolitan, and assured like his slim figure and expensive clothes. He was urbane, amusing, passionate. His appearance was deceptive, and Massinger suspected the ambitious Party functionary beneath the silk shirt and the skin. Pavel drank more cognac, then passed his glass to the young man. It was generously refilled. More applause, then immediately another Schubert song, one of overblown romantic longing.

I have that, Massinger told himself. I have achieved what that song aches for. The sensation was warming, like drink. Pavel silently toasted Massinger once more, then ostentatiously sniffed the cognac and sighed with pleasure. And I daren't risk losing it, Massinger added to himself.

"Did you enjoy the opera?" he asked.

"Enjoy—what is *enjoy*? It is—so pale, so Western, my friend. I lived it, *lived* it!"

"Good for you."

"And this song is like the opera, mm? So unreal. A romantic dream." Massinger had forgotten that Pavel spoke German as well as French and English. "Operas of power interest me more. Like Wagner. Though I trust you not to report me to the Central Committee for my pro-Nazi sentiments!" He roared with laughter, creating little whirlpools of conversation as guests were distracted from the singing in the next room.

"Power—yes," Massinger murmured. Then he saw Margaret at the door, having detached herself from the party around the piano. Her finger made circulating motions in the air, and he nodded, smiling. He was neglecting his duties as host. Escort, he thought, might have been a more accurate description. Nevertheless—

"And falls from power," Pavel added as Massinger was on the point of excusing himself. "Like that of your poor friend Aubrey."

He watched Pavel's eyes. Slightly glazed, the pupils enlarged. His trim frame was unsteady, beginning to rock with the current of the alcohol.

"Yes."

"Tears, idle tears," Pavel quoted.

"Quite." Massinger's back felt cold, his mind as icy as the pendants of the chandelier above them. "Maybe we ought to shed tears, even for an enemy?"

Pavel shook his head and spread his arms. Cognac

slopped onto his wrist, staining the cuff of his white silk shirt. His face was red. Then he laughed.

"Not one," he said, vehemently. "Not one for him. These people here aren't crying. Why should I—why should we?" He laughed again. "They've abandoned him, haven't they?"

"I'm afraid they have, Pavel." Then Massinger said, quickly and lightly: "But you should mourn him as one of yours—surely?"

Massinger sensed the moment, as clear to him as the befuddled, slightly out-of-focus stare with which Pavel regarded him. "He is one of yours, after all—isn't he?" he asked quickly.

Pavel's eyes cleared, hardening into black points, like chips of coal. Then he laughed once more with what appeared to be genuine amusement.

"How should I know? Am I a spy?" he roared, mocking the question." Am I a member of the Politburo, that I should know the answer? Besides, if I denied it, would you believe the word of a Russian diplomat? I'd be bound to deny it if he was an agent of the KGB!" His laughter boomed. Massinger felt hot, and disappointed. He glanced around the room, as if afraid Margaret might be watching, listening.

Pavel swallowed more cognac, then said with hearty, amused confidence: "I heard all about the arrest, you know," he said. "From my—colleague in Vienna. My opposite number there tells a most amusing story—quite anecdotal." His features sharpened around his gleaming eyes. Massinger sensed triumph exuded like an odor. His arm waved his glass around the room. Massinger tensed himself for revelation. Pavel was on the point of indiscretion, already certain of Aubrey's fate. "Aubrey has been gathered in like a good harvest," he said. "My colleague saw his face, at the moment of his arrest. Quite, quite crestfallen! It must have been so dreadfully embarrassing for poor Aubrey," he added venomously.

"Yes," Massinger said after a long silence. Why am I doing this? he asked himself. I have abandoned him, too.

Paul raised his glass once more, and murmured something inaudible. He knows all about it, Massinger recited to himself. He knows. His—the Vienna Rezident was *there* . . . ? If the Vienna Rezident was watching, then Aubrey's arrest was *expected* . . . and if he was there, why was there no attempt to save Aubrey, *their agent*? Massinger's head whirled, as if he were drunk. Realization struck him like a drug, temporarily clearing away a gathering fog. *They were observing the fulfillment of their plan!*

Aubrey was *innocent, framed!*

He raised his own glass and left Pavel, who seemed complacent at his own indiscretion, unworried. His indifference had to spring from complete and utter confidence. And it was as if he had needed to tell, to boast of it to a man who had been Aubrey's friend . . . *and,* as Pavel must know, had abandoned him in company with everyone else. Massinger felt nausea rise into his throat.

If only I could make him talk, make him tell, Massinger thought. If only I could—he knows it's all faked, that it's a setup—he knows what's going on. . . . The Vienna Rezident *saw* it all.

He realized he had left the party, glass in hand, and had walked through the dressing room into their bedroom. He studied his glass, his reflection in the dressing table mirrors, and his swirling thoughts, and decided he would not return to the drawing room immediately. He sighed, and looked at his watch. A masochistic urge prompted him to turn on the portable television on the table opposite the bed. He sat down, hearing the slither of silk beneath his buttocks. Soft lights glowed upon silver brushes, crystal jewelry trays, pale hangings, deep carpet. A late news magazine program bloomed on the screen.

He could not believe what he saw. Aubrey, in front of a monkey cage. A tall, bulky man standing next to him. Summer, blue sky. A distant, hidden camera.

". . . film sold to RTF, the French broadcasting service, which purports to show the head of British Intelligence and his Soviet controller during one of their meetings. The French television service has refused to name the supplier of the film. . . ." Massinger was stunned. He saw his blank face and open mouth in a mirror. An idiot's expressionless features. ". . . Foreign Office has tonight refused to comment on the veracity of the film. We have been unable to confirm the identities of the two men. . . ."

It was Aubrey. Body, head, build, profile, full-face—Aubrey. And the other was Kapustin, no doubt . . . *Teardrop* himself. He moved quickly to the television set and switched it off, almost wrenching at the controls. An image of Pavel's satisfied, confident features floated in front of his eyes, then melted and re-formed into the features of Sir William, then

Babbington and then the others, followed by Aubrey's shrunken, defeated old face. Finally, the professional mask of the driver of the blue Cortina.

They had him now. Aubrey. Tape, film, public exposure, trial by television and newspapers. They had wrecked him. Anger rose like a wave of nausea in Massinger.

He moved into the dressing room, piled with coats and umbrellas and raincoats and furs and capes. He had to do something, now that he knew. He had to do something to quiet his conscience—make sure Hyde contacted Aubrey, came in, told his story. . . . Christ in Heaven, Hyde must have seen everything!

First, Shelley—those files for Aubrey. That, too, he could arrange . . . nothing more, but these things he *must* do!

He picked up the telephone swiftly and dialed Peter Shelley's number. The ringing summoned, again and again. Massinger perspired impatiently, guiltily. Sir William's face appeared again in front of his eyes, but then he saw Margaret—a multiple image of her face that afternoon, before she left him and Babbington alone, and her face that evening, *glowing*.

He felt sick with betrayal.

"Come on, come on!" he urged, as if afraid that the new and unexpected determination would desert him, seep away down the telephone line. "Come on." His head kept swiveling toward the door.

Why, why? he asked himself. Why am I calling—

"Yes?" Shelley answered. He sounded the worse for drink.

"Have you seen the late news program?" Massinger demanded.

"Yes." Shelley's voice was young and bitter, almost sulky. "What do you want?"

Massinger knew he was poised above a chasm. All he had was an anger caused by some faked film and the smug, insulting, deliberate indiscretions of a KGB Rezident—and threats and bribes. They did not seem to justify this—this *commitment*. His shame had been revitalized, but even as he dialed Shelley's number, bribery and love reappeared to restrain him. At least he had resolve enough to see him through to the end of his small part in this business. He could withdraw, once these things had been done—he *would* withdraw, for the sake of his marriage, their future . . .

His call went through.

"I want that file tomorrow."

"Why the sudden change of heart?" Shelley asked haughtily.

"Never mind. Tomorrow, at eleven. Meet me outside—outside the Imperial War Museum—yes?"

"I—I'll have to have the file back by one."

"You will. Just be there, Peter. It's very important."

"Have you heard from Hyde?"

"No—you?"

"No."

"I'll talk to the woman again tomorrow. Now, good night."

The door opened as he put down the receiver. His hand jumped away from it as from an electric current. He automatically adjusted his tie in the cheval glass before turning. Margared stood there, with Pavel.

"Pavel wanted to say good night," she announced. The noise of the party swelled through the open door behind them. Her hand was on the Russian's arm like the touch of a fellow conspirator. Yet it was he who was the real conspirator, the real traitor.

"Good night, Pavel."

"Good night, my friend—good night, and thank you."

Pavel turned away as he approached, poised to be escorted to the door. Then Massinger said, before he could weigh or recall the words: "Not one teardrop, Pavel?"

The KGB Rezident's shoulders stiffened. Then he turned a bland and smiling face to him.

"Perhaps just one," he said. There was amusement in his eyes. Then he laughed. "No, I really must be going." He held out his hand. "Take care, my friend." The warning was precise. "Take good care of yourself. Good night, Margaret."

His handshake was firm and hot. He pecked Margaret's cheek, and was gone. Massinger closed the door behind him. The noise of the party loudened. His head had begun to pound. Impulsively, he put his arms around Margaret and pulled her to him, holding her tightly against him.

Eventually, she pulled gently away, smiling.

"Back to the party for you," she instructed humorously. "You're becoming much too self-indulgent."

She took his hand, and led him back toward the drawing room.

God, he thought with the fervency of prayer, don't let me hurt her. Don't let me lose her—don't let me hurt or lose her. . . .

"Hyde?"

The word seemed to hang somewhere in the air between London and Vienna. The static and distance seemed like eavesdroppers. Paul Massinger hunched over the telephone receiver in the woman's apartment as if to conceal his voice and movements from prying ears and eyes.

The call from the woman, Ros, had come while he was shaving. The dressing room extension had been nearest—the receiver of betrayals. He had picked it up fumblingly with a wet hand, the mouthpiece immediately whitened by his shaving foam. He had been aware, like a fear along his spine, of Margaret's still-sleeping presence in the bedroom. The call had not woken her.

The woman had persuaded Hyde to talk to Massinger, when could he come . . . ? Would ten . . . ? Hyde seemed nervous, on edge, wanted to talk to him urgently. . . . He had swallowed all betrayals, all fears, and agreed to come to Earl's Court before ten.

He had seen no blue Cortina; he had seen no other tail. They had accepted his surrender; they did not guess at this renewed rebellion. Betrayal . . .

Beyond this telephone call, Peter Shelley and the transcript of the *Teardrop* file lay ahead of him like an ambush in the bright, cold morning.

Then the call had come. Ros had answered, nodded, and handed the receiver to him. He had taken it like a thing infected or booby-trapped. At the other end of the connection, Hyde waited like a malevolent destiny. He was certain of it—certain no good would come of it. Then he plunged.

"Hyde?" he repeated.

"Massinger? Is that phone bugged?"

Involuntarily, he looked up at Ros, and repeated Hyde's question. Ros stood like a guardian near the sofa, arms folded across her breasts. She shrugged, and then she said:

"I'm just his landlady. He knows that, so do they."

Massinger nodded.

"We don't think so—we're pretty sure."

"Who's we?" Hyde asked in a worryingly unnerved way,

then he added: "Oh, Ros. Okay. I've heard of you, Massinger. You were CIA, a long time ago, but you've been out of things since then. What's your angle?"

Hyde mirrored his own emotions, Massinger realized. He, too, anticipated exposure, capture, perhaps worse. Why? Why was Hyde so evidently in fear of his life?

"I'm trying to help Aubrey. Why are you afraid for your life, Hyde? Who's trying to kill you?"

Ros's large, plump hand covered her mouth, too late to hold in the gasp she had emitted. Her body seemed to quiver beneath the kaftan with a sudden chill.

"You don't know, do you?" Hyde replied. Massinger sensed that he had come to a decision.

"No, I don't."

"How is the old man?"

"Aubrey? Afraid—running out of hope, I think," he replied with deliberation.

"Aren't we all, sport?"

"Hyde—why can't you come in? It is a question of *can't*, isn't it?"

Hyde was silent for a moment. The morning spilled pale sunlight across the dark green carpet of Ros's lounge. It touched the back of the sleeping tortoiseshell cat. Massinger sensed immediately that the woman had brought Hyde's cat to her flat for safety—from what she would not have been able to explain. Then Hyde blurted out:

"I'm running from our side—comical, isn't it?"

"What do you mean?"

"I mean—collusion between the KGB and SIS. Look, Massinger, I'm as good as *dead*!" Hyde's voice broke on the word, like a dinghy against a rock. Massinger sensed the utter weariness of the Australian, his collision with the brick-wall dead end of hope and will. He was at the end of his tether.

"I don't understand you. . . ."

"You don't fucking well understand?" Hyde yelled. His voice seemed to move closer, be in the room together with the scent of his fear and the desperation that must be on his face. "What's so fucking hard to understand? Vienna Station tried to terminate me—terminate, as in finish, bump off, *kill* . . . !" Massinger heard Hyde's dry throat swallow, then: "I tried to come in. . . . I knew the old man wanted help. . . . I rang the Station, gave the proper idents . . ." There was no way Hyde could stop himself talking now. He had lost control of his situation and himself, now that the faint possibility of escape had gleamed; help had whispered down the international telephone lines. "Ten minutes later, the KGB turned up, and they were loaded for bear. They wanted me dead—they must have wanted me silent on the subject of Kapustin's watching the whole arrest. . . ."

Some dramatist's instinct warned Hyde that he had laid out sufficient quantities of his mysterious wares for the present, and he left the sentence unfinished. Massinger could hear his harsh breathing down the line.

Collusion . . . Kapustin . . . Vienna Station . . . collusion . . .

"I—I can't believe it, Hyde. . . ." he managed to say.

"Kapustin stayed behind to watch the whole bloody thing—he must have set it up, for Christ's sake!"

Massinger's head spun with the information and its implications. Scraps, impressions whirled like leaves on the dangerous surface of a whirlpool, a deep well. He saw the sides of the well as if all around him, locking him within the situation this telephone call had created. He had intended to make arrangements, then simply walk away. Now that he had heard what Hyde had to say, and knowing that Hyde was being hunted and close to being caught, he could not. Margaret retreated. For the moment, he could not join her in her safe place. He could not leave this apartment, leave Earl's Court, and simply get on with his life.

Answers. He had to have answers. *He* needed the truth as much as Aubrey did. He could, yes, he could do it secretly; Margaret need not know. If he acted quickly, he could still get Hyde to Aubrey.

"You must—must . . ."

"What? Stay alive? I want to! How can you help me achieve my ambition?"

"Your papers?" They were in one of Ros's plump, beringed hands, clutched against her breast. She seemed to offer them toward Massinger. The cat stirred, then fell asleep once more, the tension in the room insufficient to disturb it.

"This city's sewn up—I need those if I'm to get out. Let me talk to Ros about that—where to send them."

Collusion—Kapustin—Vienna Station—KGB—SIS— collusion.

"I'll—bring them to you. I must talk to you," Massinger offered suddenly, surprising his rational, conscious brain, unnerving his objective self.

"You'll come . . . ?" Hyde was suspicious, and relieved.

"I'll come. I'll bring them. We must talk."

"When?"

"Tomorrow, two days—I'll have to be—careful."

"They're on to you!" Hyde accused.

"No. I've been warned off Aubrey—nothing to do with you. There's no connection between us." He saw the blue Cortina parked in Philbeach Gardens very vividly in his imagination. "I—give me a little time to cover my tracks. I have to talk to Shelley anyway—"

"No!"

"It's all right. I won't mention you. It's about Aubrey—the frame. . . ."

"How have they done it—*who*'s done it?"

"KGB—I don't know much more. Shelley has—some information for me."

"So have I. Watch yourself, for my sake. I said collusion and I meant it." Hyde had recovered something for himself. A patient who has been bled and is weakened but more clear-headed. A boil had been lanced, the pressure eased, by his outburst. He would now last, perhaps, as long as it took Massinger to reach him in Vienna. "Watch your back. Someone wants me dead and Aubrey out of the game. It could be anyone. It's someone who can give termination orders concerning his own people and expect to be obeyed, and someone who has established two-way access between SIS and the KGB in Vienna. You understand?"

"I understand the implications," Massinger murmured. Blue Cortina, Aubrey framed, blue Cortina, *collusion* . . . The word pained him like a blow. A rumbling headache had begun in his left temple. He rubbed it. "I understand," he repeated.

"You're my only hope," Hyde said flatly.

"I know. Give me a little time. Ring—ring your landlady tomorrow, at the same time. . . ." He looked up questioningly. Ros nodded. "At the same time," he repeated. "She'll have information for you. Try to stay out of trouble until then."

"Believe it, mate." Hyde paused. The connection seemed distant, unreal, tense once more. "All right," he said finally, "I'll trust you. Everyone always said you were a bit too *nice* for our kind of work, but you're Aubrey's pal. All right—I trust you." Then he cackled in an ugly, fearful way. "After all, I can kill you when you get here, can't I?"

"You can—if I'm not what you need or expect."

The connection was broken at that point. The telephone purred. Hyde was gone, almost as surely as if the call had never been made; as surely as if he had been taken.

He gingerly put down the receiver. Ros was glaring at him.

"I'll try—as hard as I can, I'll try," he said, soothingly. "Meanwhile, you know nothing. You have not heard from Hyde, you don't expect to. As his landlady, you're angry enough to let his apartment to someone else. Understand?"

Slowly, uncertainly, Ros nodded.

"Okay."

"Good. Now, I must go." He glanced at his watch. Ten-twenty. He would have to hurry to meet Shelley. The sunlight lay chill and pale across the carpet, cold on the cat's fur. Massinger shuddered, as at an omen.

"What will you do?" Massinger asked.

"Hide the car and keep a lookout." Peter Shelley's breath curled around him like gray signals of distress.

"You say you lost the tail?"

"I lost one car by hiding in a coal merchant's yard," Shelley replied without amusement. "But I only spotted one car. I'm not Hyde—not a field man. I don't trust my judgment that much. Neither should you."

"Very well. To photocopy this—" He indicated the buff envelope, thickly filled with paper, that the younger man had given him. "—I'll need at least half an hour."

Shelley looked at his watch with a feverish little gesture, fumbling back the cuff of his dark overcoat. When he looked up again, his face seemed to Massinger even paler and more drawn than before.

"I have to have that file back at Century House by one," he pleaded. "The meeting is immediately after lunch—the copies will be collected. . . ."

"Very well—I'll hurry," Massinger replied stiffly, and opened the car door, climbing out as quickly as he could from the bucket seat. He slammed the door of the BMW without looking back at Shelley.

Shelley watched him ascend the steps to the portico of the Imperial War Museum, its hugh dome threatening to topple and crush him in the now gray, low-clouded morning. His slightly limping figure was dwarfed by the two fifteen-inch naval guns in front of the portico. Bedlam, Shelley thought. The building had once housed the Bethlehem Royal Hospital for the Insane. It seemed an apt meeting place, after he had crossed the river and passed the weather-stained concrete of the South Bank buildings only to find a tailing red Vauxhall in the driving mirror. It had been a long time before he shook the tail. It was Bedlam. In this insane, dangerous situation he had volunteered his own incarceration.

Massinger entered the museum's doors in search of the photocopier in the reference library. He fitted the place, would be anonymous and unregarded inside its doors. He was old, he limped . . . he wasn't an agent, a *professional*.

Angrily, Shelley started and revved the car's engine. He paused for a few moments, foot hard down as if receiving the engine's determination into his body. He consciously had to use the gears, force himself to drive back toward the gates and Brook Drive. He had to make himself expose the car, leave it parked in the street so that his tail might pick it up again. He had to make himself want to see his tail.

He parked the car and left it, reentering the Geraldine Mary Harmsworth Park toward the museum. He unfolded his copy of *The Times* on a cold, damp bench and sat on the newspaper. The chill struck through his overcoat and the trousers of his gray suit. He slid into a lounging position, his BMW visible through the railings of the park, and considered Paul Massinger.

Was he frightened, like himself? Frightened and old and weak like Aubrey? The huge weight of class, of social context, of his marriage and friendships. Massinger could lose patronage, friendship of a powerful, beneficial kind—even his identity. He could lose his wife because Aubrey was presumed to have betrayed her father. Shelley, too, could lose everything, take the same losses—his own marriage apart—if he continued this investment in Aubrey's cause.

He wanted to walk away from it. *He saw a red Vauxhall almost immediately, hadn't really lost them, then.* He feared that Massinger's resolution could not last and he would be left holding the grenade. Massinger vacillated, saw around things, into and through them. The red Vauxhall passed the gates, *wrong car, then*. His breath sighed smokily into the cold air. It was possible that Massinger was making the appearance of an effort simply to assuage guilt and for friendship's sake. Just doing a little bit, looking good, then dropping Aubrey like a live coal when things got rough.

He kicked at a stone in disgust. It narrowly missed a pigeon, which fluttered a few feet then settled to inspect the gravel once more.

The red Vauxhall was coming back, slowly. It stopped outside the gates. Shelley drew in his long legs, hunching into the cover of a bush growing beside the bench. He'd first spotted the red car as he crossed Waterloo Bridge, the Vivaldi on the cassette suddenly becoming more chilly. He'd tried to shake the Vauxhall through the narrow, terraced, ugly Lambeth and Southwark streets, and then thought he had lost it after he had turned into the coalyard amid the blackened trucks. Now he suspected that there had been two cars, and a radio link.

He watched the red Vauxhall. A man in an overcoat got out and crossed to inspect the BMW. Almost at once, he turned and nodded to his driver. Then the passenger returned to the Vauxhall, climbed in, and the car pulled away, leaving the smoke of its exhaust to disperse in the chill, windless air. Shelley listened to its engine retreat, slow, louden, and then stop. Parked. They would wait—*who would wait?* He shivered.

He had to get the file back to Century House—it was his most urgent priority—because the JIC meeting under Sir William's chairmanship scheduled for tomorrow had been brought forward to that afternoon.

Who was in the red car? *Who . . . ?*

MI 5, SIS, KGB . . . ?

He did not know. His body felt feverishly warm beneath his jacket and overcoat. When he had the file back, and had returned to his office, that would be that, wouldn't it? No more need for red Vauxhalls, no more need . . .

His nose would be clean. Very clean. Twelve-twenty. Come on, Massinger, come on. . . .

There was weakness in Massinger, weakness in himself, too, for that matter. Weakness of the same kind, like cracks hidden behind heavy wallpaper, cracks that went down to the foundations and boded trouble.

Blue Cortina—

Massinger's blue Cortina, *his* tail?

The blue Cortina stopped opposite the BMW, then pulled forward and away. Shelley shivered violently and stood up, rubbing his arms and the backs of his thighs. He gazed toward the facade of the War Museum almost with longing. There was no one on the steps. He crunched along the gravel, hands thrust into his pockets. They had him now. Perhaps they did not know why he had met Massinger—perhaps they had not followed the American. . . . But he was under suspicion, under surveillance. His breath smoked around his head like a gauzy hood. He was breathing harshly, as if afraid or spent. He hadn't recognized any of the faces in the two cars, which meant they were more likely to be MI 5 than KGB—Babbington's troops. They had him, then.

Massinger emerged from the doors as he reached the top of the steps. Shelley turned to look back over the railings. He could distinguish the red Vauxhall, but there was no sign of the blue Cortina.

"Finished?" he asked eagerly.

"My God—yes, I've finished." Shelley snatched the buff envelope that contained the *Teardrop* transcript, its pages protected by stiff plastic. "I was careful, Peter. No one will realize it's been copied." He smiled, but some other emotion removed the expression from his lips almost at once. "I—just glances, you know. It's incredible. Even talking to Aubrey didn't prepare me for it. Nearly forty years of treachery documented there. Aubrey's being turned in 1946, being woken from his long sleep two years ago, the information he's passed, his promotion, and the prospects and plans—dismantling SIS, turning it into . . . my God, it's so—so *convincing!*"

"Especially the last two years."

"But Hyde was there—most of the time he was there."

"And Aubrey often went off by himself—unlogged. Or he wasn't wired for sound, or he didn't make full reports of his contacts. Who could defend him adequately against this?" Shelley's face was set in a stony, lifeless expression. To Massinger, he looked young, afraid, vulnerable.

"Any activity?" he asked, gesturing toward Brook Drive with the gloves he held in one hand.

"The Vauxhall's back with me," Shelley muttered, then he burst out: "Christ, I'm shit-scared at having anything to do with this!"

"What do we do?"

"Walk. I—can collect the car later. Lambeth's the nearest tube station in the other direction. Okay?"

"Okay. Who are they?"

"I—don't know."

"You suspect . . . ?"

"Babbington's people."

"Damn—you're sure they're not KGB?"

"Not sure—not sure they are, either. Veering toward MI 5." Shelley's voice was almost inaudible above the crunching of their footsteps on the gravel.

"I thought a great deal about this last night," Massinger murmured as they passed out of the gates, heading toward the Kennington Road. Massinger recollected Margaret's quietly breathing form next to him throughout the night. The awareness of it was vivid, almost a physical sensation against his arm and side. The memory pained him deeply.

They had talked for a long time after their guests had left. The glow had not left her, even though her eyes were tired. She had apologized for asking Babbington to talk to him, and he had, almost perfunctorily, forgiven her. Then she had explained her sense that he was betraying her, siding with Aubrey. He had demurred at that. He winced, even now, at recollecting her pleasure at their reconciliation, at his apparent agreement to do nothing more for the guilty Aubrey. The sense of Aubrey's innocence had nagged at him then, and later while they made love and in the aftermath, while she fell softly asleep . . . nagged, nagged, *nagged.*

Schemes had flitted in his head, solutions, desperate remedies. To hold on to Margaret yet help Aubrey? *If only he hadn't tricked Pavel into giving the Russian game away!* Knowledge weighed on him like a burden. He *could not* let Aubrey drown for want of a lifebelt thrown to him. Schemes, mad ideas, desperate solutions, crazy thoughts had flickered in his sleepless head all night. . . .

In the bathroom, shaving, he had managed to resign Aubrey to his fate, except that he would obtain the files from Shelley and arrange for Hyde and Aubrey to make contact. Now, he had already volunteered himself as the courier of Hyde's false papers to Vienna, and all the crazy schemes and solutions were back, filling his head like seductive snatches of pleasurable music.

And there was the fear, of course, growing in his imagination throughout the sleepless night. He had aroused interest. . . . Pavel would recollect what Massinger had tricked from him, would wonder, consider, watch, perhaps act . . . fear.

Margaret's anger, coldness, dislike would have to be risked. If he could prove Aubrey *innocent*, and himself to have been *right*, surely she would see he had acted properly? He had to believe that.

He had, he admitted, been drawn subtly, inexorably into Aubrey's dilemma. One unweighed step after another, choosing the placing of his feet by feeble torchlight that did not reveal what lay ahead. It was almost as if he, too, were trapped as surely as his old friend. At no time had he intended to exceed his simple, allotted task—to help Aubrey make contact with Shelley and Hyde. But things had changed. He had to go on. He was *inside* the situation now.

And there was vanity, too—mere ego. He knew it worked in him like a drug. . . . He could pull it off, he *could* . . . he had to. Pavel knew that *he* knew. He would be watched—was being watched?

He turned his head, but no red car appeared to be moving.

"And? What were your thoughts?" Shelley replied reluctantly, listening to the older man's hard breathing and the tap of his stick on the pavement. Both noises were dispiriting.

"I spoke to Pavel Koslov, the KGB Rezident, last evening."

"Where?"

"He was at the flat. A social occasion."

"And?"

They passed an eighteenth-century house with a grand door and an iron balcony to the second and third floors. It appeared aloofly unaware of the neighboring laundry and Indian restaurant. Shelley seemed distracted by the odors of tandoori cooking.

"He let something slip—drunk, of course. He knew exactly what was going on. That it was a frame. He even knew what had happened in Vienna. It amused him. His opposite number there had told him the whole story of Aubrey's arrest."

"What can we do about it?" The question surprised Shelley himself.

Massinger halted, and the two men faced one another.

Shelley knew he was being weighed and was sick with uncertainty. Why had he said that? He had to get the file back, *that* was what really mattered.

"Do you mean that?" Massinger asked finally. A turbaned Sikh brushed lightly and apologetically against them. A shopping cart dragged behind a large woman banged painfully against Shelley's ankle.

"Yes," Shelley replied reluctantly, unable to prevent the answer he gave, shrinking from it even as he did so.

"Good man."

"But what can we *do*?" Shelley protested as they walked on.

Massinger slipped on a patch of ice and Shelley steadied him.

"Do you realize we have no time left?" Massinger asked. "Already, we're both under surveillance—if it is MI 5, then we have no time at all, and if it's Pavel who's set the dogs on us, then we may have even less time. Pavel wouldn't hesitate . . ."

"I know!" Shelley snapped. "There is no need to scrawl the message on the wall. So? What hope is there?"

They had reached the entrance to the tube station. Massinger paused, facing Westminster Bridge Road. On the other side of the thoroughfare, whitewashed racist slogans had been daubed on a wall beside the poster of a cowboy smoking his favorite brand of cigarette, a packet of which obscured the grandeur of Monument Valley. Massinger received a fleeting image of John Wayne lying prostrate on the roof of a racing stagecoach, of a crowded, child-noisy movie theater. His youth.

"I realize Pavel's too well protected—and on guard," he murmured. Shelley had to bend his head to hear distinctly. "There'd be a God-awful stink if anything happened to him. But we have no *time*! There are the three of us, and one of us is trapped in Vienna with no hope of getting out. The agent—*our* field agent—cannot come to us. I have to go to him."

"What then?"

"Someone may be planning to stop us because of what we've already done. If we can do something quickly, something *decisive*—then maybe we can win. Slowly means we lose—altogether."

"I realize that. But what—?"

"Bear with me, Peter. We need Hyde, and that means

going to him. Which means Vienna. I want everything Registry has on the KGB Rezident in Vienna—the Rezident and his senior staffers."

"Why?"

"Will you get it for me?" Massinger's eyes gleamed with daring rather than reason.

"Why?" Shelley repeated.

"If we could make him talk—if we had *proof*!"

"The Rezident, in Vienna . . . madness." Shelley's anger was fueled by fear. "It's absolutely *insane*!"

"It's quick. Speed is our only hope."

"That's not hope, it's lunacy."

"And the entirely unexpected. Get me everything on the current Rezident. There must be something, some time when he's virtually alone, unattended, off his guard . . . a moment in which we can—talk to him?" Massinger's smile matched his eyes. Shelley quailed. It was the most desperate, monstrous lunacy, a four-in-the-morning solution to the problem. It should have dispersed in the light of day.

"You can't!" he felt obliged to say.

"At least we can try, man!"

"And this KGB senior staffer—he'll just answer your questions politely?"

"No. Which is why we will need pentathol and a man with a needle."

"*What?*"

"You control East Europe Desk, Peter. You must have someone, somewhere in Europe, someone you can still trust, who can inject the necessary drugs? There must be someone . . . ?"

Shelley felt himself mocked. More, he felt himself endangered. Massinger was in the process of flinging him over a precipice.

"I—can't do what you ask," he murmured. "It's too risky, leaks like a sieve. . . ."

"My God, man—don't you realize that your precious job may not exist if this goes on much longer!" Massinger stormed through clenched teeth. It was a superior, cold anger. "There is collusion between elements in your service and the KGB. Everything we know and everything that has happened to Hyde tells us that much. You *must* want to know who, and why—you have to try and stop it. We *must* establish the truth, Peter. We must discover what this awful cooperation means, how far it extends—what and who is behind it. It's your *job*, for God's sake!"

Shelley half-turned away, his hands flapping feebly at his sides. "I don't want to realize that," he muttered.

"But it's necessary—crucial. It's the reality of this business."

"I know. It's standing beside you like a bloody shadow. Duty. God, Queen and Country. I know I have to. I know it." Shelley's lips twisted in a sneer.

Massinger looked at his watch. "You'd better get that file back, Peter," he instructed gently. "And the other material—can you get it for me today?"

"Today?"

"Hyde is in constant danger. *Your* people in Vienna Station threw him to the wolves. He's running and he's afraid. He may have even less time available than we do."

Shelley nodded in accompaniment to Massinger's grave words. Then he looked up from the pavement and his shuffling feet, and said: "I'll try. I'll try, and call you tonight?" He left the statement as a question and studied Massinger's face. The American glanced at the buff envelope under Shelley's arm, then nodded.

"Yes. Do that. I—we have to go on with it—whatever."

"Yes. Now, I have to go."

Shelley turned away abruptly, and entered the tube station, leaving Massinger staring at the cigarette billboard across the street.

"You're certain it was Massinger?"

"No, sir—not certain."

"But Shelley—yes?"

"Yes, sir."

"And you lost them?"

"They shook us off, sir. Didn't use the car."

"Where are they now?"

"Massinger's at home. Shelley's at Century House. He's been there since a little after one."

"Why did they meet? I don't see the significance of the War Museum."

"Sorry, sir—can't tell you."

"Why did they meet?"

"Sorry, sir—didn't quite catch—"

"It doesn't matter. It can't add up to anything much. Old loyalties having a daytrip, chickens scratching around in the dust. Mm. Shelley will have to be watched more closely. I'm certain Massinger doesn't have the stomach for this—he'll run out of steam fairly soon."

"I see, sir."

"Maintain surveillance on both of them, until we can be certain what they're up to—if anything."

"Sir."

Hyde recognized that he had passed through both fear and the oppressive sense of isolation. They had worn themselves away, like an overfamiliar lust. Finally, he had been left with no more than a desire for action. It was his simplest emotion; whenever he encountered it, he felt he had arrived at a destination or a new beginning.

The rain slanted in the gusts of wind across the street. Car headlights glared onto the windshield of the Volkswagen van, and brake lights splashed on the road like ruby paint. He had hired the van from a small backstreet garage and had borrowed the stained gray overalls he now wore. Almost six in the evening. He was waiting for Wilkes to leave the SIS offices on the Opernring. The van was parked beneath the trees, alongside the tramlines, thirty yards from the door of the office building. Wilkes had not yet left. Impatience filled Hyde, gratifyingly, in itself a signal of purposeful activity. His fingers drummed against the greasy touch of the steering wheel.

Wilkes would tell him the truth. Wilkes, the man who had sent the KGB for him in the café, in the cathedral square. The purposeful men in the heavy overcoats. Wilkes—

Wilkes stepped from the door, turning up his collar, glancing to left and right, crossing the pavement to his parked car. Hyde started the engine of the Volkswagen with a fierce tightness in his chest and throat. Now, now it begins, he could not avoid thinking.

Wilkes's Audi pulled out into the traffic flow, and Hyde slid into the line three vehicles behind it. Was he going home, back to his apartment? Going for a drink, meeting someone? To Hyde, it did not matter. Eventually, Wilkes would be alone, and then . . .

Hyde damped down the suddenly rising anger. He had not realized, until that first moment of secret surveillance as he pulled out into the traffic behind the unsuspecting Wilkes, how much he wanted to hurt him, damage him, make him talk. He had been too isolated, too endangered and for too long. Wilkes was going to repay him for that frightened, hunted, wasted time.

Wilkes's car turned off the Opernring, into Mariahilfer-strasse, following a tram that flashed blue sparks from the wire above it. The Hofburg Palace loomed to Hyde's right for a moment, then they were passing the massive elegance of the Kunsthistorischesmuseum. Audi, Mercedes, small Citroen, then the Volkswagen. Hyde considered moving up, anticipating being caught by one of the sets of traffic lights. He decided against it, however. There were sufficient sets of lights to keep Wilkes in sight, even if he missed one of them. He would not lose Wilkes. He was there, three cars away beyond the wipers and the slanting rain.

The center of Vienna changed, the lights of modern shops obscuring then throwing into shadow the old buildings whose ground floors they had usurped. Side streets became narrower, the traffic lights less frequent. Wilkes had made no attempt to accelerate, or to turn off. He was still unaware.

The Citroen turned off, and Hyde moved up. Then the Mercedes disappeared, and he dropped back again. A Renault overtook him and filled the gap between the van and the Audi. The black, gleaming station roof of the West-Bahnhof lay beyond the grimy, streaked window of the Volkswagen, then Hyde turned into a wide cobbled street behind the Audi.

The Audi slowed, taking him by surprise. He drove past, consciously stopping the foot that had been about to transfer itself from accelerator to brake. He did not glance in the direction of Wilkes's car, but watched it stop, floating into his rearview mirror. Its headlights dimmed, and then it was nothing more than a dark shape alongside the pavement. Hyde pulled in perhaps sixty or seventy yards farther along the street, opposite a newspaper and tobacco kiosk set in the featureless ground floor wall of an apartment building. His eyes returned to the mirror. In a moment of quiet between passing cars, he heard Wilkes slam the car door. Hyde wound down his passenger-side window, and craned his head to see Wilkes crossing the street toward high iron gates. One of the gates opened and Wilkes disappeared.

Hyde scrambled out of the Volkswagen, hurrying between oncoming traffic across the street. A childish and inappropriate sense of having been cheated filled his imagination. Somehow, the rules had been changed; Wilkes was engaged in his own mystery, rejecting his role as hunted victim. The rain, flung by a gust of wind, slapped across Hyde's face. His hand reassured itself for a moment on the butt of the Heckler & Koch beneath his arm.

A wrought scroll of iron set into the tall gates announced *Altes Fleischmarkt*. Through the gates, receding into an unlit darkness, Hyde could see a large cobbled expanse surrounded by decaying, lifeless sheds and warehouses.

He gripped the cold, wet iron of the gates with one hand, slipping the gun into the pocket of his overalls with the other. He listened. There was no sound of footsteps. The gates were unlocked. One of them groaned open as he pushed at it. He left it open.

Meat market. The old meat market. Why?

The cobbles were pooled and rutted and treacherous beneath his feet. He stood, searching for light, for movement. Nothing.

His left hand touched the barrel of the torch in his pocket. Then he moved forward, across the open, rainswept cobbles. Meat market. Empty. Wilkes had disappeared somewhere, into one of the warehouses. Why?

Traffic rumbled down the cobbled street behind him. One of the gates moved protestingly, pushed by a gust of wind. There were no other noises.

He moved toward his left. Beam from a flashlight?

He could see an open door, sagging on its hinges. His feet splashed in a puddle of water. His hand touched the damp wood of the door. His hearing reached ahead of him, encountering only silence. No flashlight, then . . .

He slipped silently through the open door, into the musty interior of the warehouse. He listened once more. Nothing. He moved lightly and carefully, his shins brushing against buckets or perhaps cans. Somewhere, a rat scuttled, startling him. When his hearing was able once more to move beyond his heartbeat, it encountered the same silence. He withdrew the flashlight from his pocket with the stealth of a weapon. The pistol, almost ignored, appeared in his right hand at the same moment.

The door shifted on old hinges, but did not close. No trap, then—

Where was Wilkes?

He listened for a car engine firing, the noise of Wilkes having thrown him off his tail. Faint, whitewashed walls stretched back into darkness.

Empty?

He flicked on the flashlight, pointing it directly ahead of him. Five yards away, a huge portrait of Lenin glared at him. The sight stunned him.

Lenin?

"Hello, Patrick," he heard Wilkes say from the darkness away to his left.

He could not move.

3
For the Record

Lenin?

His mind refused to release that image, caught in the beam of the flashlight. His thumb would not move the switch to turn it off. He could not comprehend the voice—Wilkes's voice, he remembered dimly—coming from the darkness to his left. He could not move the flashlight in an arc to reveal the speaker, or move the pistol across his body to endanger Wilkes.

Trap.

But Lenin?

Joke?

He shivered, newly aware of cold and wet. The shivering would not stop once it had commenced. He had stepped into some mad theater, without his cue. He could only wait for his prompter. . . .

"Hello, Patrick," Wilkes said again. Then the door moved on its hinges. Heat stung the back of his neck as he tried to overcome tight, frozen muscles to turn his head. The door slammed shut behind him. He imagined, almost immediately, that he could hear breathing in the darkness around him. Two, three, four pairs of lungs, his imagination counted. Trap. He *knew* they were there. He did not know how many, but they were plural. Collective. They were a trap, and they had snapped shut on him. "Okay, Patrick," Wilkes added confidently, almost amused, "put down the gun. There's a good chap."

Now!

There was the single, elongated fraction of a moment in which his body would not come unfrozen, would not move—then the light was out, and he leapt and rolled, and crashed into something that gave and then toppled upon him, winding him. Beams flashed and played about him, and someone cursed. Not Wilkes's voice. He clung to something tapering and molded or carved. A flashlight beam struck as he pushed it away. A model of one of the towers of the Kremlin.

Kremlin?

He rolled away. No gunfire, only the searchlight beams licking across the dusty floor of the warehouse, seeking him. The embrace with the model had threatened the return of his paralysis, but since he could not explain it, he rejected it. He scrabbled. Others moved now, converging on the point where his light had been, where his collision with the model had taken place. He rolled under a bench, into a corner, hunching against the wall and trying to control his breathing.

Footsteps, like the slither and rush of rats. Flickering flashlights, orders—

Silence, filling the bowl of the warehouse. Some children's game, but played in the dark. *Statues*, was it? When Hyde looks, all stand still. Make a statue.

Lenin, model?

"Patrick?" Wilkes said clearly, his voice whispering in the hollow acoustic. "Patrick. I think you ought to give it up as a bad job." Silence, then: "Oh, for your information Clint Eastwood made a film here. You saw some of the set dressing, the props. A spy film. Very exciting, I believe."

"Where's the bloody main switch?" someone called out.

"In the office!" Wilkes snapped.

Someone collided with some cans or buckets, setting them rolling on the cobbled floor. As he moved under cover of the noise, Hyde heard the man cursing.

Then Wilkes was speaking again. His voice betrayed the subtle pleasure of having known it was Hyde tailing him in the Volkswagen, of having known his every move. Wilkes had trailed him behind his Audi like a kite.

"Come on, Patrick—there's nowhere to go. We'll have all the lights on in a minute. We shall all know and be known. Just don't be silly about it."

Rage enveloped Hyde.

"What the hell do you want with me, Wilkes?" he yelled, at the same time scurrying along the wall, deeper into the warehouse, almost on all fours. Weak moonlight seemed to drip with the rain from broken skylights in the roof above him. Something—

Nothing.

Wilkes's voice pursued him, and there was movement from ahead of him. He crouched silently against the wall.

"We have our orders, Patrick. We have to render you harmless," Wilkes announced dispassionately.

Hyde was shuddering with exertion, damp, cold, and terror.

"Why?" he yelled out in anguish. "*Why?*"

His body had given up, collapsing into spasm and chill numbness.

"You know why, Patrick. London says you're under suspicion." Wilkes's voice oozed insincerity. "Sorry. You've been a naughty boy." Then, as if slightly unsure of the endgame, Wilkes shouted: "Where are those bloody lights?"

Hyde's hand gripped the steel of a girder. Unwillingly, his eyes traced it aloft. It grew up the whitewashed wall like a tree. Part of the framework supporting the roof, some reinforcement of the original wooden structure.

"I've got them," he head someone call distantly. "Ready when you are."

Hyde's other hand—stuffing the pistol into its holster—climbed up the girder, involuntarily. Then his left hand climbed, then right, so that he was standing upright, pressed against the wall. Right hand encountering a handhold, left foot a foothold, left hand, right foot, right hand . . .

He was climbing, past the lower crossbeam, up toward the roof. The noises he was making were like the scrabbling of rats, perhaps discountable by the men below him. The lower crossbeam was below him now, and the weak moonlight cast the faintest sheen. The black bar of the upper steel girder was still above him. If it was more than six feet below the broken skylight, he could never exit that way—

"Everyone under cover?" he heard Wilkes ask, interrupting his doubts. *It had to be no more than six—*

The others replied; his hearing, choked with his heartbeat and breathing, could not distinguish direction. They seemed all around him. Lights—

A glare of whitish light. He scrambled across the girder, lying flat for a moment, then rising onto his haunches, hands white as they gripped the cold, wet steel. He was sitting like a waiting animal, yet the posture suggested resignation, immobility at the same moment. A pool of shadow lay below him, cast from his body by the . . .

No, not his body, Wilkes's body as the man moved out into the open. They couldn't see him, a gauze of light between him and the ground, thrown by the lamps suspended on long wires. *He was above the light—*

Rain seeped through the skylight onto his neck. His forearms and shoulders already ached with the pressure he was exerting simply to remain still and balanced on the narrow girder. Wilkes was almost directly below him. An animal would have dropped at that point, that moment—an animal would have ignored the odds of four or five to one.

"Patrick? Come on, Patrick . . ." Wilkes was regretting his bravado, regretting the open and the hard, dusty light.

Hyde looked up. Five, six, six and a half? Jagged glass, but bare wood in places—rotten wood? One jump, one stretch only. Or wait?

Perhaps for no more than a minute they would be surprised, confused, puzzled, inactive. Then the ratlike noises would take on purpose and identity, and when they had scoured the floor area and the ground-level hiding places, they would look up. . . .

Look up—

Six and a half; wet, dark, paint-peeled windowframe; jagged glass, no footholds—he could imagine his shoulders heaving up and through, legs kicking, noise of effort, of cracking wood and glass, then the surprised, upturned faces and the guns aimed at the struggling, kicking legs. . . .

A shudder ran through his aching arms and shoulders. He steadied himself, then looked down. Four of them, emerging from the shadows against the walls, collecting beneath him—Wilkes waving his gun, miming instructions now . . . one moving toward a stack of wet cardboard boxes, another back into the recesses of the warehouse, a third moving away toward a hanging-open door to some disused office.

Apart for a moment, then they'd be drawn back together again—

Now—

No movement—

Stand up.

Hands letting go, reluctantly. Thighs and calves feeling weak, rejecting the effort. Hands free, fingers numb, slow to flex. Arms aching. Legs quivering as they straighten, window not coming close enough. Arms protesting as they stretch above the head, fingers clenched to grasp. Touch—not enough. Touch; grip. Yes, close enough. Girder wet, foot slipping a fraction. Wood—wood sound enough. Grip.

Now.

Hyde heaved at his seemingly leaden body, drawing it up toward the skylight and the rain blowing in. His arms shrieked with cramp and the pain of his effort. Slowly, his head came through the skylight into a windy night, ragged clouds being scuttled and bullied across gaps of stars and the sliver of a new moon. His shoulders passed his elbows, and he kicked with his legs. The wood of the windowframe groaned loudly, and he scrambled through, leaving the skylight empty, a hole through which Wilkes's cry of surprise pursued him.

The roof sloped away from him. Splinters of wet wood pained his fingers and palms. Other shouts below him now, and the concussion of two shots striking the corrugated iron of the roof, their impact shuddering through his hands and the soles of his feet.

Quickly, quickly, his mind bullied, echoing Wilkes's cries from inside the warehouse. He scuttled down the slope of the wet, ice-cold iron roof toward the guttering. He extended his legs, using his heels as brakes. The guttering coughed in protest, and shifted, but held. Hyde lay back for a moment, pressed against the roof listening. Running footsteps, shouted orders, pauses of intent silence—the hunt. He sat up, and leaned his body over the narrow alley that ran between the warehouse in which he had been trapped and its neighbor. Empty. Ten feet . . . ?

He lowered himself over the gutter, clinging to it, wincing at every groan and squeak of protest it uttered. His legs dangled for a moment, and then he dropped.

"Here!" someone yelled, only yards away. "Come on!"

Inexperienced, some cold and previously unused part of his brain informed him. The man was slow, undecided, afraid. *Kill it—*

Hyde was on his haunches, absorbing the impact with the ground, and he fought the momentary weakness after effort and the trauma of surprise and shock. The pistol was in his hand with only a fractional delay—kill it—danger—trap closing, insisted the cold, now-admitted, now-controlling part of him. Kill it.

Hyde fired twice, and the body to which the voice had belonged bucked away against the wall of the warehouse, then slid into a patch of deep shadow, losing shape, identity, volition. Then Hyde pushed himself to his feet and ran.

Broken wooden slats over a glassless window. He clambered up onto the sill, and kicked at the rotten wood. It gave inward, instantly disintegrating into wet sawdust. He hesitated for a moment, hunched and staring into the interior of the dark, wet-smelling warehouse, and then he jumped, colliding almost immediately with cardboard that gave soggily, and rolled and tumbled through a stack of boxes and cartons.

No way back, another part of his brain informed him. The icy part had retreated momentarily. This part was nervy, feverish, close to panic. He had killed one of his own. Now, he was no longer one of their own, one of them.

They were going to kill me. . . .

No way back. It's over. You're dead. He could smell the recently fired gun in the damp warehouse air. He thrust it, warm-barreled, into his pocket.

He scrambled out of the wreckage of old packing cases and empty cartons, arms outstretched, and blundered across the warehouse. He could hear footsteps, then silence, then a curse.

Gate—

A minute, perhaps two, and then they would guard the gates against him. The only direction in which he could be certain there was not a blind alley lay toward the gates through which he had followed Wilkes. Perhaps he had less than a minute.

His claw-bent fingers collided with the opposite wall. Now he could almost see the faint gleam of its whitewash. Direction? There were no noises from outside the window, from the kneeling group around the dead thing slumped in the shadow. Door, then?

This warehouse was closer than the first to the gates; he would not have to cross their line of fire; they would be behind him from the start of his run.

He moved slowly, carefully toward the doors. To his adjusted night vision the warehouse now possessed a pallid gleam. The floor space was empty. He reached the double doors, touching them with the urgent delicacy of a blind man. One huge, rusted bolt above his head and below it the doors rested slightly ajar from one another. One bolt—

He listened. His advantage was draining away. He

touched the bolt, trying to ease it. It squeaked, then grumbled. He let it go, as if it contained a charge, held his breath, and then jerked at it. It slid noisily out and he heaved open the drunkenly leaning doors.

Voices?

Traffic, then his own footsteps beating across the slippery cobbles, splashing noisily in puddles. Other footsteps, then the first shot. He began to weave in his running, slipped once, regained his balance. The gates ahead of him wobbled in his vision, but he could discern no one outlined against the street-lamps beyond. He collided with them then propelled himself through the gap he had left. A shot struck one of the scrolled ornamentations, and careered away. Then he was in the wide, cobbled street, and a tram flashed sparks at him like a signal of assistance. He dodged one car and ran across the street, just as the tram stopped.

A very old woman was climbing painfully aboard, helped by a younger woman. Hyde, his breath escaping and being recaptured in great sobs, watched in a fever of impatience—left foot, stick, hip swung, right foot, totter, the young woman's arm braced against the weight that threatened to topple back off the platform. There was a figure at the gates, then a second shadow. *Come on, come on—*

The old woman heaved her center of gravity forward into her habitual arthritic hunch again, and then tapped a step forward. The younger woman placed her left foot on the platform. Someone—a tall figure, not Wilkes—was pointing toward the tram. *Come on, come on—*

He had to clench his teeth to keep the words in. The tall figure began running across the road. The younger woman had both feet on the platform. Through the lighted glass of the rear of the tram, two figures were moving across the road like black, shadowy fish, hunting.

Three steps, and the old woman had still hardly mounted the lowest of them.

Trap, *trap—*!

Hyde turned his head wildly, realizing his stupidity, his meek acceptance of the first assistance he had recognized. On the tram, he was trapped. There was nowhere else—

Trap, safe—trap—safe . . .

He pushed past the two women as gently as he could, squeezing past the surprised malevolence of the old woman's face and her hunched, tottering form. He passed down the tram. Now he was the fish in the lit bowl. Timing, timing. He could take them all the way on the tram, but they'd still be there when it emptied. They could wait.

Standing opposite the center door of the tram, he watched the door by which he had entered. Both doors were open. Wilkes's face, lighting up and hardening in the same moment, bobbed into view behind the two women, still not seated. Where was the other one? Wilkes's expression promised him full retribution; malevolent, full of hate, full of pleasure. Where was—?

Wilkes's smile was broadening, and the tall man was standing on the pavement opposite the center door. Hyde let his shoulders slump. The tall man stepped onto the platform, raised a foot to the step.

The driver waited. The tall man stepped back. He'd follow in the car, having blocked Hyde's escape. The driver pressed the bell, and the door moved fractionally. Hyde went through without touching it and the Heckler & Koch's barrel struck the tall man across the forehead. He staggered back, blinded by pain and sudden blood.

Inside the lit glass bowl of the tram, Wilkes's mouth opened like that of a fish. Hyde stepped over the tall man's still form, and ran, at first as if to catch the tram, then into a narrow, ill-lit street, guessing it headed toward the Westbahnhof and light and crowds.

He ran. The noise of the tram faded behind him. There was no noise yet of a car engine firing or of pursuing footsteps. It was enough of a gap.

He ran.

Peter Shelley remembered looking out across dark, light-pricked London on numerous earlier occasions from the broad windows of his office in Century House. The river wound like a black snake between two borders of light, its back striped by the lamps of bridges. Increasingly, his last, reluctant, half-ashamed cogitations of the day had come to concern Kenneth Aubrey. Aubrey and the old order—he owed them everything, including his latest and most gratifying promotion to the directorship of East Europe Desk. That office was a recognized stage on the road that led to the very top: part of the Jacob's Ladder of SIS mythology. He should repay, honor his debts to Aubrey. Yet whenever he decided that, an image came to him of a sunlit garden in Surrey, and his wife pushing the swing that held and delighted his small daughter. He was always the observer of the scene, and he seemed to himself to lurk beneath the apple trees like an intruder, someone who intended harm to that secure and loved couple. The feeling of danger posed to them was so intense it was as if he held a weapon in his hands, or the two people were naked and vulnerable and he, a stranger, obscenely desired sexual violence.

Paul Massinger had hinted darkly at SIS collusion with the KGB, on Hyde's word. Shelley trusted both men, and could not ignore them. But Babbington, with Sir William's blessing, now controlled SIS along with MI 5, and Shelley was in danger—his family was in peril along with his mortgage and his promotion and his career and his ambitions—if he did more than nothing. He must do nothing, nothing at all.

He turned from the nighttime view of the city, and the telephone seemed immediately at the focus of his vision. He all but removed his right hand from his pocket to reach for it, then relented. His breathing was audible, almost a gasp. There was one more moment of reluctance, and then he picked up the receiver and dialed an outside line. The telephone purred. He watched the door, as if afraid of being surprised in some guilty act. He *had* to, no matter what the cost. The calculation, the selfishness he had hoped would come to him, had not materialized. He was helpless before his obligations to Aubrey. He *had* to help—

He dialed his home, and waited. His wife's voice gave their number.

"Darling . . ." he began.

"Peter—where are you?" Then testiness creeping in, tones of a dinner postponed or spoiled. "You're not still at the office, are you?"

"Yes—sorry. Something's come up. Can dinner be kept?" he added hopefully.

"No!" she snapped, then: "Oh, I suppose so. Honestly, Peter, you said you'd be early this evening."

"I know," Shelley soothed. A hard lump of guilt appeared in his throat. "I'm sorry. Look, it won't take me very long. I'll be with you by—" He studied his watch, a birthday present from his wife. "—oh, eight at the latest. Okay?"

She sighed. "Okay. Don't be any later." Her voice had hardened again, as if being mollified had left her feeling cheated. "*Please* don't be any later," she repeated with heavy irony.

"I promise—"

The receiver clicked and she was gone. Reluctantly, he put down the instrument. Her testiness, he felt, was entirely justified; he felt more bereft at it than he might have done had they been more affectionate. He was betraying her, all the more so because she was not an ambitious wife, not pushing. She might even have agreed with his decision to assist Aubrey, to repay his debts. That knowledge was almost insupportable.

Swiftly, he left and locked his office, and made for the elevators. The corridor was empty except for a cleaner with a noisy vacuum. She did not look up as he passed, as if to mirror his shifty guilt. The elevator arrived almost immediately, surprising him, and it did not stop until he had reached the basement level, which housed Central Registry.

He stepped out into an echoing concrete corridor. He waved his ID quickly at the duty security officer opposite the doors of the elevator. The man nodded, even smiled briefly. Shelley was known, Shelley was senior. . . .

The refrain ran in his head like a mocking jingle. Shelley was recognizable to everyone at Century House, Shelley was a coming man, Shelley was known, Shelley was senior, senior, senior. . . .

Known came back at him out of the darkness in his head. It was easy to get into Registry, easy to fulfill Massinger's request. And easy for others to remember he was there, what he wanted.

A second duty officer, then the doors opened automatically to admit him.

The cavern of Registry retreated before him, the strip lighting in the ceiling shedding a dusty light. There was a musty, underground chill to the place, too, despite the efficient heating. Registry was a sterile, low-ceilinged library, even a cathedral nave. The confessionals of partitioned booths lay to his left, each of them containing a microfilm viewer and a video display terminal with access to the main computer files. It was a place to which Aubrey very rarely came; he dispatched emissaries if he required files, digests, or information. Shelley shivered with his own nervousness. The place repelled him, too, at that moment.

Registry retreated into shadows where rows of ceiling-high metal shelves held the hundreds of thousands of low-grade files that had not yet been sifted for transfer to computer tape or for shredding. The place was almost deserted. He showed his identification at the desk, and the clerk gestured toward an empty booth. Shelley hurried to it like a man on whom it had suddenly begun to rain.

The VDT screen was blank and coated with a film of dust. Shelley's fingers touched it reluctantly. He sat down in front of it, and switched it on. Immediately, a request for his security classification and identity code appeared on the screen. His hands poised over the keyboard. Once he tapped out his code and identity, he was logged on to the computer. On record, for anyone who looked to see, would be his name, the date, the files he had asked for. He had thought of disguising his request, approaching the information regarding the Vienna Rezident obliquely. Hurriedly, he identified himself, and a few moments later the screen accepted him with its permission to proceed.

He could still postpone, or avoid, identifying himself with any particular file, any area of information. He cleared his throat. A weak, dry little noise.

Garden swing, daughter passing through a white beam of sunlight, haloed . . . Aubrey on the rack . . . Hyde at risk . . . *collusion* . . .

He looked at the ways of escape—Reset key, Control key, Escape key—the ways out.

The screen cleared, and then the request for his orders tiptoed across the screen again.

Why do it? Why even be here? The commuter train is waiting—get on it, retreat to Surrey. Did Massinger have the nerve to go through with this? Wouldn't *he* be left, Joe Muggins, holding the baby or caught with his trousers down when the lights went on? Why be there at all?

Massinger, he understood, he had been drawn back to the secret life. There was something beyond friendship toward Aubrey or a concern with truth. Another junkie of the secret life, as Hyde had once described it to Aubrey, who had pursed his lips in disownment of the colloquial epithet. Massinger, Hyde, Aubrey most of all . . . and himself. Junkies. Secrets direct into the vein—pure, uncut, as Hyde had said. Yes . . .

It was simple to explain his being there. The smell and taste and touch of a secret. The passion that swept away reason, caution, nerves, sometimes even self.

Shelley typed in his request with eager fingers. First, the general code. Visitors. Then the more precise identification, KGB. Then, London. Then Home Base to identify the Soviet Embassy. Finally, Team Manager to identify the Rezident, Pavel Koslov. Then he typed in the request for All Information—Digest.

The screen went blank for a moment, then began spilling its information in a green waterfall. Age, place of birth, education, training—Shelley watched the past unroll with indifference. The VDT screen filled and emptied, filled and emptied again and again like a glass bowl, with green, luminous water.

The years fled—early postings, successes, contacts— Paris, Cairo, Baghdad, Washington. Each place had its appropriate reference number for extracting the full files on each period of operational residence.

Vienna—

Shelley looked at his watch after he had stopped the progress of the information. Then he entered the request for the full Vienna file. It was a childish precaution; someone inquiring into Shelley's logged use of the computer, however, might just be put off by the London Rezident's ident and look no further. Now, he had jumped sideways, into Vienna Station's records.

He was aware of the clatter of another keyboard in a neighboring booth, and could not shrug off the sense that he was being checked upon by whoever was operating that second terminal. He shivered. In the distance, the central heating clunked.

Vienna, during Pavel Koslov's period as deputy Rezident. Shelley knew that the current Vienna Rezident, Karel Bayev, had been Koslov's superior during that time, and his friend. He tapped the keys, demanding access to Koslov's biography and record in Vienna. Then, he summoned information on Koslov's relations with his superior, then information on that superior.

Finally, he called for an update on the Vienna Rezident, under contacts with Koslov in recent years. Trips by one to Vienna, the other to London, holidays, meetings throughout eastern Europe . . .

The information unrolled, canceled, sprang up again; none of it betrayed what Shelley had hoped for. He summoned surveillance reports by SIS on Koslov and the Rezident in Vienna—as recently as the previous year, a long weekend visit by Koslov.

Women—professional? Reference earlier reports, same woman? Yes. Regular visits by the Vienna Rezident, a long-term, strictly professional arrangement. A file number was supplied.

Shelley exhaled, inhaled deeply. If someone followed him this far, they would guess. If they took the next step with him, they would *know*—

And he might kill Hyde and Massinger, because he had found what he wanted, and he knew what they would put into effect on the basis of this information—Massinger's crackpot plan.

He demanded that section of the Vienna Rezident's file dealing with Social/Sexual Contacts, looking once more at his watch. His tension flickered in his mind, short-circuiting him to an image of his wife waiting to serve dinner, and the clock at eight-thirty; it wasn't important, but expressed his desire to leave Registry, get out of the place, finish this.

There it was. The girl's name, address, security check, together with the decision that she could not be used. The Vienna Rezident visited her once a week—a prostitute. No other involvement, no leverage. Payment in U.S. dollars, equivalent to a hundred and fifty pounds sterling. The girl supplied him with nothing but her body and her ersatz passion. Even the sex was uncomplicated. No deviations; no kinks. Sex without strings, sex without danger of compromise.

Shelley memorized the address and the other details, and then pressed the Escape key. He had to force himself to return the screen's interest to Pavel Koslov. His fingers trembled. It was a futile bluff, but it might just confuse a bored officer assigned to keep surveillance on Shelley. The screen supplied information concerning Koslov's relationship with the Vienna Rezident until the section of file was completed.

Shelley logged off and shut down the terminal. He had read none of it, simply sat there until the program had ended; a man waiting for the end of a previously seen and not-much-liked film.

He stood up, feeling cramped and chilled. He had to force himself to walk at a leisurely pace past the desk, to nod a good-night to the clerk, to pass the two duty men in the corridor with a neutral expression on his face, hands thrust casually into his pockets. He felt cold, suppressing an almost feverish shiver until the doors of the elevator had closed behind him.

Thursday. The day after tomorrow. The Vienna Rezident visited his whore on Thursdays, without a security escort.

Thursday.

Shelley realized he would have to hurry to catch his train.

Eldon had lost patience with him, but Aubrey could not begin to exercise any control over the situation. He had, instead, to hold his hands together in his lap to still their tremor. He was desperately tired, lost in a maze of protestations and evasions and denials. He was increasingly edgy and uncertain. It was the third day of his interrogation by Eldon—his "debriefing" as they persisted in labeling it, with manifest irony—and they had no intention of easing the pace. He was to be worn down as quickly as possible, made to admit, agree. . . .

To confess and confirm, Aubrey reminded himself as he watched Eldon's darkened, handsome features. Yes, the man had lost patience; but his anger was groomed and fresh-looking, not shirtsleeved and weary. It might be no more than pretense, but Aubrey did not think so. Eldon believed in his guilt, and he was now angry that the old man opposite him wriggled and lied and evaded evident truths—the facts of the case. During the past few days, Aubrey had seen the glow of Eldon's righteous indignation. He was passionate in his loyalty and honesty. He despised traitors, and he was convinced that Aubrey belonged to that detestable species. His passion made him the most dangerous adversary Aubrey could have encountered, and revealed how well he had been chosen by Babbington. Eldon was Aubrey himself, but younger and stronger.

"Sir Kenneth," he observed in a clipped, even tone which yet managed to sound repressed, held back, "you have prevaricated for two days. You ignore evidence that points to your complicity—you deny everything, you answer only the questions you choose." Aubrey summoned an ironic bow of the head. Eldon's eyes glittered. "You have, in fact," he continued, "no friends or allies—anywhere. . . ." Aubrey realized that the anger had at first flared up like a flashfire but was now under control and being used by Eldon. "Of course, we monitored all your calls yesterday." Eldon employed a smile.

The information did not surprise Aubrey, but to be reminded of it weighed on his weariness like an immovable stone on his chest. Increasingly desperate telephone calls, all the previous afternoon. Grasping at straws, or lifelines. The Foreign Office, the Cabinet Office, the PM's office. All had fended him off or turned him aside. Each individual, each department—not at home. Only Sir William Guest had received his call in person. That in itself had alerted Aubrey. Contempt, rejection, dislike had come down the telephone line to Aubrey; seepages from his life-support system, damage to it. Sir William had abandoned him as all the rest had done.

And this man knew it, this dangerous, clever man opposite him. Eldon knew and approved, and felt his own obligation to produce the admissions and agreements that would confirm the evidence against him.

He could not hold Eldon's gaze, and dropped his eyes. His feet shuffled irresolutely on the carpet, a signal that Eldon did not fail to notice. Aubrey was daunted—frightened, yes, he could even admit to that—by his sense of isolation. He was unnerved by the subtlety and cleverness and completeness of the trap into which the KGB—*Kapustin!*—had led him.

"It isn't quite like 1974, is it, Sir Kenneth?" Eldon inquired silkily.

"I don't understand—" Aubrey blurted, startled.

"We should have had you in 1974," Eldon said, his hand closing slowly into a fist on his knee. "We must have been within a hair's breadth of exposing you then."

"What?"

"Bonn, dammit!" Eldon snapped, his impatient contempt revealing itself again. "In April—after they arrested Gunther Guillaume. You recall the *fuss?*"

"That was a ridiculous rumor," Aubrey protested.

"It lacked proof, but not credence. Someone in your service tried to tip off Guillaume just before the Germans got to him. I became convinced of that during my inquiries."

"You were forced to clear every member of the SIS staff at the Bonn embassy," Aubrey retorted, feeling a landslide of confidence within himself. Another old bogey now to be laid at his door. It was true, there had been rumors that an officer in British Intelligence had tried to help the Russian double, Guillaume, to escape the net closing around him. Gunther

Guillaume had been Willy Brandt's closest adviser during his period as Chancellor of West Germany—and Guillaume had been a Russian spy. His arrest had caused Brandt's downfall. Eldon had been part of the MI 5 team of investigators who had been drafted to Bonn at the end of April to inquire into the truth of rumors that there was a British double agent in league with Guillaume. Nothing except the innocence of Aubrey's officers in Bonn had been proven.

"We were evidently looking in the wrong place, Sir Kenneth. You were not, yourself, subject to investigation."

"No, I was not."

"Evidently a crucial omission."

"It was never more than a foolish rumor."

"I wonder."

"I was in Bonn at the request of both the BND and the BfV—you know the circumstances. German security and intelligence required—oh, information, instruction, coaching, call it what you will. . . . They were afraid that the World Cup in Munich that year might end up inviting the same kind of tragedy that attended the Olympic Games in 1972. They did not want more dead on their hands. Representatives of almost every Western intelligence agency were in and out of Bonn that year in advisory capacities."

"And that's all there was to it?" Eldon inquired with heavy irony. Aubrey nodded tiredly.

"It was all you could yourself claim at the time." He waved a hand in dismissal. "Guillaume is back in the East now—all the matter seems to be good for now is more mudslinging. Put it aside, Eldon. There was no double agent in my service helping Guillaume to avoid arrest."

"It's a matter we shall go into again—very thoroughly," Eldon warned.

"Really?" Aubrey remarked contemptuously.

"However, for today, perhaps we should return to the events of 1946?"

Aubrey realized that the subject of 1974 had been broached to soften him, to expend yet more of his dwindling resistance and energy. This was to be the meat of the repast— Berlin, 1946.

"Very well, Eldon," he replied at last. Sunlight was reaching across the lounge, catching motes of dust and turning them to gold. "Very well. Proceed."

Eldon inclined his head in a mocking gesture of thanks.

"You arrived in Berlin, attached to the Allied Control Commission, as an SIS officer—in April, 'forty-six, yes?" Eldon made a business of consulting his notes. His briefcase lay, open-mouthed like Aubrey's Pandora's box, next to him on the sofa.

"That is correct."

"Robert Castleford was, at that time, a senior civil servant transferred from Whitehall to the Commission, and had no links whatsoever with SIS?"

"Again, correct. He did not. He was not a member, or an associate member, of the intelligence service." Aubrey's lips pursed as he finished speaking, and Eldon's eyes gleamed.

"It seems to me that even now you speak with some disparagement, Sir Kenneth. But, of course, there was friction between yourself and Robert Castleford from the very beginning, was there not?" Without waiting for a reply, he continued: "You resented the authority of any—civilian? You resented any interference with your work. With your rather high-handed methods, you crossed swords with Castleford more than once. Your various encounters are a matter of record."

"I did object on occasion, yes . . . it would seem I possessed remarkable foresight in being wary of him, considering my present situation."

Eldon did not smile. Aubrey's attempt at nonchalance irritated him.

"You immediately disliked, and resented, Robert Castleford?"

"No—"

"Sir Kenneth," Eldon breathed with evident, malicious irony. "That, too, is a matter of record. There were other complications later, but your antipathy toward Castleford was evident to colleagues from the very first. You complained, time after time, of the manner in which the civilian authorities presumed to override what you considered to be important intelligence work. You seemed to consider your work of more significance than the huge task of getting Germany back on its feet once more. Catching ex-Nazis and spiking the Russians' guns seemed of more importance to you than the rebuilding of Germany?"

"If you say so . . ."

Aubrey gripped his hands more tightly together in his lap, and averted his gaze. Castleford's dead face had presented itself to his imagination in hideous close-up, the blue eyes going blank and glazed, the head beginning to tilt backward. The noise of the revolver was in Aubrey's ears. As his eyes found the carpet near his feet, Castleford's face, too, fell sideways and the man's body was vividly before him, stretched on his carpet—so vividly that he was afraid that Eldon, too, would see it: see the flow of blood from his temple staining the white shirtfront. He shook his head and the image retreated.

"Something wrong, Sir Kenneth?" Eldon asked.

"Tired," Aubrey managed to say.

"You wanted, from the very beginning, to fulfill your own ambitions in Berlin," Eldon pursued. "You were building your own career, and you would brook no interference from outside your service. Your ambitions dictated that even a very senior member of the Commission such as Castleford was not to be tolerated if he interfered with your work." None of the observations were interrogative. For Eldon, they were merely statements of fact.

"If you say so . . ." Aubrey replied wearily.

"You went about establishing your own network, did you not, within weeks of arriving in Berlin?"

"Yes."

"Setting out thereby to prove your superiority to brother officers in SIS? You were not the senior officer there, I take it?"

"Of course not!" Aubrey snapped.

"Then why did you begin to behave in this—cavalier fashion?" Eldon's hands moved apart in a shrug. "Toward officers more senior and experienced than yourself," he added darkly.

"Because their networks were suffering from rigor mortis. Most of them were established during the early days of the occupation of Berlin. We were finding out less and less, we were catching fewer and fewer Nazis—we had no real access in the Russian sector. . . ."

"You're suggesting that you had all the right answers—*only* you, no one else?"

"Not that—simply a fresh mind, fresh links." Aubrey looked up at Eldon. There was only sunlight on the carpet now. "Surely you can understand how networks become moribund?"

"Perhaps. But you spared no one's feelings, no one's

pride, as you went about this fresh approach of yours. You made yourself deeply unpopular in intelligence circles at the time."

Aubrey shrugged. "All that summer we were afraid that the Russians would try something like a blockade of Berlin—we had to pull out all the stops to try to discover what they meant to do. In fact, they postponed their intention for two years, until 'forty-eight."

"And your new networks began to produce results?"

"Not at once. But, slowly—yes, they did."

"Castleford objected, on many occasions, to your high-handed, even illegal treatment of German nationals, did he not?"

"Yes, he did," Aubrey sighed. "There were a number of cases—"

"Where he reprimanded you for *overzealous* behavior? Such as detaining German nationals without charge—or blackmailing German nationals into assisting you? Bribery, black market goods supplied for favors and information. Castleford objected most strenuously to most of the methods you used, did he not?"

"He did."

"Increasing the antipathy between you?"

"Naturally. He—got in my way on every possible occasion. I was looking for Nazis and for Russian agents being funneled into the other sectors of the city, then to the West, under the guise of displaced persons and even German soldiers. There was little time for niceties."

Eldon's lips pursed in contempt. "Perhaps Castleford thought that the war was over by the summer of 1946?" he said with heavy irony.

"Perhaps. We simply did not agree as to priorities."

"You were caught by the NKVD in the Russian sector of Berlin in December of 'forty-six?"

"Yes."

"Why were you there?"

Aubrey hesitated for an instant. Stick to your original debriefing, he instructed himself. Eldon will have seen the reports. Give him what he expects. He said: "Following a lead—a suspected double in one of the new networks. Not a very spectacular operation. The double knew I was coming, apparently, and proved his real loyalties by turning me over to the NKVD."

Aubrey sat back in his chair. The sunlight on the carpet had reached the round toes of his black, old-fashioned shoes, lapping at them like water. A hateful vision of himself as an old man at the seashore who had slept too long in a deckchair, unaware of the incoming tide, occurred to him. He dismissed it.

"You were interrogated, of course?"

"Yes—for three or four days."

"And released?"

"I escaped."

"During your interrogation—which could not have been gentle, by any standards—you supplied information to the NKVD."

"I did not." Aubrey was suddenly too weary and dispirited to inject any force into his denial.

"But you did. . . ."

Aubrey, sensing the clear anticipation in Eldon's voice, the knowledge of surprise, narrowed his eyes and steeled himself. What—?

"What do you mean?"

"Castleford disappeared the very day you—*escaped*—back to the British sector," Eldon said. "No one ever saw him again. He vanished from the face of the earth—utterly and completely. His remains were eventually found in 1951, during the digging of the foundations for a new office block, and finally identified by a ring, his dental record, and a fracture of the leg sustained in a rugby match at Oxford. Remember, Sir Kenneth?"

Aubrey could not disguise a shudder.

"There was a bullet hole in the skull. His remains were brought home, and honorably interred. And that was the end of the story—*was* the end. . . ."

"Was?" The skull grinned up from the carpet, from the spot where Aubrey had seen the dead face minutes earlier. His hands were shaking.

"We now know what happened."

"You know?"

"Read this if you would, Sir Kenneth."

Eldon removed a number of enlarged photographs from his briefcase and passed them to Aubrey. They goldened in the sunlight, as did Eldon's hand. Aubrey took them with a premonitory shiver.

"Perhaps you would confirm that this is your signature, Sir Kenneth?" Eldon murmured.

Aubrey turned to the final print. What kind of transcript had been photographed? Old, certainly . . . yes, that was his writing, his signature. . . . He flicked back through the sheaf of prints, rapidly reading the faded Russian, the badly aligned, inexpert typing—question, answer, question-answer, answer answer answer—

It was an account of his interrogation by the NKVD—and it purported to be signed by himself as being supplied voluntarily and freely, for use in evidence at some unspecified future trial.

Fake, *fake*!

"It is, isn't it?" Eldon prompted. There was almost a purr of satisfaction in his voice. "That, of course, is part of the *Teardrop* file, supplied by our friends in Washington." He smiled wintrily beneath the moustache. "*Your* file. Experts have confirmed the genuineness of the signature. If your Russian is still as expert as it once was, you will see that you are represented in the text as having supplied Castleford's name and his current whereabouts in Berlin to your interrogator."

Aubrey looked up. "Patently a forgery," he managed to say. His chest felt tight. He could hear his racing heartbeat in his ears, feel its thump in his chest.

"I see. You will also discover, as you read on, that you explain it was Castleford who operated all your networks, presenting yourself only as a minion in SIS's organization. You deliberately suggested to the NKVD that it was of the utmost importance for them to stop him. Even to get hold of him. You claim in that document that Castleford was your senior officer in SIS. You lied so effectively to the NKVD that they had Robert Castleford murdered as a British agent!" Eldon cleared his throat, then added quietly: "It was at that point, when you had betrayed Castleford, that you decided to throw in your lot with the NKVD and become a Russian agent!"

Aubrey felt choked. He could not speak.

They had him.

The telephone rang and Massinger snatched up the receiver. Ros's plump hand hovered near his for a moment, and then she stepped away from him, as if to dissociate herself from the conversation to come. She gathered the tortoiseshell cat to her large breasts.

"Yes?"

"Massinger?"

"Yes." It was Hyde. He felt flooded with relief. He had spotted no tail on his way to Philbeach Gardens, but he wondered at the extent of his own competence. It had been too long since he had needed those old skills to be certain he still possessed them.

Hyde was evidently using a pay phone, yet there was the sound of music in the background which Massinger strove to identify. A string quartet—Mozart? "Where are you? Are you safe?" he asked.

"Just. They're getting closer. I'm at a recital, chamber music. No one would look for an ignorant Aussie in a place like this."

"You're keeping off the streets?"

"Yes. And away from bus depots and stations. Last night, it was close."

"How close?"

"Inches. A coat of varnish."

"But you're all right?"

"I'm still operational, if that's what you mean. But it can't last much longer. Vienna Station tried to kill me again last night."

"My God, you're certain? Sorry, yes, you're certain. I—must come to Vienna. I'm seeing Shelley later today. He should have some information for me that could be of use. Tomorrow. I'll arrive tomorrow."

"A room at the InterContinental, then."

"Is there anything else? Anything I should be aware of?"

"No . . ." Hyde replied reluctantly.

"*Anything?*" Massinger demanded.

"All right—last night, I had to kill one of them. One of *ours.*"

"Damn!"

"It wasn't open to choice."

"I understand. Look, I have a copy of the file on Aubrey—the frame-up. It looks very bad for him."

"It's bloody worse for me, mate!"

"Yes, I know that. I have a plan, something we might be able to do to change things. In Vienna—"

"Christ, mate, all I want to do is get out of Vienna!"

"I'll have papers to make that possible, Hyde. But, perhaps you won't be able to leave at once."

"Christ!"

"Look, hold on. This matter is—it's *so* big, Hyde, that we may have to take risks, greater risks than ever, if we're going to help Aubrey. You understand? It's not simply a question of your life any longer."

Yes, it was Mozart. One of the "Haydn" quartets. A door had opened somewhere near Hyde and the music had swelled out. The B-flat quartet, the "Hunt" . . . *door opening* . . . ?

"Hyde? Are you all right?"

"Yes. Don't get jumpy. Just hurry it up, will you?"

"Okay. Tomorrow." Aubrey's signature at the bottom of a full confession, naming Castleford. For a moment, the document he had read at his club—so that Margaret would have no idea of what he was doing—was vivid in his mind. Very clever, very tight. Nooselike. The document had taken his breath away, removed for perhaps ten minutes any facility to believe it a forgery. In Vienna, the Mozart quartet had ended. He could hear muted applause.

"Tomorrow," he repeated. "The InterContinental."

He heard Hyde's exhalation of relief.

"See you."

The connection was broken and the telephone purred. Slowly, Massinger replaced the receiver, unaware that he was not alone in the room—unaware of the room.

"Is he all right?" Ros asked.

"Mm—what?" Massinger looked up. The cat nestled against Ros's breasts like a stole. "Oh, yes. For the time being."

"Can you help him?"

"I think so."

Ros's face was restrained momentarily, then complete fear possessed it. "Then for Christ's sake do it!"

Massinger turned his back upon the sharp, cruel—and now so personalized—satire of Hogarth's *Marriage à la Mode*. His eyes caught the timeless glances of *Mr. and Mrs. Robert Andrews*, their tranquil security evident to him in a moment, before settling upon Constable's *Salisbury Cathedral*, white and green and blue, colors of an innocence he could not pretend. Room XVI of the National Gallery was quiet except for the mutterings of a troop of schoolchildren being shepherded through part of their undesired heritage.

He and Shelley stood side by side, almost caricatures in their identical dark overcoats.

"First thing," Shelley said, "Hyde's new papers. I've checked them, as you asked. They should be good for at least a few days, perhaps longer." He passed the small flat package to Massinger, who hurried it into the breast pocket of his coat. Shelley's face looked pale and strained with worry and lack of sleep. "Another thing," Shelley added, "there's a recent snap of the Vienna Rezident—his name is Karel Bayev, by the way—included with Hyde's papers."

"Thank you, Peter. I've spoken to Hyde."

"How—is he?"

"He's killed one of your people in Vienna."

"God—"

"He had to."

"I see. Are they that close to him?"

"He can't have long."

"We have to have Hyde's testimony."

"I know. But, it won't be enough. We have to have *every-thing*, Peter."

"I know," Shelley replied glumly.

"Then what do you have for me? Shall we walk?"

They began to patrol the room. Massinger regretted leaving the impossible cleanliness of Salisbury cathedral, reaching out of the placid green meadow. Even its illusory peace was something to be treasured.

Gainsborough and Reynolds portraits. Their satisfied, aristocratic eighteenth-century faces irritated him while Shelley recited what he had gleaned from Registry. Massinger nodded from time to time, absorbing each fragment of information. Turner's *Fighting Temeraire*, then the misty, swirling rush of his *Rain, Steam and Speed*. The schoolchildren trooped out of the room; silence returned. Shelley's voice dropped to accommodate itself to the renewed hush. An attendant's heels clicked on the tiles. Finally, they confronted the obscure shapelessness, the formless half-world of Turner's *Sun Rising in a Mist*. Its reduction of the world to muted color and pearly, bleared light echoed Massinger's mood.

And Shelley's final words.

". . . if, *if* you go on with this, then Cass is a good man with pentathol. He can get to Vienna tomorrow afternoon. Remember, unless you're skilled at this or familiar with the techniques—" Massinger shook his head abstractedly. "—then you can make mistakes. You can close the oyster shell as easily as you can open it. The whole thing is very risky, Professor."

Turner's wan sun struggled in the mist.

"I know."

"Then, do you think you can do it? Why not just bring Hyde out?" Massinger was shaking his head, vigorously.

"No, Peter. This has to be done. Desperate remedies. We must know what's behind it. Vienna Station is working for someone other than you. Hyde is right about collusion. We don't know friend from enemy. We don't even know if we have any friends."

Shelley shrugged. "Very well. Then you must gain this man's confidence. Pavel Koslov is his closest friend. You speak Russian, Professor—you know Koslov. When you talk to the Vienna Rezident, under pentathol, you must *be* Koslov." Shelley announced this in the manner of an examination, a test for his companion.

Slowly, Massinger nodded; the abstracted, detached agreement of an academic conceding an argument. "I see that. Very well, if that is what is required."

"But can you *do* it?" Shelley asked in exasperation.

"I have to, don't I?" Massinger smiled humorlessly. "Quit worrying, Peter. It's our only chance—isn't it?"

"Do you think it's one of their 'House of Cards' scenarios actually being put into operation?"

"It'd have the same effect, maybe, if it succeeded," Massinger replied. "Throw your service into total confusion, sow discord at all levels—I guess that's possible. But it could as easily be a vendetta against Aubrey."

"But our people are helping them to carry it out."

"The last twist of the knife. That's why I have to succeed in being Pavel Koslov. Why I have to get the Rezident to talk to me."

"Couldn't we go to JIC, even the PM, with what we have? With Hyde?"

"I've been warned off once."

"What about Sir William?"

"It was Sir William who warned me off. We wouldn't be believed. Just Aubrey's old friends and colleagues. Interested parties. No, it has to be a *fait accompli* or nothing." He looked once more at the Turner painting. "Let's walk, Peter. That picture is giving me a chill."

"You're still relying on a lunatic plan, Professor—"

"I know it. But, if we can get at even some of the truth and tape it—*then* we can go to Sir William, or even the PM, and show them what good little boys we've been on their behalf." His smile was both self-mocking and grim. "There's no other way, Peter. We must have *corroboration*."

Massinger felt dwarfed by the large Renaissance canvases lining the walls on either side of them as they moved toward the main staircase.

"What can I do while you're in Vienna?" Shelley asked, as if requiring some form of self-assertion between the huge paintings.

"Check Vienna Station—anything, any means. We must know how rotten the barrel is—and whether it's the only rotten barrel in town."

Shelley nodded. He appeared relieved to have been given some task. Relieved, too, to be obeying orders. Massinger had become a surrogate Aubrey. The weight of the realization burdened Massinger, and his feet felt uncertain on the marble steps down to the entrance hall. He felt old, rather tired, very reluctant. Ahead of him lay danger, doubt, and perhaps an unsatisfactory outcome. More than those professional risks, however, his wife lay ahead of him in time. As he envisaged her, she seemed unsubstantial, about to vanish like his own tormenting, betrayed Eurydice. If she even so much as suspected, she would never forgive him. She would not remain with him; she'd leave and never return. His certainty of that was a sharp physical pain in his chest.

He would tell her he had been invited to a Cambridge college for a couple of days by the Master—a former academic rival, a present friend. She would accept that. She had a great deal of committee work during the week; she would be relieved that he, too, would be busy, in company.

The lying had begun. He had taken the road he profoundly wished he could have avoided.

He and Shelley parted on the steps. Across Trafalgar Square, a flock of pigeons rose into the cold sunlight like a gray cloud.

"Be careful," Shelley offered. Then, as if unable to let the matter take its course, he added: "It doesn't seem sufficient!"

His protest was deeply felt, almost desperate. "It can't be enough to guarantee success—surely?"

"I don't know, Peter," Massinger replied gravely. "We simply can't sail a better course or grab a bigger stick. We have to do it this way. There isn't a choice. Take care of yourself."

The words of each seemed comfortless and empty to the other.

It was almost dark when Massinger reached the house. He let himself into the ground floor hallway, and began climbing the stairs. He had studied Hyde's new papers at the club, had sat at an eighteenth-century writing desk jotting down everything he had been told, and everything he knew and could remember concerning Pavel Koslov. And he had booked his seat on the British Airways morning flight to Vienna, and a room at the InterContinental Hotel.

The ascent seemed to become steeper as he mounted the stairs, as if a weight of guilt and reluctance pressed against his head and body. Margaret was there, waiting for him. She would have begun preparing dinner; supervising the housekeeper but preparing the sauces and the dessert herself. There was a pang in his chest that would not disperse.

He fumbled his key into the latch and pushed open the door. He listened, but there were no noises, no wisps of conversation from the kitchen. He opened the door of the drawing room.

Margaret and Babbington were both sitting, apart yet somehow subtly united, facing the door. Babbington's face was serious to the point of being forbidding. The man was charged with the electricity and danger of disobeyed authority. He was still wearing his overcoat. Massinger had passed his hat and gloves unnoticed on the hall stand.

Margaret's face was angry. Betrayed, flushed. Her eyes were hard, accusing.

She knew.

Babbington had told her.

Told what?

He was acutely aware, like some schoolboy pilferer, of the evidence of Hyde's new papers in the breast pocket of his coat.

4
Into Exile

After the initial shock, it was the tense, unaccustomed silence that struck Massinger. There was so often music in this room—records Margaret might be listening to, Margaret doodling at the piano, even singing—

Margaret burst out: "Paul, where have you been?" It was matronly yet somehow desperate. Babbington had introduced her to subtle nightmares. "What's going on, Paul?" she continued. "Andrew's been telling me all sorts . . ." She looked down, then, her voice trailing into silence. She sensed herself as part of a conspiracy against him. He saw Babbington watching her with what might have been an eager hunger—a suspicion of some former relationship between them stung him inappropriately at that moment—then the man looked up at him. His eyes were satisfied.

"What's the matter, darling?" he asked as soothingly as he could.

Her face had hardened again when she looked up. "You know what's happening!" she accused. "Andrew didn't want to tell me. I made him. . . ." She was ashamed of that. "You're still trying to help that man!"

"My dear," he said, moving toward her. Her knuckles were white against the velvet of the arms of her chair. She was wearing only her engagement ring and narrow gold wedding ring. Babbington's face indicated that Paul had been sufficiently warned, that the consequences were now of his making. "How can I have been helping him? At the club, at my stockbroker's?" The lies came fluently. He turned to Babbington. "Andrew—would you explain this, please? How have you upset Margaret?"

"I'm not *upset*! I *hate* that man!"

127

"For God's sake, Margaret!" His eyes never moved from Babbington's face. The directorships, the Quangos, the circles that might have admitted him, the *respect*—they all paled. This was Babbington's real power—*this*—a woman in tears, almost hysterical with fear and anger and hate. Babbington could, he was amply demonstrating, poison Margaret's mind incurably.

He was made aware once again of how many pictures of her father this room, other rooms, contained. The portrait watched from the wall. Castleford was here, in the room with them, assisting Babbington. He felt nausea and guilt sourly together in his throat.

Then he remembered Aubrey. The pictures stared at him, the portrait watched. Aubrey, in the back of his awareness, pleaded for, demanded help.

Castleford—

Aubrey—

"My dear," Babbington murmured, touching Margaret's hand, his large fingers tapping at the two rings, at the knuckles of her left hand. Massinger clenched his fists at his sides. "My dear, go and calm down a little. I think I may have—well, let me talk to Paul about this . . . mm?"

She looked at Babbington, nodded, sniffed, and got up. It was mesmeric, a further demonstration of Babbington's power over her mind. She left the room. Massinger pulled off his overcoat, careful of the package as he folded it and placed it across the back of a chair. The wall lights appeared gloomy, the room large and vacant.

"Well?" he accused Babbington. "What the hell are you up to, Andrew?"

He stood over Babbington, who did not attempt to rise.

"What the hell are you doing, Paul? It's *my* right to ask, I think, not yours. What are you *doing*, man?" Even then, his hand indicated the door by which Margaret had left. It was as if he had struck her. "What were you doing in Earl's Court, at Hyde's address? Who did you talk with—his landlady? Why, man? What were you doing at the Imperial War Museum, with Shelley? Why did Shelley have to throw off surveillance in order to meet you?" His eyes glinted, but Massinger suspected that he had no answers to his questions, using them as he was simply in the form of accusations. Please don't let him know, he thought, and realized the weakness of his position. He and Shelley and Hyde. The sum total . . .

Inadequate.

"I—" Careful, careful, he told himself, trying to rid himself of images of his wife, trying to press down upon his anger, create a mood of apologetic explanation. Not too weak, not too quick, but start to give in. "I don't see what it has to do with you, Andrew. I really don't think it needs you to come here and poison my wife against me—" He had walked away from Babbington soon after he began speaking, and now he turned to face him, deliberately, the whiskey decanter in his hand as he did so. "Do you?"

"Poison?" Babbington smiled. "You never possessed much sense of proportion, Paul, did you? I'm not poisoning Margaret against you. I'm just trying to establish what you think you're engaged upon, that's all." The remark invited explanation.

Not too quickly, Massinger instructed himself, pouring a large whiskey without offering one to Babbington. Margaret kept intruding, tightening his chest with a physical pain. It was difficult to concentrate on fending off Babbington.

"Do I owe you any explanation, Andrew?"

"I think you do, yes. You don't even know this man Hyde. Of what interest is he to you?"

"I—" Massinger looked thoughtful, slightly guilty, almost determined. "Aubrey asked me to check . . ." he admitted slowly.

"What?"

"Aubrey asked me to check," he blustered. "It's as simple as that. He wanted to know whether Hyde had been heard from. Does that satisfy you?"

Enough bluster, too much? Had he hooked Babbington, used the man's poor enough opinion of him? Dodged and faltered enough to be dismissed?

Babbington smiled. His eyes almost seemed to form words—errand boy, pet dog—Babbington's contempt for him was evident. Massinger wondered whether the man might not destroy his happiness simply out of amusement.

"Aubrey asked you," he repeated with heavy sarcasm. "And what, pray, did you find out?"

"His landlady hadn't heard from him."

"And the matter of Shelley—your little assignation with the head of East Europe Desk?" Babbington made it seem a very temporary appointment.

"Much the same," Massinger snapped, irked by Babbington's interrogation. "Look, dammit, I was *asked* by an old friend, a very old friend, if I would seek help for him. Can't you understand? Aubrey was desperate, isolated, afraid. I had to do as he asked. I couldn't turn him *down*!"

Yes, yes, yes, he thought, his eyes watching Babbington as he held the tumbler to his lips. Loyalty, old friendships—the futility of it was expressed in Babbington's eyes. He had successfully *placed* him now, understood and dismissed him as a sentimentalist. It confirmed what he thought of Margaret and Massinger together, and the leverage any threat to personal happiness would exercise on him. Massinger held his body unmoving, though a wave of relief swept over him. He'd done it . . .

For the moment.

"I see," Babbington murmured. "But with what result?"

"Enlistment isn't fashionable these days," Massinger replied bitterly. "Leastways, not for lost causes."

"Ah. And you—do you feel Aubrey's cause is lost?"

"I don't believe he's guilty."

"That's not what I asked."

Massinger shrugged. "There's—nothing more I can do, either way," he admitted grudgingly.

"I agree." Babbington stood up. "Thank you for being frank with me," he said, crossing to Massinger and extending his hand. Massinger held his drink for a moment, as if in defiance, then Babbington added: "I'll just have a word with Margaret. Don't worry. She'll be fine. Her father *was* a very special man, you know," he added. "Especially to her." Massinger shook his hand. "I'm glad things are—cleared up, Paul. Thank you for being so honest." There was an evident, cruel amusement in his eyes. And visible contempt—

"Margaret's been through enough already, Andrew," Massinger warned.

"Quite. Good-bye, Paul."

He exited through the door to the dining room, closing it behind him. Massinger swallowed his drink. *Yes*—the contempt of power for emotion, for sentiment—*yes*. He was warmed by the passage of the drink and by a fierce delight in his own skill and intuition. He resented Babbington's returning Margaret to him like a borrowed gift, but he waited for her to come through the doors, smiling.

"Paul," she said. Yes, she was smiling. "Paul, Andrew's explained everything! I understand what you've been trying to do." There was a superiority about her understanding, almost a maternal, comforting sense. He ignored it, holding her close against him, feeling her breathing against his throat and neck. He had beaten Babbington.

And Babbington had shown him his power over Margaret and, once more, the power of dead Robert Castleford. Babbington would use Castleford without hesitation against him as he was using him against Aubrey: to fulfill his own ambitions. What he held, he would keep—the joint Director-Generalship of MI 5 and SIS. Absolute power in the secret world. Babbington would stop at nothing to retain that power. The KGB had provided him with the means to finish Aubrey. Babbington cared nothing for the truth of the matter, for the KGB's motives, for the rot that might have set in, for *collusion*. . . .

He'd see none of it. He'd see only his chance, his success.

Massinger felt anguished. Slowly, he held her at arms' length. Her eyes were still bright with dismissed tears. Her face glowed. He ached with love for her, with fear at losing her. He *couldn't* let her go . . . *wouldn't* . . .

He had to.

Fear and anger gripped him.

Pavel *knew* . . . Aubrey tugged at him like an imploring child at his sleeve . . . he became angrier than ever at Sir William, and at Babbington's blackmail and contempt . . . Margaret's willful, unquestioning, blind loyalty to the memory of a father she had hardly known . . . all of it enraged him. He knew he would not stop now until he had established the truth . . . he would *show* them Aubrey was innocent, by God!

A part of his awareness laughed mockingly at his resolution. Nevertheless, he knew he would go on with it . . . dammit, she would *have* to understand!

"Darling," he murmured.

Her left hand, the one with the rings he had given her, the diamond flashing in the subdued lighting, reached up and stroked his temple, then his cheek. He could not help feeling this was some kind of final, parting blessing. He caught her hand as she murmured: "Darling . . ." Her lips pouted. He was aware of her sexual attractiveness in a swift, piercing way. He knew that she had begun to entertain images of their lovemaking. He could envisage her face smoothed, whitened, dreamlike at climax, and he felt aroused.

He clutched her hand, but prevented her from moving close to him again.

"Margaret," he began guiltily. "Margaret, listen to me, please."

"What is it?"

He led her to the sofa, made her sit down. She was half-puzzled, half-amused. He lowered himself into the cushion, his body separated from hers. He held her hands solemnly.

"It's not over. Whatever I told Babbington, it's not over," he murmured. She looked struck, even wounded. "No, just listen to me before you say anything, please—" He held up one hand to silence her. "Please listen before you say anything, before you judge me."

Eventually, she nodded stiffly, a little bob of her head. Her fair hair fell across her cheek, her brow. "Very well."

"This isn't about Aubrey," he began. "At least, it's not just about Aubrey. No, don't make that face, you can't hate him that much. . . ." He abandoned the argument, and continued: "I have evidence—from Aubrey's man in Vienna, and Peter Shelley's convinced too—that the KGB are behind this business. Whatever the truth of the matter, they're using it. More than that, Aubrey's man could well be killed by his own side." He paused. There was little reaction other than puzzlement, a sense of unfamiliarity; then dismissal, the light of common sense falling on this dark corner of experience and making it seem ridiculous—incomprehensible and incredible. "No one else believes it. No one else is interested. Babbington is blinded by his own ambition, Sir William is content to see Aubrey go to the wall because he's persuaded the Cabinet Office and the Joint Intelligence Committee that they want and need a unified security and intelligence service." Her eyes revealed that she was dismissing each of his statements even as he made them. He waved one hand loosely to indicate his helplessness. "You see," he pleaded, "why I can't give up on this?"

She was silent for a long time, and then she said simply: "No, I don't see."

"But, you must!"

"I *can't*! All I can see is that you're still willing to help the man who betrayed my father—who caused his *death*!"

"You don't even know if it's true!"

"And you don't care! You'll help him anyway!"

"My darling, I promise you—I *promise*, that if I find it is true, I'll abandon him like everyone else. If Aubrey helped to kill your father, then to hell with him. I won't lift a finger to help him."

"I can't bear this. . . ." she murmured.

"There's nothing else I can do."

"Why can't you talk to William about this—please?"

"Because he's convinced that Aubrey's a traitor. Just like everyone else. They don't want to look any deeper into it."

"But you do—" she accused.

"I must."

"So, only Paul Massinger can be right, only Paul Massinger's priorities are important."

"You know that isn't true!"

"*How* do I know? Dear God, it isn't even your *country*!"

He stood up, unable to bear her hot gaze, her accusing mouth. He crossed the room, then turned to look back at her.

"I'm trusting you with my life," he said quietly. "I've told you because I had to. I promised Babbington that I'll go no further. Only you know I'm continuing with it. I—have to go to Vienna for a couple of days, to see this man of Aubrey's." She averted her face. His body had taken on a supplicant's stoop, arms akimbo. "I ask you to tell no one. If anyone asks, then I'm in Cambridge for a couple of nights. Out of harm's way," he added cynically. "When I get back, I'll tell you everything. I'll let *you* decide."

She turned to him, her face reddened, her hands clenched on her lap. She shook back her hair.

"Don't come back," she said. "Just—don't come back." She, too, stood up. Her body was rigid with determination. "If you leave this apartment on that man's behalf—" He groaned inwardly. She had accepted nothing of what he had said. "—then you need not bother to come back. I don't care if I'm being unreasonable, or stupid, or even malicious—but I can't *bear* it! If you go on helping that man, then we're finished. It's over."

Paul Massinger was stung.

"My God, Margaret, but you're being unreasonable!" he flared like straw ignited by a spark.

Her face paled, then two livid spots appeared on her high, prominent cheekbones. She swept a stray lock of hair from her forehead, as if giving some contemptuous signal of dismissal.

"*I'm* being unreasonable? Me? What about *you*, Paul—

what about you? You're not Sir Galahad, Paul, you're a man of sixty with a deteriorating hip!" Her eyes were blazing. He quailed inwardly at the force of her rage. "Despite everything, despite *everything*, you're determined to go ahead with this ridiculous nonsense to help that man!"

"You don't even know he's guilty!" he shouted back at her.

"I know he killed my father—there's no question of it," she replied, breathing heavily, shoulders slightly forward, combatively. "Everyone knows it!" she added with something like triumph. He shook his head slowly. "Don't you *patronize* me!" she yelled, moving forward, leaning over him in the armchair into which he had retreated. Her hands gripped his arms with a surprising strength. "I'm not the village idiot that you have to feel sorry for me! You're the one who's wrong— *you*!" Her hands were shaking his upper arms as she attempted to bully common sense into him. Massinger stared at his wife's face, unable to perceive anything except his sentence of dismissal. It was too late now to retreat, to back off. He clung, in his misery, to the fond hope that she would see sense, listen to *reason*, if he established the truth about Aubrey . . . if he could prove Aubrey was innocent—that 1946 was just a part of the weave and fabric of the setup—then he might recover her. She would forgive him. . . .

Castleford's portrait sneered from the wall.

He had to believe he could recover her love, but the hope of doing so was like a distant, small white hand desperately trying to cross the sea of misery she was inflicting upon them both. Tears were bright and held back in her eyes, and he felt them prick in his own.

"Margaret—" he groaned.

She turned away immediately, as if he were about to trick her into some gentler mood.

"Leave now, and don't bother to come back," she announced heavily, as she turned her back on him, closing the dining room doors behind her with a firm, quiet finality.

The British Airways Trident dropped toward the snow-bound landscape amid which the southeastern suburbs of Vienna straggled out toward the pattern of Schwechat airport's runways. The scene was uniformly gray and white to Massinger's red-rimmed, prickling eyes. Bodily, he was little more than a lump that had sleeplessly occupied a hotel bed near Heathrow and then a taxi and then a departure lounge and then an aircraft seat next to a window. A lump that had previously performed, like an automaton, the tasks of packing, gathering passport, credit cards, wallet, Hyde's papers, ordering a taxi, avoiding all sense of Margaret in other rooms in the apartment, avoiding him.

His mind was numbed. Not free, or released, merely numbed. He could no longer think of her or about her. He had lost her. That realization was like a wall in his mind, closing out other images and thoughts.

The wheels bumped, and snow-covered concrete and grass rushed past the window—a moonscape produced by snowploughs. Then the aircraft was taxiing, turning right then left, back toward the strangely provincial, miniature airport buildings. Schwechat was like any airfield in Eastern Europe: a bare, flat child's model of a grown-up's real airport. He and Margaret had flown into Schwechat often, visiting concerts, operas, galleries in Vienna. . . .

The thought drifted away, as if he had no powers of retention left. The landing music switched off and the stewardess wished him a pleasant stay. People began to gather baggage hurriedly, tumbling it out of the overhead lockers as if prompted by an escape timetable limited to split seconds. He followed them slowly across the pooled, windy tarmac into the terminal building.

Passport control, luggage, customs. A largely empty hall, echoing, modern, aseptic. He tried to anticipate the events to come, the evening and night ahead, but all he gained was a sense of foreboding and weakness, and he surrendered the idea. He had begun, he knew, to lose interest, not to care. *Teardrop*, Hyde, Aubrey the old man, the KGB, all became figments of a melodramatic dream, as they had been for Margaret. There was only one thing he now cared about, one fragment of the truth upon which he must lay hold: Had Aubrey betrayed Robert Castleford, had him killed in Berlin almost forty years ago?

The answer to that question contained the kernel of his future happiness. The KGB, he had realized, must know something about 1946 to make the accusation of murder plausible. If not, they would not have used it as part of their *Teardrop* operation. A terrible, recurring fear gripped him. If Aubrey had done it, then Margaret was lost to him forever.

She would never, never forgive him . . . yet he could not *believe* it! Aubrey was innocent of the murder, and if he could prove it by unraveling *Teardrop*, then Margaret would have to forgive him, just *have* to—

Recovering her was what animated him. The question of Castleford's murder obsessed him. *That* he would pursue, whatever else. . . .

The doors slid back and he walked into the freezing air outside the arrivals hall. Immediately, a gray Mercedes displaying a taxi sign pulled out from a parking space and, jumping the line of vehicles drawn up, halted directly in front of him. He was startled into clutching his suitcase more tightly.

"Massinger," Hyde said. It was a recognition, not a question. "All right. I'm Hyde. Note the accent?" Hyde smiled grimly at Massinger's relief.

"How did you—?"

"Money. What else? Just borrowed it. Get in." He pushed open the rear door and Massinger climbed in, sliding his suitcase in front of him. The moment he shut the door, Hyde pulled the Mercedes away, down the ramp toward the main road. "I thought a taxi might come in useful—oh, better be kosher and put the clock on." He turned his head to glance at the American. "You strong on tipping, Massinger?"

"What? Oh—"

"What's the matter?" Hyde asked urgently.

"Everything," Massinger began, then noticing Hyde's alarm, he added: "And nothing. No need to worry. I wasn't spotted and followed."

"I know that. I've been here two hours waiting. No face I know, not even one I suspect I ought to know, has shown up." Hyde grinned suddenly, showing his profile once more. "You're not doing too bad for an old man."

"And you—how are you doing?"

"Ahead. Just. It's only real professionals we have to worry about. Brought my papers?"

"Yes."

On the wide empty road raised above flat white fields, they passed a gray, lumped-together factory complex. A red-and-white chimney belched dark smoke.

"Good. Well, what's the plan?" Hyde was clearly enjoying a human contact he did not have to fear or suspect. He was almost blithe.

"We—we're going to kidnap the KGB Rezident in Vienna. A simple job—"

"You what?"

Massinger was offhand, almost satiric, because he did not care. He was unable to concern himself closely with the matter. It was no more than a preliminary task to be executed before he could return to London to discover the truth concerning Aubrey and Castleford; he might even confront Aubrey, after he had dug around, yes, he might . . .

Hyde was stunned by his apparent nonchalance. "Did I hear you correctly, Massinger? Did you say kidnap the Rezident? Hands up everybody in the Soviet Embassy, all right, come with us, sunshine? You're talking through your backside!"

"There's no other way. The Rezident must know—I am certain he *does* know what's going on here. He knows about *Teardrop*, and what's behind it."

"Of course he bloody does! So what?"

"I know where he will be tonight, and I know he will be alone. Without his security men." Massinger was amused, in a detached manner, at the signals of competence and superiority he was hoisting. "Shall I go on?"

"Oh, please do," Hyde replied with thickly spread sarcasm.

"Very well."

Small, peeled-paint houses and farms, a flour mill, then newer bungalows, pebble-dashed or faced with gray concrete. Pink or light green, many of them. Then the city began rising to two or three storys and closing in around the car. The river to their left was dark and sluggish. The wheels of the Mercedes clunked over tramlines. Dingy shops bearing weather-beaten nameboards and advertisements, new cars, tall new buildings. Then the heavy, monumental buildings lining the Ring.

They were in the Johannesgasse and close to the Inter-Continental before Massinger had completed his narrative.

"Well?" he asked finally as Hyde passed the hotel and slid into a parking space fifty yards beyond it. The Australian switched off the car engine and turned, leaning his arm on the back of the bench seat. His eyes studied Massinger over the sleeve of his stained overcoat.

Speaking almost into his sleeve, he said: "So there's me, you, and Shelley. That's the entire army, is it?"

"Yes." He felt dry-throated from talking without pause or interruption, and weary from lack of conviction in what he was doing.

"And you couldn't give a bugger. What about Shelley?"

"What do you mean?"

"Your scheme is harebrained, but it doesn't seem to frighten you. You don't care enough. I can't see us getting away with it unless you wake up."

"I see." Massinger wanted to explain, but then said bluntly: "Unless you help—unless we get to the bottom of this—you're living on borrowed time."

"Sure—and interest rates are going up and up. I know. But—*you* watching my back? I don't think so, mate. Thanks all the same."

"You know Aubrey is supposed to have betrayed my wife's father to the NKVD in 1946. She believes it, anyway. Does that answer your question? I may not seem to care—but if I want my own answers, my own peace, then this has to be the first step. Now—do we go or not?"

Hyde studied Massinger's drawn and tired face for a long time, then he said: "This bloke Cass—he's laid on, is he?"

Massinger nodded. "He arrives this afternoon. He knows where to contact me."

"Do you know enough to play the Rezident's pal—just through having a couple of drinks with him and watching the opera from the same box?"

"I'll have to, won't I?"

"You will." Then Hyde shrugged. "I don't have any choice, anyway. Argument's just a lot of finessing crap. I don't have anywhere to go. The body in the alley decided that for me." He held out his hand. "Okay, Massinger—light the fuse and stand well clear."

"You understand, Professor? I'm sure Pete Shelley warned you of the dangers of pentathol interrogation—opening and closing doors?" Massinger nodded. Cass's face was a mere white blank in the darkness of the car. Hyde had left them once more to patrol the street, adrenaline-alert, senses and intelligence heightened to the point where Massinger sensed excitement, even pleasure in him. "Good. You have to *be* this man Pavel Koslov and you mustn't step out of character, not for a moment. At least, it would be wise not to."

Cass was about Shelley's age, an old school friend of the head of East Europe Desk, clever, fluent in at least five languages, apparently a good field agent, and totally lacking the other's ambitions. Madrid Station was simply another enjoyable and easy posting on a covert tour of the world. Shelley's assessment of and liking for Cass were both deserved.

"Do you think it'll work?"

"It might—I say only *might*. I won't be there to increase the dose, or direct you. Shelley made it clear that I should disappear as soon as I've filled his veins."

"Yes, you must get away at once."

"All right. First of all, I'll knock him out with sodium pentathol. Twenty minutes later, I'll inject enough benzedrine to bring him round again. Then he's all yours. I'll stay long enough to check the first couple of questions, to make sure he doesn't need any more benzedrine. He'll be somewhere between waking and sleeping, then. Almost comatose, but bright-eyed and bushy-tailed at the same time. Okay?"

"Yes."

"Good. This is a form of narcotherapy. There are other and better drugs that could be used with a greater chance of success, but they're harder to handle. I couldn't leave you to do the whole thing by yourselves."

"I see."

"Now—lull him at first by talking slowly, sleepily if you like—the old-fashioned hypnotist's voice. Mm?" Massinger nodded. "Then come across as strongly as you can in the guise of Koslov. Create an atmosphere for him, a conversation. Now, if he begins to doze off, don't slap his face or shake him about. You might start waking him up properly. I'll leave you a syringe. Ten milligrams of benzedrine if he falls asleep. Okay?"

"How long do I have with him?"

"Perhaps an hour, even an hour-and-a-half. But if at any time ten milligrams don't bring him back to you, leave it. Unless you don't mind what happens to him."

"I don't want him—harmed," Massinger replied.

"Okay, that's that, then. All we have to do now is wait."

Cass settled back in the seat, arms folded across his chest. He seemed sublimely unconcerned. Massinger scanned the street for Hyde and eventually saw him drifting back toward the car from the direction of the Michaelerplatz and the massive facade of the Hofburg Palace. The girl's apartment was on the third floor of an elegant nineteenth-century house, the ground floor of which was a jeweler's shop.

Hyde thrust his head inside the Mercedes, and announced: "Not a bloody sausage, Massinger. The street's clean for three blocks, and the square's strictly kosher. Okay? Can I get warm now?"

"Thank you, Hyde."

Hyde got into the car, looked at Cass's dozing form, then settled down in the driving seat. He had brought the smell of cold into the car, together with the scent of excitement. Massinger was aware of his own adrenaline, sluggish at first like melting ice, now prickling and prodding him into alertness. He was aware of how little he had considered Margaret in the past hours, and was abashed and grateful. Temporarily, at least, his wife had receded in his heart and mind. Now he did want this; he did want to know.

"What time do you have?" he asked Hyde.

Hyde slanted his watch to catch the light of a streetlamp.

"A couple of minutes to nine. If, as you tell me, this bloke's as regular as a sergeant-major's bowels, he'll be here in a mo."

"Quite." Massinger's smile, hidden by the darkness, was eager and almost childish. "Cass?" he whispered. Cass sat upright.

"Here's a black Mercedes—no official plates," Hyde reported. "Probably his own car."

The car passed them and pulled in at a vacant parking meter on the opposite side of the Herrengasse. It was less than twenty yards from the front of the jeweler's shop and the discreet, narrow door between its window and the next shop, where jackets and skirts, cardigans and trousers lay like the victims of a skirmish, softly lit from the ceiling. All three men leaned forward in their seats.

A short, plump man got out of the car. He was alone, and little more than a dark overcoat and trilby hat. He fed the meter and locked the car, and as he passed the boutique, they saw his face for a moment. Massinger sighed.

"That's him," Hyde said unnecessarily.

"We'll give him ten or fifteen minutes. He mostly stays

until after midnight. Her only client on Thursday evenings. Drinks first, I guess," Massinger almost drawled.

"Gives him wind while he's performing, I'll bet," Hyde murmured.

"Hyde?"

"I know. Is your joking really necessary? No, it isn't. But I haven't had many laughs lately."

The Vienna Rezident of the KGB rang the bell and the door opened a moment later. They had seen him bend forward to speak into a grille set to one side of the door.

"Damn," Massinger muttered as the door closed behind the Russian.

"Don't worry. Speak Russian," Hyde instructed. "He'll let us in if he thinks it's official. Sound annoyed at being dragged out on a night like this. It'll work wonders."

"No, I think German. The police," Massinger replied. He looked at his watch. "Ten minutes, then we'll go in while he's still drinking his second glass of champagne." His voice was light, filled with an unaccustomed excitement.

"You're the boss," Hyde said. "You're the boss."

"Anything in today's airport snaps?"

"Couple of girls with big tits—LOT hostesses."

"All right—bring them over. I'd better look them over before I initial the docket."

"There. Couple of wasted rolls. Oh, those two in that shot. KGB back from London leave. See the M & S bags full of goodies. Should guarantee them a good time in Moscow when they next go home."

"We know those two. Log them back in."

"Wilkes?"

"Yes?"

"Why are we after Hyde—I mean, really after him?"

"You don't believe he's been turned?"

"I've worked with Hyde before. He's a barmy Australian, I grant you, but he'd never take orders from some KGB control. Too bloody-minded for that."

"Look, you weren't there the other night. He didn't hesitate to kill that poor sod Philips."

"I know that—"

"There you are then. Would he do that if he *wasn't* working for the other side?"

"I suppose not."

"He's been on the run ever since they took in Aubrey. He's Aubrey's man, all right."

"I have my doubts about Aubrey, too."

"For Christ's sake, Beach! London *arrested* Aubrey. They wouldn't dare if they didn't have a good case. Now, be a good lad and pour some coffee while I glance at these snaps."

"Okay, Wilkes."

"Mm . . . nothing there . . . big knockers is right . . . Boris and Doris, the terrible twins. Caught London just right for the January sales . . . no, nothing in those two . . . thanks . . . mm, not bad for a beginner. Too much sugar."

"So sorry, Wilkes. What did your last servant die of?"

"I don't recognize him—ah, Ivan the Dreadful, on duty-go at Schwechat again, I see. It must be his boils they don't like . . . no, no . . . nothing, nothing, nothing . . . stop bloody whistling, will you, Beach, it goes right through my teeth . . . no, no, and no . . . almost done. Hello, do I know you from somewhere?"

"Found something?"

"No, shouldn't think so. Just a face I thought I knew . . . mm? Can't place it. Just a look-alike, I expect. . . . Where's that bloody glass? Ah, let's blow you up a bit . . . no? Now, who the hell is that? I'm sure I know him."

"Let's have a look, then—"

"You're too young to remember. I think this face goes too far back for you . . . there. Recognize that bloke with the small suitcase, tall one?"

"Looks British to the core. Banker? Company director? Civil servant? I don't recognize him."

"Back in time . . . years ago . . . civil servant, you said? Like us or the 'Yes, Minister' mob? Now, who the bloody hell are you? No—I don't think he's anything to do with us. Come to think of it, I don't even think he's British. But I'm just *sure* there's some connection with Aubrey."

"More coffee?"

"Oh, Christ!"

"What is it?"

"I've just remembered who this bloke is!"

"Go on, let's have another look."

"You won't know him. Paul Massinger—yes, that's right, he's a Yank—CIA years ago. A friend of Aubrey. I've seen him with the old man. Aubrey's used him unofficially as an adviser from time to time. Paul Massinger."

"What's he doing here, then?"

"I don't know—but I'll bet London would be interested. What time was this—bloody hell, he's been here half a day already. You hang on here, I'm going to signal London now. Someone's bound to think this isn't a coincidence."

The silences between their words were little islands of civilized living. As soon as either of them spoke, the mellow whiskey and the subdued lighting and the rich velvet curtains retreated, and Aubrey was once more fighting for his survival and Andrew Babbington was his opponent.

Staring into his crystal tumbler, Babbington said with finality: "I really came to tell you that JIC and the Cabinet Office and myself are to meet the PM early next week to formalize the setting up of the new Security and Intelligence Directorate. SIS and MI 5 will no longer continue their separate existences." He looked up. There was a flinty calm in his eyes. "And I have been instructed to prepare papers in your own case for the DPP as soon as possible."

Aubrey felt winded. He studied his own whiskey greedily, but did not drink. He silently cleared his throat and drew saliva into the roof of his mouth from his cheeks so that his voice would not betray him when he spoke. Then he said: "So, you have it all. King, Cawdor, Glamis, all as the weird women promised."

"Do you fear I have played most foully for it?" Babbington countered.

"No. Foolishly and dangerously, perhaps."

"How so?"

"Andrew, if you do not see that I *cannot* be guilty of these things, then I cannot persuade you. You are blinded by your own supreme ambition, and your blindness has served you well. What you may, by omission, have done to my service and your own, I can't say."

"Your service?"

"My former service. They mean to send me to trial, then?"

"Perhaps. Cooperation could forestall that. . . ."

"How can I cooperate? I do not know the script of the

play!" Aubrey snapped, getting up from his chair and topping up his whiskey. Babbington refused the proffered decanter.

"I see," he said.

"How far will they take this matter?" Aubrey asked, his back to Babbington, shoulders slightly hunched as if he were leaning heavily on the sideboard for support.

"I'm not sure—no one is at the moment."

"I don't want a trial. I don't think I could face that," Aubrey murmured.

"Then—"

"I have nothing to offer as cooperation, man!"

"Then—let me say this to you. There are elements—not necessarily in the majority—who consider a trial, *in camera*, of course, but certainly a prosecution before the law, could be useful. A cleaning of the stable, purification of the house—reconsecration, so to speak. Good for Security and Intelligence Directorate at its inception."

"And, of course, there is always the PM's stern morality to deal with. The PM would be inclined to a trial, no doubt. After all of them, *all* the old bogeymen who've been let off, allowed to go free, brushed under the carpet, kicked upstairs and even honored for treachery—the buck stops here!" He turned to face Babbington. His face was drawn and tired, but animated. "The wrong place at the wrong time. One traitor too many to stomach, mm?"

Babbington shrugged. "Perhaps . . ."

"And, of course, my background isn't quite what it might have been."

"That *is* nonsense—"

"Is it? Is it really?"

Aubrey appeared about to continue, but the telephone, ringing in the hall, silenced him. Babbington got up immediately.

"Probably for me. I gave them your number—"

Aubrey shrugged and Babbington crossed swiftly to the door, closing it behind him. It moved ajar slightly, but Aubrey had no desire to listen. There was no motive for suspicion. Babbington was keeping nothing secret from him. His end had been prescribed—etched in clean, deep lines. They were determined that he should be finished, and that he should be seen to be finished. The king must die. His ashes would fertilize the new seed. And Babbington would be Director-General of the new organization.

Resentment died, to be replaced by a hollow, deflated feeling. Emptiness.

He realized that they had succeeded in taking his life from him. Not simply his past, or his reputation and credibility; not his achievements or his probity; not his rank or his honors. His life. More important even than his good name. He was not Othello. He could no longer do as he had always done; he could no longer involve himself, belong . . .

They had taken away his reason for living.

"I warned him—I *warned* him," Babbington was saying heavily in the hall. There was a brutal power in the man's voice, a naked strength. Babbington was too strong an opponent and Aubrey had no will or allies with which to fight him. Kapustin had known all this, had known everything that would follow from the instigation of his damned *Teardrop!*

Aubrey's eyes were damp with rage and self-pity.

Damn Kapustin. He had guessed correctly at every turn of the cards, every throw of the dice. *Teardrop* was cast-iron, watertight, unsinkable. There was nothing he could do.

"You've done that? Good," Babbington was saying. "Yes—oh, no, it was no coincidence. He went deliberately, to make contact. Yes. No risks. Yes."

The receiver clicked back onto its rest. Aubrey straightened his slumping, tired old body, forcing it to replicate a former self.

Babbington entered the room again, his face dark with anger. A domestic tyrant facing a squeaking, fearful little rebellion from one of his children. Not endangered or unsettled, simply enraged at the enormity of defiant words or disobedience.

"Your friend Massinger—" he began, then swept his hand through the air in a dismissive gesture. "The man is a *fool!*"

"A sentimentalist. They are only the same thing once in a while, usually over women or small animals. Paul is no fool."

"If he tries to help you, he is."

"Has he—?" Aubrey could not prevent himself from asking.

"Inadequately, yes. There's no comfort in it, though."

"No," Aubrey admitted.

Babbington crossed to his briefcase, and removed a buff file.

"Read these," he said, pressing them into Aubrey's hand.

"They contain the details of your arranged escape from NKVD custody in Berlin, and Soviet instructions to ensure that you reach the British sector safely." The papers shook in Aubrey's grasp, and he could not prevent them doing so.

"Your ambition's blinding you to everything except the surface . . ." Aubrey began.

"You had Castleford killed. You're a Russian agent—my God, to think what might have happened if we hadn't got hold of this!—and we'll have you for that. Especially for that." Babbington collected his briefcase, and made for the door. Looking at his watch, he said: "I'll send Eldon along in a little while. I'm sure you won't object to a late night? I doubt you could sleep, anyway."

"There. He's ready for you now." Cass inspected the dilated pupils of Karel Bayev, KGB Rezident in Vienna, as his plump, still fully dressed form lolled in a deep armchair. The light of the room fell on Bayev's blank, dead-yet-alert features. The man looked capable of reason and speech at one moment, incapable even of movement at another. "Try him out," Cass suggested as he filled another syringe with benzedrine.

Hyde slipped silently back into the room through the door to the bedroom. A call from the Vice Squad had persuaded the girl to open the door, and shock had prevented her from having to be hurt or disabled as they pressed through. Hyde had gagged her with his hand and bundled her up the stairs in front of him. Bayev had been sitting idly drinking champagne, and at once called out to the girl as they opened the door of the lounge. He had recognized a type in Hyde almost immediately but Cass, holding Hyde's pistol, had quelled protest.

Simple preliminaries, Massinger reminded himself. Almost too easy. Now, begin—

Hyde had crossed to the window, almost unobserved. Bayev's pupils had not followed his progress. He was staring into some unknown middle distance.

Margaret—

Begin.

"Karel, old friend—so good to see you again!" Massinger exclaimed in Russian, attempting as close an impersonation of Pavel Koslov's ringing tones as he could. "Karel!" he tried again, catching in his memory the echo of Pavel's usual enthusiastic greeting. "It's Pavel—your old friend, Pavel!" He chuckled, imitating Pavel's delight, clear in his mind, from the darkened back of an opera box.

"Embrace him," Cass whispered. "Call his name again."

"Karel—come on, Karel!" Massinger bent forward and took Bayev by the shoulders, kissing him on each cheek. "It's Pavel. I want you to show me Vienna, old man!"

Bayev seemed to snap into wakefulness. His eyes watched Massinger, who could not but believe that the fiction would be exposed in a moment, that Bayev would protest, attempt to rise from the chair, threaten, become frightened—

"Pavel . . . Pavel . . ." he muttered, his voice thick with phlegm.

"That'll clear in a minute," Cass observed nonchalantly. "Once the station's tuned in properly. Go on."

"I've four whole days in this beautiful city, and I'm ready for anything. Just like the school vacations, eh, old man? Tallinn—do you remember Tallinn? The *girls!*"

Cass was smiling broadly when Massinger glanced up at him. He nodded encouragingly. Hyde was also smiling, then he tossed his head toward the door and went out.

"Ah . . . aaah . . ." Bayev sighed. His hands moved in slow motion, describing the female form in the air. "Yes—the girls in Vienna, too! Wait till you see some of them. *Meet* them, Pavel! Oh, yes—"

"Very well, old friend. And how are you—busy?"

"Too busy. Much too busy. But, I will give myself a special assignment for a few days—we'll enjoy ourselves!"

"Good, good." Massinger could not see the conversation unfolding any further. He had established the circumstances, the fiction of himself as Koslov, but he could not force his own imagination to ignite. He could not *be* Koslov.

"What now?" he whispered.

"You've got the script," Cass replied.

"Damn," Massinger breathed, then he said: "London is a pig, Karel, old friend. Trouble, trouble, trouble. I can't tell you how they're keeping us on our toes. . . ." His voice and ideas trailed off once more.

Then Bayev said: "*You* complain? We had that bloody Deputy Chairman here again last week! My God, that operation is never-ending!" Bayev was animated, waving his arms slowly like the sails of a windmill or the slow circling of a lighthouse beam.

"My God," Massinger whispered. Then: "Kapustin always was a real shit!"

"Too right, my friend, too r-right . . . y-es, oh . . . y-e-ss . . ."

"What's happening?"

"He's not lasting long, is he?" Cass replied. He moved toward Bayev's form, which now had slumped back in the armchair, his pupils tiny and hard like currants, his eyes staring blankly. His hands and legs lay like those of a dummy about to be folded into its case.

Cass injected benzedrine, and stood back. "He could be overtired or half cut. I can't tell. Looks like you'll have to keep waking him." He looked at his watch. "If I want to catch the Frankfurt flight, I'd better go. I'll leave you the syringe. Remember, if he doesn't come out of it at any time, leave him alone."

"Very well."

Bayev snapped awake once more.

"Kapustin's a real shit," Massinger said at once.

"Who are you?" Bayev replied in a suspicious voice.

"Oh, Jesus!"

"What is it, Wilkes? What did London say when you told them? What did they come back to you for?"

"Never mind—look, go out and get some chocolate cake, will you? I'm starving."

"Now? Everywhere's shut—"

"Not that little delicatessen on the corner. Go on, do as you're told for a change."

"Money first. I know you."

"Here—and don't be long."

"Okay. See you."

"Thank God for that . . . now, six . . . seven . . . four . . . eight . . . nine . . . three . . . one . . . five . . . Come on— Christ, if this hits the fan, Wilkes old son, you can forget a cushy berth next time out—come *on* . . . thank God—give me Savin—at once. Never mind, just put me through. Yes, yes, the bloody code of the day is *Volgograd*—bloody imaginative, isn't it? Hurry up! . . . Savin, is that you? Listen. London just signaled. If you know where your Rezident is, check up on him and keep him secure. Why? Because someone's been into our Registry files, and they've been checking on your boss. Yes, and that someone's in Vienna now—probably with Hyde . . . yes, that's right, Hyde. So, if you know where he is, I should check up on him if I were you!"

"Pavel—it's Pavel," Messinger said hesitantly.

"Pavel?" Bayev was still suspicious. Massinger had been attempting to reestablish the fiction for more than five minutes. Cass, as if supremely indifferent, had left to catch his flight—Frankfurt then onward to Madrid, his job now simply to make himself secure. Massinger's task was proving difficult, if not impossible. It had been too easy, like a gleam of sun before fog returns.

"Yes, Pavel—come on, Karel, what's the matter with you? Pissed again?"

Bayev laughed. "Pavel!" he exclaimed. "You old rat, how are you? What are you doing in Vienna?"

"Vacation—fun! And business, of course."

"Not more orders—not more of this business. Does Kapustin never sleep?"

"Thank God," Massinger breathed.

The telephone began ringing. Startled, Massinger stared at it. He did not dare pick it up. Bayev's round head swung slowly, and bobbed like a bird's on his thick neck as he attempted to focus on the ringing telephone.

"Don't bother with it!" Massinger said, inspired. "No time for business now. I want you to show me some of the sights!"

Bayev's head swung back. "But, what if—?"

"It's not Kapustin, and who else are you afraid of? *I've* got Kapustin's instructions. Come on, we'll talk as we walk, eh? I've got a hell of a thirst on me!"

Bayev laughed. The telephone stopped ringing but he did not seem to notice.

A customer, a customer, Massinger prayed in the silence, then he said: "God, I'm thirsty!"

"Same old Pavel!"

"Well, why not? I do my job. Anyway, being a party drunk is a good cover. London society loves me!"

"And so they should. I know a nice new bar—the girls are *delightful!*"

"When was Kapustin here last?"

"Two weeks ago. We were running round with our arses hanging out trying to keep up with him. He was meeting the Englishman—"

"Aubrey?"

"Of course. Who else?"

Massinger paused. Here was the Pandora's box. Aubrey's ills lay inside it. And then he wondered: Is Aubrey in there, too? Is there something more? For a moment he could not bring himself to continue the conversation. Bayev sat patiently, hands folded in his lap, body upright, a machine awaiting a current of electricity.

The door opened. Hyde, preceded by a draught of cold air, entered the room. Massinger heard his ragged breathing and turned to him at once.

"Three cars," Hyde struggled to say, clinging to the door handle. "Three cars, and they're not friendly. What the bloody hell do we do with *him*?"

5
An Evening on the Town

"Well?" Hyde repeated. "What *do* we do with him? Not to mention ourselves?"

Massinger turned his gaze back to Bayev's face. He seemed unaware, as if he had been switched off until required.

"I don't know—how close are they?"

"They're watching at the moment, cars drawn back maybe thirty yards on either side of ours. They'll be looking for our car first—then us. They'll try not to harm him, but don't you reckon on walking away."

"How did they—?"

"Christ knows—it doesn't matter! Get that bugger on his feet, Massinger."

"He can't be moved."

"He'd better bloody well be, if you haven't finished with him!" Hyde moved into the room and through rather than across the heavy white carpet. He studied Bayev's simpleton expression and vacant eyes. "Christ, he's well away. Have you got the information?"

"By no means—"

"Then we'd better keep our hands on him. We might be a little bit safer in his company. Help me get him down to the car. We can't barricade ourselves in here."

"It might be dangerous to move him."

"And fatal if we don't!" He looked up at Massinger. He was still bending in front of Bayev like an exhausted runner. "You can ask him questions in the car. He's not going to bloody well know the difference!"

"Very well—"

"Get his coat—it's hanging up in the hall."

151

Hyde crossed to the window and peered through a crack in the curtains. Their car appeared unguarded, undetected. Massinger returned with Bayev's coat.

"You talk to him in Russian," Hyde instructed. "Keep him calm."

Massinger nodded, and they bent to lift Bayev by the arms.

"Come on, Karel, old man—you've had one too many, *again*!"

Hyde raised his eyebrows in what might have been a compliment as Massinger laughed and patted Bayev on the shoulder blades. They shrugged him into his overcoat.

"Right—weight on you, please," Hyde instructed, loosening the pistol in its shoulder holster. "Just in case."

"Come on, Karel—you need a breath of fresh air!"

"It's *cold*!" Bayev exclaimed like a child.

"Where did he get that from?" Hyde murmured as they slipped sideways through the door into the apartment's small hallway. "Is he coming round?"

"I don't know. Damn! The syringe. I've forgotten it—wait here, old man! Haven't paid the bill!" Bayev sagged against Hyde and did not move, as if once more switched off. Hyde watched the front door of the flat, hand hovering near the breast of his overcoat. Massinger reappeared, thrusting a small, black case into his pocket.

As soon as Bayev saw the second figure in the hall, he said: "It's cold, Pavel—bloody cold out there!"

"You need to wake up, old man. Come on!"

"Keep the bloody noise down when we hit the street. Put your hand over his mouth if you have to. Right?"

"Right."

Hyde leaned forward and unlatched the door. He levered it open with one foot. The narrow staircase was empty.

"Right, then. Quick as you can, down the little wooden hill."

"Forward march, Karel old man!"

They bundled Bayev down the stairs, Hyde leading, the weight of the Russian across his shoulder and back, while Massinger leaned backward, taking the strain. He tried to ignore the stabbing pain in his arthritic hip. Bayev seemed drunk in his inability to negotiate the individual stairs, stumbling and giggling. He had evidently accepted the suggestion that he had drunk too much, and Massinger inwardly cursed this further complication. They leaned heavily against the front door to the street, breathing hard. Bayev was still giggling. Massinger's hip was burning with pain.

"Straight across the street to the car. The drunk act might just fool them, but don't let him start bawling in Russian. Don't stop, don't even hesitate—they won't shoot if they *do* recognize us, not with him between us. Ready?"

"Ready."

Hyde drew the Heckler & Koch. The plastic of the butt was warm from his chest and arm. He levered a round into the chamber, and then nodded.

"Okay, here goes. . . ."

He opened the street door slowly, then peered round it. The small area of the Herrengasse he could see showed his car and one of the Russian vehicles. The driver was still behind the wheel but there were no passengers. He listened—was startled by a passing car which went on, past the Hofburg— and heard one set of slow footsteps echoing. Other side of the street?

Moving away?

There was too little sensory information, and his adrenaline was already dangerously underemployed.

"Come on!" he whispered fiercely, and they dragged Bayev into the street, moving across the pavement onto the cobbles as quickly as they could. Bayev's feet slipped and skidded and stumbled on the icy road.

"It's *cold*!" he cried out, and Massinger squashed his hand over the man's mouth. His face winced with shock and the pain in his hip.

"Shit—" Hyde breathed. Bayev slipped heavily, almost bringing them down. Hyde felt the cold of the cobblestones through his trousers as he went down on one knee, Bayev's weight across his back until Massinger took the strain.

One man, two . . . three . . .

All now alerted by the brief Russian exclamation, two of them already certain of the small stationary group in the middle of the Herrengasse. The third man focused on them. Movement—

"Don't waste time, they know! Get him to the car as quick . . ." They rushed Bayev across the road, his toes dragging black snailtracks behind them. Hyde thrust the Russian against the boot of the Mercedes, then heaved open the door. "Get the bugger *in*!"

Massinger began bundling Bayev into the back of the car, heaving at him as the man protested, finally throwing himself, with a stifled groan at his own pain, on top of the Russian and wrestling him across the rear seat.

Closest man ten yards, running now, mouth open to shout—

Second and third coming fast, fourth even closer, but approaching warily, trying to outflank . . .

Hyde slammed the rear door and jumped into the driving seat, locking the door behind him.

"Lock the bloody doors or they'll—" Massinger snapped down the locks.

Hyde started the engine. A face appeared at his side window, pressed flat, smearing the glass with his lips. A gun angled across the window, held by white knuckles, threatened them. Now they could shoot him, Hyde realized, without endangering the Rezident. The Russian outside the car straightened up and stepped back a pace from the window. Rearview mirror, the second and third men closing—a bump as one of them skidded and collided with the boot of the Mercedes—now Massinger, too, was separable, easier to kill.

Hyde pressed his foot down on the accelerator, and spun the wheel. The car slid sideways, lurched, wheels spinning, and then shot away toward the Michaelerplatz and the Hofburg. The KGB man at Hyde's window staggered back and was left behind. A fourth man began running out into the Herrengasse, but Hyde swerved the car around him.

"It's all right, Karel—just some noisy drunks," Massinger was saying as firmly and soothingly as possible in the back of the car.

"Who are you?" Bayev replied suspiciously. "What are you *doing*?"

"For God's sake, stop *struggling*, Karel!" Massinger snapped.

Hyde swung the wheel—two cars already moving in the Herrengasse, threatening shapes slipping in and out of the light of successive streetlamps—and the Mercedes turned ninety degrees and roared into the narrow, dark archway of the Hofburg's entrance, beneath the cupola. A pedestrain whisked out of their way, dragging a small dog on a leash behind him. The noise of the engine was magnified by the bowl of the cupola's roof, and then they were into the principal square of the palace leading to the Ring, with traffic lights ahead.

Red.

Behind—first car turning into the archway already.

"Karel, Karel, wake up, old man! Do you feel better? Come on, you're not drunk, just tipsy!" Massinger was shaking Bayev gently, the two men now propped up on the back seat.

"I can't go back to the hotel," Hyde said, "not until I've shaken all three cars."

"This is no good—" Massinger protested. "He's totally disorientated."

"I'll drive around."

Green. The lights changed as they passed beneath the War Memorial, and Hyde turned right onto the Burgring, opposite the huge, dark, frosty bulks of the arts and natural history museums. Maybe only two of the cars would catch the light?

Radio. They'd have radio. They were as vulnerable in the Mercedes as they had been in the girl's flat.

Two cars, yes. He accelerated. Karl Renner Ring, Karl Leuger Ring, each set of lights thankfully green.

"Where?" he asked.

"*Anywhere!*" Massinger snapped.

Schottenring. Red lights ahead, strung over the middle of the wide thoroughfare. The first car was no more than twenty yards behind them, in the thin traffic. The road was shining with frost.

Green.

Hyde swung the wheel hard to the left, and the Mercedes skidded, its back end floating away, then he accelerated and the car bounced heavily over tramlines and he was into a narrower street. He took the first right, then right again. The lights of the Schottenring were ahead of him. He turned into it a block further north from where he had left it, and accelerated again.

"Aubrey's people," Massinger was saying loudly and firmly. "Aubrey's people. He's fighting for his life, Karel. He's desperate. He hasn't got a chance!"

"No chance," Bayev agreed, but there was something mechanical and listless about his voice. Massinger pressed him.

"We can't afford any slipups—the pair of us have to stay safe. After two years, we can't afford a screw-up now."

Hyde turned the car onto the Franz-Josefs Kai, alongside the Danube Canal. The traffic was almost nonexistent, the strung-bead lights of a bridge ten blocks away from them. Cross the canal, something told him. Into the narrow streets, the darker streets. Two cars still behind him. The third one would be hanging back, waiting for directions; for some pattern to be placed on the movements of the Mercedes, some possibility of a trap.

"Two years? You're a latecomer," Bayev said in the same mechanical toy's voice. "Pavel, it's been a plan for maybe *five* years. . . ." Hyde sensed that Bayev's drugged, confused awareness had slipped back into his drunk's role. His voice was slightly slurred, his tone confiding, nose-tapping. Bridge coming up.

Lights red—

He ran through them and a lorry loomed up on the right, the driver's face clearly visible as he stared down at the Mercedes rocking on its springs, leaning drunkenly to one side as Hyde spun the wheel. The car skidded, turned half around, then reversed behind the lorry, finally pulling away from it and running across its path onto the bridge. The lorry's horn sounded angrily behind them as the car shuddered across the cobbles of the bridge and jolted along the tramlines.

"Five years—my God!" Massinger exclaimed, his voice still shaky from their encounter with the lorry. "Five years. You're obviously a lot more trusted than I am, Karel."

"Gossip—only gossip," Bayev slurred. Then he yawned.

"Kapustin's always been in charge—yes?" Massinger pressed.

"Is all this on tape?" Hyde asked.

"Yes. It's still running. The recorder's in my hand."

"Thank God." He turned the Mercedes right. The rearview mirror was clear for four seconds before the first of the pursuing cars appeared. He accelerated again. The speedometer climbed dramatically. Seventy miles an hour. "We could be getting somewhere," he murmured.

"Kapustin's always been in command," Bayev repeated like a lesson he had learned.

"Brilliant—a brilliant plan. What a *mind*, what insight!"

"Balls."

"What?"

"Kapustin—balls, Pavel! Kapustin's just the operator, the controller. It's not his plan. Just 'cause you're sucking up to him at the moment, looking to stay in London. . . ." Bayev belched, so convinced was he of his own drunkenness. He was argumentative now, restless, and he moved himself into the corner of the Mercedes. His arms waved slowly once more like windmill sails. "Oh, yes, I know you. You'd kiss anybody's arse to stay in London."

"Karel, old man—" Massinger protested.

"It's not Kapustin's scheme, you stupid shit!" Bayev screamed, as if at an enemy. He was now in a violent, enraged, heightened mood, under the effects of the drugs. "Petrunin created it! Bloody Petrunin—who's a better man than you any day—*he* created it!" Bayev was screaming at the top of his voice.

"Who?" Massinger murmured in the ensuing silence.

Two cars in the mirror, slowly closing the gap. The dark, ugly hump of the Nord-bahnhof rose to their left. Hyde shuddered. Glaring, cold lights over the massive freightyards beyond the station.

"Petrunin. Tamas Petrunin," Hyde said, unnerved. "That clever bastard."

"Shelley?"

"Yes."

Peter Shelley indicated to his wife to turn down the television set. Alison Shelley pressed the remote control handset. Laughter at the comedy show softened. Shelley was still smiling at the last remark he had heard when he realized it was Babbington's voice at the other end of the line. Immediately, he was intensely aware of the back of his wife's head as she sat on the sofa, of the television beyond her, of the bay window still revealing the moonlit, snow-covered back garden. The images pressed upon him accusingly; claiming their rights.

"Shelley—I won't beat about the bush, not with one of my senior men," Babbington began, and then paused for effect before adding: "You've been working unofficially, Shelley. You have provided confidential information for people without security clearance."

Shelley drew in his breath sharply. Alison's shoulders twitched, as at the shock of static electricity in the room.

"I'm—sorry, sir?"

"Don't play games, Shelley. Massinger asked you for certain information and you provided it, from Registry."

"Sir—"

Alison looked round at the tone of his voice. Her face was immediately concerned. He waved a hand to suggest there was no need to worry. But there was.

"You're a good man, Shelley. I prefer to consider you've been misguided in this matter. Old loyalties, all that." There was a bluff forgiveness in Babbington's voice that made Shelley hopeful, yet suspicious. Babbington wore the voice like an ill-fitting mask. "You'll take a week's leave, beginning at once. When you come back to East Europe Desk, things will be different. . . ." Alison was still watching his face intently, her brow lined with guesses and intuitions. ". . . a great many things will be different. I expect you to fit into the new organization. Understood?"

"Yes, sir. Sir, I'm—"

But Babbington was gone.

"What was that?" Alison asked.

"A very severe letting off, I think," Shelley said ruefully, rubbing his chin. He put down the receiver, and sighed with relief.

"Mm?"

"A bawling out, but not the sack. As long as I keep my nose clean."

"Aubrey?"

"Partly. Partly to do with Paul Massinger—providing him with some information. . . ." Shelley straightened his legs out in front of him and rubbed his thighs. "God, Babbington's got eyes and ears everywhere. I *was* careful—"

"Is that the end of it?"

"I've got a week's leave."

"Good."

"While they get on with their shake-up of the service. When I get back, I won't recognize the old place. I wonder what Massinger's doing now."

"Do you still want to know?"

Shelley looked up. "I don't know."

"Then you'd better make up your mind, Peter. I'm not giving all this up—" Alison indicated the room around them, dwelling with unconscious humor on the fireplace. "—without a very good reason."

"Mm?"

"If you're going to be dragged into this thing again, you'd

better do it because you really want to—or I shall be *very* annoyed!"

Alison looked very serious, he thought, but her brow was clear and untroubled. Was he committed? Did he, after all, *really* want to risk everything for Aubrey? Babbington had let him off the hook. Shouldn't he accept that gratefully?

"I don't know, darling," he murmured. "I don't know what I really want."

The freightyards. Hard, cold lights, each haloed by the beginnings of a freezing fog. Power lines, overhead cables, and telephone wires were already thickened and white-leaved with frost.

The Mercedes was parked on a sloping track that led down to the finger spread of tracks and gantries and signals that constituted the Frachtenbahnhof Wien-Nord. It huddled amid a few dozen cars presumably owned by railway employees at work in the freightyards.

Hyde had driven them into the lightless, deserted Prater Park, beneath Harry Lime's ferris wheel, the Reisenrad, where memories of the film had chilled Hyde . . . *if one of those dots down there stopped moving, Holly old man* . . . because he was one of those insectlike dots. The Prater had been too empty, too exposed to stop the car for any length of time. And Massinger needed time—quiet and time.

He'd lost the two cars somewhere in the Prater, bewildering them amid the fairground and the numerous roads and tracks that crossed the pleasure park. Since he knew they would waste time searching, he immediately left the park, passing the railway station again and finding the goods yard and its string of parked cars along the track down to the railway lines. Massinger had been pressing him to stop. He considered they were still too close to the pursuit but Massinger had priorities of his own.

Hyde watched him roll up Bayev's sleeve and inject ten milligrams of benzedrine. There appeared to be no effect on the Russian. He was still slumped in one corner of the car, wet marks on his cheeks where he had been weeping openly before becoming unconscious, his eyes still open but sightless.

"Well?"

"It doesn't look good, I'll admit," Massinger said drily.

"Will he come round?"

"God only knows. It's been a rough ride for him." Bayev's face appeared a deathly color in the floodlighting falling on the freightyards. One thing that might put the KGB off the scent—it was too light to suggest itself as a place of concealment.

"His eyes rolled then," Hyde said eagerly.

Bayev appeared to be watching him. His face was disgruntled, mean.

"Karel," Massinger murmured softly in Russian. "Are you all right, old man? God, you gave us a turn, then. Passing out like that. You haven't done that since you were in school— remember, all nosebleeds and fainting fits?" Hyde looked at Massinger, baffled, but the American merely shrugged. Lies and truth, perhaps, no longer mattered. Only detail, building blocks of the fictitious, drug-perceived situation. "We used to think your periods would start any time!"

"That wasn't me, that was that little squirt Voris—Vos— Vorisenko!" Bayev snapped back. "Bloody fairy in the making, he was!"

"Yes, poor old Vorisenko," Massinger laughed. "Are you all right now?"

"Headache."

"Just the drink, I expect."

The fog was thickening around the floodlights, so that they became sheets of white light, no longer glaring circles hung in bunches. The windshield of the Mercedes was misting over outside and Hyde switched on the wipers. Through the cleared arc, he could see no one moving.

"Shut up," Bayev grumbled. "Shut up, Pavel. I'm sick of your bloody voice, sick of the sound of it. I want to sleep."

"Kapustin would be pleased with you, Karel. You must be getting old."

"Piss off. Let me sleep."

God, Massinger thought, he's slipping away. The next ten milligrams won't bring him back. He's exhausted. What could he do?

"All right?" Hyde murmured.

"I don't think we've got long."

"Christ, get on with it, then."

"How?"

"Give him a bawling out—that always works with the

KGB. They're all scared of some big Red chief sitting on their necks."

"How can I? I'm Pavel Koslov—same rank, same function. His friend."

"Tell him you're talking on behalf of someone else—"

"Kapustin?"

Hyde shrugged. "Why not? Why not Petrunin, even?" Hyde's face twisted in dislike.

"I'll try Kapustin." He turned to Bayev, leaning closer to him. "Karel, the reason I came to Vienna . . ."

"Shut up. I'm tired."

"Kapustin especially asked me to come. As a friend of yours, he thought it might be easier for me to tell you . . ." Massinger's tone was insinuating, even sinister.

A goods train shunted below them, its lamps enlarged by the thickening fog. The wagons rattled and grumbled together.

"Tell me? Tell me what?" The first spots of fear, forerunners of the infection, had appeared in Bayev's tone. Kapustin's disappointed. . . ."

"With what? In me?" Bayev was sitting upright now, his eyes wide and alarmed, though even now they remained unfocused. "What do you mean?" His reluctance, his weariness were both gone for the moment.

"I'm afraid so. You've been letting the British control too much here in Vienna." Massinger saw, from the edge of his vision, Hyde's knuckles whiten on the back of his seat as he watched them. He could hear the Australian's breathing, hard and urgent. "He doesn't want the British in control here."

"They're not in control."

"They are—the man running it, the link man . . . oh, what's—"

"Wilkes doesn't run anything. We liaise, that's all. Wilkes does as we want. That's always been the understanding."

"What understanding?"

"How the hell do I know? Kapustin doesn't confide in me! I deal with Wilkes. What else goes on I know nothing about."

"Shit," Hyde murmured slowly.

"Why haven't you got hold of this Englishman, Hyde?

Kapustin wants to know that. What are you playing about at?"

"Wilkes wanted to handle that. I thought everyone agreed they'd do it!" Bayev protested. "It isn't my fault," he whined. "He must understand that. . . ." His voice had begun to slur, and Massinger looked at Hyde, shaking his head.

"Nothing more."

"Ask him *why*, dammit!"

"What's behind it all, Karel?" Massinger demanded, still maintaining the voice but not the persona of Pavel Koslov. Bayev was evidently confused. His head wobbled slowly in puzzlement on his shoulders. His body was already sliding slowly back into the seat. Massinger realized that he was slipping away once more, and that this time he would, in all probability, remain unconscious and unreachable, despite benzedrine.

Hyde glanced at the windshield. Like the side windows, it was misting over again. He reached for the wiper stalk. The car was silent, isolated, almost unreal. In the goods yard, couplings clanked weirdly.

"What's behind it, Karel?" Massinger persisted. "Why are we running our tails off? What are we doing it all for?"

"Who knows . . . ?" Bayev replied faintly.

Hyde tensed, staring at the Rezident. His hands gripped the back of his seat, squeezing the plastic hard. Come on, come *on*. . . .

"Why? Karel—why, man, *why*?" Massinger shouted.

"Who knows . . . who . . . knows . . . Petrun . . . runin . . . i-i-i-n-n . . ."

His head lolled forward. Instantly, they heard him snoring.

"Damn—" Massinger groaned.

Hyde cursed aloud and snapped down the wiper stalk. The blades slithered frostily across the windshield.

"He didn't know—he bloody didn't *know*!" Hyde yelled accusingly. "Oh, *fuck* it, he didn't *know*!"

He turned in his seat. Through the cleared windshield, he could see the bulk of the approaching man, no more than a few yards from the car. His hand came out of his overcoat and he had fired two shots through the windshield even before Hyde began reaching for his pistol.

• • •

"You simply cannot continue to deny everything, Sir Kenneth," Eldon admonished him, in a voice that was reproving, wise, and sinister. "You have admitted your signature, you have admitted your capture, your imprisonment in the Russian sector, your interrogation at the hands of Colonel Zalozny, whose methods and successes are well documented. . . ." Eldon paused, passing his hands like a magician over the papers on his lap. Self-evident, the gesture repeated. Conclusions, proofs are here. . . .

Aubrey could no longer disguise his signals of frailty and hopelessness. Wearily, he rubbed one hand across his forehead, as if he intended soothing some fierce ache.

"You think not?" he replied softly. The tone was pale, lifeless.

"It would, of course, assist everyone—including yourself, Sir Kenneth—if you would confirm the accounts presented in these documents?"

"I can't."

"I see."

"No, you do not see. Keeping me from my bed, agitating my nerves, giving me violent indigestion—none of these things can extract additional, confirmatory information which I do not possess." Aubrey's voice soothed him. Calm, quiet, soft—as if he retained control of the situation.

"Very well, Sir Kenneth—let us go back to the *coincidence* of events—the fact that Robert Castleford was last seen alive on the very day, the very *evening*, that you made your successful return to the British sector of Berlin—mm?"

"Yes. Yes. By the time I had—recovered from my imprisonment, he was missing. No trace of him. The morning after I returned, apparently, he was not to be found."

"Did you lead the NKVD to him?"

"No."

"But you told them where to find him?"

"No."

"But—"

"Despite what it says above my forged signature there, I did not place the onus of SIS secret operations against the NKVD in Berlin and the Russian Zone of Germany at Castleford's door. Castleford was a wealthy, brilliant, ambitious civil servant making the most of his posting to the Control Commission. He aimed very high. I did not like him, we did not get on together. I did not betray him—I did not have him killed."

"But—you would agree, would you not, that if you had painted this colorful picture of Castleford as some kind of master spy, the NKVD would have had very good reason to—cause Castleford to suspend operations against them?"

"If I had, then yes. If they thought of him in that way, then yes. None of it, however, is true."

"When did you last see Robert Castleford?"

"I—I'm not certain. . . ."

Eldon consulted his notebook. The tape recorder on the coffee table continued to hum in the room's lamp-lit silence. Shadows and soft light. Aubrey could not rid himself of a persistent sense of menace. Eldon looked up once more.

"There was a meeting between you the day before you entered the Russian sector—in pursuit, as you claim, of your double agent."

"Was there? Perhaps there was. I don't remember it."

"Could you try, Sir Kenneth? Could you try to remember what you discussed at that last meeting?"

"I don't think I can," Aubrey murmured, but in his mind he clearly heard Castleford's voice. Yes, it had been that occasion; that penultimate occasion.

Damn you, Aubrey, I think you're out to ruin me!

No—

Yes! Your insane jealousy—

Mine, or yours, Castleford?

Damn you with Clara, too. You've been investigating me, you arrogant little man. Me? What do you expect to rake up about me? What can you rake up? You intend to smear me, to get me out of your way. I won't let you do that, Aubrey. I won't let a bigot like you take more power than you already have. I warn you, Aubrey—unless you drop this ridiculous, vindictive investigation of me, I'll take steps to see that you are ruined. Understand me? Finished. You'll be finished!

It was difficult for Aubrey to control his breathing; as difficult to avoid the conclusion that, almost forty years later, Castleford's prophecy of his ruination was about to come true. He watched Eldon watching him, eager for his reply. He shook his head.

"I—can't remember," he murmured. "No doubt it was another occasion for reprimand. It usually turned out to be like that, whenever we met. Castleford taking a high-handed moral line toward SIS's work."

"Yours in particular, I gather."

"Perhaps."

"You disliked each other."

"Yes. Our enmity, however, was not strong enough for me to betray him. I did not wish him dead."

They do not know about Clara, do they? Aubrey asked himself. They must know, some other part of his mind answered. It was known to others—the quarrels, the *courtship*, the victory—people in Berlin knew of Castleford's interest in Clara, of my interest—? Why hasn't it been brought up?

"I see."

"Eldon?"

"Yes, Sir Kenneth?"

"What is the mood—of your masters?" Aubrey hated himself for asking the question, but it had eaten at him from the moment that Babbington had broached the subject. "Will they require a trial? A charge of treason to be answered?"

"Yes, Sir Kenneth—I think they will."

"Rather late in the century for it, wouldn't you say?"

"Some might say long overdue rather than late."

"I suppose they might."

"You did hate Castleford, didn't you?" Eldon asked quickly.

"He hated me," Aubrey replied.

"You hated him, also."

Aubrey stared at Eldon's quietly implacable features. It was a matter of days, no more. He would know how close he was to being charged with treason the moment they gave him access to his solicitor. At that moment, his interrogation would be over and his trial on the point of beginning.

Trial, trial, his mind echoed. Zalozny had offered him that, often. In the intervals between the bouts of cold water, the bucket over his head being beaten with wooden sticks, the blows of huge peasant fists, the standing to attention in the freezing, snowbound yard of the prison, teeth chattering, body shuddering with ague. If he gave in, they promised him a quick trial and execution. The situation was an almost exact parallel.

One of his most vivid memories was of having to defecate into a bucket while an eye watched him through the spyhole in the cell door. Stained, torn trousers around his ankles, buttocks perched on the icy rim of the iron bucket—all dignity gone.

He dismissed the past. Of his present situation, he knew that whatever he had to do—except confess—he would do to avoid a trial. He would never be led into court, never hear the charge of treason, never face a jury. Whatever he had to do, he would avoid that sham.

He watched Eldon. Eldon would never understand about the trial. He would never assume that Aubrey the traitor had left to him anything with which he could not bear to part in public.

Hyde raised his head above the level of the dashboard. Glass prickled his neck and the backs of his hands and slithered from his overcoat onto the driving seat. Behind him, he knew that Bayev was dead—one glance at the doll slumped in the corner of the Mercedes had told him that. He had not even looked at Massinger. There was no time. The Russian was coming on, now, heavily jogging the last few strides between himself and the car. Hyde fired through the crazed remains of the windshield and the man disappeared sideways below the bonnet.

Only then did Hyde turn his head. Massinger was sitting bolt upright in the back, evidently in shock.

"Come on, mate! Time's up."

"What . . . ?" Massinger might have been drugged himself, so slow and unfocused were his movements. Hyde reached over the seat and grabbed his arm.

"Bayev's dead—we're next. Get out of the car!"

The top of the incline, where the road passed the freightyard, was blocked by a long, black saloon. Two men were standing by it, one of them already advancing the first few paces down the slope. A glance in the side mirror had shown Hyde that much.

"Out?"

"I can't move the car!"

Massinger began to move, groaning as he levered himself out of the door. Hyde saw the walking stick, and his chest and stomach felt hollow with foreboding. Massinger's bloody hip!

Massinger looked up the slope, appearing to Hyde to lean

heavily, breathe hard. "How many of them?" he said urgently.

"Just the one car. They didn't wait for reinforcements. Someone told them to shut Bayev up as a first priority. Tape?"

"Yes." Massinger patted his pocket. "For what it's worth, dammit! We both know it's worthless—he knew *nothing*!"

"Come on—this way."

He watched the two men who had halted at the top of the rutted, frosty incline. They were mere dark lumps in the fog, revealed only because of the powerful floodlights. Fog danced and moved around them. Twenty-five yards. The kamikaze had had to come in close in order to pick out his targets. A tactic of desperation, the impetus of a high-ranking order behind him, pushing him on. Now that he was dead, the other two wanted to wait for reinforcements.

"Down?"

"Yes, down. They're not eager to follow. Come on."

Massinger moved ahead of Hyde, who walked carefully backward, his heels seeking the ruts and frozen puddles. A goods wagon's couplings clanked in the fog, startling him. He could hear Massinger moving away, limping, sighing with effort. The cautious footsteps of the two Russians reached him, too. Then the sound of a car arriving, braking hard.

"Hurry it up," he called to Massinger. "The cavalry's arrived."

He turned his back, caught up with Massinger, and took his arm. He studied the man's face. Tired and lined, hardly handsome any longer. He nodded.

"I'm all right—" Massinger protested.

"No, you're not. Just doing all right. We're going to have to hurry."

He forced Massinger to break into a limping jogtrot. The American used his stick like a drunken, uncertain third leg, and he groaned once or twice; but he did not attempt to slow Hyde until they reached the bottom of the incline. A gate in a wooden fence, then the tracks on either side and ahead disappeared into the fog. A locomotive was moving slowly somewhere in it like a circling, invisible shark. Its headlight flashed occasionally, and its passage made the fog roll and billow. Hyde shuddered with cold.

"All right?"

Massinger nodded, recovering his breath. "I'm okay, Hyde. I'm just angry as hell."

"Never mind. They'll be consulting and planning for a couple of minutes. There's time enough."

"What do we do now?"

"Get out of Vienna. There's nothing else we can do." He pushed open the unlocked gate. Warning signs forbade them to cross the tracks. Massinger passed through the gate and Hyde closed it behind them. The incline retreated into the fog. Hyde could not see the Mercedes or the body in front of it, but nothing appeared to be moving on the slope. "Okay. Be careful—I don't know whether there are any live rails or whether it's all electrified overhead. Just watch where you put your feet."

Massinger was aware of the momentary confidence in Hyde's voice. He was a hundred yards ahead of the pursuit and shrouded by the fog. It was enough, apparently, to satisfy him. Massinger recognized Hyde's quality. He'd controlled only a few men like him all those years ago. The nerve-enders, the jack-in-the-boxes. Good field agents.

He crossed the first set of tracks, listening attentively. Scrapings, clanks, the roll of flanged wheels, the movement of locomotives. Strangely, a cow lowed somewhere in the fog and was answered by other cattle. It was unnerving for an instant, then became comfortingly innocent.

A line of freight cars loomed out of the fog.

"Underneath and through," Hyde instructed.

Massinger grasped the icy buffer of a wagon, then bent down into a crouch. His hip hurt badly, and at the center of the pain was a light, almost floating feeling of weakness. He was afraid that his hip might give out at any moment. He straightened up with great difficulty, and his breath escaped in a misty, smoky gasp.

"You okay?" Hyde asked anxiously.

"I'm all *right*, damn you!" he replied fiercely, leaning on his stick, watching Hyde with a twisted, angry face. "I'm all right."

"Okay." Hyde shrugged. "Let's keep moving."

Four more sets of tracks, snaking toward their feet and slithering, so it seemed, away again into the chill-lit whiteness of the fog.

"Hold it!" Hyde snapped suddenly.

Noise of a locomotive, coming toward them. Massinger studied his feet, his heart racing. Between tracks? Beyond, between . . . ? The fog swirled, writhed, then parted to admit a looming black shape with a headlight struggling to cut a swathe through the curtain. Massinger leaned away, feeling the rush of the air and the bulk of the engine and the thudding of it through his shoes. He could see Hyde nowhere. Wagons clanked past, allowing little slats of white light to appear between them.

The noise was deafening.

Eventually, it had gone and the fog had closed in behind the guard's van and the dim red light it carried.

"Hyde?" Massinger asked fearfully into the fog.

"Keep your voice down! Come on."

Three, four, five more sets of tracks. Sheds, repair and maintenance shops, points, gantries, lights. Then a high stone wall with frost thickly riming weeds and ivy, and the dim glow of streetlamps above and beyond it.

"Look for some steps," Hyde instructed. "And be careful."

The flight of steps was two hundred yards away, toward Lassallestrasse. Hyde climbed it first, then waved to Massinger to follow him. At the top, a gate barred their exit to the street. It was unlocked. Hyde gestured Massinger through.

Icy puddles, poor streetlights, blank-faced warehouses. A narrow, grubby, cobbled street empty of people and cars.

"Can you walk a bit more?" Hyde asked defensively, his hands raised, palms outward.

"Yes. How far?"

"The station. We'll get a taxi back to the hotel. Just take it easy and stay alert."

As they walked, Massinger's stick tapped the cobbles and echoed from the blank walls and doors of the warehouse. The noise of it reminded Hyde of the American's age, his infirmity, and his determination. Nevertheless, he could not avoid the feeling that he was carrying the older man; even though Massinger had adopted the role of his field controller almost naturally and by right. Massinger would make the decisions, but he would be left to carry them out, to put himself in jeopardy.

"Have we got anything out of that?" he asked.

"Mm?" Massinger was silent. No, no, no, his stick tapped out in the fog, then echoed its negative. "Tell me about this Petrunin," he said eventually. "You know him, don't you?"

"Too well."

"Sorry?"

"Onetime London Rezident. Later, he tried to screw me again in Australia and Spain. We don't get on—quarrel all the time!" Behind the banter, there was a quiver in his voice that Hyde could not eradicate.

"He's a field man?" Massinger asked in surprise.

"No. He's been a general in his time."

"In his time."

"Word is, he got demoted back to colonel last year. . . ."

"Because of you?"

"No. But I helped. He couldn't keep the lid on something."

"Part of the lid being your death?"

"Right."

"His scheme, apparently, wasn't discredited with him," Massinger commented bitterly.

Hyde stopped the American, then moved ahead and checked the well-lit street that lay ahead of them. Cars passed now, moving slowly in the fog, there were one or two pedestrians, dog walkers or night-shift workers. It felt to Massinger both safe and dangerous at the same moment. More, he sensed an excitement in himself. Dangerous, foolish, desperate. Hyde returned.

"It's clear, as far as I can tell. I don't imagine they've given up, but it's a big area down there behind us. They may not be covering the station yet. But be careful. If I move, you move. I shan't wait for you. Okay?"

"Okay." Massinger nodded.

"The station's just a couple of hundred yards down the street," Hyde continued. "What do we do when we get back to the hotel and the car you hired?"

"Take the autobahn to Linz, and then maybe Munich. We can get there by morning, with luck. Unless this fog lasts all the way."

"And then?"

"I must talk to Peter Shelley again. We must consult. I wish I could talk to Kenneth again . . . but that's too dangerous." He turned to face Hyde. "You see, neither of us has anywhere to go at the moment. Babbington forbade me to go on with this—someone informed Vienna I was here, someone wants me dead along with you."

"Babbington?"

"I doubt it. But—someone. Wilkes can't be the only rotten apple. Wilkes takes orders from someone else. This collusion is too smooth, too efficient and, according to our dead friend back there, too long-standing to be run by people like Wilkes. Someone, in Europe or in London—a senior officer, at least as senior as Shelley or one of Shelley's deputy directors, has to be in the KGB's pocket."

"Christ! Shelley?"

"Well?"

Hyde shook his head vigorously. "No, not Shelley."

"I thought not."

They had reached the portico of the Nord-bahnhof. A rank of taxis stood alongside the pavement. There seemed no one concerning themselves with Hyde and Massinger. Hyde's relaxation was evident to Massinger.

Obsessed with his theory, he had forgotten their narrow escape, forgotten the dead body of Bayev in the back of the Mercedes; forgotten the men who wanted himself and Hyde similarly disposed of.

He had to know. There was a KGB double in SIS, and it had to be someone fairly senior—it was the only explanation that made sense.

"Okay, in you get." Massinger struggled into the back of the taxi and ordered the driver to the InterContinental. He sighed with relief as he lay back in the seat.

"You accept the hypothesis?" he said as they crossed the Danube Canal. Hyde was silent for a moment, then he nodded.

"You have to be right. It has to be one of the high-ups. But *who*?"

"Yes, who indeed? The KGB have someone important in their pocket, helping to carry out *Teardrop*. If we knew *why*, we might know who."

"You haven't any theories about that?" Hyde asked with evident irony. Beneath that tone, there was the indifference that springs from sudden and unexpected well-being. Hyde, out of danger, was shutting himself down like a complex series of circuits and relays.

Massinger, knowing that he was doing little more than thinking aloud, said: "To make sure that Aubrey is finished off? To throw the service into confusion? To assist some huge operation we know nothing about? It could be any or all of those—and maybe other reasons. We've got who and why, and no answers to either question—"

But I have an idea, he thought. Even crazier than this

Viennese business. And it needs *you*, he added to himself, glancing sideways at Hyde's lolling form. And you won't like it, not one little bit.

Margaret returned to him, then. He shut her out.

Later, later, my darling, he told her image. This matter first . . .

Why? That's the real question. *Who* could be anybody—perhaps one of fifty, even a hundred . . . and they had no access, no leverage. There was no one who could, or would, tell them. Shelley might be able to draw up a list of possibilities, but it would be a long one.

And there was one man, just one man, who knew everything—who knew *why!* *Who knew the traitor's name.* . . . Petrunin knew everything. *Teardrop* was his creation.

He glanced at Hyde from slitted eyelids. "Do you know where Petrunin is now—in disgrace, you said?"

"More than one report's confirmed he's in Afghanistan. At the Kabul Embassy. The roughest posting they could find for him, I suppose," Hyde replied without considering the implications of either the question or his answer.

The taxi turned into the Johannesgasse. Hyde was relaxed. In a couple of hours, with luck, they'd be halfway out of Austria. He patted his overcoat pocket. His new papers lay there, against his breast like a talisman. He did not consider the future beyond the next few hours, which were decidedly hopeful.

He was getting out of Vienna, where he might easily have died.

PART TWO

The Longest Journey

. . . reassembling our afflicted Powers,
Consult how we may henceforth most offend
Our Enemy, our own loss how repair,
How overcome this dire Calamity,
What reinforcement we may gain from Hope,
If not, what resolution from despair.

Milton, *Paradise Lost*, Bk. 1

6
The Golden Road

Hyde was still dazzled by the snow gleam from the mountains as the Douglas C-47 taxied noisily along the runway at Peshawar. There was thin snow on the plain, but the yellow earth revealed itself in patches, and the foothills beyond the town were stubbornly gray. But, as the old aircraft had circled and dropped toward the airport, he had seen, disbelieving, the mountains stretching northward toward the Hindu Kush and even the Himalayas as if they would never end, never descend again to desert or plain.

It was cold in the aircraft despite the cabin pressure and the heating. Most of the soldiers who were his companions, returning from leave in Karachi and Hyderabad and the southern towns, rubbed their arms beneath their greatcoats and shuffled their feet. They had taken little notice of him almost from the moment they had left Karachi's military airfield. He was foreign—English—and they probably guessed his purposes in journeying north toward the border with Afghanistan. They were refugee-camp nursemaids and policemen; he was probably a border crosser, illegal, frowned upon, tolerated but unofficial.

As the plane taxied to a halt, Hyde could see two trucks waiting for the returning troops. Drawn up perhaps ten yards from them was a Land Rover. A Pakistani officer who managed to appear neat, small, groomed even in green combat jacket and black-and-white scarf stood beside it. To Hyde, he might have been part of some ancient and romantic war film. He presumed it was Colonel Miandad of the Pakistani Bureau for the Border, a branch of army intelligence. Hyde collected his hand luggage and followed the last of the disembarking soldiers through the huge door in the fuselage. Immediately

175

he appeared on the passenger steps, Miandad's attention switched to him. Incongruously, the Pakistani officer raised a swagger stick in greeting and moved quickly to the bottom of the ladder, hand extended. The first of the trucks was already pulling away toward the low, shacklike airport buildings.

"Mr. Hyde, I imagine?" Miandad said in clipped, almost accentless English. His features were narrow, dark, intense. His eyes glittered on either side of a hawkish, aristocratic nose. Hyde thought he appeared most like a civilized, assured pirate.

Hyde shook the extended hand, then they both replaced their gloves. "Colonel Miandad?"

"That is correct. Please come with me. Some coffee, I think?"

"Please."

Hyde climbed into the Land Rover. As Miandad got behind the wheel, he said: "You look very lost, very out of place, Mr. Hyde—if you do not mind my saying so?" There was, after all, a hint of the comic Asian inflection expressing itself in archaic colloquialisms. Hyde was almost relieved to discover it.

"I am," Hyde admitted.

"Here." Miandad passed him a vacuum flask. Hyde poured himself a strong, sweet coffee.

"It is most unusual—your visit," Miandad continued. "However, perhaps not the strangest request we have received in the Bureau since the Russians entered Afghanistan. Usually, it is the CIA who require the most outrageous assistance." He smiled with very white teeth. He looked young around the mouth, experienced around the eyes, where fine lines had begun to appear. Hyde assumed he was probably in his midthirties.

"Coffee's good."

"Excellent. I do not have great good news for you, Mr. Hyde. Not so far, at least."

"Oh."

"Professor Massinger's idea was a very clever one," Miandad admitted. "In theory. And as my old university teacher, he was sensible to think of myself, and to remember that I had been trained, at least in part, at one of your establishments in the country. . . ." Miandad's eyes seemed to stare into the distance, toward the mountains, or toward memories that were years old. ". . . by your Sir Kenneth Aubrey. Who is now in such deep trouble . . . " The comic, singsong inflections were stronger for a moment, as if Miandad parodied his English education and experience. "Yes, all that was very astute. However, it relied upon the assistance of the *mujahiddin*, and Pathan *mujahiddin* into the bargain."

"I see."

The pilot and crew of the Douglas were already in the second truck, which then pulled away after its companion toward the airport buildings.

"I don't think you do see, Mr. Hyde. And I'm afraid we should move now. There are sometimes eyes who watch, even in Peshawar."

"Russians?"

"The occasional one. No—Afghan army spies who cross over as refugees, some of them even posing as rebels. I will take you now to meet the man who is the problem. A *mujahiddin* leader called Mohammed Jan. A brave, independent, pigheaded man. Without his help, I do not think you could even cross into Afghanistan. You certainly will not be able to reach your objective." As he put the Land Rover into gear and revved the engine, Miandad watched Hyde. He seemed to be weighing the Australian, who felt his glance was clear and keen, missing little.

"What are our chances?"

Miandad shook his head. "I should say, Mr. Hyde, that they are very poor. Mohammed Jan does not send his people into Kabul any longer. Certainly, he would not send them to attack the main headquarters and barracks of the Soviet army!"

The Land Rover bumped in the rutted wake of the two trucks. Hyde did not know whether his uppermost sensation was disappointment or relief. Three days ago, he had been asleep in the hired car as they approached Munich in a gray, wet dawn. A weary yet fiercely wakeful Massinger had been driving. In the moment that a halt at traffic lights had woken Hyde, he had seen a determination that amounted to passion in the American's face. The smile that Massinger had directed at him had been ominous in its self-satisfaction and its attempt to disarm. Hyde's relief at escaping from Vienna remained, but it was severely lessened by the promise in Massinger's smile.

In the forty-eight hours that followed, Massinger never left his hotel room; rarely was he not engaged in a telephone call. Hyde supplied his drinks and his meals, and otherwise wandered the city in the chill rain to escape the hothouse atmosphere. The man burned with organizational energy, and with an almost demented sense of purpose. His face and voice and the countries and persons who received his calls continually hoisted signals of danger to Hyde, unsettling him, making the adrenaline flow, eroding his reluctance.

Shelley, of course. Call after call to the telephone booth outside the village pub. Shelley's wife had answered the telephone at first, and forestalled Massinger's identifying himself. Shelley had gone to the telephone booth and rung Munich—the first of perhaps twenty conversations between them. Then other people in London, then old colleagues in Langley and Washington or even retired to New England, Florida, or California. It appeared as if Massinger were calling his whole, lifelong acquaintance. Then Pakistan . . .

Eventually this neat, purposeful man beside him. Colonel Zahir Miandad of Pakistani Military Intelligence: an expert on Afghanistan and the guerillas and the Soviet occupation. On that first occasion a crackling, scrambled military line down which Massinger had to shout to be heard. Perhaps the first of fifteen or sixteen calls, the last of them almost the beginning of Hyde's journey. Massinger had not asked him to go, simply told him what had been arranged, having continued in the assumed role of his field controller.

He had one simple task—the capture of a senior Russian officer from his headquarters in Kabul, or from any place he was to be found. Petrunin. The creator of *Teardrop*. Hyde, with guerilla help, was to attempt to capture Tamas Petrunin of the KGB.

"I have talked to Mohammed Jan on many occasions," Miandad was saying as the Land Rover nudged and shunted its way through the maze of rutted, frozen mud streets of one of Peshawar's ugly, low suburbs. It was a shantytown, a disfigurement. Miandad's eyes were carefully intent upon the traffic—bicycles, oxen, ancient cars. Hyde saw a Morris that had been daubed orange and was probably prewar, and an old, partially roofless Leyland single-decker bus. "I have talked to him of this matter twice—no, three times—in the last twenty-four hours. He refuses to entertain the idea." Miandad turned to him. "I cannot make a bargain on your behalf. You have no weapons to supply him. He is not interested in men and what is in their heads. Only in guns—rocket launchers, especially. He would capture the Russian First Secretary for you in exchange for a half-dozen 'Red Eye' launchers and suitable missiles!" Miandad's smile gleamed. "But—it is not the case. And although I am able to assist you because I am much my own master here, I cannot offer our weapons on your behalf."

"I understand."

Was he relieved, or disappointed? He could not decide. The Land Rover broke free of the restraining traffic, and almost immediately, they were beyond the last gasoline-can and corrugated-sheet shanties and the bullocks and the wrapped women and turbaned men. The mountains that contained the border and the Khyber and the other passes into Afghanistan lay ahead of them, gray barriers climbing to dazzling white peaks and ridges. The contrast was too great, almost unbearable, burning like rage or nausea in Hyde's chest. The mountains loomed pitilessly over the river plain that was scabbed and diseased with the shantytowns and refugee camps that surrounded and clung to Peshawar. Hyde had seen the like of it in South Africa, and on a few occasions when his flight from Australia had refueled at somewhere like Bombay. The big-eyed, big-bellied children outside a tent made from a corrugated iron sheet and a length of cardboard propped against one another.

He dismissed the images, both remembered and recent. It was his task to glide across the surface, not to look through the ice at what lay beneath. A white bullock ambled across the track. Miandad slowed the Land Rover, then jarringly they accelerated again. Disappointed, Hyde told himself. Even though Petrunin had almost killed him twice, directly or indirectly, and even though Hyde feared meeting him again—he *was* disappointed.

"Where is this Jan?" he asked.

"One of the camps. One of the many, many camps," Miandad added wearily.

Before them, at the edge of the plain, the mountains gleamed with innocent snow and ice.

"But you think seeing him again will do no good?"

Miandad shook his head. "I'm afraid not," he murmured.

• • •

Alison Shelley pushed one shopping cart, Massinger the other, down the busy aisles of the supermarket. The Shelleys' young daughter, Helen, sat, legs akimbo, facing her mother from the trolley. She seemed contented with chocolate, the corners of her small mouth already stained like her fingertips. Shelley walked beside Massinger, occasionally depositing bottles or tins in the two carts. Were anyone observing them, their activities would have appeared an obvious fiction.

Peter Shelley had brought his family by hovercraft on a day's shopping expedition to Calais. Massinger had spent the wet morning patrolling the beach and seafront of the Pas de Calais like an exile, as if simply to catch some distant, half-illusory glimpse of his adopted country. His damp hair had been blown over his forehead, into his eyes, by a chill, searching, salty wind; his body had shivered and his raincoat had become sodden. Yet he had remained on the seafront until it was time to meet Shelley, because across the gray, uninviting water he could sense Margaret's existence, know precisely the distance that separated them, thereby lessening it.

He had telephoned, of course. Eager to establish his health and safety, she had, once worry had been assuaged, allowed their last meeting to flood back, filling the present. She had ordered him home; he had feared she might have spoken to Babbington; the gulf between them had yawned open again. He had put down the receiver with the sensation of a physical pain in his chest and a hard lump in his throat, which he was unable to swallow.

"Some smoked ham, darling?" Shelley asked absently. A short, dumpy woman with a thin, moustached, gray-featured husband in tow passed them, her arms laden with the weaponlike shapes of half a dozen long French loaves. The tip of one of them had already broken off. She held them protectively to her ample bosom, eying the two shopping carts malevolently. Massinger turned his aside for her to pass.

"Very well," Alison replied, tight-lipped. She had accepted the fiction of the shopping expedition, yet her tension was evident. She appeared to blame Massinger for her situation, for Shelley's situation.

Shelley pointed at a large ham. The French delicatessen assistant flung it into a bag, twisted the neck, and then priced the item. Shelley dumped the parcel in Massinger's cart, and seemed reluctant to leave the hanging rows of sausages, their skins crimped and wrinkled and provocative. Massinger read off the names of dozens of pâtés in earthenware bowls. There seemed singularly little point in the meeting, as if their tension and urgency had been separately expended and lost during their journeys to Calais, or during the past days when they had been in almost constant telephone contact.

"You think Hyde has any chance?" Shelley asked, reaching up to finger one of the dark, thick sausages.

"I don't know," he replied. "It was *some* sort of chance—he had to be sent. Besides, it keeps him out of Europe at a period when he's in great danger."

Shelley's eyes narrowed, then he nodded.

"I just don't see how—" he began. Massinger's eyes glared.

"Neither do I!" he snapped, his Bostonian accent more pronounced, as if he wished to dissociate himself from Shelley's very English doubt. "Hyde's a dead man if he's caught—maybe I am, too. Did you ever think of that, Peter Shelley?" His voice was an urgent, hard whisper. "I'm laying it out for you now, just as it is. Unless Hyde and ourselves can discover who and what is behind this—behind what happened in Vienna and what's happening to Aubrey—then we'll never be safe again. I don't intend to spend the rest of my life looking over my shoulder."

Shelley's face was smooth with disquiet, youthful and somehow incapable. After a moment, he said reluctantly: "I still can't see—"

"Look, I want Hyde to kidnap this Russian, Petrunin. Miandad knows almost all there is to know about Petrunin—dammit, it *could* happen! There are moments when the man leaves Kabul, when he's vulnerable. It could happen. . . ." Massinger's whisper tailed off into a doubt of his own. Then he shrugged off the mood, and said in a normal speaking voice: "It could, Peter. It just could."

"Perhaps . . ."

"All right—instead of that, what have you got for me? What do you think? Have you any suggestions to make?"

Shelley shook his head.

"Hadn't we better keep moving?" Alison whispered fiercely, as if afraid they would become some kind of target in the next moment. Her body was curiously hunched over her daughter, who sat unconcerned, finishing the last of the chocolate. She had left fingerprints on the glass counter of the delicatessen. Massinger wondered whether Alison Shelley might want to remove them, for safety's sake.

"Yes, perhaps we should," Massinger replied as soothingly as he could. Bottles clinked against each other as Massinger pushed his cart away from the counter. "But at least you agree that we're dealing with someone in your service who's helping the Soviets?" he said to Shelley. Alison walked a little way ahead of them now, glancing to right and left at the shelves as if they concealed surveillance equipment. Massinger felt sorry for her, dragged into Shelley's world of perpetual mistrust.

"I have to—after your account of Vienna."

Massinger nodded vigorously. Shelley deposited some tinned mussels in the cart. "Good," Massinger said. "There is a traitor, and he has to be a senior officer."

"Yes . . ." Shelley sounded alarmed. "Yes . . . I'm sorry. Yes, I agree with you. There is someone high up who wants Aubrey out of the way and is helping the KGB achieve their object."

"Then, what do we do?"

"Helsinki—could you manage that?"

"Why Helsinki?" Massinger said.

They followed Alison as she turned right, then paused as she halted almost immediately and began inspecting racks of children's clothes.

"There's someone there who might talk to us—to you, if there's anything to talk about. Phillipson used to be station chief in Helsinki, and one of Aubrey's appointments. He was always loyal to the old man. He retired six months ago. He liked Finland and the Finns, so he didn't come home. He's still there, and out of things."

"Yes?"

"But he organized some of those meetings between Aubrey and Kapustin—the one on film, the one with the soundtrack . . . ?" They moved on again. A dress had been measured against the little girl, and found acceptable. Shelley's daughter was craning round in her seat to keep it in view.

"You mean, if there was any funny business, this Phillipson might at least have suspected it—noticed something out of the way?"

"Exactly. Oh, what about funds?"

"I'll take whatever you have. Credit cards leave traces. I haven't had time to make a transfer."

"I brought—well, quite a bit. Petty cash, you know . . ."

"Good. What will you do in the meantime?"

"We need a list of possibles."

"We do."

"I can't get access—it'll have to be memory work. It has to be—someone on East Europe Desk, doesn't it?" Shelley looked crestfallen—a youngish bank manager whose head office is seriously displeased with him.

"Or higher still," Massinger said heavily.

"You'll come back to London, after Helsinki?"

"Yes, I think so." Margaret intruded, and he knew that to return to London was dangerous and inevitable. "Yes," he sighed.

"Where will you stay?"

"Hyde's apartment," he replied without hesitation.

"It might work."

"Hyde thinks it will—temporarily, at least."

Alison Shelley was absentmindedly loading long French loaves into her cart. Shelley appeared to be calculating the number of bottles of wine he might add to his present purchases without paying duty. Eventually, he reached for a good claret from one of the higher shelves.

"Look at that," he said lightly. "Less than three pounds, and perfectly drinkable. I shall have to talk to my wine merchant." He smiled. Massinger felt unnerved by the casual remark. Instead of simply dispelling their grave mood, its reminder of normality brought images of Margaret flooding back. His hands were weak as they gripped the handle of the cart. The bottles rattled softly against one another. His eyes were misty as he stared at his damp-stained sleeves. Shelley gently placed the claret in the cart. Alison was waiting for them, impatient and decisive.

"Helsinki, then," Massinger murmured.

"Better than Afghanistan at this time of year," Shelley chided, insensitive of the causes of Massinger's gloom.

Massinger pushed the cart forward with an abrupt, noisy jerk. Ahead of him, beyond the checkouts, rain streaked the glass doors of the supermarket. Ahead of him more clearly was Helsinki and a man called Phillipson. Projected upon those images, as if they were no more vivid than a blank white screen, was the sense of separation from Margaret, even her hatred. He could see no end to that, no conclusion.

The ancient, gleaming Lee Enfield rifle was inlaid with gold and filigree work. It was cradled in the Pathan's folded arms almost like the scepter of a king. The weapon, a relic or museum piece in age, was only the final assertion to Hyde that he was seated opposite one of the few men he could be certain was capable of killing him. Not desirous, not even an enemy—though certainly no friend—but simply sufficiently skilled, sufficiently strong.

Mohammed Jan shook his head once more as Miandad translated yet another of Hyde's pleas for assistance. The scarf of his green turban fluttered, emphasizing his refusal. His blue eyes were hard and expressionless, startling amid the kohl on his eyelids and beneath his eyes. It was almost as if he did not see the Australian and his Pakistani companion. His lips, within the grayed sable of his beard, were a thin line of refusal. Mohammed Jan and his Pathan *mujahiddin* were interested in Petrunin—indeed they hated him and devoutly wished his slow death—but they had no interest in any scheme that Hyde might propose. Hyde's interest in the Russian was no concern of theirs.

For two dozen SLR or NATO FN rifles, for three launchers and their accompanying missiles, they would have raided the central barracks in Kabul, where Petrunin had his quarters. But Hyde had no bribes, and therefore no leverage.

Hyde was cold. They had not even been invited into the man's lean-to hut of wood and corrugated iron, but had been required to squat on the ground outside its door. The afternoon was wearing away and the temperature dropping. The shadows across the refugee camp were long and the mountains beyond Parachinar were tipped with gold. It had been a drive of four hours from Peshawar, and the journey had been completely in vain.

"He repeats that Kabul has become a much more dangerous place," Miandad translated. Hyde tossed his head.

"I'm not asking him to go into Kabul," he replied. "You've already told him that. I want a plan of Petrunin's routine—I want to catch him away from Kabul, out in open country. God, you'd think these blokes had never set an ambush before!"

Mohammed Jan's eyes flickered at the angry frustration evident in Hyde's voice. His face, however, remained expressionless. He seemed to be patiently awaiting the departure of his uninvited guests. They had received tea, served by one of his daughters-in-law, he had listened to their arguments, and he had rejected them. Now only their departure was unaccomplished.

Hyde stood up and walked away. Miandad followed him, and the Australian turned on him.

"Can't that stubborn old goat see—" he began.

"You have given him no reason to help you."

"Christ—he hates Petrunin! What more excuse does he need?"

"You offer neither weapons nor help. You only want something from him. Something he is not prepared to give—lives."

"He's over there—the man with all the answers!" Hyde bellowed. He waved his arms. "The man with my life in his hands," he added more softly. Miandad nodded.

"And Sir Kenneth Aubrey's life, perhaps, and that of my old university teacher. I understand. But Mohammed Jan does not. Your concerns are not his. This is his concern, here. . . ."

Miandad gestured around the refugee camp. It dropped slowly away from them down the hillside, not unlike the slow slide of rubbish down the slope of a tip. It had long since lost its appearance of temporariness and become permanent—the kind of village expected amid that scenery and so close to the border with Afghanistan. Its tumbled lean-tos and tents and hovels contained the remnants of perhaps three or four different Pathan tribes, predominant among them the tribe whose chieftain was Mohammed Jan. This was his territory, this heap of refuse flung into a narrow valley that led toward the border town of Parachinar and the Kurram Pass into Afghanistan. He ruled the place and its inhabitants autocratically, and he lived to kill Russians and Afghan troops. He was an exile, more certainly and with far more purpose than Hyde himself.

"All right!" Hyde snapped, turning his back on the camp, now beginning to soften into shadow. Cooking fires were already strengthening their glows, and cloaked women moved around them. Children and goats grumbled and shouted. Armed men moved as if their only purpose was to be carriers of weapons. "All right—my life doesn't matter to him. But *I* can't help worrying about it, just a bit. If I can't do anything, then it's a question of sitting out the war—for the duration. Here, or somewhere like here."

Miandad turned to look once more at Mohammed Jan.

"They are as fierce and cruel and proud as people say they are," he murmured. "Also immovable. They simply live in another world from you. Your dislike of Russians is—well, rather like moonlight at midday. Not to be noticed beside their feelings. They are very good at hating—but on their terms, for their reasons."

"Let's get out of here."

"Very well. We should be safe, driving back to Peshawar. It is always possible we may not be, of course." Miandad smiled a small, grim smile. "Mm. Just one moment. I wonder what is happening over there . . . ?"

"What?"

"Listen. The old man talking to Mohammed Jan—I want to hear what he says."

Hyde moved away, hands in his coat pockets, shoulders slumped, eyes hardly seeing the grim reality of the camp. It did not interest or move him. He felt only his own predicament, and frustrated rage that these Pathans would not help him. He heard shouts, and saw men moving up the slope toward Mohammed Jan's hut. They passed him without taking notice. They carried long, ancient rifles and modern Kalashnikovs. All of them wore bandoliers of cartridges. Miandad was right; it was a different world. Its priorities, the depth of its hatreds and revenges, all were alien to the encounters of Hyde's professional life. He began to wonder what changes had been wrought upon the urbane, intelligent, professional persona of Tamas Petrunin since his engagement in this kind of war.

"One of Mohammed Jan's returning raiding parties is in trouble, I think," Miandad said softly at his elbow, startling him. Men continued to brush past them, flitting like shadows toward their chieftain's hut. Hyde turned to watch them gather around Mohammed Jan. The man's voice was powerful as he began speaking.

"What did you say?" Hyde asked absently.

"His eldest sons are leading a returning raiding party. The old man who arrived a few moments ago was a lookout, awaiting their return through part of the Kurram Pass. But they are pinned down and waiting for darkness—there are helicopters. And many of the party are dead, from the numbers the old man was able to see."

Hyde shrugged.

"You told me," he said, "it's a different world. What can I do?"

Men were already moving off, toward the perimeter of the camp and the long shadows from the mountains. The snow-clad peaks gleamed in the setting sun. A sprinkling of lights showed the position of Parachinar. Mohammed Jan had disappeared.

"Come," Miandad said. "Perhaps you will see what this war is all about. Perhaps it will be a good lesson for you. We will follow Mohammed Jan and his men. You may see what your old acquaintance has learned of guerilla war." Miandad's teeth flashed whitely, but not in a smile.

Below the aircraft, the scene was colorless—gray and white. The waters of the Gulf of Finland were wrinkled like a shabby gray cloth, ending abruptly where the snow-covered shoreline of Helsinki became a sheet of white. Narrow lines of snow-ploughed roads and railway lines had been lightly traced, but the overweening impression was of an uninhabited, hostile environment. Massinger turned away from the window at the recognition that the landscape and the sea lay below him like an image of his own state of mind—empty and somehow hopeless.

He could not let go, he told himself once more, though the precisely formed words in his mind echoed hollowly in a small, piping voice. Patriotism seemed ridiculous to him, an expatriate Bostonian, a cool-minded academic, especially the simple, emotional kind he seemed to be experiencing. Hyde did not have it, and he wondered whether even Aubrey possessed it. Somehow, though, he had a capacity for patriotism, like a capacity for love, and the object of that capacity could as well have been Afghanistan or the United States or, as it plainly was, Great Britain. He found that he cared, almost despite himself, that his adopted country's intelligence service was being manipulated by the Soviet Union. It was intolerable.

Or was it merely his damnable sense of right and wrong? Was that at the bottom of his heated urge to solve the mystery, clear Aubrey, defeat his enemies? It might be, and he disapproved. It was a naive aspect of his character, and he desired not to be naive.

He had spoken to Margaret again, from the airport, looking out through tall windows onto a rainswept runway, a scene reduced to monochrome like the one below him now as the aircraft dropped toward Seutula airport. He had attempted to convince her that he was safe when the very reason he could not return to her, do as she asked and give it up, was because someone wanted him safely and incuriously dead. The conversation had been painful, pointless. The chasm was still there, merely emphasized by physical distance. She had settled into a routine of hatred toward Aubrey, totally believing in his guilt; it was an orthodoxy that nothing could soften or contradict. Therefore, while he aided Aubrey he was a heretic, and damned.

Yet he knew that her belief was tearing her in two, just as he was himself being pulled apart. He could not tell her he would never be safe, never, unless he could unravel the mystery—whatever the truth concerning her father and Kenneth Aubrey.

Lastly, he had told her—trusting her with his life, as he had wanted to do, felt he needed to do—that he would be coming back, that he would telephone, that he had to see her. . . .

The telephone receiver in their apartment had gone down on those protestations, on his pleading, on his need for her. The line had crackled with static and he had listened to the emptiness for a long time before putting down his receiver.

The rain had been cold on his face as he had crossed the tarmac to the Finnair flight to Helsinki.

The wing outside his window dipped, showing him the gray buildings and the runways of Seutula. The aircraft dropped its nose, straightened, then began its final approach. Massinger settled himself to thoughts of Phillipson and the immediate future.

In the growing darkness, Hyde caught glimpses of light-colored cloth from blouses or turbans, even of dark, shadowy forms against the snow, as the Pathan raiding party moved from rock to rock, from bush to stunted tree to straggling vegetation. On the ground, it was a scene in extreme slow motion, the elapsed time so extended it was almost stilled. Above the defile of the narrow, knife-cut valley that cut through the border north of Parachinar, Russian helicopters moved like agitated insects—flies maddened by poison from an aerosol spray. Patience and urgency; hunters and hunted. To Hyde, using night glasses, it seemed that many were wounded, and by Miandad's guess the party was considerably reduced from that which had entered Afghanistan three days before.

The MiL gunships drove the valley again like airborne beaters of game, moving toward the high cleft in the rocks that concealed Hyde, Miandad, and a little away from them, Mohammed Jan and three or four of his trusted lieutenants: old, gray-bearded men with long, antique rifles. The noise from the helicopters was deafening. Then they turned, whirling as easily as dancers, the downdraft plucking at Hyde's hair and shoulders as the four MiL-24s moved away. Hyde could distinguish the 57mm rocket pods beneath their stubby wings and the four-barrel machine gun in the nose of each aircraft as they turned no more than two hundred feet above him. He shivered.

"There," Miandad shouted above the din and its ricochet from the valley walls. "There!"

Hyde lowered his night glasses, following Miandad's extended arm, focusing the glasses beyond the retreating gunships. The faint redness in the lenses swam and cleared. The scene had little color. A clear, bloodless monochrome. As the focus sharpened, it was as if something had entered an arena: something making everything else of less significance. A pike in a pool. A presence.

The helicopter must have been daubed some garish color, Hyde guessed. Certainly, it was not camouflaged like the gunships that now seemed to bob and curtsey their way toward it.

"Red—blood-red," Miandad murmured.

Hyde lowered the glasses for a moment, and looked at the Pakistani colonel. Miandad nodded. Hyde felt chilled, but he could not have explained his reaction. Petrunin?

"Him?" he asked.

Miandad nodded. "Him. You will find his style—more flamboyant?" Miandad's teeth gleamed white in the darkness of the cleft of rocks.

Hyde raised his glasses once more, again adjusting the focus slightly. The command helicopter that contained Petrunin was moving up the valley, though very slowly, as if engaged in some courtship ritual with the four MiL gunships. Its speed decreased further as it reached its four heavily armed courtiers.

Hyde moved the glasses down, twiddling the focus. He was prompted by an inexplicable fear and urgency. Below him, in the narrow riverbed, the Pathans seemed to be moving with a similar sudden speed. Wounded men were being handled more roughly, pulled and even dragged. Small, bent figures scurried ahead of them. It was dark now, and they were no more than half-a-mile from Hyde's vantage point. They had already crossed the border, even though that crossing was meaningless. Hyde returned his gaze to the black air above the valley—some stars beginning to appear, falsely bright in the night glasses—and the five helicopters. The four gunships hovered and paid homage in a slow circling dance about the command aircraft.

Hyde heard Mohammed Jan issue orders. Men below them began to move swiftly toward the oncoming party and its wounded. Away down the valley, the noise of the helicopters was magnified by the valley walls.

Then the group dissolved. The four gunships wheeled, came into line, began to beat up the valley again. The command helicopter lagged behind, the armed sportsman waiting for the game to be terrified into flight. It was sinister in the extreme, especially to Hyde, who knew the occupant of the red MiL-24. The rescuers scuttled and weaved and ran toward the returning party: flickering white and light-colored patches or swift shadows. The four MiLs closed above them, their noise a fearful clatter from the rocks. Hyde watched.

He winced as small black shapes detached themselves from the bellies of each of the MiLs. Strings of laid eggs. He followed them down, watched some bounce, roll, jump, split. None of them exploded. His shoulders and stomach relaxed. He turned to Miandad, glancing into his grim face. The Pakistani shook his head slightly. Hyde returned his attention to the moving Pathans. The two parties had met; wounded men received extra, urgent support. The tempo of their progress increased. The four MiLs banked and turned. More black eggs fell. There were no explosions. Hyde found it difficult to breathe, impossible to understand.

The retreating MiLs passed over the moving men, their

noise towed behind them like a net. Almost silence, out of which the separate and distinct noise of the command helicopter emerged, closing at a height of no more than two hundred feet. Its racket banged back from the cliffs above the valley floor. Hyde saw raised faces, bobbing, quick-moving turbans. He could begin to distinguish bodies, forms, figures. The party, augmented by the rescuers, was no more than a quarter of a mile away from his vantage point. A faint, silver-sheened mist was rising in the valley. It shone as if with dew or an inner light.

Mist?

It was thin, gauzy. Yet it glowed falsely.

The red helicopter—now Hyde could distinguish patches of other shades on its nose and flanks. Shark's mouth? Grotesque faces? Animal heads? He could not tell. Something occult, almost, about the thing, as if it was not a piece of airborne technology but something much older.

It hovered. Men ran, scattered, limped, or fell. Hunched, scuttling, they moved through the sheen of silver that seemed to cling about them, rising from the floor of the valley to a height of no more than ten or twelve feet. Petrunin's helicopter hovered.

Miandad inhaled sharply. Hyde's shoulders hunched with tension, and his neck ached. The eyepieces of the night glasses hurt him as he pressed them to his face. Men ran, closer now, almost . . .

A glowing spark seemed to drift down from the command helicopter, which instantly lifted to a greater height and banked fiercely away. The spark fell like a luminous insect, or even a cigarette end dropped from the helicopter.

The mist burst into flame. A tunnel of fire existed in an instant, a coffin of flame that contained every one of the moving men. Hyde could see them still moving, then standing, then twitching, then staggering, then falling. He could hear the roar of the ignited napalm or whatever it was. It was louder than the faint screams.

Then it began to die like the glow of a flashbulb: remaining on the retinae of the watchers still as a bright light, but dying into paleness, then shadow, then darkness. Hyde had dropped the night glasses. Heat beat against his face for a moment, then was gone and he felt chilled to the bone. A few ragged shots from the antique rifles in the rocks near him rang feebly out after the command helicopter. Hyde raised the glasses once more. He felt nauseous. Petrunin's helicopter was retreating backward down the valley, its pilot and observation windshields facing back toward the carnage, its air intakes above the windshields like huge, flaring nostrils. It looked like something gloating over its success.

"I think there were more than fifty of them," Miandad murmured. "Including the wounded." Hyde turned to him, open-mouthed. "Including two of his sons." He nodded his head at the man beyond Hyde.

"I—I—" Hyde began, but he could say nothing more. His mouth remained open, as if expecting comment. What was it? What lurked at the back of his mind like a shadow? Some book, was it? Conrad—Kurtz? *Heart of Darkness*, that was it. . . .

Petrunin had become—a savage. A murdering savage. "*The horror . . . the horror,*" Kurtz had said of his own decline into savagery—or the world's decline. Petrunin was Kurtz now. Once urbane, clever, far-seeing, professional; now a butcher, and one who gloated. The camp guard with the lampshades of Jewish skin . . .

Hyde retched, but nothing came.

There was a smell of burnt flesh, burnt people, reaching them from the floor of the valley, together with the faint aroma of chemicals. The black eggs he had seen must have burst open on impact, spreading the gas that he had been able to see as a mist. The spark dropped by Petrunin's helicopter had ignited the mist that by then clung to everything—especially to fleeing human skin and clothing. A twelve-foot-high box of fire, a prison of flame.

Mohammed Jan was standing over himself and Miandad. He spoke to Miandad in Pushtu—perhaps two brief sentences. Hyde looked up into the chieftain's face, above the cradled Lee Enfield. The whites of his eyes gleamed, but Hyde could distinguish no expression on his face. Then he turned and was gone.

"Come," Miandad said. "He wishes to speak with us. Of the Russian."

Miandad got up and brushed off his trousers. Hyde rose weakly. Turning slowly, he could see Mohammed Jan descending to the floor of the valley, moving toward the charred remains of his two sons and fifty of his Pathan subjects. Hyde dragged the cold air into his lungs. There was a black, charred swathe through the valley. Through the clean snow that blanketed the high pass. Hyde found himself shivering. He had always feared Petrunin. Now, he was terrified. He was in dark, turbulent water, entirely out of his depth.

Paul Massinger carefully stamped the snow from his shoes at the top of the steps leading to the low wooden cabin. After the cries of an unseen bird, more like a cough than a song, had faded, the taxi's idling engine behind him made the only sound. The forest of dark-boled, snow-laden pines seemed to crowd in upon the cabin, threatening its temporary occupation of the small clearing. There, no more than twenty miles north of Helsinki, Massinger felt totally isolated, utterly without resources.

He tugged at the bellrope. The noise reminded him of his own schooldays—his turn to be the bell monitor. When the heavy sound died, he could hear no noise or movement inside the house. His breath smoked, the air was chilly against his face. The clearing was almost colorless: only black and white, trees and snow. He shivered.

He rang the bell again, then shrugged at the taxi driver, who seemed uninterested, or interested only in his meter. Phillipson had answered the telephone, had agreed to talk to him, albeit with some reluctance. They had agreed the time, but now—

Footsteps?

"Who is it?" a voice asked. Its evident anxiety, even through the wooden door, chilled Massinger more deeply than the temperature.

"Massinger—Paul Massinger. We talked on the telephone—"

"I've nothing to say to you, Mr. Massinger."

Massinger heard his own surprised, quickened breathing in the silence that followed as if it were the noise of Phillipson's fear. The man was evidently afraid . . . had been frightened. . . .

Massinger ignored the idea. "Mr. Phillipson—it could be important," he said as levelly as he could, leaning confidentially toward the rough, unpainted surface of the door. A strong lock, he noticed. "It really could prove very important." He glanced behind him. No, the driver wouldn't hear, not with the engine running. "It has to do with the arrest of Kenneth Aubrey. I couldn't explain to you over the telephone line, but . . ." He breathed deeply. He could hear, above the engine of the taxi, the heavy, persistent silence of the small clearing and the forest around it. It intimidated. He continued in what seemed a small and inadequate voice: "I'd like to explain it to you in detail—in private, Mr. Phillipson." He felt like an unsuccessful salesman.

"I have nothing to say to you—please go away."

"Mr. Phillipson—what's the matter? Can I help? You can certainly help me."

"Please go away!" The voice was high enough to be described as a shriek of protest. It was the voice of a child or a very old man. Someone bullied?

"Mr. Phillipson—"

"No!"

"Please!"

"Go away!"

Massinger knew that the taxi driver was watching him, that he had heard Phillipson's desperation and terror. Yes, it was terror.

Phillipson had spoken to someone—someone in Helsinki, London, anywhere, it didn't matter—and that person had frightened him into complete silence. That someone might—

Might be behind the door, standing next to the frightened Phillipson, hand firmly upon his arm.

Massinger shivered. "Then be damned to you, Phillipson!" he called defiantly through the door before turning on his heel. The taxi driver's head flicked round and the man stared through his windshield. Massinger stamped down the wooden steps, using his stick to make as much noise as possible. The fading afternoon light between the massed pines was like darkening smoke. The clearing seemed tiny, imprisoned. Massinger wanted to hurry, to urge the driver to accelerate, but he merely gestured wearily and said: "I'm afraid I'll have to change my plans. Let's go back to Helsinki."

The driver nodded and let off the brake. The car's rear wheels slipped slightly, then gripped with their studded tires. Massinger did not turn his head to look back at the lonely cabin as they bounced down the rutted, snow-covered track toward the main road. No other tracks, he told himself. You fool. There was no one else there.

He wouldn't have talked. He was afraid for his life.

He folded his arms tightly across his chest and tried to relax into his seat. The taxi turned onto the main road. There was a hurry of traffic heading in the opposite direction, away from Helsinki. The afternoon darkened into evening, a red sun little more than a thumbnail on the horizon. The short winter day was already over. They passed through Haarajoki, then joined the *moottoritie* into Helsinki. The traffic thickened and headlights rushed at them out of the darkness.

Massinger gratefully allowed himself to doze, refusing to acknowledge that somehow he had run out of will, energy, even purpose. He hardly realized that the taxi left the highway in the outer suburbs of Helsinki, diverted because of an accident and the subsequent traffic jam. Dimly, he glimpsed the grubby edges of the city: light industry's chimneys, low factory blocks on snowbound plots that still appeared scrubby, wire fences. Bungalows, tower blocks, two-story houses filled the spaces between the chimneys and the factories. His eyes were open as they passed the circle of a concrete stadium, preyed upon by its floodlights.

He dozed again, to be woken by the coughing of the taxi's engine. It faded, caught again, then died, and the taxi began to slow down. The driver steered it to the curb, then turned to Massinger apologetically, shrugging his meaning rather than speaking. Massinger pursed his features and nodded impatiently. The driver got out and went to the taxi's trunk. Massinger saw him waving a gasoline can at the window, nodded again, and then watched him in the mirror as he began to trudge back the way they had come. Massinger had no idea when they had last passed a garage.

Massinger sighed. He had no desire to be left to his own devices in the back of a taxi in the suburbs of Helsinki. He was suddenly hungry, and he needed the satisfying narcotic of alcohol—half a bottle of good wine, if his hotel stocked any. He wanted something to stifle the procession of speculations regarding Phillipson that had paraded through his fitful dreams.

The driver had left his radio on after reporting his whereabouts and his delayed return. Its splutter of incomprehensible Finnish grated on Massinger's nerves at first, but he found a superficial reassurance in it after a while. It was normal, utterly normal. He settled further in his seat, pulling his overcoat closer around him. The car was growing cold without the heater.

There were houses and bungalows set back from the quiet road: mere slabs of darkness without feature, pricked or squared by lights. Occasionally, a car passed him. His body continued to register the rapid drop in temperature inside the car. The windshield and the windows began to steam over. He almost dozed again.

A bleep from the radio and another burst of Finnish woke him. He stretched his eyes, and saw the car, parked without lights across the quiet road from him. A pale Mercedes. He could see nothing behind the dark windshield, but he sensed people inside. It was parked on the main road, not in the service road, and he knew it belonged to neither resident nor visitor.

Then the voice on the radio began speaking in heavily accented English. It mentioned him by name. It referred to the taxi, to the taxi's delay, to the American passenger of the taxi. The voice spoke in English, which he knew he was meant to understand and fear. Involuntarily, he glanced across the road at the parked car. No lights, but then the flare of a lighter or match. Then nothing again.

There was another scratch of static from the radio, followed by mumbled messages, replies from the dispatcher, all once more in Finnish. Incomprehensible. He fumbled with the handle, opened the door, and climbed out of the taxi. The air chilled him. He stood with his hand still gripping the handle; whether for security or support he was uncertain. The darkened Mercedes remained still and lifeless, gathering menace. Two cars passed in quick succession, and then the road was silent and empty once more. Massinger was aware of the tiny distance that separated him from the Mercedes.

He stood there for minutes that had no precise shape or division. Then the headlights of the Mercedes flicked on and off three times, and the engine fired. The car pulled out and away, heading north. Massinger was gripped by a fear that it meant to make a U-turn and come back for him, but its taillights eventually disappeared over a slight rise in the straight road.

Massinger realized he was shivering with relief and with the lingering sense of menace. Someone was trying very seriously to frighten him. And it had worked. He felt perspiration growing chill on his forehead and around the collar of his shirt. He no longer wanted to go on with it or have anything at all to do with the fate of Kenneth Aubrey.

7
The Zone of Occupation

If she kept her eyes closed, tightly closed for just one more moment, her father would walk out of that bright, wet haze where her tears refracted the sunlight through the branches of the old tree. It wouldn't just be Simmonds in the Bentley, or even Mummy sitting in the deep rear seat—it would be her father, smiling. . . .

Margaret Massinger snapped upright in her chair, lifting her head, shaking it to remove the insidious past. Even many months later, she had still believed he would come. Mummy had made certain of that.

The body in the ruins that had been identified as that of Robert Castleford, in 1951, had been as much of a shock as if he had been murdered that day or the previous one. She had never been allowed to imagine that her father was dead or would not return—not for a single moment in five years. And he had indeed come back—as a hideous skeleton whose grinning, broken skull she had seen in grainy monochrome in a newspaper photograph. The newsstand placards had borne his name for days, the teachers and some of the older girls at school had reminded her by their looks and words for many weeks. Mummy had shut it out. To her, he would always, one philandering or amnesiac day, return to her—as he always had done.

After the sanatorium, the hospital, the mortuary, and finally the cemetery, her mother was buried next to the grinning skull of her father. Margaret went to live with her paternal grandmother, where her relatives had, by degrees, explained her father to her. A warm man. Unfaithful, often. Everyone had assumed, without voicing the thought, that it had been a woman in Berlin who had been instrumental in his disappearance. Even after 1951, that assumption had continued. He had been killed by a jealous husband, another lover, by an enraged or abandoned woman.

It was her mother's image of him, however, that indelibly remained: the fictitious, idealized portrait of husband and father that so suited her years and her sense of loss. And it still continued plaguing and paining her.

Throughout her adult life, she had been able to comprehend her attitude to her father, explain it rationally to herself. Like stunted growth. Yet, like dwarfism, it was impossible to grow out of or beyond. She had only her child's veneration, nurtured in the hothouse atmosphere of her mother's quiet madness. Mummy had never admitted him to be less than a saint, a minor god. Never *permitted* any other view of Robert Castleford as her reason slipped beneath dark water.

And after Mummy's death, Grandmother had taken Robert Castleford up like a beacon with which to lead her granddaughter. Her memories of her father formed an enchanted circle from which she could not escape. Had never wanted to.

It was simple, really. Paul had betrayed her past, chosen to help the man who had murdered her father. She could not forgive that, even though something strong—and growing—inside her cried out to her to do so. She wanted Paul to come back; she needed him with an aching sense of new loneliness. Revisited loneliness, come back like the recurrence of some fatal disease. But she could not, *could not*! He *must* stop helping Aubrey. If he did, then it would be all right, everything would be all right. . . .

She was being torn in two. She understood that with complete, stark clarity. But she blamed Paul for that, for helping her father's murderer. She could never forgive that, never.

Handel was being played on the radio. There were crumbs of toast on the front page of *The Sunday Times* and on the lap of her dressing gown. And the remains of a Valium sleep in her head, squeezing like a closing vise. She had never needed Valium since her marriage to Paul, and had only taken to it originally in the aftermath of a previous affair, when the pain and blackness of the first weeks had seemed like an echo of her mother's quiet madness. It was late. Almost midday.

The *Insight* article, a *Sunday Times* exclusive, became smudgy print once more. There was a damp spot where a tear had fallen. She still felt the first moment of shock at her father's picture, at Aubrey's picture, at an unidentified silhouette between the two snapshots, and at the headline MÉNAGE À TROIS? Beneath that, even more pompously, *The meaning of treason?*

A warm man. Her grandmother had ignored her questions. Her beloved and only son's sexual peccadilloes were of no significance, and obviously allowable in such an able, brilliant, ambitious man. But like dark jewels, sly and covert pieces of gossip had decorated his adolescence. His name had been associated with an abortion, an almost-expulsion from one school, desperate, ineffectual blackmail by one married woman, affairs. . . .

Robert Castleford had attracted sexual indiscretion, and had always charmed it into harmlessness.

There was something else on the front page, too—something concerning 1974 and Germany, under the headline WHO ELSE HAS BEEN BETRAYED? She had begun to read it as a distraction—World Cup, Olympic massacre, advisory role for Aubrey, investigation, Gunther Guillaume. . . . She could make little sense of it, and it possessed no interest for her. Her eyes and her mind and her memory continually returned to the *Insight* article. She could not bear to turn to page eighteen for a fuller account. The front page was sufficient—her father and Aubrey involved in some sordid sexual triangle in Berlin with the wife of a sought-after Nazi war criminal . . . ?

Lurid, melodramatic—attested to by a former intelligence agent in Berlin, someone who knew the protagonists well. Now living in retirement on Guernsey, so the article claimed. Sexual jealousy, rage, quarrels, despair, hatred, violence.

She understood the emotions. Her own sexual experience confirmed that it was possible—emotions in riot and disorder, passion amounting almost to madness. Her father could have died in such circumstances. Aubrey had killed him over a woman. It was so much more convincing, so much more real than the world of callous treasons and betrayals, of politics and intelligence work and the Cold War. And it made more sense than person or persons unknown. The latter seemed like a senseless and more contemporary piece of violence, such as the two and a half lines in the extreme left-hand column of the front page accorded to an old woman's death at the hands of muggers.

Margaret's loss had begun in 1951, and she knew she had never recovered from it. It was as if she had contracted some childhood disease as an adult when the consequences were much more serious, even fatal. Her mother had deluded her for five years, and when the truth dawned and could no longer be avoided, her mother went slowly and utterly mad and killed herself. Margaret had found herself abandoned in a way she could not have imagined possible. Since that moment of the skull grinning from the newspaper, held in some German workman's hands, she had been completely and utterly alone. Rich eventually, by report beautiful, intelligent, possessed of energy and a capacity for work and enjoyment, but solitary, isolated, bereaved. Alone.

Until Paul. Paul, in unholy, unforgivable alliance with her father's murderer. For that, for the deception of hope followed by betrayal, she could never forgive him.

She let the paper fall to the carpet. She sniffed loudly, sitting erect—she remembered her mother doing the same, in the same stiffly defiant posture and now she realized that she, too, had been fending off painful realities. She would not cry again. She would, instead, finish her toast.

The Handel was solemn, like a pathway into grief, so she left her chair and switched it off. The transistor radio—which Paul never used to listen to music, always preferring his stereo equipment in the study—was on the dark Georgian oak sideboard. Apart from the small dining table, it was the only piece of furniture in the alcove that constituted their breakfast area. The wood gleamed like satin, like a mirror. Her fingers touched it. It was carved, narrow-legged, three-drawered—a piece her father had acquired before the war. Almost everything—everything prominently displayed—had been collected by her father.

She returned to her chair. The toast broke and crumbled under the pressure of her knife. There was sticky marmalade on her fingers. Her eyes became wet—

The telephone rang.

She looked up from her plate, startled and almost as if rebuked for her poor table manners. She stood up and removed the extension receiver from the wall, flicking her hair away from her cheek before holding the telephone to her ear.

"Yes?" Only as she spoke did she realize it might be someone she did not wish to speak to, perhaps a friend appalled by the article whose sympathy was unwanted. Then she heard Paul's voice.

"Margaret—are you all right?" he asked breathlessly, as if she had been the one endangered.

"Paul!" she blurted in reply. "Are you all right?" The Valium headache tightened in her temples.

"Yes, I'm all right. I'm in London, I must see you. . . ."

Her exhalation of relief, the trembling of her body, the lump in her throat all transformed themselves, the instant after she knew he was alive and safe, into an angry echo of her recriminations. Paul was still Aubrey's ally.

"Have you given it up?" she demanded.

"What? I haven't found out the truth, if that's what you mean. Darling, can I come and see you, talk to you?"

"No, Paul—"

"Margaret, I *have* to!"

"You're in London, you must have seen—"

"I have seen. It's nonsense—utter nonsense."

"It *isn't*!"

"You don't know Aubrey!" Massinger protested. Stephens the butler opened the door, hesitated for an instant, then discreetly withdrew. Margaret could hear her own breathing, as well as the noise of a passing car. Then only the noise of the distance between herself and her husband. He was still speaking, still protesting Aubrey's innocence, but she could hear more clearly the whisper of the static and its measurement of distance. "You don't know Aubrey, darling, or you'd never believe that nonsense." There was a false, urgent attempt at jocularity; it was garish and ugly, like too much rouge on a wrinkled cheek. "You can't take that seriously. . . ." Then, "Darling? Are you there, Margaret?"

"Yes, I'm here," she replied wearily, staring at the blank wall. "You're safe, you say? You'll be safe now?"

"No," he said softly.

"What do you mean?"

"What I mean. I'm in too deep now. Whether I like it or not, I'm in. I've aroused—interest." He sounded grim. There was a tone she had not heard before in his voice: something that belonged to his past, to that world he had once shared with Aubrey—the great, stupid, heroic, filthy game of spying. He was demanding she take it seriously. To him, it was far more real than the idea that people could kill for love, out of sexual jealousy or desire.

"Oh, God . . ." The grinning skull. In her world, people could die for the change in their handbags or for the desire they could not satisfy or have reciprocated; in Paul's world, people died because they intrigued, they turned over stones, they desired the truth. The skull: her father's grinning bones.

"Let me see you," he pleaded.

"No!" She could not—yet she wanted him to be safe. Above all, safe. "You must talk to Andrew Babbington—you *must*! Tell him you're in danger—*please* talk to him!"

"I can't—Margaret, I simply can't talk to anyone about this."

"Then leave me alone!" she wailed, thrusting the receiver away from her, clattering it onto its rest on the wall, leaning her head against it as her body slumped. The receiver joggled off and the telephone purred. Paul had evidently hung up. The tears coursed down her cheeks. She stared at her future mirrored on the blank wall of the alcove.

"I must ask you, Mr. Hyde, if you have any suggestions as to how we are to capture your Colonel Petrunin?" Miandad's tone was reproving, even recriminatory.

"What the hell else could I do?" Hyde protested sullenly, squatting on his haunches, his back pressed against the wall of the earthen-floored, chilly room. The pale blue of the sky was visible through the lattice work of the broken roof. "You know damn well he had me by the short and curlies." Hyde stared into Miandad's face. It was evident that the Pakistani, too, was recollecting Mohammed Jan's words: his ultimatum. The Pathan chieftain had stood over them, tall in the firelight as their discussions ended, and he had spoken to Miandad in Pushtu. Hyde had recognized the trap in the Pathan's tone, even before Miandad translated.

He will take you to the border, and across it. He will help you, show you where to find your Colonel Petrunin, and he will show you all the difficulties. In return for his help, you will guarantee to capture the Russian and to hand him over to the justice of Mohammed Jan and his tribe. This will pay for the deaths of his sons. It is the Pathan code of Pushtunwali, where the vendetta is the highest loyalty. Mohammed Jan asks you to choose—to go or to stay. Do you understand, Mr.

Hyde? Do you know what this means? If you want his help, you must promise him the capture of Petrunin."

All the while, Mohammed Jan had stood over them, immobile as a carved figure, the long Lee Enfield rifle with its gold inlay cradled in his arms. Hyde avoided looking at him, avoided too the circle of faces around the fire, Mohammed Jan's council of elders. Nevertheless, as soon as Miandad had finished his translation and given his warning, Hyde had replied.

"*Tell him yes. I promise he will have Petrunin for his justice.*" There had been no other way. He had not dared to even hesitate. To be trusted, to gain their help, he had had to commit himself at once. He wanted them to endanger themselves on his behalf. He had had to agree.

"I agree," Miandad said. "There was nothing else you could do. But you have no idea of how to lay hands upon the Russian?"

Hyde turned to the Pakistani. "Look," he said, "there's you and me and a gang of brave lunatics. They're prepared to stay inside Afghanistan until the job's done. For the moment I've managed to stall them with the idea of an ambush." He grinned mirthlessly. "They'll get some new guns and who knows—we might get some hard news of Petrunin."

"You're an optimist, Mr. Hyde."

"Am I? I'm bloody trapped, that's what I am, sport."

"Perhaps."

"At least they'll wait. Wait until Petrunin comes out to play."

"I know much about your Russian. He is unlikely to allow himself to be captured. By helicopter, he has at least two heavily armed gunship escorts, by road he travels in a heavy convoy. He is virtually impregnable. He spends a great deal of his time at Soviet army headquarters when he is in Kabul, and the rest of the time at the embassy—very little time at the embassy, actually. You see, he knows how much he is hated, how deep the desire to punish him is."

"All right, all right . . ." Hyde sighed. "I know we're in the shit. Thanks for jumping in with me."

"There are obligations."

"To Aubrey you mean?"

"And to men who served with me. It is not only Pathans who have been burned by your Russian's napalm." Miandad's face was grim. Hyde lowered his head, looking at the baggy trousers and sheepskin jacket that were part of his disguise. He rubbed his unshaven skin and sighed.

He looked at Miandad again. The Pakistani, similarly disguised as a Pathan warrior, was softly rubbing his chest and shoulders. Hyde forced himself to concentrate on the problem of Petrunin. "How has it happened?"

"The Russian?" Miandad shrugged. "It is not a nice war here. Not cricket—not even ice hockey." Miandad smiled. "Your Russian was sent here in disgrace, was he not?" Hyde nodded. "He is a very bitter man. This is a war of bitterness. It was easy for him, I suspect. It is always easy to degenerate." Miandad shivered and stretched out his hands to the small fire around which they crouched.

They were alone in the ruin of the Afghan fort. They had crossed the border before daybreak, a party of thirty picked men, all well-armed and provisioned. After miles of high, snowbound passes they had come down, before midday, to this abandoned fort, trudging through a pine forest to reach its shelter. A bitter wind had searched their clothing throughout the journey. Hyde had reached the fort exhausted and chilled to the bone. He had eaten ravenously, then slowly thawed in front of a small fire. The wind moaned and shrieked around the partially ruined walls and barracks and stables. Mohammed Jan had seemed to find some source of satisfaction in the Australian's weariness. Then the Pathans had left, to scout the road between Kabul and Jalalabad.

"I'm getting stiff," Hyde announced. "Let's walk."

They left, passing through other rooms that might once have been offices—a broken chair, sagging wooden shelves—until they stood in the main courtyard of the fort. The snow-laden pines stretched away up the mountain slope until they petered out at the treeline. The scene was almost colorless. Hostile and lonely.

They paced the courtyard of hardened earth, ridged by old cartwheels or the ancient wheels of gun carriages. Hyde flapped his arms against his sides for warmth.

"It is a deadly game, my friend," Miandad said after a long silence filled only by the wind and their stamping footsteps.

"I know that."

"He will hold you responsible if you do not—"

"I know that!" Hyde snapped. He halted, turning to Miandad. "My life isn't worth a spit anywhere in the world unless I get hold of Petrunin and get the truth from him. In those circumstances, mate, it's easy to make extravagant promises and put your balls in the scales!"

"Very well. But how will you prevent Mohammed Jan from putting your Russian to death immediately he is captured—always supposing he is captured alive in the first place?"

"Shoot the bastard, if I have to—Christ, I don't know! Just hope, I suppose. Or threaten to kill Petrunin myself unless they let me talk to him."

"And how will you get Petrunin to talk?"

"Christ knows! Offer him a way out? Let's face it, some bastard's going to be disappointed with the outcome—let's just hope it isn't us!"

"Very well."

"You'll be safe?"

Miandad nodded. "Oh, yes. Mohammed Jan will not harm me. You see, I represent the possibility of guns and ammunition, and shelter."

"God, I wish I knew what the hell to do!"

"Perhaps you should ask Allah for inspiration? Or your own god?"

"Who? Janus of the two faces? Some hope."

"My friend, do not despair. If we find a patrol, and we can capture some of the Russian soldiers, they will talk easily enough. They will know Petrunin—he is a legend among them, one of the few they have. They will know, perhaps, his movements and his timetable. *Then* an idea may come to you."

Hyde looked up at the climbing pines and the white mountains against the pale sky. He could not shake off his abiding sense of the alienness of this country. His mission was doomed to failure. He should never have crossed the border.

A voice called out in Pushtu. They turned swiftly, Hyde bringing the Russian Kalashnikov to bear. A turbaned Pathan waved urgently to them from the main gate.

Miandad said: "They've found a patrol. We are ordered to make haste." He looked at the sky. "No more than two hours of daylight left. The patrol ought to be returning to Jalalabad or Kabul very soon. Come, my friend. Let's hope there are plenty of new guns, even a rocket launcher. Mohammed Jan will be mollified if the haul is a good one."

• • •

"Then there is nothing else you can do—you must get out of it." Shelley's face was grim as Massinger looked up. He had been staring at Hyde's telephone ever since he had replaced the receiver. He could still hear, more stridently and more affectingly than any of Shelley's prognostications and fears, Margaret's almost hysterical refusal to see him, to believe him, to care what happened to him. He was numbed by the fact that she could abandon him.

"How can I?" he asked bleakly.

"How can you? Drop it—drop the whole thing, man!" It was evident that Shelley was pleading with him for their mutual safety. The tortoiseshell cat roused itself, as if the electricity of their fears disturbed and shocked its fur. Then it settled back into its hollow in the sofa next to Massinger. "You'll have to bluff your way out."

"You've already thought this through, haven't you?" Massinger asked. He made it sound like an accusation, and Shelley lowered his eyes as he replied.

"Yes, I have." He looked up again, defiantly. Massinger thought perhaps his eyes had caught the front page of *The Sunday Times* and he had been reminded that he was abandoning Aubrey. His old chief's fate seemed settled, inexorable. Perhaps there was nothing that could be done.

He squashed the thought like an irritating insect, half-afraid of it as of some exotic, corrupt sexual temptation. He could not simply abandon Aubrey. He shook his head. "I can't."

"You *have* to! Look, I've given this a lot of thought. Whoever is running this show has closed all the doors against you. Good God, don't you realize that what happened in Helsinki means that someone knew what I'd been doing almost before I did it? I made a couple of telephone calls, I met you in Calais—and it's as if we carried placards announcing our intentions." Shelley's voice was urgent and afraid. "It's time to face the truth. There's nothing we can do. We can't keep anything hidden from them. Sooner or later, they're going to get tired of us, like buzzing flies, then—*splat!* You, me . . . families . . ." Shelley's voice trailed off.

Massinger patted the younger man's knee roughly, and said in a low voice: "Even if I did, how could I make them believe me?" He felt almost as if Aubrey could hear every word he spoke. Yet Margaret remained the light at the end of the tunnel. She would see him, come back to him, let him come back.

"It's easy!" Shelley said quickly. Massinger recognized that the conspiracy was agreed between them. "You have to convince them that you're interested in the truth of this—" His finger tapped the newspaper. Aubrey's face stared at them. Shelley's damp fingertip became smudged with print from the picture and the headline—*The meaning of treason?* Shelley rubbed his finger on his jeans. "Don't remain in hiding—don't just skulk here. Go to Babbington, even, and ask him all about this. Ask to talk to this man living in Guernsey who's quoted here—what's his name, Murdoch? Convince them that all you're interested in, all you've *ever* wanted to discover, is whether or not Aubrey murdered Castleford. If you can do that, you can walk away from this mess." Shelley's voice ended on a low, seductive note.

Massinger knew it would work. Babbington would accept it, and so would Margaret. *The Sunday Times* had opened a route to the border of the wild country in which he had found himself. He could be across that border by nightfall, safe.

"And the traitor?" Massinger murmured.

"Forget him."

"But we *know* he exists!" Massinger began.

"And we can do *nothing!*" Shelley snapped at him. "We have to stay alive. *I* want to stay alive, anyway. So do you, I suspect."

"But—"

"You don't know where to begin. You have nothing to offer, no influence, no power, no knowledge, and no leverage. You can't even protect yourself. Give it *up!*"

He could be dining with his wife that evening. He could be holding her in his arms within a matter of hours.

Safe. The route to the border was open. Safe—

"And you?" he asked.

"I'll ring this man in Guernsey—on your behalf. A half-hearted final gesture, for form's sake. Then I can go back to the office with—a clean sheet." Two spots of shame had appeared on Shelley's cheeks, but it was evident that he was determined. He had abandoned Aubrey and was already learning to live with the amputation of a small part of his conscience. "As for you," he added, "why not go and see one or two of these people I've dug up who were in Berlin in 'forty-six? It will make for conviction, mm?" Shelley picked up some sheets of paper from the coffee table. "Yes, why not? See one or two of them, and then you call Babbington. Ask to see him—seem to want to be convinced. Sound as if you want to believe everything you read in the papers." Shelley's forced jocularity was evidently acted. He was assuming his new role. "When you've spoken to Babbington, all you have to do is convince him that you're satisfied. Aubrey killed Castleford. They have to be made to believe that you believe it. Who knows—perhaps the old man did, in a fit of passion—"

"Don't be stupid!"

"Sorry."

There was a very long, strained silence. Massinger suspended all thought, almost ceased to breathe. Cross the border, he told himself again and again.

"Very well," he said eventually. "It's the only way. I agree."

As Shelley sighed with relief, Massinger encountered an image of Aubrey's old and shrunken form in silhouette at the end of a long, poorly lit corridor, abandoned and alone. Massinger clenched his fists and turned his thoughts forcibly to his wife.

It is ludicrous, Aubrey told himself, that I should be providing my interrogator, just as he is at his most dangerous, with a roast pheasant Sunday lunch accompanied by a bottle of good claret. He watched Eldon squash a portion of peas onto his fork and raise them to his lips before he refilled the man's glass from the silver-necked ship's decanter. Aubrey watched his own hand intently as the wine mounted in Eldon's glass. It was steady. He had absorbed the shock of the *Insight* article long before Eldon had telephoned and been invited to lunch. Mrs. Grey considered their dining together an act of madness or heresy, but had prepared one of her best lunches, with apple tart to follow. Aubrey had needed the normality of the occasion, false though it was, to assist the drama of casual indifference and easy denial that he knew he would have to perform for Eldon.

Within himself, controlled but evident, the turmoil of an approaching crisis brewed like a tropical storm. The subject of Clara Elsenreith had arisen, and Aubrey knew they would be looking for her. He also knew that he had to get to her first, at whatever risk.

"She seems to have quite disappeared," Eldon was saying. "Ah, thank you, Sir Kenneth. As I said, an excellent claret."

"I'm sure you regard it as a great pity that I have not continued the liaison until the present day," Aubrey remarked. He sliced neatly at the thigh of the pheasant, placing the meat delicately between his lips. He was well into the role, and was confident he could play it to the end of the interview—despite his increasing weariness, his growing desperation, and the new and sudden fear that he had to make a move. The journal that Clara had kept for him for thirty-five years must be destroyed. Now, it could well constitute the last link in the chain they would use to bind him. They felt they had a motive now—*ménage à trois*, he thought with disgust—and his confession to Castleford's murder was in the hands of the woman in the case. Find her and they would find his confession.

Eldon's eyes studied Aubrey. He smiled thinly.

"At least, Sir Kenneth, you admit the liaison itself."

"Of course. Murdoch was not the only one to know of it."

"And this woman was Castleford's mistress, too?"

Aubrey's face narrowed as he pursed his lips. "She was not."

"But—" Eldon's fork indicated the room, which somewhere contained the newspaper article and Murdoch's assertions.

"Murdoch assumed the fact."

"As did others?"

"Naturally."

Eldon's brow creased. "I wonder why that should be," he mused.

"Because Castleford's reputation in such matters was well known. Because he—actively pursued Clara Elsenreith."

"You had, then, no cause for sexual jealousy? *You* were, in fact, the victor, the sole possessor of the lady's favors and affection?" Eldon's tone was light, sarcastic, stinging. The slighting of the affair, of the woman in the case, was quite deliberate.

"I was," Aubrey replied levelly.

"We shall have to ask the lady for corroboration."

"When you find her," Aubrey remarked incautiously.

"Is there any reason you should hope we do not?" Eldon asked sharply, laying down his knife and fork.

Aubrey shook his head, sipped his claret. "None whatsoever."

"You have no idea where she can be found?"

"As I indicated—the lady belongs very much to an earlier part of my life. An episode I thought long closed," Aubrey added with unpretended bitterness. "I have no idea where you might find her." An elegant apartment opposite the Stephansdom, above a smart shoe shop, his memory confessed, almost as if he had spoken the words aloud. He sipped at the claret again. He could clearly envisage, without concentrating, the rooms of the apartment, much of the furniture and many of the ornaments, the decoration of the drawing room and the guest bedroom where he had occasionally slept. Clara owned the shop below the apartment. It sold shoes produced by the small companies in which she had an interest in France and Italy.

Thank God, he told himself, that she never called her fashion house by her own name, married or maiden. Thank God for that, at least.

Castleford had pursued her, yes. Castleford had become insanely jealous when he found her drawn toward another man. He felt himself cheated by Aubrey, insulted by the poorer physical specimen's success, by the junior man's triumph. He had pleaded with Clara, attempted to coerce and blackmail, to bribe—to possess. Castleford needed to possess women, to use and enjoy them, then put them to one side like empty bottles when he had done with them. Clara had loathed him, though Aubrey was certain that, for her own advantage, she would have become Castleford's mistress had he not appeared on the scene. Clara would have had to look after herself. From Castleford she could have obtained papers, food, money, clothes, protection, safety. Instead, Aubrey had supplied those things.

Yes, Castleford had been jealous. At first Aubrey had been jealous of Castleford, suspecting a success the man had not at that time enjoyed. But sexuality was not the motive for Castleford's murder.

No, not sex, or money, or power . . .

"You seem thoughtful, Sir Kenneth?"

Damn.

"Not at all. More claret?" Eldon demurred, covering his glass with his palm. "Then I'll ring for Mrs. Grey. We'll have the dessert."

I must save myself. Only I can save myself, Aubrey's mind recited to the tinkling of the silver bell in his hand. I have to get to Vienna. I have to destroy that stupid, stupid journal, before . . .

He looked calmly into Eldon's face.

Before *he* sees it!

"Come on, Mike—you can tell me how you got onto this chap Murdoch—surely?" Shelley's voice was strained with bluff jollity.

"Look, Pete—I told you. The man came to us. You know it happens all the time."

"And you believed him?" Shelley, sitting on his sofa, the receiver pressed to his cheek, watched his daughter patiently rolling a growing snowball around the garden. Alison, as if she felt the child required close personal protection, was standing in her fur coat, arms folded tightly across her breasts, intently watching their daughter.

"You don't think we didn't check, old boy?" the jocular, superior, knowing voice came down the line. It was as if the voice mocked not simply Shelley's naiveté but also the innocence of the scene through the bay window. The new patio doors seemed suddenly very insecure—too much glass.

"No—"

"Well, we talked long and hard to him. We even cleared it with your people. Not that we had any need to, but we did. They gave us a couple of other names. Common knowledge, old boy. Aubrey and Castleford at it like hammer-and-tongs for months, both trying to crack this Nazi widow. We couldn't trace her, more's the pity. I can't imagine your boss having that much of a yen for a bit of the other, can you?" Mike laughed.

"No," Shelley replied ruefully. He trusted Mike. He was a journalist SIS had used before, fed or pumped as the need arose. He could be trusted. And he would probably pass on the fact of Shelley's inquiry. And his acceptance of the answers he was given. With luck, Shelley was beginning his professional rehabilitation. *I just made a few inquiries for Massinger's sake*, he thought. "You believe it, then?" he added.

"I do. Don't you?"

"I suppose so. God, it takes some swallowing, though."

"The most unlikely people can get steamed up over sex, old boy. Your old boss is human after all—I think." Mike roared with laughter again. He was beginning to irritate Shelley, as if the amusement was directed at his evident disloyalty.

"I suppose so."

"Any chance of the first hint when they charge him?"

"I—yes, of course." Shelley felt sweat break out along his hairline. *He hadn't even thought of it!* Charges. They'd be charging the old man any day now. "Yes, yes—I'll be in touch," he added. "See you."

He put down the telephone hurriedly. It was growing dark in the garden. Suddenly, he did not want his wife and daughter outside any longer. He crossed swiftly to the patio doors beside the bay window. The Labrador arranged on the rug in front of the fire opened one hopeful eye. Shelley slid back the glass doors.

"Come on, you two," he called with false jollity. Alison immediately studied him.

"Just a moment, Daddy," his daughter called, intent upon the snowball, almost as tall and heavy as herself. She heaved at it and it moved toward the rosebed.

"Careful," he cautioned. Oh, come *in*, his thoughts pleaded.

"Close the doors," Alison instructed. "You'll let all that expensive heat out."

He slid the doors closed. "Oh, *shit!*" he bellowed. He'd established his alibi. Murdoch in Guernsey had reluctantly answered the telephone, spoken to him, confirmed his claims in the paper. Mike, author of the *Insight* article, had apparently satisfied his curiosity. To all intents and purposes, Shelley was satisfied with the motive for Castleford's death and the evidence for Aubrey's guilt. He had surrendered, made himself harmless—defused himself as a threat.

He was miserable in his shame. He had abandoned Aubrey for good.

• • •

The main highway between Kabul and Jalalabad lay below them. Twisted like rope between tumbled, snow-clad cliffs, it seemed to writhe like a living thing. A snowplough had passed through since the most recent fall. On the other side of the road, between its embankment and the gray skein of the river, which looked as tarred and graveled as the road itself, the snow-cloaked remains of a burnt-out personnel carrier had returned to innocence. Dawn slid softly down the face of the opposite cliffs.

The Soviet patrol had spent the night in a bombed, deserted village rather than risk an ambush in the dark on the highway. Scouts had reported, almost gleefully, the restlessness and the inability to sleep as well as the numbers, vehicles, and arms of the patrol. Mohammed Jan had decided to wait until dawn, until the patrol returned to the highway to make its way back to Kabul. The Pathans were now hidden on both sides of the narrow highway, high up in the cliffs. From his vantage point, Hyde was aware of no more than half a dozen of them, and he felt they were competitors in a race. He did not trust any of them to leave a Russian soldier alive for long enough to be questioned. He needed an officer, preferably. But, anyone—

If he was quick enough. Even then, all he could offer the man in exchange for information was a quick bullet rather than execution by mutilation. Thus his tension as he crouched in the rocks. Miandad beside him was, apparently, more diffident and relaxed. Below them, almost directly below, rocks and larger boulders had spilled across the highway, effectively blocking it to traffic. A similar small landslide had been prepared farther back down the highway, to block any retreat.

The dark air was bitterly cold. Hyde felt as if he had never been warm since he had boarded the old military transport in Karachi. The cold sunlight slid further down the cliffs. A mirrored light flashed a signal toward their position. Mohammed Jan stood up and waved in reply.

"Less than half a mile away now," Miandad murmured. Hyde merely nodded. Miandad studied the lightening sky above them. "I wonder whether they will send a helicopter from Kabul."

"Do they usually?"

"A year ago, every patrol had a helicopter escort. But now—who can say? This part of the country has been quiet for most of the winter. The Russians assume they control this highway. Perhaps there will be no helicopter—until we have finished our business, anyway." Miandad smiled, then unconsciously flicked at his moustache, parodying a British officer.

Hyde returned his attention to the road. Less than three minutes later, a green-painted BTR-40 scout car rounded the nearest bend, moving with what appeared to be exaggerated caution. Its small turret and finger-pointing machine gun swiveled from side to side. The vehicle seemed to possess a jumpy tension of its own. Then two caterpillar-tracked BMP infantry carriers, squat and green and heavily armored, appeared behind the scout car. Each of them was armed with a missile launcher and a 73mm gun. There would be eight men in each, all capable of firing with the aid of periscopes while the vehicle kept moving. The red stars on the flanks of the vehicles were hardly visible in the slow dawn. A second scout car brought up the rear of the small column.

Hyde shivered with cold and tension. Yet, however much he reminded himself of the armor and armaments of the men and the vehicles that contained them, he could not avoid the impression that this slow-moving patrol was afraid and vulnerable. Four armored vehicles—two missile launchers and two heavy cannon mounted on the BMPs, two machine guns on the scout cars, sixteen to twenty Kalashnikov AKMs inside the four vehicles, perhaps four or five handguns, grenades, perhaps one or two machine guns like the PK or the RPK . . .

The catalogue meant nothing. It could not prevent those Russian conscripts from being afraid every moment they crouched behind their armor, jogging and bucking back to Kabul. Thirty Pathans with old rifles and stolen Russian arms and American or British or Czech or Russian grenades posed a far more potent threat. The terrain and the fanaticism both belonged to them.

The leading scout car began to slow, well down the road from the small, deliberate landslide. At that moment, the officer in command of the scout car would be operating on assumptions. In that situation, and with his nerves, he would assume that the landslide was deliberate and that it was intended as part of an ambush. Perhaps less than a minute to decide, to report over the radio—

The scout car turned awkwardly on the highway and headed back toward the two BMPs. The trailing scout car also turned, making for the bend in the road. Hyde imagined that the patrol had already summoned a helicopter from Kabul, less than thirty miles west of their position; perhaps ten or fifteen minutes' flying time for an MiL-24 gunship.

The two BMPs began to turn very slowly, shunting back and forth on their caterpillar tracks, the stationary scout car near them like a sheepdog. Nothing else appeared to move on or near the highway. Hyde heard a distant rumble that might have been thunder or the echoes of a shot. Presumably, the second landslide. His hand involuntarily jumped with nerves as it rested on the chilly plastic stock of his stolen Kalashnikov. The remains of a sticker—he hadn't noticed it before, but it was lighter now—were still affixed to the gun. It was yellow, had been round, and displayed the torn remains of a smiling cartoon face. The Cyrillic command to smile had been parti-ally torn away. The image disturbed Hyde, adding to the spu-rious but intense nerves he experienced as a spectator of the almost innocent scene below.

A figure moving, crawling in the roadside ditch? He could not be certain. The second scout car, the one that had headed back down the highway, now seemed to flee back into sight, a spray of slush rising at the side of the road as it cor-nered at speed. Hyde's hand covered the torn, smiling sticker and he leaned slightly forward, drawn to the opening scene of the drama that was as inevitable as a previously witnessed tragedy. He saw from the corner of his eye that Miandad's body had adopted the same posture. He had no doubts. He'd been told the ending of this play.

A figure, yes—

A brown-robed Pathan slipped on all fours onto the gray ribbon of the road, rolled something, then ducked back into the drainage ditch. Hyde held his breath. He was captive and captivated. Four seconds, then the grenade exploded beneath the scout car. Flame billowed around its flanks and wheels, but died almost at once. The scout car appeared undamaged, apart from scorch marks on its olive drab paintwork. Hyde lowered his binoculars in disappointment. Miandad nudged him, and pointed.

Dandelion clocks. He focused the glasses. Dandelion clocks. They floated, orderly, delicate, innocent, down from the lowest rocks toward the vehicles on the road. One BMP had turned, the other straddled the highway while undoubted and furious radio contact continued between all four vehicles. The trap was dawning upon them. The grenade had been some kind of signal? Perhaps just a piece of bravado.

The dandelion clocks—

Suddenly, he knew what they were. Soviet RKG antitank grenades, hand-thrown and capable of penetrating five inches of armor. The BMP armor was 14mm thick, that of the scout cars 10mm. The white patches which had reminded him of dandelion clocks were the small stabilizing drogue parachutes which ensured that after the grenade was thrown its shaped charge struck nose first.

One of the BMPs launched a Sagger missile with a bright, spilling flame. Rock and snow and dust flew away from the suddenly obscured hillside above the road. Above the Pathans, too. Boulders began to roll toward the lower slopes. The echoes of the noise deafened Hyde.

The first dandelion clock struck, then the second. One detonated on the surface of the road, the other on the trailing scout car's back. The armor erupted like a boil, then split as if the vehicle had been unzipped. Something staggered from the ruin, ablaze, and fell to a whisper of rifle fire. Hyde could not hear screaming at his safe height. Other grenades struck one of the BMPs. Flame, noise, the tearing of armor. Hyde had never realized the hideousness of the noise of splitting armor plating. It seemed to cry out on behalf of the occupants of the troop carrier.

Another Sagger was launched by the undamaged BMP. The cannon atop the first troop carrier also opened fire. Rock and hillside boiled and shattered. The narrow gorge filled with smoke and raging noise. The surface of the gray river was pattered into distress by falling rock and metal. Uniformed men running—others lying still, sprawled down the sides of vehicles or by the caterpillar tracks or on the slush and gray tar of the highway. Hyde could hear, though he could no longer distinguish, the firing of both 73mm cannons from the BMPs. Flame lit the smoke and dust cloud from within—flickering flames from the shooting, steadier flame from one of the scout cars, burning.

The roar of the hillside being torn by another missile, the chatter of a machine gun. Then the noise of only one of the two cannons and a newer, brighter source of light within the cloud of smoke and dust.

Miandad nudged him, leaning his head toward him. "It

is time for us to make a move!" he yelled. "Otherwise, there will be no one left alive to question!"

Hyde blanched as he looked down into the boiling, dense cloud garishly lit by flame. He could not, for a moment, shake off the distance between himself and the action below. Then he nodded. Together, they scrambled down the loose-surfaced slope, entering the cloud of smoke and dust. Hyde wound his scarf around his face, coughing violently, his eyes watering. He could see Miandad only as a shadow beside him.

"Where?" he shouted, inhaling a mouthful of acrid smoke. He could smell burning gasoline, cordite, and flesh. He clambered out of the ditch—he could hear the screaming now—blundered against a Pathan tribesman, and then he was on the road, crunching over the rubble of metal and rock.

"This way!" Miandad grabbed his arm and pulled him to his left. Hyde followed the Pakistani. A gout of flame shot up somewhere ahead of them and he felt its heat against his skin. Other Pathans slipped past them, a uniform blundered near, but it was alight and Hyde ignored it. Only minutes, and he began to think it was already too late. "The other side of the road, yes?" Miandad shouted against his ear. Hyde nodded.

The leading scout car was wrecked and on its side. A body spilled out of its forward trapdoor like a leakage of fuel. Miandad bent by the meaningless form, then looked up. Hyde could see his eyes gleaming, their whites intense.

"What?" he yelled.

"Some got out—some must have got out!"

"Where?"

A burst of machine gun fire from close to them whined off the overturned body of the scout car.

"There!" Miandad yelled.

A deep, rumbling explosion, followed by the clatter of hot fragments and slivers of metal on the road around them. One piece sliced and burned Hyde's sheepskin jacket, another scorched his hand. Evidently, one of the BMPs had exploded. There couldn't be many left now. A turbaned Pathan staggered against the scout car and fell on top of Miandad. The Pakistani almost fastidiously pushed the body away. In a moment of silence, Hyde heard someone screaming like a rabbit. Then the machine gun opened up again, raking the road away to their left. Evidently, the officer who commanded it had decided that anyone still likely to come out of the maelstrom of smoke and dust would be an enemy. And if not, better to take no chances just for the sake of one or two raw conscripts.

"Come!"

Miandad moved away to the right and Hyde followed him in an awkward crouch, moving as swiftly as he could. The edge of the road appeared, gray changing to earthen brown and filthy slush. Then they were in the wet ditch, the snow soaking through Hyde's baggy trousers and sleeves.

To his left, Hyde could see—in the moment when he heard its renewed chatter—the flickering flame at the muzzle of the light machine gun. There was little other firing now. Sufficient lack of concussive noise to make movement audible. Screaming audible, too.

Dying men everywhere—

Close.

Hyde grabbed Miandad's arm in a panic of fear. Ahead of them, no more than twenty yards away, the machine gun had stopped firing. The cloud, too, seemed to thin. Struggling men. The group who commanded the machine gun had been found, were being killed—

Hyde ran, Miandad a pace behind him, both of them blundering along the uneven, rock-strewn ditch. A blank-eyed face stared up at them from the edge of the road. Hyde did not even register consciously that there was little that remained of any human shape below the shoulders. Then he was among the struggling group. Someone knocked him aside. He saw a military bayonet flicker like silver, then a curved knife at its business. Miandad blundered against him, then seemed to dart to one side. Hyde's head moved from side to side in growing desperation. He was looking for something as small, as insignificant, as collar tabs or shoulder boards. He needed an officer.

Miandad was struggling with something on the ground, dragging it along the ditch, resting it against the roadside slope. He bent to lift the unmoving legs, and as he did so a Pathan emerged from the thinning cloud, rifle at his side, knife in his hand. He hesitated only for an instant as he saw Miandad struggling with the Russian's limp legs, and then he raised his knife. Hyde did not know whether the man assumed Miandad was being attacked—a fellow Pathan—or whether he did not care. He had time only to move a single pace and swing the butt of the Kalashnikov. Its rigid plastic stock struck the Pathan just above the left eye, and he fell away from Miandad and the Russian, dropping his knife as he did so.

"Quickly!" Miandad demanded, looking up.

Visibility was improving quickly now. Hyde could see perhaps a dozen Pathan tribesmen moving among the wreckage and the bodies. He saw one Russian soldier's body buck and twist as his hands were cut off. The man did not scream because he was already unconscious.

"Help me get this one away into the rocks!" Miandad added.

Hyde shouldered his rifle, and together they dragged the Russian—young unconscious face, bruise on his temple, slight burns on his cheeks and jaw, collar tabs, an *officer*!—out of the ditch and down the slope toward the river.

They splashed through the shallow water, the Russian officer supported between them, and gained the cover of the rocks at the foot of the steep cliffs. Hyde's breath was coming in huge gulps, and he was bent almost double, resting on his knees as if vomiting. Miandad's hand rested on his arm. The sky above was pale and blue. They were out of the dust and smoke, which was now dispersing, exposing like the retreat of some tide the wreckage on the shore of the highway.

Miandad pointed toward a clutter of broken rocks.

"Help me get him over there," he said. Hyde realized he was no longer shouting. There was no longer any need. The gorge echoed now only with screaming of a decreasing intensity and horror and the occasional rifle shot. A burst of startling fire as some ammunition exploded, then only the screaming, which had begun to sound more like the noises of carrion birds than those of dying or mutilated men. Hyde nodded. "You don't have much time," Miandad added, tossing his head back toward the road.

"Okay. Let's go."

They dragged the Russian, who groaned once in a boyish hurt way, toward and behind the rocks. They were perhaps seventy or eighty yards up the slope and a hundred yards from the road.

"Work quickly!" Miandad commanded, tilting a silver flask to the young Russian's lips. The boy coughed, and his eyes opened. Opened and became fearful at the same moment as he saw Hyde's turbaned head in front of him.

"Be quiet!" Hyde snapped in Russian. The boy's eyes widened further, in surprise and shock. He turned his head and saw Miandad's narrow dark features. "Now," Hyde continued, "if you want to go on living, keep your voice down—lieutenant," he added, glancing at the collar tabs and shoulder boards.

"Who are you?" Hyde could not be certain of the accent, but it sounded Ukrainian. The lieutenant was little more than twenty or twenty-two.

"It doesn't matter. You're my prisoner, not the Pathans'. You understand the difference?" The lieutenant nodded, swallowing the fear that bobbed in his throat. "Good. Give me your papers—quickly!"

The lieutenant hesitated, as if the documents were somehow talismanic, then he reached into his jacket and removed them. His hand shook as he passed them to Hyde. There was a high-pitched scream, and his whole body twitched in an echo of the agony of the man on the road. Hyde opened the ID folder. A tiny monochrome picture of the young officer, unsmiling and perhaps a little pompous. The official stamps, the public details. Lieutenant Azimov. Yes, from Kiev in the Ukraine. Commissioned two years before, after leaving military academy. Afghanistan had been his first posting. Sergei Azimov. A white, scorched, bruised face, foreign-looking in an alien place.

A sheet of paper, much folded and unfolded, drifted to the ground. The young man's eyes followed it hungrily. Hyde picked it up. There was a snapshot, too, in the little bundle of papers that had been tucked inside a battered wallet that might once have been the boy's father's property, almost an heirloom. Hyde read the letter.

> Dear Sasha,
> I love and miss you so much. We have
> spent such a little time together. It is very hard
> for me to think about my work, about anything
> but you. I worry for your safety all the
> time. . . .

Hyde stopped reading. The girl was round-faced, unmemorably pretty, her hair tied back. Azimov's wife, Nadia. Hyde felt he had pried. He hurriedly passed the letter and the snapshot to the lieutenant, who pressed them against the breast of his uniform jacket. He was shivering now, with aftershock and the cold.

"Right, Lieutenant Azimov—you can stay alive if you tell me what I want to know—understand?" A solitary scream, hardly human, worked like a stimulant on Azimov. "You understand?" Azimov nodded. "Good. I want to know about Colonel Petrunin—understand? Colonel Tamas Petrunin. Everything you know, everything you can remember. I want to know where he is now, what his routine is, where he can be found. Help me, and I'll save your life."

You lying bastard, Hyde told himself.

Miandad tilted the flask again. The boy swallowed, cleared his throat and said: "Thank you, thank you. . . ." Hyde merely nodded. The boy evidently had no interest in who he was, in the loyalties dictated by his uniform, in anything but the fiction that he would go on living. Hyde raised his head and peered over the rocks down toward the road. The cloud had dispersed. Cold sunlight was edging like a spent wave across the gray road. The river gleamed like polished steel. The mutilated bodies had been flung into the ditches on either side of the road. The Pathans were gathering weapons and ammunition—machine guns, rifles, the RPG rocket launcher, a Pathan waving that jubilantly above his head, boxes of ammunition dragged from the burning wrecks. Two men were even dismantling the machine gun from its mounting on the overturned scout car.

They had perhaps ten minutes.

He had already begun to lose interest in the young officer, possessed as he suddenly was by an idea. The rocket launcher, with luck complete with night sight, capable of penetrating more than twelve and a half inches of armor—or a solid wall.

Uniform, confusion, disguise . . . ?

"Ask him," he instructed Miandad. "Ask him everything. If—if he's—" His excitement was evident. He snapped at the officer: "Where is Petrunin now—today, tomorrow? Do you know? Can you tell me where he is?"

"That bastard," the young officer muttered.

"Yes, that bastard. Where is he?" He was almost shouting at Azimov, who flinched at the noise and urgency of his voice.

"He's in the embassy . . ."

"Military headquarters, you mean?"

"No, the embassy. He's KGB, remember. He won't use military communications—too insecure for *him*."

"Why the embassy?" Hyde snapped.

"Who knows? Who cares? Some purge of the civil service in the wind, of the government, of the army. Who gives a toss why? He'll be there all week, so I hear."

Yes, yes, *yes* . . .

"What is it?" Miandad asked, standing up beside him.

"Find out everything. Get him to draw you a map of the embassy. I'll stall Mohammed Jan for as long as I can."

"You have a plan?"

"I think so. If he knows as much as he seems to. Find out. I'll keep them away from you." The RPG-7 launcher was being handed almost reverently to Mohammed Jan, who accepted it like some symbol of authority. Yes, Hyde thought fiercely, yes—

"I speak very little Russian, you speak no Pushtu. *I'll* stall for you while you question the boy." Hyde hesitated, then nodded.

"Okay. Give me ten minutes."

"I'll try." Miandad turned away, then looked back at Hyde. "You realize," he said softly, his eyes focused beyond Hyde, on Azimov, "you can't allow him to go, or to remain here in hiding. If a helicopter comes, he knows too much." Hyde nodded, expressionless. "And you can't hand him over to—" Hyde shook his head. "You realize, then—"

"Yes," Hyde said in a whisper. "I'll shoot him when he's told me what I want to know. In this God-forsaken place, a quick, clean death is tantamount to a mercy killing!"

8
The Capture

Miss Catherine Dawson bobbed and fussed about the bird table in her garden much like one of the tiny creatures she was attempting to preserve with bacon fat and bags of peanuts and bread. She wore gumboots and an old fawn coat, and her gray hair was wispy as it escaped from her headscarf. The snow drifted down gently from a uniformly gray morning sky. Miss Dawson seemed well able to contain her impatience with regard to her visitor.

Massinger guessed she was almost seventy, which would have made her a woman in her late twenties, perhaps as much as thirty, when she was posted to Berlin as a Control Commission translator and interpreter immediately the war in Europe ended. She had been a member of Castleford's staff for more than a year before the man disappeared.

Massinger had first telephoned the previous afternoon. There had been no reply. He had rung repeatedly, obtaining an answer from Miss Dawson only late in the evening. She had been visiting friends for the day. Yes, he might certainly call the following morning. At ten? Certainly. Thus, Massinger had remained at Hyde's apartment overnight. He realized that, while he possessed a safe route across the border, it was crucial to his continuing safety that he appear both convincing and convinced when he surrendered his quest for the truth. He needed to talk to this woman, perhaps to other survivors, before he could lay down his self-imposed task and declare himself satisfied with his discoveries and the fact of Aubrey's murderous guilt.

He had slept little. He was ashamed that impatience to be with Margaret had troubled him more than guilt at abandoning his friend. Now, at a little after ten in the morning—

Terry Wogan had been making his farewells on the transistor radio as he had passed through the kitchen behind Miss Dawson—he was at the rear of a modernized cottage in an Oxfordshire village, pursuing the charade that might save his marriage and his life. Despite his lack of sleep, he felt fresh. Impatient, too, and increasingly optimistic. A lighter, shallower person, perhaps, than he had felt himself to be for some considerable time. He could, however, sense himself putting clocks back, reordering pleasure and happiness like additional supplies for a hopeful expedition. The soft, large flakes of snow fell on his uncovered head, melted on the shoulders of his raincoat. They were chilly, pleasurably so, against his clean-shaven cheeks. He almost wanted to put out his tongue to taste the snowflakes like a child.

"It's very good of you to take the time to see me," he offered again to Miss Dawson's bobbing back. "I realize I must be intruding."

"Must you?" Miss Dawson replied, turning to face him. "What could you imagine so occupies me that a visitor would be unwelcome?" Her blue eyes twinkled. Her dentures were falsely white, but displayed in a genuine, almost mischievous smile. He wondered whether it would be wrong, even patronizing, to feel regret for her that she had never married.

"I'm sorry," he murmured.

She completed her ministrations at the bird table and came toward him. Almost at once, a robin appeared on the table. Two yellow-breasted tits followed it, dangling at once from the slightly swinging bag of nuts. A red plastic mesh. Sparrows landed. Miss Dawson turned and contemplated the scene for a moment like a satisfied Savior, then ushered him indoors as if she had only that moment realized it was snowing and he was bareheaded.

"Coffee—cocoa?" she asked, gesturing him to one of the upright kitchen chairs. He lowered himself onto it, aware of his hip. Its aching, its stabs of pain had returned with renewed vigor, it seemed, since his decision to rehabilitate himself with his wife and Babbington, as if he wore his conscience in a holster on that hip.

"Coffee would be fine," he said. Miss Dawson had studied his awkward movements.

"You should have the operation," she murmured, fussing with a nonstick saucepan at the stove. "I did—both hips."

"Yes, I should," he replied. The conversation aged him—something did, at least. "Maybe after the summer . . ."

She poured milk into the saucepan. The gas plopped alight. She removed her gumboots and coat and headscarf, patting her gray hair into shape. Her eyes were bright and sharp.

"You want to talk about dear Robert Castleford—presumably because of the newspapers yesterday?" He nodded. He was wary of the incisive tone in her voice. "I feel so sorry for your wife," she added like a warning. "How can I help you?"

He was silent for a moment, then spread his hands on the surface of the kitchen table. A check cloth, which matched the curtains. Then he blurted, only partly acting: "I—I have to know the truth. You see, I have been a friend of—of Kenneth Aubrey for some time—married to Castleford's daughter, you can imagine my dilemma . . . ?" He looked up into her face, which was pursed and narrow and studious.

"I see. You're an American, Mr. Massinger?" she asked with what seemed like keen relevance.

"Yes."

"A dilemma?" She seemed contemptuous. "I don't see why. What does your wife say?"

"She—doesn't know what to think."

"You can tell her from me, then, that your friend Kenneth Aubrey probably—almost certainly—did murder her father!"

Massinger was startled by the wizened, malevolent look on Miss Dawson's face. It was as if she had thrown off some harmless disguise with her scarf and boots. Now she was the wicked queen with the poisoned apple, not the old woman with the sweet voice. Massinger guessed she had carried some kind of torch for Castleford—one evidently still burning.

"How—how can you be certain of that?" he asked. "So certain after all this time?" Miss Dawson had her back to him, lifting the milk from the stove, pouring it into two round, daubed mugs.

"Sugar?" she asked brightly, disconcertingly.

"Please—one."

She returned with the mugs and sat down.

"How can I be certain?" she repeated immediately. "How can I be certain? Because the two of them quarreled all the time, whenever they met. Because Aubrey hated Mr. Castleford—hated his success, hated his importance, his charm, everything about him, in fact." Massinger sipped his hot coffee after stirring the sugar. There was something pat and even rehearsed about the woman's outburst. Nevertheless, he could not ignore it. He could not even regard it as part of the play in which he was acting for Babbington's benefit—for the traitor's benefit, too. The man in Guernsey had believed it—Miss Dawson did, too. Why? "Aubrey had no respect for the rules, Mr. Massinger—but I expect you know that. From past experience, if you're a friend." Massinger merely shrugged. "He was ambitious. He stood in Mr. Castleford's shadow. In fact, Mr. Castleford referred to him as someone too late to fight who wished the war was still going on. Do you understand that?"

Massinger nodded, studying his coffee. "Yes," he said. Margaret's father—had he been like her? The thought had never occurred to him before, and yet it now seemed crucial to the whole business. If he had been— "Was he a gentle man?" he asked suddenly, unable to contain the question.

"Mr. Castleford? Yes—considerate, kind, appreciative. Charming, of course, ambitious, full of energy . . . but he would never ride roughshod over anyone . . . a real gentleman, of the old school. Class, of course—breeding will out, as they say."

The woman seemed to have changed once more, to have revealed unexpected origins and prejudices. She looked up to Castleford, always had done. She was a snob on his behalf, even now. Yet she made the man seem like Margaret.

What if he had been? How could he have been the kind of man Aubrey could have ignored, or accepted? He would have been the kind of man to awaken jealousies, to have created in Aubrey, perhaps, the dark side of a triangle? Massinger felt breathless with the quick thoughts as they crowded in on him, lay on his chest like weights. He sipped more coffee.

"So—you think he might have been murdered by Kenneth Aubrey?" Massinger asked heavily.

"I most certainly do," she answered vehemently. "Please tell your wife I'm convinced of it. If the knowledge will do her any good. It must be very distressing for her."

"It is, yes." He looked up. "But why would he have done it?"

She was silent for a long time, and then she sighed. "I might as well admit it," she said. "You've no doubt guessed for yourself. I was in love with Robert Castleford. Deeply in love. I was thirty, attractive and efficient. But—"

"He thought of you as someone who worked for him?"

She nodded. A lock of gray hair fell across her forehead where the face powder was visible in the furrows of her brow.

"Yes," she admitted reluctantly. "He never noticed me—in that way. *Her*, yes, but not me."

"You mean—"

"Yes. That German woman on the make. Securing her future. She moved fairly rapidly from Aubrey to Mr. Castleford—after all, he could do more for her, couldn't he?" Her face was again wizened with malice. Thirty-seven years later, she had no intention of forgiving Clara Elsenreith.

"I see. She *was* Castleford's mistress, then. You're certain of that? After she had known Aubrey?" Miss Dawson nodded. The lock of hair bobbed vehemently. Her small body was pinched in, hunched with anger, with forever-unpurged jealousy. *Beware the green-eyed monster.* . . .

Yet he could understand it, sense the power of that emotion. He had known it in high school, even in college. He did not imagine he had grown out of it like a species of acne; rather, he had had no cause. But if someone took Margaret . . . ?

"You're certain?" he asked again.

Miss Dawson nodded once more. "Yes," she repeated, tight-lipped. "Yes. He—he told me about her, about her coming to him."

"Told *you*?"

Miss Dawson's cheeks flushed. She looked down. "I was eavesdropping. I overheard—he was telling one of his colleagues, a grubby-minded little man who asked him straight out. He told him. Told him he'd taken that woman away from Aubrey, even . . ." She did not continue. After a while, she said: "I dropped something in the next room. After that, the door was closed and their voices were lower. I didn't hear anything else."

Massinger inhaled. The noise sounded like a windy groan. He studied Miss Dawson's face. He had found the utterly unexpected in a place he had entered with closed eyes, looking for nothing. No more than a stop on an easy journey of deception. He was drawn toward believing Miss Dawson's evidence, even discounting her jealousy, her admiration for Castleford, her dislike for Aubrey and the woman. She had overheard. Castleford had stolen the woman from Aubrey.

A great rush of relief, like a chill wind or a wave of cold water, enveloped him. *Now* he could return to Margaret, ask, beg for her understanding, for her to forgive him. Somehow, he did not doubt they would be reconciled. He felt a rush of anger, too. Anger at Aubrey—for deceiving him, for almost ruining his marriage, for placing it in jeopardy.

"Aubrey was angry?"

"There was a blazing quarrel a few days later. I didn't hear what it was about, but I was told there were threats. Mr. Castleford seemed very upset, very worried, during the rest of the day—for days afterward." She swallowed. "Until the time he disappeared, in fact."

"Aubrey threatened him?"

"Yes."

"Because of the woman?" His voice was urgent. He could not avoid adding: "This is very important to me."

"What else could it have been? Mr. Castleford was very, very worried."

Massinger finished his coffee. He felt he must leave, must have time to think. He stood up unceremoniously.

"Thank you for your time," he said. "Thank you for the coffee. I'm sorry to have troubled you."

"Have I helped?" she asked.

"I—don't know," he admitted. "Perhaps you have. Well, good-bye, Miss Dawson—no, don't worry, I'll see myself out. Once again, thank you."

The woman watched him turn away and exit from the kitchen. She listened and, when the front door shut firmly behind him, her body twitched slightly at the noise. She continued to listen, as if for whispers in the air, and nodded when she heard a car start, then accelerate away from the cottage.

She sighed, and unbuttoned her cardigan. She untaped the tiny microphone from her waist, and unwound its lead. She smiled as she looked at it and, before laying it on the table, she said: "I hope that was satisfactory."

Sir Andrew Babbington shunted the folded sheaf of German morning newspapers to one side of his desk. Eldon watched the firm, satisfied expression on his superior's features. Most of the German nationals had taken up the story of Gunther Guillaume from the previous day's *Sunday Times* and had treated it fully, with unanimous speculation of Aubrey's part in the Guillaume scandal. As Eldon had firmly believed since *Teardrop* first broke, Aubrey was the mole in British Intelligence who had tried to warn the East German double agent of his impending arrest. There hadn't been smoke without fire.

"Nothing new, I'm afraid," Babbington commented. "However, it's of minor importance."

"Sir?"

"Nineteen seventy-four—not our main concern, Eldon."

"With respect, sir—I really think we should go after it. Full cooperation of the BfV . . . ?" Babbington was already shaking his head. Eldon kept his features expressionless, immobile. On his thighs, his knuckles whitened. Damn it, Babbington simply couldn't *see* it!

"I don't think so, Eldon. What we might happen to dig up wouldn't be worth the effort, in all probability. No, let's go with what we have, as they say. The last two years, Aubrey's period of *real* activity. And for my personal satisfaction and for the sake of Robert Castleford's ghost—find that damned woman who was involved with both of them in Berlin!"

"I would have thought she wasn't our main concern, Sir Andrew," Eldon observed without inflection. Babbington studied his features, his nostrils closing and dilating with suppressed anger.

"No?" he inquired lightly.

"What can she know?"

"Who murdered Castleford, for example?" The sarcasm was evident. Babbington looked immediately at his watch. "I have to see the Foreign Secretary at eleven." Eldon could see a trace of satisfaction in the corners of Babbington's mouth. Also present at that meeting would be Sir William Guest as Chairman of JIC and the Home Secretary. That small group of men would ratify the establishment of the new Security and Intelligence Directorate and confirm Babbington as its first Director-General. Babbington was less than a hour from absolute secret power.

Eldon felt no envy for the man—merely a thankfulness that SIS would at last be under the aegis of the security service; in future, its work would be properly supervised. And Eldon felt profoundly grateful that they had uncovered

Teardrop—Aubrey. The damage he had been able to do was not irreversible, not conclusive in all probability. It might take a year or two, but they would weed out everyone who had worked with him and render his betrayals relatively harmless.

Yes, it was a consummation to be profoundly thankful for.

"Very well, Sir Andrew," he replied. "What about Shelley and Paul Massinger?"

"Mm." It was evident that Babbington had already made his decision and was simply pretending to muse. "I'm pretty certain that Shelley will be a good boy in future. I think he has been somewhat misled by old loyalties . . . and of course, Massinger has been subjecting him to pressure." Babbington steepled his fingers, elbows on his desk. "As for Massinger, his conversation with Miss Dawson has left him seriously in doubt. I think we can predict he will drop the matter very soon. He's beginning to believe that Aubrey did the dirty deed, after all."

"You're certain of that, Sir Andrew?"

"No, Eldon, I'm not certain. I simply don't think we need do very much more. There is no need for us to make the whole thing more messy than it is by precipitate action. Massinger doesn't want to lose his wife. Anything that persuades him, or helps to persuade him, that Aubrey is guilty of her father's murder, will be clutched to his bosom only too eagerly. Just let the matter take its course."

"Very well, Sir Andrew. And Hyde?"

"He must be under cover somewhere—skulking on the Continent like a debtor. He'll come to light eventually. He's no problem. Incidentally, any KGB activity?"

"None."

"They've cut their losses. Abandoned Aubrey to his fate, then?"

"It appears so, Sir Andrew."

"Wise of them, in the event. Very well, Eldon. The DPP would like the papers by midweek. Naturally after they've been seen by the PM and the Attorney-General, in this extraordinary case. Can your department manage that?"

"Yes, Sir Andrew. Sir Kenneth can be formally charged this week."

"Good."

• • •

"You know where he is now?"

"Yes, Comrade Rezident General. He is returning from Oxford at this moment. He is driving—"

"Never mind. Just make sure they don't lose him in London. You presume he is planning to return to the man Hyde's flat?"

"We presume so, Comrade Rezident General."

"Very well. Dispose of him—this morning. As soon and as quietly as possible. Our friend seems to be overconfident as to Massinger's harmlessness. I am not convinced. What he knows already is too dangerous. He might—just *might*—talk to someone who will believe him. Someone like Colonel Eldon, for example. No, it is too dangerous. Massinger represents too great a threat. They lost Hyde in Vienna—*we* have found Massinger. We will make certain. Give the order—kill Massinger. I'll sign the authorization."

"Thank you, Comrade Rezident General—"

"You didn't think I'd leave you holding the baby, did you?"

"I'm sorry, Comrade Rezident General."

"Very well—get on with it. It's a pity."

"I beg your pardon, Comrade?"

"Never mind. Just see that it's done."

Hyde had been jolted by Kabul, alienated. They had approached the capital a little after noon, filtering into the city in small groups, making their rendezvous in one of the city's oldest and most warrenlike bazaars, setting up headquarters in the rear of a rugmaker's shop. Its owner was, apparently, a relative of Mohammed Jan. He bewailed the loss of Jan's sons, dropped the ritual tears, put his resources at the Pathan chieftain's disposal.

After they had eaten fragrant, indigestible nan bread and a rice dish with mutton and raisins, Mohammed Jan and Miandad set out with Hyde to reconnoitre the Soviet embassy buildings. The city was crowded, its poorer suburbs and bazaars timeless, antique. The donkeys and handcarts seemed intruded upon by the few ancient cars, the handful of military vehicles. Veiled women, turbaned men, or men wearing beaded, gold-threaded caps; then, suddenly, the InterContinental Hotel and high-rise office buildings. Earth underfoot changed to tar. The contrast stunned Hyde. A rug vendor, samples of his wares over his shoulder and at his feet on the pavement, stood in front of a department store. Hyde grinned, and Miandad returned his expression.

"Nothing changes," the Pakistani murmured.

The smell of passing donkeys, overladen with gasoline fumes. The noise of a passing Russian truck. Someone getting out of a very long black American sedan in front of the hotel; a man in a well-cut, fur-collared overcoat, a woman in furs. The squeak of cartwheels, the noise of a single-decker bus. Turtleneck women's sweaters in the nearest window of the store.

A car or a truck backfired. Hyde immediately saw Azimov's face in the moment that he had fired the single shot from the pistol. The boy had known—even as he feared, even as he experienced a terror of realization and was crushed by its weight, he had known. His eyes had retained a kind of calm. If there was forgiveness, even gratitude, in that look, Hyde could not trust to it. He might have been inventing it.

Even as Mohammed Jan had argued, had demanded the boy, Hyde had been unwilling, unable to give him up. Then a Pathan had moved to lay hands on Azimov, at Mohammed Jan's orders, and Hyde had simply turned and fired, almost without taking aim. One shot, through the forehead, knocking the boy's dead body back against the rocks. Keeping the vital, invaluable Soviet military uniform intact, unblemished, without bloodstains.

"*He was* my *prisoner!*" Hyde had raged at the Pathan chieftain. Within the circles of kohl around his dark eyes, Mohammed Jan had acknowledged Hyde's claim with a single flicker of his eyelids. Then Hyde, calming himself, had explained the necessity of the quick, clean death—the condition of the uniform. Mohammed Jan had accepted his cunning.

He had also accepted his scheme for reaching Petrunin, after listening to what Hyde had learned from the boy. Oh, the boy had been informative. He'd known a lot, remembered a lot, and he told Hyde everything because he was spending the coinage that ensured he would live. He was bribing the Pathan tribesman who spoke Russian and had light eyes and a lighter skin than the others. He had held his letter and the snapshot of his wife against the unmarked breast of his uniform jacket all the time he spoke. Hyde had put it and the letter back inside the battered wallet.

"Hyde?" Miandad asked, nudging his arm.

"What?"

Mohammed Jan was already striding away from them, toward the principal square of Kabul, where the main facade of the InterContinental Hotel outfaced high-rise offices and apartment complexes and overlooked the compound of the Soviet embassy.

"We must not loiter," Miandad instructed. Two soldiers with Kalashnikovs on their shoulders took up position on either side of the main doors of the InterContinental. Two other guards, now relieved, marched toward a troop transport, then climbed beneath the shelter of its tarpaulin. The truck roared away, black fumes belching from its exhaust.

"Okay."

They trailed after the tall Pathan, crossing the square. There were more cars, many of them Russian, with small, stiff flags on the hoods of the black sedans. Others, mostly cream or white, still possessed an official appearance. The buses were crowded. The streetlamps were beginning to glare in the afternoon air, and some illuminated neon signs gained a bolder glow. Billboards for consumer products vied with stern governmental portraits and Afghan and Soviet flags.

Flags on the Soviet embassy. Behind high black railings, across a forty-yard width of snow-patched lawn, the low bungalows of the compound were dotted around the white facade of the embassy building. An ugly, modern concrete and glass extension lay alongside the main building like a squat, utilitarian transport ship berthed alongside an elegant, superseded sailing vessel. The extension appeared sufficiently modern to have been completed after the Russian invasion. There was a guard on either side of the main gates and a red-and-white barrier pole. Ten yards farther out into the square stood a large concrete bunker, the guard post.

Hyde lounged against a lamp post while Mohammed Jan and Miandad began haggling with a rug vendor who had set up his stall on a small, grassless island amid the traffic, opposite the embassy gates. As they bargained, Hyde knew they would be assessing distances, firing positions, angles, cover. Their knowledge of Kabul and of killing Russians was compendious and impressive. For himself, he was for the moment simply the sightseer. His work lay beyond the black railings, wearing Azimov's uniform. Cars and buses swirled between

Hyde and the railings of the embassy. The square was noisy behind him.

The Pathan chieftain had guaranteed to get them out of the city once Hyde had completed the capture of Petrunin. And Hyde had repeated his promise while the adrenaline of Azimov's murder still prompted him. *I will give you Petrunin, for your justice—damn you, I'll give you Petrunin! You didn't need this poor wretch—I'll give you the man himself!* Miandad had not bothered to translate, and Mohammed Jan, without loss of face or dignity, had turned his back on him and descended the slope to the road. Hyde had watched him in a mood that was angry, jumpy, and uncertain.

Hyde surreptitiously glanced at the watch concealed by the baggy sleeve of his blouse. Four. The air was darkening. Behind the embassy buildings, where the plain ended and the mountains of the Kindu Kush loomed forty foreshortened miles north of the city, the snow-covered peaks glowed pink while the mountain flanks displayed a dull gleam already dying into darkness. He came at this time usually, the boy had said.

Dear Sasha . . .

Not *Darling Sasha*, only the more formal acquaintanceship claimed by *Dear*—Dear Sir.

Dear Sasha . . . Nadia wouldn't even get the letter and the snapshot back—unless they returned them after removing them from *his* body, not Sasha's stripped and rock-hidden corpse. She would never know exactly what happened. She would, undoubtedly, fear the worst.

Unnoticed, Mohammed Jan was at his side. Hyde jumped as the Pathan spoke.

"Your promise?" he asked lightly in very accented English, a parody of Miandad, who appeared on the Pathan's other side.

"It still holds," Hyde replied.

"Can you do it?" Miandad asked a moment later, translating now from Mohammed Jan's Pushtu.

"Can he cause enough confusion, once I've got past the gates?" Hyde replied belligerently, staring into the chieftain's face. "You can operate the rocket launcher—can you hit the embassy from here and kill the guards in that concrete bunker? Can you pin down the Russians for fifteen minutes afterward? Because if you two can't do what's needed, then all my promises won't be worth a light, will they? Just bear that in mind—*I'm* the one who's taking the risk, walking in there and relying on you two. Remind Gunga Din of that little fact, will you?"

Hyde turned away as Miandad began to translate. He itched with nerves, his skin crawling with his increasing tension, with little prickly outbreaks of sweat, even as the temperature dropped toward zero. He knew he would be all right; he'd be able to cope, get through it. He had to, anyway. It would be some kind of compensation, an apologetic risk to prove that he didn't always kill unarmed boys to save them from torture and mutilation.

Now, Petrunin and the thought and memory of him no longer made him afraid. It was Petrunin, after all, who was really to blame for the boy's death on the chilly, dawn-lit hillside. It was Petrunin who was really to blame for what had happened to Aubrey. It was Petrunin who was really, *really* to blame for Hyde's danger, for his presence in this alien country, and to blame for the fact that even his own side would kill him if they found him. He wanted Petrunin very badly.

The curfew began at ten. Darkness fell before five.

The black car was escorted by motorcycle outriders with Kalashnikovs across their backs, and by two other black sedans before and behind it. The windows of all three cars were tinted and dark. The cars were heavy, ponderous, armorplated, even on the underside of the chassis by the look of it, to prevent injury from a rolled grenade or a landmine. It was the arrival, or so it seemed to Hyde, of some hated local despot or potentate. Petrunin. *The flagless car*, the boy had said. *No emblems, nothing. And the outriders*.

The barrier swung up, the gates opened electronically. With little hesitation or slowing of its speed, the small motorcade swept through into the embassy compound. Hyde watched the cars until they halted outside the ugly extension, then his gaze transferred to the forest of aerials on the roof of the new building, then finally to the windows of the third floor. He counted.

Petrunin's suite of offices. The boy did not know how many guards, what alarms, what booby traps. There, once inside the building, he would be alone, on his own, isolated and without assistance.

"Have you seen enough?" Miandad asked softly. There were flecks of snow in the darkening air. "We have settled our matters."

Hyde nodded. "Yes, I've seen enough." *He never sleeps, or so they say*, the boy had told him. *Bad conscience*. He had even smiled at that. *He takes pep pills all the time. He can't sleep so he works all night.* "Yes, I've seen enough," Hyde repeated. "Let's go."

Massinger stopped the car and switched off the engine. The curve of Wilton Crescent had lost most of its snow. He had parked almost directly opposite his own apartment. As he looked up, he almost expected to see Margaret at one of the windows—dining room, drawing room, any one of the tall windows.

He kept his hands on the wheel of the rented Ford Granada, afraid that they would display a tremor he could not control the moment he freed them. It was past midday. He had been driving around central London, simply driving without purpose or destination, in the heavy Monday traffic for perhaps an hour. His mind had been filled with black and bitter recriminations. He blamed Aubrey, and more, he blamed himself. He viewed the past days, since that morning he had first visited Aubrey, as a kind of delirium: something heightened, feverish, unreal. A lost week, a period out of time—days stolen from his life.

Aubrey had been the thief of his time. Aubrey the murderer.

Not that he was convinced. . . . No, he was not convinced, he told himself once more. But he could not rid himself of the suspicion that it was true, might be true, could possibly be true. . . .

Massinger shook his head like an old, tormented animal smelling the already-spilled blood of the herd.

He knew, with a bleak certainty, that he had begun the process of moving toward a conviction of Aubrey's guilt. And for the moment, relief that it was over, relief that he could take up his life at the point where he had put it down like a parcel—all that was less important than the creeping horror that Aubrey *had* murdered Margaret's father. *Had done, had done it—*

Even the thought that he and Margaret would be as they had been—before all this business, before his visit to Aubrey—paled beside the betrayal that Aubrey's guilt represented. *Aubrey*—of all people, of all crimes, *Aubrey?*

He could not move from the car. Wearily, with limbs weighted with the gravity of some huge, malignant planet, he wiped at the clouded windshield.

Hyde, he thought, but the thought lost shape, tailed off. Hyde?

Probably dead.

The traitor?

Unidentified.

Himself?

He saw the concepts as words, and they appeared to him as clearly and as robbed of significance as if they had flickered onto a computer screen. And his answers were similarly robbed of importance. They were the mechanical answers of a computer.

Himself?

Safe . . .

Yes, safe. He could cross the crescent, enter his apartment, greet his wife, eat lunch after a dry sherry, then ring Babbington with a clear, satisfied conscience.

A few minutes, many words, an honorable draw. Everyone satisfied. No shame to him—Aubrey probably had done it, for whatever mad and jealous reasons.

Margaret would take him back. That was another of Massinger's certainties.

Then, get out of the car. . . .

He felt weak. The facades of Wilton Crescent beckoned. *My God—Aubrey had almost managed to destroy everything, everything he had ever cared for, everything that gave meaning!* A gray pigeon settled on the windowsill of his drawing room. Four feet from it, on the interior wall, two original Turners hung, one above the other. They had been behind Babbington's head, early on in this business.

The pigeon lifted heavily from the windowsill, gained height, seemed to become slimmer, more streamlined, rose and flew against the gray sky.

Massinger opened the door and climbed out of the Granada with a fresher resolve. Yes, all would be well.

He locked the door and looked up at the window of the drawing room. There was a face—old, rich Miss Waggoner—at one of the windows of the next apartment, and then there was Margaret's face at the correct and expected window. He could not resist waving. Her hand fluttered next to her ear, then it touched her mouth as if she regretted the involuntary action and was remembering the past week. He waved again, hurrying forward, stick tapping ahead of him. He did not look down at his feet as he had become accustomed to doing, but kept his gaze on the window, on her face. Younger lover, much younger, arriving—he should have bought flowers, wished he had now that the black moments were past.

Her eyes flickered away from him, then returned. Her mouth—he could see it quite clearly, opening into a black round O—seemed to be trying to warn him—

Noise of a car, fierce acceleration.

Noise of a car, getting nearer, some youthful, trained part of his awareness warned him.

He turned his head.

The distinct image of a dark blue Cortina—*dark blue Cortina*—and a stabbing, reluctant pain in his hip. Awareness of the polished handle of his stick, firmly in his grasp. Awareness of being stranded in the middle of Wilton Crescent. Twenty yards, fifteen, ten yards.

The blur of a cat racing across the road, disappearing beneath the wheels of the Cortina, not even a lurch from the car, nothing but the scream of the cat. He looked helplessly up at the round dark hole of Margaret's mouth, knowing she had begun to scream, as if expecting her in some way to help him, alter his circumstances. Then he hobbled, lurched, staggered, fell, rolled. . . .

The Cortina's flank bounced away from the stronger bodywork of a Rolls. An oncoming small red Renault had swerved into the curb, squashing its already blunt nose against the trunk of a low sports car. Massinger lay in the gutter, blood from a graze filling his left eye. His right eye blurred with tears or sweat as he watched, almost from beneath the front wheels of the Rolls, the professional face in the Cortina. Jagged, crumpled bodywork was close enough to his face to be out of focus.

Too many people, already too many people. His hip ached infernally, as if someone had tried to wrench off his leg. His arm and shoulder were bruised against the Rolls—the silver lady had torn the sleeve of his raincoat—and he had grazed his forehead. But he was alive.

The professional face studied him for a moment. The moment elongated, and Massinger began to realize, foggily, that he was not safe, it was not over. The driver's window began to open, rolling down slowly.

A gun?

Then the scene was blocked out; someone was kneeling by the front wheel of the Rolls, between his body and the man in the Cortina. A man's knee, a neighbor's voice murmuring something shocked and solicitous. He wanted to warn the man, then felt all energy and tension drain from him as the Cortina's engine revved furiously, the tires squealed, and the car pulled away round the curve of the crescent.

He nodded in reply to whatever the man had said. Then he could see again. He watched the neighbor's feet move away. Beyond the cramped perspective of the chassis of the Rolls, he saw the man kneel anxiously, even gravely, by the squashed form of the cat. It was the neighbor's cat; he recognized it now.

The woman who had been driving the small Renault was complaining to a gathering audience in a high, shrill, enraged voice. Massinger groaned with relief.

He looked up into Margaret's face as she touched the graze on his forehead. He grabbed feverishly at her hand, holding it to his cheek, pressing his face against her palm. He groaned again, with realization.

"What is it—darling, what was happening . . . ?"

He shook his head. "Help me up, dear." She took some of his weight. He levered himself up on the stick she handed him, jamming it like a vaulting pole into the angle of the gutter. He felt dizzy for a moment; someone unnoticed murmured an inquiry, which Margaret fended off. She helped him across the pavement, up the three steps into the house. Someone else had the ground floor, a film producer hardly ever in residence, and the second and third floors belonged to Margaret—to *them*, he corrected himself.

He allowed his body to press against her as they climbed the stairs to the first floor. Lovers, returning . . .

He sighed, cursed in a whisper.

"Are you hurt?" Margaret asked. "Shall I call Dr. Evans?"

He shook his head. "No. I—I just realized that nothing's changed."

"Oh, God!" she breathed fiercely.

"It wasn't an accident."

She thrust open the door of the apartment. "I—realized that," she announced with difficulty. "Here, take off that raincoat. I'll get some hot water and iodine. Any other damage?" She was a bluff, competent nurse—playing a role with narrow horizons for the sake of a moment's respite.

She directed him into the drawing room. "Have a whiskey. I won't be a moment." She pressed his hand fiercely, then released it, and disappeared into the bedroom. Massinger looked up the stairs to the second floor and his study, as if needing music more than a drink, but then he went into the drawing room.

He clattered the decanter against the glass as he poured a large whiskey. He swallowed greedily, coughed, and straightened his aching body against the sideboard. He breathed slowly and deeply a number of times.

They wouldn't let go. Shelley had been wrong, *he* had been wrong, to believe the illusion of escape. He knew too much, even though he knew little. He could talk. Someone, eventually, might listen.

He was safer dead.

Margaret was at his side. The iodine stung like his thoughts, bringing tears. The whiskey warmed his chest and stomach. Minutes later, they were studying each other across a space of carpet, each perched on the edges of their chairs like people in a strange room, peasants who had uncomfortably inherited a palace. Margaret's hands quarreled with each other in her lap, mirroring some internal struggle. Except for her hands, and a stray lock of blonde hair, she possessed the midday appearance of a woman of her background and wealth: groomed, confident, desirable.

But vulnerable, now, like himself.

"I—almost believe—" he began.

"What happened?" she blurted at the same moment.

Exchanged smiles turning to worry on her part, lack of resolve on his. She gestured to him to continue. Instead, he answered her question.

The smell of iodine, suggesting wounds . . .

"They tried to kill me."

"Who—for God's sake, darling, who?" There was no longer any barrier between them. He had come home, but not by the route he had planned.

"I don't know. Whoever believes I know too much."

"Do you?"

He shook his head. "I don't think I do. I met Hyde in Vienna, but he knew nothing except that Vienna Station, in full or in part, is working for the Russians."

Her eyes seemed to resist the secret world for a moment, then she merely nodded. She wished to be counted in, a convert.

"Go on."

"They tried to kill him."

"Where is he now?"

"Afghanistan—but I don't know whether he's alive or dead."

"But—*you*?"

"There's someone," he began, "someone high up, in this country's intelligence service, and it isn't Kenneth Aubrey—" He raised his hand to still a protest, but there was little reaction to the name on Margaret's face. Her white hands had stopped their fitful quarrel. "Someone who is a Russian agent, someone who's afraid of Hyde and me being on Aubrey's side . . ." He sighed. "I'll tell you everything I know," he said.

She listened without interruption. Aubrey, Vienna, Helsinki, Oxfordshire. Once or twice, when the subject of her father appeared like a broken bone through skin, her features winced or pursed. Otherwise she was expressionless, her eyes fixed on Massinger, her fears for him more evident than any other concern. Occasionally, her hands resumed their conflict in her lap, on the light blue and gray of her skirt.

He announced, after a final pause: "Obviously, they'll kill me unless I can find out who they are. Who *he* is." Then he sipped at the remainder of his whiskey. His throat was dry with speech, and with renewed fear. He had explained it all to her in unemotional terms, with simple clarity. Now, having so carefully and clearly laid out the parts of the puzzle, he saw that it possessed more potency, more ability to frighten than a crowd of vague, unformed premonitions or nightmares.

It was strange, he thought, that when he told her he had begun to believe Aubrey guilty of Castleford's murder, she had shown little in the way of expression. He had paused to allow her to comment, but she had done no more than wave him on with his narrative. Now, as he waited for her to speak, she studied him for a long time in silence. Her cheeks seemed blanched beneath the makeup, and there was a small, close-knitted frown above her nose. Then she stood up, crossed to the sideboard, and poured herself a drink. She returned to his chair and stood by it—as she had done a week ago when Alistair Burnet had stunned them with the news of Aubrey's arrest and the accusations against him, and her father's face had filled the television screen.

She clutched his hand. He did not look up. He felt the tremor running through her grip, and squeezed her fingers. She shook his hand gently. He heard the tumbler touch against her teeth as she drank from it.

"What do we do, then?" she asked.

He sighed. She shook his hand gently once more. He was indeed home. But he had returned to find that his home had been transformed into a fortress in his absence. He was no longer alone, but he had brought, close behind him, the enemies he had made. Now they threatened his wife as well as himself.

Using the number of one of Aubrey's credit cards and the telephone of a nearby restaurant, Mrs. Grey had bought a change of clothes, underwear, toilet accessories, and a suitcase to contain the purchases. A friend of hers had picked up the clothes and toiletries and the suitcase and left them in a locker at Victoria Station, bringing Mrs. Grey the key.

Now, all he had to do was to place himself in conjunction with his new and unseen luggage. A ticket to Dover was all that was missing from his arrangements—no more than a moment at a booking office window. He had only to slip from the house, find a taxi, get into it, order it to Victoria, collect the suitcase . . .

The arrangements revolved again and again in his mind like something worrying him while he was still on the edge of sleep. He could not awaken sufficiently to rid himself of it or solve the puzzle it presented.

Because such repetition was only a blind, a piece of self-delusion. Beneath it lay the extreme difficulty, the practical impossibility, of leaving his apartment unnoticed. And beneath that in the geology of his fears lay the enormous and still-enlarging sense of his imminent undoing—the despair at the possible discovery of his journal before he could destroy it. Forty-five years of service, almost seventy years of his life, would be reduced to complete and utter ruin. *It had been good for that man if he had not been born*, his memory had quoted at him throughout the day. He could not regard such an idea as melodrama, or exaggerated or out of proportion. He realized that his professional ruin would mean that much to him. He would, with foreknowledge of it, have chosen not to begin, not to have existed.

He had to go.

He knew he could not rest if he consigned a message to Clara. He trusted her, but he did not trust himself to find peace of mind without himself putting the journal on the fire or tearing it into small pieces and flushing it away. Destroying it. He had written the full and true account of the death of Robert Castleford because his accursed, punctilious conscience would not allow him to leave the truth unrecorded. It had been as if, one day far ahead, he expected to be asked to account for Castleford's murder—as now he had been.

But now, now he did not want the truth, had no use for it. The truth would be regarded as a lie, his motives overlooked or dismissed. Now, only the brute fact would have significance. Eldon would say, with triumph in his tone, *You did do it, then? We knew you had. As for the rest of it—mere nonsense. In your own handwriting, a confession of murder . . .*

He had to *see* those pages burning or flushing away! There was no other way, no help for it. He had to make the journey, escape from England.

Even that idea pained him—an indigestive, burning pain in his chest. *He*, having to *escape* from his own country, the country he had loyally served for most of his adult life, in war and peace, declared war and undeclared war.

He looked at the clock. Almost six. Heavy traffic outside, the flash of passing headlights on the ceiling of the darkened room. Through the window, if he raised himself in his armchair to see it, Regent's Park had retreated into darkness. Beyond the park, the lights of Primrose Hill receded northward into the distance beneath the orange-glowing winter sky. The first stars were out, hard and brittle. The room was warm yet; he sat in the chair in his dark overcoat, hat resting on his lap, as if he could no longer afford his heating bills.

He was ready to leave. He needed only to find the nerve to begin, to take the first step. He had prepared for the moment, perhaps ever since they had confined him to the apartment.

Compulsively, without definite purpose but with all his professional instincts, he had studied the surveillance teams: their characters, their routines, their weaknesses . . . most of all, their growing, inevitable complacency.

He had encouraged Mrs. Grey, much against her will and much to her disgust, to begin to supply the various teams with cups of tea, cups of coffee. Then with warm pies or fish and chips they had bought. To provide sandwiches on occasion. To mother them . . .

Stiffly, angrily, she had learned her part and softened into it. He, meanwhile, had watched their changeovers, especially those that came after dark. Especially this one at six. Every evening he had watched.

Sloppy. Complacent, lazy, sloppy—more so with each passing day and night. Only one old man to worry about upstairs . . . easy, cushy . . .

Tonight it was curry from an Indian take-out place. Mrs. Grey had chilled the lager they drank with it, in her fridge. She had just taken it out to them, enough cans for the two teams, new and old. She would chat, in a motherly way, for a few moments, acting like a further sedative. Then, when she judged it safest, sensed the right moment, she would return to the door and ring the bell, summoning him to begin his journey.

There would be only a moment when he might slip undetected across the street to the darker park side of the terrace. Then he might reach the corner, then the Marylebone Road and the rush hour and the taxis. . . .

They would not be expecting—

The doorbell sounded, shrill in the silent apartment. Aubrey's body twitched as if electrocuted. His hands grabbed the arms of the chair. His hat fell to the carpet. Like an automaton, he pushed himself upright, bent to pick up his hat, then moved stiffly to the door. He did not glance at the furniture, the emperor's new clothes that had been no more than an illusion, but left the apartment almost unseeingly. He descended to the ground floor. The front door was slightly ajar. He could see Mrs. Grey on the porch, hidden from the surveillance cars by deep shadow. She turned as his hand touched the latch. Aubrey could tell, by the look she gave him and the immediate, worried frown, that his face must portray wildness and inadequacy. He patted her hand fumblingly like a very old and senile man. She appeared unreassured. He brushed past her. She had no idea where he was going, only abroad, escaping—what she did not know she could not mistakenly tell.

He did not look either right or left, but crossed the road with a firm, blind, jerky step. He reached the opposite pavement. When he turned, the facades of the Nash houses gleamed orange-white in the light of the streetlamps. Aubrey began to walk away from the parked cars of the two surveillance teams. Mrs. Grey had not even had time to tell him all four men were sitting in one car, eating. He strode on, a melodramatic actor in his dotage parodying a blind man's walk.

A woman with a dog spoke to him. He raised his hat without seeing or identifying her. There was the noise of a car behind him, but it did not evoke fear. He merely walked on until he reached the end of the terrace and turned right toward the Marylebone Road.

Lights, traffic. His legs felt weak, almost without energy, paralyzed. His body had become very heavy now, glutinously restraining his emotional desire for speed, for flight. He forced his limbs to move. The noise of the traffic loudened. He reached the Marylebone Road.

Taxi, taxi, taxi—

It was cracking, like a mask upon the skin. As his resolve and his will dehydrated, the mask had begun to crack open.

The taxi stopped. "Where to, guv?"

The inquiry was like a gulp of reviving air. He fumbled with the door handle, murmuring "Victoria" in a choked voice. He almost fell forward into the taxi's interior, gaining the seat just before his legs gave way and a hot flush invested his entire body. He sighed, loosened his overcoat, lay back.

"Traffic's bad this evening," he heard someone say, presumably the cab driver, but he had no interest in replying. He merely wanted to rest now, and allow reaction and weakness their moment, then recover from them.

He had done it, he told himself. Blundered out of his captivity like a child or a blind man. He had done it.

Alison Shelley had become fascinated by the woman who sat opposite her in her lounge, still wearing her woolen coat and holding her hat in her twisting hands. The woman was perhaps ten years older than herself, distraught, pale from her various and contradictory fears, tired. Yet she possessed a calm, a sense of certainty, what could only be called authority, that Alison envied. Margaret Massinger, by virtue of her upbringing, wealth, and social milieu, had never had the slightest interest in, or need for, feminism, or equality of opportunity.

She studied, too, her husband as he talked to Margaret Massinger. Peter was afraid and kept throwing sly little guilty looks in her direction, but some covert part of him was intrigued, mystified, prompted to action. Alison knew that he was on the point of throwing in his lot with the Massingers and she knew that she, reluctantly, would do the same with her husband. She would join because she knew his current sleeplessness and irritability all derived from his self-contempt and his inability to quell his loyalty.

"There's no other line, Mrs. Massinger . . ." Peter was saying, spreading his hands helplessly. "I only wish there were. Your husband has had all the doors slammed in his face. That's the size of it, I'm afraid." Shelley looked as lugubriously regretful as a bloodhound.

"That's not a lot of help to Mrs. Massinger," Alison observed quietly, studying her sherry glass and then Margaret's face. Margaret Massinger seemed grateful for her intervention, perhaps understanding her motives.

Peter Shelley's face was dubious, then his frown cleared. He, too, realized the purpose of her interjection, even though he could not act upon it. He shrugged. "I know it isn't," he said. "But it's also true, darling."

"Surely there's some way—" Margaret began, lowering her eyes to the crumpled hat in her lap as her voice faltered. She was distraught, and evidently she felt inadequate to counter Shelley's expertise, his insider's experience. After a moment she added, not looking up: "Paul can't stay cooped up forever, Mr. Shelley."

"I—don't know what to say" was Shelley's only reply.

"Why can't we talk to Andrew Babbington?" she blurted out.

Shelley paused, then shook his head as he spoke. "We don't know," he said softly. "We don't know who it is. And whoever it is might get to hear—then . . ." He hurried on gloomily: "We don't have any proof, we wouldn't be believed."

"What about this man Hyde?"

"God alone knows where he is. He arrived in Pakistan—there's been no contact since."

"Isn't there *anything* you can do?" Alison asked in a

strained voice. She got up, pacing the room in front of the glowing fire, her sherry glass catching its lights. "There must be something, Peter. Mr. Massinger's life's in danger. He's hiding in his apartment like a criminal. He needs your help!"

"What can I do?" Shelley pleaded, resenting her interruption. He shifted on his chair almost with the squirm of an accused small boy.

"*I* can't tell you what to do, Peter. . . ." she continued, now patrolling the borders of the lounge like an inexperienced, nervous guard. *Sunday Times—Insight.* "I don't know what to suggest. . . ." The newspaper, remaining disarrayed from the previous day, lapped over the edges of a pink-upholstered reproduction chair. *Sunday Times—Insight.* Alison moved on from the exposed front page. Yesterday's news. She had pored over the articles more than once, deliberately and evidently, but after Peter had made his telephone calls, he had been reluctant to discuss it. So she had abandoned the matter.

She realized that Margaret Massinger was watching her expectantly. Alison had invited her attention by protest and movement; now she resented it, realizing she had compromised Peter.

Who else has been betrayed? Heavy type, lowercase letters. She had read that, too. She passed the fire, its warmth sudden against her calves, reminding her upper torso that it was chilly with indecision, helplessness. Peter was staring glumly through his interlaced fingers at the carpet in front of the sofa. Sideboard, standard lamp, door, bookshelves—Peter's English classics and books on sailing, her own biographical tastes—then the newspaper again. She had patrolled the room's border once again. *Who else has been betrayed?* she read.

"Peter . . . ?" she asked slowly.

"Yes?" he replied eagerly, sensing her tone. He had always admitted her intuition as a legitimate intellectual activity. He needed intuition in his work. Aubrey's was the intuition he really admired.

"Nineteen seventy-four," she announced slowly. Each syllable of the date was elongated, charged with a good-humored, almost excited mystery. "That business in Bonn."

"I know," Shelley said. "What of it?"

"Is it just newspaper talk?" Her hand reached for the paper, but she merely rearranged it so that she did not have to read the front page upside-down. 1974. Bonn. Gunther Guillaume, Willy Brandt's senior adviser, the East German spy. Rumors of an attempt to warn, even get him away, by a British officer.

"No, it isn't. Hell of a flap at the time. Everyone's talking about it at the office today. Aubrey's the prime suspect now, of course, because he was in Bonn advising the Germans on anti-terrorist security for the World Cup—after that disaster at the Munich Games. It's rubbish, of course. But the mud will no doubt stick," he ended with a sigh.

Alison was standing in front of him. "Was there any truth in it?"

"We never admitted there was. MI 5 did a job on us, just as we'd done a job on our own people. Nothing. Just a trace of woodsmoke, but definitely no fire." He smiled thinly, then shook his head. "Pity we can't ask Guillaume, now he's back with his own people."

"Isn't there anyone else?" Alison blurted out in disappointment, half-afraid at the ease with which she had been drawn unresisting into the secret world. Her relationship with her husband now was as intimate as lovemaking, yet entirely cerebral. Her body was flushed with tension. She found she had placed herself beside the chair in which Margaret Massinger sat.

"To ask?" Shelley pondered. "I doubt it."

"If—if, Peter?" Alison pressed her empty glass against her forehead and ran her other hand through her thick hair. "No, just listen—I think I'm having an intuition—" Shelley smiled involuntarily. "Look, if there was someone in 'seventy-four—a British agent working to help this Guillaume . . . couldn't he be the one who's helping to ruin Aubrey now?" She seemed unconvinced as her words trailed off.

"Yes . . . ?" Shelley asked, evidently disappointed.

"You mean, just as they're blaming Mr. Aubrey—" A small, pinched mouth signaled distaste, then Margaret continued: "If you assume his innocence . . ." She looked down, divided, then: "If you do, then, then—the someone who could have acted then, in 1974, could be the same one now. Do you see what we mean, Mr. Shelley?"

Shelley rubbed his cheeks with his long fingers and was silent for a time. Eventually, when the tense breathing of both women was audible above the occasional spitting of logs on the fire, he looked up and said: "It's thin—it's almighty thin."

"Do you think Mr. X existed in 1974?" Alison demanded.

"No, but I believe he exists now—and he isn't Kenneth Aubrey, Mrs. Massinger." She waved the assertion dismissively aside.

"I'm keeping his two guilts apart," she announced quietly, frostily. "It is *this* business which threatens Paul, not my father's murder."

Shelley nodded. "Very well."

"If he exists now, he would have to be high up, wouldn't he?" Alison asked.

Once more, Shelley nodded, but this time it was in response to some inward image or realization. "Yes, he would," he murmured. "He would indeed."

"If he's helping the Russians now—then *couldn't* he have been the one helping them in 1974?" Alison felt her hands clenching into fists at her sides, felt herself willing her intuition upon her husband. A fragmentary sense of Margaret Massinger's continuing problem, the identity of her father's murderer, was dismissed as soon as it appeared.

"He could . . . he could indeed," Shelley said, then: "It's a very long shot, though." He looked at Margaret. "But it would get Paul out of the country for a while—to Germany. He'd be safer there. Can you two do that?"

Margaret nodded, and said: "But where? Why?"

"The German security service, BfV, cooperated with Aubrey and our people, later with the MI 5 investigation. They have files. And we have the man Paul can ask."

"Who?"

"A German—" He grinned like an adolescent. "—who owes Aubrey his innocence, his career, his respect . . . just about everything."

"Who?"

"Wolfgang Zimmermann."

"The man—" Alison began.

"The man the KGB tried to frame as a double agent when the Berlin Treaty collapsed. He can repay Aubrey's efforts now. Time to call in the loan."

"But didn't the previous Chancellor sack him?"

"He resigned."

Margaret was aware that Peter and Alison Shelley were oblivious to her. She envied them their easy communication, their intuitive, quick-minded cooperation. They represented an image that contrasted with the rift that had yawned into a chasm between herself and Paul. She would take this chance now, go to Germany with him. Her father would have to wait—as he had waited beneath the ruins of that bombed house in Berlin for five years, decomposing. . . .

She shook her head. Her companions did not notice as their talk bubbled and flew. She had to forget him. Someone had tried to kill Paul. She had to help Paul, keep him alive. She could not bear the thought of his death, that new, utter, final loss—the loss of the man who had replaced her father.

"Yes," Shelley was saying to his wife as she attended once more, "when the plot was exposed, the Chancellor wouldn't take him back on the payroll, but he appointed him Special Adviser to the BfV. The man has a lot of power—he can get into the old files, rake them over for you . . . even arrange some protection for you."

"Can you do all this?" Margaret asked confusedly.

"Yes. I can talk to him. He'll do it. Ever since his own people informed him of the debt he owed Aubrey rather than themselves for being cleared, he's wanted the chance to clear the slate. He'll do it." Shelley's face darkened, then he added: "Who knows, Ally—we might find your Mr. X this way. I think we may have just found another, hidden door into the fortress. A Judas gate." He smiled directly, disarmingly at Margaret. "You should get packed for a trip—discreet departure, I think. You're probably being watched. The apartment, certainly, will be under surveillance." He paused, then added: "Believe me, Mrs. Massinger, you won't be helping the man who killed your father. Kenneth Aubrey couldn't have done that, not even for a personal motive. I swear he could not."

Margaret Massinger stood up abruptly. "Thank you, Mr. Shelley. Thank you so much." From her eyes, it was evident she disbelieved Shelley's oath testifying to Aubrey's innocence.

A burst of wailing pop music from an unlit upstairs window, farther back down the alley. Someone laughing, then a child's grizzling crying. The smell of food and dung and garbage. Even as the heavy tires of the BTR-60 armored personnel carrier squeaked as the vehicle trundled slowly into the square, Miandad was returned to his own childhood. All that was lacking from the familiarity of odors was the hot, fetid scent blowing off the mouths of the River Indus. Here, in Kabul, the night was colder, and the familiar smells changed to sharpness in his nostrils. In Karachi—

No, it was different; the illusion could not be sustained. The personnel carrier was head-on to him now in the dull fire glow on the infrared nightsight. There was a flat-helmeted head behind the black hole of the 14.5mm machine gun that was mounted on the squat turret above the two slightly open viewing ports. The rubber eyepiece of the nightsight pressed around the socket of his right eye. He could feel his perspiration becoming chilly beneath his arms and across his back. Behind him, Hyde was waiting, dressed in the dead boy's uniform—Lieutenant Azimov resurrected. Mohammed Jan was behind him, too, with two other Pathans. The rest of his men—no more than seventeen of them now, after the attack on the patrol—were in their positions around the square. Seventeen, he thought again. Enough, but perhaps only just enough. Fanaticism swelled their numbers.

The BTR-60 came on toward them, skirting the hard-lit square past the shops and the hotel as if it, too, sensed it had no place there. Now, it was no more than seventy yards from the unlit alleyway where he and Hyde and Mohammed Jan waited. Somewhere, a bell struck the hour. Three, four—four in the morning. Miandad's right hand tensed around the forward stock, his finger squeezing gently at the trigger of the rocket launcher. His left hand steadied the slim barrel on his shoulder with the rear stock. The projectile, looking like a miniature closed umbrella, waited at the end of the barrel. The personnel carrier came on. Except for the vehicle, the square was empty; it looked like a stage without performers, a great stadium in which the white light glared and smouldered pointlessly.

Except to him. To him, the square was red. Dull red, like the last of a fire, through which a dark shape composed of wheels, hatches, machine guns, approached. His target. Forty yards away now.

He squeezed the resisting trigger of the RPG-7 launcher. The tube on his shoulder bucked; noise enveloped him. Through the nightsight, he saw the projectile ignite its own internal rocket, then watched the spit of flame moving on its brief, flat, accurate trajectory toward the bulk of the BTR-60.

The HEAT shell struck the personnel carrier just below the slightly open viewing hatches, penetrating the 10mm armor immediately upon impact. The flare of the explosion was like watching a backward-run film of a gunshot. The flame from the projectile was swallowed by the bulk of the carrier, which, at the same moment, buckled, swelled like a green, squat toad, and then erupted—two, three, four times its size, then no more than wheels bouncing away, flanks disintegrating into sheets of torn metal, turret opening like flesh sliced with a sharp knife. Smoke, the thunder of detonation, the first tinkling and crashing of windows and falling pieces. Something like a dummy, arms akimbo, was thrown perhaps a hundred feet without its lower torso. Two more dummy things were flung out of the viewing hatches like jack-in-the-boxes. Exploding ammunition filled the square with panic-making firepower.

Miandad loaded a second projectile onto the end of the hot tube of the RPG-7. He glanced up at Hyde. An alarm was beginning to sound in the embassy compound. Incredibly, someone was screaming in the shattered maelstrom of flames. Miandad shuddered, then adjusted his body to comfort in his crouch. He focused the nightsight. The pale concrete of the guard bunker outside the embassy gates was perhaps a little over one hundred yards from where they hid in the alleyway.

"Begin," Miandad told Hyde. Two Russian soldiers had emerged, dazed and horrified, from the refuge of the guard bunker. Miandad could see their surprised, desperate, fearful faces, very pale even though reddened by the nightsight. They seemed very young, like Azimov. Farmboys or factory hands, not professional soldiers. "Good luck," the Pakistani added.

Hyde tapped his free shoulder and then began running down the alleyway to enter the square at a point nearer the embassy gates. Miandad adjusted the sight. The rubber eyepiece was damp with sweat. Mohammed Jan stood by him, immobile, as if despising the modernity of their attack. The old Lee Enfield was cradled in his arms.

Miandad shifted the balance of the launcher on his shoulder. An officer was ordering soldiers toward the burnt-out personnel carrier. They seemed reluctant to the point of disobedience. All of them were still close enough to be killed by the impact. He squeezed the trigger.

Ignition, the spit of flame traveling straight and flat. One hundred yards, one third of a second, slowed down by the perspective of the nightsight and the flow of adrenaline. Then, impact. The concrete above the sandbags swallowed the flame, and the roof flew off the bunker in a rain of concrete boulders. The walls collapsed outward, burying those who had left the bunker. Dust rose to disguise the violence and the murders. Patiently, swiftly, expertly, Miandad fitted the third projectile. He scorched his wrist against the hot barrel of the RPG-7, sucked it for a moment, then pressed home the folded umbrella of the projectile. He adjusted the sights, felt the sweat on his forehead, soaking into the untidy folds of his turban, felt his back tight with reaction to what he was doing—killing so many, so easily—and then he hefted the tube of the launcher on his shoulder so that it was comfortable once more.

As the dust began to settle, the embassy lights came out like huge stars. The concrete bunker was still half standing amid its own shipwreck. Bodies on the floor, one or two staggering away, parts of them evidently missing. It was, he admitted, a vision of the infernal in the dull-fire glow of the nightsight. Screaming, punctuated by exploding ammunition. The hard-lit stadium was a battlefield.

Now.

He squeezed. Ignition, one-third of a second, impact. It had been faster because he was tired. The adrenaline was running out, just as Hyde needed his. He watched for long enough through the nightsight to see that the gates hung drunkenly on their hinges, almost twisted off their supports, the huge red star broken into crazed paving. Then he passed the RPG-7 to one side, and a Pathan took it from him with a chuckle of pleasure and admiration. Miandad listened to the first Kalashnikov fire and the wail of a siren crying above the noises of other alarms, then stood up. Hyde was now on his own. He had precisely fifteen-and-a-half minutes from the breaching of the gates.

Already, less than fifteen minutes remained.

Hyde's hand gripped the railing. He steadied himself, flinching against the burst of random, dangerous fire from exploding ammunition in the ruined bunker. There were two men staring at it helplessly. The red-and-white barrier had been flung off its hinges. The smoke and dust made him cough. He looked down at his boots—a size too big, stuffed with rags—and saw with satisfaction that they were coated with dust that had settled on them while he made his way along the railings. He touched the leather holster at his hip that contained the Makarov 9mm PM pistol. Then he stooped to pick up a crumbling fragment of concrete, paused for a moment, then rubbed it viciously across his forehead and down his left cheek. He winced and hunched into himself with the pain and the stinging it left behind. He touched his forehead and cheek with his fingertips, casting the lump of concrete away from him. Blood, when he looked. Blood and dust and sweaty dirt. He adopted a limp, and shuffled the last fifteen yards to the shattered gates of the embassy compound.

The concrete guard bunker was an opened, ruined flower, the smoke rising from it obscuring much of the hard white light from the square beyond. Bodies. Some men still upright, but concussed or shocked. Wounded, too. Alarms, sirens, the roar of vehicles, exploding ammunition. The self-inflicted wounds stung intolerably.

He reached the gates. He could just hear, already, the noise of a helicopter in the distance, the whine and beat of the main rotors carried on the cold night air. Evacuation. Support, defense, evacuation—the order of things. Hyde looked at his watch. Fourteen minutes thirty before the Pathans abandoned the square and retreated to the bazaar before making their dawn exit from Kabul.

A soldier blundered into him. His jaw was missing, and his eyes begged. Hyde rested him like a plank against the railings and slipped through the gates. No one challenged him. He was clean-shaven beneath the dust and blood, armed and wearing the full uniform of a lieutenant in the Red Army. Ahead of him, the lights in the embassy extension blazed like the lights of an oncoming liner. A heavily armored BMP rumbled on its tracks around the side of the main embassy building, increasing speed along the gravel path, squeaking and crunching its way toward him. Its cannon and Sagger missile mounting were clearly outlined against the facade of the building. Hyde began running.

There were other men running—confused, frightened, challenged men, who felt they were too few and in an alien country. His boots crunched on the gravel, his shadow raced ahead of him, thrown long by the lights in the square and the burning bunker. Then a shadow began stretching behind him like a warning to turn back as he entered the field of light of the KGB block. The BMP howled past him, cannon swinging like a pedagogue's eyes looking for someone small to punish first, and he stumbled into the doorway of the glass and concrete block which reminded him of, of—

It was suddenly important, like reorientation, like disguise and bluff, as a guard rammed his body against him in the doorway.

The Czech embassy in Kensington, amid all the old and graceful and corrupted buildings the ugliest and most modern.

He snapped the guard to attention, straightened his cap, wiped at his superficial injuries, and glared.

"Colonel Petrunin wants a report—*now!* Out of my way!" The guard's eyes lost suspicion a moment after his Kalashnikov bisected his features, at attention. Then his eyes became afraid, and Hyde realized how young he was. Like 1914—the Russians were sending their youngest, their youth. . . . "That's better," he snapped, passing the guard and making for the iron-railed, mock-marble stairs, which had already begun to pull away from the wall alongside them.

He smelled burning paper. Someone had panicked and was already beginning to incinerate sensitive material, the incriminating files, as if a liberating army lay out there in the square. He remembered the SIS house joke when the Ayatollah's mobs had climbed the U.S. embassy fence in Tehran. The only prayer you could hear, so it ran, was for another box of matches. . . .

He steadied himself at the turn of the stairs. The adrenaline was out of control, running like heady wine. He couldn't restrain his thoughts. That was Petrunin's doing. Even as he saw the sleeve of his uniform jacket, he envisaged the boy's broken, bleeding head—a small thin fount of blood—bang back against the rocks before the dead body slid into a heap. He rubbed his cheek, reminding himself of the stinging pain. Stop it; stop it—

His hand was quivering, his arm shaking as he gripped the cold iron banister. Counterproductive, he told himself. Out of control. He'll kill you in this state. . . .

Helicopter noises, closing now outside—

Helicopters laying black eggs that opened to let out a mist that Petrunin had ignited—fifty men dead, charred like burnt biscuits in no more than a moment. A red helicopter that gloated its way back down the valley—

He could kill you in this state!

Two hard-faced men in civilian clothes passed him, their arms clutching bundles of files. They did not even glance at him. They were obeying an order to abandon ship that had not yet been given. The noise of the helicopter was louder still. He looked through the windows into the compound. One helicopter—only one so far, its lights smearing red-blue-white across the snow on the lawn, red-blue-white, as it descended.

In five minutes, Petrunin would be on his way back to army headquarters and be lost for good.

He clattered up the rest of the flight of steps, sprinted along the corridor, the plan of the building he had drawn for himself from the dead boy's description clear in his mind, as if he had summoned it onto a screen. Almost, in the heightened state of his senses and imagination, he could see himself like a moving dot on that screen. Other end of the building—this corner—empty corridor . . .

A narrow-skirted girl emerged from an office. Hyde sent her tumbling as he charged into and past her. He heard his boot crunch on her lost spectacles, heard her cry as he rounded another corner. Outside, now that the rotors of the first of the helicopters had slowed, he could hear the chatter of rifles on automatic, answered more distantly by the guns of the Pathans from the square.

He looked at his watch. Twelve minutes—less—remaining. Perhaps four minutes before the corridor in which he hesitated like a lost visitor was filled with rescuers, ready to escort Petrunin to that first helicopter in the company of the Soviet ambassador.

Guards in the next corridor. He could hear the nervous words flickering between them like gamblers' bids. He strode around the last corner. Carpet, suddenly, not linoleum. Petrunin's KGB suite of offices. He glanced out of the tinted windows along one wall of the corridor. The guards had their noses pressed against the glass like children at a fairground.

"Back to your posts!" he snapped.

Troops were running across the light-mossed, snowy lawn toward the main embassy building. One of them fell, killed by a bullet that could have come from either side. Other soldiers scuttled from beneath the idling rotors of the MiL-8 transport toward the KGB building.

Three minutes.

The soldiers had already sullenly shuffled back to their posts, almost forming a ceremonial guard for inspection as he passed down the corridor to the main double doors at the end. One guard, two, three, four—

"Sir—there's no admittance," the fourth guard offered, unslinging his Kalashnikov from his shoulder.

Hyde turned and glared at him. He pointed at his forehead and cheek.

"Do you think I've come for the coffee?" he asked. "Comrade Colonel Petrunin wants a full report on the situation at the gates. *I* was at the gates, unlike you lucky bastards! Understand? You want to delay my report to the Comrade Colonel?"

"No, sir."

"Then step aside. And don't admit anyone else, not until you've seen the proper authority."

"Sir."

Hyde passed swiftly on before he could be asked for papers he did not possess. He knocked once, loudly and peremptorily, on the double doors, then opened one of them and slipped into the anteroom, his hand fiddling with the holster flap over the butt of the Makarov pistol.

A male secretary on the telephone glanced up immediately, his only concern his inability to identify the features partially disguised by the cuts and bruising. One hand reached into the top drawer of his desk. His left hand still held the telephone. He continued his urgent request for more backup.

Then the Stechkin automatic came above the level of the desk and the telephone was ignored, and Hyde shot him twice, the Makarov still pressed against his hip. The secretary ducked under the table, as if looking for coins he had dropped. The telephone receiver followed him with a clatter.

Hyde swiftly crossed the carpeted, comfortably furnished anteroom to Petrunin's door. Petrunin, in his present circumstances, would be as alert as a cat. How many of them were in the room, how many guns?

He wrenched at the handle of the door, felt resistance, then flung his shoulder against it, aware of the hollow, soft stomach he presented to any bullet fired through the door. There was a muffled cry and he stepped through, closing the door behind him with his heel. It slammed shut like a call to attention.

Hyde's eyes took in the room.

Petrunin was alone. In uniform, looking much older, much more cunning. Spread-eagled by his thrust against the door, he had raised himself to a sitting position on a circular, rumpled Chinese rug. Highly polished wooden floor, Afghan, Persian, Indian rugs and wall hangings. Exotic. Not Western.

Petrunin was looking at him. And at the Makarov leveled at his stomach by a young lieutenant with his back pressed against the door. There was something familiar. . . .

"Good morning, Comrade General Petrunin," Hyde said in English and he could not help, even though his body was shaking with reaction and his voice had quavered, indulging in an almost boyish grin.

"Hyde!" was all Petrunin said. And then once more: "Hyde."

9
The Prisoners

"Hyde," Petrunin repeated once more, then added: "You've come a long way."

He exuded an easy, false confidence as he sat on the rug, almost as if welcoming a guest to some casual, even exotic party. Hyde remained with his back against the door. There was no sound from outside, but he was intensely aware of the dead body of the secretary behind his desk. Anyone who entered the outer room would sound the alarm.

"Comrade General Petrunin," Hyde acknowledged, hearing the noise of a second helicopter approaching.

Through the long window behind Petrunin's desk, he could see people being hurried by greatcoated soldiers toward the first helicopter. The ambassador, a dark coat thrown over his pajamas, waded through the patchy snow in large fur boots; a woman clutching a dressing gown around her followed him. He had less than ten minutes by the timetable they had agreed on before the raid. He had little more than a minute in this office before Petrunin's rescuers arrived.

Petrunin got up slowly, casually. He appeared unafraid. "You seem to have entangled yourself in the web quite willingly," the Russian observed, flicking the rug's fringe into greater order with the toe of his right boot. Hyde watched the man's eyes and hands and the shape and intention of his body.

Beyond Petrunin, the rescued figures were clambering or being pushed into the interior of the MiL helicopter. The noise of approaching rotors was louder now.

"Time for us to go," Hyde said.

"Of course. Then we can walk into those who have come for me." He pointed to the window. "Rescuing the ambassa-

259

dor is a matter of correct form. The helicopter has, in reality, come for me. There is no way out for you."

"Perhaps—come on." Petrunin smiled but did not move. The room was overhot. The central heating purred and clicked. Petrunin contemplated his desk. Then he turned on Hyde.

"Why are you here?"

Hyde grinned. "You know I'll kill you, don't you," he said. It was not a question. "You know I'd have killed you in Australia because I knew I should have killed you in England. You're sure of it."

"And that is why you're here?" Petrunin was watching for signs of growing impatience. Yet he was also troubled.

Hyde shook his head. "I'm here because of *Teardrop*—there, I've given you your passport. I need you alive."

Petrunin laughed aloud. "Then they've done it?" he asked excitedly. "I wondered, when I saw that Aubrey . . . but, it's *Teardrop*, you say. *My* scheme." His face darkened. "While I *rot* here!" he added with a black and utter bitterness.

"Come on."

"There's no way out for you."

"Nor for you. I'll kill you, if it comes to it. You know that—*quickly* now!"

Hyde moved closer, his eyes intently watching Petrunin's face as he brushed his hand over the man's jacket, his torso. Then he moved carefully behind the Russian, touching along the line of his belt, then brushing his back. Petrunin had no weapon. Hyde gestured to the door with the Makarov, and Petrunin hesitated only for a moment, then collected his greatcoat from the rack and picked up his cap and gloves from a small table. He passed with assured nonchalance out of his office, Hyde close behind him, the Makarov drawn as if for Petrunin's protection.

A guard blundered into the outer office. From his position, Hyde could see the secretary's legs, despite the cover of the desk. The guard saluted. Hyde closed on Petrunin, touching the small of his back with the barrel of the Makarov. Then he stepped quickly away again.

"Is my escort here?" Petrunin demanded.

"Yes, Comrade Colonel!" Petrunin's shoulders twitched at the mention of his present rank, as if it pained him that Hyde was present to witness his reduced circumstances.

"Then get on with it. Get out of the way!"

The guard's face was white, thin. He held the door open. Hyde motioned him away from it and slammed it shut behind them, just as Petrunin appeared about to issue an instruction to the guard—perhaps to assist his secretary? Hyde grinned. There was the slightest shrug from Petrunin as he donned his greatcoat. Hyde glanced through the windows. A splay of lights on the patchy snow, the noises of a helicopter's descent. In the windowed corridor stood three soldiers and an officer, the soldiers in combat fatigues and armed with AKM rifles. Crack troops. The officer saluted Petrunin.

"Come quickly, Comrade Colonel," he instructed. "The helicopter is waiting for you." His glance passed over Hyde but was satisfied by the uniform. Petrunin nodded but said nothing, then swiftly moved into and beyond the circle of the three soldiers, shielding himself from Hyde with the three bodies. Hyde realized he had lost the advantage. Petrunin—this Petrunin—had an animal's quick, alert cunning. A word—a moment of safety and a quick order—could kill him. The Russians moved down the corridor and rounded the corner. Hyde hurried after them, aware of his own danger. People were running and there was a smell of burning paper and plastic and celluloid. Hyde sensed panic. There was sporadic firing from beyond the embassy compound as the second MiL helicopter, a big transport, began to sag into view, thirty yards or so above the lawns, its lights playing over the grass and snow and the bare trees on the other side of the compound. Still Petrunin remained silent. The man was taking not the slightest chance. Hyde guessed he had begun to enjoy the situation. He knew that the tables had been turned—that now *he* had Hyde.

Hyde reached the top of the stairs. People pressed back as Petrunin and his small escort moved down the stairs, boots clattering, rifles bristling, Petrunin at the center of their tight circle. Hyde cursed himself. He had allowed himself a moment of confidence in which he had relaxed, and in that moment Petrunin had surrounded himself with a protective curtain of soldiers. The helicopters had been minutes too early, *minutes—*

A bright, false sunrise garishly lit the windows alongside the stairs, gleaming whitely on each shocked, puzzled face. The officer, Petrunin, each of the guards, each of the embassy staff. Hyde's eyes were dazzled.

Petrunin glanced back up the steps that separated him from Hyde. His expression was shocked. For the moment, the man was incapable of giving the order he might have issued an instant before. *Move*, then—

The first helicopter had been minutes early, had been left out of Hyde's calculations. Then the second helicopter, the big transport—

Gobbets of flaming metal, a burning body, flailing rotor blades scattered down on the snow and grass and the guards around the first MiL. A huge ceremonial firework. Miandad had used the rocket launcher once more, perhaps because he had weighed the odds against Hyde. Panic now—

Hyde moved, skipping the intervening steps. Petrunin watched him come, his gloved hand reaching toward the officer's arm, to turn him and his dazzled attention toward this new danger—then Hyde was alongside Petrunin and the Makarov was pressed into the flank of the military greatcoat, hard. Hyde grinned.

The remains of the transport helicopter were burning like a scattered bonfire on the embassy lawn. Soldiers were rolling in the snow, extinguishing the flames that had caught them. One or two green greatcoats lay still. Frightened faces watched from the windows of the surviving MiL. The soldiers surrounding Petrunin had begun to drift toward the glass doors of the building. One of the transport's main rotors lay buried like a sword in the lawn. A ball of flame ascended from an exploding fuel tank. The light washed the foyer. Much of the glass had shattered—Hyde felt his face and hands prickling with fragments—and the cold night air had entered, the successive waves of heat from the fire now dispelling the chill.

Hyde had regained control.

"Guard the helicopter!" Hyde yelled in a high, panicky Russian voice full of desperate authority, pressing the gun into Petrunin's side to ensure his silence. The officer in charge of the escort detail turned to him. "Do it! It's the Colonel's only way out, you fools. Move!" People were clambering into the surviving MiL—civilian staff, soldiers, clerks, and secretaries, clinging to it like the one remaining lifeboat adrift from a sinking liner. "Get everyone off that helicopter except the ambassador and his wife!" Hyde yelled in Russian. "Get them *off*!"

And they moved. The officer transmitted Hyde's orders. The Makarov pressed against Petrunin's side, just below the ribs. A BMP rolled gruntingly, cautiously past the foyer, passing a parked staff car. Petrunin moved his hands as if to restrain the now-running soldiers, but he said nothing. The soldiers spread out, moving toward the helicopter, whose rotors had begun to pick up speed. There was shouting—a woman was bundled from the interior of the MiL and flung spread-eagle on the melted slush.

"Now!" Hyde whispered fiercely into Petrunin's ear.

He pushed the man forward with the Makarov, through the main doors. The cold was more intense now that the helicopter fire was dying down. There was still some firing at the gates, their ruin almost blocked by the BMP slewed across them. Hyde saw the vehicle launch a Sagger missile. There were dozens of soldiers near the gates now, and two trucks and a personnel carrier. In the hard-lit square, buildings appeared to be burning.

They reached the staff car. Hyde opened the door. Guards watched them from the steps, undecided. Petrunin looked back at them, then at Hyde. He shook his head.

"In," Hyde said, gesturing with the gun.

Guards, suspicious now or concerned for Petrunin's safety, had begun to descend the steps. Petrunin sensed the moment, and raised his head as if to summon them. A small explosion at the gates distracted him and distracted the guards. Hyde struck Petrunin across the temple with the barrel of the Makarov and shoved his crumpling body into the rear of the staff car, arranging it as carefully as he could on the rear seat. Then he climbed into the driving seat. The keys were in the ignition of the Zil, and he switched on the engine. The noise brought the attention of the guards back to him. He waved them away, and accelerated toward the gates, the rear wheels slewing then biting into the gravel of the drive.

In the driving mirror, the guards seemed to accept the situation. The escort detail was busy emptying the MiL of its unwanted passengers while still more of the embassy staff—many of them obviously half-dressed or still in their nightclothes—streamed toward the helicopter as to a shrine. Petrunin sat propped and unconscious behind him.

Many of the Russian troops had moved beyond the gates now. Hyde glanced at his watch. His time had run out; the Pathans were beginning to withdraw and he was now racing to overtake them. He swerved around a truck, then edged the staff car alongside the green, high flank of the BMP, its cannon pumping shells into the square. He looked up, seeing flat Soviet helmets above the flank of the vehicle. Kalashnikovs on automatic were creating a dense field of fire ahead of the BMP, which had begun to move into the square.

The nearside wheels of the staff car jolted over one of the ruined gates. An infantry officer suddenly appeared and bent to glance into the car, then indicated that Hyde should wind down the window. Two soldiers barred the car's path. The BMP moved away, letting the lights in the square glare on Hyde, like a curtain being drawn. The concrete bunker was still smouldering and there were a number of bodies near the gates. Most of the square was littered with wreckage and clumps of flame and smoke. Hyde wound down the window. The lieutenant had checked the identity of the passenger. Hyde saw distaste disfigure the man's features.

"This bastard's been wounded—I'm getting him out!" Hyde explained, gambling.

"Pity he isn't dead—*bastard*'s right. Where's your escort?"

"We were going to use the chopper—but there's panic back there. Everyone wants to get on. They'll be shooting each other for a place in a couple of minutes!"

"Fucking KGB!"

"He's too afraid of getting shot by one of his own—he wants to get out the quiet way. If they've got a launcher out there, they could pick him off. . . . Come on, man! If I don't deliver him, I might as well shoot myself!"

"Too right. Running like a rat, is he?"

"You've got it. Can I go, then?"

"Okay—out of the way, you two!" The lieutenant waved Hyde on. He slid the car through the wreckage around the gates, jolting it over rubble and bodies. Petrunin slid slowly to one side behind him until he was lying slumped on the seat. Hyde ignored him. The BMP was ahead of him, its field of fire concentrated toward the shadowy streets beyond the lights. There seemed to be no return of fire. Infantry followed the BMP on foot, armed, cautious. Through the still-open window, above the noise of flames and firing, he could hear the approach of other helicopters. He pressed the accelerator after assuring himself that Petrunin was still unconscious, turning the car into the narrow street at the corner of which Miandad had crouched with the RPG-7 and opened the way in for him. The staff car bounced on uneven cobbles. In the driving mirror, the small sliver of the square that he could see was filled with soldiers and light. The attack had been beaten off.

He unbuttoned his tunic and reached into its inside pocket for the map of Kabul they had given him. He stopped the car in the narrow, silent street that was little more than an alley, and switched on the courtesy light over his head. He studied the river, the warren of narrow streets, the broad Soviet-Western thoroughfares, the suburbs, the road to Jalalabad.

A helicopter beat low over the buildings that lined the street, startling him. His finger twitched on the map where it had been tapping the location of the bazaar, his point of rendezvous with the Pathans and Miandad.

The narrow street was gray now, not black. Hanging lines of washing emerged from the featureless profiles of blocks of apartments. Many windows were lit. A helicopter made another pass over the street in the direction of the square. He laid the map on the passenger seat, checked Petrunin's unconsciousness once again, and accelerated. The map of the city's network of avenues, streets, and alleys unrolled in his head. He reached for the red light, to attach it to the roof, and looked for the switch for the staff car's siren. It would be easy. He would move in the direction of army headquarters, only turning into the warren of the bazaar district at the last moment, doubling back through the chilly, vile, winding alleys and packed-earth streets to the rug maker's shop.

He reached out of the window and clamped the red light to the roof. New York, he thought. Playing cops. Behind him, Petrunin murmured and Hyde turned, startled into a sense of danger once more. The hand that still held the red light twitched, then let go of the seeming toy that had reminded him of celluloid policemen and blank cartridges. He stopped the car at the end of the alley and turned in his seat to look at the Russian, as if for the first time.

The man was still unconscious. In the faint gray light of the first of the dawn, his features appeared sickly, unfed. There were deep lines in his cheeks and brow and beside his lips. He looked much older; he looked vulnerable and alone and someone who had become superannuated and unable to frighten Hyde any longer. Yet this was only a sleeper's mask. Hyde had been shocked by the changes he had seen in Petrunin's face the moment he had slammed shut the door of his office. Older, cunning, the eyes haunted, even totally empty until they filled with a transitory fear and then with a violent urge toward self-preservation. He had come face to face with a savage, degenerate man, someone who had taken lives indiscriminately and often—and had learned to enjoy that power, desiring and needing it. He had been certain of that from the moment the red helicopter had hovered, watching the incineration of fifty tribesmen in the narrow, snow-filled valley. Petrunin's altered, corrupted face had confirmed Hyde's certainty.

Hyde shook his head. He rubbed his throat where the uniform collar had chafed his skin after the loose robes of his Pathan disguise. Petrunin had become a wild, dangerous animal, instead of a senior KGB officer bound by the unwritten rules governing the conflicts between intelligence services. Like the Pathans he pursued and destroyed, he was without emotion and mercy.

Hyde realized that he could never trust the Pathans with Petrunin. It would mean his having to travel in the rug maker's delivery truck toward Jalalabad when it left Kabul within the next half hour, hidden in the back with the Russian. Without him, Petrunin would be a corpse by the time the raiding party took to the mountains.

Petrunin moaned again, entertaining nightmares. Hyde turned his back. The self-loathing that he could not avoid sensing in that low moan chilled and disturbed him. He felt the reality of the alien country and people around him once more. Petrunin was a prisoner of the war he fought. He had become, in essence, a light-skinned Pathan. How would he, he wondered, ever get *this* Petrunin to talk? What tortures . . . ?

Mutilation followed by an offer of the release of a quick death—would he have to use those threats, those bribes? He dismissed the Pathan thought.

Savagely, he pressed his foot on the accelerator and slewed the staff car out of the alley and onto a broad thoroughfare that might have belonged in any city of eastern Europe that the Soviets had rebuilt after the war; even in Moscow it would have been familiar. The wide road ran alongside the river, a sullen gray scarf in the first light. In the distance, the Hindu Kush was tipped with bright gold. Hyde accelerated. The mountains seemed impossibly high and end-less, and alien like the streets of Kabul.

Aubrey left the main passenger lounge of the ferry be-cause the carelessly disposed bodies of those sleeping sug-gested defeat to him, and the high, raised voices of parties of schoolchildren seemed taunting. The lights, too, were hard and unsympathetic. On deck, the wind was sharp and buffet-ing and chilly. Nevertheless, he made his way toward the stern. Long before he reached it, he felt himself to be an old, skulk-ing figure, displaced and exiled. And as if they had gathered to witness his departure from England, he could see the lights of Brighton along the coast, slipping behind the Dieppe ferry.

He had avoided Dover almost superstitiously, suspecting that any search for him would be concentrated there. He had not rung Mrs. Grey—he could not bear to discover that the hunt was up. His journey from Victoria had been uneventful, the pursuit confined to the tumbled and broken terrain of his thoughts. His fears had chased him across the landscape of his imagination.

He gripped the stern rail, which immediately struck cold through his gloves. Brighton, a town he had never much liked, now appeared infinitely desirable—the last rescue craft moored to his country, ablaze with light. The wind filled his eyes with water. He refused to acknowledge the tears for what they were. Instead, he tried to concentrate upon the ease of his escape. One bored policeman at Victoria had seemed more interested in the antics of two drunks than in looking for someone like him. The passport that he had always renewed in a fictitious name had served him well. SIS knew nothing of this falsehood. It was a private matter. Almost everyone in the intelligence service possessed at least one other, unofficial identity. It was, to Aubrey, the twitch of distrust at the very center of the animal that was always alert for the possibilities of deception. There was a subconscious comfort in possessing a secret and unused new identity. The secret world was habit forming, perhaps incurable.

He was skulking away from England. The wind now seemed like an obscuring curtain drawn between himself and the lights of Brighton. The wake of the ferry straggled away into the darkness like a lost hope.

He thought of them, then. The others. The secret others. The notorious ones, most of whom he had known or met or questioned at some time. William Joyce, sitting detached and even amused in the dock of the Old Bailey after the war. Lord Haw-Haw, voiceless. Then Fuchs, then Burgess and MacLean and Philby and Blake and Blunt, and others behind them. It was as if he had become a dream through which they paraded, much as the Duke of Clarence had seen the ghosts of those he had helped his brother to murder on the night they came to drown him in the butt of wine. He saw his own ghosts, who seemed to wish to number him among them. Traitors.

Aubrey recognized his own self-pity. He looked down at the choppy, churned water as if it offered escape, then sniffed loudly. He was filled with anger, too. More than forty years of loyalty. When Joyce and Mosley had become Fascists and Blunt and the others had become Communists in secret, he had enlisted in the service of his country.

And now his country was slipping away below the horizon, only a haze of lights to remind him of its position, its existence. He was going into exile. When they discovered him gone, they would search for him, then they would wait until the mole popped its head above ground in Moscow to collect its medals and state pension.

In the darkness, too, he heard the laughter of his father, that ugly, exultant barking at the misfortunes and comeuppances of others that had served him as a source of satisfaction for as long as Aubrey could remember. The verger had hated the secret life, and Aubrey had often suspected that he had escaped into it to put a final and complete barrier between himself and his father. Perhaps he might not have been able to keep it from his mother, but she died while he was still at school. His increasingly infrequent visits to his father had been filled with that abiding satisfaction, that his whole adult life was a secret from his vindictive parent. Now, years after his death, his laughter at his son's downfall could be heard on the dark wind.

The noises of teenage horseplay—someone threatening to throw someone else overboard, he thought—interrupted his reverie. His body was chilled anew by the wind and the company. One of the group lurched into him, reeling from the spring of one of his companions. Aubrey shrank from the contact. He clenched his lips to prevent an escaping moan of protest.

"Sorry, Grandad," a black face said, and disappeared laughing. Aubrey felt his whole body shaking. He gripped the rail fiercely. The wake seemed to fade close to the ship. Brighton was a smudge of lights, no more. He shuddered with cold and self-pity and fear. England continued to slide beneath the sea like a damaged vessel.

He turned his back on it, and went forward again, toward the lights and noise and sleepers in the lounge.

The British Airways Trident dropped out of the low, clinging gray cloud only hundreds of feet above the runways of Flughafen Köln-Bonn. No more than minutes later, Massinger and his wife were hurrying across twenty yards of cold tarmac to the terminal building from the aircraft. As she followed Massinger, who moved urgently yet without real purpose, Margaret puzzled at his strange, withdrawn mood, his constant half-smiles tinged with guilty sadness, his reassuring pats on the back of her hand. He seemed to wish to comfort her—or was it that he wished to promise something? Margaret was confused. Paul seemed distracted rather than tense or excited. For herself, she was relaxed after the tensions of their flight from Heathrow. She had not really been able to believe in Paul's elaborate precautions to ensure they were not observed or followed. Sneaking out of the house while it was dark, taking the train to the airport rather than a taxi, booking in individually at the check-in desk, boarding the aircraft separately. . . . It was all unreal, even though Paul's continued tension had begun to affect her as the Trident lifted into the anonymity of gray cloud, then through to a uniformly blue sky above a white cloud carpet. Then with a gin and tonic, she had begun to relax.

But Paul? She could not tell what seemed to be driving him. He had spent most of the night at the Australian's flat in Earl's Court, using the untapped telephone to talk to Wolfgang Zimmermann. Shelley had been there, too. Margaret had been unable to rest. She had packed and repacked in an attempt at self-therapy until Paul had returned to Wilton Crescent.

The passenger lounge was warm, as was the baggage

hall. Their suitcases inched toward them along a conveyor belt; the building around them whispered and purred in its efficiency. Paul Massinger stood near his wife, intensely aware of her even as he concentrated on their suitcases, wobbling like targets pulled on wires across a shooting range. Now that he appeared to be safely out of England, his guilt had increased sharply, like the return of a virus. He knew he had to establish the truth of Castleford's death, and that he had to persuade Wolfgang Zimmermann to help him. He had to know. By knowledge, by the truth alone, could he repay his wife's loyalty, her decision to throw in her lot with him, believing as she did that he was helping the man who had murdered her father. To repay *that* . . .

There was only one way. The truth, even if the truth damned Aubrey.

"Mr. Massinger?" a slightly accented voice inquired beside him. His body jumped with surprise. He turned. "I'm Wolfgang Zimmermann," the tall man offered, handing Massinger his ID with what appeared to be amusement. Then the German took off his fur hat, doffing it to Margaret. "Mrs. Massinger—welcome to the Federal Republic." His identification of the political reality of West Germany was formal yet intense. Zimmermann's diffidence, Massinger guessed, was little more than superficial. Massinger shook his hand warmly.

"Thank you for meeting us—thank you for your offer of help," he said, smiling.

Zimmermann released his hand. He stood perhaps two inches taller than the American. Massinger could see in him the ability and charm that had, at one time, made him indispensable to ex-Chancellor Vogel. He could also see a sleepless night in the smudges beneath his keen blue eyes. "I have made a start," Zimmermann offered. "There is, as you will imagine, a great deal of material to cover. I have my car outside. I will drive you to your hotel. I thought we might set up our headquarters." Again, there was the persistence of some secret amusement in Zimmermann, as if the disappointment of his political hopes in the collapse of the Berlin Treaty had left him detached from, and amused at, the antics of the body politic. "If Mrs. Massinger has no objections, of course?" he added.

Margaret smiled and shook her head. Then she said: "I've come to help, if I can. Paul's life is in danger until this business is cleared up." She looked at Zimmermann levelly.

"Quite," he agreed with a slight bow. "Come, I will take one of the suitcases, and we shall make our way to the parking lot." He picked up Margaret's pale blue leather case and went ahead of them.

Outside the airport buildings, the wind clipped and tousled them coldly. There was snow in the air. Zimmermann led them to a gray Mercedes and unlocked the rear door, gesturing them in.

A minute later, he turned the car southwest onto the autobahn to the Rhine and Bonn. Beside him on the passenger seat, Massinger saw a heaped, neat pile of folders, envelopes, and ring binders. As if sensing his curiosity, Zimmermann patted the heap.

"A little preliminary sifting," he explained with a chuckle. "The BfV, fortunately, do not keep as much paper from the past as the Abwehr once did. You, Mr. Massinger, were too young for G-2?"

"Postwar experience only," Massinger agreed.

"CIA. A somewhat distinguished record."

"You've checked, of course."

"My apologies. My curiosity, not my suspicious nature. My old acquaintance Aubrey is lucky to have you for a friend." He was silent for a time, as if studying the heavy midday traffic, then he added: "As I, too, was lucky to have him, a man of such skill and such loyalty. I was very saddened—even alarmed—at what recently occurred. Surely your MI 5 does not really believe it? It is quite preposterous."

"As was your own frame-up by the Chinese—and the Americans," Massinger snapped, leaning forward in his seat.

"Out of bounds—I'm sorry," Zimmermann said.

"I apologize."

"Don't mention it."

They drove on toward Bonn in silence for a time. An airport bus rushed past them. As always, the newness of most of the cars struck Massinger. They were worn on the country's roads and autobahns like badges of merit and success, even with the German economy in a recession.

Evidently, Zimmermann regarded his own experiences as *verboten*, even though they so nearly paralleled those of Aubrey. Someone was framing the head of SIS just as someone had tried to frame Zimmermann as a Russian agent. Zimmermann had survived, in part because Aubrey exposed the frame-up—but Aubrey would not survive his trap. Unless—

Zimmermann had been labeled, during his crisis, as a second Gunther Guillaume. And it was the last days of freedom of that same Gunther Guillaume that might hold the truth of *Teardrop*. Might. Just might.

Zimmermann was speaking once more.

". . . a number of areas of interest, Mr. Massinger. The World Cup was, of course, a time of detailed cooperation. My service was most concerned to avoid a repetition of 'seventy-two in Munich—at all costs to prevent such another tragedy. There were a number of people, apart from Mr. Aubrey, in and out of Bonn over a period of weeks, even months. Also, there was, I gather, some internal investigation in the British embassy, regarding accounts or funding—I'm not sure of the details. No security implications, however . . ."

Massinger listened with a polite, noncommittal half-attention while he considered how he might raise the subject of Berlin and Castleford's murder. Surely there must be people still in BfV who might have been there, people Aubrey had used? He had to do it. Now, more than ever, he owed it to Margaret.

They crossed the Rhine via the Kennedybrücke. The river was stormily gray beneath the leaden, snow-filled sky. Massinger noticed that the windshield wipers of the Mercedes had been switched to intermittent, clearing the first snowflakes. Mistily, wintrily, the group of buildings that comprised the federal parliament, the Bundeshaus, and the residences of the Chancellor and the President appeared white and isolated in their parkland on the far bank. Massinger watched as Zimmermann's head turned sharply, then straightened to look ahead once more. It was the glance of an exile.

A minute later, Zimmermann was turning the car off the Adenauerallee into the forecourt of the Hotel Königshof. Ten minutes after that, the three of them were ensconced in a spacious suite that looked toward the river—long, black barges sliding through the tactile-looking steel-gray water—the heap of files and envelopes spread out on the large low coffee table. Zimmermann, having carried the documents to their suite, showed no inclination to leave. Massinger felt himself playing a subordinate role—a fact for which he felt a strange gratitude, as if his burden had been lightened. Margaret seemed prepared to begin working under Zimmermann's direction like someone drafted in to do an unpleasant, even distasteful job. Someone stoically determined to see the matter through.

She poured drinks for them—a gin and tonic and two whiskeys. Then they seated themselves around the heaped files, as if ready to open the parcels that contained their belated Christmas presents.

"Shall we begin?" Zimmermann asked, removing a notebook from the pile. "You understand, this is only a preliminary selection of the material. I have some very enthusiastic, but not necessarily experienced, young men who work for me. I think we can make a better job than they could." He splayed his fingers on the top file. "Mr. Massinger . . . ?" he invited.

"What are we looking for?" Margaret asked, putting down her glass. A barge hooted on the gray river. Sleet melted against the window, traced snail tracks down the huge pane of glass. "Are you familiar with the actual arrest of this man Guillaume?"

Zimmermann's face pursed; Massinger could not be certain whether the reaction was a personal one, or some national distaste or hurt. "I am," he replied.

"Then, do you think there was someone here who tried to help Guillaume?" she blurted.

Zimmermann nodded. "I do. And I do not think it was Aubrey. Incidentally, with regard to your father—" Zimmermann was already turning toward Massinger, who leaned forward in eagerness.

"I'm not here to discuss that," Margaret snapped. The window was obscured by snail tracks now, themselves interrupted or made to adopt new courses as large flakes of snow burst silently against the glass. The river was hardly decipherable in the distance. The room was warm behind its double glazing. "I'm here because my husband's safety is at stake."

A glance she resented passed between the two men, and then Zimmermann said with a slight nod of his head: "I'm sorry. Let me clarify the events of April 'seventy-four. Guillaume was arrested by officers of the BfV—our security service, like MI 5 in England—on the night of April twenty-third. He had been under suspicion for some time before that. BfV recommended to Chancellor Brandt that he be allowed to continue in office as one of his close advisers, hoping that the man would eventually betray his network and his control—his pipeline into the DDR or even to Moscow. . . ."

Massinger nodded. Margaret, leaning her chin on her fist, listened intently as to a new and exciting teacher. She looked, Massinger realized, almost childlike. He realized that her untroubled, rapt features betrayed how much of her self and her past lay buried at that moment. She was working only with the surface of her mind and feelings. ". . . I would not have done that. However, what it meant was that, though the Chancellor continued to use Guillaume, even to trust him because he discounted much of the BfV's evidence for many months before April 'seventy-four, the man himself was put under very close surveillance."

"So, you have a complete record of his movements, contacts—everything?" Massinger asked.

"Indeed. The BfV calls the official record a failure—because Guillaume must have guessed that he was under suspicion. He led us nowhere. His arrest became inevitable because there was nothing more to be gained from letting him run. The BfV knew that Brandt was still reluctant to believe or to act, so it waited until the Chancellor was on a visit to Cairo, then made the arrest . . ." There was a gleam in Zimmermann's eye as his voice trailed off.

Massinger, realizing that his intuitions were being tested, said quickly: "That's not quite it, though, is it? BfV had to rush at the last minute, I guess?"

Zimmermann nodded him a compliment. "Quite so. His telephone had been tapped, his movements watched. He went about his business as usual. We expected the mouse to play while the Chancellor-cat was away—forgive me, incidentally, for using the term *we* so freely. I was, of course, not connected with the service at that time." A moment of retrospection, then he continued: "He became concerned to shake his tail. This he did on two occasions in the week before his arrest. He kept assiduously away from his network, his couriers, and his control. They, it seems, were to be kept safe. But he was meeting someone. Someone we did not know was evidently helping him. Warning him." He thumbed through his notebook, then nodded. "Yes—April twenty-second. A voice speaking German with a heavy English accent telephoned Guillaume, and was warned off the line. Guillaume immediately left his apartment, and went to a public telephone booth. Fortunately, we had bugged all of them within a certain radius. Enough of a radius." Zimmermann was enjoying himself, as if recounting a particularly pleasing episode in his own biography. Whatever disappointments he had suffered in the past two years, he had evidently flung himself whole-heartedly into his role as special adviser to the German counterintelligence service. It was as if he had recaptured, entirely and freshly, his Abwehr past.

"And?"

"There was trouble. Hitches. BfV gossip was, however, repeated to Guillaume—gossip that could only have come from us or from people liaising with BfV as part of the World Cup security studies." Zimmermann looked grave. "Papers were arranged, a car hired. There were a number of calls to different telephone booths, but we never were able to trace the caller. The flight to the DDR—by car with a false passport—was to take place on the twenty-fourth. So, Guillaume was arrested the previous night."

"Always the same caller?"

Zimmermann nodded. "Always. An Englishman with good, correct, school-taught German. BfV was certain that he was a professional intelligence operative and that he was relaying the instructions of Guillaume's masters. Whoever he was, he was working for the East Germans or the KGB. And probably still is."

Zimmermann, his narrative complete, sipped at his whiskey, smiling encouragingly at Margaret. Massinger saw her frown of concentration lighten. Her features were still smooth, however. She had hidden or otherwise temporarily disposed of whole parts of herself in order to concentrate on his safety.

The snow had eased, and the window was gradually clearing. The barges moved like flat-backed whales.

"Was there any evidence pointing at a particular individual?"

Zimmermann shook his head. "Unfortunately, no. The car hire firm was traced—a nondescript man was described. The tickets for a train journey—presumably as backup—which we found in Guillaume's apartment were bought by someone whose German sounded a little peculiar—no description. No, there was nothing to go on."

"And how many suspects?"

"Conservatively, perhaps twenty or twenty-five. There were a great many advisers, as well as the normal embassy staff."

"You have a list of names?"

"Here." Zimmermann passed Massinger a sheet of typing

paper. The list of names was neatly aligned in the center of the page. The typeface might have belonged to a computer.

"Well," Massinger sighed, "no one anywhere has found anything up to now. What have we to lose?"

"I have one other name for you," Zimmermann said, and was surprised at the hungry, guilty eagerness Massinger's face displayed. He glanced at Margaret, then back to Massinger. He saw their mutual love, sensed the anguish not yet dissolved between them. The scene was a moment of nakedness from which he wished to remain detached. Nevertheless, sensing the crisis that was imminent, he passed Massinger a small, folded sheet that he had removed from his breast pocket. "He's retired now," he explained.

Margaret realized at once the implications of Zimmermann's words. "Who is this?" she asked angrily. "What other name?"

Massinger's shoulders hunched as he began his explanation. "It's to do with—"

"My father? That's it, isn't it? You've asked Herr Zimmermann to help *me*!"

"Not you—*us*."

"No!" Zimmermann was pained by her anguish. She suddenly looked older, careworn. Haunted.

"I *can't* leave it!"

"I don't want you to—"

"I must—"

"Leave it alone!"

Zimmermann hesitated, then said: "I do not think that you will find it was—"

"I don't *care*! I don't want to *know*!" Margaret wailed.

"It cannot be Aubrey."

"Why not? Why *not*?"

"I believe it can't be." Zimmermann glanced at Massinger, then back at his wife, then Massinger again. In a hoarse voice, he said: "But you believe it could be Aubrey, Mr. Massinger. You do, don't you?"

"I don't know what to think—"

"You're wrong—"

"Stop it! Stop it! I don't want you to go on with it, Paul—I want to begin to forget it. Can't you understand that? *Please*—"

"I must," he murmured, unfolding the paper. Margaret

got stiffly up and left the room. A moment later, they heard the running of a bathroom tap, the clink of a glass.

Massinger felt Zimmermann's gaze on him, felt the man's hostility stalking the room like an interrogating officer. He looked up sheepishly.

"If I had known," Zimmermann began, "that this was your opinion—"

Massinger held up his hand. "Please," he said. "Please. I have to know. Margaret has to know. Christ, I don't know what I believe!"

"But you suspect . . . ?"

Massinger nodded miserably. "Yes."

Zimmermann shifted uncomfortably in his chair, as if he was disarmed by the American's unguarded display of misery. "I do not understand," he murmured at last. "I do not understand why you have these—suspicions. But you have the address now, whatever good it will do you. I have requested the BfV to trace this woman you claim was involved with Aubrey and your wife's father. The man whose name you have was one of the people employed by Aubrey in Berlin, one of many such who later became good BfV officers. The Allies trained many of our best people—to catch other Germans." There was no expression on Zimmermann's face. "The man lives in Cologne. You will need a car."

Massinger looked up. "What?" he asked numbly.

"The sooner you get this business over, the sooner I can begin to help you and your wife—and Aubrey and perhaps even England. I do not know. Your wife will not, I suspect, wish to see you when she has—repaired the damage?" He smiled quizzically. "I suggest that you allow me to entertain her for lunch while you pursue your demon in Cologne. Then, perhaps this evening, you can be of help to me, I to you?" There was a thin, quick knife cut in the final words, and a sense of knowledge. Massinger felt his dilatoriness, his selfishness, his guilt laid under a hard light and dissected.

"You've spoken to this man, haven't you?" he guessed.

Zimmermann smiled. "Perhaps."

"Then tell me!"

"No. Hear it for yourself."

Massinger glared at Zimmermann like a malevolent puppet for a moment, then he stood up stiffly. His hip twinged like his conscience. There was hope, too, if Zimmermann despised his doubts about Aubrey. . . . He could not tell. "Very well," he said. "Very well. I'll do as you suggest."

"There is a car booked in your name. You have only to ask at the desk." Zimmermann's handsome features twisted in contempt. "I will not wish you good luck," he added acidly.

Deputy Chairman Kapustin of the KGB watched the traffic in Dzerzhinsky Square below his window, the transcript of the coded signal from Kabul in his hand, his thumb and forefinger clenched upon the flimsy sheet of paper. Its ragged top edge suggested the urgency with which it had been torn from the pad and hurried to his senior secretary in the outer office. A small motorcade of black, official Chaika sedans turned out of the square beneath the swirl of driving snow toward the Kremlin. The Chairman and some of his senior advisers attending a select Politburo meeting. Kapustin wondered why he should feel like a boy not invited to a party. More appropriately, perhaps, he was like the mouse about to play during the cat's absence.

Snow flurried more thickly across the square. Opposite his third-floor window, the lights—burning early in the afternoon—of the KGB's own exclusive *beriozhka* shop gleamed like an illuminated hoarding. As he turned to the senior secretary who had brought in the message, he glowered with appropriate anger, and quashed the rising sense of possible failure and the fear that accompanied it.

"How positive is this identification?" he asked.

"Colonel Petrunin's team questioned the guard detail very thoroughly, Comrade Deputy."

"You checked—"

"Sir. The code clerk informed his superior—there was a full exchange of signals with Kabul before the message was sent upstairs."

"And—"

"Kabul concludes—"

"Who in Kabul?"

"Petrunin's senior KGB captain—our man."

"Very well. His conclusions?"

"The kidnapper of Colonel Petrunin was undoubtedly a British agent." The secretary appeared uncomfortable, sensing himself on a limb.

"Nothing more particular?" Kapustin asked heavily.

"Our man thinks he knows him."

"From hurried impressions—from the description here?"

The secretary nodded. "I—placed a call myself, Comrade Deputy. I considered the delay—worthwhile, in view of the implications."

"Implications?"

"Sir—Petrunin's second-in-command was *our* appointment. When Colonel Petrunin was disgraced, he asked for one of his closest confederates to accompany him when he was posted to Kabul. You, sir, thought it wiser to send someone we could trust."

Kapustin's laugh was like a dog's bark. "I remember!" he exclaimed. "Poor devil. I remember the look on his face." Then his mood darkened, and he added: "Well?"

"He claims that the man involved *is* a British agent. He claims to have identified him from interrogating soldiers on duty during the kidnapping. He says the man is Patrick Hyde."

Kapustin appeared puzzled. "Who?"

"Hyde was with Aubrey in Helsinki, and Vienna. He was with him during many of your meetings."

Kapustin's eyes widened. "*Him?*" he breathed. "In Kabul? I don't believe it. He's skulking somewhere in Europe. . . ."

"Our man is positive—he *knows* the man. Sir, if there's even the slightest possibility—"

"*Teardrop.* You think he's—"

"I don't know, sir. We can't afford to take the chance, however. In my opinion, sir."

Kapustin studied his face, then the sheet of paper in his hand. Then he looked up again. "You've checked—double-checked?"

"Yes, sir. Our man sticks by his word."

Kapustin was silent for some time. Then he said: "Then there is only one solution. A pity"—the sentiment sounded blatantly hollow—"but we have no choice. There mustn't be the slightest possibility. . . . Very well. Issue the damned army its orders. Tell our man to take full command. Get rid of Petrunin, Hyde—find them and get rid of them all."

"Sir."

• • •

It was evident to Eldon that Sir Andrew Babbington reveled in the congratulations that Eldon had felt, in duty and sincerity, he should offer his superior. Babbington had been confirmed as the first Director-General of Security and Intelligence Directorate that morning. Eldon knew he would rise with Babbington, but it had not affected the spirit in which he had offered his good wishes. There was only one small element of personal calculation—Eldon was embarrassed and angry at the disappearance of Aubrey and wished to deflect what he anticipated would be Babbington's similar anger. Otherwise, he considered SAID a satisfactory innovation and Babbington its natural DG.

"Thank you, Eldon. A pity, however, that our euphoria must be incomplete, thanks to the laxity your men displayed with regard to Aubrey."

"You'll remember, Sir Andrew, that I originally suggested a closer method of surveillance?" Eldon observed with studied lightness.

Babbington glared momentarily, then waved his hand to brush the subject aside as easily as crumbs from the white linen tablecloth. The club's dining room was almost full, but Babbington's table was well removed from its nearest neighbor. Eldon could remember occasions when Babbington the aspiring acolyte in the secret world would not have merited such a secluded corner of the dining room. The memory amused him. In some small part, the audacity of Aubrey's escape amused him, too—just as it enraged him morally to see the man escape his trial and conviction.

"Very well. As long as Kenneth's found, there will be no recriminations. Shelley obviously wasn't involved. Kenneth ran out of luck, and nerve, and time. But, Eldon, on this matter of SAID—" The tone had an element of seduction in it.

"Yes, Sir Andrew?"

"I want you as Deputy Director-General. Second Deputy, of course. I shall have to promote Worthington—temporarily."

"I understand, Sir Andrew. Thank you." Eldon sliced at his lamb cutlet. Babbington sipped at his claret. "I did not expect—" Eldon felt obliged to offer, surprised at his own lack of excitement.

"You never do, do you, Eldon?" Babbington almost sneered. "You seem quite without proper ambition, at times."

"I'm sorry, Sir Andrew," Eldon replied calmly, chewing

on the piece of lamb, his gaze level and untroubled. Babbington was irritated by his subordinate's self-possession. His own delight was tarnished by Aubrey's disappearance, but only on the grounds that its ease reflected on himself. Aubrey, per se, did not matter any longer. He had lost, was lost.

"Very well, Eldon," Babbington snapped, irritated by the lack of surprise and pleasure in Eldon, then dismissing the emotions. Eldon was good, reliable, efficient, unambitious— a perfect DDG 2. There was a wife somewhere in Hampshire who would, no doubt, see the promotion in cruder, more pleasurable terms than had her husband. "Where do you think dear Kenneth is now?"

Eldon studied the claret as if its vintage and origins were no more than a cover story. Then he sipped it, and nodded. "On his way East, Sir Andrew. He'll pop up in Moscow, no doubt, in due course—for the medal ceremony." Eldon seemed to be speaking without irony.

"I suppose so," Babbington agreed. "A damned nuisance, all the same."

"Perhaps tidier," Eldon murmured.

"Root and branch now, Eldon. Your first job. All Aubrey's old cronies, his lackeys and appointments and time servers. I want them all out."

"Of course. It makes sense."

A waiter approached as Babbington was about to reply. A silver tray was offered. Babbington took the sealed envelope. He opened it with the proffered letter opener, levering up the red, embossed wax, then waved the waiter away. Eldon watched him as he read—watched, too, his own emotions. Studied the lack of pleasure, remembered the Sunday lunch he had shared with Aubrey, and sensed an unwilling and surprising comparison of Babbington and Aubrey in his emotions. Babbington was without warmth, except when he chose to exercise it. Aubrey was charming. Gifted, intuitive, and he would have said upright before events proved that idea no more than a sham. Aubrey was what Eldon might have fancied himself to be—except that Aubrey was a proven traitor. Eldon had no wish, however, to be Babbington.

He watched Babbington's heavy features. Brutally handsome, perhaps. Elaine would have admired the strength of character they displayed, even in growing anger, as now. Fear, too, he thought quickly, even as he inwardly smiled at his wife's impressionability with regard to the superficies of human character. It was as if he had married, with subconscious deliberation, someone who could never rival or imitate his own capacity for insight.

Fear?

Why?

Babbington caught Eldon's gaze, and there was only anger. Eldon maintained a calm, expressionless exterior. Babbington screwed the paper into a ball in his fist.

"A message from the Continent," he announced with heavy irony. "Massinger has been seen in Bonn."

"One of the first fruits of SAID," Eldon observed.

"It isn't a joking matter, Eldon!"

"I'm sorry—"

"What in hell's name is Massinger doing in Bonn?" Eldon thought he detected an element of bluff, or subterfuge in the puzzlement. As if Babbington knew the answer . . . Eldon dismissed his guess. Better to be like Elaine on some occasions, he warned himself. Interrogator's paranoia. "Why the devil can't he drop this damn business?" Babbington continued. "He must be stopped."

"Does it matter? May I?" Eldon held out his hand. Babbington reluctantly passed him the ball of paper. Eldon smoothed it on the tablecloth, and read. Eventually, he said: "I don't see what we can do, since he's with Zimmermann. Ask politely, I suppose?"

"So do it. And—find Aubrey. I want him to stand trial—I want Aubrey in the dock at the Old Bailey!"

Eldon glimpsed the fear once more, lurking beneath the anger like a serpent beneath a flower. Eldon, too, squeezed the sheet of notepaper into a ball in his fist.

To have reached the abandoned Afghan fort before darkness seemed to Hyde like a race that had been won. The day had exhausted him. Not because of the distance so much as the tensions that surrounded himself and his prisoner. There were eleven Pathans still alive, including Mohammed Jan, and all of them coveted Petrunin as certainly as if he were encrusted with precious stones. Even now, in the shadows of the fort's empty, windswept rooms—a wind that plucked little drifts of snow from the corners and floors of the rooms whirled them like new showers—Hyde could sense their eyes turning continually toward the Russian, their hunger evident.

Miandad sensed some kind of approaching crisis, too, for he had positioned himself near Hyde and Petrunin, his small frame crouched and alert with tension. Mohammed Jan, after posting his lookouts, paced through the fort like a magnate who had acquired a mansion requiring extensive renovation. There was about him both an urgent need for change and a sure sense of possession. Petrunin was *his*, his stance and movements declared. His by right, his to take.

They had left the truck to continue its journey to Jalalabad less than five miles from the place where they had ambushed the patrol and Hyde had killed Lieutenant Azimov. The Pathans who had slipped out of Kabul in wagons, on bicycles, by bus, and even on foot rendezvoused with them before midday. Hyde was shocked to discover how few in number they were. There had been no time at the rug maker's to ask Miandad anything as the Pakistani had hurried him into the back of the truck with the now conscious Petrunin, then joined the driver in the cab. The staff car was driven away by one of the rug maker's sons and presumably dumped.

The truck had not been searched. They had evaded the net, perhaps by no more than ten or fifteen minutes. Confusion still aided them, and Petrunin might not yet have been missed.

The afternoon had been filled with the noise of helicopters, after they had taken to the hills—their noise and the sharklike shapes of MiL gunships dark against the snowclad hillsides. The Pathans had protected Petrunin like their dearest possession—which he was, Hyde admitted. He was the purse that held the currency of their hatred and their revenge. Bright gold coins. They had avoided detection with what had seemed like ease, threading through narrow defiles or using hidden, hair-thin tracks that clung to the sheer sides of the hills, until they reached the fort where Hyde and Miandad had rested two days before.

After nightfall, they would continue their journey. Miandad expected them to cross the border into Pakistan before dawn. Hyde associated the crossing, and the hours before it, only with crisis, not with safety at the journey's end.

Hatred. Even in that subzero temperature, its effects heated Hyde's body. Almost three-quarters of the Pathans had died for this man's capture, the last of them in the square, buried by rocket-loosened masonry or raked by bullets. Some of them might yet die of wounds, exhaustion, or gangrene.

Their efforts and their losses demanded the mutilation of Petrunin and his slow death as recompense. To satisfy their hatred, they would risk capture and death by remaining here for two or three days just to kill him slowly and with infinite pleasure.

Above all, Petrunin had burned fifty of Mohammed Jan's men; burned two of his sons.

"My friend," Miandad murmured on the other side of the apparently sleeping Petrunin, "what will you do? Have you decided?"

The wind whipped snow from one corner of the roofless room in which they huddled around a small, flickering fire, creating a tiny blizzard that lasted no more than a moment. The arms of Petrunin's greatcoat were dusted with snow. The Russian's head remained resting on his chest. Petrunin had answered none of Hyde's questions. He realized his value to the Australian and relied on Hyde's protection. Petrunin realized as clearly as the Pathans his value as a commodity. He knew Hyde would not sell him to Mohammed Jan, not even at the price of his own safety.

Hyde shook his head. "I don't know," he muttered. "Christ, I don't know!" Petrunin appeared to stir in his sleep. Hyde dug his elbow viciously into the Russian's side. "Wake up, you bastard!" he growled. As if the Pathans had been large cats huddled around them, there was a murmuring noise as Petrunin sat up—a throaty, greedy, hungry noise. "You bastard, you bastard . . ." Hyde repeated impotently.

"You can't threaten me with them," Petrunin observed calmly, though his face betrayed the effect of the Pathans' murmuring on him. "And I won't tell you, because then you would give me to them. And you can't hand me over and hope to stop it if I talk—they'd never let you."

"So how do you expect Mr. Hyde to protect you, if they are so much to be feared?" Miandad asked.

Petrunin glared at the Pakistani.

"Can *you* get us over the border?" Hyde asked.

"From here, yes—but I doubt if we could slip away unnoticed, my friend."

"Shit—"

"I am already compromised, I fear," Miandad continued. "It would do me no extra harm to help you escape. But I cannot see how we would possibly outrun Mohammed Jan—can you?"

"No, I can't. We're right in it, thanks to this bastard."

"I didn't ask to be kidnapped," Petrunin observed with an affected lightness that seemed to recapture, for an instant, a former time and place, even character.

"Aubrey didn't *ask* to be set up!" Hyde snapped. Again, the Pathans stirred. Wild, large cats. "I didn't *ask* to get shot at by my own side, or to be here."

"I did nothing more than create *Teardrop*—I didn't use it. It was an intellectual exercise, nothing more."

"What was its purpose?"

"Ah," Petrunin answered smugly, and smiled. Hyde could see his face in the failing light, somehow softened and made younger. It was haggard with effort, of course, and afraid. But it belonged to the Petrunin Hyde had formerly known. It was the face of an invalid who had recovered from a severe fever. And the face of a still dangerous enemy.

"Listen," Miandad said, his head cocked on one side. "I think the helicopters have returned."

Petrunin's eyes gleamed in the firelight as he raised his face to the darkening sky. Hyde listened, realizing that Petrunin still expected, by some miracle, to be rescued. Mohammed Jan had appeared in the doorway, then turned and moved quickly away at the first sounds overhead. Hyde got to his feet. Most of the Pathans were alert now, standing or already moving back into the shadows at the corners of the room. Someone had kicked out the fire. Petrunin's smile was almost indistinguishable. Hyde drew the Makarov and nudged the Russian's side with its barrel. The noise of rotors was loud now, and Hyde leaned toward Petrunin's ear in order that the man would hear him.

"Back against the wall. Don't be stupid in your old age." Petrunin nodded and did as Hyde ordered. They pressed back into the shadows. Hyde thought he could distinguish a thin streamer of smoke ascending from the fire's scattered remains, but perhaps it was only the smell of the fire that remained. Snow began to lift and swirl from the floor and the corners and the rooms beyond. The rotor noise was deafening, very low and near.

"Look," he heard Miandad call out. Hyde raised his head.

The MiL gunship loomed over the roofless room. Involuntarily, Hyde's body began to shudder, as if the rotors were beating at the packed earth under his feet. The helicopter squatted on the air, toadlike, and they watched it like minnows from beneath clear water. A dark, ugly shape. The snow whirled up in the downdraft, coating their clothing, flicking against their skin and into their eyes. The room was foggy with the distressed, dusty snow. Hyde, looking up, realized that the helicopter was still descending. It was perhaps no more than fifty feet above the room in which they pressed against the chilly walls, and was slowly enlarging, as if the toad were inflating itself. The snow seemed sucked toward it through the open roof. Like a roof itself, the helicopter filled the space of evening sky.

Mohammed Jan appeared, sidling through the doorway, pressing against the wall. Then a white searchlight beam struck down into the room. Hyde froze. He heard Mohammed Jan shouting above the noise of the rotors, then Miandad crying out, too.

"Soldiers! The lookouts report troops moving up the hillside to encircle us!"

Hyde jabbed Petrunin with the barrel of the pistol. "No!" he warned. Petrunin seemed to shrug. The light spilled across the floor toward their feet. Pathans were already slipping out of the doorway, sidling along the walls. The snow funnel swirled and obscured, garishly lit by the searchlight. The sky had vanished above them. There was only the dark belly of the MiL around the halo of the light. "Move!" Hyde ordered. "Move, you bastard!" He pushed Petrunin along the wall.

Sky again. The light, like a waterfall, poured over the doorway and into the next room—then back. A Pathan fixed in its glare looked up, immobile and afraid. Hyde could discern the noise of other helicopters. There was shooting from outside, in the main courtyard of the fort, perhaps beyond the walls. Miandad moved ahead of the reluctant Petrunin. The light holding the Pathan spilled over them. The helicopter began to alter its angle of hover, and its belly light slipped away from them. Another light, presumably from a searchlight mounted beneath its nose, illuminated the room beyond.

"Now!" Miandad shouted. Hyde prodded Petrunin forward and they blundered past the transfixed Pathan into the cone of light from the nose of the MiL. Machine gun bullets plucked and tore at the packed earth of the floor. Hyde heaved at Petrunin to make him run. They almost tripped over the Pathan's body. Bullets ricocheted from the stone walls.

They stumbled out into the courtyard, which was washed by moving searchlights. Something dark tumbled from one wall of the fort. Machine gun fire from two more MiL helicopters raked across the open space. Hyde saw fleeing figures, still forms.

Panic, noise, death. Three, four bodies—another Pathan falling, then the light fixed them, held them. Hyde, surprised, realized that Miandad was on his knees. He seemed to be coughing. A vertical cone of light, then a second, more glancing beam. It was as if the courtyard had become a stage, and the spotlights had focused upon the three tiny figures.

Petrunin was looking up into the light. His shadow was flung away across the courtyard by the noselight of the second helicopter, which shuffled closer through the dark air. There was more shooting. One half-ruined wall of the old fort bulged inward, and Hyde glimpsed figures and lights moving up the suddenly exposed hillside toward them.

Petrunin was waving. Hyde was distracted by a wracking cough from Miandad. Snow whirled up around him, but the snow just in front of his hunched form was red in the hard light. A patch of bright crimson. Hyde moved to him. Petrunin was waving to the helicopter. Miandad looked up at him as he clutched his shoulders, tried to smile, coughed deeply, spraying the front of Hyde's sheepskin jacket with blood, dyeing his supporting hand. Then the Pakistani slumped against him, his eyes staring into the beam of the searchlight with dilated pupils. Hyde let the body fall gently to the ground. The helicopters hung over him. He could feel the beat of the rotors. He turned his head.

Petrunin was waving and shouting. The helicopter neared. Something blundered against Hyde, and fell. Mohammed Jan's green turban was blurred by its proximity. The man's dead face fell past him; a curved knife glittered on the snow. Hyde drew the Makarov, concealing it against his stomach.

Petrunin looked up into the open side door of the MiL, arms uplifted as if in prayer. He looked, too, into the muzzle of a Kalashnikov leveled at him. Hyde swung the Makarov, realizing the entire situation subliminally, knowing without understanding. Petrunin stepped back a single pace. The marksman was bracing himself against the metal frame of the side door; the MiL was absolutely level, completely stationary. The Kalashnikov fired—Hyde saw the spit of flame—and then Hyde fired. The marksman fell through the open door, arms spread, rifle dropping ahead of him. His body thudded onto the snow.

Hyde ran. The MiL lurched away, bursting into flames. One of the surviving Pathans had used the rocket launcher, or else it was a lucky rifle shot. The MiL crashed into the wall of the fort, exploding. In the lurid light, its flames echoing on his retinas, Hyde turned over the body of Petrunin, realizing that he had lost everything.

10
The Journey
to the Border

The block of luxury apartments was no more than a few years old and stood on the east bank of the Rhine, looking across the river toward the old city of Cologne. Even seated in a deep leather armchair, Massinger was still able to glimpse beyond the windows the tops of the cathedral's three spires, sooty against the leaden sky. The whiskey he had been offered on arrival had made his stomach rumble audibly, and his host had immediately offered to make sandwiches. The plate of neat, afternoon-tea triangles of bread and German sausage now lay between them on the long coffee table.

Gerhardt Disch was ebullient, clever, alert. Recently retired, he had also become recently widowed. The pictures of his wife—mountains, skiing resorts, beaches, the Lower Manhattan skyline behind her—were rather more prominent on the walls and sideboard and cabinets than those of his children and grandchildren. The large, comfortable, warm room was overfilled with heavy furniture, much of it antique, an indication that he had once occupied more spacious premises. There was also an almost sparkling tidiness about the apartment, which denoted a fastidious man with too much time to fill. Only one or two concessions had been made to spontaneity. Massinger noticed particularly a very old sepia enlargement stuck at an angle into the frame of the ornate mirror above the gas fire. A young woman, presumably Disch's late wife, staring into the lens and into strong sunlight—squinting and smiling. Massinger suspected that Disch had found the old photograph when packing or unpacking during his recent move. What was it—first vacation together, honeymoon, just a day trip? Her dress was postwar. Disch himself was only a little over sixty; Massinger guessed his wife had been perhaps a few years younger.

He took one of the tiny sandwiches and bit into it, nodding his compliments. Disch seemed inordinately pleased with the effect of his cuisine upon his guest.

"I believe that Herr Zimmermann has already spoken to you?" Massinger said when he had finished the sandwich.

Disch nodded. "That is correct." His English was good, his accent more pronounced than that of Zimmermann. His voice rumbled. "But only for a moment—and to ask if I would help you. I know Wolf Zimmermann for some years now. I was attached to the Chancellery Security Section, you understand?" Massinger nodded. "Of course, I am pleased if I am able to help." He shook his head lugubriously. "It is a sad thing, what they say of Mr. Aubrey—my apologies, Sir Kenneth Aubrey—and, of course, it is ridiculous."

Massinger felt his heart pluck in his chest, as if uplifted by some great sense of relief. Doubt, however, immediately returned.

"Please go on," he said. "I understand you worked with Kenneth in Berlin, after the end of the war."

"Ah—that is what interests you?" Disch's eyes were bright with inquiry. Massinger felt himself studied, weighed. Retirement had not dulled the man's professional instincts or abilities. "You are in some doubt about the matter?" Disch asked sharply. "I was not told this."

"I'm sorry, but I thought—" Massinger began. Disch was studying him with bright, narrow suspicion in his eyes. The German raised his hand. "What did Herr Zimmermann say to you?" Massinger persisted.

"Only that you wished to speak to me. He explained who you were, of course. And that you were trying to help your friend, Sir Kenneth Aubrey."

Massinger felt hot with embarrassment. Hesitantly, he said: "I am not here under false pretenses, Herr Disch." Even to himself, it sounded priggish. He was surprised at the loyalty toward Aubrey evinced by the German. It was almost forty years old, and still it had not atrophied. With a cynical amusement, Massinger realized it was the same kind of loyalty that had made him visit Aubrey the morning after the fateful news bulletin.

"I wonder?" Disch said. He brushed his hand over his remaining strands of gray hair. His face was cherubic in complexion and shape, and now it appeared almost froglike with suppressed anger. "Yes, Herr Massinger, I wonder about your motives."

Massinger resisted an explanation, as if he felt the use of Margaret's name and situation would be an evasion. Yet he was not prepared to admit that it was his doubts that must be satisfied. His disloyalty . . .

"Please tell me about Berlin," he pleaded at last.

Disch continued to study him, then said carefully: "And this will help? It will help Sir Kenneth?" Massinger nodded, his features expressionless. "What will happen to him?" Disch asked then.

Massinger shrugged. "I don't know. With luck—with a great deal of luck, his name perhaps can be cleared. I don't know what will happen then."

"I see." Disch was like a man guarding a precious hoard, suspecting every caller of being a potential thief. He rubbed his round chin and pressed his jowls into froglike enlargements against his collar, as if he had bent his head to watch his visitor over half-glasses. "I see," he repeated softly.

Massinger quelled his irritation and his tension. He received a moment of insight. Behind the bonhomie and the good manners lay the cleverness and the professional training. And those elements of Disch's character were troubled. Massinger's questions posed some kind of threat. There *was* a secret, then. There was a suspicion hidden in Disch's mind. Of Aubrey . . . ?

Yes. Of Aubrey. Disch had been disloyal in his own way, perhaps only since Zimmermann had spoken to him. Zimmermann had appeared confident, but Massinger had no idea as to Zimmermann's sense of morality. The man was in debt to Aubrey, and wished to repay. He had, perhaps, made allowances, given no weight to what Aubrey might have done in Berlin. But Disch had. Disch knew or suspected something to Aubrey's detriment.

"Please tell me," he prompted.

Disch shrugged expansively, and attempted a smile. "Very well," he said with something like relief. "But Sir Kenneth, I am certain, is innocent of these charges against him. He is not a Russian agent. . . ." He hurried on: "I worked with him again in 'seventy-four, when he was in Bonn. What the press here and in your country have suggested is nonsense!"

"But, about Berlin?"

Disch nodded, and swallowed. He was obviously burdened. Massinger should have seen it earlier, played upon it. There was a confessional air about Disch, suddenly.

"Yes, yes," he said almost breathlessly.

"Kenneth was captured in East Berlin and held for some days—then he escaped."

"I believe that he *did* escape," Disch protested, angry and yet somehow relieved that he was under interrogation. "All other suggestions are nonsense."

"Why did he go to East Berlin? Wasn't it dangerous?" It had been his job. A stupid question. It was difficult to think of Aubrey as a young man, a field agent. "I have been told," he added, "that one of his networks was threatened."

Disch nodded. "Yes," he said heavily, "we agreed to that."

"Agreed? It wasn't the truth, then?"

Disch shook his head vigorously. "I did not say that—"

"Who agreed?"

"Sir Kenneth—and the others—four of us."

The voice was laden with guilt. Massinger was appalled. What kind of conspiracy was this?

"Why was it necessary to agree?"

"I do not mean *agree*—I mean, we—oh, how do you say, we were told by Sir Kenneth that this is why he had to go over . . . told to say that . . ." His voice trailed off. There had been turmoil, then. For how long? Forty years, or just since Zimmermann had spoken to Disch?

"Why?"

"For security reasons. It was a cover story—" Disch blurted out. "There is nothing unusual in that. It was our cover story from the beginning."

"But why? Why did he go?"

Disch shifted uncomfortably in his chair. The leather squeaked in the tense, warm silence.

"Very well. I persist in believing—" Massinger waved the protestation aside gently. Disch continued. "Yes. The cover story, to protect the real reason for the operation, was that Sir Kenneth suspected a double agent in one of his networks in the Russian Sector . . . ?" Massinger nodded. "You know we also searched for Nazis?" Disch asked with apparent inconsequentiality.

"Yes."

"That was his real reason."

"But I don't understand, Herr Disch. Why did he need a cover story for such a mission? Everyone was looking for Nazis then."

"I agree. Also many Germans were involved in the hunt—like myself."

"Yes," Massinger admitted awkwardly.

Disch smiled. "You need not worry. My family was killed by the Russians during the bombardment of the city. All of them." He shook his head. "I was twenty-one, and starving. I burned my uniform, and went into hiding. I did not surrender to the Allies until the city had been divided into its four sectors. I was not a Nazi, or a Communist—though my father was sympathetic until he saw what the Russians were doing to his country and his city. Sir Kenneth found me interned. He questioned me in case I was a Russian plant. Then, because I had existed in the Russian Sector for a year, and I knew people, and places, he took me to work for him. He trained me well. Mine was the story of many people—not at all unusual."

"I see. Go on, please."

"The cover story—yes. It was necessary because we had been working—for a long time working—to discover how so many Nazis were still able to escape from Berlin, even from the Russian Zone of my country. Sir Kenneth believed that they received help from inside the Control Commission itself. . . ."

Disch's voice trailed off. His face was red with embarrassment, guilt, suspicion. He wished to say no more.

"Who?" Massinger demanded in a thick voice.

Disch shook his head. "We did not know. But Sir Kenneth had a message from one of our people in the Russian Sector—some news of the source of the assistance to escaping Nazis inside the Control Commission. The contact could not come over—Sir Kenneth made his arrangements immediately to enter the Russian Sector." Disch shook his head. "He told us when he returned that he had learned nothing. The signal had been no more than a clever trap for him."

Massinger said in disappointment: "Then there was nothing? You don't know anything?" Disch merely shrugged. Then he leaned forward and selected one of the tiny sandwiches. "But—what did Kenneth suspect before he went over?"

"That the man was British, and highly placed," Disch

said hurriedly, mumbling slightly through the bread and sausage in his mouth, using the sandwich as if it would help conceal the truth from Massinger.

Massinger opened his mouth to speak as the implications of Disch's statement struck him. Without the German's evasiveness and Massinger's certainty that the man had his own suspicions, the statement would have meant little or nothing to him.

"British?" he said at last.

Disch's eyes were little more than slits. He nodded.

"He was highly placed. But Sir Kenneth told us he learned nothing in the Russian Sector, that it was only a trap for him!"

"You don't believe that, Herr Disch—"

"I am certain that there is no connection—"

"But you *do* believe it! You think this highly placed Nazi sympathizer was Castleford and that Aubrey murdered him on his return from the Russian Sector."

"No!" Disch protested weakly.

"Oh, my God, man—you *do* believe it! Ever since you spoke to Zimmermann, you've been thinking about it." Disch blanched, then nodded. "You do believe it, don't you? That Aubrey killed Castleford because he was helping Nazis to escape? Don't you?"

The central heating plopped in the silence. The room seemed hot. The cathedral spires rose against the gray sky, a sky as bleak and featureless as the landscape of Massinger's imagination.

"Yes," Disch admitted finally in a small, weak voice. "Yes, I believe it."

The second helicopter flicked up and away, its belly luridly reddened by the flames from the first. A fuel tank exploded, and a ball of white flame soared into the air, almost touching the underside of the surviving MiL. The whole of the courtyard was illuminated. Dead Pathans, sporadic movement, Miandad's body, Mohammed Jan's green turban on the snow only yards away. Hyde turned over the body of Petrunin and tugged open the greatcoat and the jacket beneath. There was a spreading stain on the front of his uniform shirt. A thin dribble of blood from the corner of Petrunin's closed mouth. Hyde groaned as if he, too, had been wounded.

The flames from the crashed helicopter died down and he almost missed the flickering of the Russian's eyelids. But he saw it, and heard the groan of pain. It was thick, as if coming through a liquid. More blood dribbled across Petrunin's cheek.

Hyde hauled Petrunin into a sitting position, then laid the Russian's weight across his back and heaved himself upright. Petrunin was draped heavily and unmoving—perhaps fainted, perhaps now dead?—in a fireman's lift. Staggering, Hyde jogged at leaden pace across the courtyard. The spotlight of the second MiL was returning, moving toward the source of the rocket that had destroyed its companion. The shooting had almost stopped. Then the four-barrel machine gun in the nose of the gunship opened up, raking the other side of the courtyard.

Hyde stopped, regained his bearings, shifted Petrunin's weight to greater comfort across his back, and then jogged through the shattered gates of the fort. Immediately, his feet blundered into thicker snow and his breathing became more labored. His field of vision was restricted, but he saw no soldiers. He was climbing before he fully realized the fact, stamping one precarious and tired footstep ahead of the next, his face bent almost to the snow under his burden. He heard a groan, but sensed no movement through Petrunin's body. Fire lit the snow around him, dimly and fadingly. He thought he could hear orders shouted above the noise of his heart and breathing, but he could not be certain it was not his own voice urging him to greater effort. The light on the snow had vanished, and he realized he was in the trees above the fort. He leaned their combined weights against the rough bole of a fir, then let the Russian's body slide into a sitting position while he rested, hands on his knees, dragging in lungfuls of freezing air. When he turned his head, Petrunin seemed to be watching him sightlessly and Hyde could only wish it had been Miandad still alive and whom he had carried out of the fort. It might have been his hatred that caused the trembling in his limbs, or simply weakness. Blood stained Petrunin's chin. Hyde knelt by him, holding him upright, his hand at his back. It felt sticky, and he realized that the bullet had passed through the Russian's body. He realized, too, that the bullet had punctured one of Petrunin's lungs and that the man was going to die.

He studied the terrain below them. Figures moved in the

light of the hovering helicopters—there were two of them again now—checking bodies. There were three Pathans in turbans in the center of the courtyard. He heard clearly on the cold air the shots that killed them. The helicopter that had crashed had almost burned out. He counted more than twenty Russian troops, disregarding however many the two MiLs carried. He returned his attention to Petrunin, who had turned his head slightly and was looking directly into Hyde's face. The Russian tried to smile, but only coughed blood. Hyde wiped the man's chin slowly and delicately with the sleeve of his loose blouse. The blood, he saw, stained his sleeve almost up to the elbow. Petrunin was dying.

Petrunin nodded, as if he guessed at Hyde's thoughts.

"They had orders to kill you," Hyde said. "You're right in the shit now, just like me." Again, Petrunin nodded. "They wouldn't take the slightest chance, would they? Not with your bloody *Teardrop*. As soon as someone laid hands on you, that's all that worried them—stop you from talking at all costs." Hyde was breathing heavily again, and leaning toward the Russian. Then he stood up. "Oh, fuck it," he growled. He looked back down at Petrunin. "Do you want to go on living—or stay here?"

Petrunin held up one limp hand. Hyde knelt by him. Then he said: "Drop them in the shit, sport. Tell me about *Teardrop*." Petrunin shook his head, the slightest but most definite of movements. Hyde glared at him, then shrugged. There was no time, now. Later, perhaps—

He dragged Petrunin's arms across his back, hefted the body—Petrunin groaned once and immediately became deadweight—across his shoulders, and rose from his squat. He staggered under the weight and the sudden assault of his own weariness, then he began climbing again, one foot slowly and carefully and numbly placed in front of the other: one, two, three, four, five, six, seven . . .

Skirting trees, resting every twenty steps, then fifteen, then twelve, as he climbed into the darkness and silence of the forest. Often, he had to drop Petrunin's unconscious body into the snow and rest—waiting until the shaking weakness left his limbs and he could return his breathing to something like normal. Then he would heft him up again, after checking the fluttering, fading pulse and the amount of blood soaking the uniform, and continue his climb.

Two hundred and forty-three . . . four, five, six . . . seven

. . . eight, nine, ten . . . eleven. . . . He dropped the body again. When he had recovered sufficiently to look around him, the fort was invisible, and the forest was lightless and quiet. Distantly, he heard the rotors of a helicopter, moving in what might have been another world or time. It hardly impinged upon his awareness, and occasioned no sense of danger in him. His body was capable of feeling only weakness, of resenting the weight that burdened it. Hyde was incapable of emotion.

Seven hundred and sixty-two, three . . . one thousand fifty, no, seventy, eighty-three . . . twelve hundred and eighty-three . . . four . . . four . . . five, six . . . three thousand forty-one . . . one, two, three. . . . six, seven . . .

Hyde lurched and fell. The trees were smaller, more straggling, upside down. Something soft was falling on his face and hands. He crawled, clawing with his hands, pushing with his feet. He touched snow, pulled at it as at a lifeline, felt rock beneath, clung to it as if on some vertical cliff face.

He drifted . . . attended . . . drifted . . . woke. His breathing was calmer, his body numb. Petrunin lay, staring upward, a few yards from him on the gentle slope. He had noticed nothing of the changing terrain. The thinner trees were stunted by altitude. Hyde turned on his back. Rock hung over him, a great shelf blacker than the sky. It frightened him before it slowly assumed the properties of safety and hiding. He listened. His fading heartbeat, his breathing, the soughing of the wind, the call of an animal. Then, silence. What was missing? What noise—

There was no noise of rotors. His hands beat the snow at his sides in applause. Of course! No helicopters. No noise. He could not consider his luck, or his direction, or why his footsteps had not been discovered. He looked at his snow-covered body, and licked his wet face. He blinked. There were no stars. Cloud?

It was snowing. He hadn't realized until a gust of wind had blown the snow under the overhang and onto his face. He raised his head. Petrunin was slowly being whitened by the snow, as with a shroud.

Shroud—

Hyde got to his knees and crawled swiftly, scrabblingly across to Petrunin, shaking him by the lapels the moment he reached him. Cough, blood, eyelids flickering . . .

"Come on, you bastard!" Hyde breathed fiercely. "Get

out of the bloody snow!" He giggled to himself as he dragged Petrunin under the overhang. He propped him against the rock, and pulled his greatcoat tightly about him, in part to hide the bloodstained shirt. Petrunin's face was white, drawn. He was dying, was already close to death.

Failure filled Hyde, as if his exhausted body was a bay that had simply waited for the tide of that emotion to engulf it. The one man who understood *Teardrop*, who had created it, was dying at his side. Bleeding to death with absolute certainty. Hyde could do nothing.

He clenched his hands into fists he could not feel, not even his nails digging into his palms. Cold or exhaustion, he could not tell. He could distinguish nothing except the sharp edges of the rock at his back and the curtain of snow falling, swaying in the gusts, moving aside, falling again. He could do nothing.

Except listen.

Petrunin was talking. His voice sounded calm, without delirium, but it was weak and interrupted by coughing. Hyde tore part of the tail of his blouse away and wiped at the man's chin after each bout of coughing. It was as if the words were mouthfuls of puréed baby food and the piece of cloth a means of removing any the baby did not swallow. Petrunin stared at the curtain of snow that must have hidden their tracks from the pursuit and was concealing them now, and spoke. It was evident he knew he was dying.

"I hate this place," Petrunin was saying. Rather, his voice spoke; it was somehow separate from the man, almost the last surviving particle of him. The tone was tired, detached, almost affected. Hyde would have dismissed it, in other circumstances, as a lack of resource in a mediocre actor. "I hate this place." It was evident that he had repeated the phrase over and over again, until it caught his companion's attention. "I hate this place. . . ."

"Yes," Hyde said quietly. It seemed sufficient, for Petrunin's strange, calm, objective voice continued:

"I hate to end like this. I know I'm dying, Hyde. I know . . ." He coughed a small, polite cough. Hyde wiped the little dribble of blood from the Russian's chin. "I am so—so angry. . . ." It was the weary anger of a corpse. Yet Hyde knew the depth of Petrunin's feelings would have wracked a healthy body. He did not look at the Russian, but merely nodded. He felt himself slipping into sleep, in and out of shallow, cold water. He shook his head and sat upright, pressing his back against the sharp creases in the rock. Petrunin's hand was waving feebly toward the swinging curtain of the snowfall. "Out there. A shithouse, Hyde. Like nothing you would know . . ." He had spoken in English as he gestured, but his voice was as expressionless as that of a translation machine. Alternately, he spoke English and Russian, at times dividing the same sentence or phrase between the two languages. "Like nothing *I've* known . . ."

Hyde knew time was slipping away as surely as Petrunin was moving toward his final evasion. Yet he could not interrogate the man, not even point his monologue in a more fruitful direction. Petrunin might simply give up, die the moment he was interrupted. Hyde had no idea how long remained. He was angry, and yet he simply listened.

"So many bodies—no rules—oh, yes, they knew what they were doing—" Hyde wiped the man's chin. The face was gray, the teeth outlined by a dark mascara of blood. Hyde looked away. Petrunin continued, thickly: "Kapustin and Nikitin and the smug, smiling, certain others—they knew what they were doing. The boy has got too smart, too big for his boots. Let's drop him right in the shit. . . ." There was a gray self-pity in the voice now, though its tone was still remote. "Let's send the smart ass to Afghanistan. It might even save us a bullet!" Hyde wiped at the man's chin, but there was only a little blood. He began to worry now that the blood would stop, that the final internal hemorrhaging would begin, drowning Petrunin before his narrative was ended. He had changed from shock into the costume of self-pity. Hyde could only wonder when he would become more confidential, ready for Hyde's voice—needing company, needing comfort.

"Two years—two years I survived it . . . God. Do you know how much I learned about killing, about slaughter, about mutilation! And the rebels taught me everything. I threw up the first time I saw a patrol of ours that had been attacked by rebels. . . ." No coughing. Nothing but a loud, choking swallow. "Napalm, burn them like rats, like dark things in corners, like lice. You can burn them all if you can find them. . . ."

"Jesus wept," Hyde breathed, but it might have been no more than impatience that prompted him. Snow flurried in a quicker wind and dusted them. Hyde tasted it, then smeared it across his face as if to wash, to freshen himself. His beard rasped. Its growth seemed more than a mere stubble—a change of identity. Petrunin, too, had suffered change. Yes, they had known what they were doing when they sent him into exile, to Kabul.

"You could burn them all if you could find them, if you had enough napalm," Petrunin repeated. "Kapustin—I can see his cunning peasant's face now—sitting on Nikitin's left, telling me I had overreached myself. . . ." His English was more regular now, its tone more clipped, educated, as if the man were reverting to some former, more urbane self as he died.

"Come on," Hyde whispered. The snow curtain swayed, flickered, swayed, fell.

"*Overreached* . . . even then, he must have been patting *Teardrop* on the head like a newly adopted son . . . even then . . . *peasant!*" His hissing voice was interrupted by coughing. Hyde almost covered his mouth with the bloodstained piece of shirt, suppressing the spillage. Hyde's lips moved silently, as if he were praying. Eventually, Petrunin's heaving chest subsided. When Hyde removed the cloth, the Russian's cheeks and chin were smeared with darker patches and stripes: an animal mask resembling the symbols that had decorated his blood-red helicopter as it hovered over the burning tribesmen. Hyde sat back, and almost at once his weariness made him close his eyes. He jolted back to wakefulness, his eyes staring at the falling snow. His boots and trousers were covered by a thin, white blanket. He heard Petrunin's teeth chattering, and knew he could not let the man wander in the landscape of his self-pity any longer.

In Russian, he said with studied deference: "They did badly by you, Comrade General—those Party hacks." The words were out almost before he could consider and weigh them; yet he knew they were right. He remembered Massinger's voice from the rear of the Mercedes, interrogating the Vienna Rezident. Something like that—a last delusion for the dying man, drugged by his wound. "You're right, sir—*peasants*, all of them."

There was a long silence, then he heard Petrunin's remote, quiet voice. "You want to know, don't you?" he said. "Hyde? You're here to find out—aren't you?"

"Yes," Hyde could not help admitting. Somehow, the proximity of Petrunin's death disarmed him.

Petrunin laughed; coughed, so that Hyde plucked up the

piece of cloth at once; continued to laugh. His amusement seemed as deep as his bitterness, as deep as his inhumanity.

"Why not?" he said finally. "Why not?" Then, after a long pause: "Why not indeed?"

Hyde glanced up at the overhang of the rock as if at the sky. His hands clenched at his sides with the relief of tension.

"It had to be your idea," he said. "So bloody devious."

"You didn't know—you found out, but you didn't guess?"

"No."

"Good. But yes, it was my idea. I created *Teardrop*. Kapustin merely stole it. After he failed to rescue me—let me drown in front of Nikitin in the juice of my failure—he simply came along and picked the whole thing up."

"Why?"

"Why? Because the time was right, that's why. Aubrey was head of the service—the time was right. For everyone in Moscow Centre, the time was right." The tone of Petrunin's voice was thin and faint, like the distant sounds of a boy treble rising from a hidden choir. Unearthly. Yet there was a satisfaction that even his closeness to death could not diminish. His scheme had ended Aubrey's career in disgrace. Petrunin's revenge was complete. The high faint tone of the voice was like a long amen. Petrunin seemed at peace.

"But—just for revenge? You created it just for Aubrey's disgrace?" Hyde's words resonated with disappointment.

"Not Aubrey—sweet, though. Anyone. The Director-General of the time . . . there were other scenarios . . . but the best, the best belonged to Aubrey. Everything fitted . . . and 1946 was a bonus. Oh, I was an avid reader of Aubrey's biography. I know more about him than anyone on earth—even himself, perhaps. Sweet . . ."

"Why? What was the *real* reason?" Hyde persisted. The curtain of snow seemed lighter now, almost transparent. Petrunin was silent for a long time. Hyde felt very cold, especially numbed in his left arm and shoulder. Then he realized that it was Petrunin's weight leaning against his side. The man's eyes were closed, his jaw was slack, and his lips hung open amid the stripes and stains of the smeared, dried blood. Hyde groaned aloud. Almost a wail. He shook the body by the shoulders, but Petrunin's eyelids did not flicker.

Then Hyde heard the distant noise of a helicopter.

• • •

Wolfgang Zimmermann felt a curious gratitude that Margaret Massinger seemed so willing to immerse herself in the sheafs of reports and surveillance digests he had given her. He was aware that the woman was somehow keeping herself in check, as if turning her past lightly page by page, an album of old photographs to which she gave hardly any of her attention—someone else's snapshots, another person's history. She seemed determined that the work should occupy her.

Zimmermann felt that Margaret understood he did not believe Aubrey to be innocent of the death of her father. He had struggled to conceal the truth of his guesses and suspicions when she questioned him about Disch, but the woman was perceptive, keen-eyed for proof of Aubrey's guilt. He did not think he had masked his intuitions sufficiently to deceive her. He did not wish to believe Aubrey guilty, but Castleford's execution as a closet Nazi helping war criminals to escape did not contradict his knowledge of Aubrey's character. He surreptitiously glanced at his watch. They had been working for almost two hours since lunch, and Massinger still had not returned. Zimmermann almost dreaded his arrival.

Margaret saw, from the corner of her eye, Zimmermann's tiny movements as he turned his wrist to check his watch. She did not look up. Paul. What had Paul learned? Was he afraid to come back? Did he *know*? She ground her teeth, certain that the noise was audible, and pressed all thought of her father into the back of her mind. Most of the time—especially whenever she reminded herself of the danger that threatened Paul—she was able to believe that concern over the truth of her father's death had become less important to her. But at moments when she was off-guard, as when Zimmermann consulted his watch, it leapt at her with unabated strength. Yet she *had* to suppress it, had to—

"I—excuse me, Wolf . . ." Zimmermann looked up and smiled. Her German was grammatical, stiff, well-learned, and recently unused. "I—I've made a list of what you could call—absences without leave during the period from February to April 'seventy-four. There are a lot of them."

She stretched forward, arm extended. Zimmermann, too, leaned toward the coffee table, and took the sheet of notepaper. He inspected it, nodding and shaking his head in turn. Then he looked up.

"I agree. It is a poor comment on the protection we offered our guests. Yes, I'm afraid there was a great deal of time unaccounted for by SIS personnel during those weeks." He sighed. "A pity—whether we can check very much of it after so much time, I'm not sure." He pondered, then asked: "Do you detect a pattern here?"

Margaret shook her head. "Some were greater offenders than others—I've starred their names. Mostly night times are unaccounted for." She smiled. "Might it mean anything?"

"Possibly. We must try."

"And you? Have you found anything?" Her gaze was direct, almost fierce. Guiltily, he glanced down at the heap of files balanced on his lap. He had kept Aubrey's material for his own examination—his movements, contacts, debriefing, subsequent debriefings of those assigned to his protection from the BfV. In it, as he had expected, he had found nothing. He shook his head gently, wisely. Margaret's features pursed at the patronizing mannerism.

"No, I have not. I did not expect to," Zimmermann said coldly in response to her expression. The woman's suspicions were suddenly irritating. "What may or may not have happened in 1946 has nothing to do with 1974, or with now," he said pedantically. "I am certain of that. There is nothing here to link Aubrey with Guillaume or anyone else."

"Do you say that only because you are in his debt, Herr Zimmermann?"

"I do not," he replied angrily. "I am in his debt, greatly so. That is true. But it is not true to make it an accusation. Do you forget that you and your husband are perhaps both in danger? *He* certainly is. The real enemy is here somewhere, in this maze, in all this old paper. Your father is dead—he has been dead for almost forty years. . . . Your husband is alive."

Margaret's face had reddened. She clenched her hands in her lap. "You don't have to lecture me, Herr Zimmermann."

"My apologies."

"I—I'm sorry. It—it's just that it's so *hard* to help the man who might have killed my father!"

"Then help your husband!"

"Very well! What do you want me to do?"

Zimmermann stood up, clutching the sheaf of files in both hands. He threw them onto the sofa beside her. "Here! You think that man killed your father—*you* find something against him. I can't! The reason I can't is that there is nothing to find." Zimmermann was visibly trembling as he stood in front of her. She disregarded the files on Aubrey.

"I'm sorry. I'll carry on with—with my own work, here."

"As you wish," Zimmermann observed coldly, turning away from her and walking to the window. The snow had stopped, but more threatened from the heavy sky. Zimmermann was angry with himself for losing his temper. Margaret Massinger was under a great strain.

He almost turned to apologize, but could not. Better to leave her, for the moment, to recover herself. He heard her shuffling through papers, and knew that she would not now look, even glance, at the Aubrey material. In a moment, he should get back to it.

Where was Massinger?

He prevented himself from looking once more at his watch. It was already beginning to get dark outside. The barges were like long, black slugs on the gray path of the Rhine. No, there was one with washing hung out even in this dreary, freezing weather, a line of it like naval signals of greeting or distress.

Where was Massinger?

Nerves took hold of Zimmermann, unformed but gathering fears. He should have provided the man with an escort, with protection.

Margaret Massinger was speaking.

"What?" he asked abruptly.

"I didn't realize that Andrew Babbington was in Bonn during that period," she repeated, undisturbed by his tone.

"Oh. Yes, he headed the team of interrogating officers that MI 5 sent over, a few days after Guillaume was arrested," Zimmermann replied absently, watching the barge, flying its signals of colorful washing, move upriver toward the Kennedybrücke.

"No, he was here before that," Margaret continued. "Some internal investigation in the Chancery section of the British embassy—misappropriation of funds, it says here."

Zimmermann turned from the window. "That is not unusual. . . ." he began with heavy humor.

The door opened, and Paul appeared.

"Well?" Margaret asked breathlessly almost at once. Zimmermann saw the certainty on Massinger's face, and quailed inwardly. Massinger believed in Aubrey's guilt, that much was evident. Just as it was evident he wished to conceal that conviction from his wife. "What did you find out?" she asked ominously.

Massinger laid his raincoat across the back of a chair and sat beside her. The man seemed to have no masks left; Zimmermann could see that any effort at deception would fail miserably.

"It's no more than speculation," he began.

"What is?" Margaret snapped.

"Your father. It's a crazy, wild guess. Aubrey was wrong, I'm certain of it. . . ."

"*What?*" Her tone was icy.

Zimmermann turned once more to the window. The barge with its hoisted washing was slipping beneath the Kennedybrücke now, bereft of color. No more than another black slug on gray. It had begun to snow once more. He remembered that Massinger's gray hair had sparkled with wetness when he came through the door. Zimmermann wished to excuse himself; he was inwardly hunched against Massinger's reply. It was nonsense that it might not have been a fate deserved. If true, Aubrey had *known*, would have been *sure*.

"No!" Margaret almost screamed. "No, no, no, *no!*" The stain was too great, the smear. What Zimmermann had divined from his own conversation with Disch had become clear to Massinger, too. Perhaps Disch himself, on reflection, had also come to believe it. Now, Margaret Massinger was trying to reject the suspicion they all shared. Not that—above all, not *that* . . . Her father could not be at one with the mass murderers of the six million, the maniacs, the slaughterers, the misfits, the thugs and torturers—not *them!* Zimmermann, as a German, could not but resent the horror in her voice, even as he sympathized with her.

She was sobbing now; he was murmuring useless comforts, having caused her distress. Zimmermann had hoped Disch might have concealed what he suspected, but had not believed he would.

"No, no, no, no . . ." she was murmuring.

Stop, he thought. Stop it. It was useless to suspect, more pointless to believe, most futile to know. It was almost forty years ago. She had to shake it off. Both of them had to exorcise her father's ghost. It might be a matter of life and death. Theirs . . .

Snow, snail tracks once more on the window, long, slow barges, the steely river. The barge with the washing, and her words at that point, just before the barge slipped out of sight beneath and beyond the bridge . . .

Babbington. Sir Andrew Babbington. The Director-General of MI 5.

Read the will, he thought. When the body is discovered in the library and the rich old lady is pronounced murdered, read the will! Who has the most to gain? Who benefits? Who becomes rich?

He smiled. Margaret's sobs and the soft, coaxing words of her husband no longer impinged upon him. He felt only an impatience to study the files.

Babbington. Read the will, Inspector, read the will. . . .

Sir Kenneth Aubrey could think of nothing other than the destruction of the journal in Clara Elsenreith's possession. Its continued existence was frightening and painful to him, but all other thought frightened and pained him more. Beyond the destruction of his confession to Castleford's murder lay nothing. An empty landscape. Perhaps he could hide with Clara for days, even weeks. After that, however, there was nothing. Only his disappearance, an act of willed disguise, anonymity, denial of his former self. He would have to find somewhere to skulk as *Herr Jones*, or *Monsieur Smith* or *Signor Smith* or *Señor Jones* for the rest of his life. He could never be Kenneth Aubrey again.

One of the Frenchmen who shared his compartment had removed his shoes and stretched his legs. His socks smelled in the overwarm, dry atmosphere. The sleeping child in the farthest corner of the compartment murmured, shifted. Her mother adjusted her arms about her. The express was less than an hour from Strasbourg. He would be in Vienna the following day.

The French newspapers carried nothing concerning his disappearance from England. Evidently, it had not been made public. There were stories, of course—peculiar and witty Gallic cruelties regarding himself, British Intelligence, Britain itself. But nothing of his current whereabouts. The secrecy did not comfort him. Instead, he saw it as a signpost on the road toward his inevitable disappearance into another identity. Already, the press had lost sight of him, and that was only the beginning. Unlike the traitors, for him there wasn't even a Moscow where he could arrive in safety and remain himself.

All he was able to do was to destroy the written evidence

of his guilt. There was nothing more to hope for. The early edition of *France-Soir*, which he had bought in Paris, lay still opened on his lap. Mitterand was in London to see the PM concerning the EEC budget—again. He could read the headline and the caption to the photograph in the brief, fleeting lights of a country station. The tired familiarity of the wrangle hurt with a physical sensation of pain in his chest. He, Kenneth Aubrey, might have been calling to brief the PM not an hour after the talks with Mitterand had ended. Or the next day, or the day after that . . .

Now, he would never do that again.

He did not love power. No, he resisted that insinuating accusation that popped out of the darkness at the back of his mind. No. But it had been forty-five years since he had begun to serve his country, since he had begun to be the person he thought himself to be. Now, he had to relinquish that country, that person.

The express rattled over points, swayed, then clicked on into the winter night. The lights of another country station. A railway employee—some guard or porter or stationmaster or signalman—watched the train pass. Aubrey recognized that he might become that anonymous man past whom the world would rush and disappear into the distance.

Tears pricked his tired eyes. Sleep would not come. The odor of the Frenchman's socks mingled with that of half-melted sweets from the opposite corner of the compartment.

Petrunin's eyes opened. They seemed, impossibly, to fall open rather than be revealed by the raising of the eyelids. The man's face was drawn and gray, but the only visible blood on his face was old and dry. Hyde's breath escaped in a ragged, elongated moan of relief. The noise of the helicopter had returned and then had faded once more as he had sat hunched against the man he thought was dead, his head listening for some betraying heartbeat against the wetness of Petrunin's blouse. It had almost stopped snowing. Hyde could see the black sticks of the nearest stunted trees against the whiteness of the ground. But Petrunin was alive. Just.

"Why?" Hyde said at once, seeing that the Russian's eyes remained unfocused, inward staring. "Why? What was the reason for it?"

Petrunin was silent for a long time. The wind whispered,

puffing snow under the lee of the overhang. Hyde was numb with cold. Then the Russian muttered in the remote voice that had become familiar to Hyde: "I don't want to be remembered as the butcher of Kabul." It was uninflected, passionless yet full of self-pity. Hyde had not reached the place where what remained of Petrunin had retreated. "I don't want to be remembered as the butcher of Kabul," Petrunin repeated exactly. Hyde did not think it was even a nickname he had been given. He was describing the state of his self-knowledge.

"*Why?*" Hyde shouted. "Why did you need *Teardrop?*"

"I was being used, even then," Petrunin said, disconcerting Hyde. "In 1941, during the nine hundred days . . ." His voice trailed off. Hyde had no idea what he meant. "Even then, scouting, carrying messages. I was no more than a boy—thirteen when the war began. They've had me in their pockets since I was thirteen. Since Leningrad . . ."

Hyde was chilled by this glimpse into Petrunin's past. As little more than a boy, he had experienced the privations and terrors of the German siege of Leningrad, which had lasted nine hundred days.

"Yes," he said.

"In their pockets. Their man, their *thing* . . ."

"But—*why?*"

Something reminded Hyde to attend to the reality beyond the tiny huddle of himself and Petrunin. Silence, except for the quiet soughing of the wind. The snow was still falling, but more lightly. He could not hear the helicopter's rotors.

Petrunin did not answer his question. Instead, his cold, remote voice said: "Leningrad . . ." It was a sigh. Its meaning had become a talisman for Petrunin, which perhaps protected him against memories of the more recent past. Hyde felt himself totally identified with the Russian, a fellow conspirator in a world of enemies. The identification was so close that Hyde could not envisage the border or foresee his escape.

"Why?" he asked again softly and without hope of any reply.

"Why?" Petrunin repeated. "Why?" He spoke in English once more, a sharper, more amused tone in his voice. "To place him. To place our man at the apex, the pinnacle, whenever we wished. When the time . . ." A slight cough interrupted Petrunin. His eyes closed as if to eradicate pain. Hyde looked at him. Only minutes now. Then Petrunin seemed to gather a new, urgent strength. "The time was right," he announced. "Sir William was the Chairman of JIC, he had your Prime Minister's ear. Your new service, combining intelligence and security, could be set up *now*! The time was right . . . and sweet . . ." He coughed, then added: "For our man . . ."

Hyde heard only that last phrase, as Petrunin's voice faded like a poor radio signal.

Their man. Hyde felt himself shivering uncontrollably. The answer was a moment, one more sentence away, and the realization of its proximity made him more sharply aware of his surroundings and his situation. Once he had the knowledge, he had to stay alive, get out—

"Who?" he asked, and before he received an answer he had pressed his palm against Petrunin's mouth. The Russian's eyes widened. Hyde could not be certain the Russian could see the soldier moving slowly across the snow, forty yards from them, clothed in winter combat camouflage, Kalashnikov carried across his chest, snowshoes lifting and clumping and flattening the snow.

Hyde felt Petrunin's lips moving against the cold flesh of his palm. It might have been the name of the traitor; it might have been a protest at being gagged. It might have been some last, futile epithet. Hyde clamped his hand more firmly over Petrunin's mouth as the soldier continued to pass across their field of vision.

11
Arriving

Two more soldiers came out of the stunted trees, bobbing into view as they climbed the last of the shallow slope. Both of them, rifles angled across their white-clad chests, appeared to be walking straight toward Hyde and Petrunin, able to make out their huddled shapes beneath the overhang. Petrunin's body slumped against Hyde once more, almost into an embrace, and Hyde knew the man was still alive because his lips kept murmuring soundlessly against his palm. His hand was warmed by the faint breathing of the Russian, but it was a fitful breeze, threatening to disappear each time it tickled his palm.

The first soldier passed out of sight and his two companions moved after him. Their exaggerated steps sifted and fluffed the light snow. There was no sound of any helicopter. Petrunin was shivering against him. Ten seconds, fifteen, twenty, a minute. Time elongated. Hyde wanted to cry out, to scream as the nerves tautened all over his body, as if the cold had left him cramped and maddened with pins and needles. A minute and a half . . .

They stopped, casting about. Hyde was convinced that he could see, with vivid clarity, the slight depressions left by his labored footsteps in the snow. He thought he could make out the shallow trough where he had slithered, dragging the Russian, toward the overhang. It must be clear to the soldiers.

They moved off, as if half afraid of being left too far behind their companion. Hyde's breathing rushed in his ears. He could hear his heart, just feel Petrunin's shallow, irregular breathing. Out of sight, out of sight. Go on, *go on.* . . .

Another few yards, yes, three, two, another step . . .

They were gone. He heard one of them call after the first soldier. He heard the quickening slither of their snowshoes. Now, the snow beyond the overhang looked smooth and un-dimpled except where they had walked. Gently, as if in apology, Hyde removed his hand from Petrunin's mouth. The lips were still working soundlessly, not so much searching for words as for an expression—perhaps a smile.

"Your man?" Hyde asked. "Who is he?"

"Babbington," Petrunin replied after the smallest hesitation. His lips found something like acceptance, then the name, finally a smile. "Babbington."

"Christ—then it's worked!"

"Of course." The voice was remote again, but in a superior, Olympian manner. "Of course."

"Jesus-bloody-Christ," Hyde breathed. "*Him?*"

"Him."

"When—how long, for Christ's sake?"

Petrunin waved his hand dismissively, weakly, as if he considered Hyde was wasting the little time left with the wrong questions. "A long story," he murmured. "It always is. Now—what will you do?"

Hyde rubbed his face. "God knows."

Petrunin cackled, and coughed. No blood, but his head lolled as if his body were sinking in something. Or filling. His whole form lolled. Ballast shifting, Hyde thought, then: *Nothing . . . I don't have . . . not even paper, no tape, no record, nothing . . .*

It was as if the Russian could read his thoughts. "You see?" he asked. "You have no proof. You have nothing. You cannot even escape, I think . . ." He leaned back, as if trying to sink into the rock. His face was colorless; his eyes, unfocused, studied the rock above their heads.

"Then *help* me," Hyde replied desperately. "Help me to screw the bastards. Help me screw the people who want you dead—who've already done for you." He leaned his head toward Petrunin until their faces almost touched. He could feel no breath from the Russian warming his cheek. "Help me. They've killed you. Help me spoil their bloody game."

"How?" Petrunin asked, and then the realization of what Hyde had said gripped him. He was afraid. Even knowing, he had not wished to hear it pronounced. Hyde had sentenced him. "No—" he spluttered. Blood poured from his lips, staining his chin, staining Hyde. It felt warm, ugly, and final. Hyde gripped the Russian's arms, almost hugging him like a lover.

"Come on, you clever, clever bastard—where's the proof? Tell me where the proof is and I'll spoil their fucking game for them. Come on. . . ." He was holding Petrunin now, the man's head against him, mouth pressed to Hyde's ear. Wet. His chin was resting on Hyde's shoulder. "Come *on*," the Australian whispered urgently, afraid of time unraveling utterly in the next few moments. Only minutes now. Less perhaps . . .

"It's all on computer—you couldn't get hold of it . . . only I could do that, from—from inside a Soviet Embassy. . . ." Hyde groaned. He wanted to push Petrunin's body away from him in protest, but some instinct made him hold on. Or perhaps it was merely sympathy. Petrunin, unnoticing and undeterred, continued to murmur against Hyde's ear. His lips were frothily wet. Hyde shuddered. His stomach felt hollow with loathing and disappointment.

Babbington was unassailable—he *was* British Intelligence, just as Aubrey had been. Hyde had nothing. In itself, without proof, the knowledge was worthless, futile. Babbington was the man in the high castle. Impenetrable. Petrunin continued, as if with some litany of confession. It was evident, in his remote and inhuman whisper, that he was mocking Hyde even as he wished him to know and to be able to do something. Revenge and amusement.

"Access is strictly limited," he said. "You would have to be me to get it. Understand—understand? Only *I* can get hold of it—you would have to be *me*! Understand?"

"Yes." Hyde did not understand.

"I—I have it on file, hidden in the computer. I saw the advantage of having an, an, an insurance policy. . . . I suborned a programmer to create a secret file, stored under their very noses. Everything's in it—dirt, operations, even your precious *Teardrop*—my precious *Teardrop*. Do you understand me?"

"Yes." Hyde still did not understand. He simply accepted that he must listen to Petrunin until he could speak no more. Hold the man until he felt the final slump of his body into bonelessness.

"Access it from any remote terminal linked to Moscow

Centre . . . any embassy abroad or in the Eastern bloc. . . . If you knew each of the passwords, you could find it. Only I know them—only me. . . ." He paused, his body shifted violently, as if some last part of his human cargo had shifted in a storm. He sat more upright, and his face appeared haunted. He could see the end now, the need to race his own collapsing body. "I killed the programmer, of course, for security— before they sent me *here*. It was to be my insurance, even my ticket to the West. I would have been the most valuable defector on earth, with just a computer cassette. . . ." His voice was lower now, but quicker, urgent.

"Listen to me, listen . . . you must access Assignment Histories in the Personnel Files of the computer . . . access my file. . . ." He paused, his eyes flickered open and closed against Hyde's cheek, as if he were trying to focus his gaze. Or remember. Then he said: "There are passwords to remember before that. Listen. Listen . . . access to the Main Menu is by the password K-2-U-7, stroke, R-S-4-K. Repeat it to me!" Hyde did so, then to himself once more. Yes. "To Personnel, access is by another password, letters and numbers again . . . C-7-3-5, stroke, D-W, stroke, P-R-X. . . . Repeat that. . . ." Petrunin sighed with what might have been exhaustion, or satisfaction, as Hyde repeated the password. "Good, good . . ." Petrunin's hand patted against Hyde's shoulder with the force of falling snow. "Assignment Histories has the password White Nights, White . . . *Russian*, White Bear, without a break. . . . After that, you request *my* assignment history. Then—then use my, last three postings, in reverse order—reverse order, without a break, to access the secret file. You, you—a poem appears next—it looks like a corrupted data file, it's meant to, put people off . . . *don't cancel it!* Let it run, all fourteen lines . . . to a girl I once knew . . . then, out comes *everything*—everything. . . ."

He paused, expecting Hyde to reply. Hyde did not understand anything beyond the urgency of the communication. Yet he memorized it. Like a recorder, he would be able to reproduce the information, if requested. If he ever talked to someone who understood.

"There is—is a shortcut to *Teardrop* . . . shortcuts to everything . . . wouldn't have much time, perhaps, to cut and run . . . had to be sure I could get at the juiciest . . . *Teardrop* espec—ially . . . *shortcut!*" He cried out, as if he saw an enemy approaching. Hyde flinched, almost turning to check his back. Petrunin began coughing. Hyde's neck and cheek were wet, slimy. "No, *no!*"

"Shortcut—" Hyde prompted, shaking Petrunin's arms lightly.

Petrunin's right hand was patting Hyde's shoulderblade furiously, emphasizing words that the Australian could not hear. Then his hands scrabbled for a fingerhold on Hyde's sheepskin jacket as if clinging at the edge of an abyss. His voice bubbled.

"Shortcut . . . short . . . cut . . . shor . . . cu—t . . ."

"Yes, yes!"

Petrunin's body slumped against Hyde, boneless and then rigid almost at once. As if he had been dead for hours, frozen stiff. Hyde pressed him back against the rock. His mouth was still daubed with blood, his chin darkly painted. Smears on his cheeks and neck. His forehead was white and dead. His hands were still shaped into claws.

Powerless. His information was as dead as Petrunin. Every Soviet embassy, anywhere in the world. The only places to have access to the main computer system in Moscow Centre. It was hopeless. Pointless and hopeless. He was almost pleased that Petrunin was dead, that the effort had shortened his life, even if only by minutes.

Yet he felt a curious reluctance to release the body, as if his chilled hands had somehow become frozen to the material of Petrunin's greatcoat. The Russian stared lifelessly at him, and past him at the still-falling snow and the stunted trees. Then Hyde removed his hands and the body slid a little sideways, to loll sloppily like a forgotten toy against the rock. Hyde breathed deeply a number of times, then crawled out from beneath the overhang. The wind and snow against his face were fresh rather than icy. He felt himself waking from a light trance, disoriented and suddenly fearful of this strange place. He remained on his hands and knees, like a dog sniffing the air. He could not hear the soldiers, but there was a distant noise of helicopter rotors, an indistinct buzzing like that of a television left on after the last program had finished.

Instinct rescued him before noises alerted him. Instinct, or memory. He remembered what had been called out by the last of the three soldiers who had passed their hiding place. Something about distance, about the limit of their patrol, about the time and about reporting in . . .

He shook his head but could not recall the words. His subconscious mind, however, had remarked a sense of limit, or *return*. . . .

They would be returning—

Hyde scrambled to his feet. Dying images of sympathy for Petrunin faded in his mind. The man who wanted to bomb and burn his way back to favor in Moscow, the man who had had to face the wild animal in himself, the shadow of the urbane, intelligent, overproud man. He began to move on sluggish, almost-giving-way, cramped limbs. He blundered like a drunk, staggered, then began to achieve locomotion. The details of Petrunin's description of *Teardrop* became unimportant the moment he heard the first voice—a call for someone to hurry, which almost at once became a yell of surprise and command and delight. He heard the scratch of a transmitter being switched on, then a gabble of Russian as his position was relayed. He ran through the deep snow at the edge of the clearing, laboring almost at once as the slope steepened above the overhang. Sounds came to him, the cry of discovery, the yell of orders to pursue, the more distant and inhuman noise of a reply from the R/T the first soldier was using. He was bent almost double, knees coming up beneath his chin, hands jabbing down into the soft snow at every step to stabilize his leaden charge up the slope. Dwarf trees crowded around him, as if he were scuttling through a toy forest. Snow flew as he brushed whippy branches; his face stung from their recoil. He became aware of the gun in his belt. More noises from behind, the half-shouts, the voices straining with bodily effort. They were climbing after him.

He was perhaps four or five miles from the border. He paused, his breath smoking around him, mouth open like that of an exhausted dog, and looked up. The mountain seemed to go on forever, white with the gray creases of bare ledges and steep cliff faces. He could not make out the peak or the fold near the peak where they had crossed from the valley to come down to the fort. The snow seemed invested with something of the approaching dawn's grayness. The noise of rotors seemed louder.

The first bullet ripped through low, closely packed branches near his head. He scrabbled away on all fours, then leaned again into his blundering run. The snow was deep and loose and he floundered on, his feet and legs numb, his chest heaving, pressed by a tightening steel band. Two more shots, both wide. Fear made him aware of every inch of flesh on his back and buttocks, even though he did not know whether they wanted him alive.

He turned to his right, running like a fairground target along a humped ridge which climbed toward a shoulder of the mountain. Underneath the snow, Mohammed Jan had assured him, were tracks, Pathan routes. Hyde knew he was following the route they had taken when they had crossed into Afghanistan, but there was no track. He could not believe in a track, did not consciously choose his path. Some detailed, trained memory guided him, prompted his changes of course, his upward movement. More shots, again wide. He heard the bullets whine in the air, skip off the bare cliff face twenty yards from him. He raised his body slightly, arms akimbo for balance. It was as if he were running across a tightrope of snow. On either side of the ridge, the mountain fell away—forty feet or more to his left, thousands of feet to his right. He wobbled forward, terrified of slowing, of losing his balance.

He was climbing again, the ridge broadening like a flying buttress at its point of closure with the cathedral. He spurred his numb, leaden legs to more effort. One, two, three, four, climbing more deeply now, he remembered this section, the ridge and beyond it the narrow path across the cliff face, then a winding, slow climb up to the fold in the mountain that concealed the entrance to the long, narrow valley where Petrunin had burned the Pathans to death.

Ten, eleven, twelve . . .

His left leg blundered deeply into the snow, up to his groin. His right leg bent, balanced him, and he thrust with it, toppling himself to his left, over the edge of the ridge, the snow pouring like a waterfall with him as he fell, his head spinning—stars, snow, grayness, snow, snow in his eyes and nostrils, in every opening and crack in his clothing. He tried to reach for balance, then like a vessel out of control he struck against a rock submerged in snow and lay winded, consciousness coming and going, his body incapable of further effort.

He paused in the secret darkness on the narrow staircase, and wondered whether the ghost of the old maiden aunt had observed his arrival. Not even a maiden aunt, he reminded himself. At the top of the staircase was an apartment that had belonged to a reclusive, aged spinster without living family.

She had died entirely alone. Her death had been unmourned, even unrecorded. Her property had never been sold. The cat and the canaries, of course, had been disposed of. The apartment provided an ideal meeting place, a safe house. On the ground floor were the offices of a small and unsuccessful importer of plastic novelties from the Far East for inclusion in Christmas crackers. A KGB cover.

Already, he could smell the mustiness of the little-used apartment reaching down the stairs toward him. Mothballs, the long-ago urinations of successive cat companions, the smell of unchanged and uncleaned bird cages, the smell of mothballs in old tweed skirts and out-of-date dresses and rubbed-bare, patchy fur coats. Yet he waited on the stairs. Upstairs, his contact would be waiting. It was not that he was reluctant to begin the meeting. Far from it. Pausing for a moment between the noise of traffic from the street outside and the pervading old-maid scents from above, Babbington was confident. Treachery was like an old, wounded elephant. Threatened, it had to blunder to its own defense, unable to move quickly or decisively. The cutouts, the drops, the contacts, the mailboxes, all the subtle means of contact, prevented speed and decisiveness. Security—the security designed to protect him—was a handicap when speed was required. Yet it needed only locomotion—a few moments for the elephant to gather its strength in order to make its enemies instead of itself seem puny and wounded. There had been shock delay, of course.

And the fact that Petrunin's scheme had been too clever. He had warned them about that. Dazzlingly clever. Aubrey, solitary as he was, had never lacked friends, willing hands. Which had brought the Massingers into the game, and Hyde and Shelley, and now Zimmermann.

And yet, it had taken the work of only a few hours—would he admit to the sweaty, uncertain, tense nature of those hours, now that he was safe again? Perhaps yes, just a little unnerving, but only a few hours to right the balance, to restore the fortunes of the board.

Tracing the Massingers had been a KGB priority—he'd had to let them take on the task because of that damned need for *secrecy*! Anger coursed. He desired the exercise of his power. He could crush them easily, all of them, and he would never be threatened again! But he could not, however much they enraged him. He dare not make any overt move against the Massingers, Shelley, this Elsenreith woman. Not yet, at least. Soon, but not yet. The KGB had found the Massingers in Bonn. And had also found the Elsenreith woman. Did she know the truth of Castleford's murder? That old murder, that unpicked-up stitch that might yet unravel the whole of *Teardrop*. Now that he knew the whereabouts of Clara Elsenreith, he knew also that the Massingers would go to her. Thank God they'd found her! Zimmermann had traced the woman, too. Massinger would soon possess the information. So . . . Babbington's hand clenched slowly into a fist . . . into the trap. Vienna Station was his; he could use them. Massinger and his wife, if he read Massinger's stupid American character aright, would go to the woman to seek the truth about Robert Castleford's demise. They would walk into a neat and certain trap: the conclusion of their inquiries. Full stop. *Period*, as Massinger might put it.

Babbington smiled to himself in the darkness. The wallpaper was old, pregnant in a dozen places with damp and time. Zimmermann would hold back so long as one frightened him sufficiently. And Aubrey—yes, Aubrey, too, might make for Vienna, for that woman with whom he had once been involved. . . .

Babbington shook his head. That was, perhaps, too optimistic a view. Whatever, Aubrey would be found soon—

And silenced.

It would be well, all manner of things would be well, just so long as he acted quickly. And he had done so.

He looked up toward the head of the stairs, the landing, and the door into the musty passageway of the apartment. Oleg would be there, the irritating portable cassette player in his lap, narrow headphones at his ears, passing the time with Mahler and modern jazz while he awaited his arrival. A man sitting in self-contained silence in a barely furnished room in need of decoration.

Oleg. His contact, for many years. A London embassy chauffeur. Now, temporarily fulfilling the role of the Rezident. Pavel Koslov had been relieved of his responsibilities, though he remained in London to prevent a report of his return to Moscow arousing *any* kind of interest. Pavel, who had precipitately ordered the death of Massinger, convincing that self-righteous humbug that Aubrey was innocent after all. Just when Catherine Dawson had put him off the scent for good! Babbington's chest tightened with angry tension. Pavel had all but ruined everything—

Fortunately, he was now out of the game. Oleg was in command, and Oleg would instruct Moscow Centre to stand back on this for two good reasons. First, they must not compromise or even expose him by violent response. And second, Oleg would regard it as a test. Could Babbington cope with this emergency? Now their man possessed the power, could he use it to protect himself?

Babbington again smiled to himself, moving one or two steps nearer the head of the staircase. Moscow Centre would be nothing if not pragmatic. Even he could be risked in order to test his quality. Well, he'd done it. This little crisis, just a hiccup, would last no more than another twenty-four hours —especially if they killed Petrunin and Hyde in Afghanistan, as should have been done with Petrunin in the first place.

He'd liked Tamas Petrunin when he had been London Rezident. *He* was the sort of KGB staff officer one could admire, admit as an equal in mind and taste and dedication. Unlike the peasant Kapustin. Nevertheless, sentiment would not have interfered. The moment *Teardrop* was activated, that should have been the end of it. No dropped clues, no loose threads. Petrunin would have disappeared.

Babbington reached the head of the staircase and looked down. There were muted noises from the traffic outside, and a ratlike scrabbling from some ground floor storeroom behind the importer's offices. Otherwise, silence. All would be well. There was no real emergency. Only individual stings, not a swarm. Pieces of little value to be removed from the board—a small matter with the power he now possessed.

But softly, softly. Oleg would have to be made to understand—the thugs who issued his orders would have to be made to understand—that *time* was required. On this side of the Curtain, gangsterism was out of the question. He couldn't simply burn Shelley and his family in their home, have the Massingers run their car over a cliff, have Zimmermann fall under a train. However sweet it all might be, it would create suspicion. And to him, suspicion might be mortal, like the bite of a snake. Time was needed. Oleg would understand that. Once sufficient time had passed, and he was confirmed in his innocence and his authority, then he would rid himself of all of them.

Poor stupid Moscow Centre. They believed him satisfied now, with his secret power his achievement of the pinnacle, but they had never understood or concerned themselves with his motives. Greed, the ache for power, the *amusement* of secrecy, money, discontentment—those things they understood. But not him.

He had joined them in the wake of Suez. In 1956. They assumed, as they always did when ideology and money were not involved—as they were not in his case—that power was the answer. The secret, convoluted, game-playing power that Philby and Blunt and the others had enjoyed, whatever their ideological protestations. Their gratification was not his. His was subtler, more refined.

The warmth of self-congratulation spread through his strong frame. He could indulge it, keep Oleg waiting a moment longer.

It was to avoid being powerful in a third-rate way. To avoid being no more than a secret, powerful cog in the machinery of a third-rate world power. He despised the pinnacle of secret power on a mountaintop where those who ruled felt the appropriate and glorious last move in the Great Game was the reinvasion of the Falkland Islands. The brouhaha of that incident had nauseated him—even made him shiver with embarrassment now, as he stood at the head of the stairs—and left him more than ever confirmed in his chosen secret path.

He might never have changed allegiances had he been born a century earlier. England would then have been able to offer him everything he wanted. He would have been vital, *crucial*, to a first-rate power, to *the* world power. . . .

In the fifties, he could not turn to America—had they been the enemy in whose ranks he could have secretly enlisted, he would have done so—and thus he had turned East, to Moscow. To the Soviet Union, to the KGB, he was as important as Kapustin, as important as the Chairman, almost as important as First Secretary Nikitin. For that secret pinnacle, for that value to be placed upon him, he had waited for almost thirty years. For that he had worked, for that he had made his original choice. He was one of the most important figures in the hierarchy of a superpower. England, now bankrupt and laughable as she was, proved every day to his immense satisfaction that he had chosen wisely.

He crossed the narrow, linoleumed landing almost blithely, and opened the door. The musty passageway was unlit, but there was a dim light from the lounge beyond. Yes, Oleg would be sitting there with his silly little headphones on, his foot perhaps tapping in rhythm.

Babbington smiled. Twenty-four hours, no more than that. That is what Oleg would want to hear, and that is what Babbington felt himself able to guarantee.

"Babbington played an uncharacteristically minor role in the ensuing investigations. His absences, his pattern of behavior—they could be regarded as suspicious with ease, my dear fellow."

Zimmermann watched Massinger carefully slicing at his portion of *apfelstrudel* with a small pastry fork. The American deliberately would not look up, nor would his wife. It was infuriating. Even their mutual choice of the homely German dessert seemed like a species of insult.

The dining room of the Königshof was almost deserted. They were some of the last guests enjoying—no, not that—*enduring* a late supper. Behind them, the river glittered with lights reflected from both banks of the Rhine. Navigation lights moved on the river apparently without solid forms beneath them. Rain pattered against the huge windows.

When Massinger did not reply, Zimmermann pursued: "I have made a great many telephone calls this evening, since I left you." He had rushed, in an unseemly way, from the hothouse of that hotel room, escaping the tense, violent emotions sparking between the American and his wife. He had plunged into the pursuit of his intuitions, regarding Babbington as into a cold, refreshing swimming pool. Babbington had indulged a brief affair with a married woman during his residence in Bonn in '74; it was the perfect cover, if it was a cover. "There is a woman in prison in Cologne. . . ."

Massinger looked up. His eyes were abstracted, hardly focused. "What?" was all he said.

Margaret Massinger continued to devote her attention to her dessert, picking at it without appetite. Zimmermann realized that the woman was determined. For her, there were no more decisions. They had all been made. Zimmermann cursed himself once more for giving them the address of Clara Elsenreith as a peace offering when he returned to the Königshof to join them for supper. The instant, greedy lights in their eyes had shocked him. They hardly wished to hear his assurances that the KGB probably had no idea of her whereabouts, hardly showed interest in the old files that had contained her name, were evidently impatient with his recital of the cold trail followed by some of his enthusiastic young men. Now the Massingers knew where Clara Elsenreith was, and wished to go to her. Thus, in this conversation he was no more than a boring pedagogue on the last day of the term, insisting on unremitting study while the sun shone outside and vacation stretched ahead.

"Prison. She was arrested two years ago, on charges arising from . . . for war crimes. She still has not been brought to trial. I intend to see her. She was the secretary assigned to Babbington during his residence here. He used her apartment for—his assignations, you see." Zimmermann spoke without pause or interruption, as if speed and emphasis would attract their deeper attention.

Massinger stared with little interest across the table. Margaret, Zimmermann could tell, was alert but stubbornly refusing to accept the importance of the subject he had broached.

"What do you expect to learn?"

"The truth of Babbington's story—what else?" Zimmermann snapped. He dabbed his lips with his napkin, his own dessert of cheesecake finished.

"You think Babbington's the man?"

"I don't think, I merely suspect."

"But that's nonsense!" Massinger burst out, as if all that had been said to him had only just impinged on his reason. "That's too fantastic to be true."

Margaret looked up, shaking her head. "The idea of Andrew being a traitor is ridiculous," she said calmly, with utter, dismissive certainty. "Impossible," she added, as she saw his expression change to one of anger.

Zimmermann remembered the murmured promises, over and over repeated, that the American had made to this woman. Now, he realized how much it blinded and determined them. Tomorrow, they would travel to Vienna to see Clara Elsenreith.

Zimmermann had sent no one, had not spoken to the woman himself. It was cowardice, he acknowledged. He did not wish to know.

But they did. More than anything. More than safety,

more than friendship, more than the future, they had to know. Who killed Castleford, and why.

Zimmermann understood the woman. She was behind it. Her whole being rejected the idea that her father could have been, might have been, was ever a Nazi. To disprove that monstrous fiction, she had to know from Clara that, if he was killed by Aubrey, it was a crime of passion. That she would accept, her father's death as an adulterer. But never a Nazi, not one of the beasts of the past.

It was hopeless. He would never convince them.

"Will you promise me to come back—once you have spoken with Frau Elsenreith—and help me?" he pleaded.

Even now they hesitated, as if they could not see that far ahead. Cautious investors in an uncertain future, machines programmed for one simple, immediate task. It was as if they mutually assumed everything would be over, ended, once they knew the truth of Berlin in 1946. He sighed inwardly. Why could they not *see*?

"We'll—yes, but we can't promise until we—we've been to Vienna," Massinger replied lamely after a long, embarrassing silence. Margaret touched his hand, as if to strengthen a flagging resolve.

God, Zimmermann thought, *God in Heaven!*

"I see," he said coldly, rebuffing them. He laid his napkin on the table. He wished to be cruel, and added: "Remember you are known in Vienna. Be careful. Employ your old *professional* instincts, my friend." He stood up, nodded a stiff little bow toward Margaret, who remained silent, then announced: "I shall go to Cologne at once. I am concerned to hear this woman's story. Good night—and good luck."

Massinger made as if to rise. Zimmermann waved him back onto his chair, and left with a firm military step.

The snow in his mouth and nostrils was choking him. His eyes were caked with snow and he was blind. He brushed at them, opened them, coughing out the snow and sneezing. He sat up quickly to clear his nose by violent blowing. He was white from head to foot, encrusted with snow.

The soldier was standing over him, Kalashnikov pointed toward the middle of Hyde's form. The Australian looked up, searching the pale young face for nerves, for apprehension and doubt and the need for prompt support. He found everything he sought, and rolled over slowly, clutching his right arm with his left, groaning.

"Stay still," the young soldier warned. Hyde continued to roll slowly until his right arm was masked by his body. Melted snow trickled down his back like a trail of fear. His chest and stomach were icy with the melted snow he had swallowed. He reached carefully behind him and drew the Makarov automatic that had once, long ago, belonged to the young lieutenant he had killed. He sat up, gun masked by his thigh, then shot the Russian soldier twice, once in the stomach, bringing his head forward, then a second time through the forehead, just above the left eye. The Russian's body sprang away from him, as if in surprise at some electric shock, and lay unmoving in the snow.

He had killed the man without calculation. He looked up the furrow of disturbed snow that indicated where he had stumbled and fallen. The flying buttress of the ridge stretched up and away from him and was empty of other troops. They'd split up, then, probably on orders from the nearest helicopter; he could hear one clattering up the side of the mountain, still well below his own altitude. The sky was now uniformly gray.

He scrambled to his feet and fought his way up the slope, slipping and staggering in the deep drifted snow, eventually reaching the ridge once more. Still no one. He skirted the hidden crevasse and climbed the buttress to the point where it joined the face of the mountain. Slowly, with caution that memory advised, he edged his way along the narrow, snow-hidden ledge that climbed around the mountainside, no wider than a goat track, its precise dimensions fattened and masked by the snow. He rubbed his back against the rock for security as he moved.

Gradually, he moved out of sight of the place where he had fallen, where the dead Russian lay. He was perhaps a couple of hundred feet above the overhang where he had left Petrunin's body. He was exposed above the tree line. After twenty minutes, he could see the more distant and higher peaks, beyond Parachinar and in Pakistan, tinted with gold. The sky had lost its leaden grayness. The cloud was wispy and thin and the snow had stopped. The ledge broadened ahead of him into a path where two men could have walked abreast, climbing steeply to the sharp crease in the mountain that gave access to the long, narrow valley at the other end of which lay Pakistan.

He began moving more quickly now, wishing he had stolen the dead Russian's R/T and so enabling himself to keep in contact with his pursuers, monitoring their progress, their distance from him. He was bent and worn, leaning forward as he jogged desultorily, his head beginning to fill with the noises of his own heartbeat and breathing, emptying of everything else. Petrunin, the computer retrieval that was no more than a pipe dream unless you were Petrunin himself or a KGB Deputy Chairman, Miandad, Mohammed Jan, the Pathans, the dead young Russian below the ridge whose Kalashnikov he had forgotten, like his R/T, his last footsteps, the noise of helicopters . . .

All faded. To each step there were numerous heartbeats. One ragged breath each time a foot was lifted and moved—the snow was thinner here, because the wind sliced it off the path like a knife, cutting through him too, freezing him—and almost ten hurried beats of his heart before each step was complete and the next one begun. He labored upward with increasing slowness, staggering from time to time, those times when he failed to lower his foot quickly enough to keep his balance. His breath came more and more quickly because the air seemed so thin. He couldn't get enough of it into his lungs with a single deep breath, and yet did not want to breathe deeply because of the searing pain caused by its coldness. His stubble was frosty where his breath had frozen on his skin and hair. He did not look at his watch—he did not even become aware of the wrist at the end of his left arm unless he needed that arm to drive on, to adjust his balance, to plunge into the thin snow and lever his body forward.

All noises outside himself faded. The path had rounded the mountain as he climbed. His hands were deathly white in the first sunlight; the snow began to glitter, hurting his eyes. He was almost there. The path narrowed but he could still move freely along it, the wall of the mountain to his left, touched often by his hand, scraped by his knuckles for reassurance or gripped by tense, clawlike fingers for support when he became dizzy or unbalanced.

He passed through the crease, the narrow gate to the valley, without realizing. He began to descend into shadow again, away from the first rays of the sun. He paused then, on his hands and knees, and looked ahead of him, out of Afghanistan.

And suddenly realized that he had no image of rescue in his imagination. He had not thought, not considered what it meant that he had lost Miandad, his courier, his secretary. Hyde did not know the arrangements.

The slope of the mountains dropped quickly, like the deep gash of a great knife, to the snow-covered floor of the narrow valley perhaps two hundred feet below him. This ran like a twisting snake through high mountains for perhaps three or four miles, until the land lifted again to the pass over which he might reach Parachinar and the Pathan camp.

He knew he could not return alone to that camp. He did not dare. Something seemed to give out and slump inside him, something more vital than mere physical energy. He shivered with weakness, on all fours, an exhausted animal. Then he fell against the cliff face, hunching into it as if into a parent's skirts, a lover's comfort. His breathing sounded like sobbing, even to himself. . . .

Until it was drowned by the noise of helicopter rotors approaching rapidly from behind him, clattering against the rock face, making his body shudder with the downdraft as it lifted into view and hung there, its tinted glass windshield like a threatening mask, its gunports like a grin. It dipped sideways. He could see faces at the open side doors. He could see a heavy PKMS machine gun on a swivel mounting in the doorway, aimed at him. He rose from all fours to his knees, pressing himself against the rock. The helicopter moved closer, perhaps thirty feet above him, where the slope of the mountain peak allowed its rotors closer access without danger. Spiderlike, huge, deafening, the MiL gunship hung over him, filling the morning sky, its racket reverberating from the mountain. It sank very slowly toward him. Hyde could not move.

He became enveloped by the whirling snow dragged up and flung about by the downdraft. The helicopter lowered itself into the writhing cloud of snow it was creating. Hyde pressed his face against the rock, feeling the pressure of the downdraft in his arms and hands—fingers slipping all the time, unable to hold their grip, grow into the rock enough— then in his body, which shuddered with increasing velocity and violence as he crouched with his back to the rotors, then in his knees and calves and feet, which shuddered, slid, began to move across the narrow ledge toward the edge and the drop beyond. He was being agitated into motion, like a compound in a chemist's jar, shaken into something else—a body falling from a high place.

He held on, trying to hug the rock. He attempted to sit, then to lie flat. His legs slid away from him like those of a baby, uncontrolled. They were dragged toward the edge of the track, toward the drop. He felt his body slip, too. He turned onto his back and dug in his heels, but could not prevent himself moving. The ground seemed alive and sandlike in its distress beneath him, the helicopter a huge black beetle hovering above him, the cloud of upflung, powdery snow obscuring everything else.

His legs scrabbled in space, then slumped, knees bent, over the edge. His buttocks moved toward the edge. He could not turn over again; his hands could not grip.

The MiL slid to one side. Blue sky where it had been, then a black something dropping from it on a rope. A smaller spider, or only the spider's thread. He lay on his back, legs over the edge, snow boiling around him, covering him, as the helicopter's winch man came to collect him. Twenty feet, fifteen, ten—he seemed to swoop in toward Hyde, who could only wait for him. He came level, hanging over the drop, then the MiL began to shunt him sideways toward the ledge.

A hundred yards, two hundred, something told him. No more than that before you reach cover. *Then three miles*, something else announced. *At least three miles.*

Two hundred yards, the other something replied.

Six feet, five, four, his eyes registered. The winch man's boots scrabbled on the edge, found purchase, his body leaning slightly away, then straightening. He was on the ledge. Hyde kicked out and the winch man danced away as the MiL shifted slightly, a puppet on the wire that had lowered him. He came swinging slowly back like a pendulum, feet scrabbling again, then gaining purchase, the rifle already coming around from its position slung across his back. Hyde rolled toward the winch man, and the MiL danced him away again. Hyde scrabbled in the snow, found frozen dirt, dug his fingernails into it, stopped the roll of his body toward the edge. He was exhausted and terrified, incapable of much more. The winch man danced back, feet touching lightly on the ledge again. This time, he was grinning, and the gun was pointing.

Did they want him?

For a while—before they kill you . . .

He made as if to roll again, and the man's feet began to dance upward—Christ, the pilot was good and they'd done this trick before—and then he hovered as if performing a strange, frozen entrechat in combat boots. The boots remained a foot or so above the path. The powdery snow settled around the legs of the man as he waited. Hyde rolled, the legs danced upward, and Hyde drew the Makarov from behind his back and fired. The winch man's smile became lopsided, and emitted blood—like Petrunin—and Hyde didn't look anymore. The MiL whipped away from the ledge, and Hyde turned and was running. The helicopter buzzed behind him, closing. He heard a terrible scream, then the scrape of metal and flesh and bone along the wall of the mountain. They hadn't even winched the man in, just left him there, alive, banging him along the cliff, trapped, ending the dance.

The PKMS opened up, scattering bullets along the track behind him, shattering the outline of a rock that had been close to his head the previous moment. Hyde dropped into the twisted, jagged, concealing trench of rocks that led to the valley floor, fear making his body flow almost as easily as the stream that must once have reached the valley by this sharp-cut course. Hyde, his body jarred and bruised and shaken, continued swiftly downward.

He looked behind him, just once. The MiL was a hundred feet up, and the dead winch man was being hauled up. His body hung grotesquely, broken, beneath the gunship. Hyde slithered downward, desperate to reach the valley floor before the MiL resumed the game.

"There could be—depositions made available, Frau Schröder. I'm sure your lawyer understands me . . . ?" Zimmermann made the statement lightly, turning his head so that he could see the reactions of the woman's legal counsel. A youngish man, running to fat, gold-rimmed glasses giving him a learned air that was at odds with the expensive, modishly cut suit and the flamboyant shirt. He would have been little more than a baby when the Schröder woman was committing the atrocities of which she was accused.

The lawyer nodded for him to continue with the bribery. Margarethe Schröder watched Zimmermann from beneath heavy eyelids. Her anger and outrage were evident, making her face appear too young for its surmounting thatch of white hair. She shrugged, as if Zimmermann bored her, but there was a gleam of calculation and alert cunning in her eyes. She had spent the last two years in prison, in her home city so that relatives might conveniently visit her, awaiting a trial that might never come. She had been a guard at Maidanek camp. The depositions that had been presented against her recited her deeds. She had killed babies, children, women as a matter of routine—something more chilling to Zimmermann when he had first read the depositions than the gratuitous, hideous way her activities had reached above and beyond the call of duty: the dashing out of brains on concrete floors or against the wooden walls of huts, the rumors of lampshades of skin, the collection of enlarged photographs that decorated her quarters.

Zimmermann had met them before—the surviving SS and Gestapo. There was still no other emotion he could feel than sick, quiet horror, at them, at their nationality, and at history.

The woman had been on vacation with a party of similarly retired women in Florida when a survivor of Maidanek had seen and recognized her. Margarethe Schröder had never denied the charges, merely dismissed them as unimportant. She did not acknowledge their criminality. Now, however, Zimmermann believed she wished to end her imprisonment. She resented the sense of blame, of accusation that surrounded her—resented it deeply and bitterly. He could offer her a speedy and innocuous trial, even if he hoped he did not mean it, preferred to think that he would renege on any deal. However, all that was for later.

"I would undertake," he continued, breaking the silence that had held only the slight noise of the humming striplight, "to ensure that the trial was brought forward—dealt with this year. . . ." Schröder's eyes watched him, burning and suspicious and afraid. Zimmermann tried to smile reassuringly. "We could ensure a very light sentence, thanks to some new depositions that contradict those held by the Federal Prosecutor's office—a sentence which, in view of your incarceration for the past two years, Frau Schröder, would ensure your release before next Christmas."

He waited then. Schröder looked at her lawyer, who appeared to carefully consider the offer that had been made. He removed his spectacles, becoming at once little more than a boy in appearance, wiped them with a silk handkerchief, then replaced them and his learned air with a flourish.

"There will be no notes," he observed. "At the moment, this is not to be considered a statement of any kind."

"Of course not."

"You will not ask Frau Schröder any questions concerning the period 1941 to '45. Do you agree to this?"

"Naturally. That part of Frau Schröder's life does not interest me—it is not important to me," he corrected himself, unwilling to antagonize the woman. Again, he essayed a smile in her direction. She was looking at her lawyer, who nodded to her. She turned to Zimmermann. Her voice was deep and hoarse. Her hands, spread on the bare, Formica-covered table, were large and unmanicured. Zimmermann might almost have called them a man's hands, had he not realized the easy platitude for what it was, and recognized the way in which he was making her fit a stereotype. In reality, there was nothing with which to compare Schröder and all the others.

"What do you want to ask me?" she said grudgingly.

"Thank you, Frau Schröder." Zimmermann sat down on the opposite side of the table. Schröder lit a cigarette and blew smoke at the humming striplight. The interview room was warm, drily stale, and unused. The prison was modern, clean, and spacious, like a huge office building, suggesting that criminals were not to be found there. Like most of those built in Germany since the war, the prison always appeared to Zimmermann like a grim pastiche of a Costa Brava hotel.

"I wish to take you back to 1974, when you worked . . ." She nodded dismissively. She knew why he had come. ". . . for an officer in British Intelligence during his residence in Bonn. You were the secretary of a man named Andrew Babbington?"

"Yes."

"I want to ask you some questions about him."

"I was always a good secretary—very efficient. There were no accus—" She colored slightly, but mostly in anger at herself. "No *reports* of inefficiency, I am certain."

"Of course, Frau Schröder. Of course not. I know that Mr. Babbington was very pleased. It is not you I wish to discuss, but him. You understand that I cannot tell you why at this moment?"

She weighed his statement while Zimmermann looked at

the lawyer, who eventually nodded his complicity. There was no need for Zimmermann to warn either of them of the security aspects of his inquiries. He returned his attention to Margarethe Schröder. She was grinding out the first cigarette, lighting a second almost at once. She nodded. Evidently, she had accepted that it was not some subtle trick, an indirect and overland route to Maidanek and her crimes, even if she could not understand the importance attached to an Englishman in 1974.

"I believe that Mr. Babbington had an affair—with a married woman who has since died of cancer—while he was in Bonn?" He studied Schröder. "You knew of this affair, of course?" His tone was carefully calculated. It implied a vague bond between them, a similarity of attitude to the business of their discussion, but it was clipped and authoritative, suggesting that Zimmermann was some kind of senior officer in the same organization in which Schröder served. She nodded abruptly in reply. "Good. Now—how often did they meet? Where did they meet?" There was guilt, at once, a sense of complicity that might now endanger her. The cigarette wobbled between her lips. She coughed. "Come now, Schröder—you have done nothing wrong. Where did they meet?"

"In—my apartment," she admitted in a small voice. "Usually in my apartment." The repetition was more defiant. She had lifted her head.

"Why? For security?" he asked nonchalantly.

"Of course," she answered scornfully. "The woman was the wife of a civil servant, someone he worked with here in Bonn." Zimmermann was nodding safely, staring at the table top and its faint geology of coffee stains and pencil scribbles, doodles and cigarette burns. "They had to be careful. I was asked—I helped." The implication was that she had been paid, too. Babbington had evidently won her over. She flicked a lock of frizzy white hair from her forehead. "They met there two, maybe three times a week."

"Can you remember exactly when this was?"

"In 1974, of course." And then her anger burst out. "When Guillaume, the traitor, was arrested. Now *he* is back in the East, after what he did to betray Germany, and *I* am here!" Zimmermann reached toward her, but she snatched her broad hands from the table. "Why do they still care about all that?" she wailed. There was iron in the self-pity, however.

"It was forty years ago—everyone has forgotten—people don't know and don't want to know! *Why am I here?*" she screamed.

Zimmermann stood up, leaning his knuckles on the table. "It is to help you get out of here that you must answer my questions, Frau Schröder. A little more help, if you please. I am a very busy man, and I have no time to waste with these— demonstrations of self-pity."

She turned from her lawyer to him, sniffed and wiped her eyes. The tone stung and impressed her. Bribed her, too. She nodded her head, vigorously.

"What can I tell you? Two or three times a week, there was never mess, the sheets were always changed on the bed, there were champagne glasses washed up, any food . . . all was washed up, put away when they had finished. I was never inconvenienced. The apartment was always empty when I returned."

"Did you know this woman?"

"Yes. By name. I had seen her once or twice."

"But never at the apartment?"

"No. They were—discreet."

Zimmermann pondered. At last he had been able to dehumanize the situation, purge it of its associations. Margarethe Schröder was now no more than a possible witness to events in 1974—a retired secretary with a high security clearance. The recipient of a civil service pension.

"Can you be specific, as to dates? When did this affair begin—when did they begin using your apartment for their meetings?"

"I went to work for Mr. Babbington—oh, in March, or perhaps the beginning of April. I am not certain. At first I did not wish to be party to it, but he was very charming, very considerate. . . ."

"Of course. And the apartment?"

"Perhaps two weeks later. At first, it was to be only for one time, then he pressed me, with such apologies . . . and so . . ." She raised her hands, almost smiling. "Then two or three times a week." She chuckled throatily.

"I see. They could not use hotels?"

"The woman was, as you know, well known in Bonn. She might have been recognized by women in her circle." To Schröder, it was self-evident that such precautions had been needed.

Zimmermann paused for a moment, then he said: "You had a telephone installed in your apartment, of course?"

"Naturally."

"The week of the traitor Guillaume's arrest—Mr. Babbington used your apartment?"

"Often. He persuaded me that I had been working too hard, that I should take a few days' leave. I went to Bavaria—it was beautiful in the spring. He bought the train tickets and booked the hotel . . . a good hotel."

Zimmermann contained his rising sense of excitement. The apartment with its untapped, unsuspicious telephone, had been in Babbington's possession for the crucial few days. Babbington's periods of disappearance had been accounted for because of the affair—they even knew where he was, so the surveillance reports and recollections claimed. Babbington had disarmed them by indulging in an affair and finding a hiding place for himself and the woman. It had excused any and all of his actions, giving them the gloss of adultery, not criminality. The telephone calls to Guillaume had begun on April twenty-second.

"You returned to Bonn—when?"

"On the twenty-fifth of April."

"And Mr. Babbington continued to use your apartment for his meetings with—this woman now dead?"

Margarethe Schröder shook her head. She even appeared saddened by the recollection. "No. Mr. Babbington was very upset. He told me that her husband was becoming suspicious—they had to part, even though he begged her—"

"You believed him?"

"You think I don't recognize unhappiness when I see it?" she challenged.

"So, the affair was over—and, of course, Mr. Babbington's new work took up all his time. He was able to lose himself in his responsibilities."

"Luckily for him. Slowly, he seemed to mend, to recover his spirits."

"Did he settle your very high telephone bill before he returned to England, Frau Schröder?" Zimmermann asked quickly, startling and confusing the woman.

"How did you . . . ?" Then she dismissed the suspicion that this was the thrust of Zimmermann's inquiries, and said: "Yes, he did. Every mark and pfennig."

"It was a high bill. Did most of the calls—local ones—come while you were on vacation?"

"Yes . . . I think so, anyway."

"But before that there were many calls—long-distance, even international?" She nodded. "But the mainly local ones were while you took your vacation?"

"There was never any attempt to deceive me—Mr. Babbington explained that he took work to the apartment, that he had to talk to London a great deal—*before* the bill arrived he told me all this."

"Ah. Of course. It was nothing." He looked at his watch. One in the morning. He felt a tired, jumpy excitement tightening his chest. This was, at the very least, a satisfactory beginning. He had method and opportunity now—perhaps he might discover motive, too, given time. He stood up. He shook hands with Margarethe Schröder perfunctorily. "Thank you," he said. "Thank you. I—shall be in touch with your lawyer, Herr Ganzer, within a matter of days. I am sure we can do something to make your next Christmas something to remember!" He tried to smile once more, and almost achieved the expression of sincerity.

"Thank you," she said bemusedly. Zimmermann shook hands briefly with Ganzer, the lawyer, nodded an assurance as he did so, and left. His footsteps clattered along the brightly lit, tiled corridor.

As he passed through the corridors and levels of the prison toward the main gates and his car, beneath the long striplights, he began to escape the pervasive sense of imprisonment. It had radiated from the woman, Schröder. She was the past that imprisoned him and his country.

He hurried into the cold air of the courtyard, turning up the collar of his overcoat. He climbed thankfully into the Mercedes, started the engine, and drove to the gates. He showed his pass and the gates opened. He was free.

He had almost reached the access road to the Cologne-Bonn autobahn before he realized he was being followed.

Babbington took the telephone call from Bonn and for once envisaged the town at the other end of the connection. He remembered, quite clearly, Margarethe Schröder's small, cramped, neat apartment and the telephone—the dozens, even hundreds of calls he had made. Sometimes the woman had been there—poor Ilse, who had died of cancer so painfully—but mostly he had been alone. Ilse had been a good cover, a good lover, but a luxury he had had to abandon as time ran out for Guillaume. He had covered his tracks, but *Teardrop* had been bound to raise the ghosts of '74, and now he was forced to exorcise them a decade later.

"It is done—everything as you ordered. Do you want to look at the stuff?" The accent was American. The KGB officer had, like so many of them, learned his English in the United States, probably as a student.

"What is it?"

"He had all the right files pulled. He was getting close. The woman in Cologne—he's seen her."

"You're certain?"

"Yes."

"Then let's hope tonight will be a lesson to him. Many thanks."

Babbington put down the receiver and rubbed his nose between thumb and forefinger, as if easing his sinuses. Oleg sat opposite him in a dowdily covered chair, a tumbler of malt whiskey balanced on its wide arm. He appeared at ease. Babbington considered.

Zimmermann had moved quickly, with insight and talent.

"Okay," Babbington announced casually. "It's been done. Zimmermann is due for a shock. It should keep him quiet—at least temporarily."

"What do you gain by that?"

"Time. Just as we gain time when Massinger and his wife fall into my hands tomorrow."

"And Aubrey?"

"My reply to that, Oleg, is—*and Hyde?*"

"Don't worry. He's alone—he can't get out."

"Petrunin *is* dead?"

Oleg nodded. Fair hair flopped across his forehead. He flicked it aside. "Yes. They're certain."

"Two years too late."

"Perhaps."

"I have the right to complain—I'm coming behind with the broom, Oleg."

"The Centre is eager for—a greater display of ruthlessness," Oleg said, almost apologetically. "I wish to caution you against it." The man's tone and manner were confiding, those of a friend. He did not intend to deceive, only advise. Babbington nodded his agreement.

"I don't need to be warned against the backlash," he replied, smiling. "But, thank you. I agree the dangers are too great, the risks too high. . . ." He ground his teeth. "Though the Centre's habitual ruthlessness *is* an attractive alternative, Oleg . . . ?"

Oleg shook his head, then wiped away the lock of straying fair hair. "What will you do with the Massinger couple, when you find them?"

"Have them brought back—what else can I do?"

"And Aubrey?"

"The same. My hands are tied. This place is worse, from the Centre's point of view, even than Poland. Too many people know. You can't just kill people, even if they are *not* Catholic priests, and assume no one will take an interest. Your people fail to understand that." Babbington's thoughts raged, even though his voice was calm. It would be easy now to use his enormous new powers, all too easy. . . . Damn the Centre, tempting him to violence. . . . Probably they advised it because they wanted to test him, nothing more. If he had proved indiscreet now, he would have failed.

As if echoing his thoughts, Oleg said softly, "It would be easy. Like swatting flies. The problem is, the squashed flies remain on the windowpane, or the white wall."

"I don't need a lecture in caution, Oleg!" Babbington snapped. A slight tic commenced at the corner of his mouth, and he masked it with the glass, sipping the whiskey.

"Very well. Might Aubrey be on his way to this woman, also? We know he had contacted her over the years—"

"Perhaps. Why should he?"

"On the other hand, why should he not? It is possible we could have them *all* in Vienna."

"Which would be convenient, and *nice*. The woman, anyway, is unimportant. Clever of your people to trace all the calls made by Zimmermann *and* to recognize the old name, Elsenreith. My congratulations."

"They are not all morons at the Centre—not the younger ones, anyway." Oleg smiled, appeared young himself. "Don't involve the woman—she's well connected in Vienna."

"I'm not interested in her . . . only as a honey trap. A pitcher plant. I'll take care of this, Oleg. Have no worries on that score. *Without* swatting the flies—"

But, he promised himself, if any of them *knew* he would swat them like the flies they were . . . if they *knew* rather than just guessed or suspected, blundering around blindfold at the party hoping to touch someone they could not see, then God help them. If they knew, then attempted to act against him sometime in the future—he would have them eliminated. . . .

He felt a justified anger swelling in his chest and stomach. It was the *Centre*'s fault, *all* this!

"Had you had Massinger killed while he was *last* in Vienna," he announced heavily, "I would not now be running this risk."

Oleg nodded. "It *was* remiss," he sighed.

"You could have finished Massinger and Hyde well away from *my* doorstep—which your people managed to foul anyway . . . hence the need for *caution* now! If those damn fools hadn't lost them!"

"I agree . . . they tried to remedy the situation—"

"Just as Pavel did, at the very moment I had convinced Massinger of Aubrey's guilt!" He swallowed whiskey, then waved the tumbler expressively. "Forget it. I shan't make the same kind of mistake. I shan't have my work wasted again, either. Tell the Centre to await *my* instructions, will you?"

Oleg smiled conspiratorially, and with genuine amusement.

"Certainly. But you will need help?"

"When I ask for it. Help, not interference."

Oleg nodded. "Agreed."

If they knew or acted against him, at any time, he repeated to himself, then—

Dead.

"Another dead one," he said, picking up the whiskey bottle and finding it empty.

Zimmermann inserted his key in the lock, and the door swung open at once, before he had turned the key. Immediately, he knew he had been burgled. There was no one in the corridor; he had passed no one on the stairs; no one had been using the lift. . . .

He listened. Nothing. Silence. The smell of liquor, of broken bottles. He stepped into the hall and felt for the switch. When the light came on, he could see the door of the lounge ajar. Furniture was overturned—a small piece of Meissen broken near the door, a headless shepherdess—and the smell of the broken whiskey and gin bottles increased. Still he heard nothing.

He hurried now. The lounge was a shambles, and the wide-open door of the bedroom as he passed it revealed the tumbled bed and the drawers hanging open like shocked mouths. His clothes were strewn about the room.

He saw immediately that the silver pieces were gone, and the porcelain. The paintings had been cut from their frames, the photographs—there was one from his own past, in the uniform in which Aubrey had captured him in 1940, grinning from beneath his peaked cap—had been smashed or ground underfoot. The liquor cabinet had been emptied—yes, a bottle of whiskey and one of gin, neckless, soaking into the carpet.

He saw that the small wall safe hung open, the picture frame that had concealed it, askew. The files were gone, every one of them, together with his savings books, his checkbook, his other credit cards, his will, and the rest of his papers. And the two thousand marks in notes he always kept there.

But it was the files, of course. The damned files . . .

He was galvanized rather than numbed by shock. He looked out of the window but the Audi that had followed him was not to be seen in the street. He crossed to the telephone, rescuing it from its entanglement with a rug, finding the receiver itself hanging over the back of the sofa. He dialed the Königshof Hotel. He had no wish for a restorative drink. The spilled whiskey was oppressive and heady. He was angry at the damage—the professional entry clumsily disguised by modern vandalism. Very angry.

He requested Massinger's room number.

"Come on, come on. . . ." he murmured, then: "Ah, Paul, my friend. I apologize for waking you at this hour."

"Wolfgang? What is it?"

"I appear to have been burgled. The files have been taken. I'm sure they were the object of the burglary. I am calling you to advise extreme caution tomorrow and for all the days that follow."

"Burglarized! God . . ."

"Please be careful. I will not caution you not to go, because you would not listen. But watch your back, my friend. You may need old instincts, old training. And hurry back. I—we need each other's help, of that I am certain."

"Yes, yes, I will. A couple of days, no more—"

"Good night, then."

He flung the telephone onto the sofa, as if to allow it to remain an integral part of the ransacked room. He rubbed his forehead as he paced the stained and littered carpet. He appeared professorial, and on the point of beginning some abstruse line of argument. His thoughts, however, were clear and simple.

KGB. Moving to protect, moving to remove proof. Carrying away on large farm forks the dungheap concealing the diamond. Protecting their own.

It had to be. Babbington. At once, they had moved to a position of aggressive defense on his behalf.

It meant caution. Extreme, almost somnolent caution, if he was to proceed. Especially, it meant doing nothing to arouse their suspicions until he had Massinger back with him from Vienna.

It also meant, he thought suddenly and scrabbled for the telephone, it also meant that Frau Margarethe Schröder might, just might, be in some immediate danger. Picking up the telephone, he began dialing the prison in Cologne, his eyes roaming over the littered, broken remains of his furniture and ornaments with a weary gleam of wisdom and cunning.

He was running into the low, just-risen sun, wintrily red, his shape black against it for those pursuing, his shadow thrown long behind him. His shadow was palpable to him, even though he could not see it. To his heightened, exhausted, almost hallucinatory senses, it dragged behind him like a lure for hounds. He was an easy black target against a red disk. He could hear the noise of the MiL gunship as it prepared to swoop once more, and he scanned the rocks for cover.

Finesse, you bastards, finesse, finesse . . . ! he had silently screamed at the helicopter, over and over, as he had reached the narrow, twisting floor of the steep valley and began running as the dead winch man was retrieved by the crew of the MiL. He wanted them to toy with him, play cat and mouse. That way, he might survive.

The snow had drifted in places in the narrow knife cut of the valley. It caused him to stumble in his fear and haste and weariness, then it was a thin, powdery skin and he ran easily from rock to rock, dodging, sprinting, bending low then run-

ning upright, head back like an athlete. It was perhaps no
more than four miles long, and he would reach the border in
less than a mile—

That was what he had announced to himself, between
the few quick, deep, preparatory breaths he had taken at the
foot of the tumbled, boulder-strewn slope, the Russian helicopter still above and behind him.

Less than a mile—

It was meaningless, of course. The border wasn't even
drawn at that point; it did not exist. Pakistan lay at the other
end of the valley, and Parachinar, which he had to avoid. And
somewhere was the army and the people who would be waiting for Miandad, under instructions that the dead Pakistani
officer had never divulged to him.

Less than a mile—

And he had begun running. Random, fast, hesitant, bent
over, upright, apparently directionless. There were one or
two shots that faded on the dry, cold morning air, their bullets
well wide. It was not Kalashnikovs he had to avoid, but rockets, cannon fire, machine gun volleys, grenades, antipersonnel mines, all the potent weaponry of an MiL-24 gunship.

Half a mile, surely half a mile by now, he pleaded with
his judgment as he heard the MiL move from the hover to the
approach as if it were a bird of prey stooping to the kill. The
noise clattered in the thin, dry air, bouncing off the rocks.
The modern Stuka, he heard some irrelevant part of his
awareness remark.

He turned, and watched the MiL. It was flying
cautiously—no, not cautiously, tauntingly was the right description. One change of acceleration, one dip, and it could
cover him like a coffin lid in no more than six or seven seconds.
But it wanted to play cat and mouse because its crew were so
enraged and so confident. Make him sweat—

Terror, advancing up the narrow valley, dragging its
wake of deafening, reverberated sound behind it. Terror. It
minced slightly, from side to side, swaying as if grotesquely
miming a woman's walk. It moved toward Hyde's shadow,
which had seemed to prostrate itself at the helicopter's approach. Hyde felt his body quivering uncontrollably.

Terror.

He turned his back on it, and began running again,
weaving as quickly and agilely as he could through the lit-

tered rocks and boulders. His legs were leaden; the noise seemed to drain them of strength. Then he heard the launch of one, two missiles from the pods beneath the MiL's stubby wings. He dived for the nearest rock, almost somersaulting over it, crouching behind it immediately. The flare from the rockets dazzled his eyes; he could feel the heat of the exhausts. The two rockets exploded twenty yards ahead of him, throwing up earth and rock and snow in front of the red sun, obscuring it. The valley appeared dark. Hyde stood up and ran into the churning cloud of debris, and through it into the glare of the sun. They'd been playing with him. He wasn't meant to die at once, not just yet.

The MiL slipped over the haze of settling earth and dust, following him, moving barely faster than he was himself. He jumped a low rock, almost twisted his ankle as he landed on a loose boulder, hopped until his balance was righted, and went on, dodging and weaving in his sprint, changing direction every few paces. Meaninglessly, he realized he must already have crossed the border. The MiL's long, fat shadow slid over him like night, and the machine was a little ahead of him. A grinning face swung the mounted machine gun in his direction, a flutter of iron butterflies emerged, fell from the belly of the MiL, bouncing and skittering ahead of him like tacks spread to ambush an approaching cyclist. Antipersonnel bombs, the toylike things that had deprived children of arms and eyes and faces in a dozen corners of the world. Play with the nice iron toy, painted dark green. Bang—

Hyde jumped onto a rock as one of the stub-winged bombs rolled toward his feet. He tiptoed like an unpracticed tightrope artist along the rock, arms akimbo for balance, then jumped to another rock, jumped again, ran and skipped three paces, jumped to a larger rock—

One lay in the fold of the rock, and his toe reached at it, but he overbalanced, tumbling onto the snow-covered ground where the tips and wingtips of the iron butterflies thrust out of the thin snow carpet, growing like strange plants. He rolled, groaning, and stopped his momentum by digging in his heels. His head swung round and he was staring at the white numbers on the squat little body of one of the bombs.

He could not tell whether they would detonate on contact or after the lapse of a precise number of seconds. Fused, or contact?

Then one exploded behind him, shattering a loaf-sized

lump from its parent rock. He got to his knees, then stood and hopped. A deadly game of hopscotch, one foot, side, forward, side, side, up onto a rock—the MiL was still ahead of him, the machine gunner grinning, waiting for him to catch up with the game—along the rock, one foot, space there, bomb there, quick, quick, *bomb!*—clear ground, hole in the snow, *avoid!*—clear, clear, bomb, clear . . .

He was out of the little cabbage patch they had sown for him, and the ground was clear. Small detonations, throwing up snow and brown earth, began almost at once. He ran, keeping close to the scatter of rocks and boulders, his breath and limbs laboring now that the going was instinctive. He must be no more than half a mile from the end of the valley. He was across the border—closer to death.

"Finesse, finesse, finesse," he kept repeating through the thick saliva in his mouth, through clenched teeth. "Finesse, finesse . . ."

The rocks were charred, even the snow looked black beneath its light, latest covering. Something had burned . . . ?

Fifty Pathans—metal balls, the strange eggs that had burst open on impact—the silver, gleaming mist . . .

It was here. The MiL was above him. He could almost see the eggs dropping, bursting open, smell the napalm mist—

Egg, egg, three, four, six, ten—fifteen . . .

He could see them!

Half-eggs, rolling, their contents spilled already. A string of eggs laid by the MiL. *They were going to burn him!*

He felt the mist cold on his face. It refracted and distorted the sunlight, enlarged the huge red disk ahead of him. It was cold, chilling, terrifying. It clung. It was higher than he was, he was *in it*—

A tunnel of silver mist, just like before, gleaming even in the daylight. It outlined his arm as the limb bobbed in front of his eyes like St. Elmo's fire. It clung to his hands, to the skin of his hands, to his Pathan clothing, to every part of him. To his face and beard and eyelids—

He wanted to scream, to stop and do no more than scream, as the MiL banked sharply and returned toward him.

He remembered the firefly glow he had seen drop from Petrunin's blood-red helicopter. . . .

A tunnel, a box of mist that would become a box of fire, consuming him—

He rubbed his clothing. The mist moved about him, closed in again. The helicopter slowly settled above him, the machine gunner grinning, signaling farewell in an exaggerated, final salute. He rubbed at the mist again where he felt it on his skin, waved his arms, shook and danced his body but the mist only stirred sluggishly then closed in, as heavy and unmoving as long curtains in a slight breeze. It surrounded him. He was trapped, already dead. The mist had formed a cell, with a roof, walls, floor. And it would consume everything within it.

Within it?

Spark?

He could see the spark, in the dark belly of the MiL—the means of ignition was about to be released.

Within it—

He ran. The mist moved, closed behind him, gleamed and shimmered, dulled the light. He ran. He ran. The mist gave but did not end. Its spread was exactly controlled. The box of mist that would become a box of flame could be escaped, but he did not know how wide it was, how deep, how long. . . . He did not look up. He ran.

Light, air, less coldness on his face and the backs of his hands. He ran.

Mist folding behind, rock ahead. He ran.

He was still covered with it!

He dived for the shelter of the rock, hearing the roar of the mist as it became flame. He rolled in the snow, hiding his face and hands, folding them into the bulk of his body. He rolled. Searing pain in his hands, on his face. He plunged them into snow, burning on his legs, he rolled and rolled in the snow, driving his body into a drift against the rocks which half buried him, filling his nostrils and mouth and eyes and driving out all sensory impressions of the burning mist. He did not want to know about his burns.

He did not want to know anything. He was finished. The snow cooled him, froze him. He couldn't move. The snow numbed his face and hands. He turned his mouth, spat out snow, breathed. It was enough. The air, even if it tasted of napalm, revived him.

But nothing more—

He would wait.

He kept his eyes closed. They were heavy with snow. He heard the helicopter, his body tensed. He waited.

The noise—he could feel the downdraft of the rotors—clattered off the side of the valley, enlarging and expanding into two, three sets of rotors. Perhaps others had come? He did not care. He could no longer even be terrified. Soon, soon now . . .

He was numb. The smell of burning napalm was dying down, the heat dissipating. He opened his eyes slowly. Half-melted snow watered in them. The helicopter hovered above him blackly, haloed with sunlight. There was another helicopter thirty yards away. Then he heard the retreating noise of rotors. Retreating . . .

Roundels, green and white. Hyde was disorientated, still waiting to die. The crescent moon and one star of Islam at the tail of the helicopter.

Green and white, no red star on the belly.

Roundels . . . ?

He could not explain what had happened, not even as the Pakistan Army Sikorsky S-61R gunship helicopter dropped gently toward the charred floor of the narrow valley, blowing snow over his body from its downdraft as it descended.

12
Truth from an Old Man

"This whole matter has gone far enough to have become something of a shambles." Sir William Guest, GCMG, Cabinet Office Chairman of the Joint Intelligence Committee and a former Head of the Diplomatic Service, appeared pleased with the opportunity to display his seniority. His leather swivel chair creaked under his considerable weight. Babbington noticed again that he had a fat man's enclosed eyes and expressionless facial flesh, which suggested slowness of mind, even stupidity. It was, of course, a mask. Sir William *was* his master, and his mentor, and his intellectual capacities were considerable. SAID was his brainchild; its birth was the fruit of his persuasion of the PM and the Cabinet Committees concerned. "A shambles," Sir William repeated with heavy emphasis. Then: "You will remember, Andrew, that I opposed the idea of lifting the press restrictions, and especially the idea of a prosecution for treason in Aubrey's case." It was not a hand-washing exercise, rather a reprimand.

"Yes," Babbington replied, waiting. It had suited his game, and that of Moscow Centre, that Sir William and others had seen him as the coming man, had assiduously encouraged his promotion and effected his seniority in MI 5. It was an express train, as Kapustin had once vulgarly put it, to the top of the mountain. The peasant Deputy Chairman of the KGB had laughed familiarly at that. The man always managed to remind Babbington that he thought of him as Moscow's man, Moscow's property, Moscow's *creature*.

Babbington suppressed his thoughts. Sir William's thick right eyebrow had moved, as if he had already seen some expression on Babbington's face.

Sir William's office was a comfortable though drably colored part of the warren of Cabinet Office rooms on Downing Street. As Sir William had said on one occasion: *You may call it the factory floor—I prefer to call it the hotel annex.* As he said it, his eyes had seemed to see through all the doors, along all the twisting, narrow corridors, toward the main house and the Cabinet Room and the PM's private office. His thoughts had then evidently returned to his own room with satisfaction, as if his description of the Cabinet Office's whereabouts was mere self-deprecation.

His chair creaked again as he shifted his bulk. "I'm glad you agree, Andrew. This isn't in the nature of a reprimand." There was cigar ash on the lapel of his dark suit, and on the Old Etonian tie. "However, be that as it may, we are now, to some considerable degree, compromised."

"I don't follow your logic."

"The newspapers have the scent, and we have to leave them baying at the moon. You let Kenneth Aubrey"—there was a hint of amusement in the gray eyes that were encircled by folds of fat—"get away, not to put too fine a point upon it. You don't know where he is, and we have a charge of treason for him to answer. And my goddaughter, Heaven help her, has gone chasing off to Germany to discover the truth about her father!" He raised his hands in the air in mock horror. They descended with a drumlike beat on his desk. He was not smiling as he continued: "I don't foresee great happiness for her there, whatever the truth of the matter. . . ." He seemed to be remembering distant events, then he shook his head. "A strange man," he murmured. "Brilliant, but strange." Then his eyes blinked into attentiveness once more. "The Prime Minister has changed her mind on this matter." His voice and facial expression implied a sense of frustration, eternally that of the civil servant at the whim of the politician. "There is to be no more fuss. Aubrey is to be found and persuaded to remain abroad. Unless he has plans to appear in Moscow in the near future."

"He has nowhere else to go," Babbington observed tartly.

"Whatever . . . we do not want him back here. Understood?" Babbington nodded, tight-lipped. "Good. It is the future we must now look to, and that will be your business, at least in part. A cleansing of the stables. That and a full inquiry. That should satisfy the House, and the press. The PM's first puritanical flush of enthusiasm—nay, her sheer exasperation after Blunt and the others that there was more bad weather coming from the direction of the intelligence service—has died down. She has listened to wiser heads, to counsels of calm." Sir William seemed to glare at that moment. Babbington, of course, had been one of the headhunters. The PM had listened with enthusiasm, had agreed. Now, Sir William's advice was being heeded.

"I see."

"Excellent. You can bring Margaret back as soon as you wish—you have my blessing on it. That *foolish* man, her husband . . . but, when have we ever expected maturity from our transatlantic cousins, mm?" Babbington was invited to smile, which he dutifully did. *He* was not still to be blamed, apparently. He would continue as Director-General of SAID, at the pinnacle. And Sir William, like everyone else, would continue to be unsuspecting in the matter of his real power. It could have been a great deal worse, he concluded.

Except for Massinger and Aubrey and Hyde and Shelley—the small party of the faithful. Sir William had made them inviolate—but they might have to be silenced.

"When I return from Washington in a few days' time, I want to have a long talk with my goddaughter. *Why* she did not come to me at once I shall never understand!" Again, he threw up his hands melodramatically. "Dashing off like that. She was to hostess a small party for me next week." His full lips were twisted with indulgent humor. A confirmed bachelor, he had been provided with an easy, comforting surrogate child in Margaret Massinger, who had never cost Sir William money, time, or tears and brought him some degree of easily gained pleasure. Parenthood without responsibility, Babbington thought sourly, an image of his own son, tie askew, dinner jacket stained, wildly drunk—a regular feature of the *Tatler*'s picture pages. Ex-Eton, ex-Oxford, ex-, ex-, ex-

Suddenly, he hated Margaret Massinger and her husband. And sensed their danger to himself. What did they know, or suspect? The old ghosts of '74 had been stirring. If they *knew*, then . . .

Even if they suspected.

"I understand your concern, Sir William." The studied introduction of cool deference stung the older man. He glowered.

"Andrew," he said heavily, "I am not concerned. I want

this foolish matter closed, like a factory without orders, like an old file. Closed. Finished with. Bring them back. Have them put on a plane home—today."

"Very well—William." At last, Babbington began to feel comfortable with his role before this audience of one. "Yes," he continued with a sigh, "I hope you can persuade her to desist in this affair. And her husband. The silly man persists in the belief that Aubrey may be innocent."

"That's ridiculous. You should have been able to convince him."

"I tried—dear God, I tried. This American *passion* for investigation . . . it blinds them to the most evident truths."

"I quite agree." Sir William's voice was lazier now, more drawling. They were two powerful members of the same exclusive club. There were no differences between them now. He smiled benevolently upon Babbington.

Kim Philby, Babbington thought. Or Guy Burgess. How they must have relished—*loved*—moments like this. Laughing into their sleeves. The cosmic joke. He trusts me, I'm on his side now that he's demonstrated his petty power. All pals once more. Club members for life.

Yes, Babbington admitted to himself, there is a tang, a *bouquet*, to moments like this. The appetizer to the feast.

"But, if we talk to him together—forbid him to continue, I think he can be brought to his senses."

"That ought not to be beyond us. Margaret will certainly have to be reminded of her duty." He snorted. "The silly woman could have put herself in danger, for God's sake. *Amateurs!*" The word was pronounced with the force of some profound imprecation. Babbington thought: You impossibly pompous, *blind* old man.

Sir William raised his hands, more limply this time. "Ah, well," he sighed, "it's done now. There are no more than a few pieces to be picked up—and your job of cleaning house. Then we can move ahead. I want it all working like clockwork before I finally vacate this chair." The voice purred, and hinted at the identity of the next occupant of that chair and that office. Babbington shrugged off the compliment, and in the same moment inwardly reviewed the prospect with satisfaction. This was beyond the laughter in the sleeve, the nod and wink of secret knowledge. In Sir William's position, his treachery would be preeminent, invaluable to Moscow. Kapustin would be little more than an office boy by comparison.

"I'll have it in hand, William, before your return from Washington. Eldon can take charge of the cleaning up."

"Let's just have it over with!" Sir William remarked with sudden and unexpected testiness. "Unpleasant, time-consuming business . . . let's get *on* with it, and then on with more important matters." His voice reproved gently and with immense authority. Babbington, like a tiresome junior boy, was wasting the Housemaster's valuable time. As if to fulfill the image that occurred to Babbington, Sir William added: "Let's not spend too much time with the juniors, shall we, and neglect the senior team? What's past is past."

"Quite." Babbington was satisfied with the self-control he had displayed during their meeting. He looked at his watch. "I have a lunch appointment, William," he explained deferentially.

"Of course, my dear fellow. As a matter of fact, so have I." Sir William stood up, and offered his large, smooth-knuckled hand. Babbington took it, smiled.

Babbington envisaged the tightrope, the knife edge. Timing would be important, daring crucial. Sir William might have to content himself with eventually learning that his goddaughter and her husband had walked into the very danger he had always feared they might meet. Unfortunate, the meddling of amateurs . . .

As for Aubrey—if they once laid hands on him, he could be shipped to Moscow and his treachery displayed there for the world to see . . . before he was quietly killed. Aubrey might yet have made his greatest mistake. He had been safer in London than he was in any other part of the world.

Yes. Who dares wins, he thought ironically. Who dares wins.

Paul Massinger was afraid. Not professionally, but in a deeper, more personal sense that he could neither quell nor ignore. Zimmermann's warning to employ his old training and instincts had amounted to no more than a half-hearted attempt to avoid surveillance at Schwechat airport when they reached Vienna. His awareness was clogged and weary with the images of his sleepless night; the turning, tossing body of Margaret lying in the other bed, pretending sleep. He had been unable to discern any surveillance. He had made Margaret walk with an American couple to the doors of the lounge while he held back, watching the passenger lounge, the stairs, the doors. It was futile—a branch of mathematics that he had forgotten and that would not return. He was no longer an agent.

He had given up the attempt and rejoined Margaret outside the glass doors in a bitter afternoon wind that seemed to mock them, and they had immediately taken a taxi.

Margaret talked quietly and obsessively in the back of the taxi. Occasionally, Massinger glanced through the rear window but saw no tailing car. The turning of his head was a duty rather than a skill. His wife's voice endlessly refuted the accusation that her father might have been a Nazi. There was Cliveden, of course, even an acquaintance with Mosley. But it was nothing, *nothing*. . . .

He had not been allowed to take a commission because of his importance in the wartime civil service. No one had worked harder; no one was more outspoken of the need to defeat Hitler and the Nazis. People had trusted him. Churchill. Sir William would laugh at the suggestion . . . it had to be the woman . . . the answer was with the woman.

Nonsense. Ridiculous. Foul . . .

Foul, foul, foul . . .

Massinger's head beat with the voice, with its almost mad intensity. Nothing had changed. His wife was still obsessed with her father's death. There was nothing else. Nothing else, nothing else, his mind began to chorus with her assertions and refutations. Nothing else. The remainder of their lives together was at stake, he admitted.

Sobs like the separate, recurring pains of violent toothache. All night. Yet, whenever he addressed her or sat up in his bed, she had not replied but pretended sleep, holding her breath in the darkness of the bedroom as if listening for the noise of intruders. Until he, too, adopted a regular rhythm of breathing that imitated sleep. After a while, the sobbing would begin again, punctuated by sighs, and occasional stifled groans. The distance between the twin beds was a gulf. He had never felt so separated and apart from her, and the sensation horrified him. He recoiled from what they might find in Vienna, even as she pursued it fervently.

His call to Clara Elsenreith as he looked out at the Rhine masked by slanting, driven rain was one of the most reluctant he had ever made. The woman had agreed, almost suspiciously, to see them, but only because he was a friend of Aubrey whose name she recognized. She did not promise help or revelation.

The Stephansdom, in the center of Vienna.

He could not recall, except with difficulty, that this was the city of less than a week ago, the city of the drugged KGB Rezident, of Hyde's danger.

It was hard to remember Hyde. He was a distant, drowning figure in the waves of Margaret's anguish, his white hand raised for help. He was, in all probability, dead.

The taxi stopped and the driver turned and indicated the imposing seventeenth-century facade of the second and third floors of the building that housed the elegant shoeshop. Beyond the broad window of the shop was a cobbled courtyard, which would contain the entrance to the apartments. Massinger paid the fare, tipping with unconsidered generosity.

Margaret got out into the wind, which distressed the hair she had perfunctorily tidied in the taxi. She was heavily made up, and the effect was to make her look older rather than to disguise the tired, drawn appearance of her features. The wind chilled and sculpted her features into an expression of hopelessness. He took her arm and, as the taxi pulled away out of the Stephansplatz, led her beneath the archway into the courtyard. A small fountain was toyed with by the gusting wind. Green plants appeared drab and hardly alive.

Massinger rang the bell. Immediately the security loudspeaker inquired his name. Then the lock was released, and they entered a wide hallway, elegantly carpeted, small tables dotting it as if items left over, superfluous. Wealth announced itself quietly and firmly in the hall and on the staircase. Massinger clutched Margaret's elbow more tightly, brushing down his ruffled hair with his other hand. Paintings, furniture, tables, sofas.

The door opened as they reached the head of the stairs. The woman, white-haired and perhaps sixty, was four or five inches taller than Aubrey. Perhaps Castleford's height— almost as tall as himself, Massinger realized. Yes, she and Castleford would have made what would have been described as "a handsome couple." But Clara Elsenreith had preferred Aubrey, hadn't she? She was dressed in a shirt and trousers perhaps too young in style but worn with definite confidence, even panache. Her eyes were intelligent, quick to observe. She smiled, introducing herself.

"I am Clara Elsenreith. You are the Massingers. Please

come in." Her cool voice might have been that of a reception-
ist. A young maid took their coats and disappeared with
them. The walls of the reception hall were crowded with
paintings, some of which Massinger recognized. The sense of
wealth clashed with the image he had had of Clara
Elsenreith, bereft and penniless and an expert exploiter of
men. She waved them through double doors into a long, high-
ceilinged drawing room. Gold leaf, gilding, and a wealth of
paintings and ornaments. A high marble fireplace and tall
windows through which the bulk and the towers of the cathedral could be seen. The room was warm.

She indicated deep, comfortable chairs while she
perched cross-legged, hugging her knee like a much younger
woman, on a high-backed, delicate chair covered with some
heavily embroidered material in blue and gold. Her shirt was
chocolate-brown silk and her beige trousers were elegantly
tailored. On her small, narrow feet were flat gold slippers.
She seemed to watch them with amusement. There was no
reluctance in her.

"I've ordered coffee," she announced after a few moments.

"Thank you," Margaret replied. Massinger sensed that
the woman regarded them with lofty superiority, as if they
were two distant country cousins who had arrived in the city
for a first visit.

"It was good of you to see us at such short notice," he
offered.

Clara remained silent while the maid brought the coffee.
Modern Rosenthal for the service, the coffeepot silver and old
and valuable. Then, when the maid had been dismissed, she
said: "I was curious. Especially since I knew that dear Kenneth was also coming to Vienna—and at the same time. I
don't believe in coincidences. . . ." Her English was throatily
accented so that it sounded almost false, the trick of an ac-
tress. "Do you?" She seemed pleased with Margaret's discom-
fiture and shock, as if it represented the last piece in a
complex puzzle she had just solved. She nodded to herself as if
to confirm Massinger's impression.

"He's coming *here*?"

"He is a—regular visitor, Frau Massinger. A very old
friend."

Margaret looked at Paul, her face suggesting she might
flee from the room at the slightest suspicion of Aubrey's ar-

rival. He tried to smile to calm her fears, but it was evident his expression did no good. She violently resented the information that Aubrey was on his way. Massinger himself realized he should have considered this a sanctuary to which Aubrey might run, if he ever had the chance. And, he added to the thought, if there was truth here, somewhere, it existed only in the woman's memory. Was it a truth dangerous to Aubrey?

His eyes roamed the drawing room. The apartment was larger than their home in Wilton Crescent, more richly appointed.

"You're wondering," Clara Elsenreith announced, following his gaze. "I began with the shoeshop on the ground floor. Then other shops, then small manufacturers. The shops sell my designs, clothes, and shoes made by my companies, all over Europe."

Massinger nodded, apologizing for his curiosity. The woman seemed uninterested. She continued: "You are Kenneth's friend—I know of you. I understand what you must have been trying to do . . . but I understand what interests your wife, also."

"Will you tell me the truth?" Margaret blurted out, the shoulder strap of her handbag twisted in her hands. Her face was sharp, urgent, demanding.

Clara considered. "What truth?"

"About my father—"

"Ah, then what about him?" She seemed amused at Margaret's anguish. Massinger suspected a deep dislike of Castleford behind the cool eyes. At twenty or twenty-two, she would have been very beautiful, very desirable. A confident, challenging air of sexuality surrounded her even now. "You wish to know what happened to your father? He died."

"And?"

"I know no more than that. If I did, it would not be my business to tell you."

"Then you do know more!"

"I said I did not." Her tone quelled Margaret's outburst. Clara was used to obedience.

"You knew my father?" Clara nodded. "You were his— lover?" Massinger remained sitting in his chair, separated from her, little more than an observer or witness. There was no part for him to play in the present scene.

"No, I was not," Clara said, smiling.

"But—"

"You believed I must be." She shrugged. "Perhaps I might have become his mistress, had I not already met Kenneth." She brushed her hands absently through her hair. "Kenneth was able to arrange matters for me to leave Berlin. Later, he arranged my papers here. He was able to help in many ways. Your father was more powerful, yes, but the choice was not left to me. Your father disappeared—died, we now know." Everything was announced in a cool, unmoved voice. Massinger could not decide whether or not the woman was acting the part they expected her to play—heartless gold digger, living on her wits. He felt she had been attracted toward Castleford's usefulness, but . . . ?

"You didn't like Castleford?" he asked gently.

"Liking did not come into it, not in those days, in that place."

"Nevertheless, something repelled you. What was it?"

"Possession," she announced, suddenly ruffled, looking hard at Margaret.

"Aubrey and my father hated one another?" Margaret asked.

"They did."

"And you—you were the cause. Possession, you said."

"No—I would flatter myself if I were the cause. In your father's case, perhaps . . . but," she added, turning to Massinger, "you know Kenneth. Passion would not disturb him so much, I think?"

Massinger shrugged by way of reply.

"It must be that!"

"Why must it?" Clara asked Margaret. "Why? Kenneth's dislike of your father was—professional. He interfered in Kenneth's work."

"And Aubrey killed him." Margaret had shifted her point of vantage. Now, it was rivalry, professional animosity.

Clara seemed to look to the far end of the drawing room, toward an alcove. Massinger followed her gaze. Aubrey stepped into the room. Aubrey, old and tired and wearing a silk dressing gown below which pajama trousers appeared. He was, however, shaved and groomed. He appeared fully at home in Clara Elsenreith's apartment.

"Paul," he acknowledged quietly. "Mrs. Massinger, I—"

"You?" It was like a curse.

Aubrey came to Margaret's chair, and studied her. She glared at him, then her gaze turned aside. Aubrey continued to regard her for some moments, then turned to Massinger. His expression was kindly, sadly wise.

"Is your wife ready for the truth she has come to hear?" he asked Massinger.

"Yes!" Margaret snapped in a hoarse voice.

Massinger pondered, then slowly nodded. Clara looked at her watch.

"Kenneth, I have appointments this afternoon. I must change. My apartment is at your disposal." Clara's lips demonstrated a fleeting smile. Aubrey nodded. It seemed that something passed between them, brief and secret like a coded message; it appeared to be affection, at least.

"Very well, my dear. It's my responsibility, anyway. I must explain everything. I need the help of these people, both of whom are dear to me."

"Then be careful," Clara warned.

"No, the time for caution is past. You run along, my dear."

Clara left the room with only a brief nod toward the Massingers. Surprisingly, she lightly pecked Aubrey's cheek. The old man seemed warmed by the gesture. He lowered himself onto the sofa as the door closed behind Clara, his gaze directed at Margaret. Then, without preamble, he began talking.

Zimmermann switched on his answering machine. His secretary was still at lunch and he had been out of his office for almost an hour. He listened to the familiar voice. Only its content was unexpected—disturbing and enraging. It was the Chancellor's senior private secretary.

"The Chancellor wishes you to take a week of the leave at present due to you, Herr Professor. This unfortunate matter of the suicide of a prisoner only hours after you interrogated her must be properly investigated. The woman's lawyers and family are prepared to make an embarrassing public display of their feelings—and of their suspicions that the nature of your questions disturbed the balance of her mind. . . ."

The message continued. There was no order for him to present himself to the secretary or the Chancellor or to make himself available to any investigation. He was to be away from the scene until the fuss died down. There was no reference to any connection between the suicide of Margarethe

Schröder in Cologne and the burglary of his apartment. A public fuss concerning a senior officer of the government, albeit one unelected, was the only thing of significance.

Zimmermann remembered another answering machine, years before, and the message, that his wife had died in the hospital, coming hesitantly from it in an official voice. It had been late, he had been dog-tired, ready for bed, knowing he should not avoid the private room for another night and day where she was slowly, certainly dying—and then there had been the message. The pain and the guilt had been equal and immediate. The guilt had remained while the pain eased during the months after the funeral.

Now, this message was meaningless. Sufficient only to raise a small anger. It was also a rope that tied him to a chair, immobilizing him. He would be unable to assist Massinger and Aubrey now, he realized that.

Someone had killed Schröder; someone had burgled his apartment. KGB, or KGB-linked—had to be. They were worried, and it wasn't Aubrey they wished to protect. It had to be Babbington.

Where was Aubrey? his thoughts demanded as he switched off the voice that had reminded him of the lonely death of his wife. The coma she was in did not excuse him, the fact that she would not have spoken, would not have recognized, not even *known him.* . . .

Where was Aubrey? If he could talk to Aubrey, he might still be able to help.

Otherwise there was no hope.

"I went into the Russian Sector of Berlin to meet Clara's husband," Aubrey was saying. "Karl Elsenreith, formerly of the SS—the department concerned with foreign intelligence under Schellenberg to be precise—and now working for new masters. The Russians. For a department of the NKVD." Aubrey studied his audience for a moment, then continued to recite his narrative toward the high ceiling and the long-chained chandelier. "Karl Elsenreith dared not return to the Allied Zone, or to the West. He was a native Berliner and his part of Berlin, or what remained of it, was occupied by the Russians. As for his wife, I am sure he thought it an inconvenience that they had become separated—but he had found consolation for his loss elsewhere."

"The Russians trusted him?" Massinger asked.

"They used him. They appreciated his talents. He had a comfortable apartment, a mistress, an income, an immunity from his former life and associates. In fact, his only problem was some of those less savory old friends, senior officers, *kameraden*, popping up now and again, asking for help. Money, papers, passage out of the Russian Sector, the Russian Zone of Germany. What could he do? He could never be certain the organization might not destroy him if he refused, so he began to help. On my *final* visit to the Russian Sector, I went at his request."

Aubrey paused and Massinger, after looking at Margaret, asked: "Why?"

Margaret flinched. She had half turned in her chair, away from Aubrey. She seemed sunk in some private world of her own.

"He had heard of my association with Clara. Evidently, he still cared something for her . . . or so I thought when I received his message. He promised me certain valuable information if I guaranteed I would do everything in my power to help her, look after her. But he could not, dared not come out—so I crossed into the Russian Sector."

"And?"

"It was a trick. I was blinded by the chance of success, and by the nobility I envisaged for myself making promises about my mistress to her Nazi husband!" Aubrey was mocking himself. Then he added: "Elsenreith was a charming, attractive, poisonous young man. I saw why Clara had been attracted to him, even though he no longer wore that obscene and glamorous uniform—and then I saw why he had really asked me to come. I was becoming too much of a nuisance to the Russians in matters of intelligence. They wanted me removed from the board—once I had given them all the names in my head, of course."

"But you escaped?"

"I did."

"How?"

"With help. People who helped me because they could not afford to see me broken. *My* people. It was during one of my transfers from prison to their headquarters—Elsenreith's office, to be exact. The car was ambushed and I was smuggled away from the scene and back into the Allied Sector."

"And that's it?" Massinger asked. "All of it?"

Aubrey shook his head softly, but Margaret caught the gesture.

"What else is there?" she challenged.

"My dear, there is no easy way to tell you this. The information that Elsenreith gave me—that he had promised me as a lure and supplied out of amusement because it was intended I should never be free to use it—was the name of the man in the Allied Sector into whose care and protection he consigned those *kameraden* who periodically embarrassed him by appearing with demands for help."

Hatred was clear on Margaret's face. "And? *And?*"

"My dear, it was your father. . . ."

"No!" she wailed, and yet Massinger knew that, hearing it from Aubrey, she had immediately begun to believe it. Believing him to be her father's murderer, she had to believe all he confessed.

"How *could* he?" Margaret sobbed, but she wished only to hear of opportunity, not motive.

"It was easy for him, my dear. He was in command of so much valuable paperwork. New identities were easy."

"Then *why?*"

"Because he was a soul in torment," Aubrey announced. The words, the compassion with which they were said, stunned Massinger. "A soul in the most grievous torment."

"Oh, God," Margaret sighed lifelessly.

"And?" Massinger pressed.

"I killed him."

The words hung in the still, warm air of the room, followed by a silence that seemed endless, inescapable. Massinger thought they would remain forever at this exact stage of emotion and knowledge. He could not see ahead, or see beyond.

Eventually, Margaret said in a stilted, dull voice: "You are his murderer, then?"

Aubrey nodded gravely. "In the struggle, it was the pressure of my finger that squeezed the trigger of his gun. Yes, my dear, I am guilty of your father's death."

Margaret seemed spent. She neither moved nor spoke in reply. Her face was turned into the armchair, her legs spread out, her feet turned awkwardly, as if she had been thrown into the chair. One shoe was half off her foot. She might have been a costume dummy rejected by a fashionable shop.

Massinger cleared his throat and said: "What hold could

they have had over him, Kenneth? How could they make him do it?"

Aubrey spread his hands. "Quite easily," he said. "What he confessed to me, I believed. He had known many prominent German diplomats and soldiers and civil servants before the war. Many of them became his friends, as they did of many Englishmen of his class in the thirties—our age of innocence. At Cliveden, in London—parties, operas, shows, brothels, hunts, shoots. The same faces. Hopeful, confident, blond young men. Castleford admired, imitated, sympathized. Oh, I don't think he did much more than many others. Certainly, there is no suggestion that he was false once war was declared, even though he thought it lunacy on behalf of Poland, and further and greater madness when we allied ourselves with barbarian Russia in 'forty-one."

"But, before . . . ?"

Aubrey waved his hand for Massinger to desist. "I think only indiscretions, loose talk—no secrets. No more than a friend at court, so to speak."

"So—what hook did they have in him in 1946?"

"A generous gesture. An old friend, one of the blond young men from Cliveden and all the other country houses, appeared. He recognized Castleford in the street. He'd been skulking about the city for weeks, a hunted man. You can hear it pouring out, I imagine?" Massinger nodded. "Castleford helped him with a set of forged identity papers which described him as a Pole—a former POW, now a displaced person. The man got away. And sent his friends, one after the other. An endless line, all wanting new papers, new identities. You see, we'd been catching a lot of the smaller fry whose papers were second-rate and poorly produced. They needed other outlets, fresh supplies. English papers, duly signed by Castleford and people he controlled who were not in the know. Elsenreith sent people, too. Probably he sent people like himself, SS now working for the Russians. I had to plug the leak, close up the hole. I don't know whether or not the first young man who approached Castleford—he'd whored with him, shot with him, ridden with him, got drunk with him, I heard all this from Castleford—was genuine or a trap. He served the purpose of a trap, anyway."

"And so it went on?"

"For almost a year. Long before I got to Berlin. I didn't know why Castleford disliked me so much from the outset. I think now he was afraid of me. Clara—our involvement with her—was a blind alley. She explains nothing, except perhaps the chance Castleford saw of winning her over and using her to keep a check on me. It never reached that stage."

"What happened—at the end?" Massinger breathed. He saw Margaret become immediately alert. The room was already becoming dark beneath the late-afternoon, leaden sky. The windows rattled slightly in the gusts of wind. Yet he could quite clearly see her shoulders tense, her head become more upright.

"A struggle for the gun. I had listened to him for what seemed like hours. I had come to charge him, arrest him. Even when I saw the gun, I imagined his suicide, so desperate and tormented did he seem. Instead, he intended to kill me. We struggled, and the gun went off. He died almost at once. It took me many hours, almost until daylight, to hide the body in a cellar and bring about the collapse of enough remaining masonry to effectively bury him. That is what happened. I have, if you wish to see it, a fuller written record which Clara has kept for me for almost forty years. I came here, desperate to destroy it." He looked directly at Margaret. She was watching him like a creature preparing to spring. "Now, you may have it, if you wish. It is yours by right, I almost think. . . ."

Margaret lunged out of her chair, her loose shoe almost tripping her. She stood in front of Aubrey, fists clenched, her whole body quivering, shoulders hunched toward him. Her small frame threatened him. Aubrey sat very still, his face tired but still wearing the sadly wise, apologetic expression it had worn during much of his narrative. It seemed to defeat any physical intention on her part. Instead, she scrabbled her missing shoe onto her foot and immediately plunged toward the doors as if escaping a fire.

Massinger stood up. "Margaret!"

She slammed the doors violently behind her. Massinger made as if to follow her, limping suddenly from the renewed ache in his hip.

"Paul!" Aubrey warned. "Paul—not yet. Let her have a little time to herself."

Massinger was halfway to the doors, alert for the noises of Margaret's retreat, then his shoulders slumped and he turned toward Aubrey.

"You're right," he admitted. "I wouldn't know what to say to her."

"The Elsenreith woman's gone out—there's only a maid in the place, apart from our friends."

"We can't take the maid or her mistress, Wilkes—not at this stage. They're Austrian citizens. You're certain all three of them are there? Aubrey *himself* is there?"

"All three."

"Then you'd better get on with it. Take them to the house. Keep them there until I arrive."

"Very good."

"Be careful with the maid. And with your cover story. For the moment, the Massingers are only being detained in connection with their attempts to aid and abet Aubrey. Nothing more than that. Whatever they think or say to the contrary, that's your story."

"Understood. When will you be here?"

"Tomorrow. I have a number of important committees and appointments. Just hold them until I arrive."

"Very good."

She was dazed by her misery and by the betrayal taking place within herself; parts of her mind—memory, thought, feeling, intuition, guilt—were already siding with Aubrey, accepting the terrible, haunted figure her father had become at the end. She had begun believing the struggle with the gun, the intention to murder that Aubrey had recognized almost too late. . . .

She struggled into her coat, dropped her handbag in the hall, gathered it up and clutched it against her, fumbling with her buttons. She pushed against the door, then remembered to pull the latch. The darkening air outside was chilly, empty. She went out into the courtyard. The fountain sprayed out almost horizontally in a gust of wind; the green plants looked dead as their leaves moved stiffly. The cold wind buffeted her, as if attempting to force her back into the house. She had seen bodies rolled into mass graves filled with lime on the grainy newsreel as Aubrey was speaking, the bulldozer's blade shoveling at the white, sticklike limbs and the lolling skull-like faces. The awful striped pajamas and the Stars of David . . .

Now the image would not leave her. She had seen it first as a child, part of a documentary history of the war on television. Now it had become personal, attached to her like a leech or a disease. She could not rid herself of it. Her father did not deserve the image, not now that she knew the whole truth, but everything to do with him was horrible, awful, foul. . . .

She scuttled beneath the archway into the Stephansplatz. The cathedral's bulk was grim and sooty in the dark air, its darkness heightened by the streetlamps. Horrible. *A soul in torment.* Even the man who had gone to arrest him, who had killed him, had said that. Everything lost—he had lost everything—helping *them!*

The voices of relatives pursued her across the Stephansplatz. Aunts and uncles, grandparents—even her grandmother on her mother's side—especially her, because her father had been anti-Semitic, that much she knew. He had admired the Nazis, befriended them—yes, she knew that, too. In the thirties, he had not been like many other brilliant young men—he had eschewed Communism from the beginning of his student days.

The voices clashed and reiterated in her head, and her shoulders and head ducked as if to avoid them. She looked, hurrying across the square in the beginnings of the rush hour, old, weak, and pursued by an invisible cloud of stinging insects.

The hardest knowledge of all was to know that he had been destroyed long before he was killed. That knowledge expunged all other images of him. He was no longer the man she remembered, the man her mother had gone mad through loss of . . . the man smiling into the camera and the sun or coming through the dappled light beneath the apple trees toward her childish swing. . . . Her dress flying up in the breeze of her upswing, obscuring the view of the Downs, his hands catching at the seat of the swing lightly, then pushing strongly—catching the ropes of the swing at last, when she was giddy and almost frightened—catching *her* in his arms. . . .

He was gone, that father. It was darker here, and musty rather than fresh. The air was still. All those fathers were gone.

Destroyed. Robert Castleford had disintegrated.

Still, musty air. The reflected glow of streetlamps

through high windows. Patterned windows. High, unearthly voices, as from the distant end of a tall tunnel.

She shook her head. More images of distress. She went on shaking her head, twisting her body as if she were held powerfully from behind. She was trying to escape the truth, deny it.

Because she believed!

She believed Aubrey. He had confessed to her father's murder. The rest of it, too, was the truth. She knew it was true. Just as she knew her father had been to Cliveden, had traveled and stayed with influential friends in Germany in 1937. She had seen the snapshots: dead boars, wooden hunting lodges, feathered green hats, and leather shorts or green plus-fours. Black uniforms, too. Her father had been laughing in almost every picture.

She believed it all.

She recognized her surroundings for the first time, as if she had only that moment opened her eyes. The cathedral, the Stephansdom. The great roof, the slender nave, the chancel, the musty, cold, still air, the boy trebles whose voices floated just below the roof.

It was something she did not believe. There was no comfort for her here, except that it was out of that apartment and out of the wind and she was almost alone. She sat wearily, perching herself on the edge of a chair, as if about to kneel on the hassock at her feet. She listened to the anthem, and the organ quietly decorating it. Dusty lights glowed faintly, running down toward the high altar. Gold gleamed dully, paint obtruded shapeless color in patches and glimpses. There was nothing for her here.

Except the almost-quiet, the almost-stillness . . .

She noticed that the choir and the organ had become silent, and that she was cold, despite her coat. Her legs especially were chilly. She looked around her, then at her watch. It was almost six-thirty. Immediately, she thought of Paul, and she looked about anxiously, as if expecting to see him close at hand. She thought, too, of Aubrey, and of the written account he had promised her. She did not want it. She would tell him so. He could destroy it, if it helped him.

For the moment, she realized, she was drained of all feeling. She accepted her emptiness with gratitude. It was over, if only for that moment or that day. She stood up after chafing her cold legs. Then she turned toward the west door and left the cathedral.

The Stephensplatz was still busy. Crowds of people seemed to disappear into the maw of the metro entrance across the square. Home goers hurried past her as she walked slowly back toward the shoeshop and the archway and court-yard and apartment that she now felt she could confront.

She turned up her collar. The wind had not lessened. It flicked and whirled around her, lifting the skirt of her coat, as she passed under the archway. The fountain had become a weak, broken peacock's tail, and the green plants rattled in the wind. She pressed the bell.

And saw that the door was unlocked, not fully closed to . . .

No one had answered the bell—she had not heard the catch released. The door had been open. She went in and up the stairs, rehearsing her manner toward Aubrey, especially toward Paul.

The double doors were open into the drawing room, af-ter the door at the head of the stairs had also been found ajar. Every door was open. The drawing room was empty.

"Paul," she called. Then, more loudly: "Paul!" Finally, hoarse with suspicions-becoming-fears: *"Paul!"*

The chair on which Clara Elsenreith had seated herself was overturned. The armchairs and the sofa still bore the im-prints of their three bodies. There were glasses, and a smell of whiskey spilt on the huge Chinese carpet. She bent down to pick up one of the tumblers, and her fingers were red when she clutched it. For an instant she imagined she had cut her-self, and then she saw the patch of blood on the pattern of the rug, almost circular and soaking its tight pile. There was a smear of it on the chair, too, and on the arm of the chair, as if someone wounded had slumped. . . .

It was the chair where Paul had sat!

She heard a faint, distant knocking, muffled and unim-portant. Paul! Where was he? Where was Aubrey? Blood?

She heard footsteps coming quickly, lightly up the stair-case.

The sunlight gleamed on the fins and flanks of the parked aircraft at Rome's Leonardo da Vinci airport. It was a bright, springlike day after the cold and mountains of Afghanistan. Yet for Hyde it was, also, a scene viewed through too much glass, too visible. It prompted suggestions of the imminence of surveillance and discovery, even though before entering the telephone booth he had swept the main passenger lounge a dozen times and found it clean of everyone except airport security.

He was still wrapped tightly in his dark overcoat. They had handed it to him in Peshawar as if it formed part of a new, enemy uniform. They had watched him with clever, sad, disapproving brown eyes and serious dark faces. Miandad's people, all of them disappointed, hurt that it was he who had come back, yet punctilious in carrying out their dead superior's orders. Medical attention, food, bath, shave, telephone provision with secure line, transport. Because he could not write with his bandaged, aching hands, they had given him the use of a portable tape recorder and an empty room. Once ensconced and securely alone, he had dictated into the recorder every clearly recollected word Petrunin had spoken concerning the retrieval of *Teardrop* from the security computer in Moscow. That and everything else had been done swiftly as if by well-trained servants, survivors of the Raj. Only their lips and eyes betrayed, at odd and quickly caught moments, their disappointments, the laying of blame at his door.

He had been bundled aboard a military jet to Karachi and put on the first commercial flight to Rome. He knew he was no more than luggage. Handled carefully and with respect because it was the property of a wealthy and powerful man, but nevertheless done in a remote and detached manner. His debriefing had been skeletal, concerned mainly with the way in which Miandad had met his death. Even the demise of Petrunin seemed of little interest to them. It seemed that nothing that had occurred was deemed worthy of the sacrifice of Colonel Miandad. Petrunin was the bane of the Pathans and the other *mujahiddin*. His death might console the families for the loss of Mohammed Jan and the others.

Thus, they had dispensed with his company as soon as they were able. Officially, he had never been in the country, had never crossed the border with Miandad. They had repeated many times during his period with them, Miandad's last words as reverently as if they had come from the Koran. *Mr. Hyde must be given every assistance, whatever the circumstances, whatever the outcome.*

It was why their helicopter had spotted him, picked him up.

He had spent more than an hour on the telephone to Shelley, whom Ros had summoned to the apartment in Earl's Court. He had been fully debriefed, even to reciting once more Petrunin's useless retrieval instructions. Shelley had been shocked by his revelations; bemused by the computer jargon; numbed by their incapacity to do anything against Babbington.

On the flight from Karachi, Hyde had slept because there was nothing else to do. Nothing left to do. He knew, and his knowledge was useless to him, useless to Shelley. He had measured progress only by the decreasing pain in his hands and face.

Clumsily, with his bandaged right hand, he dialed the number of his apartment, and waited for it to ring four times. Then he put down the receiver, picked it up, and dialed again. On the third ring, Shelley picked up the receiver in Earl's Court.

"It's me," Hyde announced. "What's the news?"

"Catastrophic, Patrick—nothing short of disastrous." Over the telephone, Shelley sounded lugubrious in an almost comic way. Yet Hyde sensed shock and fear beneath the gloom.

"What?"

"Babbington's got the old man, and Massinger."

"Christ, how? When? You didn't even know where they were yesterday."

"Vienna—"

"Massinger went back *there*?" The glass around him was acquiring the faint opaqueness of his tension. "I don't *believe* it!"

"I thought they were in Bonn, with Zimmermann, just as I told you yesterday. But, they got a lead on what happened to her father in 1946, in Berlin—"

"What the hell are they doing bothering with *that*, for Christ's sake?"

"His wife's obsessed by it—poor woman. But the old man was there, too—in the apartment of a woman he knew in Berlin, and one Castleford knew, too." Shelley's voice was very quiet and distant, a long way away. "I've spoken to her— got her number from Zimmermann. He's been suspended from his post, by the way. The word from on high—"

"So, Babbington got the lot of them? They all walked right into the cage. Christ, while I'm out in Apache country, the old man's revisiting one of his old flames and the bloody Massingers are worrying about dear dead Daddy's spotless reputation! What a fucking mess, Shelley! What a God-awful fucking screw-up!"

"Feel better now?" Shelley asked after a few moments of silence.

"What else is there?"

"They didn't get Massinger's wife, or this Clara Elsenreith woman. Both of them were out of the apartment when the two men were taken. There was blood on the carpet, and the maid locked in a wardrobe. This Elsenreith woman's a hard one but she's scared, too. She knows what's at stake—Aubrey must have confided everything to her."

"Where's the Massinger woman now?"

"Stored safely."

"And the old man?"

"I don't know. I do know Babbington's booked to Vienna this afternoon."

"Then he's going to see the old man. What are you fucking well doing about it?"

"There's—nothing I can do. Who would listen?"

"Sir William—he's got a pipeline straight to the PM."

"He's been Babbington's patron for years. He wanted the

new setup, SAID, and he wanted Babbington to run it. He might look at proof, but he would never listen to assertion. And once a breath of what we know gets out, we're both dead."

"I'm dead anyway when they catch up with me—remember? Babbington will know where I've been by now, and he's bound to believe Petrunin told me everything before he died."

"Well, we can't try Sir William. What chance do you think there would be of finding Massinger and the old man alive if we tell anybody? Babbington would know in five minutes."

"Screw Massinger! He's a silly fool anyway. What does 1946 matter when you could be pushed under a bus any minute?" Hyde paused, and then asked: "How could Babbington get rid of them without questions being asked?"

"His KGB pals could take care of it for him. They might take the old man to Moscow for all I know, so they can send back pictures of his emergence there before they kill him. As for Massinger, he could be driving a hired car when it leaves the road and goes over a cliff—how the devil do I know? But he'll do it."

"The bloody crunch, then," Hyde murmured. "The bloody crunch."

"What can we do about the old man, Patrick?"

"God knows. Where is he?"

"Somewhere in Vienna—there's no one in Vienna Station I dare trust, no one I can even send out."

"There's only us?"

"Yes."

"Christ . . ." Hyde breathed. "Then, for God's sake, think of something—someone. Anyone. You must be able to trust someone who knows computers!"

"There's no one. God, I've racked my brains, but I can't come up with a single name—not one I can be certain of."

"Then tell someone—without the proof—just tell someone!"

"I can't! It's too dangerous. Look, your job is to go to Vienna and talk to Mrs. Massinger—"

"Now I'm supposed to commit suicide—Christ!"

"She's desperate, she's afraid. She may know something—she may be able . . . look, Patrick, Sir William is her godfather—"

"And Babbington's a family friend. I know the setup."

"She could be your only chance," Shelley said softly and calculatedly.

"You bastard," Hyde breathed. "All right, all right. But *you*—you think of something else. Backup. This won't be enough, and you know it."

"All right—I promise. But if you can get her out, do it. Put her somewhere safe. We could need her."

"Shelley, what about the old man?"

"Forget about the old man, Patrick—we can't get near him for the moment."

"For Christ's sake, Shelley—*thinking* is *your* bloody job! So *think*! The old man could be in Russia by tomorrow or the day after—find some way to stop it happening. You owe the old man *everything*." His anger had provoked a return of the pain in his hands, especially his left hand as it awkwardly clutched the receiver. His cheek, too, burned once more.

"All right, all right. You don't have to remind me. I'll think."

"Find an answer. Now, give me the number of this Elsenreith woman in Vienna."

"How—dammit, *how*?"

Shelley stood before the huge map of Europe, the Middle East, and Asia that he had tacked to one wall of the lounge of Hyde's apartment. Ros watched him with undisguised disapproval. Hyde was untidy, yes—but during his frequent absences she was always able to restore the apartment to an approximate perfection.

And she fussed and tutted about it now because Shelley had told her where Hyde was and the danger he was in and she did not wish to think about either subject.

"I've brought you some lunch," she said, offering a plate of sandwiches and a large can of Foster's to Shelley's back. Peter Shelley turned, attempting a smile. His brow was furrowed and his face pale. He looked almost debauched by tension and failure. She witnessed fear, too, in his eyes, above the dark smudges. He was afraid for himself and attempting to ignore the feelings.

"Thanks, Ros." He took the plate and flopped on to the sofa. He drank greedily at the beer, staring at the torn sheets from his notebook scattered on the coffee table and the carpet beneath. The cat had toyed with his felt pen, wiping it in a thin trail across the green carpet, leaving a broken, blue, wobbly line. As if apologizing, the tortoiseshell rubbed itself against Ros's jeans. She gently pushed it away with her foot. Unoffended, the cat jumped on to the sofa next to Shelley, attracted by the scent of the tuna sandwiches.

"These are good," Shelley remarked. There were cat hairs on the lap and calves of his dark suit. Ros forgave him for his patronizing tone.

"Will he be all right?"

Shelley looked up, startled. "I hope so."

"He could always go back to Aussie. Nobody'd find him there. Not that he'd want to . . ."

"Do you want a sandwich?"

"I've had my lunch, thanks." Nevertheless, she sat opposite him in an armchair that fitted her large frame snugly, even tightly. She watched him, then looked at the map spread on the wall behind him. He had scribbled on it in several places—rings, crosses, names, dates. Pieces of torn notebook, frayed-edged, were also pinned to the map, obscuring much of the Mediterranean, some of the North Sea, parts of the Soviet Union, and the Middle and Far East. It looked like the creation of a peculiar, fastidious, regimented man planning his holiday or even writing a travel guide. "What is it?" she asked, nodding toward the map.

He glanced at it almost guiltily, as if embarrassed that it should represent hours of work. His stomach rumbled and he apologized. He looked at his watch. It was after three. No wonder he was hungry.

"It's every Soviet embassy in Europe and most of them elsewhere, and everything I can remember about them—and about our people in the same places." He grinned. "It's all highly secret, of course."

"Sure," Ros replied.

Shelley had told her some, but by no means all. She had needed to be assured concerning the importance of what Hyde was doing, that all would eventually be well, and had then seemed satisfied. Shelley did not understand her relationship with Hyde, or her feelings for him. And he did not have the time to spare to consider the situation.

His face must have appeared impatient, for she stood up and smoothed the creases from her jeans. "I'll leave you in peace," she said.

"There's just no way in," Shelley murmured, his finger-tips pushing the separate sheets of his notebook like pieces on a board, with deliberation and intensity.

"What?"

Shelley looked up. "Oh, sorry. Talking to myself."

"It—it is dangerous, isn't it?" Ros blurted out suddenly. Her large, plump hands held each other for comfort beneath her huge bosom.

Shelley nodded. "It is. Not for you—"

"I didn't mean that!" she snapped. "I meant him—and you, and that Massinger bloke . . . and your boss. It's a stupid bloody game to begin with, and bloody worse when you find out it's for real!"

"I'm sorry."

Ros snorted, then left the room. The cat squeezed through the door just behind her feet. Left alone, Shelley stood up and walked around the sofa to confront the unyielding map once more, the can of Foster's still in his fist. His other hand was thrust into his trouser pocket. He began toying with his car keys. The car was even parked two streets away, just in case. Alison had gone to stay with her mother in Hove—he'd taken that precaution immediately after Hyde's call from Peshawar. She'd argued all the way to the coast, but he had managed to return to London without them.

He had used the excuse of having caught a cold in order to leave his office less than an hour after reporting that morning. He had returned to Hyde's flat to await his call from Rome and to tell him the damaging, possibly fatal news of Aubrey and Massinger. He had spent the greater part of the previous night on the telephone in his flat, and the last few hours before dawn trying to sleep in Hyde's bed, which he found too hard. He was camped out, homeless.

Hiding, he reminded himself. I'm on the run like Hyde. I am hiding. No one knows it yet, but I'm already on the run.

He studied the map once more, his eyes roaming at first over whole continents, then reading his notes attached to those embassies and consulates he considered most vulnerable to a penetration operation.

He'd run all kinds of penetration ops from Queen Anne's Gate and from Century House, plenty of times. But he'd never held Aubrey's safety in his hands before, and the concentration required to play this kind of esoteric chess—this war game—would not come. He sighed and swallowed more beer. It was gassy. He belched politely. The room was warmer now, with the central heating turned up.

Come on, come on. Make a beginning, he told himself. Alison was safe in Hove, perhaps walking with their daughter, the dog, even her mother's spaniel along the beach. He, too, was safe for the moment.

Safe until he talked to someone. He could not approach Sir William without Hyde, without Margaret Massinger. Whatever he said would be transmitted directly to Babbington, and he would have endangered himself for nothing. Sir William was leaving for Washington that evening. If he spoke to him now, he would pass the matter to the Cabinet Office or JIC, and they would immediately inform Babbington. No, that way Aubrey's final disappearance was certain, and time would run out for the Massingers.

He was Aubrey's only hope. He and the annotated, scrawled-upon map on the wall. He flinched at the responsibility, convinced as he now was that Aubrey would be shipped to Moscow as soon as it could be arranged. It made sense. A drugged, bewildered Aubrey would pose for pictures in Moscow, the world would believe his treachery, and Babbington would be safe.

Shame about poor Massinger, dying in that car crash. His wife was terribly upset—she committed suicide, you know . . . poor woman. It wouldn't take long, or much of an effort, to clean the stable and ensure the continuation of Babbington the Russian agent as controller of all British intelligence and security.

Pictures of Aubrey. Babbington must already have thought of it and needed only to arrange the delivery of the package to Moscow Centre . . . Aubrey wearing his new medals, Aubrey in his new Moscow flat . . .

Before Aubrey died and was forgotten.

Come on, come *on!*

He moved closer to the map. London was out. Too well guarded, impenetrable. And he didn't have the people. Likewise Paris, Rome, Stockholm, Helsinki . . .

The Middle East. SIS was thin on the ground there, anyway. He'd dismissed Baghdad, Cairo, Amman almost at once. The Far East. They wouldn't have the computer links to Moscow Centre in some places; in others they'd be too well guarded, too secure.

His long fingers caressed the map, smoothing it, stroking countries, whole continents. Nothing. All his notes, almost every one of them, registered hopelessness. The men he could trust were pitifully few, those he could still trust in senior posts even fewer. None of them promised the kind of expertise required for handling a computer terminal, gaining access using Petrunin's instructions, and coping satisfactorily with ingress and egress. And already, almost all of them would have accepted Babbington as DG, and the reorganization of SIS into SAID. Aubrey was no more than an unfortunate part of their collective past.

An irrelevant sense of fastidiousness made him lift the bottom corner of the map and look to see whether he had marked the wall with his pins and jottings. Yes . . . stabs of felt pen, little stains, the pricks of pins—damn!

Map—curtain—map—Curtain . . . Curtain . . .

He had lifted the map like an old lady peering from behind her net curtains, glimpsing adultery or a marital quarrel or new furniture being moved into the house across the street. But the image of a political curtain, the idea of the capital letter, had come to him instead.

Behind the Curtain . . .

He'd noted one or two of their embassies in Eastern Europe already. A preliminary listing of Aubrey's people, the still-loyal, the ones who would act word of mouth from him without official orders, without explanations . . . where?

He knelt at the coffee table, a vague progression of thoughts unrolling in his mind, but shapeless and changing as soon as he examined them. So he moved with them, instinctively, quickly. *Where?*

He shuffled the papers, casting them aside because they seemed no longer relevant—a foolish speculation. Yes, here it was. A handful of people—lower echelon as before, SIS personnel who owed everything to the old man, as he did.

Berlin, Warsaw, Prague, Sofia, Belgrade, Budapest, Bucharest.

He had to look at them on the map. He got up, the sheet in his hand—locals, unofficials, businessmen, SIS officers, clerks and cleaners and secretaries—inside and outside the Soviet embassies.

Berlin. His pen tapped at the city, at head height on the wall. Berlin. Everything was kosher between the Russians and East Germans—the old pals act. East German Intelligence was used by the KGB; they shared lots of work; security would be sloppier. . . .

Berlin. Babbington would have Berlin Head of Station on his side already. Macauley would see the main chance, a London posting to East Europe Desk, Shelley's own job. . . . Who else was there? Clerks, ciphers—might do, might not? Shelley didn't know the men and therefore couldn't risk trusting them. Plenty of cleaners and secretaries on SIS's hooks in and around the Soviet embassy but no field officer capable of being trusted with the job.

He sighed with disappointment. Shapeless, changing ideas scudded through his mind. It was only their movement, their suggestion of energy that he obeyed. He anticipated nothing.

Warsaw. Nothing, not since martial law. SIS people had been picked up in the nets that caught the Solidarity leaders and so had many of the locals SIS employed. Warsaw, he noted with grim acceptance, was a blank piece of paper that he ought to affix to the map.

Bucharest—no. Too far, too many unknowns—possibly no high-grade traffic with the Moscow Centre main computers. Budapest—now, Budapest?

A network had been rolled up there six months before. It had never been reestablished. An indiscreet junior minister had been on the hook, right inside the Interior Ministry. He gave the names of all the others, of his contact officer, of the occasional visiting field controller, and they'd all gone into the bag.

They'd got two back, three were still in prison—two businessmen and an exchange student—and the native Hungarians had all been shot. Budapest—blank sheet, then . . .

Belgrade. Tight, because of Yugoslavia's nonaligned status. Just like a foreign country to the KGB. Plenty of Yugoslavs, but little to show for their efforts.

Prague. Another old pals act. The KGB used the STB, Czech Intelligence, as its messenger boys, its hit men on occasion. The heavy mob. That obscenity of a Czech embassy built of gray concrete and smoked glass in Kensington Palace Gardens carried more high-powered aerials and receiving dishes than the Soviet embassy itself. The KGB and the STB played footsie all the time with one another.

Shelley remembered a report from a low-grade source that much of the communications network used by the KGB in Prague now existed inside the Hradcany castle rather than in the Soviet embassy. As he recalled the information, he remembered himself as a tourist, years before, on vacation in Prague, and immediately his mind was filled with images of the huge, looming cathedral of St. Vitus, part of the Hradcany. He'd waited in line for hours to get into its garish, almost oriental interior—Cologne cathedral tarted up for a pop concert, Alison had said of it.

He'd seen—they'd both seen—the big black Russian sedans parked like a defensive barricade around the government buildings in the castle. That had been before 1968. Now, they were back with a vengeance. Hand in glove, almost incestuous, the relationship between KGB and STB.

It was so pally it was downright sloppy.

Shelley looked at the map. He tapped the city on the Vltava with his forefinger. He studied his list, then looked back at the city almost with longing. Who could he trust, out of all the SIS personnel in Prague, other than Godwin? Godwin was Aubrey's man. But he was useless. Godwin had been wounded in Germany protecting the life of a fake Chinese defector. He'd taken two bullets in the back and now he walked on crutches, moving two dragging, useless legs with their aid. Aubrey had not pensioned him off, as he should have done. Instead, the old man had posted him to Prague as a cipher clerk. Poor bloody Godwin.

Two crippled, dragging legs. No go. No penetration op in prospect there. Worse, Godwin had the qualifications. He was trained in computers, had used them at Century House before his Hong Kong posting, where he had agreed reluctantly to go and only because of the sunshine, since there was little or no computer work for him. He would understand—be able to analyze and explain—everything Petrunin had told Hyde. He would *understand!*

"Damn! Oh, damn, damn, *damn it!*" he shouted. *Godwin, fit and healthy, could have done it!*

The ideas in his mind seemed to drain away toward a distant horizon, like clouds seen in a speeded-up film covering the passage of a day or even a week in mere seconds. Dead end. He touched the map once more, his fingers spread as if he were about to use some secret combination that would open a wall safe.

Godwin had useless legs; Godwin couldn't even hobble without both heavy metal crutches.

His mind began softly chanting the formula over and over. Useless. Dead end. His fingers stroked the map, as if trying to coax some solution from its colors and contours and boundaries. Slowly, heavily, they stroked southward—

Vienna?

Hopeless. It was called the city of spies. Everyone was secure and no one was to be trusted in Vienna. Impossible to mount something against the embassy there, even though Hyde was there, too. In Vienna, agents changed allegiance with every remittance—Queen's face, Presidential features, German philosopher, hero of the people—they obeyed only the faces on the banknotes. And Vienna Station itself was now being run on Babbington's behalf. No go. Definitely no go.

And then he thought—

Hyde. Hyde-hydro . . . Hyde—hydrofoil.

There was a hydrofoil trip up the Danube for tourists from Vienna to Bratislava which took less than an hour, no papers required. Bratislava in Czechoslovakia. He could get Hyde into Czecho easily—

The clouds rolled back through his mind as if the film had been reversed, moving more swiftly than ever, radiant with energy. Yes, it was possible. It could be done.

Danube. January. Ice.

The hydrofoil ran only in the summer months, for the tourists.

Immediately, he was defeated, his schemes shrunken. But almost at once, because the racing clouds of his ideas did not stop, he thought—Zimmermann. Even as he realized that Hyde could not cross into Czechoslovakia without papers and knew that he could not supply them, he understood that Zimmermann would have contacts in Vienna.

Skiing. A skiing holiday. Visas were settled at the border, not required in advance. All Hyde needed to get into Czecho was a hired car, a roof rack, and a pair of skis as his cover. And an Austrian or a German passport supplied by Zimmermann. And he could get out by the same route.

Hyde knew the what, Godwin the how. Hyde had legs—ingress and egress were his business. Godwin could coach him to approach the computer, Godwin would know the precise location and nature of the computer link between Prague and Moscow Centre . . . Hyde and Godwin, not Godwin alone.

Yes.

He would have to return to the office to get off a long, coded signal—EYES ONLY Godwin—whatever the risk to his security . . . and however much the desperation that had formed the scheme kept nudging him. Babbington was on his way to Vienna by now. Shelley glanced at his watch, then at the window. It was already getting dark outside. The street-lights were on. The map was washed with an orange glow, as if lit from within.

Desperate, but he had to take the risk of going to Century House, just as Hyde and Godwin had to take the risks he intended for them. Then he would disappear back here, to hide out. Godwin would know an untapped telephone and would be able to call him at Hyde's apartment.

He sat down immediately. He wanted no truck with qualifications, with the minutiae of planning, the sense of the many dangers that pushed at his awareness like a madman at a door. Vast scope for error and failure.

No. *No!*

He began at once, in an almost blithe, superficial mood that he knew would not last, to draft the signal to Godwin in Prague.

Margaret Massinger was huddled into the passenger seat of the hired Ford as they waited near the exit of the carpark beside the access road from Schwechat airport to the autobahn. It was a few minutes after four in the afternoon, and the orange lights made the sky behind them prematurely darker. Clouds scudded in the wind, threatening snow if they but slowed in their passage across the sky. The windows of the Ford were misty with their breathing. The instrument panel glowed because Hyde had the ignition switched on so that the heating warmed the car. She felt uncomfortable with Hyde, her rescuer. He seemed an essential component of the trap into which her husband had been led by loyalty, by friendship—and by her. She blamed herself, over and over without respite, fearing he might be dying or even dead by now, and the blame spread like a patch of damp to include everyone connected with Aubrey and his downfall. Hyde was, therefore, a prime target for her outrage.

Hyde had found her sitting on a camp bed used occasionally during stocktaking or by the manager of a small dress shop owned by Clara Elsenreith. The woman had taken Margaret there less than an hour after she had discovered her fingering the small patch of blood on the Chinese rug, and told her to remain there. Once Hyde had been directed to Margaret's hiding place, he instructed Clara to leave Vienna.

Where? she had challenged.

Have you got a summer place?

St. Wolfgang, but . . .

Go there. Now.

The woman had agreed to do so. Hyde himself had witnessed her departure. He saw, also, the surveillance. Russian, he thought, rather than Wilkes and the other corrupted souls. They were evidently waiting for Margaret to return. Clara's Porsche would be followed, of course, but so would the tail car. Clara had important friends in the Viennese police hierarchy. She had told her story to one of them—*she was certain that someone was watching her apartment, following her car.* She would be guarded all the way to St. Wolfgang.

A pity her friends couldn't solve the problem of Margaret Massinger, her husband, and the old man. Vienna was Liberty Hall as far as intelligence services were concerned. The police just did not see, hear, or speak. At best, they would expect to hand Margaret Massinger over to Babbington as his problem.

Hyde glanced at her. Guilt had made its inroads on her eyes and coloring. She was guilty now, disproportionately so, blaming herself for the entire situation and its outcome. And afraid they'd already killed her husband. She'd exorcised her father, for certain, but she believed it had taken her husband's life to achieve it. Because of the situation in which she had placed Aubrey, drawing Babbington's heavy mob after her to Vienna and Clara Elsenreith's apartment, he could feel no sympathy for her. She was an encumbrance, and a reminder that attending to her safety was the only task he was competent to tackle. For Aubrey, he could do nothing.

"He was on the plane," he said. He had returned to the car from the airport observation lounge only a few minutes before. "And he's being met." He had glimpsed Babbington hurrying across fifty yards of windswept runway toward the airport buildings. It would have been an easy shot for a rifle.

Hyde had no gun. He patted his waistband. Almost no gun. A small .22 Astra that belonged to Clara Elsenreith, and one spare six-shot ammunition clip. A lady's gun with only close-range stopping power. He had never used one before. Those few field men and armorers he knew who had used the Astra advised that it required half the magazine to ensure immobilizing any enemy. The gun did not provide a great deal of comfort. It was marginally better than nothing. He settled down behind the wheel in silence. The gun might be next to useless, but he had unwrapped some of the bandaging from his right hand so that he could hold it more easily. It had been painful, closing his hand experimentally around the butt. Driving the car, too, hurt his hands, but the pain was now retreating.

When the first escorting car passed them, followed by the limousine that had to contain Babbington behind its tinted windows, the sight startled Margaret Massinger. She sat bolt upright in her seat, turning to Hyde, who at that moment switched on the Ford's engine.

"What will he do to them?"

"Who? Your old family friend and escort to the opera?" Hyde sneered. A third car was bunched up behind the limousine. It looked like a KGB procession. It was, he reminded himself.

Margaret's face was pinched with anger. "Yes. Him."

"I hear the KGB Rezident in London got pissed at your place a few times, too. That right, is it?" His hands touched the wheel gingerly, then gripped. A stabbing pain, then almost at once a steady ache he could ignore. He rolled the car gently down the on-ramp, accelerating once he reached the autobahn. The traffic was already heavier with the first of the rush hour. A caterpillar of lights rushed toward them. They were invisible in the thinner stream of traffic heading into the city. Away to their left, the landing lights of an aircraft flickered and winked.

"Yes," Margaret admitted miserably. Hyde desisted from further comment. Accusations, reminders only fed her guilt. Guilty, she was useless, even dangerous. "What will he do to them?" she repeated after a mile or more of silence.

"If it hasn't occurred to him yet, then it soon will."

"What?"

"The old man on display in Russia."

"How could he—"

"Easy. Drug the poor old wretch up to the eyeballs, take

a few snaps, then get rid of him. Babbington would be safe then, because the old man's treachery would have been confirmed."

"And Paul?"

"An accident."

"No . . ." Margaret's voice shuddered, and she covered her face with her hands.

The three cars ahead had left the autobahn into Vienna and were climbing and twisting through the maze of a major junction. Hyde closed the gap between them, aware of the plethora of signs and distances and directions. The cars braked and turned, and Hyde followed them onto Autobahn 23, heading southwest. He wondered for a moment whether he had been spotted, since the three cars appeared to be retracing their journey, and then decided it was merely a precautionary move. He let the Ford drop back into the stream, half a dozen cars behind the trailing car.

He was alert at every on-ramp and junction. They passed through Favoriten and Liesing before the autobahn turned south and became the E 7. The three cars left the autobahn at Vosendorf, turning west onto Aubobahn 21. By this time, Margaret had a road map on her knees, and periodically switched on the courtesy light.

"It looks like the Vienna Woods," she said, switching off the light immediately.

"He's not likely to go further afield. I wonder who owns the property—us or the Red Terrors?"

The cars left the autobahn outside the village of Perchtoldsdorf and Hyde slowed, widening the gap between them and himself before he, too, took the winding minor road. Now that they had left the tunnel of lights, they could see the low hills rising against still-blue gaps in the clouds. Vineyard lines and trellises flanked the road. The village was quiet, glowing, tiny. Hyde saw the doors of an inn swing open, could almost imagine he heard accordion music and singing. Yet there were modern houses, too. New wealth moving to picturesque suburbs, enlarging villages. He saw a Porsche parked outside a converted barn, a BMW outside a modernized mill, a Ferrari standing next to it. They crossed a tiny stone bridge, and as they did, the three cars ahead turned off the narrow road into trees. He saw their lights dancing ahead of them on a rutted track. He drove beyond their turning point, noticing the narrow drive and the lights of a large, low house perhaps a

hundred yards beyond. They were just outside the village.
Hyde stopped the car.

"Welcome to King Babbington's regal hunting lodge," he
remarked. "Who says crime doesn't pay? It must belong to the
opposition. *We* couldn't afford it." He gently touched his
hands together. Just aching . . . not too bad.

"Are they inside?" Margaret asked, the first tiny note of
hysteria in her voice. It disturbed Hyde.

"Oh, yes—they're inside."

"What are you going to do?"

"I don't know. I really don't know."

A log fire blazed in the huge fireplace. The lighting was
subdued, warm. The shadows of the men who got quickly to
their feet as he entered loomed and swayed on the walls and
ceiling. Deep, old chairs, a sofa, gleaming block flooring covered by thick, bright rugs. Babbington realized the appearance and furnishings probably corresponded to someone's
image of a senior Party official's dacha in the woods outside
Moscow. However, he liked the house. Always had. It was a
safe house in more senses than intelligence jargon implied. He
nodded to the three men in the room. More shadows loomed
as his escort trooped in behind him. One of them took his dark
overcoat. He shook hands warmly with Wilkes, who had
crossed the room to greet him. Wilkes *was* Vienna Station;
Wilkes was entirely necessary, even irreplaceable. The others
were locals, one of them even an emigré Bulgarian, one of the
mercenaries of the secret world. The dog soldiers.

"You've kept them apart?" Babbington asked, letting go
of Wilkes's hand. Wilkes nodded.

"All the time."

"Good."

Babbington crossed to the fireplace. The heat from the
logs leaped to his cold face. He rubbed his hands together
then offered his palms to the fire, bending slightly forward.
He appeared intent upon pictures in the flames, but for Babbington there were none. He had his objective clearly in mind
and there was no margin for error or imagination.

When his hands were warm again, he turned his back to
the fire and studied the men in the room with him. They appeared, amusingly, like stark-shadowed passport or prison
pictures of themselves against the white-painted stone walls

of the room. *His* people. Vienna Station. Wilkes, of course, had been the beginning of it, approaching the KGB when he was first posted to the city. A greedy man, a man who sought money and also loved the challenge of betrayal. Eventually, Babbington was made known to him, and Babbington began using him. By that time, Wilkes had enlisted most of the people in the room. He was running Vienna Station by then, even though the Head of Station, Parrish, was nominally his superior. Parrish allowed Wilkes, as senior field officer based outside the embassy, to control the operation of the Station: to pay, to contact, to mount operations, and to recruit—most importantly, to recruit. Wilkes had recruited the locals and the emigrés, even two of the men posted to Vienna from London. He'd done a very good job during the past three or four years. He had provided Babbington's communications base, and his eventual means of trapping Aubrey.

Briefly Babbington recollected approaching the small, self-important figure of Aubrey in the Belvedere gardens. Only two weeks ago. Another forty-eight hours would see it finished with.

Them finished with, he corrected himself.

"How badly is Massinger hurt?" he snapped at Wilkes. "I couldn't obtain a clear picture from—your colleagues." There was evident irony. Wilkes's expression did not change.

"Not bad. He's been patched up. A doc our friends use from time to time. Silly bugger wanted to be a hero. He'll live. Just lost a lot of blood, that's all." Wilkes affected boredom.

"And Aubrey?" Babbington could hardly mask the gleam of satisfaction in his voice.

"Grumbling, threatening, full of bull, about covers it."

Babbington's face registered disappointment. Evidently, Aubrey was not yet a broken man. He wondered whether he should see him, or let him stew a little longer.

"No news of the woman?"

"Which one?"

"Massinger's wife. Oh, dismiss your colleagues, Wilkes. . . ."

Wilkes waved his hand toward the others. Obediently, and perhaps with indifference, they filed from the room. Once outside, Babbington could hear the subdued murmur of their voices as they made for their own quarters, even a burst of coarse laughter. The usual assortment: the greedy, the stupid, the sadistic. He breathed more easily. His stomach had been queasy in the car, and he realized now that it was not travel or tiredness or tension. It was the demeaning proximity of the lower echelons, the infantry of the secret world. Wilkes, of course, was tolerable—usually. . . .

"Massinger's wife's nowhere in sight. The other woman—the German—she's taking a short holiday at her place outside St. Wolfgang."

"You had her followed—yes, I will. Scotch. Neat." Wilkes had crossed to a highly ornamented cabinet and removed a bottle and glasses, gesturing toward Babbington with them. He poured two whiskeys, bringing Babbington's glass to the fireplace.

"Yes. The police were there, too."

"Why?"

"She's got influential friends in the Viennese police. She's looking after herself."

"What will she have told the police?"

"We're checking on that. Not much, I think. Even if she had, there's nothing they're likely to do. If she mentioned Aubrey by name, they'd back away with a horrified expression. They don't get mixed up with us—you know that."

"I know it. Would the police look for Margaret Massinger?"

"They might. If they find her, we'll hear about it. Don't worry. I doubt they'll look very hard—not in this case."

"What if she goes to the police?"

"She can't tell them anything. And they'll be their usual reluctant selves. We could even get to her after she goes to them, if that's what you want."

Babbington sipped at his Scotch and moved a little away from the blazing fire. "I don't know yet. I want her out of the way, but I'd prefer her to be found by our people. Then we can arrange matters."

"What are you going to do with them?"

Babbington grimaced. "It's difficult, Wilkes. . . ." His voice faded, as if he sensed an admission of weakness rather than caution—as if the warmth of the room had made him soporifically lax, kindly or indecisive. "Time is running away with us," he said, more firmly, sitting more erect in his chair. "Later, we can do as we please with them. For now, I'm not going to raise a cloud of suspicion by getting rid of the entire cast!" He laughed, encouraging a nod of agreement, a grin of anticipation, from Wilkes.

"It's always the other side who have all the fun," Wilkes sighed.

"You'd have been on trial with the others in Poland, given the chance, Wilkes."

"Oh, Father Whatsisname, the priest, you mean?" He grinned. "Just football practice for some of the lads, I expect. Mind you, there's a few I'd like to do the same to, I must admit."

"In time, Wilkes. Just give it time. Settling dust, short memories, that sort of thing. You will have your chance." Babbington, amused as much by the completeness of his knowledge of Wilkes as by the man's remarks, once more relaxed. His tone was that of an indulgent housemaster; he recollected the tones of *his* housemaster, sensing he had somehow imitated them as he spoke. Wilkes gave confidence off like a scent, soothed like a masseur just by being present, by being *certain*.

"What about Aubrey?"

"Ah," Babbington sighed expansively. Now, he could see no drawbacks, no disadvantages. "There, we shall have to do something straight away, I'm afraid." Mentally, he saw his housemaster looking up from a sheaf of papers, eyes gleaming over half-glasses. Avuncular, clear-sighted, amused. All would be well. . . .

"What?"

"The others can wait. Even Zimmermann presents little danger, in the short term. But dear old Kenneth is going to appear where everybody expects him to appear. I envisage an effective, dramatic little scene which will have the effect of silencing all suspicions—at least until we have time to act. Kenneth's going on a trip. He's going over the border!"

"Moscow, you mean?" Wilkes's face shone with amusement, even admiration for the daring Babbington had displayed. Babbington basked in Wilkes's confidence. "That's clever. Yes, I can see that doing nicely," Wilkes added, raising his glass in a toast. "I'll drink to that. But will Kapustin agree?"

"He'd better. It's too good an opportunity to miss, don't you think? It simply needs to be arranged. Make contact tonight and get a message to Kapustin."

"What shall I tell him?"

"Just tell him I want to talk. Urgently." Babbington frowned. "I'm not going to let that peasant ignore the opportunity. They can dispose of Kenneth after they've taken their pictures and spread the news he's in Moscow to collect his medals and be promoted to the rank of a full general in the KGB! And *we*, Wilkes, will be endlessly and completely secure. Oh, no, Kapustin can't be allowed to pass up this opportunity."

"Do you want to see Aubrey?"

Babbington looked at his empty glass. "No. I think another drink first, don't you? Kenneth's flavor will increase with a little keeping." He smiled.

"It might at that," Wilkes replied, taking Babbington's glass.

"There'll be a car, a brown Skoda, waiting for you in the Zidovska, near the cathedral, a knitted cardigan with reindeer on the pockets lying on the passenger seat. The keys will be under the—"

"No! For Christ's sake, for the last time—no! It's impossible."

"For Heaven's sake, Patrick. You don't have any choice. Godwin has the background in computers, *you* have the skills. . . ." Even distantly down the telephone line, Shelley sounded as if he were pleading. His earlier objections to Hyde's intransigence had sounded like the disappointment of someone who has failed an examination despite being convinced of their own cleverness. Now, however, Shelley was angry, and selfless. It was no longer his scheme that mattered; it was Aubrey. "You have to do it." The words were soft and final.

"No. You have to be able to mount some kind of rescue attempt. It's a matter of calling the cops, for God's sake!"

"And they'd believe you and not Babbington?"

"But Aubrey would be alive," Hyde protested. His voice was an intense whisper, as if the telephone cubicle at the rear of the village inn was incapable of preventing the carry of his words.

"For how long? And you—how long would you be alive?"

"Mate, I can't just hire a car and skis and drive to Bratislava to collect another car that might or might not be waiting for me!"

"You can. *And* you can get into the Hradcany. And Godwin can instruct you—"

"God—"

"Look, you don't have to tell me it's desperate remedies. I know it already. But there's no other—"

Shelley's voice had stopped speaking with unexpected suddenness, almost as if he were in the inn with Hyde and had paused to listen to the music that had just struck up from an accordion, a violin, and drums. A folk song, indistinguishable from a hundred others.

"Shelley?"

"I'm just having a look out of your window, Patrick. I thought I heard the doorbell downstairs." Apologetically, Shelley added: "Getting a bit jumpy myself. . . ." Again, his voice trailed off, this time more slowly, as if his attention had become absorbed elsewhere.

Hyde waited. Tension jumped in his fingertips. He knew the conversation could have only one conclusion. Already the guilt was beginning to appear. But, he *couldn't*—it was impossible.

"Shelley?"

"Yes, Patrick."

"What is it?" Hyde asked, suddenly alert, as if an enemy had walked into the warmly lit, already smoky inn. The door had opened, in fact, and smoke from the log fire had billowed into the room. A stranger who was greeted by other customers had entered. *Danger*— "What's wrong?"

"I—think they must have found me. There're a couple of cars in the street outside. Must have found my car, put two and two together. I think they're already in the house."

"Are you sure?" Hyde felt himself sweating. He hunched into the telephone booth, the mouthpiece closer to his lips.

"Oh, yes—I'm sure. Listen, then. Brown Skoda in the Zidovska, cardigan on passenger seat, keys under the driver's mat, papers locked in the glove compartment—everything you need. It'll be there tomorrow morning—" Shelley broke off, evidently listening. Hyde imagined he could hear a knock at his door. "Got that?"

Hyde wanted to reject the information. "Yes," he said.

"Tuck the woman away somewhere safe—then see Zimmermann's chap for the Austrian passport. Change cars and papers in Bratislava, then drive to Prague. Godwin will meet you at one of the bus stops on the E 15, once the road reaches the suburbs. Look out for him—" His voice broke off suddenly. Hyde distantly caught the repeated knocking, loudening in the silence. Shelley's breathing, too.

"Are they in?"

"No. But soon. I've given you Zimmermann's number in Bonn. *Call him.* If anything goes wrong and you need a fallback plan, call him—" Shelley broke off.

"Are they in, Shelley?"

"Yes. Good evening, gentlemen," he added, addressing the visitors to Hyde's apartment. Hyde heard Ros's strident protests from somewhere outside the room. Someone spoke to Shelley, but Hyde did not catch the words. Then Shelley said to him: "You see how I'm fixed, darling. I shall be away for some time, I should think. Ring you when I get back. Take care. . . ." The voice faded on that as the telephone receiver was snatched from Shelley.

Hyde listened to the humming silence, then to the breathing that came on the line. The exhalations of someone's effort and anger. He heard someone ask Shelley who was on the line, but there was no reply. Involuntarily, Hyde turned his head so that he could watch the door, so much had Shelley's danger worked on him. The door remained shut. The breathing went on for a few moments, then: "Who is that?"

Hyde did not recognize the voice. He held his breath. In his mind, the seconds ticked away. He had been on the telephone for almost twenty minutes arguing with Shelley. Ros was still protesting somewhere in the background. The man who had spoken to him demanded silence.

"Who is that?" he repeated, the softness gone from his tone.

Twenty minutes. All meaningless now. Shelley had been cut off from him, would be taken into custody, interrogated. There might even be evidence in the apartment to suggest Shelley's scheme—he couldn't have planned it without maps, notes.

Then the voice said: "You're interested in a vacation in Czechoslovakia, I gather." There was self-congratulation in the voice, and Hyde's breath exploded. "Ah," the voice said. "Who is it?"

Shelley had had maps, notes—how much for God's sake—how much? Enough to kill his agent?

He'd called Shelley, Shelley had rung back when Hyde ran out of coins. Now, Shelley was under arrest, and they might even guess it was him on the other end of the line. . . .

"Everything's down the pan," he heard Shelley announce clearly. His voice sounded hopeless, then Hyde sensed the message in the resignation. Shelley had got rid of almost everything, then . . .

He clattered the telephone onto its rest, hurting his raw hand, and left the phone booth swiftly. The smoke billowed out from the log fire as he opened the door then slammed it behind him.

The night was cloudy, the moon obscured. The temperature chilled him and he began to walk back toward the car, which he had parked by the bridge, leaving Margaret in the passenger seat. He began to jog slowly for comfort, for the illusion of fitness and freedom, for the paramount illusion of escape. He was enraged with the anger of a trapped animal.

There was nothing he could do except follow Shelley's plan, knowing that, at each turn of the path, they might be there ahead of him, waiting.

He reached the car, startling Margaret as he dragged open the door, climbed heavily into the seat, breathing hard, then slammed the door. He ignored his protesting burns. He glared at her almost wildly, malevolently.

"What does he say?" she asked in an apologetic but firm voice. She had applied some fresh makeup and looked younger. Hyde, however, saw only a greater competence that at once disappeared beneath his stylized view of her as an inconvenience, a dangerous liability.

"Who? Shelley?" She nodded. "He's just been fucking well arrested—that's the message from London! All right now? You've bloody done for everyone now! Satisfied?"

Even though the movement was awkward, and the blow without real force, Margaret slapped Hyde across the face. "Don't *speak* to me like that!" she shouted, a lock of hair falling free across her pale forehead. Anger did not make her beautiful in the lights of an approaching car, only narrow-faced and dangerous. "Stop blaming *me* for everything!" she added when the car had passed them. "Well, did he talk to William?"

"Your esteemed godfather is in Washington for a few days. Just our bloody *luck*!" His hands banged the dashboard shelf heavily. He winced at the pain. "Not even you can talk to him at the moment," he added.

"Blast . . ." she murmured, staring through the windshield back toward the hidden house where, for all she knew, her husband might be dying.

Yes, Hyde said to himself. I've already accepted it. It's happened somewhere between the pub and here. He looked carefully, appraisingly at Margaret Massinger. Her perfume was inappropriately seductive in the tense atmosphere of the car. "What state are you in?" he asked bluntly.

"All right. Why?" she retorted, turning her face to him. *"Fine."*

"I have to find somewhere to leave you . . . somewhere safe. You'll be on your own, maybe for a few days." He, too, looked toward the trees that masked the house. Go on, he thought. Volunteer.

"Why?" she asked, again staring through the windshield.

"Something that may work—might help. Shelley's option. I'll have to try it now."

"And I'd obviously be in the way," she observed. Then she added: "But what about this place? If everyone's confined, then who will you have watching the house?"

Good, he thought. "There isn't anyone," he said.

"But they could—could move them," she said fearfully.

"Maybe."

She was silent for a few moments, and then, after nodding decisively to herself, she said: "Then get me a camera, one that takes pictures night *and* day, and give me this car and find me an anonymous hotel . . ." She had been looking through the windshield until that point, and now she turned to him. ". . . and I'll get you proof that they're in there."

"You're on," he said, surprising her.

"You don't object?"

"You're the only girl in the world, right now. We are the entire army. So—" He switched on the ignition. Then he looked very levelly at her. "—don't get caught. If they try moving either or both of them, or there are comings and goings, then get it on film. And *make* Sir Bloody William listen to you! Even if he's in Timbuctoo, get hold of him and tell him everything you've seen and photographed. Then pray he can stop it before it's too late. If you can't get through to him and can't persuade him to listen to you—you can tail the car they're in until it's pushed over a cliff!"

Margaret's face was unnaturally still as she struggled to control her emotions. She nodded violently, decisively.

"All right," she said, then more firmly: "All right."

Ghosts in the Machine

. . . our better part remains
To work in close design by fraud or guile
What force effected not.

Milton, *Paradise Lost*, Bk. 1

14
No Country
for Old Men

Hyde emerged from the low wooden hut, closing the cover of his Austrian passport on the weekend visa that allowed him entry into Czechoslovakia. Immediately, his eyes sought, and found, the hired Ford and the fur-coated woman standing beside it. He tapped his cold cheek with his passport, then descended the steps toward a dirty, gray Volkswagen Beetle, its roof rack displaying skis and ski poles. Manfred Eicher, Hyde's cover name, was going skiing at one of the resorts in the Little Carpathians, north of Bratislava. There were at least a dozen other cars displaying skis in the line to cross the border at Petrzalka, on the main autobahn between Vienna and Bratislava.

And yet he fought to calm his breathing—sending up little cold, grey, puffs of air like distress signals—as he watched Margaret Massinger climb into the Ford, reverse, turn, and head back toward Vienna. He had no sense of her danger, only of his own. He glared at the retreating Ford, then turned his head to stare balefully at the border crossing and the grey, urgent river beyond.

And the city beyond the river and the bridge. Inside Czechoslovakia.

You've crossed borders before, he told himself as he massaged his gloved hands slowly together. The healing skin was still tender. The palms and backs of his hands were still lightly bandaged. It was a reminder of fragility and, strangely, of isolation. He turned his head, watching the plume of the Ford's exhaust disappearing into the hazy gray morning. When he returned his gaze to Bratislava, it seemed in the snow-threatening air that the castle had crept closer to the river, like a guard anticipating his attempt to cross the border.

393

Hyde shivered, opened the door, kicked the slush from his boots against the car, then climbed into the driving seat. He started the engine. The pole began to swing up. An armed guard waved the lined-up cars forward. He rubbed the clouded rearview mirror. There was no longer any sign of the Ford. Briefly, he was aware of Margaret Massinger as another person, real like himself, at risk like himself with her instructions and the camera and film they had bought. Then she retreated in his mind. He gripped the steering wheel, pressing his palms down upon it to pain them. He shuddered. He could not shake off the sense of impending failure or ignore the hurried desperation that had impelled him to this border crossing.

The arrangements had been easy. A call to Zimmermann, an address in a quiet old Viennese street, Margaret Massinger watching him intently while the lights glared in his eyes and his passport photographs were taken, the hours of work, the fake stamps, the resulting Austrian passport and the new identity. The skis and sticks, the goggles, the winter clothing, the boots . . .

The clockwork, hectic rush for a surprise holiday or business trip.

To end here, he thought, putting the Volkswagen into gear and letting off the handbrake. Bratislava looked as cold and inhospitable as the Danube beneath the cloudy, snow-filled sky. He revved the engine and shuffled the car forward in the line. To end here, nerves frayed, confidence ebbed like a tide. Dry like a riverbed, he told himself. He was in poor shape. Everything depended upon him. The weight of that dependence pressed down on him.

The back wheels of the Beetle slithered in the rutted slush at the end of the road, then he was passing beneath the raised barrier. He glanced up at it, then down to look through the windshield. Steeples had joined the castle on the lumpy, indistinct horizon. They appeared like upthrust rifles or spears. Hyde felt there was no comfort to be derived from his papers, from the ease of his passage, from the car awaiting him in Bratislava, a gun taped to the underside of its chassis in a waterproof bag. No comfort. The thing was hopeless from the beginning. . . .

The river slid beneath the bridge, its surface like dirty glass, yet suggesting movement as quick and dangerous as the body of some great snake.

"Alive."

"Recovering, I trust?"

"Yes, I think we can say he is recovering very well. . . ."

"Every blow—every *blow* was delivered by you—*your* malice was in all of it!" Aubrey raged, surprised by his own outburst. His body quivered. "Because he tried to help *me!*"

"I'm sorry you feel that, Kenneth," Babbington murmured. "Please sit down—my dear Kenneth, do sit down." He indicated one of the two narrow armchairs, and the bed. "Please," he soothed.

Aubrey watched the man's eyes. Did he know? Was he here to learn?

Babbington sat in one of the chairs. Wilkes tugged aside the curtains. The daylight was gray and snowy. "Bring Sir Kenneth his breakfast, Wilkes," Babbington instructed. Before Aubrey could say anything, Wilkes had left the room. Aubrey sank into the depression in the bedclothes he had previously made. Babbington leaned forward in the chair, hands touching as if at the commencement of prayer. "Believe me, Kenneth, I am sorry about Massinger—but he brought the whole thing upon himself. You realize that, surely?"

"They clubbed him down and enjoyed doing so."

Babbington flicked one hand impatiently, then it returned to accompany its twin in further prayer. "I have said I'm sorry, Kenneth. Zeal—and anger. Yes, justified anger, perhaps. Your American friend has caused us a great deal of inconvenience—"

"I see."

"Good."

"I take it he is already in the hospital?" Aubrey asked with calculated innocence.

Babbington hesitated, and Aubrey knew that the crucial moment had arrived. Babbington would never return him to England. Babbington must know about Zimmermann, must know how close suspicion was to him! Aubrey understood his hesitation, the vague shadow of a desire to solve the problem without further violence. Perhaps he, too, had been shocked by the bruised, broken face and the gunshot wound?

"He will be," Babbington replied eventually, and by his tone Aubrey knew that Babbington had relinquished any hope of their ignorance, of their survival. His glance apologized for his decision. Then he added, sighing: "There really isn't anything to say, is there?"

"Perhaps not."

"In the car—Wilkes heard, you see. . . ." Babbington explained heavily, guiltily.

Aubrey turned and switched off the bedside lamp, whose light was more sickly than ever. With his face averted, he murmured: "I understand."

"You couldn't have hoped—" Babbington began in a tone of protest.

"No," Aubrey snapped, turning to face him. "What will you do about Zimmermann? No doubt you realize how much he knows?"

Babbington bared his teeth, but could not summon the confident smile he desired. "Yes," he said in an ugly voice.

Aubrey held up one hand, fingers spread. He counted off the names he recited. "Shelley, Hyde, Zimmermann—what has begun can't be stopped, Andrew. You must see that. . . ." Aubrey's voice trailed off. Babbington was shaking his head in disagreement, and his smile had become more confident.

"Your own fate will settle matters nicely, Kenneth," he announced. There was still something of bluff, of self-deceit in the voice, but it was evident that Babbington's confidence was growing. Soon, he would command the conversation.

"My fate?" Aubrey inquired.

"Your fate. And that of the American, naturally."

"Naturally." Aubrey's face twisted at the mockery in Babbington's voice. He snapped: "I cannot—simply *cannot* comprehend your treachery!"

Babbington blushed. His lips tautened, as if his face had been struck. His eyes were chilly. "Don't be so ridiculously naive, Kenneth."

"Naive?"

"Patriotism—with your experience of the world? With your knowledge of the skeletons in the closets? *Patriotism?*" There was a stinging contempt in the tone. Babbington had mastered his voice now. "You're as naive as that American in the next room, Kenneth. I thought we could safely have left the flag and the anthem to our colonial cousins—this late in the day. I'm surprised at you."

"I'm a little surprised at myself." Aubrey was slowly shaking his head. His lips were formed in a smile.

"Which is why I could never have released you, or allowed you to go free," Babbington announced. "You are even more dangerous than I thought."

"Why, Andrew?" Aubrey asked immediately, unbalancing Babbington, whose cheeks flushed. He smoothed them with his hands, removing evidence.

"Why?"

"Why treachery? You have—*everything*. You gained the high ground by your own abilities. What can you possibly have gained from *them*?"

"Unlike yourself, the secret life has never been all in all to me." Babbington smiled, catlike.

"I repeat—what on earth did they have to offer *you*?" He paused, and continued with biting irony: "For someone with your advantages—your background, education, influential relatives, intellectual promise? What was it? A taste for the kind of danger that makes a prominent figure in public life who happens to prefer men to women take to haunting public lavatories?" He smiled. "Is that it? The danger in the deceit—the risk of the policeman's footsteps and voice outside a grimy, odorous cubicle in a public urinal?"

Babbington's cheeks reddened. Then he waved the insults aside. "Perhaps," he admitted. "More to do, I think, with the public lavatory to which you offer up your naive patriotism." His face darkened, and he leaned forward. "This country, Kenneth. This country since the war. Look for the answer there, in the piddling little American aircraft carrier we have become over the years. The whining, useless voice wailing in the corridors of the UN!" Babbington's rage was sudden, surprising, and genuine. Aubrey was shocked by it. Shocked, too, by the contempt at the core of the man, the lonely peak his ego had climbed. Babbington's clenched fist banged his thigh. "You remain loyal to it? To *our* masters? How can you? How *can* you?"

"As you said—naiveté."

"It was not sufficient for me—I couldn't be naive."

"No. You never could. And what did they offer?"

"Eminence. No, not your sort of secret eminence, unregarded even by yourself—" He broke off. "You never really *sought* the Director-Generalship after Cunningham, did you?" Aubrey shook his head in agreement. "Eminence," Babbington repeated. "Eminence within the most powerful secret organization in the world. Do you understand?"

"I think so. A monkey requiring a larger audience for its tricks."

"You foolish old man," Babbington hissed.

"What can you do to me? More than you intend?"

Babbington shook his head. "No—not more than I intend already." He smiled. "You don't display much curiosity in that direction, Kenneth?"

"Should I?"

"I think perhaps you should."

"My appearance in Moscow would clear the field for you. I also think the idea would have a certain appeal for you. As for poor Massinger, I presume quick disposal will suffice for him." Aubrey was studying his hands as they lay inertly in his lap. He would not give Babbington the satisfaction of looking into his face and showing him his fears.

"You have no country now, Kenneth," Babbington announced. "No country whatsoever. Not much to show for forty years of loyal service."

Aubrey's head snapped up. His pale eyes were hard. "I have the small satisfaction of knowing that for forty years I have occupied time and space that might otherwise have been filled by someone like you," he delivered in a waspish, superior tone. He was satisfied with the flinch of reaction in Babbington's eyes.

"It is *now* occupied by me," Babbington replied after a moment. "And consequently your forty years has been a complete waste. Your whole life has been meaningless."

Babbington stood up. Aubrey said: "Why now?"

"What?"

"*Teardrop*. Why now, at this precise moment?"

"The time seemed right. The scenario was available. Once you took the bait from Kapustin, the whole thing gained a momentum of its own. It rolled downhill like a great smooth stone. You were so *greedy* for Kapustin's defection, Kenneth!"

"I know it."

Babbington crossed the room. "I'll leave you for the moment—" he began.

Aubrey interrupted him. "When, Andrew—when did they get hold of you? Tell me that."

Babbington paused for a moment, then shrugged. "Very well. After Suez. I'd begun in security by then. Yes, Suez seemed to clinch matters for me. That *farce!*"

"I see."

"I could see nothing ahead—humiliation, decline, bankruptcy in the world's court . . . and we have it."

"Thus go all Fascists," Aubrey murmured with withering contempt, "down the aisle of that broad church, worshiping order. Was that it, Andrew? Order. The attractions of nothing more than *efficiency*?"

"You do not even begin to understand," Babbington replied, shrugging.

"Much like Castleford, then—you admired brute force. You chose Hungary rather than Suez."

"Perhaps." It was evident Babbington disliked any comparison with another. "Mm, Castleford . . ." he murmured. "Poor Castleford. I'm quite sure he deserved to die—however, we pay for our sins, Kenneth. At least, you will."

Babbington smiled, and opened the door quickly. He exited, but the door did not close. Instead, Wilkes appeared, carrying a tray. Aubrey smelled tempting bacon, toast, marmalade, almost as if his sense of smell was artificially heightened. He glared at Wilkes.

"Take that away and get out!" he cried. Wilkes grinned, shrugged, and left the room, hooking the door shut with his foot. Someone else must have locked it, for Aubrey heard the key turn almost at once.

He listened to the retreating footsteps, then to other noises. A distant car buzzed like an insect. A dog barked. He remained sitting on the bed, head slumped on his chest, utterly weary. He was too drained by defeat to feel anger, or resentment at Babbington for his present captivity and his brief and violent future. Nor was there any professional regret regarding the fate of British Intelligence headed and controlled by Moscow's man.

The first face that came at him out of the darkness behind his closed eyelids was that of Castleford, as he knew it would be. The man was smiling in his habitually, infernally superior way. Aubrey shuddered at what he had come to, absorbed with self while Babbington trampled upon his service and his country. Yet he could not consider that. There was only Castleford's face from forty years ago, grinning at the prospect of his rival's demise.

Hyde had watched the brown Skoda for almost an hour. It was parked in the Zidovska, almost at the Danube end of the street, loomed over by the Gothic tower of St. Martin's Cathedral. Through the steamed-up window of the small, cramped bar, he had an uninterrupted view of both sides of the street and of the cathedral square. Snow fell desultorily into the Bratislava street. People trudged through rutted brown slush on the pavements. Passing cars splashed the dirty flank of the Skoda with gray-brown, half-melted snow.

He had parked the Volkswagen, skis hidden beneath the car, in an underground parking lot. It would reside there, dirty and anonymous, until he returned from Prague. It was his escape route. He would simply be returning from his skiing trip when he left Czechoslovakia.

In a strange, almost hallucinatory way, he was certain that Kenneth Aubrey was slouched, legs wrapped in a tartan blanket, in the rear seat of the Skoda, waiting for him to climb into the driving seat. The clarity and insistence of his imagination unsettled Hyde. The pressures of his task were mounting. He was unable to close his mind to the background, to the necessity of a successful outcome. Aubrey had assumed an almost physical presence, and he was nervous of crossing the street to the Skoda. He knew by now that it was not being watched, that the STB were not waiting for him. Yet he clung to the safety of the steamy, murmuring bar.

If I stay here, if I don't get into the car . . . don't get into the car . . .

He was warm, hunched into the padded anorak, his chin still half hidden by his scarf. The dark Czech beer was numbing. The brown Skoda, anonymous and drab, was like a parcel that might contain a bomb.

Don't get into the car . . .

Aubrey was there. It was as if the old man might open the passenger door and beckon him at any moment. The detonator. The wires and explosives were the travel visas, the false identity papers, car license and the other documents that waited beneath the driver's seat. And the pistol taped to the underside of the chassis. He would have to stop on the outskirts of the city and untape the gun—safer with the gun in the glove compartment—much safer, just in case—

Don't get into the car!

The dark beer slopped near the rim of the glass. He gingerly put it down on the shelf beneath the window. He studied his hands. They were quivering. He glanced helplessly at his gloves beside the beer glass, as if they might assist him. He thrust his hands deep into the pockets of his anorak.

He knew the car was clean. No tail, no watchers. Whatever they had gleaned from his apartment, and from anything Shelley had left lying around, they had no idea where, or why. He was ahead of them. They simply would not *think* of this scenario!

Don't—

Go, he told himself. Go now.

He glanced around the bar. Cigarette smoke, gray as the sky beyond the fuggy windows. Pale, lined faces. Laughter and somber, striking loneliness. The barmaid looked tired—washed-out fair hair and deep stains beneath her eyes. For yourself, he told his clenched hands, still pocketed. Told his legs, which seemed watery and a long way below his mind. For yourself.

Or run forever.

He did not wish to dramatize, would have despised it in others, or in himself had he thought or uttered the words in other circumstances. But it was true. Nowhere would be safe, ever.

Unless—

He snatched up his gloves, sending an ashtray spinning with a clatter to the floor. It startled him into a hasty exit from the bar almost before people glanced up at the noise. He saw that the pipe-smoking dominoes players near the door remained oblivious to him, then he was in the street, the door creaking shut behind him, his feet suddenly betrayed into uncertainty by the pavement's slush. He stepped warily to the curb. A bulky, almost shapeless woman in an old check coat bumped into him, then moved on without glancing at him. Hyde shivered. He glanced up and down the Zidovska, judging the traffic. The cathedral's black steeple against the heavy, smoky gray sky intruded itself behind the overhead traffic lights as they changed from red to green.

He hurried to the car. The backseat was empty. He urged his hand to the driver's door handle, opened the door, bent his head and shoulders, aware of the space between his shoulder blades, almost anticipating the heavy descent of someone's hand.

The home-knitted cardigan, reindeer on the pockets. As Shelley had promised. He'd seen it first, on the front passenger seat, an hour ago. Identifying the car. Now—?

The *Beano Annual*, on top of the wardrobe in its thin, cheap wrapping paper. Biffo the Bear on the stiff, shiny cover, together with the old, fat, red-garbed gentleman sitting in his sleigh, a cartoon reindeer in the traces, its antlers decked with Christmas baubles. The first time he had really noticed an image of snow, an image of reindeer, of winter . . .

Hyde grinned. Aubrey's specter was banished from the car. He felt warmer now, safer. The memory signaled a returning self-awareness. *He* was the priority, *his* life was at stake. On those terms, he could cope.

He climbed into the driver's seat, felt underneath it for the wrapped package of papers—yes. Was aware of the gun taped beneath the car, protected from the slush by clear plastic. He knew it would be there, just as he knew Godwin would be waiting at a bus stop on the outskirts of Prague.

He had two hundred and fifty miles to cover. He started the engine.

The young man, whose name was Voronin, described himself as the Deputy Rezident, temporarily fulfilling the office of the dead Bayev, shot while being interrogated by Hyde and Massinger. Yet to Babbington he had about him something akin to prison pallor, the sense of having newly emerged from Moscow Centre. He was evidently Kapustin's man, and Babbington despised himself as he hastened to reassure, moved and spoke briskly from bluff rather than authority. The young man's eyes were chilly, intent and clever, and he said very little, forcing Babbington to fill the cold silences with ever more exaggerated expressions of confidence.

The gardens of the Belvedere. Had this man, on Kapustin's orders, deliberately chosen the meeting place? Aubrey had been arrested here. Was this a reminder, and a call to duty? Or a demand for payment, for results? The paths were slippery, glazed with the hard frost. The hedges were stiff and thick with rime, and the lawns—whenever they emerged from one of the hedge-lined avenues—smooth white carpets. The statuary seemed lighter than stone against the gray sky.

Voronin kept pace with Babbington, while Wilkes and the young man's principal bodyguard walked a few paces behind them. Voronin looked curiously old-fashioned in his brown trilby and heavy dark overcoat, but not innocuous. Babbington was aware of the dampness of his scarf as it lay upon his chin and throat. His smoky breath had condensed like cold perspiration. Other watchers moved to the right and left of them, also ahead and behind them. Babbington, however, felt the open nakedness of the Belvedere gardens. Was he intended to? Anyone might see him here. Yet the young man had insisted on this outdoor meeting.

"It still does not answer the question of the woman, and of Hyde," Voronin pointed out, without rancor or impatience. The voice of a not-unkindly pedagogue. Babbington heard Kapustin's tones, even those of Nikitin, through the lips of the young man. He controlled a slight shiver, and looked at Voronin. He was taller than the Russian—whole inches taller, bulkier. He tried to believe his own significance.

"That is simply a matter of time. Both are simply a matter of time," he asserted.

"Yes, yes," Voronin snapped, and now there was impatience. "The man is not important, I agree. Somewhere, at some time, he will show his head above ground and will be taken. But the woman. She is another matter. . . ." He paused in his step, facing Babbington. "She has connections, she is familiar with powerful people. She cannot be allowed to remain at liberty."

"Then agree to my request," Babbington replied angrily. "Agree to my proposals for the disposal of the bodies."

Voronin shrugged, almost as if ignoring Babbington, and began walking ahead. Babbington uttered what might have been a growl of protest, and then hurried to his side. The Russian said at once: "Your solution does not, at the moment, include the woman. Where is she?"

"I've told you, Voronin, I don't know! She has only one ally in this city. She *must* be with Hyde."

"If Hyde is here."

"I have no doubt he is. Why else would Shelley be concerned with Czechoslovakia?"

"Why *is* Shelley concerned with Czechoslovakia?"

"Heaven alone knows! Perhaps Hyde wants to hide out. Where better, mm, than under *your* noses?"

"Had you bugged the telephones in that house, you would have discovered exactly why Shelley was so interested in Czechoslovakia."

It was a patent rebuke. Babbington flushed angrily and snapped: "Unlike your own dear country, Voronin, security operations require records, permissions, signatures, *authorizations*. I decided it was better to keep a low profile. It was extremely unlikely that Hyde would ring his own apartment—the woman upstairs was merely his landlady, according to our information." He recognized apology in his tone and said with steely indifference: "Forget it, Voronin. It's unimportant."

"The Massinger woman?" Voronin insisted.

"Vienna Station is looking. Your people are looking. Will you be patient and give your attention instead to my proposal?"

"What can *I* do?"

"Signal Moscow Centre—Kapustin. Tell him what I have told you. Aubrey is to be taken to Moscow. Massinger is to be disposed of. I don't care how—the woman, too. Perhaps they should all be taken to Moscow? It would prevent the slightest possibility of their remains being discovered. . . ." Babbington broke off for a moment. A vivid image of Castleford's body being discovered, years after his death, had forced itself upon his awareness. He thrust it aside. "Yes. That would be best. Take them to Moscow and dispose of them at once. In any event, Aubrey *must* appear in Moscow.

"It will silence all doubts. A matter of cutting off the head to ensure the death of the body . . ." Babbington became exasperated with his own even tone, with Voronin, with the necessity to persuade others. Why wouldn't they *see*? He burst out: "It will give us *time*—time to tie up the loose ends in a subtler fashion than your people would ever deem necessary. Time for cautious action, for *effective* caution. Good God, surely you can see that?"

They came to the end of the avenue, and the lawns stretched away from them, up toward the Belvedere. Babbington saw the windows not as dull, lightless panes, but as he had seen them on the last occasion he had walked in the gardens—lit by the last of the sun, glowing deep orange in color. He saw Kapustin leaving the gardens, and saw Aubrey's overcoated figure. He shook his head as if to clear it.

"To me it seems a very risky thing to do," Voronin remarked, gazing toward the Belvedere.

"Risky?" Babbington snapped. "What risk is there for you?"

"Risky for you, I mean."

"It was risky for me that First Secretary Nikitin and Deputy Chairman Kapustin let Petrunin live a single day after they initiated *Teardrop*. Do you realize that?" Anger, and its undercurrent of fear, gave him the authority he sought.

Voronin's eyes now displayed uncertainty and loss of confidence.

"Perhaps," the Russian offered in reply.

"It's the only satisfactory solution," Babbington pressed.

Voronin shrugged. "If you had the woman—" he began.

"With or without the woman!" Babbington turned to Voronin, his face mobile with rage. "I must be back in London tomorrow, without fail the following day. I must have, before tomorrow, your agreement to my proposal. I want *Kapustin's* agreement. You will organize and execute a rescue of your agent Aubrey, who will be spirited to Moscow by Aeroflot and then subsequently appear at some kind of staged interview with selected members of the Soviet and Western press. My God, man, you have the drugs to make him do handstands and sing soprano for the cameras if you care to use them!" One hand had emerged from his pocket, clenched into a fist. He appeared to threaten Voronin with physical violence. "Now. Will I have Kapustin's agreement? Time is pressing."

"The raid," Voronin murmured, shaking his head. "I don't know—"

"How else will you explain my *losing* Aubrey?" Babbington taunted. He was inwardly satisfied. Voronin was unsettled, out of his depth. And half persuaded.

The fear returned, churning at his stomach, tightening his chest. He breathed in slowly, exhaled the warmer, smoky air carefully, calming himself.

"Well?" he prompted.

Voronin hesitated, then nodded reluctantly. He sighed audibly. "Very well," he said. "I will signal Comrade Deputy Chairman Kapustin at once, informing him of your proposal. Perhaps he will agree—"

"He has to agree. There's no other way. I want Aubrey out of Vienna and on his way to Moscow within forty-eight hours at the outside. I want it to be seen and understood as a desperate KGB rescue operation on behalf of their blown agent."

"For the sake of realism, some of your people will have to—suffer?"

Without glancing behind or around him, Babbington nodded. "Naturally. Some of the Vienna Station personnel who will be guarding Aubrey must inevitably be killed in action. Very regrettable."

"Very well." Voronin seemed pleased at the display of ruthlessness. It was as if Babbington had correctly answered the final question of a long and searching interview. "Very well. Shall we go, Sir Andrew Babbington?"

Babbington smiled.

"Yes, Comrade Voronin—let's go."

Babbington turned, nodded to Wilkes, who seemed relieved, and began to stride confidently down the avenue toward the Lower Belvedere, the gates, and his car. Voronin hurried after him and the screen of watchers seemed trawled in their wake—a small shoal of overcoats and trenchcoats being hauled in.

Margaret Massinger watched the leading man, the one closest to her, turn as at an invisible signal and move away. She felt immediately cramped, cold, and weak. She watched the man's retreating trenchcoat, less white than the snow covering the lawns, as it passed one of the ornate fountains. When it emerged once more, it was distant and small. The eyepiece of the camera seemed cloudy, her eyes wet. The telephoto lens scraped on the stone of the balcony. She looked up, away from the camera, at the features of Maria Theresa worn by one of the stone sphinxes. She felt light-headed as she crouched behind the balcony of the terrace in front of the palace.

Her imagination was filled with photographic stills, as if she were watching some clever, tricky sequence in a film. People moved in her mind, stopped, were photographed, moved again. Stop, move, stop, snap, move, stop, snap, move.

She rubbed her frozen cheeks with her woollen-gloved hands. She was utterly cold inside her fur jacket. She rubbed her aching, chilled thighs. Her feet were numb. She felt too weak to stand.

For wildlife photography, Hyde had said, and grinned at her. The smile had been transparent, and she had seen the uncertainty behind it. The assistant in the camera shop had nodded, displaying a range of telephoto lenses to accompany the Nikkormat camera. She had tried to attend. The sleepless night in the anonymous hotel had not helped. Hyde's presence was that of a stern examiner. Yet she had eventually understood, simply by reading the literature that accompanied the camera and the lenses.

Babbington clenching his fist into the unidentified man's face, the faces clear in the eyepiece, everything else blurred and unrecognizable behind them because of the small depth of field of the 1000mm lens. She had used the largest of the lenses because she was afraid. She wanted the greatest distance between herself and—

And him. Babbington. Not so much the watchers in the white trenchcoats and the dark overcoats—the small fish—rather the one man. She was afraid of him, even in the artificial close-up of the telephoto lens—as if he might turn in her direction at any moment and be in reality as close to her as he seemed through the eyepiece. And recognize and apprehend her. So she had protected herself behind the shelter of the balcony.

Slavic cheekbones and lips beneath the trilby hat—picture, picture, picture, the motor whirring the film forward. Babbington and the Russian, their nearest bodyguards no more than blurred outlines beyond them. Adjusting the focus, taking shot after shot, fumbling to change the film with cold, frightened fingers. More shots, more, more, more—

Proof, proof, proof, the motor recited as it whirred on. More, more, more, proof, proof, more proof, more proof . . .

When they turned, the second roll of film was finished and she was spent. Babbington's heavy, handsome features filled her mind.

She raised her body slightly and looked through the eyepiece of the camera. Nothing. Babbington, the Russian, their guards had all disappeared from the gardens. The light seemed diminished. She looked at her watch. Three-ten. Immediately she began to worry about the aperture setting, the quality of the pictures she had taken—

Out of focus, too dark? Would they be able to identify Babbington? The other man, the Russian? Jerkily, she stood up, slapping her body to warm it. She stared at the camera. There had been too much haste, too little time to think, to plan. . . . After watching Hyde cross the border, she had returned to observe the house where Paul was kept prisoner. Little more than twenty minutes later, Babbington had climbed into his car and had headed for Vienna, unescorted. She had kept well back. The camera and lenses had lain on the passenger seat like a challenge. She had waited, daring no more than a sandwich, while Babbington had lunched at the Hotel Sacher. Finally, he had been driven to the Belvedere, part of a small convoy of cars. She had parked in the Prinz

Eugen strasse, scrabbled up the camera and lenses, and hurried into the palace gardens.

Exposed, clearly visible, she had sought the terrace and the balcony in a terror at her own fears and her amateurishness. Even now, as she walked up and down and warmth and feeling returned to her legs and feet, she hardly dared believe it had worked. Her camera lay like an abandoned weapon on the balustrade. She had succeeded. Two rolls of film with Babbington's face in almost every frame. Once his companion was identified, the process of saving Paul would begin.

She could not believe how easy it had been, could not avoid a sense of triumph. Hyde need not have crossed the border, put himself in danger—

Danger. Paul. The blood in the apartment. Paul.

She ran to the camera and snatched it up. The gardens were deserted except for a black, overcoated speck seated on a wooden bench, surrounded by hungry pigeons. An arm moved periodically in a scattering gesture. The tiny spots of gray bobbed and moved, as if conducted by the arm. She ran. She had to talk to her godfather, to Sir William. He had to listen to her.

Hyde sensed the weight of Godwin's body resting on the two crutches the moment he saw him at the suburban bus stop. The man was wearing a heavy overcoat and a fur hat, and his face was wreathed in a bright tartan scarf. Otherwise, there was no sense of color or even life about him. His stillness and his slump of weight expressed endless patience, a sense of defeat. Hyde steered the car reluctantly toward the small, glassed-in bus shelter. Godwin had, for some reason— perhaps only to be seen more easily by Hyde—chosen to stand in the falling snow. His shoulders in their frozen shrug of acceptance were thickly white. His fur hat, too, was mottled from its normal black to a badger's fur. He stared through the passenger window at Hyde, who tugged on the handbrake and opened the door.

Godwin, seeing him emerge and sensing his purpose, growled: "I don't need help. Is this door unlocked?" His hand was on the passenger door handle. Hyde, already at the hood and rounding the Skoda, merely nodded. Godwin's features scowled with rancor, and a hatred of pity and of his disability.

Hyde retreated to the driver's side, as if from a wounded animal.

Godwin leaned heavily against the door frame. He heaved the two crutches—old and heavy, with metal clasps and stout rubber grips—into the rear of the car, then almost fell into the passenger seat. Hyde shuddered, for Godwin and for himself. Godwin lifted his legs into the car and immediately adopted another frozen posture, staring through the windshield, his fur hat on his lap, leaking snow down the front of his coat and the corduroy trousers that covered his despised legs. On his shoulders, the snow glistened as it began to melt. Hyde slipped into the driving seat with unobtrusive and very conscious leg movements.

As a placatory gesture, Hyde said: "Petrunin's dead." It was crass, but the silence in the car pressed against his temples.

"Did you kill him?" Godwin replied after a short silence. The windshield in front of his face was already misting, as if the man exuded some violent heat.

"No. His own lot did that for him."

After another, longer silence, Godwin merely said: "My legs don't feel any better."

"Look, Godwin—" Hyde began, but Godwin turned to him. His face was wan, chilly with rage. It was as if he had been waiting at the bus stop for days, perhaps ever since he had been shot, just for Hyde's arrival.

"Christ, Hyde—why does it have to be *you*?" he spat out. He looked years older. He had lost weight—wasted rather than dieted, it seemed to Hyde. His eyes were darkly stained beneath the small, hard pupils. His hair was thinner, and lank. Hyde avoided glancing at the man's legs. "You and the old man? Why the two of you, of *all people*?" His lower lip quivered as he finished speaking. Hyde saw the self-pity and could not despise it. "I was burying myself here, nice and quietly. I wasn't forgetting, I was quietly and satisfactorily dying. Turning into a vegetable. Then *you*!" His eyes glared at Hyde as he looked up from the wet fur hat in his lap. It looked like some drowned beloved pet, the cause of Godwin's rage and grief.

"Fuck off, Godwin," Hyde said quietly, forcefully. "Take your bloody self-pity and stuff it." Godwin stared at him, his mouth working silently, his eyes angry slits in his white face.

"You're *alive*. I don't have the time or the range of sympathy to care in what condition, because if you don't help me and I can't do what's necessary, neither I nor the old man will be anything but dead. Now, if you'd like to change places, give me your fucking crutches and I'll learn to use them."

Godwin's jaw dropped. His mouth was a round, black hole from which eventually emerged a shocked, small, defeated voice, "Oh, you bastard—Christ, you bastard." Hyde did not reply, and Godwin turned his face away. Slowly, his head subsided onto his chest. Hyde listened to his stertorous breathing, as if the man were laboring up an endless flight of stairs or a steep hill; surmounting his own self-pity, Hyde hoped. Eventually, Godwin sniffed loudly.

It was almost dark in the car. The snow lay thickly on the front and back windshields, and the daylight was fading outside. There was no one at the bus stop. Traffic had begun to pass them, leaving Prague for the suburbs. In the headlights of one oncoming vehicle, Hyde saw bright wetness on Godwin's cheeks.

"Okay," Godwin said heavily, nodding. "Okay. I'm sorry."

Again, Hyde did not reply. Already, his interest in Godwin's reaction was diminishing. His words had had the desired effect. It was difficult to concern himself with anything larger than Aubrey's survival. . . .

Rare moment of absolute honesty. *His own survival.* It was that which absorbed his attention. Unless that was the case, Aubrey, Godwin, Massinger, and all the others would not survive. The priority of self might just keep others alive— on this occasion.

"It's not you," Godwin eventually continued. Hyde had to force himself to attend. Godwin was emerging slowly, like a dragonfly, from the chrysalis of his disability.

"Yes?" he demanded, almost impatiently.

Godwin's head twitched, then he said: "It's not you I blame—God knows, not the old man . . ."

"No," Hyde said carefully. Traffic passed, flowing more strongly now.

Godwin looked at Hyde for a moment, as if reminding himself of his companion's identity. Then he said: "I don't know and I don't care whether you understand this . . ." Hyde winced, wanting to stem the flow of what he sensed was a confession, but said nothing. ". . . but I want to say it." He swallowed, then Hyde heard a dry, chuckling, ironic noise in Godwin's throat. "You brought back a world I'd had to leave behind. Fuck you for that."

Hyde turned, surprised. Godwin was looking at him. His cheeks were still pale, but dry. His mouth was open in a small, cynical smile. Hyde nodded.

"Okay," he said. "Now, where to?"

"What? Oh . . . my apartment."

"Secure?"

"They leave me alone." His hands slapped his thighs. "Walking wounded. They accept my cover for the real thing. How could I be SIS, on crutches?"

"No one else knows I'm here—that I'm expected?"

"No one. Shelley's signal was very specific. What's going on, Hyde?"

"Babbington—he's Moscow's man. The proof's in the computer."

"Babbington? Bloody hell—"

"He framed the old man . . . and it was Petrunin's scenario from the beginning."

"Petrunin told you all this? You trust that bastard?"

"He was dying—and trying to pull the house down around him. He wasn't lying."

"Who's on our side?"

"Us. Just the two of us." Hyde did not mention Margaret Massinger. There was little or no point. She wouldn't be able to cope. He knew it would have been better for her if he had ordered her to lie low, merely keep out of sight. She wouldn't last five minutes trying to tail Babbington and keep that wooden house in Perchtoldsdorf under surveillance. He had doubted her ability to survive even as he briefed her, even as they bought the camera and lenses. Thus, he had been deliberately vague in explaining his own task to her. What she did not know she could not reveal when they caught and questioned her. "That's the whole army," he added. "Shelley's already in the bag."

"Christ—" Godwin breathed.

"Are you in?" Hyde asked impatiently. His hands stroked the steering wheel. He was tempted to grip it fiercely, to still the tremor he sensed beginning.

Then Godwin said: "I'm in—it's bloody hopeless, but I'm in."

Hyde looked at him. Just for a moment, a younger man

glanced from behind the bitter, older mask that Godwin wore.

"Okay. Which way?"

"Straight on. My apartment's in the Old Town. I'll direct you."

"My dear friend, I'm so sorry, so sorry. . . ."

Aubrey patted Massinger's hand as he spoke. It lay like a limp white fish on the coverlet, then it enclosed Aubrey's hand slowly. Massinger's eyes were bright, but empty of fever. His face was puffy and misshapen with dark, livid bruises that were the color and texture of raw offal.

"It's okay," he murmured, his lips working loosely like those of someone whose jaw has been deadened in preparation for dental work. His lips were swollen and split. He shook his head gently. "Okay," he repeated.

"How is the leg?"

"Someone patched it up. There's no bullet in the wound. Hurts like hell, Kenneth." He tried to sit more upright in the narrow bed, and groaned as he moved his injured leg. No doubt, Aubrey thought, the dressing on his thigh was temporary. A temporary dressing for a temporary circumstance.

He realized that Babbington had reached a decision; otherwise he would not have allowed Aubrey and Massinger to meet. There was no longer any need to keep them apart. What they knew would die with them. Thus, when Aubrey had surrendered to his hunger and eaten lunch, and then had asked after Massinger's health, Wilkes had merely grinned and taken him to the wounded man's room.

One of Massinger's eyes was almost closed with a puffy, raw swelling. His various cuts had, however, been bathed and disinfected and covered with plaster.

"I want you to understand, my dear Paul, how—how grateful I am for your efforts on my behalf."

Massinger shook his head and tried to grin. "Even though all it got me was here and now, uh?" he said. "Don't take it to heart—" He winced with pain again as he moved, then added: "I couldn't help myself. Thank God they didn't get Margaret. Thank God for that!" Massinger was almost blithe.

"Yes, thank goodness," Aubrey breathed, inwardly grateful. He hoped the woman would keep her head down, keep out of things until they were resolved. Whether she might be able to influence the course of events in any way . . . police, William Guest, the press . . . ? No, he thought decisively, no. She is out of the game. She can do nothing. He cleared his throat, watching Massinger as he did so. "You—Paul, you realize what Babbington intends . . . ?" His voice failed him.

Massinger gripped his hand more tightly as he nodded. Then he said urgently: "They don't have her, do they? They don't know where she is?"

Aubrey shook his head. Massinger lay back on the pillows as if exhausted. He murmured something which might have been "Thank God for that," once more. Aubrey realized that the man's relief at his wife's safety anaesthetized him to his own situation.

After a long silence, he said: "You've talked with Babbington?"

"Yes."

"Why—why did he? When?" Then the American opened his eyes. "It doesn't matter. None of that matters. What's he going to do with us?"

"Moscow, I think." Aubrey nodded. "Yes, Moscow. I'm certain of it. I—I'm sorry—"

"Sure. You'll survive, for a little while maybe—but not me. He has to bury the bodies, our friend Babbington. Does he have to bury the bodies!" His eyes studied Aubrey, then slowly became unfocused once more. He stared at the ceiling, and Aubrey knew the man was staring at an image of his wife. He murmured again. Again, Aubrey did not catch the words.

"I'm sorry. . . ." he repeated. Massinger did not appear to hear him.

Thank you—sorry. There was nothing else to say. Their knowledge of each other and of their situation was complete.

Aubrey's past began to press upon him once more. It would mean little or nothing to Massinger. The gallery of images parading before him formed his private collection. And each of the scenes angered him. Every voice, moment, room, person, operation, mission, committee. Angered him—

His past had been utterly refashioned by Babbington. Everything—*everything*! Completely, utterly changed—made ugly and twisted. That was why he hated Babbington. Not for the man's own treachery—that feeling had passed away. No—but because the man had robbed him of, of *reputation*! Of probity. *Othello's occupation's gone*, he remembered bitterly.

The door opened.

It was Wilkes, who immediately said: "He says you've had long enough." Aubrey glared at him. "Come on, *Sir* Kenneth—back to your own room, if you please." He used the voice of some psychiatric nurse, mocking him with orders.

Aubrey stood up and released Massinger's hand. It returned to the coverlet. Returned, too, to its former, limp-fish state, white and unmoving. Massinger's one open eye winked at him. Aubrey tried to smile.

"Do you need anything?" he asked. Massinger shook his head.

"Hardly worth it, is it?" Wilkes inquired.

"Isn't it?" Aubrey snapped.

"It isn't."

"When?"

"Less than forty-eight hours," Wilkes said. "He has to be back in London within the next two days. Look funny otherwise, wouldn't it?"

"God, Wilkes!" Aubrey hesitated, his mouth open. He had no idea what he had intended to say.

"Come on," Wilkes ordered.

Aubrey passed through the door without glancing back at Massinger. In the corridor, as Wilkes closed the door, it was as if someone had switched on a powerful light and shined it directly into his eyes. He was dazzled by his illuminated past. Each separate memory stung and hurt. He swayed with the shock of their impact.

Zimmermann and he, face to face—his first captured German officer . . . those first interviews in the small, bare upstairs apartment somewhere off the Strand, only months after he had come down from Oxford . . . the diplomatic service, he had thought, and had then felt a deep and abiding delight when they had indicated the secret world, intelligence work—

Berlin, after the war—Castleford's face intruded, still alive, smiling . . . come back like a ghost, to gloat. Aubrey dismissed him in the rush of images. Reams of paper and files passing across a desk beneath hands which he recognized as his own. The hands aged as he watched, as if his whole adult life were passing in moments—the speeded-up film of some flower's life cycle . . . the files became more important, more secret—

"You all right?" Wilkes asked. Aubrey hardly heard him,

as memory shifted like ballast in his head and he staggered. Wilkes held his arm to keep him upright.

A man of probity. There were moments of ruthlessness, of utter disregard for the lives in his hands. But he had attempted to be a man of probity in the secret world. *Othello's occupation's gone*—

Hands upon a desk. Faces across a table. Men with secrets to yield, men to be dismantled or repaired. A dozen languages, a thousand small rooms for the breaking of will, resolve, courage.

Aubrey shook his head, shook off Wilkes's supporting hand, and walked as quickly as he could the length of the corridor. He entered his room and Wilkes locked the door behind him. When the man's footsteps had faded, Aubrey began rubbing at his damp eyes with the creased sleeve of his soiled shirt.

There was no telephone in her room at the pension. She had to use the pay phone near the cramped reception desk. The foyer was empty except for the night porter, who sat reading the evening paper, his head framed by pigeonholes and hanging keys. His uniform collar was open at the neck. A half-drunk glass of beer and a sandwich of smoked sausage on a paper plate rested on the desk. Margaret turned her head into the hair dryer globe of clear plastic that enclosed the telephone.

She dialed the international code for London, then Sir William Guest's home number. Hyde had told her Sir William was in Washington; it was stupid to try his number. Yet his answering machine might disclose the means of reaching him in the States. How else could she reach him? She tugged anxiously at the looped cord of the telephone as she waited for the connection, envisaging the comfortable, paneled study in which the number was ringing. Sir William maintained an apartment in Albany, just as his father had once done. As a child, she had been overawed by the dark, heavy paneling, the grimy, looming paintings. Whenever her father had taken her there, she remembered Sir William had acted the part of a jolly, generous relative. Yet he expected good manners, long silences, then adult replies to his questions. Sir William had awed her.

"Come on, come on," she breathed. She glanced round at

the night porter. He refolded the newspaper and continued to read. "Come on—oh, please, come on!"

The tone stopped abruptly. No one answered the telephone, but she sensed a listener.

"William?" she asked hesitantly.

"Who is that, please?" a polite, assured, unfamiliar voice inquired.

"Who is speaking?" she asked, surprised. "Where is Mrs. Carson?" Then, more insistently: "Who are you?"

"Mrs. Carson—oh, Sir William's housekeeper. I'm sorry, she's away for a few days. As is Sir William."

"Then who are *you*? How do you come to be in William's apartment?"

"Lucky to have caught me here, really. . . ." The voice was light, cultivated, almost a drawl. She could picture a bright young Whitehall type. One of William's staff—but why?

"This is Margaret Massinger," she announced with mustered authority and ease. "It's urgent I speak to Sir William at once—"

"Ah, Mrs. Massinger. My apologies. My name is Renfrew, a member of Sir William's Cabinet Office staff. . . . He asked me to collect some papers from his apartment—needs to consult them, through me, while he's in Washington. As a matter of fact, I was just about to leave. But you said it was urgent, Mrs. Massinger. Can I take a message?" The question lay helpfully, easily on the air.

She hesitated. Then: "Can you give me his number in Washington? Where can I reach him?"

"I'm afraid not. His movements are rather fluid. Timetable's very crowded, I'm afraid. Look, I tell you what. Why not give me your number? Sir William is bound to contact the Cabinet Office either tonight or tomorrow. I can ensure that he calls you. What do you say?"

The voice was calm, almost offhand. Helpful.

"Yes," she began. "I'm in Vienna—"

"Vienna? Good Heavens! A vacation, Mrs. Massinger?"

"Vienna—the number is . . ."

She paused to study the number printed on the telephone's dial.

"Yes?" the voice said, eagerly. "Yes? Your number in Vienna is . . . ?" She was puzzled by the voice. Her further hesitation caused it to speak again. "Mrs. Massinger—please give me your number in Vienna!" It was an order. Unmistakably.

"Who are you?" she snapped.

"I told you, Mrs. Massinger—" The voice was more angry now.

"*Who?*"

"One of Sir William's staff—"

"One of—you're one of Babbington's people, aren't you? I know you are!"

"Mrs. Massinger. Please give me your Vienna telephone number—" The voice was unpleasant with imminent failure and threat.

"No!"

She clattered the receiver onto its rest. Her hand was shaking. She dropped the earring she had been holding in her right hand, and scrabbled for it on the worn, dimly patterned strip of foyer carpet. When she straightened, the night porter glanced incuriously at her, then bent his gaze to the newspaper once more. He looked sinister, dangerous.

She had almost told them! She could not believe it of herself, could not believe that Andrew Babbington had someone in Sir William's apartment.

She breathed deeply, raggedly, trying to calm herself. At once, her overriding priority returned. It had been growing through dinner, through the three whiskeys she had drunk to occupy the time before she had thought of reaching Sir William via his answering machine.

Paul.

Now that she had evidence, and there was no one to see it, she was like a machine that had run down. Out of fuel and motive power. Now, she could only worry, with an increasingly frantic urgency, whether Paul was still alive.

She had to know. She had to go out again, she had to drive to Perchtoldsdorf—*she had to see him!* Whatever the cost, she had to know!

15
Rites of Entry

Babbington watched his fingers, remote, detached objects drumming on the desk top beside the two oblong black boxes of the audio-encryption unit and line adaptor connected to the telephone receiver. Kapustin's voice, despite the complex rearrangements of his words by his own encryption unit, was only slightly mechanical in sound, only slightly hazy in enunciation. His tone of reluctance was not robbed of its anger and command. Babbington, with the utmost clarity, comprehended the Russian's mood.

He was alone in the room. It was warm, from radiators and the blazing log fire. A whiskey glass, half-filled, rested on the desk near the high-security encryption unit. To an observer, he might have seemed at ease. Yet he was not.

"I am not in favor of *accidents*," the Deputy Chairman announced. "Especially to the woman. Should you be fortunate enough to capture her. She has connections. Voronin, I believe, warned you of this. Her death would cause—a *fuss*?"

"I understand that, Kapustin." The room was hot rather than warm. His fingers were not remote. They drummed more quickly now, reflecting his rising anger. "Of course there is a risk. *Everything* is a risk. You should have rid yourselves of Petrunin the day this business appeared on the operations board! As it is, people *know*, people *suspect* . . . but only a handful of people. They must be removed. It is the only logical course of action."

"There is the German, too."

"I realize that—"

Snow pattered softly against the window. Babbington turned his head to stare at the square of darkness streaked with wriggles of melted snow, then returned his gaze to the fire. The large Afghan rug in front of it offered up a tiny, thin trail of smoke where some spark from the fire had landed. The ascending wisp looked like incense burning.

"What do you suggest in his case?" There was mockery in Kapustin's tone. The wisp of smoke faded. Babbington could not see the tiny hole the spark must have burned in the rug, but for a moment he imagined his wife clucking over the damage.

"There is nothing that can be done. At the moment. Except that the single, bold stroke which I propose will silence him, as it will everyone else. Aubrey's appearance in Moscow will forestall any further questions. Surely you understand that much?" His tone was one of exasperation. Almost helplessly, he continued as if some dam within him had been breached: "For twenty-eight years you have had my loyalty. You and the rest of Moscow Centre have waited twenty-eight years for the present moment! It was your impatience— Nikitin's impatience—that would not allow Aubrey to remain in his post until he retired and I succeeded by right. *Very well! You* dictated the timing of *Teardrop—you* see it through! It must be *now*, while Guest has the PM's ear and confidence and while he supports the idea of SAID and myself as its head. Don't quibble about disposing of one American and his well-connected wife!"

Babbington looked at his fingers on the desk. They had ceased to accompany his rage, and now merely quivered. He touched his fingertips against the whiskey glass, against the smooth black case of the encryption unit. He felt perspiration prickle his forehead. It was foolish, but he had been helpless against the outburst. Didn't they realize what was at stake, for God's sake? He clenched his free hand into a fist and waited for Kapustin to speak.

Eventually, the Russian said: "Your anger is understandable. I agree, with hindsight, that we should have disposed of Petrunin."

"Then make up for it now."

Kapustin was silent again for some time, then he said: "I cannot decide at once just to put your mind at rest. This must be discussed."

"Who with? Nikitin? Remind the President of the investment, and the dividend, won't you?" His hand now toyed with the whiskey glass. The crystal caught the warmth of the lamps in the room, held the flames of the fire, miniaturizing and fragmenting them.

"There is the problem of the woman. Where is she now?"

Babbington did not hesitate. "I promise you her confinement within twenty-four hours. That means you could mount the operation tomorrow night."

Kapustin seemed only to have been waiting for the moment of bluff, for he said at once: "Then you can have your raid, your dramatic rescue of Aubrey—tomorrow night, providing you have the woman in your hands before then!"

Babbington's fingers quivered the moment he put down the heavy crystal glass.

"You mean—"

"A bargain. Your rescue attempt in exchange for the woman."

"You'll take her and the American to Moscow and dispose of them there?" His words sounded almost breathless with excitement.

"Providing I can persuade the President of the wisdom of such a course, persuade him it is necessary to your survival. Yes." Babbington held back his sigh of relief. "We will dispose of the Massingers—and parade Aubrey before the cameras."

The sleety snow blew against the window like a handful of gravel thrown in warning against the pane. Babbington was startled, then very consciously looked back at the fire, considering what Kapustin had said. Considering, too, his boast concerning the capture of Margaret Massinger.

Margaret Massinger pressed her body against the bole of the fir tree. The illumination from Babbington's window spilled toward her hiding place like a flashlight searching for her. She had been able to see his head turn at the sound of the gust of snow. She had ducked aside at once. He couldn't have seen her, couldn't have . . .

She could hear her breathing above the noise of the wind. The snow blew against her collar, against her woollen beret. Now, she had seen two of them—Aubrey and Babbington. One behind a desk, using the telephone, and the other one— the one she could no longer hate—sitting in an armchair behind barred windows, staring down at his feet, as immobile as if he had died. She shivered with the cold. Next to Aubrey's room were more barred windows. The curtains were drawn across them, the room in darkness. She knew that Paul must be confined there, and she could not rid herself of the idea that the drawn curtains indicated death. Her mother had never signaled her mourning because she would not believe that Robert Castleford was dead—but Margaret had used that semaphore when her mother died. They had done the same thing here, because Paul was dead. . . .

She felt childlike, locked out of some loved place, alone in the windblown, snowy dark. Her eyes were wet, her cheeks numb with cold. She wanted to be, *had* to be, inside—

She had to know. Nothing else mattered. She had fulfilled her obligations to Aubrey, to Hyde. Now, she could choose. Everything else, all other considerations, had dropped from her as she had placed the two rolls of film, in their padded bag, in the mailbox in the foyer of the pension. Her aunt in Bath would receive the undeveloped film with precise and definite instructions to deliver it by hand to William in London. The old lady would go up by train, the whole journey spent horrified at the prospect of spending time in William's company—in the company of the man and his awful cigars.

Nevertheless, William would receive the film. And he would act. He would read her note, see the film, and act. Babbington would be stopped. She had done her duty.

She had to believe that now, shivering with cold and desperate to be discovered on the grounds of the lodge. Just as she had to believe that Paul was not dead and that she could somehow be reunited with him simply by an act of surrender.

Curtains drawn across the windows.

She would convince Babbington that she still hated Aubrey, that she still believed he was a Soviet agent and was guilty of her father's murder. Murderer, traitor, villain, abomination—anything that would persuade Babbington that Paul and she were not dangerous to him, that Paul could be allowed to live. . . .

She would know nothing. Hyde? Who was Hyde? She could tell him nothing; she knew nothing. . . . Anything that Paul may have said would be no more than delirium, the wildest imaginings, hysteria caused by loss of blood, by his wounds.

Aubrey was unhurt. It had been Paul's blood—but Paul wasn't dead; he was alive and hurt, alive and hurt. . . . He could be saved, if she could play her part to perfection. She could keep him alive for long enough—she had told Sir William where they could be found, where she would be—

If Aubrey had to die, so be it. She must save Paul.

She eased her body from behind the tree. She could see Babbington's gray hair as he sat behind the desk, still making his telephone call. She waited. The patrol would return in a few minutes, the two men preceded by the flickering flashlight. She need only step out in front of them and pray they did not fire without flicking the light toward her face. She waited, her teeth chattering, her legs and body weak with anticipation. Yet she felt no renewed desire for concealment. All that was behind her now. She stood just where the spillage of warm light from the window reached her boots, as if waiting for a tide to advance.

Should she even have met Hyde? Should she even know his name? Perhaps from Paul? Would Babbington believe her, believe even one word of it?

He must. . . .

She listened. Footsteps on the gravel. Light on the gravel. They were coming—

She mustn't look as if she were waiting for them; she must be caught!

Cautiously, bent almost double, she crept to Babbington's window. *If Paul was dead, she was meekly surrendering*. She crushed the rebellious thought. She reached the window, touched the sill with her fingertips, and raised her head to look into the room.

Light on her face, light on the gravel around her, footsteps on the gravel.

Snarl of a dog!

Dog—light—gravel—voice. She was frozen with terror. Footsteps running. She listened in horror for the dog's paws beating on the gravel. She heard it growl—footsteps, the noise of heavy boots, running. She waited, frozen, for the dog's attack.

Then she turned her face into the flashlight's beam. The man who held it laughed with surprise and pleasure. The dog, still restrained by the second man, growled, then barked viciously. She glanced away from the torch. Babbington's head had turned. His face seemed white and somehow broken open, as if he were confronted by an accusing ghost. Snow blew against Margaret's cheek, against the window. Babbington appeared shaken from a deep trance by the noise it made, perhaps by the dog's continued barking. Then, slowly and with growing pleasure, he smiled.

And spoke into the telephone, quickly and urgently and with evident triumph on his features. He had seen her held by the man with the flashlight, his hand gripping her arm. Her captor said: "Good evening, Mrs. Massinger. So nice of you to drop in."

She turned her head to stare at the dog's open mouth, its white teeth and pink tongue kept away from her by the strained-tight choke chain and leash. She sagged with relief and weakness against the man who held her arm.

"Margaret—Massinger's wife—she's here!" Babbington blurted into the telephone, unable to consider disguising his relief and surprised delight. "We've got her! Now, you keep *your* side of the bargain, Kapustin!"

"Very well," Kapustin replied at once. "Very well. Ignoring your remarkable good fortune—I shall try to persuade both the President and my Chairman to adopt your plan."

"Excellent!"

"The scheme will not be popular, but I expect it will be adopted. Yes, I expect so. Have everything ready for tomorrow night. Aubrey and the Massingers. We will dispose of them for you."

Godwin watched the neighbor's thin black cat as he might have watched an enemy. Then, he collected his crutches from either side of his chair and struggled upright, finally shuffling away from the dining table to the corner of the kitchen. Someone must have brought the brand name cat food back with them after a London leave, Hyde thought. It wouldn't be on sale in Prague. Godwin unwrapped the tin from a plastic bag that contained its odors and knived chunks of it onto a yellow saucer. Then he placed it on the floor for the cat, which had, during his careful preparations, rubbed with a sense of the frantic against the legs that could not sense its body. Occasionally, Godwin looked down at its protestations. And smiled.

Hyde wiped his mouth with the back of his hand. The cat, stroked by Godwin—how much pain in that bending to the cat's arched back and erect tail?—had begun to eat. Gulping delicately. Hyde pushed back his own chair with a mounting reluctance. He had to bully Godwin, again. And disliked the work. Godwin had almost solved the problem—but communicating it had a price of anger.

He turned on Hyde with a white face and snapped: "I've worked like an animal since I got here —from the moment I got here!"

He had been preparing the outburst throughout the well-cooked meal, perhaps ever since he had admitted Hyde to his cloistered, lonely rooms. Up thinly carpeted stairs, the walls pregnant with age and damp, to a loosely fitting door with English security locks. And the smell of heated, packaged meals and East European vegetables stubbornly cooked, the scent of the neighbor's cat, and the ozone of often-used electrical equipment—the hi-fi and the desk-top computer. Godwin's thin, eked-out life. Hyde understood, far too well, that only a pair of functioning, fit limbs separated himself from Godwin and his environment.

But Godwin had it, had the answer—part of it, even almost all of it—

"—like an animal," Godwin repeated almost apologetically.

"Sure," Hyde replied.

Godwin had been restraining himself for hours controlling himself, as he taught Hyde familiarity with the Cyrillic keyboard he would eventually encounter, taught him the jargon, and educated him in the small talk of computers and security and the Hradcany. Hyde's knowledge of computer terminals and keyboards was minimal. Godwin seemed determined to make him not only skilled, but educated. Hour upon hour, time after time, until he stopped making mistakes, avoided errors, *understood* what he was doing. And all that time, Godwin had been building to his overriding, urgent purpose: this outburst. Hyde prepared himself.

"Yes, like an animal!" he stormed, as he plugged in the coffee percolator with the wifely nonchalance of an enforced bachelor. "Do you realize what you and Shelley want from me? Do you?" He ushered Hyde back into the small lounge. The electrical smell was still strong from the keyboard and VDU resting on the old dining table that Godwin used as a desk. The crutches thumped behind Hyde, the legs shuffling behind them.

Hyde sat down quickly, reducing his own importance. In

the kitchen, the percolator plopped. The cat began to lap the milk that Godwin had also put down.

"The biggest laugh is, Shelley wants everything for Aubrey—for the old man!" Godwin glared. "For the old, blind, stupid bugger who wanted nothing to do with the thing I offered him!" Godwin's frame leaned toward Hyde. The small keyboard and screen peeped like a hint of revelations to come from behind his crooked elbow. "He put it to one side. Do you know what he told me? Do you?" Godwin's body echoed in miniature the movements of a fit body in an easy chair, bobbing forward. "'It can't possibly work, Godwin—once we tap in, we've given the game away.' That was it. His judgment and the opinion of the tame experts he consulted. He consigned *Open Weave* to the dustbin without a second thought! And now he wants me to resurrect it to save his skin! What a laugh. What an absolute fucking hoot!"

"What's *Open Weave*?" Hyde dropped into the charged silence, almost expecting the breath expelled with his words to spark in the heavy atmosphere.

Godwin's gray face narrowed. "Don't pretend you don't know."

Hyde shook his head. "I don't."

"Don't give me that! Shelley's briefed you!" Hyde rejected interruption. "Do you even begin to understand, either of you, what Petrunin *did* when he fixed the computer in Moscow Centre? Do you have even an inkling of what he had to do to make *Teardrop* available to you?" Godwin's body slumped on the crutches, almost as if he had fallen backward into a comfortable chair. The cat appeared, indifferent, licking its mouth in the kitchen doorway. The percolator reached a breathless climax behind the cat.

Godwin dropped his body into the chair opposite Hyde. Breath emerged, strangled and painful. Godwin plunged on, undeterred by the massive interruption of seating himself.

"First," he offered, marking the point on the index finger of his right hand, "he had to subvert an expert of near-genius—a programmer who was exceptionally smart. Before that, he had to *see* the possibility! He had to be really far-sighted when he served on that committee to see the chance and take it. Clever . . ." Godwin was wistful for opportunity for a moment, then continued. "Petrunin had to alter the original database, when the central records computer was first fully programmed—back when they started computerizing their entire records system. Even then he was watching his back—and aware of the best, most up-to-date way of doing it. . . ."

Godwin's face was flushed with insight, more than with the thin wine they had drunk with their pork. His eyes were inward-looking, staring after a figure following a road he could not take. Hyde realized how thwarted Godwin was by his crippled legs. Perhaps Aubrey had done him no good turn, keeping him inside the service? A big computer firm might have satisfied his ambitions much more completely.

Godwin cleared his throat, and said: "Teleprocessing showed him the ease with which he could store information under Moscow Centre's inquisitive long nose and be perfectly safe. And the method of computer access—through landlines—suggested how easy it would be to recover the information he'd stored, for any terminal in any Soviet embassy or consulate or mission, in any emergency. He'd need no more than a few minutes with a remote terminal keyboard and his special passwords. He could go straight to the stuff he'd stored, just like that—" Godwin clicked his fingers. His eyes studied the ceiling. The cat hunched its back toward the one radiator. Hyde got up and passed Godwin's chair toward the kitchen. Godwin seemed almost relieved. Immediately, in a raised voice, he began talking over the noises of coffee cups and pouring liquid.

"He must have altered the schema of the database—just in case someone stumbled onto his material by the purest fluke . . . when you dial up his doctored file, you get almost the same thing, except that the normal channels to the personnel records have been bypassed and you're really getting the prologue to all the dirt he's stored away."

"Sugar?" Hyde asked.

"No. But when they sent him to Afghanistan as persona non grata, he must have added a low-level patch to the compiler. . . ." Hyde handed him his cup. "Thanks." Godwin appeared relaxed. He had adopted the momentum and the confidence of his monologue. Here, he was the expert, the fit man. Hyde regained his seat.

"He must have killed the poor bastard who assisted him straight afterward—or could he have added this—this *patch*?" Godwin nodded. "After he'd killed the programmer?"

"He might have been able to. He'd have had to study manuals and dumps of the application programs to find a way of bypassing the computer's security. What I think he's done, from your description, is to add a patch to the compiler which translates password routine in the database management system. This would have the effect of adding an extra line to the normal password routine in the machine code version. . . . I'll show you later. It would have been easier for him, since he wouldn't have had much time after they decided to send him to Kabul, if the programmer was still alive."

"Perhaps he anticipated disgrace, along with everything else?"

"He was that clever?"

"He was."

Godwin shifted painfully in his chair.

Hyde stood up and went into the kitchen and placed his cup in the crowded sink. Then said: "You have to teach me, Godwin. Everything I need to know."

Godwin called: "How much do you know about *Open Weave*?"

"Nothing."

"Shelley told you nothing?"

"No."

Godwin's anger was quashed. Hyde raised his face to the kitchen ceiling and held back the sigh of relief that threatened to escape from his chest. Godwin was hooked. When he walked into the lounge, Godwin's face greeted him eagerly, almost wanton with excitement.

"Tell me about it," Hyde said.

"Later. It's just a way of tapping into the landline that links the computer room here to Moscow Centre."

"What—" Hyde began, hardly needing to act surprised.

"Later," Godwin repeated with affected modesty. "It'll help you into the computer room in the Hradcany as a system tester. We'll set up a fault on the landline . . . later. I'll keep you in suspense for a bit." He grinned. Godwin's face was animated with something akin to triumph: the face of an eminent actor, assured of the applause that would greet his entry from the wings.

Hyde smiled. "Okay. Keep me in suspense, then."

"You sure you wouldn't like a little nap before we begin?" Godwin asked jokingly. "This is going to take the rest of the night. Are you sure you're ready?"

"When you are. My cover's as a system tester. Who or what gets me inside the Hradcany?"

Godwin waved the question aside. "That's taken care of. You'll be helped in—and concealed."

"Okay. I'm inside."

"They'll be expecting you. That's the beauty of it. They'll want a system tester. Not a technician, you understand, just someone with a high security clearance. From the Soviet Embassy. Your clearance will be higher than that of most of the people you'll run into. They'll be wary of you."

"Why do they want this—system tester?"

"The fault on the landline. It'll be such that they'll have to check that their datafiles taken from remote terminals aren't at fault—been corrupted or damaged. They'll be worried—they'll need you to check responses from Moscow to requests you make in sensitive areas . . . Okay?"

"Okay."

"So—you're in the main computer room. With guaranteed use of one of the remote terminals—keyboard, printer, backup peripherals . . . everything."

"You're pretty sure of this—"

"I am sure, mate—bloody sure! You're using the best stuff I've got—people, ideas, cover. I'm giving you everything."

"Okay."

"The computer terminals in the Hradcany are standard stuff—they use a pirated version of IBM's CICS system—Customer Information Control Systems, that means. The terminal is permanently linked to Moscow Centre and the computer is continually asking for its services to be used. It's called polling. All you'll need—apart from enough time to yourself—is Petrunin's passwords when the computer asks you for them."

"Why do I *need* to be a system tester?"

"Because that way—" The cat had moved, and was rubbing against Godwin's legs. As if his excitement had animated his senseless shins, Godwin looked down, smiled, and lifted the cat onto his lap. It padded as if shaping his lap like a pillow, and then settled itself. Godwin's large hand stroked methodically, firmly along the cat's back. "—that way you can get into the personnel records. Education, military, criminal, anything you like, while checking that the landline, the modems, and scramblers have not affected the data or the data transfer. If that's happened, they'd need to use backup to restore the files. You can be there for perhaps three or four hours, all night if the job takes that long . . . and no one, *no one* at all, will be asking you to leave or asking you what you think you're up to! Can't you see what a *gift* it is?"

Three hours—

Hyde nodded. Godwin's scenario was daring and brilliant, and too dangerous.

But unavoidable, Hyde concluded, suppressing his rising fears. Too late for an alternative. But *Christ—*

"Good," Godwin said. "I'm glad you approve. Your Russian will hold up, I suppose?"

"Probably. But not my Czech."

"You're Russian, not Czech."

"Okay, I'm Russian."

"You're afraid, Hyde."

"No—"

"You don't like it. You don't think it'll work."

"It's not that—"

"It is, Hyde. Just sit and listen. I've thought of everything. I promise you—*everything.*"

"Okay. Tell me."

"Because they'll be expecting you. Their tame post office engineer will call the embassy for a system tester when he's finished checking the landline—when the temporary fault's disappeared."

"So, I turn up and the real one's right behind me."

"You're already on the premises. . . . You appear in the computer room before he finishes work and calls the embassy. The embassy will already know all about the fault on the landline, but they'll wait until the engineer reports before sending the system tester. You forestall that, and just take over when he finishes."

"And the fault—it just disappears?"

"It will—believe me. We set that up tomorrow morning. You go in during the afternoon. The fault actually occurs about eight or nine. The engineer won't finish before eleven—you should be out of there by twelve. And on your way home."

"Who's the post office engineer?"

"He's genuine. Has to be. But he expects you, remember. A Russian system tester. Only *you* will make you suspicious— if you can't act the part well enough."

"I need written proof."

"No cameras. Too risky, snapping away at the screen. The hard copy coming out of the printer will be too bulky. You'll use the recorder that's already wired in. They call it a streamer tape drive. Think of it as a cassette recorder. You switch on and it's just like recording a movie on TV!" He grinned. Almost boyish, for the first time that evening. Godwin as Hyde had previously encountered him. A man of promise and good nature. "Guest can play it back in the comfort of the Cabinet Office with no trouble at all. Most of the Czech equipment was made by ICL, or IBM under another label, anyway! Government contract some years ago."

"Okay. And when I've finished, I just walk out again the way I came in?"

"Yes. Just walk out. You'll pronounce your tests complete, sign a few forms, and pack your bag and go."

"And if I blow it?"

"You'll shoot your way out, I should imagine, with your usual subtlety."

"It's as easy as that?"

Godwin nodded. "Computer security needs a genius to set up—and a crooked moron in possession of one or two vital passwords to break down. Even you can do it, Hyde." He rubbed his chin. "You'll need luck. What Petrunin was about to tell you—the moment he passed on to the great Centre in the sky—was a shortcut to *Teardrop*. We don't know what that was. You'll have to sit through everything that comes out of his secret file until you hit the right stuff."

"How long?"

"Can't be too long. Petrunin would have thought of that. He might have needed the stuff himself in something of a hurry. He might have been like you—somewhere he shouldn't have been, accessing a security computer's records." Again, Godwin grinned.

Hyde nodded. "I don't have any choice, anyway." He stood up. "All right—show me what to expect on the screen, then tell me what a system tester does and how he does it." He held out his hand to Godwin, who moved his own hand forward. Disturbed by the movement, the cat leapt lightly from his lap. Hyde gripped Godwin's hand and felt the hard skin on the palm—a badge of long service with his crutch. He pulled Godwin from the armchair and handed him the crutches. Godwin stumped heavily toward the table and the computer that rested on it.

"Come here," he said. "Come on. I've got it ready for you." Hyde followed him. "Sit down, sit down—" he was impatiently instructed. "Now, on the screen you've got the—" He tapped at the keyboard. A list unrolled on the small screen in luminous green letters. "—the usual Menu. That's what you'll see on the terminal in the Hradcany—on all of them. Waiting for you to request something. . . . That's where you use the first password."

Godwin leaned over Hyde's shoulder, his thick finger pointing almost with accusation at the screen. His breathing was stertorous. Hot against Hyde's cheek. "See here—from everything we know about the way the Central Records computer works, this Menu is accurate. Everything's stored in a database, and material is accessed by choosing one of these items from the Menu—Personal Records, Military, Education, Criminal, Career Details, and so on."

"Criminal?"

"Every scrap of information on everyone, *anyone and everyone* who's ever had anything to do with the KGB—or the MVD and the NKVD, even as far back as OGPU, if they had the records—is in the database. Millions and millions of items of information . . . all there, waiting to be accessed even by an idiot like you. Dissidents, psychopaths, thieves, and murderers—and that's just the enlisted personnel—" Godwin chuckled.

"Okay. How do I find what I want?"

Godwin tapped at the keyboard. The screen requested more information from him. He typed once more. The screen cleared and then a graphic display appeared. What was it like? A family tree, Hyde decided.

"There," Godwin said with studied nonchalance, straightening up on his crutches. "That's something like the schema they'd have. See, this is the driver, as it were, that controls the database represented by this top box here." It was labeled System. Lines connected it with other boxes below. More lines connected the second, third, and fourth rows of boxes, to the System and to each other. The box below System was marked Name Identification, below that three boxes labeled Assignment History, Education History, and Personal Background. Near the bottom of the screen, below perhaps another half-dozen boxes, all labeled, were two that remained blank. "Clear?"

"Yes. What about these?"

"I can label these now, from what you've told me. Let's call them"—he tapped in his instructions—"*Teardrop* and, oh, *Dirt*, mm?" The words appeared in their boxes after a few moments. "This is a simplified model—there are hundreds, thousands of these boxes of information in the schema for Personnel Files."

"What do the connections mean—they're numbered, why?"

"They mark the sets, the pathways whereby you retrieve the information. These two boxes, the ones Petrunin added secretly, are linked only to each other and to his Assignment History—see? That's how I imagine he did it. Once you've requested information on Tamas Petrunin and given the correct code to access the information, you'll have to provide the *legitimate* password, just to prove you're kosher. Then you ask for his assignment history, and so on . . . if you *are* kosher. But since it's *you*, when you access his assignments you'll use *his* password, those postings in reverse order—and this calls up a completely different access program, and your request will follow this route." His forefinger traced the line from the System box to Name Identification, then to Assignment History, then to the box he had labeled *Teardrop*. "Except," he said heavily, "you'll have the password to *Dirt*, which you'll have to run all the way through before you can get to *Teardrop*. From what Petrunin was about to tell you, I'm sure he had shortcut passwords to each part of his secret files, but you'll have to access the lot to make sure you find *Teardrop*. Okay?"

Hyde nodded. "Okay." He felt a tremor in his hands, and pressed them between his thighs, thrusting them out of sight. "How long could it take?"

"Depends. On how much he had stored and whether he's been adding to it over the past few years. Minutes, perhaps."

"All displayed on the screen or coming out of the printer?"

"Yes."

"I might have to be alone for—"

"Ten minutes. You don't know how to go to *Teardrop* directly through all the other dirt he stored away."

"A real Chance card—go directly to jail, do not pass Go," Hyde murmured.

"It's the safest way."

"I think," Hyde began, looking up at Godwin, "that bastard Petrunin might have the last laugh—don't you? He could kill me yet. And the bugger's been dead for days already!"

Godwin said nothing except: "Let's do a test run on accessing the computer, shall we? I've set it up for that."

Hyde looked down at the keyboard of the small computer. Godwin had patiently stuck small pieces of address label on each of the letter and function keys. On each, the letters of the Cyrillic alphabet had been inscribed. Russian words now indicated the functions of the computer. He had made Hyde practice over and over, before their meal and while he noisily prepared it, in order to become familiar with the Cyrillic keyboard he would meet in the Hradcany. Now, Hyde stared at it in profound mistrust as Godwin canceled his graphic and reinstated the Menu on the screen. Thanks to Godwin, he could cope with the jargon, with the tasks he would be set to access the information he sought. But he did not think he could cope with the situation, its danger and isolation.

He would be too alone, too exposed for too long. . . . Passing time was a series of tripwires. It was going to take too long, too long—

"Ready?" Godwin asked. "Then begin."

The moment she saw him, still seated at his desk, the telephone now replaced on its rest, Margaret quailed at the prospect of deceiving Babbington. The room was warm against her cheeks, flushing them the color of confession and guilt. The guards still held her arms, and the dog scrabbled on the wooden floor of the corridor behind her. Restrained by its choke chain, its breathing was loud and threatening. Babbington was smiling broadly.

Her lies seemed pale and unsubstantial now. Babbington knew everything and would not be persuaded of her innocence.

"Margaret. My dear Margaret!" he said, rising. One of his hands signaled her release. Her arms fell numbly to her sides. Was there hope? No. The tone was mocking, confident. Babbington came toward her, hands held out. Her body flinched from his embrace. "Margaret?" His eyes hardened as he studied her face. Then he turned from her and said:

"You've caused me a lot of concern, Margaret—a great deal of pointless worry." The mockery of a stern parent's voice.

"Andrew!" she blurted out, her body trembling as if the hot room were cold. He turned on his heel.

"Yes?"

He made another gesture with his right hand, and she heard the door close behind her. Even through the wood, she could hear the reluctant slither of the dog's heavy paws as it was tugged away down the corridor. It barked once as if to remind her of her danger.

"I—" she began. Then: "Where's Paul—Paul's alive, isn't he? You've got Paul here, haven't you?"

Babbington looked grave. He gestured her to a seat and she moved nearer the fire to avoid his touch. The armchair invited, insisted. Her legs seemed without strength. Babbington sat opposite her.

"I'm afraid—" he began.

"No!" she wailed immediately, then thrust the knuckles of her right hand into her mouth. Her eyes misted. Babbington's gaze glinted. "Oh, no . . ." she breathed. "No, no, no . . ."

"I'm sorry—"

"He didn't know anything—he couldn't have been any harm to you!" she protested, finding the deception she had planned now available as something to fend off reality. "We didn't *know* anything! We didn't, I swear we didn't, I swear we didn't know anything, we didn't know . . ." Her voice subsided into sobbing. It was as if she wrenched at the hands of a great clock. Heaving time backward. If she went on protesting, on and on, Paul would be alive. "We didn't . . . nothing . . . nothing . . ."

It was difficult to see Babbington's expression when she looked up. She wiped her eyes, and saw that his face was moved only to a clever smile of satisfaction.

"I'm sorry, Margaret—it won't do." He sighed. "I toyed with the idea. I didn't believe you couldn't know. I hoped it, at first. Believe me. Then I hoped I might delude myself into such a belief . . . but, all to no avail. I can't escape the truth. You know everything. About Aubrey. About myself."

She wanted to protest, to stop him. He'd gone too far, too swiftly. There were moves to be made, gambits to deploy. Not this, this *nakedness*, beyond which Paul's death was utterly real.

"No," was all she said, dropping the hand she had extended to try to silence him.

"I'm afraid it has to be, Margaret." His voice was soft, almost a caress. She saw his bulk move from the chair toward her. Slowly, she looked up. Again, it was difficult to see his expression clearly. He cupped her chin in one large hand. "Paul's alive, my dear. Wounded, but alive—"

"What?"

He struck her, then. Her head twisted, her jaw was shot through with pain, her neck burned with the jolt from his closed fist. She heard him walk away, heard the fire grumble and spit like an old man. She touched her jaw, tasted blood in her mouth, spat.

"He's alive, and will stay alive if you tell me why you're here. Tell me where you've been, what you know, who's with you, and he lives. Understand me?" He turned to her and shouted: "Do you understand me?"

"Yes, yes!" She caught the blood that spilled from her open mouth in the palm of her hand. Blood and saliva. She stared at it, horrified, then returned her gaze to his face. He did not seem to regret the violence, or shrink from it.

"Good. Where's Hyde?"

"Who?"

He moved swiftly toward her, and she flinched. "Hyde!" he barked. "Where is Hyde?"

"I don't know."

He hit her again. The gobbet of blood in her palm flew into the grate and sizzled on the logs. She cried out with renewed pain.

"Where is he?"

"Czech—Czechoslovakia," she sobbed.

"Why?"

"I don't know!" she screamed at him. "He didn't tell me anything—just in case this happened!"

Babbington lowered his clenched fist. He seemed satisfied. "What did he instruct you to do in his absence?" he asked in a thick voice. "What?"

Margaret watched him. She must not tell Babbington anything more! She had already told him too much, far too much while the blows and the shouting were in control of her. She glanced guiltily at her handbag, at her hands, her feet. She hunched into herself, retreating from Babbington. He would kill Paul and herself once he knew everything—

"What did he instruct you to do? Follow me? Watch me?"

She was prepared for the questions to continue, yet they still acted with the naked shock of icy water, so that she flinched, appeared guilty, seemed to choke off confession by putting her shaking hand to her lips.

Babbington snatched at her handbag and tipped the contents onto the bright rug in front of the fire. He stirred the compact, the keys, the hairbrush, the paper handkerchiefs, the purse, with the toe of one shoe. Then his shoe touched the instruction booklet on how to fit and use the telephoto lens, and finally the small plastic canister in which the second roll of film had been contained before she loaded it.

Like a delicate footballer, he kicked the small canister across the rug with a flick of his toe, then separated the instruction booklet from the litter of other objects. He bent and picked them up, his face gleaming from triumph, suspicion, and the firelight. His eyes were hard when he looked at her after opening and reading the booklet. His big hand clenched upon the plastic canister, squeezing it.

"What?" he breathed softly. "My, but you have been an *industrious* little thing, haven't you." Then his voice hardened once more. "What was the purpose of your photography, Margaret? Where are your vacation snapshots?"

She remained silent, quivering like a sapling at the first wind of an approaching storm. She could not prevent her head from shaking, as if to defy him. She flinched as he stood up.

"What did you photograph?" he roared at her. She huddled into the chair. He grabbed her arms, bruising them, and dragged her face close to his. She was terrified of the hard chips of light in his eyes, of the mouth that appeared hungry. "Tell me, Margaret—or he dies now. Do you understand me? He dies *now!*" He flung her dramatically back into the chair, even as she cried out:

"No!"

"I give you my word—*now!*"

He snapped his fingers, moved toward the door.

"No!" He did not stop.

"I followed you—to a meeting—in the *Belvedere!*"

He turned on his heel. She heard his breath sigh out like sexual release. It was hot, heady in the room. Fetid, a place for exotic plants.

"You have evidence of that meeting?"

She nodded.

"Two rolls of film . . . telephoto lens . . ."

He moved heavily toward her.

"Where are those rolls of film?"

She flinched from his raised hand.

"Mailed them—"

He grabbed her chin and jerked her face upward. His thumb and forefinger pressed her jaw painfully. "Where are they? When did you mail them?" He shook her face between his fingers like something utterly fragile and breakable. "Tell me, Margaret. *Tell me!*"

She blurted out the name of the pension and the time she had mailed them. He released her chin at once and glanced at his watch. Then he moved quickly to his desk, snapping on the intercom. He barked orders into it, ending with:

"They won't have been collected yet. Yes, of course police IDs for you and whoever you take! And hurry!"

He flicked the switch and turned to her. She felt something loosen and slide within her: will, resolve, she could not tell. Perhaps even hope. She had made a final move in the game. Left herself open to checkmate. Her hands flitted at her bruised jaw, at her quivering lips. She'd lost everything, everything.

It had been ridiculous to assume she could alter events. Ridiculous from the first. All that mattered, really mattered, had been Paul's life. And he was alive. Babbington had given him back. She looked up as Babbington addressed her.

"Now, you must see your husband, Margaret." He rubbed his hands lightly together, dusting them. "I'm sorry for—well, that's in the past. I had to trick you, even hit you, to save time. I do not have that much to spare. However—" He was buoyant with triumph now, and his cold munificence chilled her more than the streak of sadism and vengeful rage he had earlier shown. "—perhaps now there is a little more time. . . ." He took her arm and lifted her from the chair. She felt unreal, a sacklike object being moved. "A pity you know nothing of Hyde's exact whereabouts or his motives—but I believe you don't know. He's clever enough not to have trusted you." Babbington smiled. They were at the door. She flinched as if anticipating that the dog lurked beyond it. Babbington opened the door. The corridor was empty. "Come," he said. "I'll take you to Paul."

She clung to that statement, blotting out the scene that preceded it. The voice had been almost warm, the hand that held her arm supported rather than imprisoned her. She moved into the fragile fiction with each step on the polished floorboards. She felt her body lean against Babbington for support.

He lied to you then hit you to disorientate you, something announced in her head. You went straight to pieces, to little pieces. . . .

She bit her tongue, as if she had voiced the words aloud. Her father's face, Aubrey's face, Babbington's face—twisted in cruel satisfaction—Paul's face . . .

Grainy picture. The skull separated from its skeleton by a workman's spade. The skull blown open by Aubrey's accidental bullet. She shuddered and pulled away from Babbington.

"No," she murmured.

"But here we are," Babbington announced with mocking breeziness. There was someone else there, an armed guard. "This is Paul's room—open the door." The guard turned a key and threw the door ajar. "A pleasant reunion, Margaret, my dear," Babbington said and thrust her forward. The door closed loudly behind her.

Massinger looked up distractedly, as if a stranger had burst in upon some scene of ordinary domesticity. The paperback remained in his hand. The small transistor radio they had provided continued to play. It wasn't food, not the right time for supper, or for the one large Scotch they served him late in the evening.

What, then—

He felt the shock of recognition. Beneath it, a further shock of his imprisonment was made real to him again. He saw the bruises in the same moment that he observed the open mouth and wild eyes.

Margaret stood by the door, trembling. Pain stabbed in his thigh and hip as he tried to move his injured leg and climb awkwardly from the low bed. He dropped the novel he was reading and heaved himself to his feet, tottering erect.

She moved toward him then. The Handel on the radio changed inappropriately from andante to allegro. Sliding into something that might have been gay. He was disconcerted. She was murmuring, one word over and over again, even as he pressed her against him and felt her whole frame shaking.

"Sorry, sorry, sorry, sorry . . ."

He did not understand the need for apology.

And then did, as he brushed her hair, as his hand moved gently to her cheek and she winced at the thought of further inflicted pain. She, too, was a prisoner. She had—yes, she had come to find him. Reckless, narrow-minded, *single-*minded . . .

He knew, with a sick certainty, that she had told Babbington everything she knew.

He lifted her face and kissed her very carefully and softly. Resenting the stubble that might pain her bruised jaw. She was looking at him with the face of a child. He sensed her body through the material of his shirt as his arms enclosed her. The fur jacket was wet with melted snow. For a moment, he almost wanted to thrust her away. To make her stand apart from him while he told her what a fool, what a mistake, what a *fatal* error . . .

But she knew it. All.

She had ceased murmuring her apology and simply clung to him, her face against his chest. He looked over her blond hair at the closed, locked door of the small room. It was as if he could quite clearly see the armed guard posted outside. He brushed absently at her hair, even at the shoulder of the fur coat. Stroking a small animal that could not be blamed.

"It's all right now, it's all right now, my darling," he began softly, gripping her more tightly in the circle of his arms. "It's all right. . . . You're safe. I've been out of my mind with worry about you. It's all right, it's all right. . . ." What she had done, she had done out of love. Killing herself as well as him. He swallowed. "It's all right now, everything's O.K." She was sobbing softly, and swallowed continually. He had to ease her guilt away. "Don't worry. It just got messed up, but—everything you've done, everything you've said or felt, has been honest. Don't blame yourself. . . . It's all right now, all right."

He continued to murmur into her hair, stroking her face and shoulder and upper arm gently. "I shouldn't have—my fault, getting you into this mess." Did he believe that? Yes, yes. "My, my stupid, ridiculous shining armor, my blindness, my stupidity." He ground the words slowly out. "I had to try and help and I didn't think about you—forgive me for that. I didn't think about you. . . ."

He continued to stare at the locked door, even as he sensed the desperation of her need for comfort. Her hands eventually opened and stilled against his back, pressing harder and harder, returning his close embrace. She swallowed. He could hear her breathing become more regular, quieter. He continued to stroke her hair and face.

Hyde distracted himself from Godwin's slow, noisy progress onto the escalator by glancing once more at the small picture in his hand. He stepped onto the escalator behind the hoarsely breathing Godwin, hefting the haversack of tools on his shoulder. The snapshot was small, monochrome—a flash picture. Wiring flared behind an opened panel surrounded by darkness. Someone other than Godwin had scribbled with a ballpoint on the surface of the photo. Two words in Czech near the bottom and an arrow pointing at one of the cables exposed to the camera.

The landline that linked the remote stations of the Hradcany's computer room with Moscow Centre.

He slipped the snapshot into the breast pocket of the oily overalls he was wearing over corduroy jeans and a check shirt. He had not shaved. Rubbing the stubble on his chin and cheeks, he reminded himself of his almost-sleepless night. Like rubbing some legendary lamp, he evoked smoky fragments of the night's information—and quashed them by concentrating fiercely on his feet as he reached the bottom of the escalator and stepped off. Godwin readjusted his crutches and leaned his weight more assuredly on them. There was no time now to consider the coming afternoon and night. . . .

People brushed past them, crowding into the warmly lit underground concourse of the Mustek metro station. Snow shone wetly on their shoulders and hats and headscarves as it melted. The mosaics were stained with muddy footprints as the morning rush hour crowds moved through the shop-lined concourse.

"All right?" Hyde muttered in Czech, leaning toward Godwin. Godwin merely grimaced and nodded.

Hyde adjusted the haversack on the shoulder of his dark blue donkey jacket. Another manual worker on his way to his job. He joined the orderly procession to the platform, Godwin following him. Hyde felt the tension rising in him like sap, sensed the lack of reserves in himself—the lack of sleep that now prevented him from using his intelligence as if it were some separate part of him. His nerves affected his ability to think.

Godwin rested on his crutches beside him as they waited for the metro. One station down the line: Muzeum. At the other end of Wenceslas Square. Then a walk down a long tunnel to a sealed inspection hatch set in the wall. The distances came to him as measured paces as he stared at the track, at three rails, one of them live. A measured distance alongside a live rail. He could think of it in no other way. He glanced involuntarily toward the tunnel, where the lights disappeared and the live rail vanished into ambush. And shuddered.

"You all right?" Godwin hissed.

Hyde nodded violently. "Shut up," he snapped.

Timetables, distances, tools, the snapshot, the imagined noises of the tunnel tumbled together in his thoughts. He clenched one hand in his pocket, the other gripped the strap of the haversack tightly, so that his knuckles were white. He felt sick, despite the croissants and rolls and coffee Godwin had made him eat. Self-confidence was a wafer-thin, puncturable envelope around him, threatened by his surroundings.

The Russian-built train sighed into the platform on rubber wheels, its lights and crowded faces slowing after the moment in which they had made his head jolt and spin. The crowd moved him forward into the carriage like a reluctant representative of some complaint they wished to voice. Godwin lumbered behind him.

The doors closed, the train jerked away from the platform. The walls of the tunnel were suddenly close—much too close—behind the row of faces opposite him. Faces with too-little sleep, fed by basic, unvarying diets, older than they should have been, little makeup on any but the youngest of the women.

Then light again, and the train slowing, coming to rest. Doors opening, *Muzeum* emblazoned on the billboardless walls. Clean cream tiles, the face of Dvorak and bearded Czechs from prehistory. The crowd moved him out of the carriage, Godwin behind him. Now, he resented their pressure against his back.

The platform emptied. The train rushed away. Hyde followed it with his eyes. He envisaged his body flattened against the tunnel wall, curving with the shape of its huge tube as a train rushed toward him, too close to the wall—

"What is it?" Godwin whispered hoarsely. The platform was almost empty. Two uniformed railwaymen, a cleaner with mop and bucket, perhaps a dozen passengers filtering along the platform.

"All right," he said thickly. Nodding. "All right."

Beginning to be all right, he told himself as Godwin studied his pale, unshaven face. Beginning to be. . . . Noticing people, eyes, distances—

"Okay," Godwin said at last, as if telepathically aware of Hyde's returning resolution. "Let's go." He began to stump away along the platform—now that it was more crowded, where were the two uniforms? One there, the other vanished. Hyde followed and caught up with Godwin, absorbing the scene. The tunnel slowly enlarged as they approached it.

"Distance?"

"Four hundred yards."

"Cable?"

"Third from top."

"Sequence?"

"Panel off—drill out lock—say three or four minutes—induction coil—next train—flip-flop transistor and battery, clock . . . before the next train."

"Okay. That's it. Set the timer for eight." Hyde nodded. They had reached the end of the platform. Hyde glanced at the clock. A minute to the next train. The platform had filled. He could see no one in uniform. No one was looking in their direction. In his imagination, he saw his feet treading carefully in the beams from his flashlight, saw the hatch, the working of the drill, the rigging of the induction coil—then nodded again.

Godwin's face was tight and calm. A case officer's noncommittal expression. Then he grinned, nervously and boyishly. Hyde backed away from him. Could he hear the approach of the train? He reached the edge of the platform, hard against the wall. He stared for a moment at the live rail, and at a cigarette packet, crumpled into a ball, between it and the outer rail. He glanced up the platform. Faces turned to the far end. A quiet, distant rumble?

Godwin had moved to the edge to mask him. He slipped his body off the edge of the platform. Aware of the sleepers and his trouser leg inches from the live rail. Then he strode swiftly but carefully into the tunnel. He heard no cry, no murmur of detection behind him. He flicked on his torch. The sleepers quivered beneath his feet and he heard the train enter the platform, come to a halt. He felt impelled to hurry, even to run. He flicked the flashlight beam along the wall of the tunnel, back to the sleepers and his feet stepping into the pools of light, to the walls, counting the seconds. Light on the wall, on his feet, aware of the fragility of ankles and the price of stumbling—seconds, wall, feet, breathing—noise, noise. The jerky sigh of acceleration, the quiver returning to the sleepers, the hiss of rubber wheels, the hum of current—

The fireplace, the fireplace and the chimney!

He stepped over the live rail and pressed himself into the inspection arch set in the tunnel wall. The train cried and bellowed past him, his lips quivered almost to the rhythm of the carriage lights splashing over him. He pressed his cheek to the rough brickwork. Silver blur of the flanks of the carriages, a solid rushing wall, a metal blizzard passing the shallow niche of the inspection shelter and the ventilation shaft that rose from it like a chimney above a fireplace.

Then silence, except that his ears rang with the noises of the train. A deafness into which the hum of the live rail insisted after a few moments. Seconds going. He pushed himself away from the wall, stepped over the live rail—five minutes now—and began to walk on weak, trembling limbs down the curving tunnel.

Second inspection shelter, third. Three hundred and fifty yards into the tunnel. He counted his measured paces, his legs marking distance and the passage of time. Each step a yard, each step a second—

He washed the thin beam of the flashlight over the tunnel wall. Instructions, conduits, fuse boxes. A *metal plate, unmarked*. He walked on. Six paces. There, just on the edge of the beam. Metal plate, like the door of a first aid box, but unmarked. He hurried to it, stepping over the live rail. Shined the flashlight. Drew out the snapshot, checked the dimensions scribbled on the back together with the distance from the platform. Yes, yes—

A heavy security lock.

The landlines that linked the terminals in the Hradcany with Moscow Centre had been buried in the tunnel walls of the metro system when it was constructed. Under KGB supervision. Just as the rock outcrop on which the Hradcany stood was bomb proofing for the cellars of the computer room, so the deep tunnels of the metro afforded similar protection to the secure communications channels.

Hyde touched the lock, then removed a drill from his haversack. He waggled the flashlight beam until he located the heavy-duty power points and plugged in the drill. He switched on—and sensed the whine of the drill funnel along the darkness to reach the platform and alert—

He pressed the drill bit against the door of the terminal box, felt it jump aside, pressed it with both hands, and began to drill into the lock.

The flashlight nestled under his chin, jammed against his hunched shoulder. Its weak beam wavered, jumped, seemed tenuous. Hyde was aware of the darkness around him, around the metal box he was attacking. Aware of the hum of the live rail behind him. It was thirty yards farther along the tunnel to the next inspection shelter. He had to listen above the whine of the drill for the next train—

He stopped and dropped into a crouch, unstrapping his watch quickly from his wrist. Then he fished in the haversack at his side, withdrew a roll of black insulating tape, and straightened up. He held the door in the flashlight beam and taped his watch to it. Its face hung there in the pale light. Two minutes forty-seven since he had stepped out onto the tracks behind the last train. Two minutes—two-nine before the next train. The second hand jerked across the face of the watch. He wedged the flashlight beneath his chin once more and placed the drill bit against the lock. One hole, two, three—one minute twenty left, one minute and ten—three, four holes. He punctured the metal, withdrawing the drill with a jerk before its tip could contact any of the cables inside the hatch. Then again—forty-five seconds. Five holes. Two more, three?

Thirty seconds. Sweat was running down his cheeks and into his eyes, even though his breath clouded around him in the flashlight beam and damply misted the face of his watch. Clouded the metal of the door. He was wet with perspiration. Twenty-five seconds. He listened after the drill's noise had trailed off. The bend in the tunnel obscured the platform. He began to drill again.

Twenty, fifteen, ten.

Six holes, beginning the seventh. On schedule. Five seconds. Train should be drawing into the station, time to begin to move—

He lowered the drill.

The sigh preceded the train, a rushing wind. He dropped the drill nervelessly. Light on the opposite wall, and a quiver in the sleepers. Hyde ran.

The train bellowed its way around the curve of the tunnel, pursuing him. He flicked the flashlight ahead of his feet, then to the tunnnel wall, then his feet—

The shallow arch was caught in the flashlight beam. He threw himself into it, his back to the train as it yelled past him and the metal blizzard of its flanks roared inches away from him. Then it was gone, and he slumped against the brickwork. The train had been perhaps thirty seconds early.

Slowly, his breathing stertorous, he returned to the junction box and the drill. Flicking the flashlight with intense nervousness until he discovered it, lying at the side of the track. *Outside* the track. It had not been damaged or its wires snapped or crushed. He picked it up, tested it. His breath was noisy, visible around him like a fog. He wedged the flashlight, checked the watch, and drilled out the last two holes with frantic, careful haste.

Then he drew a thin, long screwdriver from the haversack and levered at the lock. Heaved against it, tearing the tiny patches of metal between each of the holes—snapping out the useless lock. It clattered on the nearest rail, bounced—a flare of sparks, illuminating him briefly, robbed him of his night vision. The live rail glared on his retinas as he returned his gaze to the door, which now hung open. He waited until the hands of the watch diminished into clear focus, then studied the terminals and cables in front of him.

Third from the top. One, two—he grinned. The red one. The big red one. He bent once more to the haversack. Straightened, replaced the watch on his wrist, then touched his fingertips around the red cable. Enough room. He began to feed the length of coil around the cable, encircling it six or seven times.

How do you know?

Unofficials—

Who? Who told you about this?

He snapped off the length of coiled wire with a pair of pliers, then raised the flip-flop transistor into the beam of the flashlight. An intermittent noise on the line, interrupting the flow of data from Moscow Centre. Scrambling and altering, disrupting. . . . But not a consistent noise that could be rectified quickly. One difficult to trace because it occurred at imprecise, lengthy intervals.

He began to attach the transistor.

Chartists, people with a grudge, the greedy and the needy, Godwin had replied with a slight smile over the rim of his coffee cup. *They sell it, offer it, give it. There's a whole black market in anti-Soviet information out there, if you bother to look. . . .*

But this stuff?

Engineers, designers, surveyors—a lot of them signed the Charter in 'seventy-seven, lost jobs, need to eat or hate the Russians . . . a lot of clever people were students in 'sixty-eight . . . the trauma froze most of them—their feelings come up brand new every time. . . .

And you trust them?

I trust their hatred.

Hyde checked that the contacts were good, then drew the battery from the haversack and connected it. Watch, *watch—*

Three minutes ten already gone. Careful *this* time—

He stretched out a length of insulating tape and fixed the short-life battery to the hanging door, making certain that it was solidly held. Then he eased the door closed. When he released it, the door swung open once more. Hyde fumbled in the depleted haversack for the timer and set its hands in the beam of the flashlight.

Three minutes fifty gone—

He glanced involuntarily down the tunnel toward the hidden platform of the Muzeum station. Silence. The air was cold on his heated face. He shivered, aware of the temperature around him. Straightening up once more, he swiftly wired the timer to the circuit. At eight o'clock that evening, the timer would trip the completion of the circuit and the transistor would begin to disrupt the impulses passing through the landline, garbling the flow of information between the Hradcany and Moscow Centre. The intermittent fault would be difficult to trace and cure. The post office engineer would be on the point of giving up when Hyde arrived to test the system. Soon after that, the short-life battery would fail and the fault would disappear.

And he'd be left alone with a computer terminal—screen, keyboard, printer, recorder, all the equipment—and *Teardrop*—

Four minutes twenty . . .

Careful.

He checked the coil, the transistor, the wiring, the battery, then closed the door and taped it shut. Four minutes forty—

He shined the pale light of the torch over the junction box. At a glance—yes? Yes—at a glance it appeared closed and locked—

Lock, where was the lock?

He flicked the flashlight over the track but could not locate the lock that had bounced on the live rail. At least he was satisfied it was not visible to any workmen or repair team who might walk through this section of tunnel before midnight—when his work would be finished or he would be finished—

Stop that—

Four minutes fifty-eight, nine, five minutes . . .

He hurried along the track, flashlight pools at his feet, his hearing alert for the noise of the next train.

In this country, they almost line up to pass you information, he heard Godwin saying. *The trouble is, hardly anyone bothers to listen.* He reached the inspection shelter and pressed his body into it. The track had begun to tremble once more beneath his shoes. He waited, switching off the flashlight. At once, the darkness was icy, thick-frozen around him. He heard the metro train approaching.

Collect the drill and the haversack on your way back, he reminded himself. And shivered. The metal storm of the train rushed past him.

"You're not eating your Chateaubriand, Voronin."

"I prefer my meat to be more cooked, thank you."

"Wilkes, give our friend more claret—it might help his palate to accept rare beef. It can't be the suggestion of blood, can it?"

"You seem in a very comfortable frame of mind, Sir Andrew Babbington."

"I am. Tell him, Wilkes, how industrious you have been this morning."

"It's all arranged. Parrish, Head of Station, takes official custody of our friends this evening. Eight on the dot. They'll be taken to the safe house, and the rest is up to you. Only five or six men on duty. I'll be around. You'll get updates during the course of the evening and a disposition of forces just before you go in. Okay? I'll leave by the back door. . . ."

"I would prefer that you did not."

"What? Not on your—"

"Please listen. The safe house has monitors and surveillance cameras both inside and out?"

"Yes, but—"

"And a security room?"

"Yes—"

"Then, Sir Andrew Babbington, I propose that Wilkes remains in the safe house—in the security room itself—and he can observe our progress. You speak some Russian, Wilkes?"

"He does."

"Then over the R/T, he can inform us of the movements of his unfortunate colleagues."

"Wait a minute, chum—"

"A good idea, Voronin. That's settled, Wilkes. Drink your wine and don't sulk."

"Vienna Station was not curious as to how and where you captured these desperate criminals?"

"Of course. Wilkes bluffed it out with them, in my name. Because of Aubrey's treachery, no one can be trusted. I have had to use local unofficials and people I've drafted in— and a top-secret location. . . . Parrish swallowed it more or less whole, didn't he, Wilkes?"

"Like a greedy trout—silly old fart."

"And for your part, my dear Voronin?"

"Everything is arranged. We will go in at eleven-thirty. A strong force of men. Aubrey and the others will be transferred to the embassy, then to the airport. An Aeroflot diplomatic flight will take them to Moscow, leaving at . . . but that is not your concern. They will be safely in Moscow and no longer a threat to you before daylight tomorrow."

"Good. I'm glad that Kapustin has had the sense to accept my scenario."

"Now, I would like to see a scale drawing of the safe house, please."

"You still haven't finished your Chateaubriand."

"I still prefer my meat to be more cooked—what do you say? Well done?"

"Yes. Quite correct. Well done it is."

"Well, there it is. Castle Dracula. You all right?"

"Stakes and garlic—check."

"Just walk straight in through the gates, past the guards. Just like that busload of schoolkids."

"Bit late, isn't it? Getting dark?"

"Never too late for a bit of Party history."

"Christ—they're forming up in a crocodile—and I can't hear any noise! Something to be said for the Party after all."

"Make sure you buy the official guide book to the Hradcany. From the Cedok office in the First Courtyard. Then you can wander through the Second and Third Courtyards to the cathedral. Across the courtyard from the cathedral is the President's Chancellery. Down below the building and the courtyard are, among other things, the computer rooms. Wander over for a closer look at the architecture. You'll be looked for and spotted."

"The supervising cleaner?"

"That's him. He'll use your name. No, he knows nothing else about you, only the name. Then he'll conceal you until tonight."

"You're certain he'll know—"

"When the post office engineer arrives—yes. When an hour has passed, he'll come and tip you off. Then you're on—the big finale, all singing, all dancing."

"Why is he doing it?"

"Oh, he wants to be a bit better off financially. . . . He's bitter as well. He used to be an electrical engineer until he signed the Charter one night when he was pissed out of his mind. Now, he supervises the Mrs. Mops in the Hradcany. Someone's idea of a joke. But he wouldn't do it without the money—it's also true you can trust him. . . ."

"And I get out this way?"

"Your Soviet ID's okay—I double-checked. And the guards will change at about ten. When you come out, they won't expect to have checked you in—they'll be new."

"Okay—I'm off."

"Good luck, Hyde. I mean it."

"Don't go cold on your brilliant planning now, Godwin—that's all I need!"

"I'm not cold on it. It'll work, if you keep your head."

"I intend to."

"And remember—Moscow Centre will expect to hear from you before you start testing—and maybe during. If they ring you—*at any time*—you've got to be able to bluff it out. You have to convince them that you're doing nothing wrong, that you need to access the information you've requested to check the system thoroughly. If you don't, they could isolate your terminal at any time they choose, just like that! Your screen will go blank, the terminal will shut down, and you'll never get hold of *Teardrop*."

"Sure. Here's another busload of kids for the funfair. I'm off."

"I'll be here, waiting for you. You'll be finished before midnight and on your way to Bratislava, with any luck. You could be back across the border before daylight."

"Let's hope it's soon enough."

"Good luck."

"Sure."

Babbington's bruised knuckles as he thrust his right hand into the black glove; Margaret Massinger's swollen lips and crooked, reluctant smile; Massinger's limp and his own weariness all confirmed Aubrey's growing realization of the complete, successful power of an implacable opponent. Margaret's hurt mouth and jaw were like badges of ownership placed on them all by Babbington.

Then they were outside. Massinger shivered immediately in the thin raincoat he wore over his shirt. Margaret hunched into her fur jacket. Aubrey felt the wind whip at his sparse hair, blow coldly around his collar. The sky was bright with stars where racing clouds did not obscure them. Gravel crunched beneath their feet—draggingly in the case of the limping Massinger. Margaret supported his weight as well as she was able. Their guards walked beside them, unworried. Aubrey felt his attention drawn toward the moving, changing, unreal clouds. His thoughts drifted.

He ducked into the rear of the black BMW, and a guard followed him. In the headlights, he saw haloes of breath like signals of distress around Massinger's head as the others were put into a Mercedes for the drive to the safe house. Then the driver slipped into his seat, and Babbington settled heavily into the front passenger seat, obscuring Aubrey's view of the other car.

Babbington ordered the driver to move off. The BMW bucked down the narrow track toward the road through the village, headlights swaying and jolting, illuminating the Massingers' heads in silhouette pressed almost together in the leading car. Reconciled, accepting.

Aubrey was envious, and angry. Babbington's head obscured his view of the other car when he sat back in his seat. The guard was silent at his side, hardly watchful, already assured of the old man's harmlessness.

Yes, the Massingers had achieved acceptance, had settled for the consolation of their reunion. It was to be envied, for he, after all, would die alone.

The lights glared as the BMW hit the final, slush-filled rut in the track, and dirty, half-frozen water splashed the windshield. Then, out of the lights and the action of the wipers, knowledge emerged.

From what Babbington had said, his scheme had the attractions of simplicity and effectiveness. Everyone would see the KGB recapture their supposed agent. The Massingers would go with him to Moscow. . . .

A fault there—

Aubrey swallowed drily. No fault, only ruthlessness. Whoever was detailed to guard them at the Vienna Station safe house when they were handed over was to die. The Massingers would not be accounted for. The dead bodies would be irrefutable proof that the KGB took back their own. As for the Massingers, there were no witnesses to the fact that they had ever been in Aubrey's company.

And even if someone were to survive, no doubt Babbington's explanation to Parrish as Head of Station—and to Sir William Guest and anyone else—would be that the KGB took away the Massingers to silence them. Innocents. Victims of circumstance.

It did not even have to be *tidy*; loose ends could remain. No one would regard them as significant once the bodies were counted and Aubrey had vanished in company with his *friends* from the KGB!

He clenched his hands into useless fists and swallowed the hard lump of bilious anger with difficulty, as he might have done a lodged chicken bone.

He closed his eyes. They were out of the village now, and the oncoming evening headlights hurt his eyes. An image of Elsenreith smiled in the flaring darkness, as if his face were outlined by the explosions of an artillery barrage. Clara appeared more faintly behind him, her face thin, undernourished, waif-like, as he had first seen her. And because of Clara—love? Yes, perhaps. Certainly regard, friendship unlike with any other woman . . .

Because of Clara, Castleford.

He glimpsed the flicker of constant oncoming lights through his pressed-shut lids. They had turned onto the autobahn. He opened his eyes, confirming his guess. Glimpsed then the two silhouetted heads in the leading car, leaning together.

He shuddered, almost expecting their heads to loll away from one another in death and disappear from the rear window of the Mercedes. He closed his eyes once more.

Elsenreith, Clara, Castleford.

He had never felt as defeated, as alone and without hope while in East Berlin—the Russian Zone as it was then called, he pedantically announced to himself. The Russian Zone. Not as helpless as now, not as bereft of expectation.

His people had got him out—dragging him from the back of the car after they'd crashed a small truck into it as he was being transferred from one prison to another—moving up the ladder of interrogation and torture. . . .

He had not expected them to rescue him, but even so he had hoped. Now, he did not, could not.

Castleford's face. His whining, pleading, ashamed face—then his slow-cunning, wary, treacherous, dangerous face. Then his dead face, lying in a spreading pool of blood on the floor of his apartment.

His face in the bombed cellar—no, first his face lolling slackly and abruptly out of the backseat of the car—then his face in the weak flashlight beam in the bombed-out, ruined cellar as Aubrey obscured it with shovelfulls of rubble. Aubrey remembered the effort, the strain, of levering the fragment of wall so that it fell into the hole of the cellar, burying Castleford's stiff, white, staring face.

They were traveling northeast through the Landstrasse district of Vienna, toward the Danube. Clara had been in Vienna, they had met once more, he'd helped establish her there in business, and—

Memory disallowed success. Instead, he heard Castleford's broken voice, confessing. Voicing the trap that had closed about him when one of the bright, scintillating, glamorous young men, now with broken fingernails and a starved look about him, had pleaded to be saved from the authorities. Then another of the group Castleford had known at Cliveden and other great houses during the thirties had come, and then a third—

And then Elsenreith had come and announced the conditions of Castleford's new employment. And he had done the work because there was no alternative—helping war criminals escape, evade justice and revenge.

The trap had closed on Aubrey now just as certainly as it had shut upon Castleford.

The Massingers—he glimpsed their shadowy heads once more as the cars crossed the river by the Praterbrücke—had achieved their calm, all passion spent, and for that, too, he envied them. It would be better to lie down and wait quietly for the inevitable.

In a matter of hours, a few hours at most, they would come for him. Killing those left, duped, to guard them at the safe house. Or leaving one survivor, like Ishmael, to tell the tale. And he and the Massingers would board the flight to Moscow before dawn.

The river gleamed with lights and then the BMW left the bridge and turned north. He began to watch the passing buildings, the oncoming lights. Numbing his mind with fleeting sensations.

In the darkness, Hyde held the luminous dial of his watch close to his face; it clouded with his breath. He wiped the glass to read the passage of time. Suk, the supervising cleaner, had been gone too long—far too long. The sour smell of drying mops, of half-closed old polish tins, of dust and cold, was the room's only reality.

The odor of detergent was strong and acrid. His stomach was watery. He had been waiting too long for Suk, waiting too long to be taken down to the lower levels of the building. . . . the penetration operation was on the point of being aborted. . . .

However often he tried to dismiss that idea, it returned insidiously, always with greater strength. He was nothing more than a child playing hide-and-seek in an old, dark house. But the game was long over, no one had come to find him, and the darkness was growing more and more intense—

He shook his head, almost vehemently, clearing it. He knew that around him in the dark lay the tools of Suk's trade. Old vacuum cleaners, mops, brooms, buckets, tea chests, shelving. The pistol lay near his thigh as he sat with his back against the wall.

He looked again at his watch. Time was running away. Suk had been gone three-quarters of an hour now on his scouting job—it should have been fifteen minutes maximum before he came back to report. The engineer would have been in the Hradcany computer room for more than a half hour by now, perhaps more than an hour. . . . *Where was Suk?*

The corridor outside was silent, empty.

Suk had screwed it up, got himself suspected, caught . . . even chickened out. Delaying until it was too late, anyway.

It isn't going to happen, he heard his mind announce with solemn clarity. It isn't going to work.

It isn't going to work—and you're trapped. . . .

16
In the Labyrinth

Light switched on—

Hyde, startled into movement, slid upright against the wall, the gun coming up immediately, the barrel quivering slightly from reaction until he stilled it, aiming it at—

—at Suk's stomach. *Suk's* stomach!

His legs felt weak. Suk's face mirrored his own shock and relief.

"For *Christ's* sake!" Hyde hissed venomously. "Where the fucking *hell* have you been?"

"Come, come quickly," Suk urged, pressing his thin, stooping form against the door he had closed furtively behind him. "Please—"

"It's over an hour since you—Christ, man, where *were* you?"

"You must come at once, please, you must come now!" the supervising cleaner pleaded.

Hyde moved on stiff, deadened legs.

"Why? What's gone wrong?"

Suk shook his head vehemently. "No, nothing is wrong. I—"

"What?"

"It—it was difficult for me to approach, to know . . . eventually, I—I did not tell you this, but when I came last, the engineer. . ."

"Yes?"

"He had already arrived—I did not know how long before—I had to find out, I could not come sooner—"

"And?"

Suk seemed to stoop to Hyde's height, as if to diminish himself as a target for blame or blows. He was sweating.

457

Hyde smelled him, too, intruding upon the smells that had filled his nostrils for the past hours.

"Only ten minutes before—I swear it, only ten—" Suk cowered.

Hyde nodded, then looked at his watch.

"One hour and twenty—okay, take me down." He stared at Suk, but a threat seemed superfluous, even wrong. And his own tension threatened to interfere with his articulation, and he merely added: "Come on, Suk—take me down."

Hyde climbed into the white lab coat Suk had provided, clipping the ID card with his name, photograph, and details enclosed in clear plastic, to the breast pocket. He pocketed the pistol, and tested the weight of his briefcase filled with files and forms in his left hand. Then his right hand fiddled for the other documents in his pocket. The cover seemed as thin and unprotective as the white coat. Joke scientist—did they really expect him in that guise? Godwin nodded, smiling sardonically in his mind. Suk opened the door with exaggerated caution, almost comically. Then slipped through the crack into the corridor. Hyde followed.

Suk's whisper enticed him like the tune of a snake charmer along the corridors, down the flights of stairs to the cellars of the Chancellery building where the KGB had installed their high-security computer room, protected by the rock of the high Hradcany ridge.

Now the man wanted to talk, to babble away tension, letting it leak out in words.

"The engineer was delayed by a job outside Prague—a military installation, I think . . . complained much, but I did not think he was coming, sorry, but I missed him. . . . I have glimpsed the room only once since his arrival. . . . It seems he is still occupied. . . ."

Hyde wanted to order him to keep quiet, but was afraid of a crack in his voice. Suk's words were like a strong light, making the weave of the operation transparent and fragile. Shut up, man, shut up—

Then, the last flight of steps. The shoulder of a uniformed guard at the bottom, jutting beyond a turn in the corridor. Hyde dodged back out of sight, feeling Suk's shallow, quick breathing on his neck and cheek. He shivered, turning to face the supervising cleaner.

Then looked at his watch.

"He was delayed?" Suk nodded. Already, the beads of

perspiration on his pale forehead were drying. He had completed his role. In a moment, he would be able to retreat from this location, this tension. Count the money—

"Then the fault on the computer should have disappeared by now," Hyde said. He remembered turning the hands and setting the clock in the darkness of the metro tunnel.

He saw the shoulder of the guard, the first obstacle of his course. Even if he passed him, there would be others; beyond them, he might only find that the engineer had already left, the fault had vanished, his presence unnecessary and immediately suspicious. The guard's shoulder twitched like an organ of sense detecting something amiss. Hyde gripped the material of Suk's suit above the breastbone.

"I'm walking into a trap because you couldn't do your fucking job properly!" he hissed, leaning his lips to the man's ear. He heard Suk's ragged breathing, loud as an alarm signal, and immediately released the thin, coarse material of the jacket. Suk was vigorously shaking his head, and sweating once more.

"No . . ." he protested.

"Get lost."

He shrugged Suk aside. The man backed away like some cowed, theatrical servant, then muttered in a whisper: "I— will wait."

Way out, *exit*, his mind warned, and he placated Suk with a nod. Then dismissed him from his thoughts. He heard the hesitant footsteps vaguely—something that did not concern him.

Down the green wall to the next basement level, parallel with the handrail of the stairs, was painted a red stripe. It signified an area of maximum security. They had passed stripes along every wall, down every set of steps. They had gone from green to yellow to blue and now to red. Indications of growing security, of greater and greater restrictions to access. Increased warnings to Hyde of his danger, of the distance back from the computer room to the castle above.

Red stripe. Absolutely no unauthorized personnel. Strictly no admittance without the correct papers and identification. He looked again at the guard's shoulder. The red stripe down the wall was at the level of the marksman's badge on his upper sleeve. The tip of his rifle barrel jutted beyond his shoulder, as if searching for him; waiting.

Twelve steps—then he had only the ID clipped to his breast pocket and the other papers with which to confront this first guard. And, if he passed him, he would be between the rifle tip he could see and the Kalashnikov of the next guard farther along the corridor. In a cross fire if they so much as suspected . . .

Twelve steps.

He took the first step, body steady, temperature endurable, legs okay, breathing controlled.

His left foot fumbled at the third step. Already, the guard's shoulder flashes and arm badges were more significant, larger in his vision. It was as if he were on the point of tripping, of stumbling the short distance to a collision with the uniform. He hesitated, felt the perspiration beneath his shirt, then almost at once he was two-thirds of the way down the striped wall toward the guard's shoulder. He felt light-headed, as if with fresh, chill air. Better. Under control. Better.

His foot touched the bottom step and the guard, startled, turned to him. Hyde stared into the young, freckled, open features, knowing that if anything went wrong, if he were suspected or even exposed, he would have to kill this guard in order to get out. The narrow corridor and the flight of stairs were the only exit he knew from the cellars of the Chancellery.

Marksman's flashes, KGB stripe. "Good evening, Comrade," Hyde said casually, presenting his breast pocket ID for inspection, airily waving his other documents in his right hand, as if beginning the theatrical hypnosis of the young guard.

He waited on the edge of the precipitous moment. The guard took his papers, read them carefully, compared face with picture with face with picture clipped to his pocket. . . .

And nodded. Hyde's hand—fingers, at least—had touched the small of his back where the pistol was now concealed in his waistband. The guard looked down, incongruously, at the faded jeans and the three-striped training shoes he was wearing. And seemed more than ever convinced. Hyde's right hand regained his side, then touched the square briefcase, flicking the catch. The guard peered. His ear was close to Hyde's face, as if expecting a whispered confession. His fingers—bitten nails, but clean—riffled the folded sheets of continuous paper, the pamphlets and reference books, the ring-bound notebooks, the manuals.

"Thank you, Comrade," the guard announced at last with a slight, familiar deference. Members of the same side, the same club. Russians in Czechoslovakia—KGB Russians. Godwin had said the papers would stand up to inspection. They had.

Hyde said: "I hope this doesn't take all night."

"I'm off at twelve," the guard replied with complacency and a grin.

"Lucky bastard. I won't be out before then—" He almost wanted to cross his fingers as he said that.

He ambled with studied indifference down the red-striped corridor toward the guard at the end of it, a man relaxed by his observation of the first guard's inspection of his papers. Already, there was the smell of ozone and air conditioning. There were staircases running down farther into the cellar complex. The corridor ended, opening out into a glass-paneled area with chairs and a vending machine. An incongruous rubber plant and magazines on a glass-topped table. The reception area of a new company out to impress visitors. Beyond more glass paneling, which reached to the high ceiling, lay the computer rooms. Men in white coats and foot coverings, No Smoking signs, security warnings—the guard.

A flick of the papers, a glance at the breast pocket ID, and the guard stood aside from the door. Hyde felt breath and heartbeat hesitate, even though he hardly paused in his stride as he pushed the first door open and passed through. Ten fifty-three, he saw, glancing at his watch as he pushed open the second door then let it close behind him. Constant temperature, high level of noise—chatter rather than hum of the machinery. Perhaps three people mincing and sliding between the metal cabinets—one carrying a clear plastic disk pack, loading it onto one of the computers. The shift manager and an operator were watching the job stream unfold on a console. The night shift.

High ceiling, a long room retreating beneath bright white lighting. Rows of VDTs. Controlled air came up near his legs through one of the hundred grilles set in the suspended floor. Thick bouquets of cable and wiring emerged from the floor directly into the boxes that stood like ranks of filing cabinets, most of them orange and bearing the legend ICL. Just as Godwin had said. British computers.

"Where's the post office engineer, Comrade?" he called out. A bearded young man looked up from a sheaf of printouts, pencil held daggerlike in his teeth. He merely nodded in acknowledgment of what he guessed to be Hyde's role and business and waved an arm vaguely. Hyde followed the direction, moving more quickly now. If the fault had disappeared because the short-life battery had run down, if the engineer had called the Soviet embassy and requested a system test and the genuine tester was on his way, if, if, if—

Someone glanced at him without interest, assuming his business there. The noise of the room was almost unnerving. The temperature was dry, dead like the air. Carpet, wiring, air ducts and grilles, glass walls, racks of tapes and disks, printers, VDTs. Hyde moved through an alien, mechanical landscape toward the highest-security area. He saw guards, relaxed though in uniform, armed only with holstered pistols, an officer, and one man in overalls, incongruous as a plumber might have been in those aseptic surroundings.

A guard moved, merely glanced at his ID, and nodded. "Still giving trouble?" Hyde asked the post office engineer's back as he bent over an oscilloscopelike sophometric measuring set, toolbox open beside his swivel chair. The man waved him to silence. Hyde shrugged; someone grinned and indicated the importance of the telephone call in which the engineer was engaged.

The highest-security area was glassed off from the rest of the computer room. Unnecessarily, but with habitual, obsessive KGB thoroughness. Status, too, played its part. KGB officers who could operate a remote terminal but who did not understand, and therefore despised, computers and their programmers and operators, would enjoy this sense of separation, of distance from the people in white coats. *Civilians.*

The engineer was talking over the telephone landline to Moscow Centre's Records Directorate. In his hand, flapping like a fan, was a transistor board he must have just changed. In a similar room another trusted, security-cleared engineer would be checking the line at his end. From terminal to scrambler to modem to telephone line—the two men hurrying the miles toward each other. Feeding signals of known frequency down the line and through the system and checking the readout at each end.

The fault was less than a mile of telephone line from the Hradcany, Hyde thought. He should have found it. . . . *Intermittent*—calm down, it's not staying around to be found. *Should already have disappeared*, he reminded himself. Ten fifty-six.

The engineer put down the telephone and turned to Hyde. His round face was red and he was perspiring. His lips formed an obscenity in silence before he realized that he, rather than Hyde, remained the outsider of the group around the remote terminal. Yet he persisted in his anger, saying: "Not as much fucking trouble as that lot!" He pointed to the telephone. On the screen, green symbols—a simple piece of information, perhaps? Yes, soccer scores from Moscow. Hopelessly scrambled. A jumble of Cyrillic letters, gaps, half lines.

Then, as if by magic, resolved. At the engineer's nod, the KGB officer canceled then resummoned the scores, and they unrolled obediently. Dynamo Tblisi 2, Dynamo Kiev 1.

"See?" the engineer said demandingly. "See? What a bloody screw-up, Comrade system tester! It's too intermittent to trace. They keep telling me the fault's here, not in Moscow—not even in the Russian section of the line—but here in Prague! I ask you, how can they know that? Just bullshit!"

"Calm down, Jan," one of the guards told him. "Want another coffee?"

It was obvious they knew the man well. His freedom of expression and abuse appeared to be tolerated, even amusing to the KGB personnel. The officer appeared a little disapproving, but wished not to appear prudish or petty.

"My insides are silting up with that muck out of the machine!" the engineer grumbled.

"I'm making some real stuff now—won't be long," the guard bribed.

"Bless you, Georgi!"

Hyde saw a Moulinex coffee maker on a desk top in a glass cubicle. "For you, too, Comrade?" Georgi asked Hyde, startling him. His expression melted into a grin.

"Thanks." Hyde yawned theatrically. "How long, mate?"

"I've been here an hour—dragged off a military job for this, and even then the bastards wouldn't let me leave until I'd spun them ten miles of bullshit. . . . Nothing so far. Comes and goes."

"What's it doing?"

"You saw—can't reproduce anything properly one minute—then the next, perfect."

"I came over," Hyde began, tasting his cover story like the bitter stickiness of envelope gum on his tongue, "because we got your report. . . ." He looked at the officer, who nodded. "About eight, was it?"

"Eight-five." The officer was punctilious but not unlikable. His men evidently kept him human. "I got one of our senior managers to look at what was coming out, and he suggested it was a fault on the landline. So, we let you know at the embassy, and sent for the reluctant Comrade Zitek here." He smiled. Hyde returned the expression, and waited. "We haven't met before," the officer observed lightly, with mild, polite curiosity.

Hyde shook his head, sucking his cheeks in to moisten his dry throat. "Just got here—duty roster's got my name on it and I'm here—all night by the look of things."

"Bad luck. I'm Lieutenant Stepanov."

"Radchenko," Hyde murmured in reply, shaking the lieutenant's hand. The familiarity folded itself about him like a drying leather shroud. It would suffocate him if he wasn't careful. "Yuri Radchenko." *Tread carefully*, he warned himself. Acquaintance is as dangerous as lack of sleep or the shit-and-sugar interrogators working in harness. Watch what you say, what you think.

"Zitek?"

"Yes?"

"Any time factor—any regularity . . . ?"

"Don't waste time asking. I haven't learned a bloody thing since I've been here. An hour and a half! Didn't even get the bloody dinner they promised at the barracks! Typical of your fucking army, Lieutenant!"

Stepanov smiled thinly, genuinely trying to be amused and aloof. "I'll get some sandwiches made up for you, if—"

"Bullshit to sandwiches, Lieutenant," the engineer muttered, checking the reading on the measuring instrument. Shaking his head, muttering, raising his hands in dramatic gestures.

Georgi had moved into his glass booth and was smoking slyly. His hand waved the blue smoke periodically toward the air vent set high in one wall—the one plastered wall of his booth—while he watched his coffee percolate. Hyde was mesmerized by his watch.

Eleven, eleven-two, eleven-three, four, five. . . . Priceless minutes vanished as he listened to Stepanov.

Finally, Stepanov broke off from a description of his last leave on the Black Sea coast, and smiled at Zitek. The engineer checked his watch once more, then picked up the telephone. He dialed the Moscow number, consulted briefly with his Russian counterpart, nodding vigorously as he spoke, then turned to them as he replaced the receiver and announced: "That's it! Good luck to you, but that's it! Eight minutes without a single problem. That's twice as long as any other remission. I am announcing that the bug in the system has gone away."

"You hope," Hyde remarked, grinning, holding his hands firmly together to prevent an outburst of nerves. To listen to Stepanov, to sip at the coffee, to watch Zitek's broad, overalled back—to wait, *wait*, *wait*! Had been close to intolerable. Worse than the storeroom, this public control of nerves and imagination.

"I hope? My word as an employee of our wonderful post office service. It's gone."

"I suggest—" Stepanov began, but Hyde interrupted him.

"Give it another five minutes, okay? I'll run the first test in five minutes."

"Okay," Zitek replied in a grumbling tone.

The telephone rang, making the engineer's hand jump with surprise. Dampness was chill on Hyde's upper arms and sides.

"Bloody Moscow," Zitek growled, making faces at the receiver as he lifted it to his ear. "Yes, it's Zitek—what?" He held the receiver toward Stepanov. "It's for you."

Stepanov's face was thinned, prepared as if to confront a superior officer in person. His back was straight. He adjusted his uniform tie.

"Yes? Yes, Comrade Colonel, yes, yes . . ." His ear, in profile to Hyde, had reddened. Hyde carefully rubbed his hands down his cheeks, easing away the tension of facial muscles. "It—it appears that the fault may have—may have rectified itself. Yes, I understand—of course I realize the importance of speed. . . . Yes, he's here—" Stepanov had turned with evident relief toward Hyde, who expressed nothing more than reluctance in his features. His hand jumped in the pocket of his lab coat. Stepanov offered him the receiver like a poisoned drink.

"Y-yes," Hyde said, clearing his throat. "Radchenko,

Colonel—yes, system tester." He waited. The voice from Moscow Centre was brusque, authoritative. Radchenko was indeed on the complement at the Soviet embassy, a recent posting. *There's a lot of to-ing and fro-ing in security computer circles throughout the Eastern bloc embassies. . . .* Godwin's reassurances seemed transparent now. Hyde felt more thoroughly scrutinized by the voice of the KGB colonel than when he had entered the computer room.

"System test—I want Prague back on-line tonight. In the next hour. Understand?"

"Comrade Colonel—a *full* test will take more than three or four hours—"

"Don't give me that! Do the test in stages. Then we can get terminals back into use quickly. Begin with—Education Records. You have such a test?"

"Yes, Comrade Colonel. The embassy staff roll call—"

"Very well. Try that. I want to know how much work we're going to be involved in, and I want to know within an hour. Understand?"

"Yes, Comrade Colonel."

"An hour to be back on-line. Say midnight. No, I'll be generous. Five minutes after midnight. And keep in constant touch. Understand, Radchenko?"

"Sir."

The telephone in Moscow clicked down onto its rest. The secure line crackled, then purred. Hyde replaced his receiver.

"You heard the man," he said, smiling and shrugging.

Zitek stared at the VDT. Its screen registered a column of football scores with unerring accuracy. "Good luck to you, son," he murmured. He looked ostentatiously at his watch. "That's fourteen minutes since the last noise on the line. I told you—the fault's gone off somewhere else."

"But, what was it?" Stepanov asked.

"Who knows?" Zitek shrugged. He stood up and stretched. "Anyway, I'm off. They've got my number if you need me—*don't* ring unless it's an emergency, mate!"

"I'll try," Hyde murmured. "Eleven-twelve." He slid the cuff of his lab coat over his watch. "I'll try." The soccer scores remained unaltered, unaffected. The short-life battery had at last died, in the metro tunnel. The operation was still running.

He watched Zitek pack his equipment, kneeling by his tool box. It was old, even ornately carved, and beautifully jointed. His father's? Grandfather's? It was incongruous on the carpeted floor near an air inlet grille and a bouquet of wires. Scraps of Stepanov's irritating, half-heard account of his Black Sea leave floated in Hyde's mind, but there was nothing else there. Only Godwin's voice, the terminal keyboard and screen, and the small group of people around him. Begin—

Zitek stood up, nodded to his companions, winked at Hyde, and left. Stepanov turned expectantly to Hyde. Godwin said in his head: *The chances are you'll be expected to start with Education Records. Something low-security, innocuous. That's why you've got the roll call of Prague embassy personnel. It's one of their standard system tests—*

Eleven-thirteen.

Hyde lifted his briefcase onto the table and opened it. He removed a thick sheaf of printout paper and a metal ruler. Stepanov said: "More coffee?" and Hyde shook his head. "I think I will," the Russian murmured, staring into his empty mug. "And perhaps make use of the smoking room." He smiled disarmingly. Hyde was again suddenly alert to the danger he presented. Urbane, intelligent, pressured by his superiors in Moscow. He would remain in the vicinity, watching. Hyde felt the hair rise on the backs of his arms, on his wrists and neck. *Education Records. Neutral area.* Innocent. *The password*, Godwin had added with a broad grin, *is easy. Everyone knows it. Dominus illuminatio mea—Latin. The motto of Oxford's coat of arms. They used to use Cambridge's motto, but now, since Blunt dropped dead, they've updated it. For the next generation of recruits. Not without a sense of humor at Moscow Centre, are they? Every defector we've had for the past couple of years has told us that joke.*

Hyde placed the ruler across the top sheet of printout. Checked that the tape streamer and the printer for hard copy were both on-line. Then the screen. He canceled the unchanged, unchanging soccer scores. The screen became empty. Pale green. Georgi was seated in a chair beside him. The other guard had joined Stepanov and they were smoking in the glass booth, behind the No Smoking sign in Cyrillic. The red circle of the sign hid part of Stepanov's face like a birthmark.

Begin. Log on using the embassy code.

The guard, Georgi, was unwrapping sandwiches—some thick Czech sausage that smelled of garlic and was pressed in slices between doorstops of white bread. And unfolding a copy of the evening newspaper. He was comfortable, in a satisfied mood. Easy work. Hyde glanced back down the long room. Two figures moving distantly beyond the glass of the highest-security area. Inside the glass, only figures in uniforms. One, Stepanov, alert and intelligent.

He used the password to gain access to the Main Menu, then summoned the Education Records from the Menu presented to him on the screen. As Godwin had said, these remote terminals were permanently on-line to Moscow Centre for ease and speed of access to the records. After all, no one expected an illegal, someone unauthorized like himself, to tap at this keyboard. Access was only given to permitted staff and only permitted staff knew the passwords.

The room stretched away on his right, toward the corridor and stairs. To his left, perhaps fifty feet away, Stepanov was smoking and drinking coffee. Georgi bit into a thick wedge of bread. He smelled garlic sausage once more, until the air conditioning whisked the odor away.

Hyde typed the first of the names on his list, Abalakin, I.P. A moment, then the screen spilled his education record and qualifications. Hyde checked them against his printout, Godwin's own compilation supplemented by the official SIS roll call for the Soviet embassy in Prague. Correct. He typed the next name, Aladko, I.A. Waterfall of facts. Correct. Antipin, V.V. Correct. Baranov, I.K. Correct.

Georgi munched, rustled the newspaper. Hyde studied his watch as Boyko's mediocre educational achievements appeared on the screen. Eleven twenty-one. He selected the hard copy option, and the printer startled Georgi in midbite. Hyde stood up, leaned over the printer, and checked the information against that on the screen. Boyko was dim, but his record was flawlessly presented. Chobotov, Dedov, Didenko, Fatayev, A.G. Correct, correct, correct.

Georgi folded his sandwich bag with fastidious care. Hyde turned to him. Grim Party faces stared up at him from the newspaper.

"Sorry, Georgi," he said. "You're not allowed to see this. Not cleared, mate. I'll even have to shred it myself." Hyde shrugged. "I have to check up on their assignment histories now. Sorry."

Georgi glanced at his officer, still smoking, enjoying some kind of joke behind the birthmark of the No Smoking sign. Smoking Absolutely Forbidden, it read. The smoke did not escape into the computer rooms, thus they ignored the sign. *Absolutely Forbidden*. His hands hesitated over the keyboard. He had to make the transfer before Stepanov returned; he *was* cleared to supervise.

Before Stepanov, before Moscow discovered, before the telephone rang—go on, *go on*!

Georgi got up slowly, wiping his mouth with a gray handkerchief. He nodded, cleaning his teeth with his tongue, bulging his right cheek into an abscess. "I'll get the lieutenant," he muttered thickly and walked away casually. As slowly as some ruminating animal.

Fifty feet.

Godwin had warned him to be prepared to snatch at any chance that offered itself. But not to make a mistake—

Now?

Now. He stared at the Cyrillic keyboard, momentarily baffled by the strange alphabet. Then it was as if he had refocused his gaze; the keys swam into clear meaning. *Last three assignments, in reverse order, without break*. He could almost hear Petrunin, feel his blood-wet lips against his cheek and ear. He shivered.

He canceled the Education Records. The Menu presented itself, requesting usage of the Centre's records computer. For Assignment History, he needed the passwords that Petrunin had given him—his thread into the labyrinth. Forbidden, *Absolutely Forbidden*. He requested Assignment History, and the screen requested the passwords that would indicate his security clearance. What—

He typed: WHITENIGHTS WHITEBEAR WHITE RUSSIAN.

ERROR, the screen replied, and requested he submit the correct password. Three times, Godwin had said—you get only three chances. He heard Petrunin's voice, dammit! That awful, empty whispered growl. Hatred, delight in destruction, fear of his imminent death. The bastard had lied!

He glanced toward the glass cubicle, which was misty with blue cigarette smoke. Georgi was pointing at him and Stepanov was nodding. Then the lieutenant studied the amount of coffee left in his mug and the length of cigarette yet to be smoked. Hyde, sweating freely, waved in a casual, delaying manner in their direction.

Cancel it. Back away. . . .

He wasn't lying.

He typed: WHITENIGHTSWHITEBEARWHITERUSSIAN—
without breaks, just like the final secret password to what Petrunin had stored in the computer. Without breaks!

ERROR, the screen offered implacably. Hyde felt his temperature rise, his body quiver. Critical, the reactor out of control, the organism terrified. Georgi, Stepanov, the telephone . . . Moscow couldn't cut him off now, they had to let it run—

He concentrated, screwing up his eyes and face as if in pain. Bending his head over the keys, as if about to begin some intense recital. Petrunin's voice whispered hollowly, as if echoing in the abandoned cave of his own body. What—

Hyde listened, then, as if he had communicated with some lost spirit rather than his own memory, he typed trancelike on the keyboard.

WHITENIGHTSWHITERUSSIANWHITEBEAR

The screen cleared. He opened his eyes. PASSWORD CORRECT. The screen asked him what he wished to know, how he wished to be helped, what he required.

He typed in Petrunin's name, then rank, then given names. Then KGB number. He glanced at the glass booth. Stepanov showed no sign of movement, other than the lifting of his mug to his lips. To his right, the outer room stretched away into vagueness—his distance to run. Petrunin's assignments appeared on the screen, in summary. Hyde did not even glance at them. He knew the last three. London, Moscow First Directorate HQ, Kabul. Yes, Petrunin would have used Kabul, savoring and hating the irony. Or would he? Would he? When had he corrupted the computer?

In response to another password request, and in place of the valid password, Hyde typed: KABULMOSCOWLONDON.

Blank. Blank screen!

He knew, almost by telepathy or spiritualism, that Petrunin had used Kabul as his final assignment. He would have changed the password sequence to include it, if necessary. Oh, yes, he would have—

Come on, come on, *come on*—

Behind the blank screen, Hyde sensed the bypass occurring, felt the computer seek for the tumor that Petrunin had lodged within it. Seek, seek, seek—find!

A poem. Not information. A poem in Russian. Petrunin's record continued to unfold, and then it broke off. Became these fourteen lines of verse rolling down the screen like gentle green water. Malfunction, of course. Petrunin had warned him. Even so, his hand hovered over the keyboard. He wanted to depress the Break key and return to the Menu, as anyone stumbling across Petrunin's secret by accident would now have done. This was the disarmer. *Tears*, was that? A sad parting. Something about career and love, and the conflict thereof. Petrunin in a maudlin, self-indulgent mood. Hyde had no doubt of the poem's authorship. A younger Petrunin. Much younger. A single tear, the scenery about the lovers, a swan gliding into the distance. Hyde wrinkled his nose.

Stepanov's hand upon the door. Fourteen lines. *To Lara*. His finger still hovered over the Break key. Yet Stepanov appeared to be in no hurry. The poem vanished. Hyde pressed the button on the streamer, to begin recording. *Don't use the printer, no hard copy*, Godwin warned him in his head. He drew his hand away from the printer as if from a flame. Closing of the glass door behind Stepanov, footfalls on the carpet. Cancel—

No! Not yet . . .

Lettering. The words began to flow on the screen, as if hurried by Petrunin rather than himself. Politburo dirt. Family scandals, nepotism, immorality, jewelry, dachas, furs, everything . . .

Stepanov was smiling and unsuspicious. Hyde waited to press the Break key, his eyes hurrying from the lieutenant to the telephone to the screen.

. . . houses, mistresses, bank accounts abroad, boyfriends, money, money, money, pedophilia . . .

There was no shortcut. *Teardrop* was in there, but Petrunin had died before he could supply the individual passwords for the separate sections of his secret file. The dirt continued to spill down the screen like the front pages of cheap newspapers. Dirt on the Politburo, dirt on the Secretariat, details of current First Directorate foreign operations, agents-in-place . . . all of it useful, much priceless—but Hyde wanted one name, one man's name connected with one operation.

Teardrop.

Come on, come on—the name, the *name* . . .

Please—

The telephone rang. Hyde's hand jumped, as if electrocuted.

• • •

Paul Massinger slumped onto the edge of the vast iron bath with its ball-and-claw feet, staring at his reopened leg wound. His breathing was ragged. Margaret, who had helped him along the corridors, appeared exhausted. Her pale hair flopped over her drained, bruised face. His leg ached deeply. His hands clutched the edge of the bath to steady his shaking body. Beach, standing near the door, appeared genuinely distressed. His gun was drawn, he appeared alert—but he was concerned. He did consider Massinger's pain unfortunate, even unnecessary. Aubrey, too, had been surprised that the wound had suddenly reopened. But the old man was sunk in a profound despair. He seemed incapable of volition, regret, or even fear. As if lightly hypnotized by desperation.

"Can you—Margaret, help me get my pants off. . . ." he whispered hoarsely. There was no necessity for pretense. His leg hurt like hell. He glanced at his watch. Eleven-twenty. Couldn't be long now, have to hurry.

Margaret moved to his side. "Can you raise yourself, Paul? Take your weight on your hands and arms . . ." She undid his belt, kneeled to help his trousers down around his ankles so that the wound could be washed and repatched. Massinger felt the pain of the table edge against which he had thrust his wound, to open it again. And winced.

"I—Christ, I'll try. . . ."

Come on, Beach! The man moved, involuntarily, as if the mental command had reached him. Come on—

Massinger groaned. Margaret cried his name in fear. Beach moved closer, reaching out a supporting hand, gun hanging at his side—

Massinger struck Beach with his fist, high on the side of the head. Margaret heaved at the man, tilting his body over the bath. Massinger's left hand grabbed for the gun, touched, gripped, held. Beach's face distorted with rage. He struggled, lashing out with his fist at Massinger, then at Margaret, who stumbled away from the struggle, colliding with the wall behind her. Her hair fell across her eyes and she wiped it feverishly aside. Beach had twisted against Paul and was bending him back over the bath. Paul's face was white with effort and weakness. Beach had the upper hand, was stronger—it wouldn't work, wouldn't—

What could she do? She was aware of her own weakness, her lack of height and bulk measured against Beach's trained muscles and reactions. He hit Paul again, his fist striking her husband's chin. Paul's whole face seemed to sag.

Jug. Pattern of shepherds or a hunt. Horses, eighteenth-century costumes on the men and women.

The jug and basin stood on a bathroom stool, dusty, unused. She touched the handle. Paul groaned—

She grabbed the handle, moved forward with a sob, swung the jug, which seemed suddenly lighter, not heavy enough—

It cracked, split on Beach's head, near the right ear. Beach groaned with what might have been surprise, released Paul's shirt, his body, then subsided into the empty bath. Immediately staining the white porcelain with a thin, bright smear of blood from his bleeding head. His breathing was like a groan of protest and surprise.

Margaret leaned heavily over the bath, as if to vomit. She was gasping for breath. Massinger heaved the gun from Beach's grasp and slipped off the safety catch.

"Go!" he said urgently. "Quickly, love—quickly!" She straightened, flicking back her hair. Her face was ashen around the bruises, older. "Can you?" he asked, and she nodded at once "Good girl—be careful. If they—if they—just don't do anything, please. Put down the telephone and go quietly. Don't fight—" Again, Margaret nodded. And smiled, shakily. Like someone leaving an intensive care unit, knowing there was no hope for a relative but trying to evade the inevitable or remember some better time.

She bent and kissed his cheek, glanced at Beach, who was almost snoring in the bath, then left the room. Massinger heard her footsteps patter away like someone fleeing. He stared at the gun, held loosely in his hands, object rather than weapon, and then at Beach.

The Massingers' last stand. He grinned, and then winced at the pain in his leg. And at his fear for Margaret. Stupid move, he told himself. Stupid, dangerous move—

An act of desperation. He was terribly afraid for her safety. The gun quivered in nerveless fingers. Beach snored. Others moved about the house. All of them threatened Margaret.

Margaret hurried down the corridors, wincing inwardly at each creak of a floorboard, her breathing light and shallow, her arms and hands trembling, fingertips damp so that she sensed the betrayals of smudged fingerprints left on the wall. Her heart raced.

Another long corridor. She had noted, counted, each of the closed doors as she struggled to help Paul toward the bathroom, her mind reaching forward like a reluctant hand to the violence and danger to come. She opened the first door carefully, just a crack, fumbled for the light switch, listening to the room's emptiness—

No telephone.

Next door, next room, light, no telephone, just packing cases and floorboards and an empty table. Down the corridor another room, then another, her temperature rising at each pause, each eased opening of a door, each switching on of a light. Five rooms now, then a staircase leading down to the first floor of the tall house near the Wiener Gaswerk-Leopoldau, stranded in a scrubby industrial suburb. She hurried down the stairs to a landing, peered over the banister into an empty hallway with checkered tiles half-hidden by dusty, faded carpet, then tried the nearest room.

Door, switch, light, and the moment of caught breath as she anticipated a challenge. Carpet, chairs, desk—telephone on the desk! She closed the door silently behind her. The curtains were drawn across the windows; there were cigarette butts in an ashtray and still-wet rings on a low table near an empty glass. Beer froth coated the sides of the glass. The room had been recently occupied—abandoned for only a few moments? She hurried behind the desk so that she could face the door. There had been no key in the lock. She fumbled the telephone to her cheek. It purred with an outside line. She dialed quickly, noisily. Watching the ashtray and the wet rings on the table. Watching the door.

Ringing. Guest's apartment in Albany. Their only slim chance, that Sir William had returned from Washington. . . . Ringing out. No answer. The room still smelled of cigarette smoke, as if she had entered only a moment after it became unoccupied. Then the ringing stopped.

"Sir William Guest's residence," a voice announced as if in the role of a stage butler from a period play. It was *the* voice, the *same voice*—

"No!" she could not help exclaiming: a protest that became a moan of disappointment.

"Mrs. Massinger—Mrs. Massinger, it's you, isn't it?" the voice replied. "How the hell—"

"Oh, God, *no!*" she cried.

"You're—*where are you?*"

She had lifted her head. She did not hear the question because her glance had been caught and held. All her attention became concentrated upon a box with a short tube attached that was incongruously bolted to the wall, high up near the ceiling. In shadow at the far corner of the room. A television camera. For surveillance. Shops and supermarkets. A security camera.

"Oh, no . . ." she murmured. Failure oppressed her. The voice insisted, demanded, threatened in her ear, but she hardly heard it. She stared, hypnotized and unnerved, at the camera.

She put the telephone receiver down quite calmly, almost nonchalantly, as Wilkes entered the room, his face angry yet confident. He crossed the room swiftly, as if hurrying to obey some summons, and struck her across the mouth with his open hand. She winced, cried out, staggered. He hit her again, slapping her face, opening her bruised lip, making her eyes water, her nose ache. Then he grabbed her against him like some violent lover, pressing his lips against her ear.

"Who did you talk to? *Who? Who?*"

He was shaking her. She was limp in his grip. "Guest," she murmured.

"What?" He held her away from him, shook her again. There was fear in his eyes now.

"Guest!" she shouted at him. "Guest!, Guest, Guest, *Guest!*" She felt the hysteria rising in her like adrenaline, helping her. "I spoke to *Guest!*"

He hit her then, harder than before. She fell away, against the unresisting curtains, twisting against them, gripping them as she fell to the floor. Her jaw ached; pain lights flickered on a dark screen at the back of her head. She moaned.

She heard him dial, wait, check, then laugh and reassure. Then she was dragged to her feet. Wilkes was grinning.

"Come on, lady—back to your room in the East Wing! Where they always lock the loony wife!" He thrust her in front of him across the room, through the door, along the landing to the stairs. "Where is he?"

"The bathroom," she announced without hesitation, breathless from the way he had banged her body against the wall before he spoke.

"Come on. We'll go and surprise him!"

He dragged her up the stairs, along the corridor, pushed her round a corner, propelled her down another corridor. "This bathroom—on this floor?" She merely nodded, and he pressed her more feverishly ahead of him, as if his timetable were making its own irresistible demands. He was beyond malice now. Merely urgent.

He knocked on the door. "Massinger—don't waste my time, mate—I've got your wife here and I'll kill her unless you come out quietly. I haven't got time to waste." He paused, then said: "What's the matter—don't believe me?" He squeezed her shoulder with iron fingers. She cried out. "Hear that? Shorthand form of negotiation, I admit—but it is her."

The door opened. Paul's ashen features appeared. Seeing her, absorbing the sight, he stepped back, leaving the door wide. Beach was sitting on the bath, a handkerchief, dyed red, held to his head.

"You stupid cunt!" Wilkes snapped, entering the doorway. "Get off your ass and get them back to their room." Wilkes glanced at his watch while Massinger meekly surrendered the gun to Beach. "Quick!" Wilkes ordered.

Breaking glass. A door smashed from its hinges by a heavy blow. Other noises. Glass again. Wilkes appeared unsurprised, but said: "What the hell was that? Beach, get down there and find out—go on, man! I'll take care of our friends. *Quickly*, man!"

Beach hurried past him and down the corridor. A shot? Wilkes grinned.

"It's begun?" Massinger asked, holding Margaret tightly against him.

"Oh, yes, mate—it's begun. Come on, back to your room. They'll be expecting to find you there. Come on—move!"

Hyde depressed the Break key. The screen cleared. The Menu requested he make use of it. Stepanov's shadow fell across the keyboard as Hyde picked up the telephone. He again sucked moisture from his cheeks to dampen his parched, tight throat. Stepanov hovered, as if indulging a child in a brief telephone conversation with a friend. The lieutenant flicked at the sheaf of printout, lazily interested. Comfortable.

"Yes?" Hyde asked. *No!* Bluff it out—be *stronger*, impatient. You've been interrupted. "Yes? What is it now?"

"I—why have you been accessing Assignment History, Comrade?" the voice asked. "*How* have you been accessing Assignment History? Which files are you accessing?"

"Why? What's the matter, Comrade?" Hyde asked with evident sarcasm. The tone of a superior—whether rank, class, or security clearance remained unrevealed.

"You were accessing Education Records, then you switched—"

"And you decided to interfere! Listen, Comrade—I'm trying to find out whether the fault that just went away has damaged the datafiles in any way. You expect me to do that tooling through a list of embassy staff names, without cross-referencing, without shifting from section to section of the files? Just do me a favor, will you? Keep your long nose out until I've finished—otherwise your colonel is going to have both our heads! Understand?"

Stepanov was openly grinning as Hyde glanced up at him. The Australian threw in a theatrical toss of his head, rounding out his portrait.

"But, system tests don't usually—"

"Listen! Don't usually what? Dig so deep? Just skate along the surface of security? I'm cleared. Are you? I'm testing the system, not you. You're just the operator. Tomorrow, you can have the system back to play with. Tonight, it's mine. Now, go away and don't bother me anymore!"

"I—" A pause, then: "I'm sorry, Comrade. Please continue." The telephone clicked then hummed. The operator from Moscow Centre was gone—and with a flea in his ear, as Hyde's mother might have said.

Hyde sighed with impatience. His tension had been expelled in the execution of his bluff. It had worked. A slight delay. But the operator would think, talk, perhaps ask the colonel—

Stepanov. Why didn't he go away?

"Found something wrong?" Stepanov asked lightly, companionably. "Anything I can do?"

Hyde shook his head. "Since your engineer couldn't tie down the fault, if there is one, I'm doing a much wider and deeper test than they might have expected. Bloody little bureaucrats in lab coats!"

"And everything's in order, so far?"

"It is." Hyde glanced at his watch. Eleven twenty-six. Too long, it was taking too long. . . . Buzz *off*, Stepanov! For Christ's sake, buzz off. . . .

"Carry on, Radchenko—I'll not interfere. I promise!" There was laughter in Stepanov's voice. He had attached himself like a lonely schoolboy—a new and unwanted friend, clinging like a limpet. Buzz *off*!

In Moscow Centre, they knew when he accessed the computer exactly what area of the records he was summoning. They would not know who or what was under scrutiny. But they could find out . . . trace his inquiry like a telephone call might be traced. And if they did that—more likely, *when* they did that—the telephone would ring and the screen would go blank as they isolated his remote terminal, amputated it from the computer's memory banks.

He had perhaps minutes, probably less. Seconds. And he had to work through all Petrunin's information until he found Babbington's name and it was recorded on the data cassette and he could run . . .

"Okay. You needn't hang about if you don't want to. Makes me nervous anyway, someone hovering behind me."

"Sorry about that. I'm not getting caught not doing my job, Radchenko, even if you are a nice bloke."

Hyde turned to face the lieutenant, feeling the passing seconds pumping in his arm like an intravenous drip— measuring his danger.

"How much are you cleared for?"

"You won't be going that deep."

"Why not?"

"Because *I* can't—so you certainly can't." Stepanov pushed his cap a little farther back on his head. He was still smiling.

"Anyone for more coffee—you, sir? You?" Georgi called out, adding: "Comrade Radchenko—coffee?"

Hyde began to quiver uncontrollably, as if he had received an unexpected shock. He'd blown it—already, he'd—

"You all right?" Stepanov asked. "Not for me, Georgi!" To Hyde, he added: "You look as if you need a coffee—or something stronger. Are you feeling okay?"

"Yes! Look, just let me get on with my job, will you?"

"I'm not stopping you—"

"You're not *cleared*!"

"Then neither are you—not for more than a system test!"
Stepanov's features had darkened, his gaze was squinted and
intent. "What *are* you doing, Radchenko?"

Damn—oh, damn it!

"Look, don't get bloody stupid, Stepanov—"

"I'm not. Let's see this great, ocean-deep clearance of
yours, shall we? Just for a giggle. . . ."

Damn—

As if with a gesture of failure rather than aggression,
Hyde slipped the pistol from his belt and presented the barrel
to Stepanov, keeping the gun below the level of the keyboard.
He heard the door close behind Georgi—the silly old bastard
would bring coffee as soon as it was ready, whether asked or
not. Hyde was trapped by kindness, unnerved and exposed by
companionship. Stepanov's eyes widened, his face folded into
creases of understanding and capture.

"Just sit down, Lieutenant. Please sit down next to me."
The pistol waggled, just a little—a small, innocent wave from
a toy. Stepanov removed his cap, as if attending an interview,
and sat stiffly on the chair next to Hyde. "Try to relax, Lieutenant. You're making it look obvious."

"Who are you? *What* are you?"

Hyde smiled. "Don't be silly."

"What do you want?"

"Something you won't want to see. . . . In fact, I'll do you
a favor. . . ." His voice became strained as he twisted his body
to request Assignment History once more. The demand for
the passwords. He typed them in, his fingers touching across
the keyboard as if seeking braille, his eyes flickering from keys
to Stepanov to keys to . . . "A real favor," he continued. "You
just avert your eyes. If you see what's about to come up . . ."
The poem. A tear for Lara, whoever Lara had ever been, if
anyone outside Petrunin's imagination. ". . . you won't be
very popular at home or abroad. In fact, your future won't be
worth a cork-fringed hat . . . understand? You're a dead man
if you peek!"

The gun waggled Stepanov's gaze aside. He selected the
tape drive, his eyes flickering to the screen. First Directorate
operations in progress in Europe . . . a goldmine from which
Hyde desired only the one nugget. As the information appeared, it was recorded on the data cassette.

"You seem very afraid," Stepanov said with a level, controlled voice.

"I am."

"What is it?" the Russian hissed.

"Look and you'll get turned to stone—or fertilizer. Just as soon as they know you know."

"You won't get away with this—"

"I hope to."

"You're not sure, then—"

"I'm not sure. No, don't turn around!"

Hyde glanced toward the glass booth. Patchy steam on part of the glass. The coffee maker was ready. Georgi had made his coffee. Hyde could see him bent over the table, arranging mugs, spooning sugar.

Come on—

The telephone rang. Stepanov's body twitched, and his lips parted in a smile. He half turned.

"Don't move. Just let it ring—*let it ring!*"

He glanced at the screen. First Directorate operations— Libya and Chad. Names of illegals, guerilla unit commanders, Soviet advisers. Come on—

The bloody shortcut—what the hell was the password? *Dominus illuminatio mea,* for Christ's sake!

The telephone insisted. Hyde stared at it helplessly.

"I left my heart—in San Franciscooo. . . ."

Wilkes sat down before the bank of twelve monitors— two rows of six. He continued humming the tune he had begun to sing, failing to recollect the next lines of the lyric. His eyes flickered from screen to screen—a patient, absorbed, satisfied spectator of the scenes presented to him by the remote cameras located throughout the old house. For years, it had been variously used for training, interrogation, courses in interrogation countermeasures. The district around had been leveled and made late twentieth-century and the house had become too noticeable, too easily observed to fulfill many of its former functions.

". . . little cable cars climb halfway to the stars . . ." Wilkes burst out, remembering a detached, floating line of the song.

Vienna had meant bigger business, way back when the house had been fully utilized—then it was always crowded with people. Front line, like Berlin in the sixties. Wilkes whistled the tune of the song through his closed teeth. Watching the screens. The old house, stranded between the freightyards and the gas works, began to fulfill some of its old functions.

"I left my heaaaart—in San Franciscooooo . . ."

Voronin and Babbington had agreed, decided, concluded. No margin for error or misunderstanding. The three of them—alarmed and on their feet now—would soon be on their way to Moscow. The Massingers would never be seen leaving the aircraft—go out probably dressed in overalls and carrying plastic bags full of rubbish from the galley—but Aubrey would get the pop star treatment. And they'd all be dead within a week: the Massingers the same day they arrived, Aubrey as soon as the masquerade had worked. Heart attack. Easier than risking TV appearances, press conferences, and the like. Heart attack.

Wilkes grinned. "I left my heart—in the Lubyanka!" he bawled at the top of his voice, then added: "Your last TV appearance, old boy, old chap." He leaned toward the screen, which displayed the three prisoners. They'd roused Aubrey; he didn't look so thunderstruck now, so much in a daze. Wilkes could see the cogs grinding in the old man's brain. Too bloody clever by half—

On another screen, Beach organizing checks and barriers and cross fire. On the first floor. The cameras strained to pierce the darkness that Beach had ordered, the screens glowing gray-blue with the effort to register faces, movement, patches of light skin.

There—ground floor, rear passage. Someone wrapped in dark wool. Face dyed with polish. They meant business. The camera watched the crouching Russian move past and down the corridor toward the kitchen and the hallway beyond it.

Wilkes leaned over and pulled an R/T toward him. Its thick, short aerial quivered as he picked it up and tuned it to the frequency he had been told the Russians would be using. Whispers in Russian immediately leaked from it. One of the screens—he imagined he could lip-read and match voice to face—showed the KGB man in command issuing orders, crouched in the well of the main staircase to the first floor.

Wilkes continued to hum. The prisoners huddled at the door, as if eager for their fate. Beach moved—he was registered on a screen showing the back stairs. He'd anticipated, then . . .

Wilkes was drawn into the tension of the twelve screens. The secure room of the house, in the attic, was silent and aseptic around him, filled with the ozone smells of electricity and static and charged or burnt dust. A screen crackled as he ran his finger across it, canceling Beach.

For a moment, before the rattle of gunfire and the fall of a body away into the darkness of a staircase, his imagination seemed to throw onto the screen newsreel shots of Vietnam. Protest marches with the Capitol building behind the line of idiots melted in and out of staring-eyed pictures of fatigued, beaten, hashed-out American faces. Then he blinked away the images as his attention was drawn to another screen.

"I left my heart . . ." he ground out through his clenched teeth.

The body finished falling, came to rest and silence, in a patch of darkness that the cameras could not penetrate. Then a woollen-jerseyed Russian with a blacked-up face climbed the staircase warily, toward the camera.

"S-waneee, S-waneee, how I lub, how I lub yuh!" Wilkes burst out, almost giggling. Who was that who'd been killed? He didn't know the name. One down, and the Russians had already moved to the second floor back. Another blacked-up minstrel followed the first up the stairs, teeth gleaming as he whispered urgently into the R/T clamped to his cheek. Wilkes heard his voice like static hissing behind a broadcast.

Wilkes hummed. Beach moved quickly on one screen, two more Vienna Station staffers on another, crouching together, looking scared in the darkness. Russians moved in the main hallway, on the back landing, pressing down the first of the corridors—

To be met. Wilkes jumped to attention in his swivel chair, startled and surprised—the involved, vicariously thrilled observer of the drama. Shots, ducking bodies, one cry over the R/T near his hand, that of a wounded Russian. Shots in singles, doubles. Two screens revealed the log jam, the crouching bodies at either end of the corridor—a single flight of stairs and a corridor away from the prisoners' room.

Come on, come on—don't get stuck now, Wilkes pleaded. He glanced at his watch. Three minutes, a little more. His call would be logged exactly at the embassy. He had to call Parrish now and tell him what was happening. It was his reason—his excuse—for being in the secure room.

And to switch on the alarms!

He reached over and threw the switch, hearing the bells

begin to ring in muffled and distant parts of the house. Then he picked up the telephone. They'd been ordered not to cut the wires, even though they knew the location of the terminal box for the landline. The convincing lie, the final mounting of Aubrey in his gilt frame, began with this telephone call.

He dialed. Shots through the R/T, a body slumping too quickly back out of sight. Two down. A fusillade, then a rush at the stairs by the black-jerseyed group that had gathered in the stairwell, in shadow. Someone at the top of the stairs, outnumbered and running to save himself or to get help.

It was Parrish's direct number. Wilkes blurted the emergency code, screamed for assistance, acknowledged futile orders from the Head of Station, looked at his watch, put down the telephone. He reassumed his passive role before the bank of screens. They held the whole second floor now. Beach and his group were retreating toward the prisoners and the secure room.

Come on, come on—

He had given the operation its time limit—too soon? Had to. Look suspicious otherwise—

Who was that—Davies? Moving away from the prisoners' door toward the turn in the corridor and the staircase up which Beach and another man were retreating. One, two, three left—and himself, Wilkes: the full complement.

All the screens were empty now, except for those revealing the staircase, the corridor, and the prisoners' room. Davies appeared to be calling out. Above the noise of the alarm on the wall near his head. Then another screen and another revealed the hurried, crouched run of two men in black. Down that corridor—which?—*that* corridor, yes, Davies beginning to turn, but they had him and then they had the door handle to the prisoners' room, then Beach and the other man—who? Liske, was it? Liske. Surrounded. Angry, frightened, letting guns drop, hands and feet spread as they were searched, leaning toward the wall. Beach's face looked up at one camera and stared at Wilkes from the screen. His expression was puzzled, confused. He was wondering where Wilkes had got to, why he hadn't come down. . . . Beach's head shook, then hung defeatedly against the wall as the prisoners were hurried past him. Pleasure, congratulation, delight came in a chorus from the R/T. The bluff was evident, overplayed, easy to interpret. He watched Aubrey and the Massingers moving across the various screens as he measured their progress toward the door, toward the gravel drive and the cars now pulling up to await them.

Aubrey tired and ill and white. Massinger angry, wincing with rage and with the pain in his leg. The woman bruised and weak. For a moment, on every screen, he thought an afterimage lingered. His imagination lit each of the screens with flickering memories. Tanks rolling into Prague's Old Town Square and across the Charles Bridge; napalm in Vietnam; Russian MiL-24s in Afghanistan. Black arms raising aloft Kalashnikovs in a sugar cane setting. Red Square parades. The weak, compromising faces of Presidents and PMs. The row of implacable faces and stances along the top of the Lenin Mausoleum, the tanks and missiles passing beneath their gaze.

Then the hard-lit night, the faint whirl of snow in the wind. Aubrey and the other two huddled and bundled into the black cars. The black-garbed team hurrying now, the exhausts smoking in the spotlights. Burgeoning smoke, roaring engines over the still-open R/T—

Then movement, then the message.

"Okay, Wilkes," the R/T said, then clicked into an ether-whispering silence.

Finished. Wilkes gazed at the bank of screens. At Beach and Davies and Liske beginning to move, to clatter down the staircase. Almost time to join them. He quite clearly saw images of El Salvador on one screen, on another a retinal image of Sadat's funeral. That inevitable motorcade and the blood on a fashionable pink suit—miniskirted—on a third screen. The cradled, ruined head in Jackie's lap.

"I left my heart—" he began, but the song faltered. Joke over. The cars had vanished out of the gates of the house. On the screen Wilkes could see the gasworks in the distance.

The West was finished, he had decided. Decided long, long ago. Finished, washed up, a waste of everyone's time. Losers.

He'd stuck by that insight, and the decisions that followed it, and had been satisfied. No complaints. He flicked off the screens, one by one. No images now. Only Beach and Davies and Liske running around like chickens with their heads cut off—Liske wounded.

The only thing he'd ever disliked was the KGB's *total knowledge* of him. They'd understood him, utterly and completely understood him, from the moment he'd first approached them with—with the offer of his services. As if they'd always expected him to turn up.

Working for winners. For those who were ruthless, not half-baked. The winners.

He walked to the door of the secure room, shaking his head slightly. They'd understood him too easily; he was too much like them. . . . He dismissed the idea.

"I left my he-aaart in San Fran-ciscooo. . . ." he whispered intensely, then composed his features to concern and worry as he locked the secure room's door behind him.

The ringing stopped. Stepanov's body, erect and stiff, seemed to shudder with the impact of the silence. Hyde's temperature jumped. He felt beads of sweat along his hairline and a cold sheen across the small of his back and beneath his arms. The pistol quivered in his left hand. The screen continued to unfold the contents of Petrunin's insurance policy; the streamer stuttered, recording each piece of data, then pausing for the next buffer full of information. Already, Hyde had enough to guarantee his own safety. A coup—

Get out—

Without destroying Babbington, he had nothing. Wasted, used computer recording tape. His eyes flickered to the screen—still First Directorate current operations, still within the sphere of Ninth Department—Africa. There was so *bloody much* of it! And a shortcut password to each and every section and no way to short-circuit the parade of secret information. He looked down at the pistol, glanced at Georgi, who was looking up wondering why the phone hadn't been answered, glanced back at the screen, at Stepanov, who had now absorbed the shock of silence. He was beginning to smile at Hyde's failure. Glanced then at the vz.75 pistol in his hand. Fifteen rounds between himself and Hradcany Square.

Silence. Shortcut, *bloody shortcut!*

The operator in Moscow would be reporting to his superior, perhaps at once to the colonel. If they became alarmed, they could ring anywhere—*everywhere* in the Chancellery or the whole of the Hradcany complex. Hyde was two floors beneath the Third Courtyard, like a rat in a sewer. . . .

They could block every exit without his being aware of what they had done until he ran into the gunfire.

Stepanov made to turn to him, a remark forming itself silently on his full lips.

"Don't!" Hyde warned in a shaky voice, and Stepanov sat staring ahead of him. The weakness of Hyde's voice seemed a sufficient and satisfactory answer to the inquiry Stepanov had intended.

Then he glanced at Georgi, who was emerging through the glass door, fifty feet from them, carrying two steaming mugs of coffee. Hyde stared at the screen. Nothing yet. Forty feet away—as soon as Georgi reached them he would see the gun and, and, and . . .

He could not even complete the thought, the certainty that he could not control two men and the screen as time ran out. Couldn't control *himself*—

Georgi stopped, half turned, half the distance to them. The telephone was ringing in the glass cubicle. Above the hum and mutter and conversation of the machines, Hyde could hear it dimly calling for attention. It seemed whispered, but urgent. Demanding. Georgi glanced very slowly at the mugs in his hands, at Hyde and Stepanov, then shrugged and turned on his heel. Stepanov's tense smile faded, then reappeared as he realized the nature of the call, the probable identity of the caller. Moscow Centre—

First Directorate—damn, damn, damn—

Georgi had reached the glass cubicle, opened the door, gone in, picked up the telephone.

"Not long now," Stepanov murmured with exaggerated confidence.

"Shut up!"

He watched Georgi, the pistol pressed against Stepanov's side to prevent a sudden move. The guard was almost at attention, one hand fiddling with his unbuttoned collar. Moscow Centre. Then Georgi glanced toward them, speaking as he did so—describing the two men he could see, explaining, painting a picture. Nodding. Face suspicious, puzzled. Soon the orders—

Shortcut, shortcut, *shortcut—Dominus illuminatio*!

And then—

He did not even pause to consider the idea because, at the back of his mind, he could see Petrunin smiling, his lips painted with blood, but smiling. . . .

Break.

MENU.

He typed in ASSIGNMENT HISTORY, praying that the screen would not go gray and blank, listening intently to Georgi's door, waiting for the noise of its being opened, of the first question the guard would ask of Stepanov—

Watching Stepanov, feeling his rigid, unmoving and confident frame against the hole at the end of the vz.75's short barrel.

WHITENIGHTSWHITERUSSIANWHITEBEAR, he typed furiously.

The screen cleared. He typed in Petrunin's name and rank and KGB number. Then, almost at once, with drops of sweat falling on the keys, making them treacherous, slippery—

KABULMOSCOWLONDON.

Georgi had a pistol in his hands! Stepanov was watching Georgi, willing him to move. Telephone clattered down. Door opened, banging back against the glass wall. Georgi hurrying—

Poem to Lara. Tear for Laura.

He typed LARA.

A tear for Lara. A bear's tears.

TEARDROP, he read in Cyrillic. *Teardrop*.

He drew in a deep breath, sobbing almost, nearly choking on the aseptic, dust-free air. Georgi was hurrying, hurrying—phone left off the hook, *please report at once, discover what is happening, bring your officer to the telephone*—

Hyde raised the pistol and shouted. Georgi halted, his hands feebly gripping the air level with his shoulders, fingers fumbling into surrender. His gun barrel was raised to the ceiling.

"*Throw the gun away, sit on the floor—do it!*" Hyde yelled at the top of his voice.

Georgi almost tumbled into a cross-legged position on the carpet, the gun yards away from him, sliding harmlessly to rest. The telephone began to ring next to the VDT. Hyde glanced at the screen.

. . . *implemented when conditions favorable to place him in unassailable position within hierarchy* . . .

The name, Christ, the *name*!

. . . *operational order given. Proposed merger of two services, security and intelligence, suggests optimum chance of success for operation within ensuing twelve months* . . .

The name!

. . . Cabinet opinion favors new combined service . . . Chairman of JIC will provide favorable conditions for promotion of our agent . . . Deputy Chairman Kapustin to begin overtures . . . documents in preparation for eventual defection of agent Smokescreen . . .

Stepanov, Georgi, the telephone. Noise, urgency, fear. He felt himself out of control, weak and trapped.

Babbington.

Blank screen.

Illusion? He touched the gray surface of the screen, smoothing out its charge of static. Illusion?

Babbington. He'd seen the name in the instant that the screen was isolated and Moscow Centre cut off his terminal from the main computer. The telephone continued to ring. Babbington.

He had it. Had Babbington and Wilkes and the others. Had Babbington—

Then Stepanov moved. The gun had strayed from his side and when the pressure of numbness had diminished he had realized the fact—and grabbed for it, twisting the barrel upward. For a moment, Hyde was reduced to utter, feeble panic. Stepanov's breathing was hot on his face—the man's lips were twisted with effort; Georgi had begun to move into a crouch from his cross-legged squat and the movement distracted Hyde further; alarm bells began to sound very distantly, as if along deserted concrete tunnels and corridors. Hyde's arms were weak, unable to struggle.

Then he leaned toward the Russian officer and butted his head into the man's growing-triumphal face. Heard the groan, sensed the resistance of bone. Then struck with his right hand, at the point where blood was seeping from Stepanov's nose. The officer slumped from his seat, knelt as if in prayer for a moment before falling sideways, then lay curled on the carpet as if sleeping. Georgi's boots had reached him before he lay still, but the guard halted as he saw the gun reasserting its freedom of aim. Hyde wiped his nose on his sleeve and grinned shakily.

"Forget it, Georgi," he muttered. "Just forget it."

He motioned with the gun and Georgi backed away and resumed his sitting position. Its yogalike posture was reinforced as he placed both hands behind his head. Some compressed Buddhist statue or penitent.

Hyde flicked open the streamer's drive door and snatched out the data cassette. He gripped its clear plastic tightly in his hand like an award for effort, for winning. He turned, then, and looked down the long, bright tunnel of the outer room. Two or three individuals in white lab coats, immobilized and confused by the alarm. No figures in uniform—not yet. Time . . .

Time was looping out ahead of him, too thin to become a lifeline, but something to cling to—or to follow out of the labyrinth. He stood up, and his legs did not feel weak, only cramped by tension. He stamped his feet, as at the beginning of a race.

Then, uniforms. At the far end of the long room.

He thrust the cassette into the pocket of his lab coat. Fished in the briefcase and, after unclipping the plastic cover of a narrow compartment, withdrew what might have been an aluminum rod shaped like a small, thin truncheon. He jammed the pistol into his belt in the small of his back, patted the cassette, and walked to the door of the inner security room. Georgi remained silent and unmoving behind him. He opened the door, passed through, and the alarms assaulted him as he closed the door behind him. The noise of the computers in the main room was louder.

The guards, three of them, had halted. Seeing him in his lab coat, they appeared, even at the distance of half the length of the huge room, disarmed, unconcerned. One of them was already questioning one of the operators, who was pointing toward Hyde and the highest-security area. Hyde glanced behind him. There was no sign of Georgi. Playing safe.

Hyde began walking slowly down the room, glancing from side to side—not too casually, the alarms *are* ringing, there *is* something wrong—looking for a wheeled wastebin filled with printout that had not yet been sent to the shredder, looking for the fuse boxes high on the walls. One of the guards began to hurry toward him, still uncertain, unsuspicious. Hyde fingered the aluminum truncheon in his pocket as if it were a weapon of close-quarter assault.

Bin—yes. Full—almost. Fuse box—no, no . . . yes. . . . He gripped the tube in his pocket more tightly, levering open the small, hinged handgrip with his fingers. The guard was twenty feet away and already demanding his ID. Hyde smiled disarmingly and stroked the barrel of the Flammpatrone, Hand DM 34. Touched the handgrip, touched the now-freed trigger. Apart from the Czech pistol, it was the only weapon Godwin had given him, with precise instructions on its use—*in emergency only, Hyde*.

Hyde reached carefully into his pocket and withdrew his papers. Georgi opened the door and shouted a warning. The two distant guards turned to him, absorbing the information that he was their target. The guard in front of him moved the vz.61 Skorpion machine pistol toward Hyde's stomach. Hyde drew and fired the flame cartridge launcher over the guard's head, toward the fuse box on the wall.

The guard's surprised expression became a small, round hole through which his breath was punched as Hyde bulled into him, heaving him aside and down. Then he ducked behind one of the orange ICL cabinets as the incendiary charge struck the fuse box.

Dark—light—light glaring from the walls, the hissing of a shower of fragments at 1300 degrees Centigrade, cries of shock and temporary blindness. Hyde scuttled through the ranks of cabinets toward the scarred wall where the burning, molten remains of the fuse box, a damaged computer cabinet with sparks leaping and crying, and the burning droplets of cartridge formed a messy, brilliant bonfire almost obscured by the smoke generated by the charge.

He crouched, face averted, behind a wheeled wastebin, then heaved it ahead of him. It gathered speed as he ran. Shots flicked off the wall after murdering his growing-diminishing-leaping shadow, until he twisted and heaved the bin over. Its contents, great bundles and sheafs of printout paper, spilled toward the burning fragments—then scorched, curled, ignited.

Bullets from a Skorpion chipped a ragged contour across the wall above his head. Plaster dusted his hair. The printout sheafs were well alight. Within the smoke, gouts of orange flame were rearing toward the ceiling, sinuous as snakes. He doubled back the way he had come, moving in a swift, aching crouch, using his hands often as if four-legged to speed his progress and keep his balance. He weaved through the cabinets and the ranks of computer equipment. A printer chattered as he passed it like some lookout bird alerting the guards. The whole of the room was full of long, glaring, melting and reforming shadows. The lights had fused. Sparks protested from some of the cabinets. The guards shouted.

He glanced across the room and saw the billow of CO_2 from an extinguisher, the thin spurt of inert foam from another. The whole of the wastebin's contents were fully alight. The fuse-box dripped molten fragments down the charred wall. The smoke was rolling, dense, and clinging. Guards moved near it, through it. He had less than thirty seconds before the steel shutters locked all of them in the room. Already, the air-conditioning system would have automatically shut down. In—nineteen seconds—no, *sixteen* now, no more . . . the room would be pumped full of inert gas that would stifle the fire. And kill himself and the guards as it forced every particle of oxygen from the computer room. In seconds, the guards themselves would hurry out. . . .

Hyde regained his bearings and moved swiftly toward the doors and the corridor—

And the guards, and reinforcements and firefighters and civilian staff and security men. Stepanov and Georgi would be running by now, desperate to get out before the steel shutters slammed down, locking them in—

He straightened up. The smoke persisted, seemed even thicker. He felt it in his throat now, unnoticed before. He heard coughing, and an order to get out, leave the fire—*shutters*, he heard in a high voice, a panicky warning. *Gas*—

Go now! He had only seconds before they would block his escape, or be no more than a pace behind him. Flame spurted and coiled, CO_2 puffed and hissed, smoke rolled thick and heavy.

He brushed at his lab coat—smeared with greasy dirt, scorched in one or two places—and touched the cassette in his pocket. Then he burst through the glass doors, adopting a wild, frightened look, his arm extended to indicate the chaos behind him.

No one. No one . . .

In disbelief, he hurried through the reception area. Incongruously, a small green watering can stood beside the pot in which the rubber plant was growing. He pushed open the outer door. The corridor was empty—

No. A guard at the corner, at the bottom of the stairs. *His* guard. The alarms beat their noise down at his head, shrilled away like startled, fleeing birds down the corridor. Take the stairs to his left, downward?

No. Not deeper—

He hurried toward the guard, already shouting in panic

at the top of his voice: "For God's sake, man, isn't there any organized response to a *fire* in this place?"

The young guard's mouth opened. His rifle was held slackly across his chest. The stairs were empty. Hyde hit him in the stomach, then across the chin, then on the side of the neck as the man fell away from him. He kicked the guard's legs after him, thrusting them out of sight from the stairs. The rifle had slid away down the corridor, but he did not want it anyway. It declared his violence, obviated bluff of any kind. The adrenaline coursed. He dashed up the stairs, taking them two at a time—

To be confronted by uniforms, white coats, suits, extinguishers, rifles, a fireman's helmet. Slow, slow—

"It's chaos in there!" he screamed. "Absolute chaos! For Christ's sake—*hurry!*"

He leaned against the wall to let the group pass. One man snapped at him: "What about the security breach? The security alarm sounded first!"

Hyde shrugged. "I don't know—all I know is—the fuse box blew—fire everywhere—" He coughed, for effect, hanging his head in weariness, his eyes fixed on the man's groin as he awaited the necessity for violence.

"How many still inside? Quickly, man! How many?"

"God knows—two, three—security personnel, not computer—"

"Warn security control of casualties. I want a manual override on the shutters and the gas until everyone's out! Quickly!"

Hyde heard a bellowed reference to a security telephone, and then they had passed him on their way toward the computer room.

He turned and ran, before they discovered the unconscious, obviously beaten guard at the bottom of the stairs.

Moment of reorientation, a turn, short run, then turn right, then more stairs, up, up . . .

Suk's hand grabbed him and regretted the act as Hyde turned on him, fist raised. They were in a wide corridor, just as the memorized diagram that Suk had supplied had shown. Hyde knew where he was and how far from the clean air in the Third Courtyard—

"You're in the wrong damn place!" he snarled in a whisper. People hurried past them. Now, he could hear the noise of fire trucks moving into the courtyard. Through a window, their headlights bounced and glared. Like hunting search-lights.

"I came—I was worried when the alarms—"

"Where now?"

"Come—this way."

They were on the ground floor of the Chancellery. Already, people were being moved out of the building—cleaners, clerks, security guards, KGB and STB officers. Men in white lab coats similar to the one he wore. Suk guided him toward a tall narrow door. A guard perfunctorily inspected their breast pocket ID cards, and they were out into a windy night that snatched at Hyde's breath and lowered his temperature immediately so that his teeth began to chatter and his body shivered uncontrollably. Fevered.

"Are you—"

"Just bloody cold!" he snapped.

Firemen in yellow waterproof leggings and dark uniform coats hurried across the scene in front of them. Men with guns ran, directed by other men in uniform greatcoats or leather topcoats. Panic. The organism had been wounded in some vital part. The antibodies were in flight, hurrying to the scene. Rather, he thought, the wasps' nest, stirred with a stick. Someone had damaged the *secret* stuff, the valuable stuff—

He patted his pocket.

"Here," Suk offered, and handed him his short, dark coat. "Give me the white one."

Hyde removed the dustproofing coat and donned his own overcoat, placing the cassette in his pocket. The gun still nestled in the small of his back.

"Across this courtyard," Suk began, whispering close to Hyde's ear, pausing until the man nodded, "around the east end of the cathedral, into Vikarska—yes? I showed you on the map?"

"I remember," Hyde snapped impatiently.

"Good," Suk replied, his face pinched by cold and offense. "You will find the workmen's ladders where I showed you. With them you can climb the main wall into the garden there—and the other wall. . . ."

"I know. I can climb that with my hands and feet. I only hope you're right, mate."

Hyde looked at the man, looked through the open door into a scene that had suddenly become more ordered, drilled,

slower-moving. More brown uniforms, many leather and mo-
hair topcoats. A man with black smears on his face, as if he
had been close to a fire. . . .

They were searching now. They knew he had got out of
the cellars. Time was diminishing, being reeled in by the pursuit. He glanced into Suk's face.

"Thanks," he murmured, and then turned his back. Suk
watched him until he disappeared into the shadows near the
statue of St. George, making for the cathedral. He simply disappeared into the deeper shadow behind a spilling pool of
blue, revolving light from a fire truck. By that time, he was
already running.

17
A Consignment for Moscow

Voronin watched each of them, arranged like exhibits on the three upright chairs on the other side of the Rezident's desk. He had requisitioned Bayev's office at the Soviet embassy with a casual authority, confident of his own role at the hub of the drama. He was alone with his three prisoners—alone, except for the frowning Party portraits that stared down from the walls, unchanging, rather forbidding. He noticed them, perhaps for the first time in a number of years—since they were no more than the normal furniture of a KGB Rezident's office—with the eye of the three foreigners in the room. Lenin, Brezhnev, Nikitin, and the others sternly indicated to Aubrey and the Massingers that they were already seated in the anteroom of an alien way of life. Voronin watched them, eager for signs of stress, of defeat, and confident that they would appear as tangibly as the spots associated with chicken pox or measles.

Aubrey had combed his remaining hair and buttoned his shirt. He had tightened his narrow, striped tie. His jacket had been flung at him by one of Voronin's men as he was forced into the limousine outside the safe house. Voronin remembered it with satisfaction as a dismissive, final gesture. Aubrey wasn't wearing it now.

Massinger sat stiffly upright, his injured leg thrust out in front of him—the too-small trousers they had supplied at the lodge before he was transferred were strained over the bandage, and stained on the thigh with drying blood. His wife looked dowdy and middle-aged with her hair disheveled and makeup smudged. Defeated by her bruises and swollen, split lips. She seemed little more than a mirror of her husband's dejected and weakened condition, and it was difficult for

Voronin to reconcile the woman he saw with the well-connected, troublesome image that Babbington and Kapustin had feared.

Voronin was satisfied that the Massingers were disorientated, frightened, clearly aware of the brevity of their future. They knew they would die quite soon. Aubrey, however, the third member of the consignment for Moscow, disappointed him.

He was tired, unshaven, old. But he had the appearance of a pensioner suddenly roused from sleep rather than that of a captured intelligence officer. Voronin felt cheated. Aubrey's appearance should have mirrored that captivity. On the contrary, it belied what he must surely be feeling. It was an unreasonably lame conclusion to the days, weeks, months, years of effort of which Voronin had been an important part. Hidden cameras, microphones, doctored film and tape, lighting, scripts, actors. A complete, elaborate, marvelous forgery, all to entrap Aubrey. Entrap this one old man who seemed incapable of understanding what was happening to him. Voronin remembered the smoky rooms, the endless whirring tapes, the hiss of film sliding through projectors. He remembered Aubrey in front—*in front of the monkey cages at Helsinki Zoo*—

That day, perhaps of all days, they knew—the whole team had sensed it—they had Aubrey. That was the film they'd released to the French, that had been shown all over the world. They'd all known they had him then, that he couldn't escape them. . . .

And yet now he seemed to have done so. He looked drugged, weary, indifferent.

Voronin dismissed his disappointment and picked up the telephone. It was the reason he had had them brought to this room, rather than spend the intervening hours before their transfer to Schwechat airport in tiny, separate cells below ground. As he waited after dialing Kapustin's number at Moscow Centre, he checked the dials and lights on the encryption unit's face. Was Aubrey glancing slyly at him? Perhaps not. It was a superfluous call, merely confirming their success. But he wanted these people to hear it. It was a call for the benefit of his prisoners.

He glanced at his watch. Twelve-five. They'd be transferred at four to the airport. Aubrey with false diplomatic papers—he must be seen by witnesses who would later recall that he went willingly, not under arrest—and the other two as diplomatic passengers. Their departure would remain secret—forever. Like their later executions in Moscow.

He heard the connection being made and leaned forward to switch on the desk speaker, clamping the receiver to it. Aubrey's eyes wandered vaguely, hardly aware. The Massingers were distracted by his movements from their intent perusal of the monochrome faces looking down at them from the white office walls.

Aubrey and his companions would disappear. SIS in Vienna was in total disarray, and controlled by Babbington. There would be no effective search, no possibility of counter-measures. The Austrians would want nothing to do with it except, at a safe distance in time, to make the appropriate empty diplomatic noises. There was this room, then a limousine to Schwechat, then the cabin of the Tupolev, then another car, then another room. That was all that lay in front of the Massingers; Aubrey had little more to look forward to.

"Comrade Deputy Chairman!" Voronin announced, to attract Aubrey's attention. The eyes seemed to focus. The Massingers appeared unmoved, their attention having wandered as easily as that of children. Aubrey twitched once like a small animal receiving a shock from a buried electrode. Then his attention, too, seemed to cloud.

"Is it done?" Kapustin asked.

"Of course, Comrade."

"Casualties?"

"One on our side."

"Only one? Good."

"What are your orders, Comrade Deputy Chairman?" Was Aubrey even paying attention? Damn the old man. He could not rid himself of the sense that Aubrey had somehow reversed their positions, become the superior by his inattentive silence.

When Kapustin replied, Voronin realized that the Deputy Chairman sensed Aubrey could hear the exchange. There was a silky pleasure unusual in the Deputy Chairman's gruff voice as he said: "Do I need to repeat them, Voronin?" Momentarily, Aubrey's face narrowed to an expression of hatred. "Very well. I shall repeat your instructions. The aircraft will depart at four-thirty. Before dawn, your guests will be in Moscow. Tell them the weather promises to be fine. Arrangements here are in order. All matters will be dealt with speedily. Please assure them—but perhaps they can hear my voice,

Voronin?" The young man did not reply, merely smiled into the room. Aubrey refused to attend! "In which case," Kapustin's voice continued, "*I* can assure personally that no time will be lost in dealing with their—problem. No time will be lost." The repeated words were purred out. "Is there anything else, Voronin?"

"No, Comrade Deputy Chairman. There is nothing else."

"Then good-bye." And then, because Kapustin could not resist the temptation, he added: "Good-bye, Sir Kenneth," in a mocking, triumphant tone. Aubrey's eyes were hooded, but bright with attention. Good, good—at last!

Voronin switched off the speaker and replaced the receiver. Then he sat back in his chair, studying the faces arranged before him once more. He adopted a relaxed and confident air. They'd got to Aubrey. He knew; he understood. His inattention was no more than an act, a pretense. He was suffering—oh, yes, he was suffering. Knowing that, Voronin cared little or nothing for the others. They had retreated farther from him, but that did not matter. Their hands were linked on the woman's lap, but clearly not for the purpose of mutual comfort. Rather, in a union that suggested that the present moment satisfied them.

Satisfied?

Did Aubrey's suffering satisfy him, Voronin? Did he possess all the feelings, the strength of feeling, appropriate to this moment?

He could not say that he did.

Why not?

He knew why not. Babbington. He disliked the man intensely—always had done, the past two days more than ever. Arrogant—feudally arrogant, the sort you wanted to frighten with a gun or a club, shake out of his complacent superiority. . . .

Babbington was the hero of the hour. Hero of the Soviet Union. They'd keep the medals for the day he finally came home. Sickening. Voronin felt himself to be a child, excluded from some adult celebration party. It was Babbington's moment; all the satisfaction, the sense of success, belonged to Babbington. He and all the others had been no more than servants, scurrying to do what Babbington ordered. Saving Babbington's precious skin.

Aubrey watched Voronin. He saw the man's pleasure pall and understood the reason. He was no more than a cog, a part of Babbington's machine. Aubrey saw a discontented young man of pale complexion and sharp, bright eyes. Not fashionably dressed but dowdy and clerklike, his suit old-fashioned, a piece with the overcoat and trilby hat he had now discarded. The shirt and tie were drab. Voronin's hair was limp and straight, a dirty blond in color.

A catalog of mediocrity. Yet—and Aubrey could not avoid or escape the impression—this mediocrity held their lives in his hands. And would dispose of them all when the time came for him to do so.

Aubrey's attention retreated. What use were the pretenses, the masks? He was beaten and knew it. The Massingers were as good as dead. He, too, after a short, shameful interval, would cease to exist—

Fear came then. He knew why he had hidden his attentiveness from Voronin. The effort had occupied him sufficiently to keep the fear at bay. But now, the fear clutched at his stomach and heart and lungs, almost stopping his breath.

Voronin smiled greedily. He saw. He knew, and appeared satisfied.

The empty street, cobbled and steep, sloped away from him, pooled by shadows that filled the spaces between the lamplight. The sgraffito-work facade of the Schwarzenberg Palace seemed ghostly, luminescent. The other buildings massed silently and lightless in the square: the palaces and the town hall and the Swiss Embassy. The carved saints leaned over their madonna directly ahead of him. He felt as jolted as if he had collided with the statuary or with the wall of a building. Winded and disorientated. Godwin wasn't there.

A cripple, unable to run, but he wasn't there, wasn't there. . . .

His lungs and heart pumped out the refrain. Godwin wasn't there. . . .

He listened for the sounds of pursuit, watching the square's pools and bays of shadow for the movement of waiting men. As the strain of his efforts faded, another stronger chorus emerged. Stop it, stop it, *stop it*—

Routine questioning, slipped on an icy pavement and ly-

ing in the hospital, too cold for him to come out at all. . . .
Hyde hadn't wanted him there, and perhaps Godwin had
done no more than change his mind.

The alarms were ringing, distantly and continuously, in
the castle. The guards at the closed gates of the First Courtyard were almost invisible to his left, but he sensed their increased alertness like a scent on the cold air. He pressed back
against the wall, feeling chilly carved stone against his cheek.
He tried to control the little puffed signals his breath made in
the icy night. He began to feel cold as the sweat dried. Lights
sprang on in the castle's nearest building: neon lighting, flickering on like burning torches hurried from room to room by
the men searching for him. The group of stone giants in combat above the gates loomed over the square, black backs and
arms muscled and dangerous in the light thrown down from
the windows.

The guards had turned their backs to him as they looked
back through the gates. Already puzzled, becoming dangerous. Headlights flickered across the walls surrounding the
Second Courtyard, illuminating the frozen beard of the fountain.

Now—

Lights above him in the government offices of the old
Archbishop's Palace. More alarms, louder as if someone had
opened a window to let the sound escape. Lights coming on in
the Swiss Embassy, reducing the shadows in which he hid. A
car starting farther up the cobbled hill. More headlights in
the inner courtyards, more lights in the room surrounding the
square. By now, the fire in the computer room would have
been extinguished, and be understood as no more than a di-
version. They would be single-minded now, their attention
entirely focused on himself. They did not know what he had.
But if they had him, Godwin would tell them, and soon—

Running feet, heavy and booted—

Now!

He touched the chilly stone with both hands, as if about
to hurl himself away from it, studied the pavement and the
cobbles—and ran.

The gates were swinging open, the guards were moving
toward the leading car. He saw this as he knelt by one of the
parked black limousines in front of the Archbishop's Palace,
his heavy breathing clouding the car's polished flank. Booted
feet, voices, the alarm shrill, joined by others as if nesting

birds had been roused. He got off his haunches and ran, crouching and wary, across the cobbles to the group of figures carved around the madonna. He pressed against the base of the statue and watched the leading car roar out of the gates into the square—wheels spinning, rear of the car sliding sideways, then the drift corrected—and away up the hill toward the Strahov. Only seconds left now. An officer was instructing the guards at the gates; someone yelled down from a high window. A mechanical voice through a public address system began to rouse the whole castle. Only seconds—

He scuttled across the last pool of light, last bay of shadow. A truck with a searchlight mounted on the back trundled into the square, its brakes protesting as it stopped. Immediately, its beam began bouncing and sliding in the square like a great golden ball striking the walls of the buildings.

He doubled up in shadow, gasping for breath. Skidded slightly, dragging his cheek against cold stone. The shadow opened up in front of him like a cliff's edge. The Castle Steps. Voices, public address, the bouncing ball of light, heels clicking on frost, the roar of engines.

Godwin?

His car was near Godwin's apartment, damn.

He looked at the steps for a moment, clutching the stone of the wall as if affected by vertigo. Light bounced over him and he hunched his shoulders as if under a weight. The light moved on, someone shouted; it bounced back toward him, slithering along the wall and pavement. Orders were bellowed. He ran.

In tens. His gloved hand skated down the frosty, deadcold railing. Steps were in tens. He skipped down them, reached the level, then the next ten steps before the next level. Old streetlamps threw a muted, dusty light, making his shadow enlarge to monstrous size then quickly diminish. Blaring his shape against the walls.

He paused to look back. Flashlight, noise—they'd seen him, damn. He ran on, hearing the first pairs of boots clattering in pursuit. The noise of a rifle dropped? The glow of a television set through open curtains as he passed the window of a tall, narrow house. A door opening—

He cannoned into someone, the body soft and yielding, perhaps that of a woman. He heard breath escape like an explosion, smelled a strong, cheap perfume, then hurried past, hearing the breathing begin again and the abuse commence. The steps zigzagged, and he lost the sounds of the woman's voice and the footsteps of the pursuit.

Another ten steps, then the level, then another ten steps. Level, steps, level. Streetlight, looming shadow, shrunken dwarf on the peeling stucco of the wall, darkness, steps, level, shadow, giant, dwarf, shadow, steps, level—

Crumbling stucco, treacherous, icy steps. His breath was labored, legs almost gone. He was slowing and was aware of it. A pool of light seemed to open fuzzily ahead of him, like the opening of a door into a brightly lit room. He hesitated, afraid of what might be a searchlight. Then he plunged on, hearing once more the clatter of boots and the scraping of metal funneled down the Castle Steps toward him.

He staggered as he reached the bottom of the steps, clinging to the railing as a bout of coughing seized him. A narrow street, more light at the end of it. He forced himself to run, his feet noisy on the cobbles. Then he turned the corner into Little Quarter Square. The church of St. Nicholas rose in front of him. A rank of black cars stood outside the palace that had become the Regional Party School. The headquarters and the church outfaced one another across the cobbles. Hyde crossed the square into the deep shadows beneath the church—

Shadows?

Lights, suddenly, as if they had waited in ambush for him. He gazed about him wildly, clutching the gun in his pocket, clutching the tape cassette. The doors of St. Nicholas swung open. Noises, footsteps, and talk. An audience emerged. A notice board near his head advertised a recital that evening. He shook with relief as he began pushing into and through the audience as it descended the steps, dispersing into the square. He crossed the facade, the west door, bumped and hidden by people talking in loud, delighted voices. The recital had been a success.

He eased ahead of the small crowd and his shadow began to jog with him along the southern wall of the church as he turned into Mostecka Street. He loped easily, almost with a lightness of mood. A car passed him innocently, its color a drab fawn. People were behind him, others ahead, emerging from what might have been a club—yes, raw music, a saxophone and drums behind a wall of chatter as he passed the closing door. He slowed, then. Looked back. People. Overcoated, hatted, scarved. Cover. A few cars moved at a sedate pace along the narrow street, the cobbles jolting their axles. Sirens in the distance, but no uniformed men in the Mostecka. They'd been caught up by the crowd from the church. They'd have to block the exits from Little Quarter Square as a first priority. The pursuit was diluting with each second that passed. Hyde walked on, not too quickly, hands thrust into the pockets of his overcoat, scarf wound round his face, partly to mask his hard, strained breathing. The bridge stretched away ahead of him across the Vltava. One gloved hand gripped the cassette in his pocket. *Teardrop*—

He'd done it. He had Babbington, clutched in his gloved hand. Everything; the whole scenario; and Babbington's name. The frame, the predicted consequences that perfectly matched the reality, the double agent who was Moscow's man. He'd done it. The knowledge made him catch his breath, bare his teeth in a triumphant grin.

He hurried beneath the dark tower at the end of the Charles Bridge. The wind from the river was icy and he hunched against it. The lamps on the bridge glowed, sleet flying through the haloes of chilly light. The black statues lining either side of the bridge leaned over him, hurrying his pace as if they whispered his lack of time to him. His hand gripped the cassette more fiercely. Now that he possessed the proof, he realized with a growing, gnawing urgency as palpable as extreme hunger, that Babbington would waste no time. Margaret Massinger he no longer considered or cared about. She could well have gone into the bag with Aubrey and her husband. There was only himself, blown across the bridge like a black scrap of paper beneath the gloomy, magnificent crucifixion figure, the gold of its crown and of the inscription gleaming in the sleety lamplight. There was only himself now. The bridge tower loomed over him and he passed through its arch into the Old Town. The wind disappeared. He walked through rutted slush on the pavement, unpursued but hurrying more than before. There was only himself.

Within minutes, he had reached Old Town Square, had passed the astronomical clock and reached the shadows of the Tyn Church. Then he paused, studying the Celetna Street. Neon lights, hard. Traffic thin, pedestrians few. He could see the bulk of the Powder Tower at the other end of the street. Where was Godwin? He could pick out the darkened windows of his apartment. At the back, in the kitchen?

Hyde knew the apartment was empty. Hunching his

shoulders, he began to drift along the street, looking for surveillance—ready to run and feeling the Celetna close in on him and the weight of the streets through which he had come press like a net trawling him in. He was alone. He could go to no embassy. He had a tape, nothing more. They wouldn't believe—

Stop it—

He drew level with the Skoda and passed it. The doors and windows did not look as if they had been forced, but he could not check those on the driver's side. He glanced up at the dark windows of Godwin's apartment, almost bumping into a young man, who apologized to him at once. Hyde, shivering, mumbled something to the young man's retreating back. Then he continued walking.

He crossed the street a hundred yards beyond the apartment and two hundred from the Skoda, then retraced his steps back toward the square. Then once more toward the Powder Tower—the driver's side doors and windows had looked intact—then back toward the apartment. There were no parked cars containing waiting men, there were no open windows, no drawn-back curtains. One hand clutched the tape, the other Godwin's spare key. He reached the doorway, almost passed it, then ducked into its shadow. He fumbled for the lock and turned the key. The door creaked slightly as he touched it open. He glanced back at the street, then passed quickly into the narrow hall and mounted the stairs. He listened ahead of him as he reached the second floor. There, he paused. Nothing. No noises from the street, either. Where *was* Godwin?

He paused again at the front door of the apartment, then reached the key tentatively toward the lock, inserted it, held his breath, turned the key—kicking open the door the moment he did so, bundling himself inside the apartment and pressing himself against the wall, the gun in his hands. The vz.75 pistol was close to his face, barrel pointed at the ceiling. His thumb moved the safety catch. Fifteen rounds. He listened, holding his breath.

Nothing. He reached out and silently closed the door. Then he moved the few paces to the main room. He banged open the door, gun extended, his weight supported by the door frame. The room was lightless, empty. He flicked on the lights. Neat, orderly—unsearched, no signs of a struggle. Where *was* Godwin? Swiftly, he checked the other empty rooms. No crutches, no overcoat hanging in the hall. Bed undisturbed, empty coffee mug in the kitchen sink. Godwin had left the apartment of his own volition—to keep his appointment at the Hradcany. Where *was* he?

And who was asking him questions, and what was he saying? Hyde's mind continued with nervous inevitability, completing the scenario. Someone had Godwin under the lights by now—

And he had only the time it took for one mistake, one contradiction—or a confession because they had become impatient with evasion and lies and used force.

He went back into the kitchen. The rear of the building was two stories lower than the part that contained Godwin's apartment. Its roof stretched back on a level with Godwin's kitchen window. He slid the window up and checked the sill and the slope of the roof and the width of the gap between this roof and its neighbor. Then he went back into the lounge and picked up the telephone. He tensed immediately, but there was no betraying double click. Godwin kept his telephone swept clean of bugs. It was as secure as his apartment. He placed the pistol carefully near the telephone and slumped onto the edge of an armchair, immediately feeling the last strength in his legs drain away and his calves begin to tremble with weariness. He dialed the long series of digits with a quivering forefinger. The apartment was already growing cold from the open kitchen window.

London. Should he move the car now, while there was time? London. He dialed the final digit of Sir William Guest's number in Albany, which Margaret Massinger had given him, and wondered again about the car. The connection was made; the number began to ring. Three, four—come on . . . the car? He listened to the noises from the street. A vehicle passed, he held his breath, but it did not stop or turn. Five, six, seven . . . *come on*—go and move the car! He felt trapped now, as if bound to the chair and the telephone, unable to free himself. Then—

"Sir William!" he blurted before his caution stopped him. Relief flooded him, making him weak and shaky, even as he warned himself to say nothing more until the recipient of the call identified himself.

"Who is that?"

The voice is too young!

"Get me Sir William."

"Who is that?"

Did he recognize the voice? Did he, or was it just the tone, the accent? Who?

"Is Sir William there?" he insisted.

"You sound as if you've been rushing, old man," the voice drawled. "I'm afraid Sir William's not yet returned. We're expecting him sometime today. Can I help you?"

"Who are you?" His free hand clutched the cassette in his pocket, as if to crush it. Useless now—

"One of his staff. He asked me to call, collect some papers . . . lucky to have caught me, really. Who is speaking? Where are you calling from?" The words were affectedly indifferent, no more than a polite inquiry, yet Hyde sensed the tension beneath the facade.

"Fuck you," he whispered and slammed down the receiver. It didn't matter who it was, Babbington's man or Sir William's flunky. It wasn't Sir William. . . .

Useless. He bit his knuckles, enacting his rage as he stared at the telephone. Useless—

Before Sir William returned, the old man would be in Moscow, ready to go on show, maybe even dead.

"Oh, *fuck* it!" He slumped back in the armchair, his eyes pressed tightly shut and damp in the corners, his face raised to the ceiling. He was deeply, utterly weary. He had the evidence—and now they knew it, or they would know it soon. Babbington would be told before morning. Then he'd waste no time in getting rid of Aubrey and the Massingers. The consignment for Moscow would be on its way east. Babbington would know it was him and Aubrey would disappear, just as if he, Hyde, had given them a warning, time to act. Babbington would want to be on Guest's doormat to explain Aubrey's disappearance the moment Sir William returned. He'd speeded them up, hurried them to a final course of action—

He sat for whole minutes, still and silent, face raised and eyes pressed shut. His hands gripped the arms of the chair, his body slumped into its sagging container.

And he'd be done for himself, too. They knew he was here, they knew what he'd done, and he wouldn't be able to get out the way he came in. He'd not get as far as Bratislava, in all probability. They'd shut the country up to keep him in.

He continued to sit in silence, unmoving. There seemed no point to activity, movement, decision. Part of his awareness listened beyond the apartment to the noises from the street, the noises above and below him in the house. Normal. All normal. Someone playing a radio upstairs, walking from lounge to kitchen and then returning to the lounge. His heartbeat settled, his breathing calmed.

He sat bolt upright in the chair.

Zimmermann. Hyde stared at the telephone, then at his watch. Fifteen minutes since he had entered the apartment. *Fifteen!* He cursed himself. He had to get out. Survival. Continued living and breathing. They'd kill him, not just put him in the bag. They'd kill him for certain—

Zimmermann. *Call me if anything goes wrong—very wrong.* The German had volunteered his services as emergency case officer. *If it's too much to handle, and you can't get out . . .*

He listened. Normal. He dialed feverishly. Godwin could be talking now, could have talked already! The last three digits, what were they? What? What, damn you? His finger quivered over the dial, then he remembered. Four, two, seven.

He waited. Was Zimmermann in the bag, too, by now? Would a younger voice answer the call, smooth and dangerous? He waited. The receiver at the other end was picked up.

"Yes? Zimmermann," he heard. The voice checked with his memory.

"It's me—Hyde."

"What is it?" Zimmermann asked immediately and in English. "You are in trouble?"

"Listen—I may not have much time. Godwin's disappeared—he must have been picked up. They can't be far behind me now."

"I understand. But, you have—"

"I've got everything. The computer threw up the whole meal. Everything . . . Babbington's name, even. Even his *name*. I've got the whole elaborate frame. . . ."

"Can you get the information to me in any way?"

"No. It's on a tape. And I can't rely on the post, can I? Listen, Zimmermann—I can't go out the way I came in. They'll be waiting for me everywhere. Any suggestions?"

Hyde felt the hand that held the receiver begin to pain him. He studied the other hand. Raw new skin, still healing. It seemed a badge of his fragility, his uselessness. He waited, willing Zimmermann to provide an escape route.

Eventually, Zimmermann said: "Yes. You have to get out. Do they know what you have done?"

"Yes. I was almost caught."

"And Godwin, of course . . . mm." Zimmermann paused for a moment. "There is precious little time, if any. I can do nothing, *we* can do nothing, without the physical evidence. I am suspended. An inquiry is to begin soon. I am to speak to no one. However, I can help you. There is a plumber, a German, living in the small border town of Mytina, south of Cheb. Less than three hours from Prague. You have a map?"

"Yes."

"Mytina. You will find him at this address. . . . Do you wish to write it down?"

"No. Go ahead. . . . Okay, I've got that."

"He has acted unofficially for us on a few occasions. There are others like him, but not so close to the border or Prague. But he needs money. His name is Langdorf, and he does nothing without money. Also, you will need to explain that you have his name from me. You have money?"

"Godwin must have standard issue Krugerrands in the apartment somewhere, or there's a cache of Swiss francs here. I'll find them. I can pay."

"Then go at once. You must cross tonight—before dawn. I will be waiting for you. . . ." There was a pause. Zimmermann was evidently studying his watch, making his calculations. "Yes, I can be there before dawn. Very few people know of my suspension at the moment. I will be waiting. Try very hard to be there, Mr. Hyde. For all our sakes."

"I'll try. Thanks."

"Before dawn, remember. We do not have tomorrow."

"Yes."

Hyde put down the receiver and gently rubbed the hand that had held it. He listened to the street outside, then crossed to the window, lifting the curtain gently to one side. Traffic thin, pedestrians few, as if midnight had hurried them home. Man loitering in the dark doorway . . . no, girl there, too. No one suspicious. No curtains wide for surveillance, no muted lights. Hyde breathed deeply, clouding the cold windowpane, expelling the air like a decision made.

He turned from the window to face the room, his mind flicking through the rooms of the apartment like a sequence of still pictures projected upon a screen.

Urgency returned like the onset of a renewed bout of fever. Now, he was aware of the apartment, of the street, of the roof that might have to serve as his escape route. . . .

And of Godwin, under a bright light, fending off the anticipated moment when he would let something slip or would have to tell what he knew.

The rooms were illuminated in his mind as starkly as if he had shined a flashlight rapidly over the contours and contents of each of them. Where? Godwin would have concealed his Krugerrands or Swiss francs like every other agent posted abroad. The Sinking Fund, they called it in London. A lifeline. A way out. To be used when not waving but drowning. In this case, where?

Begin—come on, begin, he ordered his body. His hand flicked the curtain aside once more. The Skoda, a hundred yards away on the opposite side of the Celetna, was passed, light thrown upon it for a moment, by a late bus. At the far end of the street, beneath the Powder Tower, blue sparks flashed from an overhead cable as a tram rattled its way toward the river. Nothing else—there was still time; Godwin was holding out or remained unsuspected. There was time, time—

Little or no time, little or no time, no time . . .

He got onto all fours and scrabbled around the circumference of the room, his hands feeling the carpet like those of a blind man searching for something dropped. Nothing. He glanced under the dining table. He touched the undersides of the chairs, tilted the armchairs and the sofa. Godwin would, might need the money quickly, so it would have to be easy for a cripple. No bending or lifting or crawling or climbing . . .

Hyde smoothed the curtains, but there were no lumps, no rustlings. No weights that might have been coins. The old sideboard—his fingers touched and caressed the backs and undersides of drawers, lifted the clock and the tray on which Godwin's bottles of whiskey and gin stood. He began, perhaps prompted by the clock, to glance at his watch after handling or moving or touching each object—punctuating his search.

Bathroom. Cistern dirty but otherwise empty. No waterproof package. Shower offering no place of concealment. Back of the washbasin—twelve-twenty—edges of the thin, weary carpet on the bathroom floor. Nothing.

Kitchen. Undersides of the wall cupboards, just the right height for Godwin the cripple—twelve twenty-one—the stove, the pedal bin, dust and dead flies and a mummified spider on top of the wall cupboards. Buckets and mops in a cupboard, tins of food, including those for the neighbor's thin black cat. Behind the fridge—twelve twenty-two, no -three— freezer compartment of the fridge, only ice cubes and a slim package that contained some cold meat left from a meal.

Hallway. Cupboard. Hands slipping between folded sheets, shirts, smoothing down the ironing board as if searching a spread-eagled suspect. Suitcases in the bedroom, on top of the wardrobe. Bedroom. Twelve twenty-five. He was missing things, he couldn't afford to be really thorough, but he was still taking too long. . . .

Gambling on Godwin holding out because he knew, with utter certainty, that they had him and by now they would have become suspicious. Some STB man would make the connection, bring the questioning round to—

Twelve twenty-six. Nothing in the suitcases or their linings. Nothing on the underside of the narrow bed that looked like a cot from some institution. Nothing in the dressing table or at the backs of the drawers. Carpet—nothing. Twelve twenty-seven. Hyde's forehead was damp and prickly despite the cold of the apartment. He felt his body heating up inside his clothes. He could smell the dust from beneath the bed and in the carpet. Curtains—nothing. Nothing, nothing, *nothing*!

Twelve twenty-eight. He had been in the apartment for two minutes over half an hour. There could be no more than a few minutes now. Godwin would have had to supply his address—they'd know it anyway, from his file—and a police or STB patrol would be dispatched—routine in a workers' paradise. They'd be here for certain, and soon. They were already overdue. He was sweating freely now, and he could hear his own panting breaths. The exertion of tension, of frustration, was as great as that of his flight down the Castle Steps.

It had to be within easy reach, easy reach—twelve twenty-nine. Easy reach. Godwin couldn't even kneel easily, couldn't climb onto chairs to reach up, couldn't overturn or move heavy furniture without a huge, time-devouring effort. *It had to be within easy reach!*

A car drew up in the Celetna. He heard the sound through the drawn curtains. He had heard it subliminally as it moved down the street, coming from Old Town Square, but had fought to ignore it. Now, he couldn't. He heard one of its doors close quietly and moved to the window, lifting the curtain very gently. Two men. Uniforms. Police car. Looking around, then beginning to lift their heads to look up—he dropped the curtain. Routine patrol, diverted to check out Godwin's address—twelve-twenty, no, twelve-thirty. *Where?* He heard, or imagined, boots on the pavement's rutted slush, and the murmur of voices. He listened. No other cars. A tram clanged over points in the distance.

Where—easy—where, easy for Godwin—where?

And then he knew, as he heard the doorbell ring in the apartment below. The apartments were too few and cramped to have a concierge. Tenants answered their own bells. But they'd rung the ground floor to confuse and mislead anyone in Godwin's apartment.

Godwin had given up. Hyde saw him as he had seen him at that bus stop in the suburbs. Waiting out the remainder of his crippled existence. He'd never have expected or tried to escape. He would have sat waiting for them whenever they came. No run for the border for Godwin—he'd given up.

Hyde flung the old sofa over on its back as if wrestling with an intruder. He ran his hands along the edges of the sacking covering its base. Blood. A prick of blood on one finger. He heard the street door open, and quiet voices. He sucked his finger, knowing that Godwin had broken a needle that had been too light to perform the task of resewing the sacking to the material of the sofa. Its broken-off end had remained embedded in the frame. And the stitching was less neat, newer. Godwin had really hidden the money—buried it. He ripped the sacking away and the noise hid for a second the sound of boots ascending the stairs. His hand fumbled with horsehair and springs, then withdrew the expected package. He tore the brown paper. Swiss francs, high denomination.

The doorbell rang. A voice immediately called out Godwin's name, using the English prefix *Mister*. They'd seen lights, they expected someone—perhaps even him. He stood up, shaking with relief, and thrust the package into the inside pocket of the overcoat. He snatched up the pistol from the table, and hurried into the kitchen. Heavy knocking, then the short, ominous silence before forced entry. He climbed into the sink and over the sill, hearing the lock tear free of the doorframe as they entered the apartment. His hands gripped the window frame, and his arms quivered. He tested the frosty tiles with one foot, then stepped out onto the roof. Voices called behind him, but not yet to him, at him.

He scuttled, bent almost double, along the sloping roof, concealing himself in a crouch behind a bulky chimney. Sleet whisked round him; the clouds glowed from the lights of the city. Voices at the window, issuing orders, then the crackle of an R/T as assistance was summoned. Boots clattered on the sill, on the roof. He peered between the pots.

There were only two of them—until help arrived. He withdrew the pistol from his pocket, feeling its barrel brush against his thigh and side. He shuffled on his knees away from the chimney, saw the policeman's face in light from the kitchen as the man's mouth opened. Hyde fired. The Czech policeman buckled, fell onto his back, scrabbled with dying hands, and then slid down the roof and off, disappearing. Hyde heard the dull concussion as his body landed in drifted snow in the alley at the side of the building. He fired twice more, and the second policeman ducked out of sight.

Hyde, hunched over, scampered cautiously down the roof. When he reached the gutter, he paused to look down. The snow was ghostly, heaped in the alley. He could see a dark shape spread-eagled on a mound some yards away. He crouched, then jumped. Air rushed, his feet sank in, his body was chilled instantly, then he was rolling down a drift. He was winded, still struggling to breathe, as he got to his feet, his teeth chattering, his dark coat patched with lumpy snow.

Ankles? Yes, okay. Breath coming back—he gulped in air, his lungs burned, he exhaled. The second policeman's R/T crackled somewhere out of sight above him, uttering indecipherable orders. Hyde looked up. Nothing. Twelve thirty-three. He possessed the lapping athlete's sense of passing time. Three minutes since he had ripped open the sofa. He ran past the dead policeman toward the end of the alley. A car passed, making him huddle in sudden terror against the wall. It moved away down the street. He listened. A distant siren. He peered round the corner at the door of the house. No one emerged.

He hurried down the street, past the Skoda, observing the empty Celetna Street. Even the lovers had gone. His breath smoked like signals of desperation. He crossed the street, unlocked the Skoda's door, and climbed into the driving seat. The curtains in Godwin's lounge remained undisturbed. The second policeman was playing it safe until help arrived.

Twelve thirty-four. He started the engine. It caught at the second attempt. Rearview mirror empty; nothing coming toward him from the Powder Tower. He turned the wheel. Pain back in his hands as the icy cold of the drifted snow faded and allowed feeling to return. He grimaced, watching the mirror and the windshield, and drove past the police car outside the apartment, then immediately turned off the Celetna into a narrow sidestreet. Moments later, a wailing siren sounded behind him, but the mirror remained empty. He turned left, then left once more. A wide boulevard, tall streetlights at regular intervals. Wenceslas Square. People, traffic. He was becoming anonymous.

As he headed for the motorway to Kladno, Karlovy Vary, and Cheb—his route to Mytina—he began to think about Aubrey. Once out of immediate danger, self receded. Twelve-fifty. Into a scrubby industrial suburb with few lights and no traffic and an abiding sense of gray, dirty stone and uncleared slush. He could not fend off the growing fear that he was already too late. Babbington must know by now; Babbington wouldn't waste a moment, not a single moment, in disposing of the evidence against himself. He would be too late to save Aubrey's life. His journey to the border was meaningless. Hopeless.

Twelve fifty-nine. Aubrey would be gone before daylight. On his way east, perhaps even dead along with the Massingers. One o'clock. It was too late to save them.

"Where are they, Voronin?"

The question was involuntary. The Russian's features were burned out in the center by the retinal image of the lightbulb above the narrow cot, into which Aubrey had been staring. Aubrey moved his head. The glowing filament, haloed in yellow-white, moved aside from Voronin's face. The man's sallow complexion was pinked with pleasure. He stood near the door of the tiny cell, watching Aubrey. Aubrey rubbed his eyes. How long had he been staring at the bulb? The retinal image was still as fierce as an eclipse.

"They are being made ready for transit to the airport," Voronin replied.

"How?" Aubrey's voice croaked. His throat was dry and

constricted. He cleared it. "How will you smuggle them aboard?"

Voronin shook his head. "That has been taken care of—diplomatic luggage. No one will see them. Absolutely no one."

"But then, no one can be allowed to see them, can they? They are—"

"Never to be seen alive again—yes."

"You've killed them!"-something made him cry.

Voronin shook his head slowly. "As yet, they are alive."

Aubrey felt the rising guilt choke him. "How—how do they travel?" he asked, fending off other, darker thoughts.

"As part of the luggage of a returning trade mission. It is not a problem. No one searches the transport we use." Voronin smiled, moving forward to stand at the side of the bed. Aubrey was made to feel vulnerable in his shirtsleeves, prone and old. "I remember some scandal in your own country, some years ago. When the American President Carter visited—oh, where was it?—ah, Newcastle-upon-Tyne, the Secret Service and the CIA tried to drive a tractor trailer full of—*souvenirs*?—directly onto the runway and into a transport aircraft. Our people are known to do the same. No one cares."

"I remember the incident," Aubrey replied softly. "Unfortunately, someone forgot to inform the local constabulary and Customs that that sort of thing always happens." He nodded sagely, with fierce concentration. "Of course it will work. . . ." He looked up at Voronin and blurted out: "Do you have to have them killed once they're in Moscow? Do you *have* to do it?" Immediately, he recognized the utterance as merely another bandage for his conscience. He was going to have to live with the guilt, and knew he was trying to erect sandbags against an expected flood. It would be terrible, *terrible*, to face himself after they had been disposed of. He shook his head.

"You see," Voronin said. "You realize quite clearly that nothing else can be done. They know everything. It will be—quick and painless."

"Oh, jolly good!" Aubrey snarled, surprising the Russian. "And me? What about me?"

"You have an important job to do—in Moscow." Voronin grinned. His face was still tinged with color. The retinal image had faded now, and Aubrey could see the narrow, confident features clearly.

"You're sure of that?" It was blurted out, and it was nakedly fearful.

The Russian nodded. "Of course."

"What Babbington said—his threats. You're going to use me to protect him, yes?" Again, Voronin nodded. Aubrey loathed himself, but it was like pentathol. He could not control the rush of his words. "You *need* me? You do need me, don't you?"

His lips were trembling. He wiped at them.

Voronin looked unconcernedly at his watch as he said: "Of course, Sir Kenneth Aubrey. You are very necessary." The meeting was over. For whatever reason the man had come, that reason had been satisfied.

"Kapustin—" he began, but did not continue. The drug of fear had lost its overpowering effect. He sat more upright on the bed, leaning on one elbow. "What time do we leave?" he asked with forced lightness.

"It is now three-fifteen. We leave for the airport in thirty minutes. Do you wish shaving materials, hot water?"

Aubrey nodded. "Yes," he said breathily. Thirty minutes! "Yes," he repeated, more strongly.

"Good. I will have them sent to you." Voronin nodded, almost clicked his heels together, and left the cell. Aubrey heard the key turn in the lock. He felt perspiration spring out on his forehead, despite the temperature of the cell. Felt his hands begin to tremble. Felt nauseous, sick as a dog. He fought it. Fought the nausea. Fought his own cowardice, and faced the fact of his death. He had been terribly afraid, seated before Voronin, so afraid he had been on the point, several times, of pleading to be told that, unlike the Massingers, he at least was safe, would be allowed to live. Thank God he had not fallen quite that low! Thank God . . .

He wiped the already chilly sweat from his forehead. Rubbed his bald head.

And resolved.

He squeezed his eyes very tightly shut. In the darkness, some ghost of the lightbulb's filament still glowed. It had been a bad moment. His worst moment. Perhaps worst ever. But a moment. *Only* a moment—

Yes. He would try. If they were to keep him alive for a short time for their benefit, he would try to resist. . . .

Try, in front of a sea of strangers' faces and in the flash and wink of lights, to dredge up the truth. Try to struggle through the chemical bonds with which he would be tied, and say something—create some tiny suspicion, some sense of the truth, some sense, semblance, fragment, sliver, *atom* of the truth! Try to regain, if only for a moment, one fragment of himself.

He would owe the Massingers more than that, but it would be the only coinage in which he could make any repayment.

He heard footsteps outside and the key turn in the lock. His hands gripped one another and became still. Stronger, even as the door opened. Steam. A bowl of hot water. A towel.

A beginning.

Hyde watched the policeman get out of the patrol car and saunter across to the empty Skoda. He had been in the process of dialing Sir William Guest's flat when he had seen the car turn onto the forecourt of the all-night garage outside Karlovy Vary. His free hand touched his overcoat, smoothing across his chest to reassure him. Package of Swiss francs. Pistol. Pockets—spare clips of ammunition, cassette tape. *Teardrop*. The map was still in the car. . . .

Useless to assume he could run. He was still thirty-five miles from Mytina.

Kill them if you have to. The policeman had reached the Skoda. He rubbed at the driver's window and peered into the car. Inside the patrol car, the flash of a cigarette lighter. Hyde remained inside the telephone booth, half turned to watch the Skoda.

The patrolman straightened and walked back toward his car. Wait, wait—

His companion got out, stretched away stiffness, offered his packet of cigarettes. Then the two of them walked toward the dimly lit office where Hyde had paid for his petrol. He forced himself to continue dialing. The moment the number began to ring, he returned his gaze to the two policemen. The receiver rang in his ear, an empty sound. He glanced at his watch. Three-fifty. There was no cover between the telephone booth and the office. They would walk toward him, clearly exposed but able to see his every movement inside the glass box. He must wait, and when they moved, he must walk slowly, *slowly* and unconcernedly toward the Skoda. Then turn and kill them. Two shots, perhaps three before fire was returned. His free hand twitched, as if it had already entered the future. He drummed on the coin box. Mirror—

Yes, leaning on the coin box casually, he could see the office in the mirror. The telephone continued to ring. The two policemen were talking. An arm pointed toward the Skoda; the garage manager pointed in Hyde's direction. One of the policemen turned lazily, then looked away again. Toward a cup he was raising to his lips.

Hyde sighed, clouding the mirror. Furiously, he rubbed it clear. No, they hadn't moved, both drinking with the manager. A regular nightly call. There was a little time left—

Go. The telephone rang unanswered. Go.

Little time—

He knew it was close. Almost over. They didn't need to monitor Guest's telephone any longer. They'd almost finished whatever they had in mind for Aubrey. Babbington was sure of himself.

Policemen smoking, drinking coffee or tea. The manager leaning on his counter. Go now—

He canceled the number and began to dial at once. He had to know. Two men might have to be killed; he might have to run. He had to know. He finished dialing SIS's Vienna Station. The number began ringing. Three statues in a close group under the dim bulb in the manager's office. Still time.

"Yes?" Hyde did not recognize the voice.

"Listen to me," he blurted out. "It's Hyde—who the bloody hell are you?"

"Beach," came the surprised reply. Then: "What the hell do you want? You've got a fucking nerve calling—"

"Shut up and listen, you stupid bastard!" Hyde snapped. "I haven't got time for the niceties. Just tell me what's happened to Aubrey."

"My God—his *Russian pals* have got him, that's what!"

"What?"

"Two good men died tonight, you bastard! *Two good men!* All because the fucking KGB wanted their ball back! Do you understand, Hyde? His pals came and took him back! And they killed two of my mates doing it!"

Christ—

Too close. Already too late—

"Listen to me, you moron! It's not Aubrey—it's Babbington! Don't you understand, *Babbington* is Moscow's man!"

"What? You're crazy, Hyde. Babbington *caught* Aubrey. Handed him over for us to guard—and we screwed it up. Lost him. Understand? He's going back to Mother Russia, and good fucking riddance to him!"

"*What's happening to the old man?*" Hyde yelled into the telephone.

Rub the mirror clear. Smoking, drinking in the office. Heads lifted in laughter.

"He's already left for the airport—just had the report." Beach was calmer now, almost pleased.

"Then stop him!"

"Babbington's letting him go, Hyde. Your mate's not to be touched. Better for everyone. Even you—"

"Christ—don't you *listen?*" Mirror. Small, tight, relaxed group in the office. New cigarettes being lit. The sense at the other end of the line that someone else had taken—snatched?—the receiver.

A pause, then: "Hyde?" He recognized Wilkes's voice. "It's Wilkes, Patrick." Then: "Okay, Beach, I'll deal with this. Get some coffee up here, will you?"

"Wilkes—where's the old man?"

"Where are you, Hyde?" Wilkes's tone was amused, certain.

"Never mind. I've got it all, Wilkes. Everything. Even his *name*. Of course, no one mentioned anyone as small time as you."

"Everything, eh? Still in Czecho, are you? You won't get out, old son. That's certain."

Mirror!

Group breaking up, one of the two policemen nearer the office's glass door, turning back to speak, hand outstretched to the ear-shaped handle of the door. Time—

No time. All over. Hyde ground his teeth audibly as he struggled to contain his rage.

"You know what I've got," he said, certain that Babbington already knew of his interference with the computer. They'd have tracked down and run Petrunin's program themselves by now.

"You don't matter, Hyde. You're a dead man. You won't get out."

"And your boss is running for London already, is he? Wiping his shoes on Guest's doormat, full of the news that he's lost the old man to his Russian friends?"

"First businessman's flight this morning to Heathrow. Your pal Aubrey's just about to leave. He'll be in Moscow before it gets light." Wilkes chuckled.

One policeman through the door, the second replacing his cap and following. The manager's hand raised in farewell. Too late to move now. Wait until they get close—

"And then?"

"He goes on show, old son. Press call—the whole shocking story. Terrible ordeal for the poor old wretch. Can't say the same for the Yank and his wife, of course. They'll just disappear on arrival."

"I'll have Babbington, Wilkes. I swear it. And you. I don't care how long, or when and where. I'll have you both."

Both policemen near their car. One, hands on hips, staring toward the telephone booth. Cap pushed on the back of his head. Glance toward the Skoda, then back to Hyde—

"If you hurry, Hyde, you'll catch him before he boards the seven o'clock to Heathrow. First-class lounge, of course. I'll give him a call, shall I, tell him to be expecting you?" Wilkes laughed.

Seven o'clock. Heathrow arrival time, nine-thirty. He glanced at his watch as he cut off the call with his free hand. Retaining his grip on the receiver to allay suspicion. Policemen unmoving. Aubrey would be in Moscow even before Babbington's flight reached London.

Three fifty-five. Five and a half hours. Guest must be arriving from Washington on the early-morning flight.

Mirror—

The patrol car's engine started, the car moved, rounding the pumps in a wide arc, heading toward him. His free hand moved to the lapel of his coat. The policeman in the passenger seat stared at him. The patrol car did not stop. Hyde felt the wall of the phone booth hard against his side as he slumped in relief. The rear lights of the car moved off toward Karlovy Vary, climbed windingly up the hill, then dropped over the brow and disappeared.

Hyde slammed down the damp receiver and opened the

fogged glass door. He hurried toward the Skoda. He fumbled in his pocket for the car keys. Dropped them, then scooped them out of a pool of gas-rainbowed water on the point of freezing.

He wanted Babbington arrested as he got off the flight from Vienna. He wanted it. If he could talk to Guest, persuade him—

Before the old man disappeared. Why *should* they put him on display at a press conference like an old bear at the zoo? That could backfire. Everyone knew the old man had been taken to Moscow. A few snaps of him getting off the plane would be enough.

He wrenched open the door, climbed into the driver's seat, started the engine. The windshield clouded immediately. He rubbed it clear, turned the wheel, pulled away from the garage.

Aubrey wouldn't live. He knew that with a sick, inescapable certainty. Whatever Wilkes said or believed, the KGB wouldn't risk it. It could go wrong. The photographs of him getting off the aircraft, looking old and tired and ill, and then—

Heart attack. Eulogies in the papers, on Soviet TV and radio. Medal awarded posthumously. Much safer.

Aubrey was a dead man the moment he left the aircraft in Moscow.

Hyde accelerated. The lights of Karlovy Vary were spread out below him as he descended the hill toward the spa town. Four o'clock. He had five and a half hours. After that, Aubrey was lost. Irrecoverable.

Kenneth Aubrey had been surprisingly grateful when he saw the guard carrying his small suitcase containing the clothes Mrs. Grey had purchased for him immediately before his flight from London. To dress in something that fitted, something uncreased and clean, delighted him. Strengthened his resolve. It wasn't until he reached Schwechat airport that he realized the image was part of Babbington's purpose.

The black limousine, accompanied by two similar cars, and the van containing the luggage, turned off the main road from Vienna, skirted the passenger terminal, and drew up at the gates leading to the cargo and airline hangars. It was evident they were expected. Politeness from the officers at the gates, some joviality. Aubrey watched Voronin casually hand over a bundle of diplomatic passports and visas. And felt himself watched by the man beside him. Sensed the unnecessary gun jutting near his own rib cage.

The Austrian officer passed down the line formed by the three cars and the van. Aubrey tried to shrink back into the upholstery, but the man beside him, abandoning the gun he held, gripped his arm and forced his features into the hard light shining down from above the gates. A moment of hesitation without recognition, a glance at the appropriate false papers supplied by Voronin, and then he moved away. The grip on Aubrey's arm relaxed. The gun's barrel touched his side almost at once.

The officer would remember him. Yes, Kenneth Aubrey or a man answering his description was seen arriving at Schwechat, traveling under a Soviet diplomatic passport. Yes, yes, yes—

He glanced down at his suit, his modest tie, his dark overcoat. He would be remembered, as they intended. A man goes willingly in a well-pressed suit and a clean shirt. With false papers. He would step out of the aircraft at Cheremetievo— or at Domodedovo or Vnukovo, whichever airport the flight used—and he would be photographed in that same pressed suit and clean shirt and overcoat and hat, surrounded by smiling men who could be later identified as those who carried out his rescue and who were officers in the KGB. Evidence of his perfidy.

The gates opened; the cars moved forward. One of the officers touched the peak of his cap in a half-salute, as if conniving at his kidnap.

The cars followed the road toward a row of huge hangars. A tail-fin jutted from one of them, its symbol familiar, coincident with the Cyrillic lettering blazoned above the hangar. Aeroflot. They turned alongside the Tupolev Tu-134 airliner. Aubrey glanced back at the night outside the glaring hangar almost with longing. It had been so *easy*!

Doors closing behind him. He heard them in his head. Retreat cut off. The car drew to a halt. The van passed it and drew up at the far end of the hangar. There were perhaps a dozen people visible to Aubrey, mostly overalled, one in Aeroflot uniform. So *easy*. He was helpless. He glanced up at the airliner. One or two faces looking down in curiosity from the windows in the fuselage. Dummy passengers? Genuine diplomats? It did not matter.

The door was opened by the driver and Aubrey was motioned out. He climbed out slowly, blinking in the hard overhead lights, which seemed to shine through a haze of dust. He glanced at the watch they had returned to him. Four-twenty. What had Kapustin said?

Four-thirty. What was the matter; why was the aircraft still in its hangar? Engine cowling lying beneath the wing, men on a dolly working on the port engine. Something wrong with the aircraft!

Voronin was talking urgently to the uniformed man. Paul Massinger and his wife were being led from the back of the van, blinking, half dazed, frightened. He watched their reactions as they saw the airliner, understood the proximity of takeoff, of Moscow, of . . . He did not continue, but looked away from them. His hands quivered in the pockets of his overcoat. Clunk of a heavy spanner against metal, a curse in Russian. He glanced up at the mechanics working on the port engine.

Why? What rescue was possible?

Voronin had turned away from the Aeroflot officer—presumably the pilot—and was heading toward him. His face expressed irritation. "A fault in that engine—a delay of perhaps one hour, maybe more," he announced in a clipped tone.

"I see," Aubrey replied. "It makes little difference—wouldn't you say?"

"Little difference. That is true. Sir Andrew Babbington is unlikely to come to your rescue, I think." Voronin's irritation had vanished. "You will please get aboard the aircraft," he said.

"In a moment."

Voronin's features darkened. Then he said: "As you wish."

Aubrey walked away from him toward the Massingers. The Russian fell in behind him. The Massingers had seated themselves on a trunk—perhaps one of the trunks in which they had been transported to Schwechat?—dazed and silent, their hands linked on the woman's lap. The image persisted. It seemed to be a pose they had adopted for some portrait. This is how they would like to be remembered, Aubrey thought, feeling his throat constrict with guilt.

He paused and turned to Voronin. "Is there no way?" he asked.

Voronin shook his head. His eyes appeared bleak. Yet he rubbed briefly at his chin, as if pondering some statement. Then his eyes were alight with amused malice. "No way," he said. "But you will not have long, Sir Kenneth Aubrey, in which to be—sorry for them?"

Aubrey was aware, beyond Voronin's shoulder, that the Massingers were both watching him. There was something like pleasure, comfort on their faces. He felt very cold. He wished for a walking stick upon which to lean. The Massingers' faces displayed common cause with him: companionship. And he loathed it.

Voronin nodded stiffly and quickly. "I must now attend to other matters. You may join your friends."

He walked away toward the aircraft. The man who had sat beside Aubrey in the limousine hovered alertly. Aubrey felt the hard-lit scene lurch, as if he were fainting. He could not become warm.

Every time there was scandal in the service, every time an intelligence matter became the concern of the Western media, they would use the clip of film. Himself, descending the passenger ladder alongside this aircraft.

Coming home to Moscow.

He knew the fear would begin soon, and not leave him. For the moment, however, a seething rage possessed him. Always, for fifty or even a hundred years, he would be wheeled out into the lights like Burgess, Maclean, Philby, and the others. Photographs, details, comment—and the clip of grainy film of his arrival in Moscow. Flashing bulbs, the dying noise of aircraft engines, and his white, startled face.

Coming home to Moscow. His immortality.

Massinger raised his arm in a tentative invitation. Aubrey hurried toward them with the eagerness of a fugitive seeking shelter.

Place of Execution

When the child brought him a bowl of steaming, spicy stew, its dumplings like small boulders amid the meat and vegetables, he felt defeated, drained of all remaining energy and will. He felt he no longer possessed the strength to persuade Langdorf. The man's small, flaxen-haired, narrow-faced, well-mannered daughter had disarmed him. She was perhaps eleven or twelve. Her name was Marthe—after her mother, Langdorf had informed him. His almost-in-focus watch showed five. No—that was the second hand at twelve. It was already five-thirty. He had been in the plumber's flat for half an hour, to no purpose. Langdorf continued to refuse his help, even though his eyes were drawn again and again to the small, neat paper brick of Swiss francs lying between them on the check tablecloth.

Langdorf was wary of his own safety. Perhaps because of his child. "It is too late today," he kept repeating. "Already it is too late. It would be almost dawn before we reached the border. I cannot take you now." He had added, after the second or third refusal: "You can stay here until it is dark again. Then, I will get you across." Marthe had stood at the table's edge, watching Hyde intently. When Langdorf had made his offer, her head had moved slightly, indicating agreement. Now, she stood in the same spot, waiting for him to lift his spoon, taste the stew. He did so.

It scalded his throat and made his eyes water. Langdorf's face, seen through Hyde's tears, wore an amused expression. Marthe seemed to take the matter much more seriously, and he felt compelled to nod approval, and to say: "Thank you—yes, great. Lovely." His stomach resented the heat of the food, but its hunger was evident, and he ate—accelerating with each mouthful, blowing on the meat and vegetables in the spoon.

Eventually, his stomach seemed satisfied. Immediately, he said: "You have to take me—now. Whatever the risks, I must get across before first light." He tapped the little brick of high-denomination notes, knowing it was probably more than Langdorf had ever been offered before for such a crossing. "You have to." Half of Godwin's money lay on the table, the other half in Hyde's overcoat pocket, with the pistol, which might become necessary.

Except that it would probably be fatal to threaten his lifeline. His guide. Stupid—a last resort. He groaned inwardly at the prospect that it might come to such a desperate solution. *Take the money, you stupid bastard!*

"What's the matter?" Hyde sneered deliberately. "Isn't the money your motivation? Zimmermann told me it was."

Marthe lifted the empty bowl from between Hyde's planted elbows. Her narrow, pale face was filled with reproach, and Hyde realized that she spoke good English. Either that, or she was alive to every nuance of negotiatons such as the present one. Practice. She'd seen it all so many times before.

"She speaks English," Langdorf explained, lighting his pipe, streaming blue smoke toward the apartment's low ceiling. "I pay for the lessons. It is part of her education." Marthe smiled at her father: in gratitude, it appeared to Hyde's unpracticed eye. He felt moved by the exchange of looks, a conspiracy of affection where he might not have looked for it. "Yes," the plumber continued, still dressed in his shabby woollen dressing gown and slippers. Thick, striped pajama bottoms protruded from below the hem of the long dressing gown. "Yes—money is my only motivation, as you say." Blue smoke rose in puffs, signaling contentment, even superiority. Langdorf's features and his relaxed posture at the table suggested that he could not be surprised, taken aback. He knew himself; he could not be insulted or goaded.

Hyde heard the child washing up in the tiny kitchen. She was singing softly to herself. Unlike her father, she had dressed—even brushed and braided her hair—before appearing before their visitor. Probably, she was standing on something in order to reach into the sink. He heard cups and a plate rattle in the hot water, and looked at his half-finished glass of black Czech beer. *Just one*, he had announced to himself. Even so, it had further tired him. The child had glanced at the glass, perhaps hoping he would finish quickly so that it might be washed up with the other things. The clink of a spoon on a metal draining board—

Hyde was tired. Drunk-tired, bone-tired. Utterly weary. Five-thirty. Four hours, and he was on the wrong side of an enemy border. Perhaps the old man had already taken off for Moscow?

Langdorf's face was still, complacent. Hyde knew that his weariness was about to become acceptance. In a few minutes, a bed for the rest of the night and most of the day would become irresistible. . . .

Schliemann, he thought, rousing himself, his fuddled mind trying to embrace the trigger word, just as his training had intended. Schliemann. That was what they called it on those occasions when they trained you to the point of exhaustion and beyond. Some classical scholar's choice of a trigger word. Schliemann, the discoverer of the ruins of Troy. When you were bone-weary, ready to give up, wanting nothing but sleep, ached for rest. . . . Sleep is the last escape, they said. The last thing *you* want is to sleep. Be like Schliemann. Dig down into yourself, down through level after level until you find your reserves.

How many levels were there of the ruins of Troy, city piled on city for thousands of years? Seventeen, eighteen, thirty—infinite . . .

Use the Schliemann principle. Never give up. He didn't. There's something down there you can find and use. *Schliemann*. Trigger something, anything in yourself—*don't go to sleep!*

He groaned aloud, and looked up from the nest he had made of his folded arms. Langdorf was watching him through a billow of blue smoke. The clink of something picked up, banged against another utensil in the process of being wiped. Marthe practicing to be the perfect housekeeper—

He had dozed. Almost fallen asleep. *Schliemann*. Dig. *Dig*. Wake up, use anything—other people, anger, insults— anything. Bend events to your pattern.

"What are you grooming her for?" Hyde asked, nodding toward the kitchen. "Miss World?"

He leaned on his arms, studying Langdorf. The plumber had taken the pipe from his mouth. His full lips were now twisted with anger. His eyes had narrowed. His pale brow shone below the receding, graying hair.

"What do you say?" he asked, his eyes flickering nervously toward the kitchen door. The room, like the rest of the apartment that Hyde had seen, conformed to the gray, weatherstained concrete block that contained it. Tiled fireplace with an inadequate gas fire, thin carpet, poor furniture. Yet Langdorf was probably the wealthiest man in the tower block. All for the child—

"I said—what's the money for?"

Use anything, they said. *Schliemann*. Dig for victory.

Hyde felt tense, strained, but alert. The adrenaline, unexpectedly, began to flow. A high. What it would cost him, he did not pause to consider. He needed Langdorf's assistance. He had to cross the border.

Schliemann.

"For her," Langdorf admitted after a silence. The smoke of his pipe was now a screen, masking his expressions.

"What do you want for her?" Hyde pursued.

The child had entered the room. As if aware she was being discussed, she hovered in the doorway. She wore a small pinafore, and rubbed her hands in the material. Langdorf was aware of her. Hyde sensed an advantage. He leaned forward and whispered: "What do you want for her? What's the money for, Langdorf?"

Langdorf hissed: "She goes to the West. Eventually. I have distant relatives there, in the Federal Republic. When she has enough money, she goes. Money, education, cleverness—she goes."

"Is that your weakness, Langdorf? How much does it take? How much do you have? What do you *want*?" Hyde grinned at the plumber's confusion. His features were mobile, disturbed. *Dig for victory*. Hyde said: "I want something, *you* want even more than that. How much? *How much?*"

Langdorf's eyes expressed hatred. Hyde's cynicism had caught him unaware. Neither of them cared much for anything, anything at all. Langdorf had assumed that when he had opened the door to a tired man who was evidently a professional. But this man cared for *nothing*—

Hyde saw the almost-fear and said: "Come on, German plumber with dreams above his station. Give me a clue. Tell me how much you want." He glanced at Marthe, whose head still turned as she looked from face to face. "I won't tell you what I've been through, Langdorf. You wouldn't be interested. You're only interested in money. Everyone believes that about you. So, how much money? Not for freedom, or for the future, or for anything except yourself."

Langdorf had no chance. Hyde said: "What will she need in the West, Langdorf? How *much* will she need? A lot. How will she turn out, Langdorf? You don't want Marthe—" The girl's eyes gleamed at the sound of her name. Her face was twisted in concentration as she tried to follow his rapid English. "—to end up working in a poky office, typing. Do you? How will she turn out? Will she need her teeth fixed? What about her tits, when they arrive? Will she need them fixed, too? Clothes? Clothes cost a packet in the West, Langdorf, even if you shop at Marks and Sparks!" Hyde stood up, leaning on the table, knuckles white, his face glaring down toward the plumber. The unregarded pipe had almost gone out. "She's going to need *so much* if she's going to have a head start, Langdorf. Don't you realize that?" He leaned closer. He felt the sweat prickle on his forehead—dig!

He had him. He had Langdorf. One more rung on the ladder to Babbington.

He had him.

"Don't you realize?" he hissed. "She's going to need *everything* you can give her, and more. *More*. You want more? Is that what you want? Then take it out of my coat—go on, dip in the inside pocket and pull out your daughter's future!"

Langdorf's dislike, even hatred, of Hyde was evident. Yet he looked older, too—once more like a man roused from sleep. Hair ruffled, eyes slow to focus and darkly stained beneath. Stubble, gray skin. Hyde glanced at the man's small, plain daughter, hands buried in the folds of the pinafore. There was a picture on the tiled mantelpiece of a woman who must have been her mother. Thin-faced, her hair blond and parted in the middle, tied back. Squinting into the sun as she smiled at the camera. Hyde felt he had blundered into a situation, damaging it. Only he was truly cynical here. He shook his head and the moment passed.

He had four hours to get to Babbington before it was too late for the old man—

Old man? It might already be too late.

Langdorf laid down his pipe and stood up. Immediately, Marthe went to his side and took his rough hand, which gripped the child's thin fingers. The dirt beneath his finger-nails was highlighted against her white skin. Then he reached for Hyde's coat.

"The gun's in there, too," Hyde remarked, sitting down.

Langdorf appeared not to hear, yet Hyde saw his hand twitch as it brushed against the butt of the pistol. Then the hand withdrew the torn packet, and a thumb stained from the pipe riffled the edges of the banknotes. Marthe hovered uncertainly. Langdorf looked at Hyde, then said:

"This is someone's emergency money, I think? Not yours."

"He won't be needing it."

"Marthe—put the money away," Langdorf announced, sweeping up the little brick of notes on the table and tucking them into the elastic band around the packet. He handed them to the child, and she took the bundle without word or expression and left the room. Langdorf followed her. A light went on across the narrow hall. Surprised by his own curios-ity, Hyde got up and went into the hall.

In her bedroom, Marthe was locking the money into a tin strongbox which lay in the bottom drawer of a chest. The room had pink walls, pink lampshades. It appeared at odds with the rest of the apartment. The small bed was covered with a brightly colored duvet. There were a number of small, soft toys lying on either side of a depression in the pillows. Waiting for Marthe. A cassette-playing radio—Japanese—a small television set, West German. Langdorf looked round and saw Hyde. His face was angry, as if he had surprised an intruder or a Peeping Tom. Then he looked around his daugh-ter's room, and his features relaxed. Something in him wanted Hyde to see, to approve and admire. Hyde nodded and attempted a smile. He had seen Langdorf's dream. The child was being spoiled, or prepared for life in the West. He saw a new, large, expensive doll's stroller, a shelf of souvenir dolls from different countries. A hamster in a cage; goldfish in a tank, lit and heated. Marthe closed the drawer and smiled nervously up at her father. She looked, momentarily, like an unwilling accomplice.

"Go to bed now, Marthe. Ask Mrs. Janovice downstairs to take you to school with her boys—understand? Tell her I had to go out on an emergency job." Marthe nodded. "Don't be rude, remember to say thank you. Don't be late—"

He kissed his daughter. Hyde saw her thin arms around

the man's neck, and then he returned to the sitting room. He felt an intruder, yet tension once more gripped him. He was becoming angry with the delay.

He looked up as Langdorf came back into the room. He appeared calm, satisfied, his face younger and less tired. He picked up his pipe, struck a match, and puffed smoke across the table. Hyde was relieved. The man was now businesslike, no longer reluctant. He took his pipe from his lips, and announced:

"When she finishes in school, she goes to the West. I have maybe five or six years more. She will be wealthy when I take her across."

"And that's it, is it?"

Langdorf nodded. "That's it. That is why. You had enough for me to be unable to refuse. That is all."

"You could go any time. You could find work."

Langdorf shook his head. Blew smoke. "Not for me," he murmured. Even though his head did not move, the hushed intensity of his voice drew Hyde's attention toward the framed photograph on the mantelpiece. Between two cheap statuettes that stood stiffly erect like candles beside a votive picture. "I will not go."

"Christ, you can't *like* it here!"

Langdorf shrugged. He began to unfold the map he had brought back with him from Marthe's bedroom. He smoothed it like a new cloth over the table.

"It doesn't matter. I give no trouble, I am not troubled. They do not know what I do. Agreed, for that I would be shot. But, otherwise . . ." He looked up, pipe clenched in his teeth: competent, intelligent, almost amusedly in control of the situation. "Communism, capitalism, freedom—who cares? The system does not matter if the price is right—mm? You see, I am a cynic." He looked at his watch.

"Not quite," Hyde replied.

"I would have gone, if the three of us could have gone. But now—ach, I would not fit in over there. My family has been here for generations—longer than the Party! Marthe goes alone. A wealthy young woman. Then I stop this business, and no one will be able, by any means, to persuade me to continue." His pipe stem tapped at the map. A border line wriggled from north to south through shaded land, indicating mountain and forest. "It could have been cigarettes, or electrical goods, or the best sort of sanitary napkins. But people like you—professional people—pay better."

"You don't help dissidents—the Charter 'seventy-seven people?"

"Only if they can pay—then, with reluctance. They talk too freely. Many of them are good Marxists, you see. They object to—private enterprise is what you call it, mm? They would be lining up outside the door if I helped them regularly. All with sob stories and insufficient money. No, not them, unless your sort of business is very slack!" Again, he tapped the map with his pipe stem. "Now, pay attention, please. We have perhaps less than two hours if we are to act in safety. Here is Mytina. We drive up into the hills here, to the point where this track ends—near the border. There is wire— not too many towers, but dogs, and occasionally the helicopter. The wire runs beside this river here . . . you see?" Hyde nodded. "A fast-running stream. It is not much used as a crossing point, except by those who know the area well. Your poor dissidents on the run from Prague or Brno or Plzen wouldn't come here. They can't get maps or pictures of this area to help them!" Langdorf chuckled. "Herr Professor Zimmermann knows of this crossing point. He will be here, near the road to Waldsassen." Langdorf stood up. "Study that map—and these photographs." He fanned out a sheaf of color prints toward Hyde. "I took them with the Japanese camera I bought for my daughter. Learn the terrain. I will dress now. We must leave immediately, otherwise it will be light."

The Tupolev-134 moved onto the taxi way preparatory to takeoff. Babbington dispensed with the binoculars and handed them to Wilkes, who stood beside him in the upstairs lounge at Schwechat. Two more SIS staff from Vienna Station stood on either side of them at a few yards distance. Viennese police officers hovered at a short distance, also awaiting the Tupolev's departure.

Babbington glanced at his watch. Six-ten. The Tupolev's engine had been repaired. Babbington recalled the cold sense of shock he had experienced on arriving at Schwechat, to witness from this very window the tail unit of the Soviet airliner still jutting from the Aeroflot hangar. And the police cars, lights turning and washing over the aircraft's tail and the open hangar doors. And the remonstrations between the Viennese police and airport authorities and the identifiable figure of Voronin on the gleaming runway. Eventually, the police had given up. The airliner had diplomatic status; it was Soviet territory. The police had retired, having satisfactorily displayed their helplessness. A senior officer reported to Babbington that Aubrey had been identified as having arrived in a limousine from the Soviet embassy, traveling under false papers. He was definitely on the aircraft. Babbington had demonstrated anger, then acceptance.

But the shock of seeing the aircraft still grounded, in that first moment . . .

Now, the scene around him possessed all the necessary ingredients. A group of men posed, as if for some painter, expressing a communal mood of disappointment and relief.

The wingtip and belly lights flickered on the Tupolev. The aircraft passed along the wall of glass enclosing the upstairs passenger lounge. Drawn up on the runway below, the British Airways flight to Heathrow waited for its cargo of businessmen. As soon as the Tupolev had taken off, Babbington would board the Trident.

Only the persistent thought of Hyde marred his satisfaction at his own nerve and daring. Hyde—

He'd received a long report of events in Prague, from the Soviet embassy. Hyde had rifled the Moscow Centre computers, gaining access to some secret database that Petrunin had hidden in the computer—evidence concerning *Teardrop*, hidden like incriminating documents or photographs for future use. Hyde had the whole thing—even his name. He must be stopped. How, where? He'd been identified as having entered the country through Bratislava on a tourist visa. They were waiting for him now—though Hyde was too clever to come out by the same route. He had to be stopped. Now it was the only loose end—

The Tupolev turned tail-on to the windows, moving away from him toward the single main runway. Its lights winked in farewell. Babbington's satisfaction was marred. This, this very moment, should have been some kind of fulfillment: a climax, a conclusion. The Tupolev turned again, side-on to his view, pausing at the end of the runway. Kenneth Aubrey was about to fly east. A talisman to protect him. A *guarantee* of Babbington's future.

"Wilkes," he snapped.

"Yes?" Babbington glared at him. "Yes, sir?" Wilkes added in a less casual voice.

"Come with me." Babbington led Wilkes perhaps ten yards or more before he turned to him and said: "You have to lay hands on Hyde—eliminate him. He won't return here—not now that he knows Aubrey is on his way to Moscow. But he will try to get out with what he possesses. You're certain Godwin knows no more than he's told?"

Wilkes nodded. They would not be overheard, he realized, but spoke nevertheless in little more than a whisper. "They know their business. He's told them everything he can. He doesn't know Hyde's plans, unless they're for Bratislava. He doesn't know anything except that Hyde's pinning his hopes on Guest."

"Guest is the only one with the authority to do anything—except create doubt. *Anyone* could create doubt—even Hyde, if he can get some rag or TV station to listen to him. Anywhere in the world. He has to be stopped. And," he added almost casually, "ask your friends in Prague to get rid of Godwin. He mustn't appear in public again."

"That's easy. Hyde—a little more difficult. Sir."

The Tupolev appeared like a dog held back on its leash. Then the brakes were released and the aircraft jerked forward across the first yards of concrete, swiftly gathering speed. Aeroflot. Aubrey was safe. Babbington breathed more easily.

"What about Zimmermann?" Babbington asked. "You've checked on him?"

"We're still checking. He doesn't appear to be in Bonn. Don't worry, we'll find him."

"Hyde might go to him—yes, he might well go to him. As soon as you locate Zimmermann, put on full surveillance. Hyde could show up."

"Agreed."

The Tupolev had reached takeoff speed. Babbington studied it intently. The pool of color from the belly light was spreading and diluting as the fuselage lifted away from the concrete. Nose up, further up, stretching—

The Tupolev heaved itself toward the sky. The muffled noise of the engines grew fainter. Aubrey was gone.

Immediately Babbington's tone was threatening.

"It's up to you, Wilkes. I'm relying on you to coordinate with our friends. Find Zimmermann—above all, find Hyde. Meanwhile, I'll deal with Guest. He'll be entirely satisfied by the time I've finished." He grinned suddenly, staring down at the British Airways Trident. Passengers were straggling out of the terminal toward the aircraft. Luggage on a tractor-towed trailer had arrived alongside its cargo doors. He could smell coffee brewing behind the bar of the passenger lounge. A few more small, careful steps. The end of the tightrope, and safety, beckoned him. "Yes," he sighed. "The immediate disposal of Aubrey along with the Massingers is the safest step." He shrugged his shoulders. "As long as we can put our hands on Hyde." He turned once more to Wilkes. "Purchase Hyde's eternal silence, Wilkes. Today!"

"From here, we walk," Langdorf announced, turning round in the driver's seat.

Hyde stretched his legs, which were too stiff and weary to be supple. The journey in the back of the plumber's dirty, oil-smelling, tool-laden van had been uncomfortable. The suspension and the climbing tracks they had taken had conspired to jolt him continually from the sleep that threatened.

Hyde grunted.

"You all right?"

"Great." He pushed open the rear doors and dropped to the ground. He could smell the pines on the cold, damp air as the misty cloud almost settled on his head and face. It was lightless beneath the crowding trees. Langdorf closed and locked the doors of the van. It was parked deep under the trees. The thick carpet of pine debris and the thin layer of snow registered little trace of its passage. And the van was parked too far down the mountain to immediately arouse suspicion.

Langdorf flicked a flashlight beam onto Hyde's face, then switched it off. He breathed deeply.

"Good. Now, we go."

He turned and headed into the trees, immediately climbing upward. Certain and unhesitating; on a familiar journey. Hyde hunched into his overcoat against the raw, chill damp that had folded around him, already pearling his shoulders and hair, and followed. Twigs crunched dully beneath the snow. He trod warily in the plumber's wake, his eyes gritty, his head heavy. His own movement was now keeping him from the sleep he craved. Thirty hours—more—since he had slept properly.

He shivered almost-awake, and stumbled, sprawling full-length on the ground. Ankles, ankles! he warned himself, jarring his elbows to save his hands and wrists from sprain.

"What?" he heard Langdorf whisper before moving back. The flashlight flicked on, off. In the new, deeper darkness, he heard Langdorf say: "You must stay awake. You *must* try to stay awake."

Hyde got to his knees. Langdorf lifted him by his elbow until he was steady on his feet.

"Sorry."

"Come. We have a long climb ahead. Perhaps thirty minutes. Soon it will be getting light. Very soon."

"Yes, I know!" Hyde snapped. "I'm all right now. Get moving."

His night vision had returned. He saw Langdorf shrug, then turn and move off. Hyde plodded carefully in his wake. The trees above him were like low white clouds, heavy with snow.

Time clamped down like a fog. He measured his steps, but continually lost count. With Petrunin, he had registered each step, remembered the total, even with the dying man on his back. But not here. His hand went numb around the shape of the cassette in his pocket, the knuckles of his other hand ceased to register the presence of the pistol against them. His breathing was labored. Occasionally, he bumped into Langdorf, colliding with him as the man halted to check his hand-drawn sketch or to listen intently for suspected sounds. Langdorf seemed impatient with him, yet not afraid. Having accepted the commission and agreed to the price, he was more professional than Hyde.

Hyde remembered the man's reports as they drove through the small town and out into the countryside. More patrol cars . . . at one time, a helicopter overhead . . . a roadblock that recognized his van and almost hurried him through. Time closing in. *More activity than usual, much more* . . . They didn't stop the plumber, except at the one roadblock. Motorcycle police recognized the legend on the van; so did the car patrols.

The advantage of working for Party members, Langdorf had told him almost gaily as another car speeded up and passed them on a narrow country road. *When they want their German bathrooms and Swiss double sinks fitted, they want it done quickly and they want them to work! They don't use*

*the approved plumbers—all the other poor bastards get their
services. They need someone like me. . . . I go all over—
Marienbad, Karlovy Vary, Cheb. . . . They allow me to be a
capitalist. Work for myself—private enterprise, yes?*

Hyde stumbled awake, steadied himself on the bole of a
pine, and watched Langdorf's retreating back a little way
ahead. He could see the man's outline, now possessing more
depth and solidity than mere shadow. He looked at the luminous dial of his watch. Seven-twenty. Time closing in—
running out—

He plodded on.

*. . . even work for the STB, police, Party officials, their
mistresses and wives, army, athletes—all the cream. They
think I'm one sort of crook, but really I'm a different kind
altogether. I can be out all hours of the day and—*

"Quiet!" Langdorf hissed. For an instant, Hyde believed
the plumber was speaking in his memory, then the man's
hand gripped his arm, forcing Hyde to his knees at the base of
a pine trunk.

"What is it?"

"I heard something—listen!"

Hyde shook off the effort of memory that had kept him
awake. He crouched beside Langdorf. The man's hand still
held his forearm, and the quiver in it was transmitted to
Hyde. The plumber's face was a white patch beginning to
acquire features, his shape in the overalls almost possessing
color.

"How far—" Hyde began.

"Shhh!" Langdorf hissed.

Crack? Shuffle through pine debris? Hyde's senses
seemed dull, approximate. Sight was unfocused, hearing
muddy as if under water. Shadow? Noise?

The crack of a twig muffled by fallen, brown needles and
snow. The tiny clink of metal against metal. Then the muted
gleam of a flashlight. Hyde shivered with cold and the effort
to remain still. Langdorf seemed as tensely contracted as a
wound spring.

A four-man patrol. Armed with rifles, each man carrying a small pack on his shoulders. The patrol moved in a single
file, crossing the path they were using. As they came closer, he
could make out their uniforms. Border guard. They passed
within ten yards and moved slowly off, routinely alert, waiting for daylight to assist them.

When they had gone, Hyde said: "Will they find the van?"

Langdorf shook his head. "No. It is unlikely—if we hurry."

"Why are they—they know, don't they?"

"I do not know—" the plumber began.

"But you suspect?"

Langdorf nodded. "For some reason, they are very protective of this part of the border, tonight. It is not usual." Langdorf shook his head. It was still too dark to see any emotion displayed by his features. "Not usual," he repeated. Then he stood up. "Come," he whispered. "We must hurry."

Hyde climbed to his feet. Weariness had dropped away like a blanket he had left on the ground. His eyes ached, but his body was alive with the myriad small shocks and prickles of tension. He hurried after Langdorf. The ground climbed more steeply, rock jutted through the snow and pine debris; the trunks were thinner, farther apart. The damp, low cloud seemed to have lifted. Perhaps it had been no more than a mist.

Ten minutes later, Langdorf again motioned him to stop. They were at the edge of the trees. Their twisting route had always seemed to be ascending, yet now they were on the edge of a sloping stretch of grassland. An alpine meadow. Trees bordered it on all sides, except where a swathe had been cut to make a forest ride. A watchtower that was not intended for ornithology loomed at the far end of the meadow. Beyond it, a mountain climbed out of the trees, its face masked with snow. The meadow was white, ghostly.

Huts and barns huddled in the snowbound meadow. An animal snorted audibly across the white silence. In the distance, an engine coughed into life. There were lights on the watchtower, but no sweeping searchlight.

"The border wire runs alongside a stream," Langdorf explained, "on the other side of this meadow. We must follow the trees. The stream is in a narrow bed. The wire is on this bank. Soon, the stream turns west and then it is in the Federal Republic. The wire no longer follows it. Come."

They skirted the meadow warily and swiftly. In another six or seven minutes, without the aid of his sketch, Langdorf located a narrow track that might originally have been made by deer. He hurried Hyde along it, the meadow now behind them, the slope of the land dropping away, becoming rocky.

Langdorf's nailed boots scuttled and scraped ahead of Hyde.

The trees opened as Hyde heard the rush of water. Pebble and rock stretched down to a foaming, narrow stream that pushed and grumbled through its channel. Langdorf's hand restrained him. The pebbles were light, betraying. The top of the watchtower could be seen. The wire was visible on the Czech side of the stream.

"Is it deep?" he asked.

"Here, no. You can wade across. The current is strong, however. You must be careful. Strong."

The watchtower rose like a pit's winding gear against the slowly lightening sky. Patches of snow grew among the rocks and large pebbles. Snow sheathed the rolls of wire.

"Do I have to cut the wire?"

"No. You can wriggle beneath it. Directly ahead of you, the wire is in poor condition."

"Electrified? Mines?"

"Neither. This is a cheap border." Langdorf chuckled, but the nervousness was mounting in his voice and breathing. He wanted to leave. "They rely on patrols with dogs, and on the tower."

There was no wind. No movement in the trees or along the stretch of rocks. Only the noise of the stream. Above that, the growing beat of a helicopter's rotors. Hyde waited.

The helicopter slid into sight, a black insect no more than a couple of hundred feet up. It followed the course of the stream, heading north, passing over the watchtower, which signaled to it with a flashing lamp. Then its noise faded beyond the trees as it crossed the meadow.

"Now you must go," Langdorf urged. "Cross here, then follow the course of the stream. To this road here, which climbs into the hills." He flashed his flashlight on his map sketch. "Here, there is a stone bridge. Herr Professor Zimmermann will be waiting at this point. If he has come."

Hyde nodded. Silence except for the stream. Thirty yards to the wire, wriggle under and through, ford the stream, then run. Getting colder and colder. But run.

He looked at his watch. Seven-forty. In less than two hours, Babbington's flight would touch down at Heathrow. Babbington would be back at the center of the web, issuing orders, covering up, persuading—tidying up. He thrust the cassette into the breast pocket of his coat. At Langdorf's insistence it had been wrapped in a plastic bag, like the pistol. He looked at Langdorf—

Noises. Boot studs on rock, the beams of flashlights. Langdorf was startled, and immediately stood up.

"Good luck!" he snapped, and pushed at Hyde as he squatted on his haunches.

The heave was a strong one. Hyde rolled out of the trees, tumbling over and over, disorientated. Langdorf had known exactly what he was doing. Hyde would distract the patrol from himself. As he sat up, he saw Langdorf disappear into the trees, moving swiftly and certainly. Unobserved.

A dog barked. Hyde could almost hear safety catches being released, the inhalation of surprised breaths. The dog barked again, then growled. Straining at the leash. Then barking more frantically.

They were fifty yards away, coming out of the trees. Two of them and one dog. As he turned his head to the watchtower, he saw forms pass in front of the lights, then a searchlight flared and began stepping and jumping along the rocks toward him. He got to his feet as they called on him to stop.

He danced across the rocks and pebbles, arms akimbo for balance, awareness rooted in his calves and ankles, prickling across his shoulders. A shot. He winced. The one warning shot. Ten yards to the wire. Now, now the dog—

He skidded onto his belly, skinning his palms. The raw skin beneath his thin gloves protested, crying out. His knees were bruised. The roll of wire was buckled upward. The snow was shaken off as he wriggled, revealing the barbs. He crawled on his stomach. Two more shots, plucking away off the pebbles. The dog, the dog—

Get into the wire, *get under the wire*!

The dog howled at his release. He heard it coming. His pained right hand fumbled at his side, fumbled for the pocket of his coat. Snow fell on him from the dancing curls of wire tugging over his back. The dog was close—

He touched the gun in its plastic bag. The dog's growl was almost on top of him, he heard it begin to slither expertly on its belly. Boots, running. Calls to halt, to remain still, not to move. *The dog's breath on his exposed ankle, he was certain of it!*

The gun twisted in his grip. He tried to turn onto his back, but a strand of wire caught in his coat and he could not move. The dog raised its head, pulling at the cloth of his coattail. Heaving against his body weight and the restraint of the wire. Holding him. The men were twenty yards from him, still running. He half twisted, craning his neck, lying on his left side, tearing his coat open across his shoulders, feeling the barbed wire rip his skin. Felt the trigger awkwardly through the thin plastic. Moved the safety catch. Held then squeezed the trigger's vague outline. Fired, deafening himself. As one of the two shots passed through the dog's shoulder, it howled, releasing the coattail.

Hyde heaved forward regardless of the wire. The searchlight bounced onto his prone form, passed, returned. Held him. Almost immediately, a machine gun opened fire. The dog, screaming because it had become trapped in the wire in its pain, fell silent after a single long whimper. The two border guards were flat on their stomachs, out of the line of fire. Stone chips flew, bullets ricocheted. Hyde wriggled out from beneath the wire and flung himself forward into the water. Immediately, the cold stunned him, numbing his legs and trunk to the waist. The current flung him off his feet because he was too cold to move forward. He cried out at the shock. Floated, was pushed then dragged by the current. Machine gun fire swept back and forth across the stream behind him, but the searchlight had lost him. It bounced forlornly from bank to bank, picked out the two border guards on their knees, both trying to draw a bead on his bobbing head. He swallowed icy water, moved his arms in protest, but the stream thrust him on. His feet dragged on the rocky bed, his leg banged numbly against a hidden rock, then he was out of his depth.

And the searchlight was gone. The guards, running along the shore, also vanished. The wire was just visible. He collided with a midstream rock and was too winded and weak to grasp its gleaming surface. He was hurried on by the current. The banks of the stream narrowed, rose on each side. His whole body was numb, too numb, dangerously—

A rock ahead. He tried to steer for it, tried to reach it, able only to push feebly against it with his feet as he passed. He saw foggily. Drew in one breath with enormous effort. Hands, feet, legs, trunk numb. He tried to stand, touched rocks, was swept onward, touched rocks again, tried to stand, drew in a huge breath, and ducked beneath the surface. Gripping rocks with numb hands, dragging the rocks toward him as his legs and torso were swept sideways. The water's current stretched him out, refloated him. Dragged him at another rock, slimy and hard. Another, then another—

He crouched against the current as it swept to both sides of a jutting rock. Knees on the pebbly bed, hardly registering the painful, hard lumps—his head was above water! He waited, then heaved himself at the bank.

He crawled out of the icy water, heart pumping, breath absent, strength gone. Rolled onto his back, coughing weakly, waiting for the effort to subside and allow him to find the strength to draw air.

And saw Zimmermann's face. Framed by two other faces. They might have been those of the border guards. His hand flapped on his chest. Could he feel the wrapped cassette? Could he? He patted weakly. Zimmermann understood and bent down beside him. He withdrew the cassette and held it for Hyde to see. Hyde nodded. Which started him coughing again. He had begun breathing shallowly and quickly. Flashlight beams danced around his body. Men spoke in German. He realized with difficulty that he had crossed the border.

"Wrap him up well," he heard Zimmermann say. "Get him on his feet as soon as you can." He patted Hyde's shoulder softly. Hyde could hardly feel the gesture. "Well done, Mr. Hyde. We came upstream from the bridge because of the activity in the area. Particularly the helicopter. But it was a good thing you got ashore by yourself. We would not have seen you in the water."

Blankets laid on him, one after another, heavy as earth. Someone rubbing his legs, his thighs roughly. Arms, too. A hand raised his head. Brandy. He coughed, losing most of it down his chin and collar.

"Listen—" he began.

"Say nothing at the moment," Zimmermann instructed. Behind his head the sky was beginning to gain color. West German Frontier Guard—Grenzschütz—uniforms moved around him. Hyde wanted to vomit. His heart would not slow down. They continued to rub at his limbs and body. More brandy. This time he swallowed.

He coughed and said: "Not much time—have to talk to London. *Have to*, Zimmermann!" He was pulling at the German's sleeve.

The helicopter was away to the left, across the stream. Tree-top height, watching them. Heads turned to observe it.

Hyde's head ached with cold, but ideas flashed and bloomed in his mind, as if he had drunk much more of the brandy. And then, for certainty's sake, the helicopter's small searchlight flicked across the river and spotlighted them for perhaps five seconds. Then it blinked out and the small helicopter rose and slipped over the trees. Hyde lost sight of it.

They knew.

Already, Zimmermann was saying: ". . . suspected they were following from Nuremberg. Someone must have seen me when I landed. . . . They knew from my whereabouts that you—"

Hyde shook Zimmermann's sleeve, and spluttered: "Get me to a phone. If they warn London, then Babbington disappears as soon as he lands. Understand? We have to have him—have to have Babbington to save Aubrey. No swap, no—no Aubrey. Understand?"

Zimmermann's face darkened. He glanced at the sky, as if to pick out the now-hidden helicopter.

"Yes," he said. "Yes, of course—of course!" He stood up. "They will carry you down to the car." Then in German, quickly and with authority: "Pick him up. Quickly—we must return to Waldsassen at once. Quickly!"

Aubrey glanced at his watch. Nine-seven. The unbroken snow lay like a frozen white sea lapping up to the hills of Moscow. The city was revealed like cast-up wreckage: spars and towers, broad avenues, blocks of apartments, ornate, miniature churches and palaces. Railway lines and highways spread in all directions from the city; once noticed, the scene became transformed into a vast spider's web heavy with snow and with Moscow at its heart.

The three of them—Margaret Massinger kneeling on her seat like a child, her head above the back of it—stared out of the windows of the Tupolev as it lazily circled the city, awaiting landing instructions. A small delay, the pilot had informed them over the intercom. Volume of air traffic for the southern international airport of Domodedovo. Aubrey glanced up. Margaret was looking at him intently. He tried to smile and she nodded, as if she understood his intention and his difficulty.

Now, near the end of it all, he was unable to speak to her. Or to Paul Massinger. The three of them had exchanged

scrappy, broken phrases, single words, the occasional platitude but nothing more throughout the flight. Guests at a
party, the earliest to arrive and strangers to one another. The
dozen or so Russians aboard the aircraft ignored them. The
hostesses served them breakfast and drinks in bland silence.
Their guards relaxed. Each of the three seemed grateful for
silence, and for the proximity of the others. Aubrey was
pleased that their relationship did not exclude him.

The city slid beneath the wing. Traffic on the huge highway ring, tinier than miniatures. Two trains visible, rushing
into the city. The river, the Kremlin.

Aubrey had not been in Moscow since before the war. Yet
it had formed the enemy fortress for so long that it was familiar. Any map of the city he had ever seen immediately became
an architect's three-dimensional model or a series of aerial
photographs. He knew the modern city, but until now it had
belonged in his imagination. London and Moscow had been
like Rome and Carthage, made unreal by distance and history. Sites of ancient battles. Now, below him, he saw the enemy camp. And it was also the enchanted castle, the home of
the wicked. . . .

He smiled to himself. Moscow, for the past forty-six
years, had been both as real and as imaginary as a child's
dream. Fairy tale. Ogre's castle.

Now, the place of execution. All three of them knew that.
Already, the Massingers had been forced to dress in mechanics' overalls so that they could be smuggled unrecognized from
the aircraft long after he had left it in a gleam of publicity and
identification. They had perhaps a couple of hours remaining
to them.

The river glinted, frozen and silver in the morning sunlight. Gold glowed on roofs and onion towers. Apartment
blocks remained unwarmed, stubbornly gray and drab beneath the clear sky.

The aircraft began to drop slowly southward toward the
airport. Its nose angled more steeply. Aubrey glanced at Margaret Massinger. She patted his gnarled, liver-spotted hand as
it rested on the back of her seat. The Tupolev continued to slip
through the clear air toward the ground. Moscow, drifting
away behind them, was still a huge, intricate child's model of
a fortress. And Aubrey was grateful for the unreal images of
Moscow his imagination provided like a sedative. Miniature.
Map. Unreal.

• • • •

"There's thirty minutes, and they *know!*" Hyde all but wailed.

He was huddled in a striped blanket, his hands grasping a mug of coffee as if to still the constant shuddering of his arms and shoulders. His hair was once more wet where ice had melted in his matted curls. The only noise in the small room was the constant sound of his chattering teeth.

Zimmermann stood near the door of the office that had been put at their disposal by the commanding officer of the Grenzschütz HQ at Waldsassen. Sir William Guest's apartment in Albany was still unoccupied. The clock on the wall displayed nine for another moment, then its minute hand jerked forward. Babbington was due to land at Heathrow in thirty minutes. Zimmermann entirely agreed with Hyde. Once he disembarked, he would be warned off, taken swiftly into hiding and smuggled out of the country. No exchange, no return of Aubrey.

"Is there no one else?" he asked softly.

Hyde shook his head violently. The green blotting pad on the desk was sprinkled with damp spots as the melted ice flicked from his hair. He swallowed his coffee greedily, then wiped his mouth.

"No, there's no one else."

"Not even the very top?"

Hyde looked up in disbelief. "Me ring the Prime Minister, or something?" he asked scornfully. Then he shook his head more reflectively. "I'd be sidetracked. One of Babbington's people—I'd never get to anyone who could act. There's only Guest."

"You are certain they will dispose of Aubrey at once—without delay?"

"Aren't you?"

Zimmermann rubbed his chin, then sighed. "Yes. In their place, I would not allow him to be seen again, by anyone, once he left the aircraft. Anything else would be a risk." He nodded, as if some inner self had finally become convinced of the argument's inevitable logic, then raised his arms in a gesture of helplessness. Hyde merely continued to stare at the telephone clamped to the desk amplifier, his hands kneading the pottery of his mug as if to reshape it.

Nine-three.

"Are you trying that number?" Hyde snapped in English at the intercom.

Zimmermann walked swiftly to the desk and issued instructions in clipped, precise phrases. The Grenzschütz switchboard operator offered assurances of his best efforts. Zimmermann looked up at Hyde.

"I have instructed them that the number is to be left ringing. Continuously."

Hyde was about to reply when the door opened. The features of the Grenzschütz Kapitan were clouded with doubt, even embarrassment. His eyes displayed a sense of having been deceived and there was a stiff, ominous rectitude about his lips. He closed the door behind him.

"Herr Professor Zimmermann," he began formally. "I must ask you to accompany me, please."

"What is the matter?" Zimmermann snapped back, his eyes angry and affronted. Hyde sensed that he had already weighed the situation, completely understood it. "I do not understand, Kapitan."

Immediately, the Frontier Guard officer was at a disadvantage. But he persisted: "You have deceived me and my men, Herr Professor. This is not a matter of Federal security. You are at present—" He hesitated, as if once more embarrassed, then added: "You are not officially recognized, Herr Professor. You do not have official status."

Hyde, turning his head from face to face, realized that someone had acted without hesitation to inform Bonn of Zimmermann's whereabouts and intentions. The ramifications did not bear consideration. The immediate was dangerous enough. This captain could stop them simply by denying them access to a telephone. The thread was that fine, that fragile. Hyde forced himself to say nothing, closing his eyes like a child against something frightening or dangerous.

"Please, Herr Professor," the captain pleaded. "This is a very embarrassing moment. Please, you will accompany me now—"

Immediately, Zimmermann replied in a raised, authoritative voice: "No! Captain, I will not leave your office. I will not do as you ask."

The captain's dark, rounded features scowled, and his eyes glanced momentarily down as if seeking a reminder of his rank and authority. "Herr Professor—" he warned.

"Captain—you are responsible for a stretch of border perhaps fifty miles long—yes?"

Puzzled, the officer nodded. "Yes—"

"Good. You have light and heavy armored cars at your disposal. You conduct patrols. You are one of twenty thousand." Zimmermann hesitated, then pounced with biting sarcasm. "I could get ten, fifty, a hundred officers to do your job—*this moment*—from the ranks of the Bundeswehr or the Grenzschütz or even the Territorialheer reservists!" The captain's face opened in surprise, his jaw dropping beneath cheeks growing pink and eyes that signaled his sense of outrage. Zimmermann hurried his words, his tone studiedly angry and dismissive. Hyde appreciated the performance, even as his eyes glanced at the clock. "Do you understand my meaning, Captain? Do you understand what I am saying? On my side, there is myself and this Englishman—no one else. I cannot be replaced; neither can he. Nor will we be. What could you expect to understand about security? About *our* world!" He gestured in Hyde's direction. "You receive a telephone call from someone in Bonn you have never heard of, and you jump to do as he says? Do you think we dragged this man out of the river for humanitarian reasons? Do you? I suggest you spend some time—perhaps thirty minutes—checking your instructions. Meanwhile, you will leave us here, in the safety of your office where the door and the windows can be guarded, *with the use of the telephone* and the services of your switchboard operator, and we shall promise not to attempt to escape!" The climax of the sentence was mocking, superior.

Zimmermann, to emphasize his assumed, false control of the situation, immediately placed himself behind the captain's desk, apparently relaxed and comfortable in the officer's own chair. Rights of occupation, Hyde thought. Nine-six. Twenty-four minutes. Hyde once more squeezed his eyes shut. His teeth had ceased to chatter. The electric fire near his legs now gave out an appreciable warmth. He felt the last of the coffee warm in his stomach.

"I—" the captain began, his face flushed, his eyes now calculating behind the anger.

"Well, captain? Well?" Zimmermann persisted. "If we are a danger to the state, you have us well controlled—in custody already. Haven't you?"

The captain's hands were bunched at his sides. His dislike of Zimmermann became masked and hidden. His eyes moved rapidly as if he were dreaming where he stood. What if— What chance— Hyde saw the questions dart and flicker. Could he avoid offending Zimmermann and Bonn at the same time? Zimmermann was a powerful man, his authority only suspect, not ended. Eventually, he nodded.

"Very well. This room will be placed under guard, Herr Professor—in twenty minutes, I shall return. You will then be placed in proper custody until I receive further orders. Any use you make of the telephone will, of course, be monitored." Zimmermann shrugged as if indifferent, and the captain, hiding his anger at the further insult, turned on his heel and left the office. They heard him barking orders in the outer room.

Nine-eight.

"Jesus!" Hyde began.

Zimmermann waved him to silence. "It was nothing," he observed with assumed modesty and a smile. "But they are moving very quickly. They have excellent communications. They will definitely attempt to save Babbington when he lands in—in twenty-one minutes." His fingers drummed on the desk. Through the window a high pale sky retreated beyond hills dark with pine. A guard ostentatiously took up position in full view outside the window. Zimmermann laughed. "Ridiculous."

"Anything yet?" Hyde asked the intercom, flicking the switch up for the switchboard operator's reply.

"Nothing, sir."

"Sir," Hyde remarked ironically.

"He is playing even safer than his officer."

"And in twenty minutes' time?"

"That could be—awkward? I do not know what will happen. I will be in trouble with my ministry, of course. Whether any—more permanent measures might be taken, I cannot say. It depends on what power they can wield. And who could be certain about that?"

Nine-eleven. Nineteen minutes. The KGB might even meet Babbington on the runway. Come on, *come on*—

"Christ!" Hyde exploded, hurling the empty mug at the clock on the wall. It struck below it and shattered. Hyde had begun shaking once more, and tugged the blanket more tightly around him. His feet shifted, his teeth ground with rage rather than cold. *"Come on, damn you!"*

"Sir?"

Zimmermann immediately reached for the intercom switch and flicked it.

"Yes?"

"Sir, I have your call. I gave your name, sir—was that—"

"Yes, yes—put the call through, man!" Hyde's head came up. His whole frame was quivering.

"Is it—" he began. Zimmermann clipped the receiver to a desk speaker so that both he and Hyde could hear Guest and speak to him without having to pass the receiver back and forth.

"Sir William Guest? Am I addressing Sir William Guest?" Zimmermann asked breathlessly, his voice light and strange.

"Who is this? My telephone has been ringing ever since—" With a silent movement of his lips, Zimmermann queried the voice with Hyde. He had slumped in the chair, the blanket falling open, disregarded. He nodded. His clenched fists beat at his thighs. His head bobbed. It was Guest, was Guest— impossibly, it *was*—

Zimmermann identified himself to Guest in a formal, polite manner. Then he said: "I have someone here, Sir William, who must speak with you—only with you. It is of the utmost urgency. You must listen to him—" Zimmermann's tone had changed to one of pleading. He was no longer able to control his voice.

Nine-twelve.

"Yes? What is all this, Herr Zimmermann? Of course, I understand *you*, but not the mystery you seem intent on creating. I have just arrived after a very unsatisfactory airplane journey, I am very tired—"

"Shut up and listen!" Hyde shouted into the telephone, leaning forward on his chair, his face bent toward the receiver. "It's Hyde—Patrick Hyde. And I want to talk about Aubrey. Now, listen—"

"Hyde!" Sir William's voice blared from the receiver. "Hyde—how dare you—" Hyde grinned at Zimmermann. His teeth had begun to chatter once more, and his shaking seemed well beyond control. Zimmermann realized that the Australian was without reserves. He was forcing himself not to subside completely. Zimmermann prepared to take command of the situation. Hyde pulled the blanket back around his shoulders and hunched his body. Somehow, diminishing the physical space he occupied seemed to assist him, as if he were squeezing some sponge within him that still held a few last drops of energy. "This conversation must end at once, Hyde," Sir William continued, his habitual tone of authority fully recaptured. "There are channels—and *you* are persona non grata, as you are only too well aware."

"For Christ's *sake!*"

"Sir William," Zimmermann interjected, waving Hyde to silence. The Australian glared at him. And obeyed. "Sir William—time is very short, as you will understand once you have heard what we have to tell you. I *beg* you to listen." Zimmermann's tone was edged with obsequiousness, which Hyde loathed. The German adopted the role of a subordinate, but one with his own degree of rank and authority. "I really must insist—" he continued.

"What is it, Herr Zimmermann? Really, what is the cause of this unexpected, uninvited conversation?"

"Proof!" Hyde exclaimed. "Proof that Aubrey's innocent and your pal Babbington's been a very naughty boy behind your back! And from the same fucking school, too!"

"Hyde! Be silent!" Zimmermann barked. He pressed his finger to his lips, then pointed to himself. "I'm sorry, Sir William. Mr. Hyde's loyalty is not in question, as you can—"

"But it is, Herr Zimmermann—I don't know what tale he has told you, but I'm afraid you are in the company of a renegade. One of our rotten apples, I'm sorry to say—"

"Forgive me, but I don't think so."

"Really. With the kind of accusation he appears to be making? You surely don't believe him?"

Nine-fourteen. Both of them glanced in the same moment at the clock on the wall, the coffee from Hyde's mug an elongated, drying splash beneath it on the cream paint.

"I am afraid that I am forced to do so," Zimmermann replied with studied deference and conviction.

"Herr Zimmermann—I really am very tired—"

"Please, Sir William! You have been in Washington for a matter of days now. . . ."

"Yes?"

"You are then not familiar with what has happened—that Sir Kenneth Aubrey is in the Soviet Union at this moment?"

There was a silence, then Guest said: "The news does not surprise me. I will, no doubt, be receiving a report in due course. From Andrew Babbington."

"He'll be on your doorstep within the hour, mate, with his version of events. You can bloody count on it!"

"Sir Andrew has been in Vienna. Aubrey was captured by your intelligence service there—"

"Ah."

"But they lost him. He was *allowed* to fall into the hands of the KGB. They spirited him at once to Moscow. His flight will have landed by now."

Nine-fifteen. Yes, Hyde admitted, banging his thighs with clenched fists. Landed by now. Zimmermann had checked with Vienna before leaving Waldsassen for the border. The Aeroflot flight had left Vienna at six-fifteen. Three hours to Moscow. It was down by now. Red carpet, the boys in the band, the forced handshakes and back pattings, the black car—finis. Gone. Tomorrow, all you have to look forward to is a heart attack and the obituary in *Pravda*.

"And?"

"Sir William, I am convinced that Sir Kenneth is in the gravest danger—"

"From his own people?" Guest remarked with studied irony.

"No—from the Soviets. He is *not* one of them."

"But Andrew Babbington is? Preposterous!"

"Hyde has evidence, Sir William. The man is named specifically. The whole—scenario, shall we call it, whereby Sir Kenneth was made to appear a Soviet agent. Mr. Hyde has this on a computer tape. He has obtained definitive evidence of Sir Andrew Babbington's treachery and the Soviet attempt to disgrace Sir Kenneth and replace him with their own agent."

"I promoted Andrew Babbington," Guest replied. The tiny click of the clock's minute hand moving was audible in the room. Zimmermann's words had fallen emptily, with a dull, hollow noise. The cassette lay, still wrapped in plastic, on the captain's desk. It was mute; it might have been blank for all the use it appeared to be.

Zimmermann shrugged, lacing his fingers, unlacing them. He appeared at a loss.

Guest said: "Preposterous. Quite preposterous. What

kind of twisted mind invented this rubbish? Hyde? Aubrey? The Russians? It really is ridiculous, you know, Herr Zimmermann."

Nine-sixteen.

"Christ, I'm cold," Hyde murmured.

Zimmermann looked up from his fingers quickly. Hyde's face was pale; the skin quivered on his cheeks, his lips echoed the constant movement of his clenched teeth. His hands, gripping the edges of the blanket and folded on his chest, were bloodless and shaking.

"It is *not* preposterous!" Zimmermann snapped.

"I beg—"

"Listen to me, Sir William. Please listen—" He lowered his voice. Nine-seventeen. "That was obviously the factor that dictated their timing . . . your support of Sir Andrew. The new service you have conjured into existence . . ."

"You suggest I have played into Soviet hands?"

"No, no—believe me, no. Merely that Babbington and his masters took advantage of the circumstances you helped to create. The scenario had lain idle for some years—"

"And how, precisely, did *you* learn of it?"

Hyde moaned softly, but whether with cold or something akin to despair Zimmermann could not tell. The man's head was hanging. Wrapped in his blanket, he looked like a refugee or a prisoner who had been beaten.

"I—the evidence is here, Sir William, with us. Please believe that we have the evidence."

"From a *computer*?"

"From Moscow Centre itself. Everything . . ." Zimmermann sighed. He could not grasp the next word or phrase. There seemed no more he could usefully say. Guest did not believe him. Nine-eighteen. Twelve minutes. Guest could not act now, even if he believed—

"This—I think I should begin by making reference to your ministry in Bonn, Herr Zimmermann. And perhaps I should listen to Andrew Babbington's account of the affair. . . . Frankly, I don't believe a word of it. Not one word—"

"For Christ's sake, shut up!" Hyde's eyes were wide, bright as if feverish. He was shaking inside the blanket. "If you wait another bloody minute, sport, you'll kill Aubrey!"

"Don't be ridiculous."

"And you'll kill your precious goddaughter, mate. Aubrey, Massinger, and Massinger's wife. They're all on the flight."

"What?"

"Don't you ever fucking listen to anything anyone says?" Hyde almost screamed, stretching forward toward the receiver, the muscles and veins standing out in his neck. "I said Massinger and his wife are on that bloody plane to Moscow! Babbington's making sure there's no one left to testify! He's cleaning house, mate. *Tidying up!* Understand? You're making sure he kills her—kills Margaret Massinger along with Aubrey!"

He slumped back into his chair, almost tumbling it and himself to the floor. Zimmermann started from his seat, but Hyde waved him to sit down. There was a gleam of calculation replacing the wild look in his eyes. His teeth chattered as he tried to grin. Then he said:

"It's up to that pompous old fart, now." His voice was loud enough for Guest to hear. "It depends if he give a monkey's ass or not."

In the silence, the minute hand of the clock moved audibly. Nine-twenty.

Eleven seconds later—they had both counted them off—Guest said: "Assuming, perhaps only assuming . . ." He cleared his throat. "I must assume . . ." Again, he dried up. They heard him cough. "*If*—what do you suggest, Hyde? Zimmermann—what do you suggest?"

Hyde dragged his chair to the desk. The blanket fell away once more.

"Heathrow—Special Branch must grab Babbington and hold him. Just hold him—and warn them to watch out for interference."

"Yes—"

"Use *all* your emergency authority and make Euston Tower and Cheltenham transmit Priority Black signals to the embassy in Moscow, *and* Moscow Centre. They have to do that now. You have to try to stop them taking Aubrey off the plane. If you've got Babbington and they've got Aubrey, there's only one thing to do. Tell them you'll do a swap—exchange their man for ours. Understand?"

"But—"

"Look, if they agree, you've already got the proof you need! They wouldn't agree to hold the operation if Babbington wasn't their man—would they? Once they go on hold, it doesn't matter how long the tidying up takes!" Hyde growled. "Just make sure they know you've got Babbington. They'll *have* to have him back—too bad for morale if they let *him* go to the wall. It'll work. It happens with small fry—and big fish. Get them to agree to a trade."

"Euston Tower can—" Guest began.

"Don't ask—they can talk to Moscow Centre any time they choose. Priority Black, remember. Just tell them to do it. Inform the Chairman you've got his favorite toy. He should choke on the news!"

Nine twenty-one.

"Very well—this is all provisional, of course. But under the circumstances surrounding . . . surrounding the *other people* involved, I am prepared to go along with your suggestions to the extent—"

"Do it! And while you're at it, get Godwin free in Prague. If the poor wretch is still alive. Do it."

Zimmermann said quickly, efficiently: "We will ensure that the computer tape, the *irrefutable proof*, will be flown by helicopter to our computer center in Munich at once. Our computer will talk to yours at Century House. An hour after Sir Andrew reaches London, you will have confirmation of everything we have told you." As soon as he had finished speaking, he cut the connection with a brisk, decisive movement of his right hand. Hyde slumped his head on his folded arms and lay still, his damp hair staining the green blotter. Zimmermann watched him for a few moments, then said softly:

"Is there time, I wonder?"

"There'd better be," Hyde mumbled into his sleeve. He was wearing a Grenzschütz uniform shirt that was too large for him. "I don't even want to think about it." He did not look up as he added: "There's nothing we can do about it now, anyway. Nothing."

Zimmermann glanced at the clock. Nine twenty-two.

"No," he agreed. "Nothing."

As he descended the passenger steps, Babbington experienced a sensation that might have originated in some television news item. Speed, movement, action; the viewer relying upon the camera's point of view, that camera held by a running man. Vigorous panning—left, right, left, right—a desperate attempt to define the real, crucial focus of the scene.

He was three steps from the bottom of the passenger ladder. There was the expected black Mercedes and the uniformed civil service driver—this one with small arms expertise and myriad emergency driving skills. Eldon was there in his military fawn overcoat, present as one of the new influential deputies of SAID. He was standing erectly by the black car, and had not yet begun to react to the new arrivals.

Two other cars. Almost a traffic jam. One of the cars—another Mercedes—was slightly nearer, and had arrived in more of a hurry. The second new car was—Special Branch. He did not even need to think about it. Two mackintoshes, two trilbies. Caricatures. The morning sunlight glanced off the windows of the terminal, highlighted the arrogant tail planes of perhaps a dozen airliners. Gleamed on the windows of the three cars. Left, right, left, right—point of focus? Babbington was unsettled.

It would be the act of the next few moments. After that, events would be beyond his shaping. The two Special Branch men began their ponderous progress toward him across thirty yards of runway. Eldon began to absorb the scene, his left hand already gesturing to the security driver, who began reaching for his shoulder holster. Yet Eldon was confused, made compliant by his recognition of the Special Branch officers.

And the Russians. He recognized his contact, Oleg, inside the car. A hand beckoned him down the last few steps toward the opened door of their Mercedes. One young man in a well-cut suit displayed by his opened overcoat—a gun there, too—

And he believed, for an instant, that *they* would kill him rather than allow Special Branch near him.

Babbington shivered. Passengers from first class pressed behind him on the steps, their respectful stillness because of the array of cars already evaporating. The air was chilly in his nostrils, scented with aviation fuel. His chest seemed to pound. Left, right, left, right—the mad panning continued.

Eldon raised his hand in a confused, troubled gesture of welcome that might have been a signal to bar his admission to some club.

Hyde—

He had time to think that. It couldn't have been Aubrey. He was already dead, prepared for death at the very least. Poor Margaret and her stupid, persistent husband were, without doubt, no longer living. But *Hyde*—

His hands clenched into useless fists. The Russians gestured more frantically. He saw the sweep of the young man's arm, his readiness to risk even gunfire to salvage the focus of the scene, the focus of *Teardrop*. . . .

A car chase, the embassy in Kensington or some hidden safe house, a light aircraft to the Continent, then Moscow . . .

The things with which he had mocked Aubrey. The Special Branch men were fifteen yards away now. The medals, the *Pravda* eulogy—and the bitter, never-forgotten taste of failure. The daily reminders that his rank, *his* rank, was little more than a joke, albeit a respectful joke, while their uniforms demonstrated the real power and authority—

Everything was clear to him. Eldon had started forward now, confused but with some intuition that he should be acting *against* Babbington. Both he and the driver closed upon the Russian Mercedes—closing that exit, unless he ran—

Ran, ran, run, run—

Special Branch were five yards from him. *And he was already at the last step, as if to greet them with his surrender!*

"Sir Andrew Babbington?" one of them began, questioning and polite and final. His hands gripped the sides of the passenger steps. "Sir Andrew, would you please accompany us. . . ."

He heard no more. It had begun. The young Russian diplomat was already climbing into his Mercedes. Eldon was at its door, as if saying farewell to a departing guest. Then his face turned toward Babbington, the confusion in his eyes giving way to shock. The two Special Branch officers—senior officers by their age—blocked the gangway, and the passengers behind him pushed at his back, insisting he move forward.

The security driver had turned against him. His hand lay snugly inside his jacket, awaiting events. Special Branch, Eldon, the driver—blue exhaust smoke from the Russian Mercedes as it prepared to leave.

Hyde.

He choked. One of the Special Branch officers gripped his arm like a stern nurse.

He staggered forward, and the other policeman was on

his left side. He was walking toward their black Granada, un-resisting. Eldon—he turned away from the look of disillusion-ment and contempt on Eldon's face.

That Moscow apartment—

He had promised himself *never*, never that—even in '56, when he put his foot to this road, he had promised himself it would never be that.

Now, it was the best he could hope for. His only hope. That apartment, those false, powerless ranks, the bench in Gorky Park, feeding the pigeons and watching the men in uniform strut where he shuffled—

Hyde, Hyde, *Hyde—*

At least Aubrey was dead. At least that.

He ducked his head as he climbed into the rear seat of the Ford Granada.

There would be no words. Looks, gestures, impressions, visual images of lurid clarity—but no words. Nothing spoken.

Kapustin had hurried aboard the Tupolev as soon as it came to a halt near the principal terminal building of Do-modedovo airport. He was large and brisk in the seemingly cramped first-class cabin of the airliner. And delighted. There was barely concealed pleasure on his square, broad features. The face he had shown Aubrey when he had lied about meet-ing a woman, the moment before Aubrey's arrest in the gar-dens of the Belvedere in Vienna. Now, Aubrey understood the source of the secret, satisfied smile. The man had been antici-pating the arrest, as now he anticipated the final humiliation of Aubrey and his subsequent demise. No hatred; that was impermissible, unprofessional. But certainly the satisfaction of a web woven and an insect trapped.

He had uttered a few words of ironic welcome. The Rus-sian diplomats had disembarked. Through his window, Au-brey saw the herded, arranged cameramen and journalists—the audience for his farewell appearance. Once they were alone on the aircraft, Kapustin fell to inspecting the Massingers as if checking luggage, murmuring inaudibly to already briefed guards, checking through the windows for cars and cameras. Then he paused before Aubrey.

Overcoat swelling over his stomach, gloves held before his paunch in a military gesture. Fur hat tucked beneath one arm. Woolen scarf at his throat. He was monolithic and irresistible as he gestured Aubrey from his seat.

A KGB officer held Aubrey's coat, helped him into it. He glanced down the cabin at the Massingers. Paul raised his hand in a tired, slow wave of farewell. His face was pale and drawn, and his other arm was around Margaret's shoulders. Aubrey could bear to look at them for only a moment. The sense was of—betrayal? No, not quite that. Guilt certainly. Pity, too. He had not been responsible for the deaths of very many amateurs—outsiders—in more than forty years. Hardly ever for the death of a friend. Now, he was. It was to be part of his epitaph, like the photographs and television shots those outside were waiting to capture.

He turned away from the painful image of the Massingers, unable to cope with the unfamiliar emotions that gripped him. He cauterized them by staring instead at the stewardess standing at the door of the aircraft. And with the knowledge of the lessening distance between himself and the cameras. Cold, bright air crossed the threshold of the aircraft like an intruder.

Kapustin was behind him—did he speak, whisper? No—but propelled him gently, firmly toward the door. Sunlight, a stiff, ambushing little breeze, the expanse of gray concrete with heaped snow beyond it, the glitter and dazzle of huge glass windows. Faces in and behind the dazzle, watching him. The air he drew in choked him with its coldness. He coughed, as if to clear his throat before addressing the broad scimitar of cameramen and journalists at the foot of the passenger steps. Roped back, the perched, portable TV and film cameras bobbing behind them. Guards, rope—the distance of deception. He could not call to them; they would not hear. They would see him, see what Kapustin wished them to see and record and believe, and then he would be hurried into one of the waiting black cars—to disappear.

He could not have addressed them. The cough had left his throat dry, inoperative. Kapustin crowded onto the top step of the passenger ladder behind him. A murmur like wind through tall, dry grass, then the stutter of lenses and the whir of automatic winders. The dry, awful chorus of crickets in a burned landscape. Aubrey hated it. The cameras went on and on pointing, on and on exposing yards of negative and video tape and film stock.

Kapustin's satisfaction enveloped Aubrey like a heavy, suffocating blanket. Kapustin held his arm, keeping him to the pose.

Then nudged him. He began to descend the steps. The chorus of the cameras loudened, became almost frenzied. Preying on his treachery, devouring the deception. They did not expect him to smile—Kapustin would, no doubt, prefer the scowl he gave the lenses. It would later be taken to be a sign of illness and strain. A harbinger of his death. At the least, the opening of millions of newspapers the following day would lead to the conclusion that he still possessed perhaps a modicum of shame and therefore could not summon a smile.

The day after that, they would read of his death and consider, all in all, that the world was well rid of him.

Someone moving, elbowing through the edge of the semicircle of the press, from the line of black cars. Guards opening a way for a man in uniform. KGB. A major. Hurrying. For one terrible moment, Aubrey lurched sideways, as if the hurrying figure had blundered into him, or intended to do so. It was the hurry of his assassin, just for the moment.

The major did not pause at the bottom of the steps. The guards were herding the cameras and pressmen away from the cars, so that no one might speak to Aubrey or be within hearing distance of anything he might blurt out. The crickets continued their dry chorus.

"What?" in Russian from Kapustin. It was the first spoken word since he had donned his overcoat. The major gabbled. Aubrey turned almost lazily, like a very old and frail man, to this new epicenter of the scene. The crickets retreated, to become the noise of a log fire crackling in a distant room. The major's words were difficult—it was as if Aubrey had forgotten his Russian.

He concentrated instead upon Kapustin's face. The chorus of shutters and winders further diminished, more hesitant now as if suspecting some kind of pretense or swindle. He did not listen to the major's words, or to Kapustin's denials, or his growing impatience and anger. He saw the major's hands—one flapping glove held loosely by the other gloved hand, making repeated, emphatic little slaps on the rail of the passenger steps. He saw Kapustin's face. He glanced along the airliner's windows but did not see the Massingers—

He registered the other aides near the cars: a desultory, motiveless, chattering group. He heard the shutters falter, almost die. As he turned, he glimpsed the stewardess's smile die at the top of the steps, and two KGB men bulk behind her.

Turned again, and saw glass dazzle, snow stretch away across the airport, whiteness bordered by dirty slush. Saw an aircraft taxi, then begin its rush down the main runway. A Western airline's symbol blazoned on the flank and tail. It lifted, blue and white, into the sky. Air France—

Saw Kapustin, watching him. And knew.

Something, something, something . . .

His head spun. He gripped the rail of the steps, tottering slightly. Instinctively, the major's ungloved hand held his elbow, supporting him. The gesture seemed to enrage Kapustin.

"Inside with you!" he snapped in English. "Inside—back *inside!*"

Aubrey did not hear the words, but acted upon them, with the major's not-unkind help. Whatever, whatever had gone wrong—no—gone right, *gone right!*—it must be over. Before long he would be calm enough to guess at it, even to listen to any explanation they offered. But for the moment it was enough to know that it was over. Finally over.

He ducked his head unnecessarily as he reentered the door of the Tupolev. His eyes immediately, mistily sought the Massingers. Their faces, above the backs of their seats, had turned to him, afraid.

He smiled. Kapustin was raging behind him. Babbington? Hyde?

He did not understand. There were no real words being spoken there behind his back. He understood only that it was over. Margaret returned his smile, hesitantly, her swollen, discolored lips finding the expression difficult. Paul's face opened into a grin. Perhaps he understood—he spoke Russian, did he not? It did not matter. He sat down carefully, weakly in one of the seats. The Massingers were coming toward him. He had to sit still, just for a moment.

Time had become unimportant. It no longer mattered how long the delay, how long they simply sat aboard the aircraft, for eventually it would be refueled, and they would be cleared to take off on their return journey to . . . to Vienna. Yes, they would return to Vienna, not London. He would wait for that, just wait for the aircraft to take off. . . .

Massinger's hand fell again and again on the sleeve of his coat. A comforting, relieved gesture. It lulled Aubrey. He felt very tired. Margaret sat opposite him, across the narrow aisle, smiling at him, the tears beginning, her throat bobbing almost continuously as she attempted to swallow her welling feelings.

Aubrey nodded, in rhythm with the pats of Massinger's hand. Yes. It was over.

ABOUT THE AUTHOR

CRAIG THOMAS was born in Wales and educated at University College, Cardiff. He is the author of six previous novels: *Firefox, Firefox Down!, Rat Trap, Wolfsbane, Snow Falcon,* and *Sea Leopard.* Craig Thomas is married and currently lives in Lichfield, Staffordshire, England, where he is at work on a new novel.

THRILLERS

Gripping suspense . . . explosive action . . . dynamic characters . . . international settings . . . these are the elements that make for great thrillers. And Bantam has the best writers of thrillers today—Robert Ludlum, Frederick Forsyth, Jack Higgins, Clive Cussler—with books guaranteed to keep you riveted to your seat.

Robert Ludlum:

☐	24900	THE AQUITAINE PROGRESSION	$4.50
☐	26011	THE BOURNE IDENTITY	$4.95
☐	26094	THE CHANCELLOR MANUSCRIPT	$4.95
☐	26019	THE HOLCROFT COVENANT	$4.95
☐	25899	THE MATARESE CIRCLE	$4.95
☐	26430	THE OSTERMAN WEEKEND	$4.95
☐	25270	THE PARSIFAL MOSAIC	$4.95
☐	26081	THE ROAD TO GANDOLFO	$4.50
☐	25856	THE SCARLATTI INHERITANCE	$4.50
☐	05905	THREE BY LUDLUM	$12.95

    a Bantam Omnibus edition including:
      THE AQUITAINE PROGRESSION
      THE PARSIFAL MOSAIC
      THE BOURNE IDENTITY

Frederick Forsyth:

☐	25113	THE FOURTH PROTOCOL	$4.50
☐	25526	NO COMEBACKS	$3.95
☐	25522	DAY OF THE JACKAL	$4.50
☐	26490	THE DEVIL'S ALTERNATIVE	$4.95
☐	25224	DOGS OF WAR	$4.50
☐	25525	THE ODESSA FILE	$4.50

Robert Littell:

☐	05097	THE SISTERS, a Bantam hardcover	$16.95
☐	25416	THE DEFECTION OF A. J. LEWINTER	$3.95
☐	25457	MOTHER RUSSIA	$3.95
☐	25432	THE OCTOBER CIRCLE	$3.95
☐	25547	SWEET REASON	$3.50

Prices and availability subject to change without notice.

Buy them at your local bookstore or use this handy coupon for ordering:

Bantam Books, Inc., Dept. TH, 414 East Golf Road, Des Plaines, Ill. 60016

Please send me the books I have checked above. I am enclosing $_____ (please add $1.50 to cover postage and handling). Send check or money order —no cash or C.O.D.'s please.

Mr/Mrs/Miss _____

Address _____

City _____ State/Zip _____

TH—11/86

Please allow four to six weeks for delivery. This offer expires 5/87.

WHAT IF ... John Preston hadn't made a copy of his report on the Russians' attempt to breach the Fourth Protocol?

WHAT IF ... he hadn't succeeded in removing the bomb detonator from the Glasgow Police Station?

WHAT IF ... **you**, as John Preston, had to defuse the bomb yourself ... ?

WHAT IF ... the fate of the free world were in **your** hands?

THE FOURTH PROTOCOL

NOW IN SOFTWARE

Experience in a new way the intrigue-filled novel you've just read ... as Bantam Interactive Fiction, on your personal computer.

Attempt to match John Preston's performance in a suspenseful, sophisticated adventure game based on THE FOURTH PROTOCOL's plot, developed under the direction of the master storyteller himself, Frederick Forsyth.

Names, places and events have been changed, guaranteeing a challenging experience for all players!

☐ *Commodore Version*
Hardware: Commodore 64
Other equipment: one disk drive and monitor or television (printer with interface card is optional)
Memory: 64K
50027-9 $34.95 ($44.95 in Canada)

Use this handy coupon for ordering.

Bantam Books, Inc., Dept. EP7, 666 Fifth Avenue, N.Y., N.Y. 10103

Please send me _____ copies of THE FOURTH PROTOCOL software for the Commodore, order number 50027-9. I am enclosing $_____ (please add $3.00 per order to cover postage and handling). Send check or money order—no cash or C.O.D.'s please.

Mr/Ms _____

Address_____

City _____ State/Zip _____

EP7—10/86

Please allow two to three weeks for delivery. This offer expires 4/87.

Commodore and Apple are registered trademarks of Commodore Electronics Ltd., and Apple Computer, Inc., respectively.